Of Time and the River

Of Time and the River

BOOKS IV-VIII

A LEGEND OF MAN'S HUNGER
IN HIS YOUTH

by

Thomas Wolfe

*"Who knoweth the spirit of man that goeth upward, and
the spirit of the beast that goeth downward to the earth?"*

CHARLES SCRIBNER'S SONS
NEW YORK

To

MAXWELL EVARTS PERKINS

A GREAT EDITOR AND A BRAVE AND HONEST MAN, WHO STUCK TO
THE WRITER OF THIS BOOK THROUGH TIMES OF BITTER HOPELESS-
NESS AND DOUBT AND WOULD NOT LET HIM GIVE IN TO HIS OWN
DESPAIR, A WORK TO BE KNOWN AS "OF TIME AND THE RIVER" IS
DEDICATED WITH THE HOPE THAT ALL OF IT MAY BE IN SOME WAY
WORTHY OF THE LOYAL DEVOTION AND THE PATIENT CARE WHICH
A DAUNTLESS AND UNSHAKEN FRIEND HAS GIVEN TO EACH PART OF
IT, AND WITHOUT WHICH NONE OF IT COULD HAVE BEEN WRITTEN

*"Crito, my dear friend Crito, that, be-
lieve me, that is what I seem to hear, as
the Corybants hear flutes in the air, and
the sourd of those words rings and
echoes in my ears and I can listen to
nothing else."*

Contents

BOOK FOUR

PAGE

Proteus: The City   405

BOOK FIVE

Jason's Voyage   599

BOOK SIX

Antæus: Earth Again   795

BOOK SEVEN

Kronos and Rhea: The Dream of Time   851

BOOK EIGHT

Faust and Helen   901

Of Time and the River

"Kennst du das Land, wo die Zitronen blühn,
Im dunkeln Laub die Gold-Orangen glühn,
Ein sanfter Wind vom blauen Himmel weht,
Die Myrte still und hoch der Lorbeer steht,
Kennst du es wohl?
          Dahin! Dahin
Möcht' ich mit dir, O mein Geliebter, ziehn!

Kennst du das Haus, auf Säulen ruht sein Dach,
Es glänzt der Saal, es schimmert das Gemach,
Und Marmorbilder stehn und sehn mich an:
Was hat man dir, du armes Kind, getan?
Kennst du es wohl?
          Dahin! Dahin
Möcht' ich mit dir, O mein Beschützer, ziehn!

Kennst du den Berg und seinen Wolkensteg?
Das Maultier sucht im Nebel seinen Weg,
In Höhlen wohnt der Drachen alte Brut,
Es stürzt der Fels und über ihn die Flut:
Kennst du ihn wohl?
          Dahin! Dahin
Geht unser Weg; *O Vater, lass uns ziehn!"*

BOOK IV

PROTEUS: THE CITY

XLVI

As the train was pounding north across New Jersey, another train upon the inside track began to race with it, and for a distance of ten miles the two trains thundered down the tracks in an even, thrilling, and tremendous contest of steel and smoke and pistoned wheel that blotted out everything, the vision of the earth, the thought of the journey, the memory of the city, for all who saw it.

The other train, which was bound from Philadelphia, appeared so calmly and naturally that at first no one suspected that a race was on. It came banging up slowly, its big black snout swaying and bucking with a clumsy movement as it came on, its shining pistons swinging free and loose, and with short intermittent blasts of smoke from its squat funnel. It came up so slowly and naturally, past their windows, that at first it was hard to understand at what terrific speed the train was running, until one looked out of the windows on the other side and saw the flat, formless and uncharactered earth of New Jersey whipping by like pickets on a fence.

The other train came slowly on with that huge banging movement of the terrific locomotive, eating its way up past the windows, until the engine cab was level with Eugene and he could look across two or three scant feet of space and see the engineer. He was a young man cleanly jacketed in striped blue and wearing goggles. He had a ruddy color and his strong pleasant face, which bore on it the character of courage, dignity, and the immense and expert knowledge these men have, was set in a good-natured and determined grin, as with one gloved hand held steady on the throttle, he leaned upon his sill, with every energy and perception in him fixed with a focal concentration on the rails. Behind him his fireman, balanced on the swaying floor, his face black and grinning, his eyes goggled like a demon, and lit by the savage flare of his terrific furnace, was shovelling coal with all his might. Meanwhile, the train came on, came on, eating its way past, foot by foot, until the engine cab had disappeared from sight, and the first coaches of the train drew by.

And now a wonderful thing occurred. As the heavy rust-red coaches of the other train came up and began to pass them, the passengers of both trains suddenly became aware that a race between the trains was taking place. A tremendous excitement surged up in them, working its instant magic upon all these travellers, with their gray hats, their gray, worn city faces, and their dull tired eyes, which just the moment before had been fastened wearily on the pages of a newspaper, as if, having been hurled along this way beneath the lonely skies so many times, the desolate face of the earth had long since grown too familiar to them, and they never looked out windows any more.

But now the faces that had been so gray and dead were flushed with color, the dull and lustreless eyes had begun to burn with joy and interest. The passengers of both trains crowded to the windows, grinning like children for delight and jubilation.

Eugene's train, which for a space had been holding its rival even, now began to fall behind. The other train began to slide past the windows with increasing speed, and when this happened the joy and triumph of its passengers were almost unbelievable. Meanwhile their own faces had turned black and bitter with defeat. They cursed, they muttered, they scowled malevolently, they turned away with an appearance of indifference, as if they had no further interest in the thing, only to come back again with a fascinated and bitter look as their accursed windows slid by them with the inevitability of death and destiny.

Throughout, the crews of the two trains had shown as keen and passionate an interest, as intense a rivalry, as had the passengers. The conductors and porters were clustered at the windows or against the door in the car-ends, and they grinned and jeered just as the rest of them had done; but their interest was more professional, their knowledge more intimate and exact. The conductor on the train would say to the porter —"Whose train is that? Did you see John McIntyre aboard?" And the Negro would answer positively, "No, sah! Dat ain't Cap'n McIntyre. Ole man Rigsby's got her. Dere he is now!" he cried, as another coach moved past, and the grizzled and grinning face of an old conductor came in sight.

Then the conductor would go away, shaking his head, and the Negro would mutter and chuckle to himself by turns. He was a fat enormous darkey, with an ink-black skin, a huge broad bottom, teeth of solid grinning white, and with a big fatty growth on the back of his thick neck. He shook like jelly when he laughed. Eugene had known him for years because he came from his native town, and the Pullman car in which he rode, which was known as K 19, was the car that always made the jour-

ney of 700 miles between his home town and the city. Now the Negro
sprawled upon the green upholstery of the end seat in the Pullman and
grinned and muttered at his fellows in the other train.

"All right, boy. All right, you ole slew-footed niggah!" he would
growl at a grinning darkey in the other train. "Uh! Uh!" he would
grunt ironically. "Don't you think you's somp'n, dough! You's pullin'
dat train yo'self, you is!" he would laugh sarcastically, and then sullenly
and impatiently conclude, "Go on, boy! Go on! I sees you! I don't care
how soon I loses you! Go on, niggah! Go on! Git dat ugly ole livah-
lipped face o' yo'n out o' my way!"

And that grinning and derisive face would also vanish and be gone,
until the whole train had passed them, pulled ahead of them, and vanished from their sight. And their porter sat there staring out the window,
chuckling and shaking his head from time to time, as he said to himself,
with a tone of reproof and disbelief:

"Dey ain't got no right to do dat! Dey ain't got no right to run right
by us like we wasn't here!" he chuckled. "Dey ain't nothin' but a little
ole Philadelphia local! Dey're not supposed to make de time we is! We's
de Limited! We got de outside rail!" he bragged, but immediately, shaking his head, he said: "But Lawd, Lawd! Dat didn't help us none today.
Dey've gone right on by us! We'll never ketch dem now!" he said
mournfully, and it seemed that he was right.

Eugene's train was running in free light and open country now, and
the passengers, resigned finally to defeat, had settled back into their
former dozing apathy. But suddenly the train seemed to start and leap
below them with a living energy, its speed increased visibly, the earth
began to rush by with an ever-faster stroke, the passengers looked up and
at one another with a question in their eyes, and an awakened interest.

And now their fortune was reversed, the train was running through
the country at terrific speed, and in a moment more they began to come
up on the rival train again. And now, just as the other train had slid by
them, they began to walk by its windows with the calm imperious stride
of their awakened and irresistible power. But where, before, the passengers of both trains had mocked and jeered at one another, they now
smiled quietly and good-naturedly, with a friendly, almost affectionate,
interest. For it seemed that they—the people in the other train—now
felt that their train had done its best and made a manful showing against
its mighty and distinguished competitor, and that they were now cheerfully resigned to let the Limited have its way.

And now their train walked up past the windows of the dining-car of the other: they could see the smiling white-jacketed waiters, the tables covered with their snowy-white linen and gleaming silver, and the people eating, smiling and looking toward them in a friendly manner as they ate. And then they were abreast the heavy parlor cars: a lovely girl, blonde-haired, with a red silk dress, and slender shapely legs crossed carelessly, holding an opened magazine face downward in one hand, and with the slender tapering fingers of the other curved inward towards her belly where they fumbled with a charm or locket hanging from a chain, was looking at them for a moment with a tender and good-natured smile. And opposite her, with his chair turned towards her, an old man, dressed elegantly in a thin, finely-woven and expensive-looking suit of gray, and with a meagre, weary, and distinguished face that had brown spots upon it, was sitting with his thin phthisic shanks crossed, and for a moment Eugene could see his lean hands, palsied, stiff, and folded on his lap, and the brown spots on them; and he could see a corded, brittle-looking vein upon the back of one old hand.

And outside there was the raw and desolate-looking country, there were the great steel coaches, the terrific locomotives, the shining rails, the sweep of the tracks, the vast indifferent dinginess and rust of colors, the powerful mechanical expertness, and the huge indifference to suave finish. And inside there were the opulent green and luxury of the Pullman cars, the soft glow of the lights, and people fixed there for an instant in incomparably rich and vivid little pictures of their life and destiny, as they were all hurled onward, a thousand atoms, to their journey's end somewhere upon the mighty continent, across the immense and lonely visage of the everlasting earth.

And they looked at one another for a moment, they passed and vanished and were gone forever, yet it seemed to him that he had known these people, that he knew them better than the people in his own train, and that, having met them for an instant under immense and timeless skies, as they were hurled across the continent to a thousand destinations, they had met, passed, vanished, yet would remember this forever. And he thought the people in the two trains felt this, also: slowly they passed each other now, and their mouths smiled and their eyes grew friendly, but he thought there was some sorrow and regret in what they felt. For, having lived together as strangers in the immense and swarming city, they now had met upon the everlasting earth, hurled past each other for a moment between two points in time upon the shining rails, never to meet, to speak, to know each other any more, and the briefness of their days, the destiny of man, was in that instant greeting and farewell.

Therefore, in this way, they passed and vanished, the coaches slipped away from them until again they came up level with the cab of the other locomotive. And now the young engineer no longer sat in his high window with a determined grin, and with his hard blue eyes fixed on the rail. Rather, he stood now in the door, his engine banging away deliberately, slowed down, bucking and rocking loosely as they passed. His attitude was that of a man who has just given up a race. He had turned to shout something at his fireman who stood there balanced, arms akimbo, black and grinning, as they moved up by them. The engineer had one gloved hand thrust out against the cab to support him, he held the other on his hip and he was grinning broadly at them, with solid teeth edged with one molar of bright gold—a fine, free, generous, and good-humored smile, which said more plain than any words could do: "Well, it's over, now! You fellows win! But you'll have to admit we gave you a run for your money while it lasted!"

Then, they drew away and lost the train forever. And presently their own train came in to Newark, where it stopped. And suddenly, as Eugene was looking at some Negroes working there with picks and shovels on the track beside the train, one looked up and spoke quietly to the fat porter, without surprise or any greeting, as casually and naturally as a man could speak to some one who has been in the same room with him for hours.

"When you comin' back dis way, boy?" he said.

"I'll be comin' back again on Tuesday," said the porter.

"Did you see dat ole long gal yet? Did you tell huh what I said?"

"Not yet," the porter said, "but I'll be seein' huh fo' long! I'll tell yo' what she says."

"I'll be lookin' fo' you," said the other Negro.

"Don't fo'git now," said the fat black porter, chuckling; and the train started, the man calmly returned to work again; and this was all. What that astounding meeting of two black atoms underneath the skies, that casual incredible conversation meant, he never knew; but he did not forget it.

And the whole memory of this journey, of this race between the trains, of the Negroes, of the passengers who came to life like magic, crowding and laughing at the windows, and particularly of the girl and of the vein upon the old man's hand, was fixed in Eugene's brain forever. And like everything he did or saw that year, like every journey that he made, it became a part of his whole memory of the city.

And the city would always be the same when he came back. He would rush through the immense and glorious stations, murmurous with their million destinies and the everlasting sound of time, that was caught up forever in their roof—he would rush out into the street, and instantly it would be the same as it had always been, and yet forever strange and new.

He felt as if by being gone from it an instant he had missed something priceless and irrecoverable. He felt instantly that nothing had changed a bit, and yet it was changing furiously, unbelievably, every second before his eyes. It seemed stranger than a dream, and more familiar than his mother's face. He could not believe in it—and he could not believe in anything else on earth. He hated it, he loved it, he was instantly engulfed and overwhelmed by it.

He brought to it the whole packed glory of the earth—the splendor, power, and beauty of the nation. He brought back to it a tremendous memory of space, and power, and of exultant distances; a vision of trains that smashed and pounded at the rails, a memory of people hurled past the window of his vision in another train, of people eating sumptuously from gleaming silver in the dining cars, of cities waking in the first light of the morning, and of a thousand little sleeping towns built across the land, lonely and small and silent in the night, huddled below the desolation of immense and cruel skies.

He brought to it a memory of the loaded box-cars slatting past at fifty miles an hour, of swift breaks like openings in a wall when coal cars came between, and the sudden feeling of release and freedom when the last caboose whipped past. He remembered the dull rusty red, like dried blood, of the freight cars, the lettering on them, and their huge gaping emptiness and joy as they curved in among raw piney land upon a rusty track, waiting for great destinies in the old red light of evening upon the lonely, savage, and indifferent earth; and he remembered the cindery look of road-beds, and the raw and barren spaces in the land that ended nowhere; the red clay of railway cuts, and the small hard lights of semaphores—green, red, and yellow—as in the heart of the enormous dark they shone, for great trains smashing at the rails, their small and passionate assurances.

He brought to it the heart, the eye, the vision of the everlasting stranger, who had walked its stones, and breathed its air, and, as a stranger, looked into its million dark and driven faces, and who could never make the city's life his own.

And finally he brought to it the million memories of his fathers who were great men and knew the wilderness, but who had never lived in cities: three hundred of his blood and bone, who sowed their blood and sperm across the continent, walked beneath its broad and lonely lights, were frozen by its bitter cold, burned by the heat of its fierce suns, withered, gnarled, and broken by its savage weathers, and who fought like lions with its gigantic strength, its wildness, its limitless savagery and beauty, until with one stroke of its paw it broke their backs and killed them.

He brought to it the memory and inheritance of all these men and women who had worked, fought, drunk, loved, whored, striven, lived and died, letting their blood soak down like silence in the earth again, letting their flesh rot quietly away into the stern, the beautiful, the limitless substance of the everlasting earth from which they came, from which they were compacted, on which they worked and wrought and moved, and in whose immense and lonely breast their bones were buried and now lay, pointing eighty ways across the continent.

Above the pounding of the mighty wheels their voices had seemed to well out of the everlasting earth, giving to him, the son whom they had never seen, the dark inheritance of the earth and the centuries, which was his, even as his blood and bone were his, but which he could not fathom:

"Whoever builds a bridge across this earth," they cried, "whoever lays a rail across this mouth, whoever stirs the dust where these bones lie, let him go dig them up, and say his Hamlet to the engineers. Son, son," their voices said, "is the earth richer where our own earth lay? Must you untwist the vine-root from the buried heart? Have you unrooted mandrake from our brains? Or the rich flowers, the big rich flowers, the strange unknown flowers?

"You must admit the grass is thicker here. Hair grew like April on our buried flesh. These men were full of juice, you'll grow good corn here, golden wheat. The men are dead, you say? They may be dead, but you'll grow trees here; you'll grow an oak but we were richer than an oak: you'll grow a plum tree here that's bigger than an oak, it will be all filled with plums as big as little apples.

"We were great men and mean men hated us," they said. "We were all men who cried out when we were hurt, wept when we were sad, drank, ate, were strong, weak, full of fear, were loud and full of clamor, yet grew quiet when dark came. Fools laughed at us and witlings sneered at us: how could they know our brains were subtler than a snake's? Because they were more small, were they more delicate? Did their pale sapless flesh sense things too fine for our imagining? How can you think it, child? Our hearts were wrought more strangely than a cat's, full of deep twistings, woven sinews, flushing with dull and brilliant fires; and our marvellous nerves, flame-tipped, crossed wires too intricate for their fathoming.

"What could they see," the voices rose above the sound of the wheels with their triumphant boast, "what could they know of men like us, whose fathers hewed the stone above their graves, and now lie under mountains, plains, and forests, hills of granite, drowned by a flooding river, killed by the stroke of the everlasting earth? Now only look where these men have been buried: they've heaved their graves up in great laughing lights of flowers—do you see other flowers so rich on other graves?

"Who sows the barren earth?" their voices cried. "We sowed the wilderness with blood and sperm. Three hundred of your blood and bone are recompacted with the native earth: we gave a tongue to solitude, a pulse to the desert, the barren earth received us and gave back our agony: we made the earth cry out. One lies in Oregon, and one, by a broken wheel and horse's skull, still grips a gunstock on the Western trail. Another one has helped to make Virginia richer. One died at Chancellorsville in Union blue, and one at Shiloh walled with Yankee dead. Another was ripped open in a bar-room brawl and walked three blocks to find a doctor, holding his entrails thoughtfully in his hands.

"One died in Pennsylvania reaching for a fork: her reach was greater than her grasp; she fell, breaking her hip, cut off from red rare beef and roasting-ears at ninety-six. Another whored and preached his way from Hatteras to the Golden Gate: he preached milk and honey for the kidneys, sassafras for jaundice, sulphur for uric acid, slippery-ellum for decaying gums, spinach for the goitre, rhubarb for gnarled joints and all the twistings of rheumatism, and pure spring water mixed with vinegar for that great ailment dear to Venus, that makes the world and Frenchmen kin. He preached the brotherhood and love of man, the coming of Christ and Armageddon by the end of 1886, and he founded the Sons of Abel, the Daughters of Ruth, the Children of The Pentateuch, as well as twenty other sects; and finally he died at eighty-four, a son of the Lord, a prophet, and a saint.

"Two hundred more are buried in the hills of home: these men got land, fenced it, owned it, tilled it; they traded in wood, stone, cotton, corn, tobacco; they built houses, roads, grew trees and orchards. Wherever these men went, they got land and worked it, built upon it, farmed it, sold it, added to it. These men were hill-born and hill-haunted: all knew the mountains, but few knew the sea.

"So there we are, child, lacking our thousand years and ruined walls, perhaps, but with a glory of our own, laid out across three thousand miles of earth. There have been bird-calls for our flesh within the wilderness. So call, please, call! Call the robin red-breast and the wren, who in dark woods discover the friendless bodies of unburied men!

"Immortal land, cruel and immense as God," they cried, "we shall go wandering on your breast forever! Wherever great wheels carry us is home—home for our hunger, home for all things except the heart's small fence and dwelling-place of love.

"Who sows the barren earth?" they said. "Who needs the land? You'll make great engines yet, and taller towers. And what's a trough of bone against a tower? You need the earth? Whoever needs the earth may have the earth. Our dust, wrought in this land, stirred by its million sounds, will stir and tremble to the passing wheel. Whoever needs the earth may use the earth. Go dig us up and there begin your bridge. But whoever builds a bridge across this earth, whoever lays a rail across this mouth, whoever needs the trench where these bones lie, let him go dig them up and say his Hamlet to the engineers."

So had their hundred voices welled up from the earth and called to him, their son and brother, above the pounding of the mighty wheels that roared above them. And the memory of their words, their triumphant tongue of deathless silence, and the full weight of the inheritance they had given him, he brought back again out of the earth into the swarming canyons and the million tongues of the unceasing, the fabulous, the million-footed city.

And all that he had seen, all that he remembered of this earth he brought to the city, and it seemed to be the city's complement—to feed it, to sustain it, to belong to it. And the image of the city, written in his heart, was so unbelievable that it seemed to be a fiction, a fable, some huge dream of his own dreaming, so unbelievable that he did not think that he should find it when he returned; yet it was just the same as he had remembered it. He found it, the instant he came out of the station: the tidal swarm of faces, the brutal stupefaction of the street, the immense and arrogant blaze and sweep of the great buildings.

It was fabulous and incredible, but there it was. He saw again the million faces—the faces dark, dingy, driven, harried, and corrupt, the faces stamped with all the familiar markings of suspicion and mistrust, cunning, contriving, and a hard and stupid cynicism. There were the faces, thin and febrile, of the taxi drivers, the faces cunning, sly, and furtive, the hard twisted mouths and rasping voices, the eyes glittering and toxic with unnatural fires. And there were the faces, cruel, arrogant and knowing of the beak-nosed Jews, the brutal heavy figures of the Irish cops, and their red beefy faces, filled with the stupid, swift, and choleric menaces of privilege and power, shining forth terribly with an almost perverse and sanguinary vitality and strength among the swarming tides of the gray-faced people. They were all there as he remembered them—a race mongrel, dark, and feverish, swarming along forever on the pavements, moving in tune to that vast central energy, filled with the city's life, as with a general and dynamic fluid.

And, incredibly, incredibly! these common, weary, driven, brutal faces, these faces he had seen a million times, even the sterile scrabble of harsh words they uttered, now seemed to be touched by this magic of now and forever, this strange and legendary quality that the city had, and to belong themselves to something fabulous and enchanted. The people, common, dull, cruel, and familiar-looking as they were, seemed to be a part, to comprise, to be fixed in something classic, and eternal, in the everlasting variousness and fixity of time, in all the fabulous reality of the city's life: they formed it, they were part of it, and they could have belonged to nothing else on earth.

And as he saw them, as he heard them, as he listened to their words again, as they streamed past, their stony gravel of harsh oaths and rasping cries, the huge single anathema of their bitter and strident tongues dedicated so completely, so constantly, to the baseness, folly, or treachery of their fellows that it seemed that speech had been given to them by some demon of everlasting hatred only in order that they might express the infamy and vileness of men, or the falseness of women—as he listened to this huge and single tongue of hatred, evil, and of folly, it seemed incredible that they could breathe the shining air without weariness, agony, and labor—that they could live, breathe, move at all among the huge encrusted taint, the poisonous congestion of their lives.

And yet live, breathe, and move they did with a savage and indubitable violence, an unfathomed energy. Hard-mouthed, hard-eyed, and strident-tongued, with their million hard gray faces, they streamed past upon the streets forever, like a single animal, with the sinuous and baleful convolutions of an enormous reptile. And the magical and shining air—the strange, subtle and enchanted weather, was above them, and the buried men were strewn through the earth on which they trod, and a bracelet of great tides was flashing round them, and the enfabled rock on which they swarmed swung eastward in the marches of the sun into eternity, and was masted like a ship with its terrific towers, and was flung with a lion's port between its tides into the very maw of the infinite, all-taking ocean. And exultancy and joy rose with a cry of triumph in his throat, because he found it wonderful.

Their voices seemed to form one general City-Voice, one strident snarl, one twisted mouth of outrage and of slander bared forever to the imperturbable and immortal skies of time, one jeering tongue and rumor of man's baseness, fixed on the visage of the earth, and turned incredibly, and with an evil fortitude, toward depthless and indifferent space against the calm and silence of eternity.

Filled with pugnacious recollection that Voice said, "'Dis guy,' I says, 'dis friend of yoehs,'" it said, "'dis bastad who owes me fawty bucks—dat yuh introduced me to—when's he goin' t' giv'it to me?' I says." And derisive, scornful, knowing, it would snarl: *"W'ich guy? W'ich* guy do yuh mean? Duh guy dat used to come in Louie's place?" And bullying and harsh it would reply: *"Yuh* don't know? Watcha mean yuh don't know!" . . . Defiant, *"Who* don't know? . . . *Who* says so? . . . *Who* told yuh so?" And jeering, "Oh *dat* guy! . . . Is *dat* duh guy yuh mean? An' wat t' hell do *I* care wat he t'inks, f'r Chris' sake! . . . To hell wit' him!" it said.

Recounting past triumphs with an epic brag, it said: "'You're comin' out of dere!' I said. 'Wat do you t'ink of dat?' . . . 'Oh, yeah,' he says, 'who's goin' t' make me?' So I says, 'You hoid me—yeah! . . . You're goin' to take dat little tin crate of yoehs right out of deh! You'll take yoeh chance right on duh line wit' all duh rest of us!' . . . 'Oh, yeah,' he says. . . . 'You hoid me, misteh'—an' he went!" In tones of lady-like refinement, it recounted romance into ravished ears as follows: "'Lissen,' I says, 'as far as my boss is consoined it's bizness only. . . .

An' as far as Mr. Ball is consoined it's my own bizness' (hah! hah! hah! Y'know that's wat I tol' him. . . . Jeez: it handed him a laugh, y'know!)—'An afteh five o'clock,' I says, 'I'm my own boss. . . . At duh same time,' I says, 'deh's duh psychological side to be considehed.' "

And with the sweet accent of maternal tribulation, it admitted, "Sure! I hit her! I did! Oh, I hit her very hahd! Jeez! It was an awful crack I gave her, honestleh! My hand was boinin' f'r a half-oueh aftehwads! . . . I just blow up, y' know! . . . Dat's my on'y reason f'r dat! I jus' blow up! Dis fellah's in duh bathroom callin' f'r his eggs, duh baby's yellin' f'r his bottle, an' I jus' blow up! . . . Dat's my on'y reason f'r *dat!* Dat's duh on'y reason dat I hit her, see? I'm afraid she'll hoit duh baby, see? She bends its fingehs back. So I says, 'F'r God's sake, please, don't do dat! . . . I gotta headache' . . . an' then, I jus' blow up! Sure! I hit her hahd! . . . Duh trouble is I can't stop wit' one slap, see! . . . Jeez! I hit her! My hand was boining f'r a half-oueh aftehwads!"

Hot with its sense of outraged decency, it said, "I went upstairs an' pounded on dat doeh! . . . 'Come out of dere, you s of a b,' I says— Sure, I'm tellin' yuh! Dat's what I said to her, y' know! . . . 'Come out of dere,' I says, 'before I t'row you out,' " and regretfully it added, "Sure! I hate to do dese t'ings—it makes me feel bad lateh—but I won't have dem in my place. Dat's duh one t'ing I refuse t' do," it said. And with a passionate emotion, it asserted, "Sure! . . . Dat's what I'm tellin' yuh! . . . Yuh know how dat was, don't cha? Duh foist guy—her husban'— was passin' out duh sugah an' duh otheh guy—duh boy-friend—was layin' her. Can yuh ima-a-gine it?" it said.

Amazed, in tones of stupefaction, it would say "No kiddin'! *No!*" And with solemn reprehension it would add, "Oh, yuh know I think that's te-e-ri-bul! I think that's aw-w-ful!"—the voice of unbelieving horror would reply.

Finally, friendly and familiar, the great Voice of the city said, "Well, so long, Eddy. I'm goin' t' ketch some sleep," it said, and answered, "Well, so long, Joe, I'll be seein' yuh." "So long, Grace," it added with an accent of soft tenderness and love, and the huge Voice of the city murmured, "O. K. kid! Eight o'clock—no kiddin'—I'll be deh!"

Such were some of the million tongues of that huge single Voice, as he had heard them speak a thousand times, and as now instantly, incredibly, as soon as he came back to them, they spoke again.

And as he listened, as he heard them, their speech could not have been more strange to him had they been people from the planet Mars.

He stared gape-mouthed, he listened, he saw the whole thing blazing in his face again to the tone and movement of its own central, unique, and incomparable energy. It was so real that it was magical, so real that all that men had always known was discovered to them instantly, so real he felt as if he had known it forever, yet must be dreaming as he looked at it; therefore he looked at it and his spirit cried:

"Incredible! Oh, incredible! It moves, it pulses like a single living thing! It lives, it lives, with all its million faces"—and this is the way he always knew it was.

XLVII

THAT year—the first year that he lived there in the city—he was twenty-three years old. After these months of frenzy, drunkenness, and arrest, he was at the last gasp of his resources, and the eighteen hundred dollars a year, which was his salary at the university that had employed him as an instructor, seemed to him a wage of princely munificence—a stroke of incredible good fortune.

And although his position as instructor had been given to him in one of the usual ways, through the recommendation of the teachers' bureau at Harvard University, and the letters of some of the professors there, he was tortured constantly by the thought of his inadequacy and ignorance, and by the horrible fear that his incompetence would be discovered and that one day he would be suddenly, peremptorily, ruinously, and disgracefully discharged.

At night, when he went to bed in his little cell at the cheap little hotel nearby where he lived, the thought of the class he had to meet the next day fed at his heart and bowels with cold poisonous mouths of fear, and as the hour for a class drew nigh he would begin to shake and tremble as if he had an ague; the successive stages of his journey from his room in the Leopold, to the class room at the university a few hundred yards away—from cell to elevator, from the tiled sterility of the hotel lobby to the dusty beaten light and violence of the street outside, thence to the brawling and ugly corridors of the university, which drowned one, body and soul, with their swarming, shrieking, shouting tides of dark amber Jewish flesh, and thence into the comparative sanctuary of the class room with its smaller horde of thirty or forty Jews and Jewesses, all laughing, shouting, screaming, thick with their hot and swarthy body-smells, their strong female odors of rut and crotch and arm-pit and cheap perfume, and their hard male smells that were

rancid, stale, and sour—the successive stages of this journey were filled
with such dazed numbness, horror, fear, and nauseous stupefaction as
a man might feel in the successive stages of a journey to the gallows,
the guillotine, or the electric chair: the world swarmed blindly, nau-
seously, drunkenly about him. He looked at the faces in the hotel lobby,
the brawling, furious, and chaotic street, and the swarming and rancid
corridors, with dizzy swimming eyes and a constricted heart; a thousand
unutterable and horrible premonitions and imaginings of ruin and
shame swarmed through his mind—every day he felt the impending
menace of some new and fatal catastrophe, some indefinable and crushing disgrace with which each hour was ominously, murderously pregnant.

What these fears and forebodings were he could not have told, but
they occasionally found articulate expression in some scene of frightful
insubordination and rebellion, in which he found himself faced with
forty brawling, mocking, swarthily jeering faces who, like savage and
untamed horses that have sensed the fear and incompetence of their
driver, have now broken the last feeble thread of restraint and are running free and wild before him. The terror and menace of such a disgrace was heightened by the intrusion into the scene at the apex of such
a moment of riot and rebellion, of one of his employers, the Dean, the
head of the department, or a creature with a wry lean face, a convulsive
Adam's apple, a habit of writhing his lean belly and loins erotically as he
spoke, and a mind of the most obscene puritanism, who was employed
to oversee the work and methods of the instructors: he could visualize
the moment of their fatal entrance into the class-room, and hear their
words of stern, curt and immediate dismissal as they drove him out
and gathered the reins strongly into their own parched and freckled
hands.

A thousand such images of disgrace and terror swarmed through his
mind, and at the same time there began to smoulder in his heart a
dogged resentment and hatred of this nameless fear, this wordless and
sourceless shame, impalpable, causeless, maddening, which pressed upon
him from the sky, which hovered in the vast unrest and dissonance of
the air he breathed, and which at length crept poisonously through all
the rivers of life, corrupting the healthy music of the blood, the sweet
exultant music of the heart, curdling men's bowels with fear and wither-
ing their loins with sterile impotence. What was this gray lipless shape
of fear that stalked their lives incessantly—that was everywhere, legible

in the faces, the movements, and the driven frenzied glances of the people who swarmed on the streets. What was this thing that duped men out of joy, tricked them out of all the exultant and triumphant music of the world, drove them at length into the dusty earth, cheated, defrauded, tricked out of life by a nameless phantom, with all their glory wasted?

Already, in the city, he had begun to see how life was duped and menaced by this cheat: a thousand images of cruelty, violence, cowardice and dishonor swarmed about him in the streets. As the sparkling and winey exultancy of October, with its grand and solemn music of death and life, of departure and return, moved on into the harsh, raw, green implacability of winter, one could observe the death of joy and hope, the barometric rise of hate and fear and venom in the city's life: it got into the faces of the people, it wasted their flesh and corrupted their blood, it glittered in the eyes of the instructors at the university, their flesh got green and yellow with its poisons, the air about them was webbed, cross-webbed, and counter-webbed with the dense fabric of their million spites and hatreds. They wasted and grew sick with hate and poison because another man received promotion, because another man had got his poem printed, because another man had eaten food and swallowed drink and lain with women, and lived and would not die; they sweltered with hate and fear against the professors who employed them—they grew pale and trembled, and spoke obsequiously when their employer passed, but when the man had gone, they whispered with trembling lips: "Has he spoken to you yet? . . . Has he said anything to you yet about next year? . . . Are you coming back next year? . . . Did he say anything to you about *me* next year? . . ." They greeted him with sly humility and a servile glance, but they snickered obscenely at him when his back was turned. And they smiled and sneered at one another with eyes that glittered with their hate: they never struck a blow but they spoke lying words of barbed ambiguity, they lied, cheated, and betrayed, and they sweltered in the poisons of their hate and fear, they breathed the weary hatred-laden air about them into their poisoned lungs.

Around him in the streets, again, as winter came, he heard a million words of hate and death: a million words of snarl and sneer and empty threat, of foul mistrust and lying slander: already he had come to see the poisonous images of death and hatred at work in the lives of a million people—he saw with what corrupt and venomous joy they seized on every story of man's dishonor, defeat, or sorrow, with what vicious jibe and jeer they greeted any evidence of mercy, honesty, or love.

By night, the hard and sterile lights of their glittering, barren and obscene streets fell lividly over the pale and swarthy faces of a million rats of the flesh, and by day, in the weary and hatred-laden air of the university, the harsh and merciless light shone on the venomous faces of the rats of the spirit.

In his heart a dogged and furious resentment was beginning to glow and moulder—a savage hate of hate, a fear of fear, a murderous intensity of desire to strangle the shapes of death and barrenness—a resistance, still passive, but growing in bitterness and pugnacity with every passing day, as he saw how uselessly and horribly men allowed themselves to be duped, cheated, and beaten by the living rat and by the fraud of fear, and that was being strengthened momently now by an implacable conviction, a dogged and incontrovertible memory that, incredibly sharpened by his fury and desire, awoke and netted out of the sea-depths of the past, the shining fish of a million living moments. The sound of forest waters in the night, the rustling of cool corn-blades in the dark, the goat-cries of a boy into the wind, the pounding of great wheels upon a rail, the sound of quiet casual voices at a country station in the night, and the thorn of delight, the tongueless cry of ecstasy that trembles on the lips of the country kid as he lies awake for the first time in the night in the top berth of a pullman car while the great wheels pound beneath him toward the city, and he hears the good-looking woman in the berth below him stir languorously and move, in a gesture of heavied and sensual appeasement, her milky thighs.—These things had been upon the earth, past all the mockery of the old scornmaker's pride, and would endure forever. These facts, together with a thousand more—the incredible magic of the peach bloom in the month of April, the smell of rivers after rain, the wordless glory and first green of a young tree seen in a city street at daybreak in the month of May, the bird-song breaking into light once more, a cry, a leaf, the passing of a cloud—these facts, as bright as herrings in a shining water, as literal as nails to fix the hides of falsehood to the wall, as real as April and all magic whatsoever, returned now under the furious light of his awakened and incontrovertible memory.

A murderous hatred against the haters, the mockers, dupers, cheaters, and all of the walking frauds of death rose up in him. He resolved to kill the phantoms of this fear and shame which pressed upon him namelessly, he swore that he should not starve in the midst of plenty, batter his knuckles bloody on the four walls of a little cell, break the great shoulder of his power and strength against a barren wall, prowl ceaselessly and damnably a million sterile streets, in which there was neither pause nor curve nor stay, nor door, to enter: he knew there was earth for his feet, food for his hunger, liquor for his thirst, the exultant reality of strong golden joy for all the savage passion of his conviction and desire, and he swore that he should come at length to doors and harbors, he knew he would not starve and sicken in the wilderness, and that the venomous rats of the flesh and of the spirit should never gnaw his bones in triumph in the desert.

Yet, the sense of drowning daily in the man-swarm returned to him. Each day there began anew one of the most ancient and fatal struggles that was ever waged—the struggle of man against the multitude: each day like a man who is going into battle, he would brace himself with savage resolution, and gird his spirit to the sticking point each time he went out in the streets, and each day, beaten, driven, trembling and inchoate, drowned in horror and oblivion, he would at length retreat into the four walls of his cell again, conscious only of having passed through a maelstrom of sound, movement, violence, and living tissue—of living tissue from which all of the radiant and succulent essences of individual character and memory had been extracted—and which flowed constantly back and forth along the beaten pavement in a lava-like tide of tallowy flesh, dark dead eyes, and gray felt hats. The gray felt hats, in particular, those machine-made millions of neat cheap cones of crisp gray felt, all worn in the same way, and tilted at the same angle, and for the most part shading faces of the same tallowy texture—those million points of changeless gray that bobbed and moved incessantly through a thousand streets—drowned him with their tidal flow of weariness and sterility: they seemed to be the badge, the uniform, of a race of mechanical creatures, who were as essential and inhuman a part of the city's substance as stone and steel and brick, who had been made of one essential substance and charged with one general and basic energy along with the buildings, tunnels, streets, and a million glittering projectiles of machinery, and who flowed by incessantly, were poured into tunnels or driven through streets, were added to here, and thinned out there, were portioned, doled, and celled out in a million destinations, a thousand swarming heaven-daring hives, the mindless and unwitting automatons of a gigantic and incomprehensible pattern.

But if he retreated daily, out of this savage and unequal struggle with the Herculean forces of the city, if he returned trembling, beaten and exhausted to the hermitage of his own small cell, it was with no sense of final defeat, no desire for ultimate escape. His pride and fury grew from every beating that they got, his faith grew stubborn on adversity, his spirit fed upon humiliation, and spat into the face of failure, his soul plunged darkly to the sea-floor of blind horror, swarming desolation, and came up dripping with a snarl of hatred and defiance: daily they beat him with their blind appalling mass, daily they drove him livid, shaking, blind with horror, back into his cell, so stunned and stricken by the savage, obscene, and mindless fury of the streets that he could no longer think, feel, or remember; and hour by hour his soul swam upwards out of the jungles of the sea! And every night, the merciful anodyne of dark restored him; sunk deep, at length, in midnight, beastwise aprowl in all the brooding silence of the night, his spirit swept out through the fields of sleep, he heard the heartbeats of six million men: within their million cells sleep crossed the faces of six million sleepers and in the night-time, in the dark, in all the living silence of the night, the sleeping faces of Snodgrass, Weisberg, and O'Hare were strange and dark as his. He saw the city with the great giant webbing of its thousand streets, he heard the long deep notes of warning and departure, from the great ships in the harbor; and then he saw the city as a whole, six million sleepers celled in sleep and walled in night, and girdled by the bracelet of two flashing sea-borne tides that isled them round: he held them legible as minted gold within his hand, he saw them plain as apples in the adyts of his brain. Exultant certitude and joy welled up in him, and he knew that his hunger could eat the earth, his eye and brain gulp down the vision of ten thousand streets, ten million faces, he knew he should beat and eat them all one day, and that a man was more than a million, stronger than a wall, and greater than a door, and taller than a ninety-storey tower.

They swept around him on the rootless pavements in drowning tides of gray abomination, of numberless depth and horror, and like the memory of a bird-song in the wood, the memory of all his people who had lived and died alone for two hundred years within the wilderness, and whose buried bones were pointing eighty ways across the continent, returned to him in a rush of savage resolution, and he swore that he would beat death and nothingness and all the abominations of a sterile and nameless fear: he swore it with a sick heart, a trembling lip, and a nauseous gut in which the rancid wash of a sour distressful coffee growled and rumbled queasily—for in those months, this sense of nameless fear and dread, impending ruin, disgrace and menace, was so great each time he went to meet a class, its damnable victory over all the clean and healthful music of the flesh, the exultant joy of thirst and hunger, so complete and devastating, that he was unable to touch a mouthful of food for hours in advance.

Thus, while a thousand such images of disgrace and terror swarmed through his mind, he stood before each class on a small raised platform three or four inches in height, trembling on limbs from which every vital essence of blood and bone and marrow had been drained, staring at the faces that seethed and swarmed below him, with dead glazed eyes, nauseous, and sick, and palsied, left only with something clear and small and shining at the bottom of his mind, one pure small note of conviction and belief at the bottom of this horrible sea-depth of phantasmagoric chaos, of desolation and fury. Then, in a voice that was remote, unreal, and hollow in his throat and ears, he would attempt to silence them, he would begin to speak to them, and one by one, each in his accustomed place he would see the dark, ugly, grinning faces in their seats below him and become aware of the pale sweatshop tailors sitting cross-legged on their tables in the buildings just across the street—buildings which the university was acquiring as class-rooms, year by year, and one by one, as the numberless thousands of these dark and brawling hordes, there by God knows what blind fantasticality of purpose, increased.

And then, faint and far, sunken below the furious glare and clamor of the city's life, fantastic and unreal at first in these machine shops of the brain, the old words, the undying words, the deathless bird-song in the city street returned, and he spoke to them again out of the lips of Herrick, Donne, and Shakespeare, of all the things that never change, of all the things that would abide forever.

"When to the sessions of sweet silent thought I summon up remembrance of things past—" Clang—a lang—a lang—a lang a lang! Hard and harsh with the violence of an unexpected blow, the bell that marked the ending of the period rang pat upon the last word of the sentence and as it died, all of his senses rudely shocked out of the potent enchantments of the music, he gave a violent start, as if he had been prodded from behind, stopped reading, and looked up quickly from his book with an angry and bewildered face. The class, which had tittered, now burst into a roar of laughter: even Mr. Abraham Jones from his accustomed seat on the third row to the right smiled, wearily, cruelly, and contemptuously behind the winking glitter of his glasses. Eugene lost his temper completely, lifted the heavy book above his head with both hands and banged it down upon the table. "Quiet!" he shouted, "I tell you to be quiet!" The command was unnecessary, for they had become instantly and craftily silent in response to his violent gesture, they stared at him meekly and dumbly, with a kind of stricken dullness, and already ashamed of his outburst he picked up the heavy book again, fumbled with trembling fingers for the poem, and said: "You can go after I've finished reading the poem: it won't take but a moment more!"

The class stirred restlessly, there was a little mutter of protest, Abe smiled bitterly, shaking his head with a slight sigh of weary indifference. He glanced up quickly and caught them in a series of sly communications: at the back of the room Sadie Feinberg, her fat neck half-turned to the right, was whispering out of the corner of her mouth to Miss Bessie Weisman; to the left Mr. Sidney Osherofsky was whispering rapidly and cynically behind his hand to Mr. Nathan Shulemovitch; and on the right-hand side of the room Mr. Sol Grebenschik was carrying on a guttural but animated conversation with Mr. Sam Vucker. Almost every one in the class of thirty people, in fact, was either engaged in conversation or preparing to engage in conversation. Only Abe Jones and Mr. Boris Gorewitz remained faithful. Mr. Boris Gorewitz always remained faithful. He sat on the front row close, very close, ah fragrantly, odorously close, too, too close to his teacher! He took notes. When beauty was revealed he smiled murkily, showing large white wet-looking teeth. When passion was indicated he looked stern and thoughtful: he was deeply stirred and polished his glasses. When some stupid question had been asked, or some opinion expressed with which he did not agree, he smiled contemptuously, shook his head violently from side to side, saying, "Nah, nah, nah, nah, nah!" quite loudly and thrust his short dirty fingers vigorously and impatiently through the dry crinkly mass of hair that rushed back sproutily from his bulbous forehead, while Abe turned and glanced at him angrily, bitterly, mockingly, turning his cruel grinning Yiddish face to Eugene with a soft "Oh-ho-ho-ho-ho!" of contemptuous laughter.

The class had now become so absorbed in its private conversations that it was not for a moment aware of its instructor nor of the fierce accusation of his glance. His face would grow dark and swollen with a rush of blood and passion, he would begin to tremble with rage, veins stood out on his forehead. Then in a very extraordinary way, through a sort of comical intuition, silence would come upon the class again: Mr. Osherofsky, who had turned in his seat and was talking behind his hand to Mr. Shulemovitch, gradually became aware that something was amiss from the expression of Mr. Shulemovitch's face, which altered so subtly that almost without changing a muscle, it indicated that it was no longer aware of Mr. Osherofsky, that it was not listening to him, that it did not know him, that it wished he would go away, and that it was absorbed in its own meditation. Abruptly Mr. Osherofsky ceased talking, his small bright eyes shifted around rapidly at Eugene, and immediately his gaze plunged intently into his book, while his face took on an expression of sly humility.

Meanwhile, Miss Feinberg, who was now so completely absorbed in her conversation with Miss Weisman that she had twisted around almost completely to the back, received a sharp warning prod and a meaningful frown from her companion, accompanied by a significant lifting of the eyebrows. Miss Feinberg at once flopped heavily around in her seat, her heavy face fixed upon Eugene in an expression of vacant and insolent meekness. A loose smile faintly touched the corners of her lax heavy mouth: her jaws ruminated slightly at a wad of gum. Mr. Gorewitz during this commotion had turned in his seat and swept the faces of his comrades with a glance full of scornful reproof. Now he hissed loudly at them: "Sh-h! Sh-h! Sh-h!" Then, as a heavy silence fell upon the room, he turned in his seat and looked up at Eugene with an expression of understanding and commiseration. He shook his head pityingly, with a scornful smile, as he thought of these souls living in darkness, and unwilling to admit the light! Then his own face darkened! Let them wallow in ignorance if they liked, but let them remember that other people were seeking for truth and beauty! Let them show some consideration for others! Then his gaze softened, a glow of tenderness suffused his oily features, as he gazed upon Eugene's infuriated face: he looked at him now with love, with reverence, with adoration, and with the sympathy of a kindred spirit! His eloquent glance said:—"The poet, the prophet, the seer such as you, has at every time in history been mocked and misunderstood by the philistine mob. Why should you suffer so, dear teacher? You are above them. They can never know you or appreciate you as I do. Despise them, beloved master. Cast not your pearls before swine."

OF TIME AND THE RIVER

This devoted and tender message had been lost, however, on his instructor: Eugene's face was set in a fixed glare of rage as he regarded his class. For a moment he was absolutely speechless.

"If any one thinks," he began at length in a voice that was small and choked with fury, "that I am here—" apparently some one did think so for at this moment, slowly, craftily, the knob of the door began to move, slowly the door swung open as if propelled by a ghostly hand. He paused again, and this time murder sweltered in his heart and was legible upon his face. Softly with the tread of a cat he stepped toward the door, and paused as if getting ready to spring, while it opened: the class waited tensely with held breath. Then, as slowly as the door had opened, a face was thrust in through the opening: it was the face of one of the hall guards, the face of an old man, a face of unutterable melancholy and of the most dismal sourness: the old dull face, with its dry sagging flesh, and its small watery eyes turned slowly on its scrawny neck, surveying Eugene, the class, and the four walls of the room in a glance full of dislike and suspicion. Then slowly and craftily, as it had come, as if it had been thrust forward on a stick by some unseen hand, the face withdrew, and the door swung to silently once again.

For a moment Eugene stared at the closing door with an expression of stupefaction. Then suddenly a surge of humor, powerful, choking, explosive, and tongueless in its unutterable and wordless implication, welled up in his throat. He cast the book from him with a roar of laughter in which the class joined.

"Get out of here," he shouted. "I'm through! That's enough. Go away! Leave me alone!"

XLVIII

THE Hotel Leopold, where he now lived, was situated on a short and grimy street about two blocks from the university, northward, in the direction of Union Square.

The Leopold, although one of the city's smaller hotels, was not a single building, but a congeries of buildings, which covered an entire block. The central, and main building of the system, was a structure of twelve stories, of that anomalous stone and brick construction which seems to have enjoyed a vogue in the early nineteen hundreds. To the left was a building twenty or thirty years older, known as "the old annex." It was eight stories high, of old red brick, and the street floor was occupied by shops and a restaurant. To the right was a building of six stories, which was known as "the new annex." This building, more simple in design than the others, was constructed of basal stone of the rough, porous, light-hued kind which was predominant in many of the new architectures throughout the nation. The building, neat, compact, and for the most part unadorned by useless ornament, somehow gave the effect of having been stamped out, with a million others of its kind, by a gigantic biscuit cutter of such buildings—and hence to speak, how or in what way it was hard to say, yet instantly apparent, the mechanic spirit of a "newer" or more "modern" scheme—the scheme of "the 'twenties," of 1922 or 1924.

It was hard to know why one found fault with the building, but somehow it left one without joy. In many obvious ways this would be apparent at once, not only to the architect, but to the layman—it was superior to its companion structures. Although not a building which combined simple grace with use—as the old colonial structures of New England do—it was at least a building lacking in the clumsy and meaningless adornment which disfigured the surface of its two companions. Moreover, the rough, porous-looking brick had a look of lean and homely integrity: it was hard to know why one disliked the building and yet one did—the other two, with all their confusing and unreasoning decoration, were the warmer, better, and more cheerful places.

What was it? It was almost impossible to define the quality of "the new annex" or its depressing effect upon the spectator, yet its quality was unmistakable. It belonged, somehow, to a new and accursed substance which had come into the structure of life—a substance barren, sterile, and inhuman—designed not for the use of man, but for the blind proliferations of the manswarm, to accommodate the greatest number in the smallest space—to shelter, house, turn out, take in, all the nameless, faceless, mindless manswarm atoms of the earth.

The transient population of the Leopold, comparatively, was small. The great tidal fluctuation of brief visitors—business men, salesmen, newly wedded couples on their honeymoons, people from small towns out for a spree or a week or two of bright-light gayety—which swarmed in unceasing movements in and out of the city, had scarcely touched the life of the Leopold. The hotel, set in a quarter of the city that was a little remote from the great business and pleasure districts, depended largely for its custom on the patronage of a "permanent" clientele. It was, in short, the kind of place often referred to as "a quiet family hotel"—a phrase which the management of the Leopold made use of in advertising the merits of their establishment, on the hotel stationery.

But that phrase, with its soothing connotations of a tranquil, felicitous and gentle domesticity, was misleading. For the Leopold was decidedly not "quiet" and although it contained within its cell-like rooms almost every other kind of life, of "family life" there was almost none and what there was, so desolate and barren, that one felt himself to be looking at the museum relics of what had once been a family rather than at the living and organic reality. And because of this, one felt constantly about the Leopold the spirit of defeat—either of lives still searching, restless and unfound, or of lives which, in the worst sense of the word, had fallen upon evil days.

And curiously, in spite of the hotel's pious assurance of its "quiet family life," its boast of permanency, there hovered about the place continually, indefinably but certainly, a feeling of naked insecurity, a terrifying transiency—not the frank transiency of the great tourist hotels with their constant daily flux of changing faces—but the horrible transiency of lives held here for a period in the illusion of a brief and barren permanence, of lives either on the wing or on the wane.

Here, for example, among the three or four hundred beings who inhabited the motley structure of these conjoined walls, were a number of young people who had only recently come from smaller places and were still stunned and bewildered by the terrific impact of the city upon their lives, or who, after a year or two of such bewilderment, were just beginning to orient themselves, to adjust their lives to the city's furious tempo, and to look around with a bolder and more knowing calculation for some kind of residence a little closer to their true desires.

To young people of this sort, the Leopold had offered, when they first came to the city, its spurious promise of warm asylum. Many of them had landed here—or rather popped in here like frightened rabbits—after their first terrified immersion in the manswarm fury of the city's life, and the feeling of desolation, houseless naked loneliness, bewilderment, and scrambling, scuttling terror which the sudden impact of that ruthless, sudden revelation had aroused in them.

For this reason, those barren walls, those terrible, hive-like cells of the Hotel Leopold were not without a glory of their own. For in those cell-like rooms there could be held all of the hope, hunger, passion, bitter loneliness and earth-devouring fury that a room could hold, or that this world can know, or that this little racked and riven vessel of desire, this twisted tenement of man's bitter brevity, can endure.

Here, in these desolate walls, on many a night long past and desperately accomplished, many a young man had paced the confines of his little cell like a maddened animal, had beat his knuckles bloody on the stamped-out walls, had lashed about him, a creature baffled and infuriated by the million illusions of warmth, love, security and joy which the terrific city offered him and which, tantalus-like, slipped from his fingers like a fume of painted smoke the instant that he tried to get his grasp upon it.

Again, if the Hotel Leopold had housed all of the hope, joy, fury, passion, anguish, and devouring hunger that the earth can know, and that the wild and bitter tenement of youth can hold, it also housed within its walls all of the barren and hopeless bitterness of a desolate old age. For here—unloved, friendless, and unwanted, shunted off into the dreary asylum of hotel life—there lived many old people who hated life, and yet who were afraid to die.

Most of them were old people with a pension, or a small income, which was just meagrely sufficient to their slender needs. Some of them, widowed, withered, childless, and alone were drearily wearing out the end of their lives here in a barren solitude. Some had sons and daughters, married, living in the city, who came dutifully to stamp the dreary tedium of waning Sunday afternoons with the stale counterfeits of filial devotion.

The rest of the time the old people stayed in their rooms and washed their stockings out and did embroidery, or descended to the little restaurant to eat, or sat together in one corner of the white-tiled lobby and talked.

Why could they never make it come to life? Why was no great vine growing from the hearts of all these old and dying people? Why were their flesh, their sagging, pouch-like jowls and faces, so dry, dead, and juiceless, their weary old eyes so dull and lustreless, their tones so nasal, tedious and metallic? Why was it that they seemed never to have known any of the pain, joy, passion, evil, glory of a dark and living past? Why was it that their lives, on which now the strange dark radiance of million-visaged time was shining, seemed to have gained neither wisdom, mystery nor passion from the great accumulation of the buried past —to have been composed, in fact, of an infinite procession of dreary moments and little mean adventures, each forgotten, lost, and buried, as day by day the gray sand of their lives ran out its numberless grains of barren tedium.

This, indeed, seemed to be the truth about them: as they sat together in one corner of the lobby talking, all their conversation seemed made up of dreary dialogs such as these:

"How do you do, Mrs. Grey? I didn't see you in the restaurant to-night."

"No—" the old woman spoke triumphantly, proudly conscious of a sensational adventure—"I ate out tonight at a new place that my son-in-law told me about!—Oh! I had the most *dee*-licious meal—a *won*-derful meal—all any one could eat and only sixty cents. First I had a dish of nice fruit salad—and then I had a bowl of soup—oh-h! *dee*-licious soup, Mrs. Martin—it was vegetable soup, but oh-h! *dee*-licious!—a whole meal in itself—and then—" with a ruminant satisfaction she continued her arid catalogue— "I had some nice lamb chops, and some *dee*-licious green peas—and a nice baked potato—and some salad—and some rolls and butter—and then I had a nice cup of coffee—and a piece of apple pie—oh-h! the apple pie was simply *dee*-licious, Mrs. Martin, I had——"

"I'd think you'd be getting hungry by that time," said another of the group, an old man, who was their humorist, with a wink around him at the others. They all laughed appreciatively, and he continued: "You're sure you didn't miss anything as you went along—" he winked again and they all laughed dryly, with appreciation.

"No, sir!"—firmly, positively, with an emphatic nod of the head—"I ate every bite of it, Doctor Withers—oh-h it was so *dee*-licious, I just couldn't bear to see *anything* go to waste—only," regretfully, "I did have to leave my apple pie—I couldn't finish it——"

"What!" the humorist exclaimed in mock astonishment. "You mean you left something behind! Why you hardly ate enough to feed an elephant! You'll be getting all run down if you starve yourself this way!"—and the jester winked again, and the old women of his audience cackled aridly with appreciative laughter.

"—Well, I know," the glutton said regretfully, "I just hated to see that good apple pie go to waste—oh-h! I wish you could have tasted it, Mrs. Martin,—it was simply *dee*-licious— 'What's the matter?' the girl says to me—the waitress, you know— 'Don't you like your pie?—I'll go get you something else if you don't like it.'—Oh! yes—" with sudden recollection —"oh, yes! she says to me, 'How'd you like some ice cream?—You can have ice cream instead of pie,' she says, 'if you'd rather have it'— 'Oh-h!' I said,"—spoken with a kind of gasp, the withered old hand upon the meagre stomach— " 'Oh-h!' I says, 'I couldn't!'—She had to laugh, you know, I guess the way I said it. 'Well, you got enough?' she said. 'Oh-h!' I said,"—again the faint protesting gasp, "'if I ate another mouthful, I'd pop open! Oh-h!'—Well, it made her laugh, you know, the way I said it—'I'd *pop* open!' I said 'I *couldn't* eat another mouthful!'—'Well, just so long as you got enough!' she says. 'We like to see every one get enough. We want you to be satisfied,' she said. 'Oh-h!' I said," the faint protesting gasp again, "'not another *mouthful,* my dear! I *couldn't!*'—But, oh-h! Mrs. Martin, if you could have seen that apple pie! It was *dee*-licious! I was sorry to see it go to waste!"

"Well," said Mrs. Martin, rather tartly, obviously a little envious of the other's rich adventure— "we had a good meal here at the hotel, too. We had some celery and olives to start off with and then we had some good pea soup and after that we had roast beef and mashed potatoes— wasn't the roast beef we had tonight delicious, Doctor Withers?" she demanded of this arbiter of taste.

"Well," he said, smacking his dry lips together drolly, "the only complaint I had to make was that they didn't bring me the whole cow. I had to ask George for a second helping. . . . Yes, sir, if I never fare any worse than that I'll have no kick—it was a very good piece of beef— well-cooked, tender, very tasty," he said with a dry, scientific precision, and again he smacked his leathery lips together with an air of relish.

"—Well, I thought so, too," said Mrs. Martin, nodding her head with satisfaction at this sign of his agreement "—I thought it was delicious— and then," she went on reflectively, "we had a nice lettuce and tomato salad, some biscuit tortoni and, of course," she concluded elegantly, "the demy-tassy."

"Well, I didn't have any of the demy-tassy," said Doctor Withers, the droll wit. "None of your demy-tassy for me! No, sir! I had *coffee*—two big cups of it, too," he went on with satisfaction. "If I'm going to poison myself I'm going to do a good job of it—none of your little demy-tassys for me!"

And the old women cackled aridly their dry appreciation of his wit.

"—Good evening, Mrs. Buckles," Doctor Withers continued, getting up and bowing gallantly to a heavily built, arthritic-looking old woman who now approached the group with a stiff and gouty movement. "We missed you tonight. Did you eat in the restaurant?"

"No," she panted in a wheezing tone, as, with a painful grunt, she lowered her heavily corseted bulk into the chair he offered her. "I didn't go down—I didn't have much appetite and I didn't want to risk it. I had them bring me something in my room—some tea and toast and a little marmalade . . . I didn't intend to come down at all," she went on in a discontented tone, "but I got tired of staying up there all alone and I thought I'd just as well—I'd be just as well off down here as I'd be up in my room," she concluded morosely.

"And how *is* your cold today, Mrs. Buckles?" one of the old women now asked with a kind of lifeless sympathy. "—Do you feel better?"

"—Oh," the old woman said morosely, uncertainly, "I suppose so. . . . I think so. . . . Yes, I think it's a little better. . . . Last night I was afraid it was getting down into my chest but today it feels better— seems to be more in my head and throat— But I don't know," she muttered in a sullen and embittered tone, "it's that room they've given me. I'll always have it as long as I've got to live there in that room. I'll never get any better till I get my old room back."

"Did you do what I told you to do?" asked Doctor Withers. "Did you go and dose yourself the way I told you?"

"—No—well," she said indefinitely, "I've been drinking lots of water and trying a remedy a friend of mine down at the Hotel Gridly told me about—it's a new thing called Inhalo, all you got to do is put it up your nose and breathe it in—she said it did her more good than anything she'd ever tried."

"I never heard of it," said Doctor Withers sourly. "Whatever it is, it won't cure your cold. No, sir!" He shook his head grimly. "Now, I didn't practice medicine for forty years without finding out *something* about colds! Now I don't care anything about your Inhalos or Breathos or Spray-Your-Throatos, or whatever they may call 'em—any of these new-fangled remedies. The only way to get rid of a cold is to have a thorough cleaning-out, and the only way to get a thorough cleaning-out is to dose yourself with castor oil, the way I told you, too.—Now you can do as you please," he said sourly, with a constricted pressure of his thin convex mouth, "it's no business of mine what you do—if you want to run the risk of coming down with pneumonia it's your own affair— but if you want to get over that cold you'll take my advice."

"Well," the old woman muttered in her tone of sullen discontent. "—It's that room I'm in. That's the trouble. I've hated that room ever since they put me in there. I know if I could get my old room back I'd be all right again."

"Then why don't you ask Mr. Betts to give it back to you?" said Mrs.

Martin. "I'm sure if you went to him and told him that you wanted it, he'd let you have it."

"No, he wouldn't!" said Mrs. Buckles bitterly. "I've been to him—I've asked him. He paid no attention to me—tried to tell me I was better off where I was, that it was a better room, a better bargain!—Here I've been living at this place for eight years now, but do you think they show me any consideration? No," she cried bitterly, "they're all alike nowadays—out for everything they can get—it's grab, grab, grab—and they don't care who you are or how long they've known you—if they can get five cents more from some one else, why, out you go! . . . When I came back here from Florida last spring I found my old room taken. . . . I went to Mr. Betts a dozen times and asked to have it back and he always put me off—told me there were some people in there who were leaving soon and I could have it just as soon as they moved out. . . . That was all a put-up job," she said resentfully. "He didn't mean a word of it. I see now that he never had any intention of giving me my old room. . . . No! They've just found that they can get a dollar or two more a week for it from these fly-by-nights than I could afford to pay—and so, of course, I'm the one that gets turned out!" she said. "That's the way it goes nowadays!"

"Well," said Mrs. Martin a trifle acidly, "I'm sure if you went to Mr. Betts in the right way you could get your old room back. He's always done everything I ever asked him to do for *me*. But, of course," she said pointedly, "you've got to approach him in the right way."

"Oh-h!" said old Mrs. Grey rapturously, "I think Mr. Betts is the *nicest* manager they've ever had here—so pleasant, so good-*natured, so willing* to oblige! Now that other man they had here before he came—what was his name?" she said impatiently. "—Mason, or Watson, or Clarkson—something like that——"

"Wilson," said Doctor Withers.

"—Oh, yes—Wilson!" said Mrs. Grey. "That's it—Wilson! I never liked him at *all*," she said with an accent of scornful depreciation. "You could *never* get anything out of Wilson. He never did anything you wanted him to do. But Mr. *Betts!*—oh-h! I think Mr. Betts is a lovely manager!"

"Well, I haven't found him so," said Mrs. Buckles grimly. "I liked Wilson better."

"Oh, I don't agree with you, Mrs. Buckles," Mrs. Gray said with a stony and somewhat hostile emphasis. "I don't ag-*gree* with you at *all!* I think there's no *comparison!* I like Mr. Betts *so* much better than I like Wilson!"

"Well, I like Wilson better," said Mrs. Buckles grimly, and for a moment the two old women glared at each other with bitter hostile eyes.

"—Well," Doctor Withers broke the silence quickly in a diplomatic effort to avert an impending clash, "—what are your plans for the winter, Mrs. Buckles? What have you decided to do? Are you going to Florida again this winter?"

"I don't know what I'll do," old Mrs. Buckles answered in a tone of sullen dejection. "I haven't decided yet. . . . I had planned to go down to Daytona Beach with Mrs. Wheelwright—that's my friend at the Hotel Gridly—she had a daughter living in Daytona, and we had planned to spend the winter there in order to be near them. But now that's all fallen through," she said dejectedly. "Here, at the last moment, when all my plans were made, she decided not to go—says she likes it at the Gridly and it will be cheaper to stay on there than to make a trip to Florida and back. . . . That's the trouble with people nowadays," she said bitterly, "you can't depend on them. They never mean anything they say!" And she lapsed again into a sullen and dejected silence.

"Why aren't you going to St. Petersburg?" said Mrs. Martin curiously after a brief pause. "I thought that's where you always spent the winter."

"It was," said Mrs. Buckles, "until last winter. But I'll never go back there again. It's not the same place any more. I've been going to the same hotel down there for more than twenty years—it used to be a lovely place—when I went back there last winter I found the whole place changed. They had ruined it," she bitterly concluded.

"How was that?" said Doctor Withers curiously. "What had they done to it?"

Mrs. Buckles looked around cautiously and craftily to make sure that in this sinister melting-pot of a million listening ears, she would not be overheard, and then, bending forward painfully, with one old arthritic hand held up beside her mouth, she muttered confidingly to her listeners:

"—I'll tell you what it is. It's the *Jews!* They get in everywhere," she whispered ominously. "They ruin *everything!* When I got down there last winter the whole place was over-run with Jews! They had ruined the place!" she hissed. "The place was *ruined!*"

At this moment, another old woman joined the group. She advanced slowly, leaning on a cane, smiling, and with a movement of spacious benevolence. Everything about this old woman—her big frame, slow movement, broad and tranquil brow, silvery hair parted in the middle, and her sonorous and measured speech, which came deliberately from her mouth in the periods of a cadenced rhetoric, had an imposing and majestical quality. As she approached, every one greeted her eagerly, and with obvious respect, Doctor Withers got up quickly and bent before her with almost obsequious courtesy, she was herself addressed by every one as "Doctor," and her position among them seemed to be one of · secure and tranquil authority.

This old woman was known to every one in the hotel as Doctor Thornton. She had been one of the first woman physicians in the country and a few years before, after a long and, presumably, successful practice, she had retired to spend the remaining years of her life in the peaceful haven of the Leopold, and to bestow on man, God, nature and the whole universe around her the cadenced and benevolent reflections of her measured rhetoric. She became, by virtue of this tranquil and majestic authority that emanated from her, the centre of every group, young and old, that she approached. She was known to every one in the hotel, every one referred to her as "a wonderful old woman," spoke of her brilliant mind, her ripe philosophy, and her "beautiful English."

The respect and veneration in which she was held was now instantly apparent as, with a benevolent smile, she slowly approached this company of old people. They greeted her with an eager and excited scraping of chairs, the welcoming tumult of several old voices, speaking eagerly at once: Doctor Withers himself scrambled to his feet, pushed a large chair into the circle and stood by gallantly as, with a slow and stately movement, she settled her large figure into it, and for a moment looked about her over the top of her cane with a tranquil, smiling and benevolent expression.

"*Well*, Doctor!" said Mrs. Grey, almost breathlessly. "Where have you been keeping yourself all day long? We've *missed* you."

The others murmured agreement to this utterance, and then leaned forward with eager attentiveness so as not to miss any of the gems of wisdom which would fall from this great woman's lips.

For a moment Doctor Thornton regarded her interlocutor with an expression of tolerant and almost playful benevolence. Presently she spoke:

"What have *I* been doing all day long?" she repeated in a tone of sonorous deliberation. "Why, my dear, I have been *reading*—reading," she pursued with rhythmical sonority, "in one of my favorite and most cherished volumes."

And instantly there was for all her listeners a sense of some transforming radiance in the universe: an event of universal moment: the Doctor had been reading all day long. They looked at her with an awed stare.

"What," Mrs. Martin nervously began, with a little giggle, "—what was it you were reading, Doctor? It must have been a good book to hold your interest all day long?"

"It was, my dear," said Doctor Thornton sonorously and deliberately. "It *was* a good book. More than that, it was a *great* book—a magnificent work of genius to show us to what heights the mind of man may soar when he is inspired by lofty and ennobling sentiments."

"What was this, Doctor Thornton?" Doctor Withers now inquired. "—Something of Tennyson's?"

"No, Doctor Withers," Doctor Thornton answered sonorously, "it was not Tennyson—much as I admire the noble beauty of his poetry. I was not reading poetry, Doctor Withers," she continued, "I was reading —*prose*," she said. "I was reading—*Ruskin!*" As these momentous words fell from her lips, her voice lowered with such an air of portentous significance that the last word was not so much spoken as breathed forth like an incense of devotion. "*Ruskin!*" she whispered solemnly again.

And although it is doubtful if this name conveyed any definite meaning to her audience, its magical effect upon them was evident from the looks of solemn awe with which they now regarded her.

"—*Ruskin!*" she said again, this time strongly, in an accent of rapturous sonority. "The noble elevation of his thought, the beautiful proportion and the ordered harmony of all the parts, the rich yet simple style, and above all, the sane and wholesome beauty of his philosophy of art—what nobler monument to man's higher genius was ever built, my friends, than he proportioned in *The Stones of Venice*— itself a work of art entirely worthy of the majestic sculptures that it consecrates?"

For a moment after the sonorous periods of that swelling rhetoric had ceased, the old people stared at her with a kind of paralysis of reverent wonder. Then old Mrs. Grey, gasping with a kind of awed astonishment, said:

"Oh-h, Doctor Thornton, I think it's the most *wonderful* thing the

way you keep your mind occupied all the time with all these deep and
beautiful thoughts you have! I don't see how you do it! I should think
you'd get yourself all tired out just by all the *thinking* that you do."

"Tired, my dear?" said Doctor Thornton sonorously, bestowing upon
her worshipper a smile of tolerant benevolence. "How can any one
grow tired who *lives* and *moves* and *breathes* in this great world of
ours? No, no, my dear, do not say *tired*. Rather say *refreshed, rejuve-
nated,* and *inspired* by the glorious pageant that life offers us in its unending beauty and profusion. Wherever I look," she continued, looking, "I see nothing but order and harmony in the universe. I lift my
eyes unto the stars," she said majestically, at the same time lifting her
face in a movement of rapturous contemplation toward the ceiling of
the hotel lobby, "and feast my soul upon the infinite beauties of God's
heaven, the glorious proportion of the sidereal universe. I turn my gaze
around me, and everywhere I look I see the noble works that man has
fashioned, the unceasing progress he has made in his march upward
from the brute, the noble aspiration of his spirit, the eternal labor of his
mighty intellect towards a higher purpose, the radiant beauty of his
countenance in which all the highest ardors of his soul may be discerned!"

And as she pronounced this sonorous eulogy her glance rested benevolently on old Doctor Withers' soured and wizened features. He lowered his head coyly, as becomes a modest man, and in a moment the
rhapsodist continued:

"'What a piece of work is man! How noble in reason! How infinite
in faculty! In form, in moving, how express and admirable! In action,
how like an angel! In apprehension, how like a God!'"

And having sonorously pronounced Hamlet's mighty judgment, the
wonderful old woman, who had herself for thirty years been one of the
most prosperous abortionists in the nation, looked benevolently about
her at all the specimens of God's choice article who were assembled in
the lobby.

Over behind the cigar counter, the vender, a fat Czechish youth with
a pale flabby face and dull taffy-colored hair, was industriously engaged
in picking his fat nose with a greasy thumb and forefinger. Elsewhere,
in another corner of the lobby, three permanent denizens of the Leopold,
familiarly and privately known to members of the hotel staff as Crab-
face Willy, Maggie the Dope, and Greasy Gerty, were sitting where they
always sat, in an unspeaking and unsmiling silence.

And at this moment, two more wonder-works of God came in from the street and walked rapidly across the lobby, speaking the golden and poetic language which their Maker had so marvellously bestowed on them:

"Cheezus!" said one of them, a large man with a gray hat and a huge, dead, massive face of tallowy gray which receded in an indecipherable manner into the sagging flesh-folds of his flabby neck— "Cheezus!" he eloquently continued with a protesting laugh that emerged from his tallowy lips in a hoarse expletive mixed with spittle— "Yuh may be right about him, Eddie, but Cheezus!"—again the hoarse protesting laugh. "Duh guy may be all right but Cheezus!—I don't know! If he'd come in dere like duh rest of dem an' let me know about it—but Cheezus!— duh guy may be all right like you say!—but Cheezus! Eddie, I don't know!"

Doctor Thornton bestowed on them the benevolent approval of her glance as they went by and then, turning to her awed listeners again, declared sonorously with a majestic and expressive gesture of her hand:

"Tired? How could one ever grow tired, my friends, in this great world of ours?"

XLIX

At the end of his classes, the final end, when all had spoken, when that hot wave of life and turbulence had withdrawn, the last clattering foot-falls had echoed away along the corridors, the last loud aggressive voices had faded into silence, leaving, it seemed, an odor of exhaustion, use, and weariness even in the walls, boards and benches of the room, so that the empty classroom had a tired but living presence of fatigue, the indefinable but sharply felt character of a room with people absent from it, and seemed somehow to relax, settle, and respire with relief and weariness— at this final, fagged, and burned-out candle-end of day, Abraham Jones, as relentless as destiny, would be there waiting for Eugene. He waited there, grim, gray, unsmiling, tortured-looking behind an ominous wink of glasses, a picture of Yiddish melancholy and discontent, and as Eugene looked at him his heart went numb and dead; he hated the sight of him. He sat there now in the front rows of the class like a nemesis of scorn, a merciless censor of Eugene's ignorance and incompetence: the sight of his dreary discontented face, with its vast gray acreage of a painful Jewish and involuted intellectualism, was enough, even at the crest of a passionate burst of inspiration, to curdle his blood, freeze his heart, stun and deaden the fiery particle of his brain, and thicken his tongue to a faltering, incoherent mumble. Eugene did not know what Abe wanted, what he expected, what kind of teaching he thought worthy of him: he only knew that nothing he did suited him, that the story of his inadequacy and incompetence was legible in every line of that gray, dreary, censorious face. He thought of it at night with a kind of horror: the ghoulish head which craned out of a vulture's body swept after him through all the fields of a distressful sleep, a taloned fury filled with croakings of hoarse doom. Never before had Eugene been driven through desperation to such exhausting intensities of work: night by night he sweated blood over great stacks and sheaves of their dull, careless, trivial papers—he read, re-read, and triple-read them, putting in all commas, colons, periods, correcting all faults of spelling, grammar, punctuation that he knew, writing long, laborious comments and criticisms on the back and rising suddenly out of a haunted tortured sleep to change a grade. And at the end, the inexorable end, he was always faced with the menace of Abe's weekly paper: with dread and quaking he tackled it. He wrote the best papers that Eugene got: the grammar was flawless, the spelling impeccable, the vocabulary precise and extensive, the sentences cleanly and forcibly shaped. The thought was sound, subtle, and coherent—by every standard the work was of an extraordinary grade and quality, its merit was unmistakable, and yet Eugene approached a four-page paper with fear and trembling, before he had gone beyond the first paragraph great sobs and groans of weariness and despair were wrung from him, he stamped across the floor with it like a man maddened by an aching tooth; he began again, he flung himself upon the bed, got up and walked again, doused his head in basins of cold water—but it was no use: to read the paper to the end, as he did and must, was weariness and travail of the spirit—it was like eating chalk or trying to suck sweetness out of paving brick, or being drowned in an ocean of dishwater, or forced to gorge oneself on boiled unseasoned spinach. Abe wrote on a great range and variety of subjects and everything he wrote was good: he wrote about the plays of Pirandello, of "Six Characters in Search of an Author," and of "three planes of reality" therein: he estimated and analyzed those three planes with the power of a philosopher, the delicacy of a subtle-souled psychologist, and all of this to Eugene was as weeping and wailing and gnashing of teeth, because it was so good, and he did not know what was wrong, and he could not endure to read it. He could not write upon his papers that he found them intolerably dull unless he knew wherein the reason for that dullness lay, and he did not know the reason: accordingly the highest grade he ever gave to any one—the grade of "A"—was week by week wrung from trembling and reluctant fingers. But no matter what the grade was, or how flattering the comment, Abe protested. Gray, dreary, tortured, discontented, Yiddish, he would be waiting for Eugene at the end of every class, clutching his paper in his impatient fingers, armed and eager for the combat of dispute that was to follow.

The class met at night and they would walk rapidly away together along the empty echoing corridors, and turning clatter down the stairs that led to the main entrance. The vast building was deserted and full of weary echoes: they could hear the solitary clang of an elevator door, and the dynamic hum of its machinery as it mounted. Some one was walking in the big corridor downstairs: they heard the echoing ring of his footsteps on the slick marble flags, and the noisy rattle of a cleaner's bucket on the floor. The whole building was charged with a weary electric quality—with the quality of a light which has gone dim. And the taste and the smell of this weariness was in Eugene's mouth and nostrils; it was as if he had stuck his tongue against a warm but burned-out storage battery; it was like the smell that comes from the wheels of a street car when they have ground around a curve, or like the odor from a smoking hot-box on the fast express. His body also had this feeling of electric weariness, as if the vital currents were exhausted: his flesh felt dry and juiceless, his back was tired, his loins were sterile, the acrid burned-out flavor filled him.

The big ugly building breathed slowly with the fatigue of inanimate objects which have been overcharged with human energy: it was haunted with its tired emptiness, with the absence of the thousands of people who had swarmed through its every part that day with such a clamorous, hot and noisy life. The lifeless air in its passages had been breathed and rebreathed again and again: the walls, the furniture, the floors—every part of the building—seemed to exude this sense of nervous depletion.

As he hurried down the stairs on such an evening with his unshakable companion, his implacable disputant, he hated the building more than he had ever hated any building before: it seemed to be soaked in all the memories of fruitless labor and harsh strife, of fear and hate and weariness, of ragged nerves and pounding heart and tired flesh: the building brooded there, charged with its dreadful burden of human pain, encumbered with its grief; and his hatred for the building was the hatred of a man for the place where he has met some terrible humiliation of the flesh or spirit, or for the room in which a man has seen his brother die, or for the dwelling from which love and the beloved have departed. The ghosts of pain and darkness sat in the empty chairs, the spirits of venom and sterility brooded over the desks: dry hatred and the poison of the brain were seated in the chairs of the instructors; fear trembled in their seats, it made a hateful cold around the heart, it made the bowels queasy, it made swallowing hard, it slithered at the edges of the desk, it fell and crawled and wobbled like a boneless thing. And the gray-faced Jew beside Eugene made the weary lights burn dim: he gave a tongue to weariness, a color to despair.

They hurried down the steps and left the building almost as if they were in flight. The heavy door clanged to behind them making echoes in the halls, they reached the pavement of the Square, and immediately they halted. Here, they were in another world, and their weary bodies drank in a new vitality. Sometimes, on a cold still night in winter, the sky had the peculiarly frosty clarity that comes from a still, biting cold. Above the great vertical radiance and cold Northern passion of New York, it was a-glitter with magnificent stars, it was a-glitter with small pollens, with a jewelled dust of stars that seemed to have been sown drunkenly through heaven, and as Eugene looked his weariness was cleansed out of him at once, he was filled with an overwhelming desire to possess beauty and all things else, and to include all things in him. He would learn to be all things: he would be an artist and he would find a way of living in the maelstrom. The darkness filled him with a sense of power and possession: his spirit soared out over the city, and over the earth, he was no longer afraid of the gray-faced Jew beside him, peace and power and certitude possessed him. He drank the air into his veins in great gulps, he saw the huge walled cliff of the city ablaze with its jewelry of hard sown lights, he knew he could possess it all, and a feeling of joy and victory rushed through his senses.

Under the furious goad of desperation, a fear of failure and disgrace, a sense of loneliness and desolation, and a grim determination to go down into the dust of ruin only when he could no longer lift a hand or draw a breath, he learned his job, and found his life again, he did the labor of a titan, the flesh wasted from his bones, he became a mad, driven zealot, but he was a good teacher, and the day came when he knew he need no longer draw his breath in fear or shame, that he had paid his way and earned his wage and could meet them eye to eye. He took those swarthy swarming classes and looted his life clean for them: he bent over them, prayed, sweated, and exhorted like a prophet, a poet, and a priest—he poured upon them the whole deposit of his living, feeling, reading, the whole store of poetry, passion and belief: he went into the brain of a dullard like a surgeon, and he blew some spark of fire into a glow in even the least and worst of them, but that gray-faced Yiddish inquisitor hung doggedly to his heels, the more he gave, the more Abe wanted; he fed on Eugene's life, enriching his grayness with an insatiate and vampiric gluttony, and yet he never had a word of praise, a sentence of thanks, a syllable of commendation.

Instead he became daily more open in his surly discontent, his sour depreciation; his insolence, unchecked, grew by leaps and bounds, he exulted in a feeling of cruel crowing Jewish mastery over Eugene's bent aching spirit, he walked away with him day by day and his conversation now was one long surly indictment of his class, his teaching, and his competence. Why didn't Eugene give them better topics for their themes? Why didn't they use another volume of essays instead of the one they had, which was no good? Why, in the list of poems, plays, biographies and novels which Eugene had assigned, and which were no good, had he omitted the names of Jewish writers such as Lewisohn and Sholem Asch? Why did he not give each student private "conferences" more frequently, although he had conferred with them until his brain and heart were sick and weary. Why did they not write more expository, fewer descriptive themes; more argument, less narration? Why, in short, did he not do everything in a different way?—the indictment, merciless, insistent, unrelenting, piled up day by day and meanwhile resentment, anger, resolution began to blaze and burn in Eugene, a conviction grew that this could no longer be endured, that no life, no wage, no position was worth this thankless toil and trouble, and that he must make an end of a situation which had become intolerable.

One night, when Abe had accompanied Eugene from the class to the entrance of the hotel, and as he was in the full course and tide of his surly complaint, Eugene stopped him suddenly and curtly, saying: "You don't like my class, do you, Jones? You don't think much of the way I teach, do you?"

Abe was surprised at the question, because his complaint had always had a kind of sour impersonality: it had never wholly dared a final accusatory directness.

"Well," he said in a moment, with a surly and unwilling tone, "I never said that. I don't think we're getting as much out of the class as we should. I think we could get a lot more out of it than we're getting. That's all I said."

"And you have a few thousand suggestions to make, that would improve it? Is that it?"

"Well, I had to tell you how I felt about it," Abe said doggedly. "If you don't like it, I'm sorry. You know we fellows down there have got to pay tuition. And they charge you plenty for it, too! . . . Don't let them kid you!" he said with a derisive and scornful laugh. "That place is a gold mine for some one! The trustees are getting rich on it!"

"Well, I'm not getting rich on it," Eugene said. "I get $150 a month out of it. Apparently you think it's too much."

"Well, we've got a right to expect the best we can get," he said. "That's what we're there for. That's what we're paying out our dough for. You know, the fellows down there are not rich guys like the fellows at Yale and Harvard. A dollar means something to them. . . . We don't get everything handed to us on a silver platter. Most of us have got to work for everything we get, and if some guy who's teaching us is not giving us the best he's got we got a right to kick about it. . . . That's the way I feel about it."

"All right," Eugene said, "I know where you stand now. Now, I'll tell you where I stand. I've been giving you the best I've got, but you don't think it's good enough. Well, it's all I've got and it's all you're going to get from me. Now, I tell you what you're going to do, Jones. You're going out of my class. Do you understand?" he shouted. "You're going now. I never want to see you in my class again. I'll get you transferred, I'll have you put in some other instructor's class, but you'll never come into my room again."

"You can't do that," Abe said. "You've got no right to do that. You've got no right to change a fellow to another class in the middle of the term. I've done my work," he said resentfully, "you're not going to change me. . . . I'll take it to the faculty committee if you do."

Eugene could stand no more: in misery and despair he thought of all he had endured because of Abe, and the whole choking wave of resentment and fury which had been gathering in his heart for months burst out upon him.

"Why, damn you!" he said. "Go to the faculty committee or any other damned place you please, but you'll never come back to any room where

I'm teaching again. If they send you back, if they say I've got to have you in my class, I quit. Do you hear me, Jones?" he shouted. "I'll not have you! If they try to force me, I'm through! To hell with such a life! I'll get down and clean out sewers before I have you in my class again. . . . Now, you damned rascal," his voice had grown so hoarse and thick he could hardly speak, and the blind motes were swimming drunkenly before him. ". . . I've had all I can stand from you. . . . Why, you damned dull fellow. . . . Sitting there and sneering at me day after day with your damned Jew's face. . . . What are you but a damned dull fellow, anyway? . . . Why, damn you, Jones, you didn't deserve any one like me. . . . You should get down on your knees and thank God you had a teacher half as good as me. . . . You . . . damned . . . *fellow*. . . . You! . . . To think I sweat blood over you! . . . Now, get away from here!" . . . he yelled. "To hell with you! . . . I never want to see your face again!"

He turned and started toward the hotel entrance: he felt blind and weak and dizzy, but he did not care what happened now: after all these weeks of heavy misery a great wave of release and freedom was coursing through his veins. Before he had gone three steps Abe Jones was at his side, clutching at his sleeve, beseeching, begging, pleading: "Say! . . . You've got the wrong idea! Honest you have! . . . Say! I never knew you felt like that! Don't send me out of there," he begged earnestly, and suddenly Eugene saw that his shining glasses had grown misty and that his dull weak eyes blinked with tears. "I don't want to leave your class," he said. "Why, that's the best class that I've got! . . . Honest it is! No kiddin'! . . . All the fellows feel the same way about it."

He begged, beseeched, and almost wept: finally, when good will had again been restored between them, he wrung Eugene's hand, laughed painfully and shyly, and then took off his misted glasses and began to shine and polish them with a handkerchief. His gray ugly face as he stood there polishing his glasses had that curiously naked, inept, faded and tired wistful look that is common to people with weak eyes when they remove their spectacles; it was a good and ugly face, and suddenly Eugene began to like Abe very much. He left him and went up to his room with a feeling of such relief, ease and happiness as he had not known for months; and that night, unhaunted, unashamed, unpursued by fears and furies and visions of his ruin and failure for the first time in many months, he sank dreamlessly, sweetly, deliciously, into the depths of a profound and soundless sleep.

And from that moment, through every change of fortune, all absence, all return, all wandering, and through the whole progress of his city life, through every event of triumph, ruin, or madness, this Jew, Abe Jones, the first manswarm atom he had come to know in all the desolation of the million-footed city—had been his loyal friend.

It was not the golden city he had visioned as a child, and the gray reptilian face of that beak-nosed Jew did not belong among the company of the handsome, beautiful and fortunate people that he had dreamed about, but Abe was made of better stuff than most dreams are made of. His spirit was as steady as a rock, as enduring as the earth, and like the flash of a light, the sight of his good, gray ugly face could always evoke for Eugene the whole wrought fabric of his life in the city, the whole design of wandering and return, with a thousand memories of youth and hunger, of loneliness, fear, despair, of glory, love, exultancy and joy.

L

ROBERT WEAVER appeared suddenly one night about seven o'clock as Eugene was sitting in the lobby at the Leopold: he had not seen Robert since their arrest. His visit to the hotel was the result of a sudden impulse on Robert's part: immediately, without greeting or any preliminary whatever, he began to ask all sorts of questions about the Leopold —How long had Eugene been there? Did he have a good room and how big was it? How well did he like living at the hotel? Then he insisted that Eugene show him his room. Eugene got his key at the desk and took him up: at the sight of the small room with its piles of books and stacks of student themes Robert burst out laughing. Then he began to ask all manners of questions in a serious and earnest tone— Where was the bathroom?— Eugene showed him— Did they give him plenty of towels?— Eugene told him— How much did he pay?— Eugene said the rent was twelve dollars a week.

He received these answers with an air of astounded surprise, his manner became even more earnest and excited, he began to say, "You don't mean it!" "Well, I'll be damned!" "Well, what do you know about that?"—as if the most astonishing revelations were being made to him. Eugene looked at him with misgiving, because he was obviously caught in the full surge of one of his impulses and, sure enough, all at once he said with an air of complete decision: "Damned if I don't do it! It's the very place I've been looking for all along! Why, look at all you get for the money! Damnedest bargain I ever heard of! I've just been throwing my money away up there!"—he had been living at the Yale Club— "Damned if I don't get me a room and move in right away!"

This sudden prospect of having Robert as a neighbor did not attract the other youth: he was working very hard with his classes and trying to complete a play he had begun to write, and he had no intention of becoming the companion or nurse of Robert's drunkenness or the confessor of his fevered despair and unrest: he told him he would not like the Leopold, that the people were old and stodgy, and the rules of propriety very strict. Further, he made the mistake of emphasizing the difficulty of getting a room there, although there really was no difficulty: he told him the place was a quiet family hotel, that the management wanted regular tenants of quiet habits who intended to live there permanently, that the preference was given to middle-aged married couples, and that there were no vacancies anyway—that a long list of applicants were waiting to get in. All this merely whetted Robert's eagerness: he now said that he fulfilled all the requirements save marriage, and that this deficiency would soon be remedied: he said he had completely reformed his old habits of life, and that a quieter, steadier, more sober and industrious man did not exist: he said he was determined to live there, and he demanded that Eugene take him to the manager and plead for him without delay.

When Eugene saw that he was really determined, he agreed: they went downstairs to see the manager. He came out of his office with the habitual defensive look of caution and suspicion on his sour meagre face, and listened with his usual unwilling and disparaging air, not facing them or directly looking at them, but with his small parsley face averted and his eyes turned downward, while Eugene praised up Robert to the skies, said he had known him all his life, that he was the scion of an ancient and distinguished family in the South, a brilliant young attorney in a New York firm, and one of the steadiest and most proper youths that ever lived. Robert also put in from time to time with his deep voice and impressive manners, and at length Mr. Gibbs began to shake his head dubiously, to say he didn't know, to tell how difficult it was to get admitted to the Leopold—until Eugene almost laughed in his face—but that in a case like this, because it was Eugene and he knew if he recommended a man he must be all right, and so on—he would see what he could do: he began to thumb over the pages of a meaningless ledger, peering at it and squinting along his parched finger as it moved across the page and chattering and mumbling like a monkey: at length he straightened with an air of decision, took four or five keys from their boxes and gave them to the negro captain with instructions "to show this gentleman these rooms." They all got into the elevator and went upstairs again with Robert and the negro: they looked at several rooms and at length, after great indecision, appeals for advice and guidance, and innumerable questions, Robert selected a room in the old annex—a selection for which the other youth was grateful, since his own room was in the new one.

Robert moved in promptly the next day: they had dinner together; he was in a state of jubilant elation. Then no more was seen or heard of him for a week; when Eugene did get news of him it was neither welcome nor reassuring. The phone in his room rang one morning as he was dressing: a voice from the office asked him curtly to see Mr. Gibbs when he came down. He went downstairs with a sense of ominous misgiving: Mr. Gibbs came toward him with a puckered and protesting face as if he had just tasted something sour and unexpected, he began to speak at once in a tone of shocked and astounded indignation: "In heaven's name!" he rasped; "who is this man Weaver that you brought here? What kind of man is he? *You* brought him here," he said accusingly. "*You* recommended him. We thought he was all right. We took *your* word for it? What's wrong with the man? Is he crazy? Is he out of his head completely?"—his face was soured and wrinkled like a persimmon, his small pinched figure trembled with excitement and indignation, he looked at the boy with an expression of horrified reproof —he was a comical sight, but the boy was in no temper at the moment to appreciate the humor of his appearance.

"What is it, Mr. Gibbs? What's the matter? What has he done?"

"Why," he said, trembling with anger at the very thought of it, "he tried to burn us all up last night. He came in here at three o'clock in the morning, raving and carrying on like a crazy man. Then he went upstairs and set his room on fire."

"On fire!"

"Why, yes!" said Gibbs. "We had to call the fire department to put it out. Why, it's a wonder any of us are left alive—all of these people sleeping in the hotel and this crazy man yelling and screaming at five o'clock this morning that the place is on fire! Why, we can't have anything like that in this hotel," he said with the air of one who describes the desecration of a temple. "We can't have a man like that here. Why, he'll drive the other people out, we'll lose all our guests: people aren't going to stay in a place with a crazy man. There's no telling what a man like that is liable to do. Now!" he said with an air of abrupt and pugnacious decision, "he's got to get out: I won't have him here! I'm not going to have a man like that in my hotel a moment longer"—his small jaw hardened meanly, his face shrank, and his eyes narrowed, as he turned away, "and some one's got to pay for all the damage that was done! Now I don't care who pays it"—his face was averted—"but it's not going to be us! Now you can tell him," he snapped curtly, and he left.

Eugene went upstairs at once to Robert's room in a state of choking anger and resentment: he felt that Robert had tricked him and taken advantage of him, that he was being held accountable for Robert's misbehavior, and that now his own standing in the hotel had been jeopardized and he would be forced to leave this delightful and charming establishment at which he had cursed and mocked so bitterly many times, but which now, in his resentful spirit, took on a peaceful and home-like glamour it had never had before. He walked into Robert's room without knocking: the room was a wreck, a negro maid was mournfully and sullenly gathering up from the floor the charred and blackened remnants of a pile of bed linen and blankets; the mirror had been smashed by a drinking-glass which Robert had hurled at it, he said, when he saw his image reflected in it, the remnants of a chair lay on the floor, the heavy glass plate upon a writing table had been broken, there was a large brownish stain upon one of the walls where he had hurled a whiskey bottle, and one end of his bed lay tilted on the floor where he had stamped or kicked the slats and boards to splinters. Robert was standing in the midst of all the ruin he had made, with a nervous and rueful expression on his face: when his friend came in he looked at him uneasily and laughed in a feeble and foolish manner, without conviction.

"Now, damn it, don't stand there laughing about it, Robert," the other said. "You may think it's funny as hell, but it's no joke for me. Of course," he went on bitterly, "I'm the goat. I'm the one who's got to suffer for it. I'm the one they hold responsible. Now you've just fixed it so that I can't stay here in the hotel any longer: they're going to put me out!"

"You!" Robert said, in a protesting tone. "Why, it's not your fault. You didn't have anything to do with it."

"You're damned well right I didn't," he answered. "And you're going to tell them so. Now, I was a fool once, but you won't catch me that way again: I begged and pleaded to get you in here and you go and play a dirty trick like this. And you're going to pay for it, too."

"I'll pay, I'll pay," Robert said hastily. "I know it was my fault. I'll pay whatever they ask. Have they said anything to you about it?" he said nervously. "What do they say?"

"They say you've got to pay for all the damage that you've done and get out of the hotel at once."

"Oh, I'll pay!" he said earnestly, and with a pleading note in his voice. "I don't want to leave the hotel. . . . I'll never act like that again. . . . Does Gibbs want to see me?" he said nervously.

"You can just bet your balls he does! And right now!"

"Come on!" said Robert coaxingly. "You go with me. . . . He'll listen to you. . . . Tell him how it was."

"Tell him how it was! Why, he knows damn well how it was! And so do you! You were lousy and crazy-drunk, that's how it was. . . . No, I won't do it: I've been your goat long enough. You'll have to fight it out with him for yourself. . . . And don't you bring my name into it, either, Robert, this was a hell of a thing to do!" Eugene yelled furiously. "In God's name, what's got into you? Have you gone mad?"

"Ah," he said in a brooding, sullen tone, "you know what it is. . . . It's that woman. . . . It's Martha! I can't get her off my mind, I think about her all the time. . . . My God, Eugene, if something doesn't happen soon, I will go crazy, sure enough."

"Happen! What do you want to happen?"

He beat himself, suddenly and savagely, on his breast.

"Christ knows!" he said. "Something's got to break loose . . . here . . . here . . . here!" His eyes were shot with tears and a madness of desperation: in this baffled and infuriated gesture there was something that was really painful, tortured, and deeply moving: all at once Eugene felt sorry for him; he did not know why Robert wanted to stay at the hotel any longer, he did not know what he found there in that shabby and sterile life to attract or interest him, and perhaps it was nothing except a sense in him that he was disgraced, an outcast from the ranks of orderly society: he wanted to stay in order to subdue the fear and shame he felt, and to soothe, in whatever way he could, his lacerated pride. Therefore, Eugene resolved to help him.

"Robert," he said, "if you really want to stay here, why don't you go and see old Gibbs, and talk to him. Tell him you're sorry for all the trouble you made and the damage you did, and that you're willing to pay whatever he says is fair. Then let him rave. He's a sour old bastard and he'll bawl you out, but let him rave. He enjoys it. Then tell him if he'll let you stay, you'll never act like this again. And if I can help out any, I'll do it."

He agreed to this at once, and Eugene left him and went to his own room: when he went downstairs a few minutes later on his way to his first class, Robert was standing at the desk, submissively attentive to the tongue-lashing Gibbs was giving him. The little man was in a state of trembling denunciation, he squinted and peered at Robert's face, and wagged an indignant finger at him; his shrewd, sour, nasal voice carried to all parts of the room, and Robert listened apologetically and sorrow-fully, putting in a word of penitent assent from time to time, in a deep, respectful voice:

"I quite agree with you. . . . You are absolutely right, sir. . . . It was a terrible thing to do. . . . I'll never do it again as long as I live, . . . I'll pay you for every bit of damage that I did"—and he took out his check-book and opened it upon the counter. Eugene went over and joined them: the old man was beginning to simmer down somewhat into occasional howls and blasts of fury, like a hurricane which has spent its fiercest violence and is in process of abatement: Robert began to talk smoothly, entreatingly, and charmingly—he swore to a complete and abject repentance, spoke touchingly and mysteriously of great storms and tragedies in his recent life which had driven him to this mad and violent explosion, and gave his solemn oath never to repeat the experience again if he was only allowed to remain in the hotel: Eugene put in a word of agreement here and there when he thought it might help—the upshot of it was that Gibbs finally began to speak to Robert in a tone of almost paternal affection, a kind of radiance was given off from his meagre soul, he bent towards Robert intimately, he even laughed—and when they departed, to their astonishment, he even gave the repentant sinner a warm squeeze of the hand, and a friendly pat upon the shoulder.

Within a period of three furious months Robert made trips to Colo-rado seven times: he got on trains and was hurled 2000 miles across the continent as casually as a man would make the subway trip from Times Square to Brooklyn Heights. Sometimes he would leave New

York on Friday night and be back within four or five days, after spending ten hours with Martha Upshaw: sometimes he would be gone a week, and once he did not return for three. On this occasion Eugene received a telegram from him when he had been absent about five days: the message curtly bade Eugene to send all his mail to a hotel in Colorado Springs until further notice, and said he would explain on his return.

Eugene was sitting in the lobby one evening two weeks later, when Robert came in. He walked with a limp and his face seemed to have undergone a curious angular distortion: he came toward Eugene with a kind of frozen grin and when he spoke to him he began to mutter something incoherent between set teeth and to point with his finger at his jaw. In a few moments, Eugene was able to decipher his jargon sufficiently to understand that his jaw and nose were broken, that most of the teeth had been extracted, in order that the jaw-bone might be wired together, and that he could not open his mouth now, either to speak or eat, because of wires that bound the fracture. In addition, his nose, which had been strong and straight, now curved sideways in a wide broken arc.

Robert was shockingly thin and wasted, he said he had bled a great deal, and had been unable to eat any solid food since his injury: it was obvious he had about reached the limit of his strength, the whole contour of his skull was visible, his eyes were sunken and burned with a more furious and fatal glow than ever before.

But he laughed at Eugene's look of stupefaction when he saw him, and laughed again, morosely and indifferently, as he told him the cause of his injuries: he said he had been driving with Martha Upshaw the night he got to Colorado Springs, both had been to a roadhouse and were drunk and neither, to use his description of their feeling, "gave a damn." The girl was driving, the hour was late, they had come around a curve in a mountain road at great speed, the car had left the road, plunged down a steep embankment, and turned over three times before it smashed up against a tree. The girl had been badly cut by broken glass and had several stitches taken in wounds on her face and head, but she broke no bones. Robert had been hurled twenty feet from the car, he was unconscious and bleeding horribly, and it had been thought at first his injuries were fatal.

But here he was, at least a vital piece of him, smashed and broken, but still fiercely living. It was obvious, however, that this final catastrophe had hardened his spirit in a resolute desperation: the suicidal fatalism—that hunger for death which all men have in them and which is perhaps as strong a driving-force in man as the hunger for life—and which had been strongly marked in Robert only when he was drunk— had now become the habit of his soul. He no longer cared whether he lived or died, in his inmost heart he had grown amorous of death, and it was evident that living flesh and bone could not much longer endure the cruel beating he had given it. And this fact—this shocking, visible, physical fact—as much as anything—sealed him in fatal desperation, confirmed him in his belief that everything was lost.

LI

MAN's youth is a wonderful thing: It is so full of anguish and of magic and he never comes to know it as it is, until it has gone from him forever. It is the thing he cannot bear to lose, it is the thing whose passing he watches with infinite sorrow and regret, it is the thing whose loss he must lament forever, and it is the thing whose loss he really welcomes with a sad and secret joy, the thing he would never willingly re-live again, could it be restored to him by any magic.

Why is this? The reason is that the strange and bitter miracle of life is nowhere else so evident as in our youth. And what is the essence of that strange and bitter miracle of life which we feel so poignantly, so unutterably, with such a bitter pain and joy, when we are young? It is this: that being rich, we are so poor; that being mighty, we can yet have nothing, that seeing, breathing, smelling, tasting all around us the impossible wealth and glory of this earth, feeling with an intolerable certitude that the whole structure of the enchanted life—the most fortunate, wealthy, good, and happy life that any man has ever known—is ours—is ours at once, immediately and forever, the moment that we choose to take a step, or stretch a hand, or say a word—we yet know that we can really keep, hold, take, and possess forever—nothing. All passes; nothing lasts: the moment that we put our hand upon it it melts away like smoke, is gone forever, and the snake is eating at our heart again; we see then what we are and what our lives must come to.

A young man is so strong, so mad, so certain, and so lost. He has everything and he is able to use nothing. He hurls the great shoulder of his strength forever against phantasmal barriers, he is a wave whose power explodes in lost mid-oceans under timeless skies, he reaches out to grip a fume of painted smoke; he wants all, feels the thirst and power for everything, and finally gets nothing. In the end, he is destroyed by his own strength, devoured by his own hunger, impoverished by his own wealth. Thoughtless of money or the accumulation of material possessions, he is none the less defeated in the end by his own greed—a greed that makes the avarice of King Midas seem paltry by comparison.

And that is the reason why, when youth is gone, every man will look back upon that period of his life with infinite sorrow and regret. It is the bitter sorrow and regret of a man who knows that once he had a great talent and wasted it, of a man who knows that once he had a great treasure and got nothing from it, of a man who knows that he had strength enough for everything and never used it.

All youth is bound to be "mis-spent"; there is something in its very nature that makes it so, and that is why all men regret it. And that regret becomes more poignant as the knowledge comes to us that this great waste of youth was utterly unnecessary, as we discover with a bitter irony of mirth, that youth is something which only young men have, and which only old men know how to use. And for that reason, in later years, we all look back upon our youth with sorrow and regret—seeing what a wealth was ours if we had used it—remembering Weisberg, Snodgrass, and O'Hare—finally remembering with tenderness and joy the good bleak visage of the pavement cipher who was the first friend we ever knew in the great city—in whose gray face its million strange and secret mysteries were all compact—and who was our friend, our brother, and this earth's nameless man. And so Eugene recalled Abraham Jones.

This ugly, good, and loyal creature had almost forgotten his real name: the "Jones," of course, was one of those random acquisitions, which, bestowed in some blind, dateless moment of the past, evoked a picture of those nameless hordes of driven and frightened people who had poured into this country within the last half-century, and whose whole lives had been determined for them by the turn of a word, the bend of a street, the drift of the crowd, or a surly and infuriated gesture by some ignorant tyrant of an official. In such a way, Abe Jones's father, a Polish Jew, without a word of Yankee English in his throat, had come to Castle Garden forty years before and, stunned and frightened by the moment's assault of some furious little swine of a customs inspector, had stood dumbly while the man snarled and menaced him: "What's yer name? . . . Huh? . . . Don't yuh know what yer name is . . . Huh? . . . Ain't yuh got a name? . . . Huh?" To all this the poor Jew had no answer but a stare of stupefaction and terror: at length a kind of frenzy seized him—a torrent of Polish, Jewish, Yiddish speech poured from his mouth, but never a word his snarling inquisitor could understand. The Jew begged, swore, wept, pleaded, prayed, entreated—a thousand tales of horror, brutal violence and tyranny swept through his terror-stricken mind, the whole vast obscene chronicle of immigration gleaned from the mouths of returned adventurers or from the letters of those who had triumphantly passed the gates of wrath: he showed his papers, he clasped his hands, he swore by all the oaths he knew that all was as it should be, that he had done all he had been told to do, that there was no trick or fraud or cheat in anything he did or said, and all the time, the foul, swollen, snarling face kept thrusting at him with the same maddening and indecipherable curse: "Yer name! . . . Yer name! . . . Fer Christ's sake don't yuh know yer own name? . . . All right!" he shouted suddenly, furiously, "If yuh ain't got a name I'll give yuh one! . . . If yuh ain't got sense enough to tell me what yer own name is, I'll find one for yuh!" The snarling face came closer: "Yer name's Jones! See! J-o-n-e-s. Jones! That's a good Amurrican name. See? I'm giving yuh a good honest Amurrican name that a lot of good decent Amurricans have got. Yuh've gotta try to live up to it and desoive it! See? Yer in Amurrica now, Jones. . . . See? . . . Yuh've gotta t'ink fer yerself, Jones. In Amurrica we know our own name. We've been trained to t'ink fer ourselves over here! . . . See? Yer not one of them foreign dummies any more! . . . Yer Jones—Jones—Jones!" he yelled. "See!" —and in such a way, on the impulsion of brutal authority and idiot chance, Abe's father had been given his new name. Eugene did not know what Abe's real name was: Abe had told him once, and he remembered it as something pleasant, musical, and alien to our tongue, difficult for our mouths to shape and utter.

Already, when he had first met Abe Jones in the first class he taught, the process of mutation had carried so far that he was trying to rid himself of the accursed "Abraham," reducing it to an ambiguous initial, and signing his papers with a simple unrevealing "A. Jones," as whales are said to have lost through atrophy the use of legs with which they once walked across the land, but still to carry upon their bodies the rudimentary stump. Now, in the last year, he had dared to make a final transformation, shocking, comical, pitifully clumsy in its effort at concealment and deception: when Eugene had tried to find his name and number in the telephone directory a month before, among the great gray regiment of Joneses, the familiar, quaint, and homely "Abe" had disappeared—at length he found him coyly sheltered under the gentlemanly obscurity of A. Alfred Jones. The transformation, thus, had been complete: he was now, in name, at any rate, a member of the great Gentile aristocracy of Jones; and just as "Jones" had been thrust by violence upon his father, so had Abe taken violently, by theft and rape, the "Alfred." There was something mad and appalling in the bravado, the effrontery, and the absurdity of the attempt: what did he hope to do with such a name? What reward did he expect to win? Was he engaged in some vast conspiracy in which all depended on the *sound* and not the *appearance* of deception? Was he using the mails in some scheme to swindle or defraud? Was he carrying on by correspondence an impassioned courtship of some ancient Christian maiden with one tooth and a million shining dollars? Or was it part of a gigantic satire on Gentile genteelness, country-club Christianity, a bawdy joke perpetrated at the expense of sixty thousand anguished and protesting Social Registerites? That he should hope actually to palm himself off as a Gentile was unthinkable, because one look at him revealed instantly the whole story of his race and origin: if all the Polish-Russian Jews that ever swarmed along the ghettoes of the earth had been compacted in a single frame the physical result might have been something amazingly like Eugene's friend, Abraham Jones.

The whole flag and banner of his race was in the enormous putty-colored nose that bulged, flared and sprouted with the disproportionate extravagance of a caricature or a dill-pickle over his pale, slightly freckled and rather meagre face; he had a wide, thin, somewhat cruel-looking mouth, dull weak eyes that stared, blinked, and grew misty with a murky, somewhat slimily ropy feeling behind his spectacles, a low, dull, and slanting forehead, almost reptilian in its ugliness, that sloped painfully back an inch or two into the fringes of unpleasantly greasy curls and coils of dark, short, screwy hair. He was about the middle height, and neither thin nor fat: his figure was rather big-boned and angular, and yet it gave an impression of meagreness, spareness, and somewhat tallowy toughness which so many city people have, as if their ten thousand days and nights upon the rootless pavement had dried all juice and succulence out of them, as if asphalt and brick and steel had got into the conduits of their blood and spirit, leaving them with a quality that is tough, dry, meagre, tallowy, and somewhat calloused.

What earth had nourished him? Had he been born and grown there among the asphalt lilies and the pavement wheat? What corn was growing from the cobblestones? Or was there never a cry of earth up through the beaten and unyielding cement of the streets? Had he forgotten the immortal and attentive earth still waiting at the roots of steel?

No. Beneath that cone of neat gray felt, behind the dreary, tallowed pigment of his face, which had that thickened, stunned, and deadened look one often sees upon the faces of old bruisers, as if the violent and furious assault of stone and steel, the million harsh metallic clangors, the brutal stupefaction of the streets, at length had dried the flesh and thickened the skin, and blunted, numbed and calloused the aching tumult of the tortured and tormented senses—there still flowed blood as red and wet as any which ever swarmed into the earth below the laurel bush. He was a part, a drop, an indecipherable fraction of these gray tides of swarming tissue that passed in ceaseless weft and counter-weft upon the beaten pavements, at once a typical man-swarm atom and a living man. Indistinguishable in his speech, gait, dress, and tallowy pigmentation from the typical cell-and-pavement article, at the same time, although ugly, meagre, toughened, gnarled and half-articulate, angular as brick and spare as steel webbing, with little juice and succulence, he was honest, loyal, somehow good and memorable, grained with the life and movement of a thousand streets, seasoned and alert, a living character, a city man. In that horrible desperation of drowning and atomic desolation among the numberless hordes that swept along the rootless pavements, in Eugene's madness to know, own, intrude behind the million barriers of brick, to root and entrench himself in the hive, he seized upon that dreary, gray and hopeless-looking Jew.

This was his history:

Abraham Jones was one of the youngest members of a large family. In addition to two brothers, younger than himself, there were three older brothers, and two sisters. The family life was close, complex, and passionate, torn by fierce dislikes and dissensions, menaced by division among some of its members, held together by equally fierce loyalties and loves among the others. Abe disliked his father and hated one of his older brothers. He loved one of his sisters and was attached to the other one by a kind of loyalty of silence.

She, Sylvia, was a woman of perhaps thirty-five years when Eugene first saw her, she had not lived at home for ten years, she was a febrile, nervous, emaciated, highly enamelled city woman—a lover of what was glittering and electric in life, caught up in the surge of a furious and feverish life, and yet not content with it, dissonant, irritable and impatient. Like the rest of her family she had been forced to shift for herself since childhood: she had been first a salesgirl, then a worker in a millinery shop, and now, through her own cleverness, smartness, and ability, she had achieved a very considerable success in business. She ran a hat shop on Second Avenue, which Abe told him was the Broadway of the lower East Side: she had a small, elegant, glittering jewel of a shop there, blazing with hard electric light and smartly and tastefully dressed with windows filled with a hundred jaunty styles in women's hats. She did a thriving business and employed several assistants.

The first time Eugene met her, one day when Abe had taken him home to the flat where he lived with his mother, two of his brothers, and Sylvia's child, he thought she had the look and quality of an actress much more than of a business woman. There was a remarkably electric glitter and unnaturalness about her: it seemed as if the only light that had ever shone upon her had been electric light, the only air she could breath with any certitude and joy, the clamorous and electric air of Broadway. Her face belonged, indeed, among those swarms of livid, glittering, night-time faces that pour along the street, with that mysterious fraternity of night-time people who all seem to speak a common language and to be bound together by some central interest and communication, who live mysteriously and gaudily without discoverable employments, in a world remote and alien. Sylvia was a woman of middling height, but of a dark and almost bird-like emaciation: all the flesh seemed to have been starved, wasted, and consumed from her by this devil of feverish and electric unrest and discontent that glittered with almost a drugged brilliance in her large dark eyes. Every visible portion of her body, hair, eyebrows, lashes, lips, skin and nails was greased, waved, leaded, rouged, plucked, polished, enamelled and varnished with the conventional extravagance of a ritualistic mask until now it seemed that all of the familiar qualities of living tissue had been consumed, and were replaced by the painted image, the varnished mask of a face, designed in its unreality to catch, reflect, and realize effectively the thousand lurid shifting lights and weathers of an electric, nocturnal, and inhuman world. Moreover, she was dressed in the most extreme and sharpest exaggeration of the latest style, her thin long hands, which were unpleasantly and ominously veined with blue, and her fragile wrists, which were so thin and white that light made a pink transparency in them when she lifted them, were covered, loaded—one vast encrusted jewelled glitter of diamond rings and bracelets: a fortune in jewelry blazed heavily and shockingly on her bony little hands.

Her life had been hard, painful, difficult, full of work and sorrow. Ten years before, when she was twenty-five years old, she had had her first—and probably her last—love affair. She had fallen in love with an actor at the Settlement Guild—a little East Side theatre maintained by the donations of two rich æsthetic females. She had left her family and become his mistress: within less than a year the man deserted her, leaving her pregnant.

Her child was a boy: she had no maternal feeling and her son, now nine years old, had been brought up by Abe's mother and by Abe. Sylvia rarely saw her son: she had long ago deserted the orthodoxy of Jewish family life, she had a new, impatient, driving, feverish city life of her own, she visited her family every month or so, and it was then, and only then, that she saw her child. This boy, Jimmy, was a bright, quick, attractive youngster, with a tousled sheaf of taffy-colored hair, and with the freckled, tough, puggish face and the cocky mutilated pavement argot and assurance of the city urchin: he was nevertheless excellently clothed, schooled, and cared for, for the old woman, Abe's mother, watched and guarded over him with the jealous brooding apprehension of an ancient hen, and Sylvia herself was most generous in her expenditures and benefactions, not only for the child, but also for the family.

The relation between Sylvia and her illegitimate child, Jimmy, was remarkable. He never called her "mother"; in fact neither seemed to have a name for the other, save an impersonal and rather awkward "You." Moreover, the attitude of both mother and child was marked by a quality that was hard, knowing, and cynical in its conversation: when she spoke to him her tone and manner were as cold and impersonal as if the child had been a stranger or some chance acquaintance, and this manner was also touched by a quality that was resigned, and somewhat mocking—with a mockery which seemed to be directed toward herself, more than toward any one, as if in the physical presence of the boy she saw the visible proof and living evidence of her folly, the bitter fruit of the days of innocence, love, and guileless belief, and as if she was conscious that a joke had been played on both her and her child. And the boy seemed to understand and accept this feeling with a sharp correspondence of feeling, almost incredible in a child. And yet they did not hate each other: their conversations were cynically wise and impersonal and yet curiously honest and respectful. She would look at him for a moment with an air of cold and casual detachment, and that faint smile of mockery when, on one of her visits home, he would come in, panting and dishevelled, a tough and impish urchin, from the street.

"Come here, you," she would say at length, quietly, harshly. "Whatcha been doin' to yourself?" she would ask, in the same hard tone, as deftly she straightened and re-knotted his tie, smoothed out his rumpled sheaf of oaken-colored hair. "You look as if yuh just crawled out of some one's ash can."

"Ah!" he said in his tough, high city-urchin's voice, "a coupla guys tried to get wise wit' me an' I socked one of 'em. Dat's all!"

"Oh-ho-ho-ho!"—Abe turned his gray grinning face prayerfully to heaven and laughed softly, painfully.

"Fightin', huh?" said Sylvia. "Do you remember what I told you last time?" she said in a warning tone. "If I catch yuh fightin' again there's goin' to be no more ball games. You'll stay home next time."

"Ah!" he cried again in a high protesting tone. "What's a guy gonna do? Do you t'ink I'm gonna let a coupla mugs like dat get away wit' moidah?"

"Oh-ho-ho-ho!"—cried Abe, lifting his great nose prayerfully again: then with a sudden shift to reproof and admonition, he said sternly: "What kind of talk do you call that? Huh? Didn't I tell you not to say 'mugs'?"

"Ah, what's a guy gonna say?" cried Jimmy. "I neveh could loin all dem big woids, noway."

"My God! I wish you'd listen to 'm," his mother said in a tone of hard and weary resignation. "I suppose that's what I'm sendin' him to school for! Loin, woids, noway, t'ink! Is that the way to talk?" she demanded harshly. "Is that what they teach yuh?"

"Say *think!*" commanded Abe.

"I *did* say it," the child answered evasively.

"Go on! You *didn't!* You didn't say it right. I'll bet you can't say it right. Come on! Let's hear you: *think!*"

"T'ink," Jimmy, answered immediately.

"Oh-ho-ho-ho!"—and Abe lifted his grinning face heavenward, saying, "Say! This is rich!"

"Can yuh beat it?" the woman asked.

And, for a moment, she continued to look at her son with a glance that was quizzical, tinged with a mocking resignation, and yet with a cold, detached affection. Then her long blue-veined hands twitched nervously and impatiently until all the crusted jewels on her wrists and fingers blazed with light: she sighed sharply and, looking away, dismissed the child from her consideration.

Although the boy saw very little of his mother, Abe watched and guarded over him as tenderly as if he had been his father. If the child was late in coming home from school, if he had not had his lunch before going out to play, if he remained away too long Abe showed his concern and distress very plainly, and he spoke very sharply and sternly at times to other members of the family if he thought they had been lax in some matter pertaining to the boy.

"Did Jimmy get home from school yet?" he would ask sharply. "Did he eat before he went out again? . . . Well, why did you let him get away, then, before he had his lunch? . . . For heaven's sake! You're here all day long: you could at least do that much—I can't be here to watch him all the time, you know—don't you know the kid ought never to go out to play until he's had something to eat?"

Eugene saw the child for the first time one day when Abe had taken him home for dinner: Abe, in his crisp neat shirt-sleeves, was seated at the table devouring his food with a wolfish and prowling absorption, and yet in a cleanly and fastidious way, when the child entered. The boy paused in surprise when he saw Eugene: his wheaten sheaf of hair fell down across one eye, one trouser leg had come unbanded at the knee and flapped down to his ankle, and for a moment he looked at Eugene with a rude frank stare of his puggish freckled face.

Abe, prowling upward from his food, glanced at the boy and grinned; then, jerking his head sharply toward Eugene, he said roughly:

"Whatcha think of this guy? Huh?"

"Who is he?" the boy asked in his high tough little voice, never moving his curious gaze from Eugene.

"He's my teacher," Abe said. "He's the guy that teaches me."

"Ah, g'wan!" the child answered in a protesting tone, still fixing Eugene with his steady and puzzled stare.

"Whatcha handin' me? He's *not!*"

"Sure he is! No kiddin'!" Abe replied. "He's the guy that teaches me English."

"Ah, he's *not!*" the boy answered decisively. "Yuh're bein' wise."

"What makes you think he's not?" Abe asked.

"If he's an English teacher," Jimmy said triumphantly, "w'y don't he say somet'ing? W'y don't he use some of dose woids?"

"Oh-ho-ho-ho!" cried Abe lifting his great bleak nose aloft. "Say! . . . This is good! . . . This is swell! . . . Say, that's some kid!" he said when the boy had departed. "There's not much gets by *him!*" And lifting his gray face heavenward again, he laughed softly, painfully, in gleeful and tender reminiscence.

Thus, the whole care and government of the boy had been entrusted to Abe and his mother: Sylvia herself, although she paid liberally all her child's expenses, took no other interest in him. She was a hard, feverish, bitter, and over-stimulated woman, and yet she had a kind of harsh loyalty to her family: she was, in a fierce and smouldering way, very ambitious for Abe, who seemed to be the most promising of her brothers: she was determined that he should go to college and become a lawyer, and his fees at the university, in part at any rate, were paid by his sister—in part only, not because Sylvia would not have paid all without complaint, but because Abe insisted on paying as much as he could through his own labor, for Abe, too, had embedded in him a strong granite of independence, the almost surly dislike, of a strong and honest character, of being beholden to any one for favors. On this score, indeed, he had the most sensitive and tender pride of any one Eugene had ever known.

At home, Abe had become, by unspoken consent, the head of a family which now consisted only of his mother, two brothers, and his sister's illegitimate child, Jimmy. Two of his older brothers, who were in business together, had married and lived away from home, as did Sylvia, and another sister, Rose, who had married a musician in a theatre orchestra a year or two before; she was a dark, tortured and sensitive

Jewess with a big nose and one blind eye. Her physical resemblance to
Abe was marked. She was a very talented pianist, and once or twice he
took Eugene to visit her on Sunday afternoons: she played for them in a
studio room in which candles were burning and she carried on very
technical and knowing conversations about the work of various com-
posers with her brother. Abe listened to the music when she played
with an obscure and murky smile: he seemed to know a great deal about
music: it awakened a thousand subtle echoes in his Jewish soul, but for
Eugene, somehow, the music, and something arrogant, scornful, and
secretive in their knowingness, together with the dreary consciousness
of a winter's Sunday afternoon outside, the barren streets, the harsh
red waning light of day, and a terrible sensation of thousands of other
knowing Jews—the men with little silken mustaches—who were coming from concerts at that moment, awakened in him vague but powerful
emotions of nakedness, rootlessness, futility and misery, which even the
glorious memory of the power, exultancy and joy of poetry could not
conquer or subdue. The scene evoked for him suddenly a thousand
images of a sterile and damnable uncertitude, in which man groped
indefinitely along the smooth metallic sides of a world in which there
was neither warmth, nor depth, nor door to enter, nor walls to shelter
him: he got suddenly a vision of a barren Sunday and a gray despair,
of ugly streets, and of lights beginning to wink and flicker above
cheap moving-picture houses and chop-suey restaurants, and of a raucous
world of cheap and flashy people, as trashy as their foods, as trivial and
infertile as their accursed amusements, and finally of the Jews returning
through a thousand streets, in that waning and desolate light, from
symphony concerts, an image, which, so far from giving a note of hope,
life, and passionate certitude and joy to the wordless horror of this
damned and blasted waste of Dead-Man's Land, seemed to enhance it
rather, and to give it a conclusive note of futility and desolation.

Abe and his sister did not seem to feel this: instead the scene, the
time, the day, the waning light, the barren streets, the music, awakened
in them something familiar and obscure, a dark and painful joy, a certitude Eugene did not feel. They argued, jibed, and sneered harshly and
arrogantly at each other: their words were sharp and cutting, impregnated with an aggressive and unpleasant intellectualism, they called each
other fools and sentimental ignoramuses, and yet they did not seem to
be wounded or offended by this harsh intercourse: they seemed rather
to derive a kind of bitter satisfaction from it.

Already, the first year Eugene had known him he had discovered this strange quality in these people: they seemed to delight in jeering and jibing at one another; and at the same time their harsh mockery had in it an element of obscure and disquieting affection. At this time Abe was carrying on, week by week, a savage correspondence with another young Jew who had been graduated with him from the same class in high school. He always had in his pocket at least one of the letters this boy had written him, and he was forever giving it to Eugene to read, and then insisting that he read his answer. In these letters, they flew at each other with undisciplined ferocity, they hurled denunciation, mockery, and contempt at each other, and they seemed to exult in it. The tone of their letters was marked by an affectation of cold impersonality and austerity, and yet this obviously was only a threadbare cloak to the furious storm of personal insult and invective, the desire to crow over the other man and humiliate him, which seemed to delight them. "In your last letter," one would write, "I see that the long-expected *débâcle* has now occurred. In our last year at high school I saw occasional gleams of adult intelligence in your otherwise infantile and adolescent intellect, and I had some hope of saving you, but I now see my hopes were wasted—your puerile remarks on Karl Marx, Anatole France, et al, show you up as the fat-headed bourgeois you always were, and I accordingly wash my hands of you. You reveal plainly that your intellect is incapable of grasping the issues involved in modern socialism: you are a romantic individualist and you will find everything you say elegantly embalmed in the works of the late Lord Byron which is where you belong also: your mother should dress you up in a cowboy suit and give you a toy pistol to play with before you hurt yourself playing around with great big rough grown-up men."

Abe would read Eugene one of these letters, grinning widely with Kike delight, lifting his grinning face and laughing softly, "Oh-ho-ho-ho-ho!" as he came to some particularly venomous insult.

"But who wrote you such a letter?" Eugene demanded.

"Oh, a guy I went to school with," he answered, "a friend of mine!"

"A friend of yours! Is that the kind of letter that your friends write you!"

"Sure," he said. "Why not? He's a good guy. He doesn't mean anything by it. He's got bats in the belfry, that's all. But wait till you see what I wrote *him!*" he cried, grinning exultantly as he took his own letter from his pocket. "Wait till you see what I call *him!* Oh-ho-ho-

ho-ho!"—softly, painfully, he laughed. "Say, this is rich!" and gleefully he would read him his answer: five closely typed pages of bitter
insult and vituperation.

Another astonishing and disquieting circumstance of this brutal correspondence was now revealed: this extraordinary "friend" of Abe's,
who wrote him these insulting letters, had not gone abroad, nor did he
live in some remote and distant city. When Eugene asked Abe where
this savage critic lived, he answered: "Oh, a couple of blocks from where
I live."

"But do you ever see him?"

"Sure. Why not?" he said, looking at Eugene in a puzzled way.
"We grew up together. I see him all the time."

"And yet you write this fellow letters and he writes you, when you
live only a block apart and see each other all the time?"

"Sure. Why not?" said Abe.

He saw nothing curious or unusual in the circumstance, and yet there
was something disturbing and unpleasant about it: in all these letters
Eugene had observed, below the tirades of abuse, an obscure, indefinable,
and murky emotionalism that was somehow ugly.

Within a few months, however, this strange communication with his
Jewish comrade ceased abruptly: Eugene began to see Abe, in the halls
and corridors of the university, squiring various Jewish girls around
with a sheepish and melancholy look. His lust for letter-writing still
raged with unabated violence, although now the subjects of his correspondence were women. His attitude towards girls had always been
cold and scornful: he regarded their cajoleries and enticements with
a fishy eye, and with a vast Jewish caution and suspiciousness, and he
laughed scornfully at any one who allowed himself to be ensnared.
Like many people who feel deeply, and who are powerfully affected by
the slightest and remotest changes in their emotions, he had convinced
himself that he was a creature whose every action was governed by the
operations of cool reason, and accordingly now that his feelings were
powerfully and romantically involved in thoughts about several of
these warm and luscious-looking Jewish wenches, he convinced himself that he "cared only for their minds" and that what he really sought
from them was the stimulation of intellectual companionship. Accordingly, the love-letters which this great-nosed innocent now wrote to
them, and read to me, were extraordinary and unwitting productions
of defense and justification.

" . . . I think I observe in your last letter," Abe would write, "traces of that romantic sentimentality which we have both seen so often in these childish lives around us but from which you and I long ago freed ourselves. As you know, Florence, we both agreed at the beginning that we would not spoil our friendship by the intrusion of a puerile and outmoded romanticism. Sex can play no part in our relations, Florence: it is at best a simple biological necessity, the urge of the hungry animal which should be recognized as such and satisfied without intruding on the higher faculties. Have you read Havelock Ellis yet? If not, you must read him without further delay. . . . So Myrtle Goldberg really thought I was in earnest that night of the dance. . . . Ye Gods! It is to laugh! Ha-ha! What fools these mortals be . . . I laugh, and yet I do not laugh . . . I laugh and observe my laughter, and then there is yet another level of reality which observes my laughter at my laughter. . . . I play the clown with an ironic heart and put on the grinning mask these fools wish to see. . . . O tempora! O mores!"—*et cetera.*

And yet these same letters, in which he protested the cold detachment of his spirit, his freedom from the romantic fleshliness which degraded the lives of lesser men, were invariably tagged and embellished by little verses of his own contriving, all of them inspired by the emotion he pretended to despise. He always had a number of these little poems written down in a small note-book of black leather which he carried with him, and in which, at this time, with a precise and meticulous hand, he noted down his rarest thoughts, excerpts from books he had been reading, and these brief poems. At this time Abe was in a state of obscure and indefinable evolution: it was impossible to say what he would become, or what form his life would take, nor could he have told, himself. He walked along at a stooping loping gait, his face prowling around mistrustfully and with a glance full of tortured discontent: he was tormented by a dozen obscure desires and purposes and by a deep but murky emotionalism: his flesh was ugly, bowed, and meagre—conscious of a dreary inferiority (thus, in later and more prosperous years, he confessed to Eugene that he loved to abuse and "order around" brusquely the waiters in restaurants, because of the feeling of power and authority it gave him), but his spirit was sustained by an immense and towering vanity, a gloomy egotism which told him he was not as other men, that his thoughts and feelings were too profound and rare to be understood and valued by the base world about him. At the same time he was secretly and fiercely ambitious, although the energy of his ambition was scattered in a half dozen directions and could fasten on no purpose: by turn, he wanted to be a teacher and a great investigator in the sciences—and in this he might have succeeded, for he showed a brilliant aptness in biology and physics—or an economist, a critic of literature, an essayist, a historian, a poet, or a novelist. His desire was high: at this time he did not want to make money, he regarded a life that was given up to money-making with contempt, and although he sometimes spoke of the study of medicine, he looked at the profession of law, which was the profession his sister and his family wanted him to follow, with horror and revulsion: he shrank with disgust from the prospect of joining the hordes of beak-nosed shysters, poured out of the law school year by year and who were adept in every dodge of dishonorable trickery, in working every crooked wire, or squirming through each rat's hole of escape and evasion the vast machinery of the law afforded them.

Such a man was Abe Jones when Eugene first knew him: dreary, tortured, melancholy, dully intellectual and joylessly poetic, his spirit gloomily engulfed in a great cloud of Yiddish murk, a gray pavement cipher, an atom of the slums, a blind sea-crawl in the drowning tides of the man-swarm, and yet, pitifully, tremendously, with a million other dreary Hebrew yearners, convinced that he was the messiah for which the earth was groaning. Such was he in the state of becoming, an indefinable shape before necessity and his better parts—the hard, savage, tough and honest city sinew, hardened the mould—made a man of him, —this was Abe at this time, an obscure and dreary chrysalis, and yet a dogged, loyal, and faithful friend, the salt of the earth, a wonderfully good, rare, and high person.

LII

"Where shall I go now? What shall I do?" A dozen times that year he made these tormented journeys of desire. Why did he make them? What did he expect to find? He did not know: he only knew that at night he would feel again the huge and secret quickening of desire to which all life in the city moved, that he would be drawn again, past hope and past belief, to the huge glare, the swarming avenues of night, with their great tides of livid night-time faces. He only knew that he would prowl again, again, each night, the thronging passages of rat's alley where the dead men were, that the million faces, forms and shapes of ungraspable desire would pass, would weave and throng and vanish from his grasp like evil figures in a dream, and that the old unanswered questions which have foiled so many million lives lost there in the labyrinthine maze and fury of the city's life, would come back again, and that he never found an answer to them.

"What shall I do now? Where shall I go?" They returned to mock his furious prowling of kaleidoscopic night with their unsearchable enigmas and when this happened, instant, mad, and overwhelming the desire to burst out of these canyoned walls that held him in, this Tantalus mocker of a city that duped his hunger with a thousand phantom shapes of impossible desire. And when this blind and furious impulse came to him, he knew only one desire—to escape, to escape instantly from the great well and prison of the city; and he had only one conviction—wild, mad, overmastering in its huge unreason—that escape, fulfilment, a fortunate and impossibly happy fruition lay somewhere out across the dark and lonely continent—was somewhere there in any of its thousand silent sleeping little towns—could be found anywhere, certainly, instantly, by the divining rod of miraculous chance, upon the pounding wheels of a great train, at any random halt made in the night.

Thus, by an ironic twist which at the time he did not see or understand, this youth, who in his childhood, like a million other boys, had dreamed and visioned in the darkness of the shining city, and of the fortunate good and happy life that he would find there was now fleeing from it to find in unknown little towns the thing that he had come to the great city to possess.

A dozen times that year he made these mad and sudden journeys: to New England many times, to Pennsylvania, or Virginia; and more than once at night up the great river towards the secret North.

One night that year, in the month of March he was returning from the wintry North—from one of those sudden and furious journeys of caprice, which were decided on the impulse of the moment, towards which he was driven by the goadings of desire, and from which he would return, as now, weary, famished, unassuaged, and driven to seek anew in the city's life for some appeasement.

Under an immense, stormy, and tempestuous sky the train was rushing across the country with a powerful unperturbed movement; it seemed in this dark and wintry firmament of earth and sky that the train was the only fixed and timeless object—the land swept past the windows of the train in a level and powerful tide of white fields, clumped woodland, and the solid, dark, and warmly grouped buildings of a farm, pierced scarcely by a light. High up, in the immense and tempestuous skies the clouds were driving at furious speed, in an inexhaustible processional, across the visage of a wild and desolate moon, which broke through momently with a kind of savage and beleaguered reprisal to cast upon the waste below a shattered, lost and fiercely ragged light. Here then, in this storm-lost desolation of earth and sky the train hung poised as the only motionless and unchanging object, and all things else—the driving and beleaguered moon, the fiercely scudding clouds, the immense regimentation of heaven which stormed onward with the fury of a gigantic and demoniacal cavalry, and the lonely and immortal earth below sweeping past with a vast fan-shaped stroke of field and wood and house—had in them a kind of unchanging changefulness, a spoke-like recurrence which, sweeping past into oblivion, would return as on the upstroke of a wheel to repeat itself with an immutable precision, an unvarying repetition.

And under the spell of this lonely processional of white field, dark wood and wild driven sky, he fell into a state of strange waking-sleepfulness, a kind of comatose perceptiveness that the motion of the train at night had always induced in him. In this weary world of sleep and wakefulness and all the flooding visions of old time and memory, he was conscious of the grand enchantments of the landscape which is at all times one of the most beautiful and lovely on the continent, and which now, under this wild spell of moon and scudding cloud and moving fields and wintry woods, forever stroking past the windows of the train, evoked that wild and solemn joy—the sense of nameless hope, impossible desire, and man's tragic brevity—which only the wildness, the cruel and savage loveliness of the American earth can give.

Thus, as he lay in his berth, in this strange state of comatose perceptiveness he was conscious first of the vast level snowclad fields of the Canadian boundaries, the lights of farms, the whipping past of darkened little stations; then of a wooded land, the foothills of the Adirondacks, dark with their wintry foresting, wild with snow; the haunting vistas of the Champlain country, strange as time, the noble music of Ticonderoga, with its tread of Indians and old wars, and then the pleasant swelling earth and fields and woods and lonely little towns set darkly in the night with a few spare lights; and pauses in the night at Saratoga, and for a moment the casual and familiar voices of

America, and people crowding in the windows of the train, and old familiar words and quiet greetings, the sudden thrum and starting of a motor car, and then dark misty woods, white fields, a few spare lights and houses, all sweeping past beneath the wild beleaguered moon with the fan-like stroke of the immortal and imperturbable earth, with a wild and haunting loneliness, with tragic brevity and strong joy.

Suddenly, in the middle of the night, he started up into sharp wakefulness. The train had slackened in its speed, it was slowing for a halt at the outskirts of a town: in the distance upon the flanks of low sweeping hills he could see a bracelet of hard bright lights, and presently the outposts of the town appeared. And now he saw the spokes of empty wintry streets, and hard street lamps that cast a barren light upon the grimy façades of old houses; and now old grimy blocks of buildings of brown stone and brick, all strange and close and near and as familiar as a dream.

And now the train was slowing to its halt; the old red brick of station warehouses, the worn rust and grime of factory walls abutting on the tracks with startling nearness, and all of it was as it had always been, as he had always known it, and yet he had not seen the place before.

And now the train had slowed to a full halt; he found himself looking at a wall of old red brick at one of the station's corners. It was one of the old brick buildings that one sees in the station section of almost any town: in the wall beside the tracks, there was a dingy-looking door and above the door a red electric bulb was burning with a dim but sinister invitation. Even as he looked, the door opened, a man stepped quickly out, looked quickly to both sides with the furtive and uneasy look men have when they come out of a brothel, and then, turning up the collar of his overcoat, he walked rapidly away.

And at the corner, in the first floor of the old brick building, he could see a disreputable old barroom, and this, too, had this dreamlike, stage-like immediacy, it was so near to him that he could almost have touched the building with his hand, a kind of gigantic theatrical setting, overpowering in its immediacy, as strange and as familiar as a dream.

Without moving in his berth he could look through the windows of the bar, which were glazed or painted half way up, and see everything that was going on inside. Despite the lateness of the hour—the round visage of a clock above the bar told him it was just four o'clock —there were several people in the place, and it was doing an open thriv-

ing business. Several men, who by their look were probably railway
workers, taxi drivers, and night-time prowlers of the station district—
(one even wore black leather leggings, and had the fresh red complexion and healthy robust look of a country man)—were standing at
the old dark walnut bar and drinking beer. The bartender stood behind
the bar with his thick hands stretched out and resting on the bar, and
with a wet cloth in one hand. He wore an apron and was in his shirt-
sleeves; he had the dead eyes and heavy sagging night-time face that
some bartenders have, but he could be seen talking to the men, respond-
ing to their jests, with a ready professional cordiality that was nevertheless warily ready for any situation that might come up. And further
down the bar, another man was drinking beer and with him was a
woman. She was one of the heavy coarsely friendly and experienced
whores that one also finds in railway sections, she was drinking beer,
talking to the man amiably and with coarse persuasiveness, and presently she took his arm with a rude persuasive gesture, and jerking her
head towards the stairs, pulled him towards her. Grinning rather sheep-
ishly, with a pleased but foolish look, he went along with her, and they
could be seen going upstairs. When they were gone, the other men
drinking at the bar spoke quietly to the bartender, and in a moment he
could see them shaking with coarse guffawing laughter. Behind the
bar, in old ornately carved walnut frames, there were big mirrors, and
at the top of the central mirror there was an American flag, fluted and
spread fan-wise, and below this there was a picture of the beetling eyebrows and nobly Roman features of the President of the United States,
Warren G. Harding. The whole place looked very old and shabby,
and yet somehow warm; dingy with old lights, and stained with
drink and worn with countless elbows, and weary and worn and brutal
with its memories of ten thousand nights of brawls and lust and drunkenness—its immeasurable age and dateless weariness of violence and
desire.

Then the train moved slowly on, and left this scene forever; it passed
the street, and there were lights here, taxis, rows of silent buildings, and
then the station, the sight of the baggage room big with trunks, piled
with mail sacks, crates and boxes, and there were also a few people, a
yardman with a lantern, a conductor waiting with a small case in his
hand, a few passengers, the brick sides of the station, and the concrete quays.

Then the train stopped again, and this time it stopped across the street at the other end of the station. And again, from his dark berth, he could see without moving this whole immense and immediate theatre of human event, and again it gripped and held him with its dream-like magic, its unbelievable familiarity. At the corner, in another old brick building there was a little lunchroom of the kind he had seen ten thousand times before. Several taxicabs were drawn up along the curb, and from the lunchroom he could hear the hoarse wrangling voices of the taxi drivers, joined in their incessant and trivial debate, and through the misted window he could see the counterman, young, thin, sallow, wearily attentive, wearing a dirty apron, and in his shirtsleeves, leaning back, his thin white arms humbly folded as he listened.

And on the corner, just below the window of his berth there stood a boy of eighteen or twenty years. The boy was tall, thin, and rather fragile-looking, his face had the sullen, scowling almost feverish intensity that boys have on such occasions, he stood there indecisively, as if trying to make up his mind, resolve himself, towards his next action; he put a cigarette into his mouth and lighted it and as he did so, his hands trembled. He turned up the collar of his overcoat impatiently, glanced grudgingly and nervously about him and stood there smoking.

Meanwhile a young prostitute, still slender and good-looking, came out of the back room, strolled over to the corner and stood there indolently, looking around with an innocent and yet impudent look, appearing not to look directly at the boy, or openly to invite him, but plainly waiting for him to speak to her.

And all the time his efforts to make up his mind, to come to a decision, were comically evident. He kept puffing nervously and rapidly at his cigarette, glancing at the girl out of the corner of his eye from time to time, pretending not to notice her, and all the time steeling himself to a decisive action.

But even as he stood there in this temper, trying to focus his wavering decision on a conclusive act, another man came up and took the girl away from him. The other man was much older than the boy; he was in his middle thirties, he was powerfully built and well, though somewhat flashily dressed. He wore a gray felt hat, set at a smart angle on his head, a well-fitting and expensive-looking overcoat cut in at the waist in the "snappy" Broadway fashion, and he looked like a prosperous Greek; he had a strong, swarthy, brutal face, full of sensual assurance, he came walking along the narrow sidewalk beside the tracks, and when he saw the girl, he approached her instantly, with a swaggering assurance, began to talk to her, and in a moment walked away with her.

And again, the effect of this incident upon the boy was comically, pathetically, apparent. He did not appear to notice the girl and the Greek as they walked off together, but when they had gone, his lean young face hardened suddenly, the scowl deepened, and with a sudden angry movement he flung his cigarette into the gutter, turned, and with the sudden resolution of a man who is ashamed of his cowardly procrastination and indecision, he began to walk rapidly along the dark and narrow little sidewalk that ran down beside the tracks and along a row of shabby station tenements.

And again, that strange and stage-like panorama of human comedy was fantastically repeated: the train began to move, and the boy kept pace with it, below the windows of the berth. Immediately they began to pass the row of shabby old wooden brothels that bordered on the tracks; the windows were closely shuttered, but through the shutters there flamed hot exciting bars of reddish light, and in the doorway entrances the small red lights were burning. At the third house, the boy paused, turned, ran swiftly up the wooden steps and rang the bell, almost instantly a small slot-like peep-hole in the door was opened, an inquiring beak-like nose, a wisp of blondined hair peered out, the door was opened, the boy entered in a glow of reddish light, the door was closed behind him, and the train, gathering rapidly in speed now, went on, past the police station where the night-time cops were sitting, past spokes of brown streets, old buildings, warehouses, factories, station tenements, the sudden barren glare of corner lamps—the grimy façade of old rusty buildings—the single substance and the million patterns of America!

And now the train had left the town, and now there was a vast and distant flare, incredible in loveliness, the enormous train yards of the night, great dings and knellings on the tracks, the flare and sweep of mighty rails, the huge and sudden stirrings of the terrific locomotives.

And then there was just loneliness and earth and night, and presently the river, the great and silent river, the noble, spacious, kingly river sweeping on forever through the land at night to wash the basal cliffs and ramparts of the terrific city, to flow forever round its million-celled and prisoned sleepers, and in the night-time, in the dark, in all the sleeping silence of our lives to go flowing by us, by us, by us, to the sea.

That vision haunted him. He could not forget it. That boy who
stood there on the corner in that lonely little town at night became
the image of his own desire, of the desire of every youth that ever lived,
of all the lonely, secret, and unsleeping desire of America, that lives forever in the little towns at night, that wakes at times, a lively, small, and
savage flame, while all the sleepers sleep, that burns there, unimprisoned
and alone, beneath immense and timeless skies, upon the dark and
secret visage of the continent, that prowls forever past the shuttered
façades of the night, and furious, famished, unassuaged and driven as
it is, lives alone in darkness and will not die.

That urge held and drew him with a magnetic power. Eight times
that spring he made that wild journey of impulse and desire up
the river. Eight times in darkness over pounding wheel and rod, he
saw the wild and secret continent of night, the nocturnal sweep and
flow of the great river, and felt the swelling of the old, impossible and
savage joy within him. That little town, seen first with such a charm
and dream-like casualness out of the windows of a passing train, became
part of the structure of his life, carved upon the tablets of his brain
indelibly.

Eight times that year he saw it in every light and weather: in blown
drifts of sleeting snow, in spouting rain, in bleak and wintry darkness,
and when the first gray light of day was breaking haggardly against its
ridge of eastern hills. And its whole design—each grimy brick and edge
and corner of its shabby pattern—became familiar to him as something
he had known all his life.

He came to know its times, its movements, and its people: its station workers, railway men, and porters; the night-time litter of the
station derelicts and vagabonds themselves, as he was blown past this
little town in darkness.

And he came to know all the prowlers of the night that walk and
wait and wear the slow gray ash of time away in little towns—and this
too was like something he had known forever. He came to know them
all by sight and word and name: the taxi drivers, lunchroom counter-
men, the soiled and weary-looking night-time Greeks, and all the others
who inhabit the great shambles of the night.

Finally, and as a consequence of these blind voyages, he came to
know all the whores that lived there in that little row of wooden tenements beside the tracks. Eight times, at the end of night, he came again
into the last commerce of their fagged embrace; eight times he left

those shabby, shuttered little houses in gray haggard light; and eight times that year, as morning came, he again made the journey down the river.

And later he could forget none of it. It became part of a whole design —all of its horror and its beauty, its grime and rustiness of stark red brick, its dark and secret loneliness of earth, the thrill and magic of its casual friendly voices, and the fagged yet friendly commerce of the whores, the haggard light of morning at the ridges of the hills, and that great enchanted river greening into May—all this was one and single, woven of the same pattern, and coherent to the same design— and that design was somehow beautiful.

That spring, along the noble sweep of the great river he returned at morning to the city many times. He saw April come, with all its sudden patches of shrewd green, and May, with all its bloom, its lights of flowers, its purity of first light and the bird-song waking in young feathered trees, its joy of morning-gold on the great river's tide.

Eight times that spring, after all the fury, wildness and debauch of night, he rode back at morning towards the city in a world of waking men: they were for the most part railroad men—engineers, firemen, brakemen, switchmen, and train conductors, on their way to work. And their homely, seamed and pungent comradeship filled him with the health of morning and with joy.

And his memory of these journeys of the night, and these wonderful returns at morning, was haunted always by the vision of a single house. It was a great white house, set delicate and gleaming in frail morning light upon a noble hill that swept back from the river, and it was shaded by the silent stature of great trees, and vast swards of velvet lawn swept round it, and morning was always there and the tender purity of light.

That house haunted his memory like a dream: he could not forget it. But he did not know, he could not have foreseen, by what strange and dreamlike chance he would later come to it.

LIII

LAUGHING, and breaking at once into the loud harsh accents of the city, the class scrambled to its feet, and began to gather up its books. Eugene walked rapidly to his table which stood upon a little platform a few inches above the floor and stationing himself behind it, he began feverishly and untidily to stuff away into his brief-case text books and themes and the pile of examination papers in which were written out the results of the short "quiz" he had given them that night. But he knew without looking what those results would be. Miss Feinberg would tell him that "Christabel" had been written by "Keiths," and that "it was sort of an epic or narrative poem of a very romantic nature such as they had in those days." Mr. Katz would assure him that "The Eve of St. Agnes" had been written by "Wadsworth," "and you might say there is something very mysterious and peculiar about the atmosphere of the poem." Mr. Harry Fishbein would explain that a sonnet "is a kind of poetry they have, usually of a short nature. The first part of a sonnet is called the octrave. Shakespeare wrote some sonnets, as did also Wadsworth and Keiths!" Only Abe—Abe alone, the merciless and relentless and unfaltering Abe, Abe with his dull, gray, scornful face would make no errors. As for the others, what difference did it make? Would these garbled renderings of what their ears had dully heard make any change for good or ill in the garbled chaos of their lives, the glare and fury of the streets? Would Herrick sing his sweet bird-song to Mr. Shapiro as he roared down to work each morning in the Bronx Express? Would Miss Feinberg think of Crashaw as she ate her noonday cream-cheese sandwich in the drug store? Would it matter much to Katz whether "Wadsworth" or "Keiths" had written "La Belle Dame," so long as he "got by," so long as he "got his," so long as he "got what was comin' to 'm"?— Eugene could not think it. He had heard all the reasons for this folly, and the words that had been used were very fine—"a larger vision,"—"a sense of the larger life," and so on—but the bewilderment of these turbulent and raucous young people was scarcely greater than his own.

At the end of each class, jostling, thrusting, laughing, shouting, and disputing, they would surge in upon him in a hot, clamorous, and insistent swarm, and again, as Eugene backed wearily against the wall and faced them, he had the maddening sense of having been defeated and overcome.

For the weariness of flesh was like the weariness a man has after a great burst of love with a potent and adored mistress—the back was drawn in, half-broken, toward his trembling, wrung, depleted loins, his limbs faltered and his fingers shook, his breath came heavily, his body respired slowly in a state of languorous exhaustion, but where the weariness of triumphant love brings to a man a sense of completion, victory, and finality, the weariness of the class brought to him only a feeling of sterility and despair, a damnable and unresting exacerbation and weariness of the spirit, a sense of having yielded up and lost irrevocably into the sponge-like and withdrawing maws of their dark, oily and insatiate hunger, their oriental and parasitic gluttony, all of the rare and priceless energies of creation: he thought with a weary and impotent fury of great plans and soaring ecstasies of hope and ambition—of poems, stories, books which once had swarmed exultantly their cries of glory, joy, and triumph through his brain—and now all this seemed lost and wasted, flung riotously and fruitlessly away into the blind maw of a headless sucking mouth, a dark brainless, obscene and insatiate hunger.

As he looked at them, a horrible memory returned of the great fish which once he had caught in deep-sea water outside Boston harbor: he could feel again the sudden heavy living tug, the wriggling vitality, at the end of 200 feet of line, and then the wet line slipping harshly through his fingers as exultantly he drew the great fish upward to the surface. Then he remembered the sense of loss and disgust and horror when he saw it: it swam upward wriggling heavily in a flail of heavy dying protest, through a thickened murk of greenish water, and he saw that to its brain was fastened some blind horror of the sea, a foul snake-like shape a foot or more in length, a headless, brainless mouth, a blind suck and sea-crawl, a mindless abomination, glued implacably, fastened in fatal suck in one small rim of bloody foam against the brain-cage of the great dying fish. How often, in a mad fury of escape and freedom, it had lashed its brain to bloody froth against some razored edge, some coral stype upon the swarming jungle of the sea, he did not know; but the memory of it had returned a thousand times in abominable waking-sleeping visions of the night to haunt him with its blind and mouthless horror, and now he thought of it again, as they drew in on him their sucking glut of dark insatiate desire.

Their dark flesh had in it the quality of a merciless tide which not only overwhelmed and devoured but withdrew with a powerful sucking glut all rich deposits of the earth it fed upon: they had the absorptive quality of a sponge, the power of a magnet, the end of each class left him sapped, gutted, drained, and with a sense of sterility, loss, and defeat, and in addition to this exhaustion of the mind and spirit, there was added a terrible weariness and frustration of the flesh: the potent young Jewesses, thick, hot, and heavy with a female odor, swarmed around him in a sensual tide, they leaned above him as he sat there at his table, pressing deliberately the crisp nozzles of their melon-heavy breasts against his shoulder, slowly, erotically they moved their bellies in to him, or rubbed the heavy contours of their thighs against his legs; they looked at him with moist red lips through which their wet red tongues lolled wickedly, and they sat upon the front rows of the class in garments cut with too extreme a style of provocation and indecency, staring up at him with eyes of round lewd innocence, cocking their legs with a shameless and unwitting air, so that they exposed the banded silken ruffle of their garters and the ripe heavy flesh of their underlegs.

Thus, to all his weariness of mind, the terror and torment of his spirit, a thousand erotic images of an aroused, but baffled and maddened sensuality, were added: they swarmed around him like the embodiment of all the frustrate hunger, desire, and fury he had come to know in the city, with a terrible wordless evocation of men starving in the heart of a great plantation, of men dying of thirst within sight of a shining spring, with a damnable mockery, a nightmare vision of proud, potent and hermetic flesh, of voluptuous forms in hell, forever near, forever palpable, but never to be known, owned, or touched.

The girls, the proud and potent Jewesses with their amber flesh, schooled to a goal of marriage, skilled in all the teasings of erotic trickery, with their lustful caution and their hot virginity pressed in around him in a drowning sensual tide: with looks of vacant innocence and with swift counter-glances of dark mockery, they pressed upon him, breathing, soft and warm and full, as they cajoled, teased, seduced with look or gesture, questioned trivially, aggressively, uselessly—those with a body, and no mind, intent alone upon seduction spurred on perhaps by some belief that promotion and reward in all the business of life could best be got at in this way; and those with minds and bodies both, intent upon some painful mixture of sharp protest, struggle, and seduction which made erotic musings in their soul: "Oh, but I don't—ag-gree with you at aw-ull! That's not the meaning that I saw in it, at aw-ull! I think you're being very supe-er-fish-al. I don't ag-gree with you at aw-ull!"—the rich voices, aggrieved, injured, hen-like and sensual, omened with deep undernotes of ripe hysteria, rose and fell with undulant cluckings of yolky protest—the rich sensual voices of the Jewesses receiving, giving, returning and withdrawing, rose and fell in curved undulance of yolky hen-clucking protest, with omens of a ripe hysteria. Receiving, clucking, and protesting with their warm hen-feathered cries, they seemed to say, "Oh, come and take me, break me, but I don't ag-ree with you at aw-ull; Cluck-cluck-cluck-

cluck-cluck! Oh, do, oh, don't, we will, we won't, but we don't ag-ŕee
with you at aw-ull!"—the rich injured undulations of aggrieved protest, the omened menace of impending hysteria awoke in an alien spirit
a powerful surge of desire and humor, a wave of wild choking laughter
mixed with love and lust as one listened to the sensual, aggrieved, hen-
clucking protest of their souls.

The Jewish women were as old as nature, and as round as the earth:
they had a curve in them. They had gone to the wailing walls of death
and love for seven thousand years, the strong convulsive faces of the
Jews were ripe with grief and wisdom, and the curve of the soul of the
Jewish women was still unbroken. Female, fertile, yolky, fruitful as
the earth, and ready for the plow, they offered to the famished wanderer, the alien, the exile, the baffled and infuriated man, escape and
surcease of the handsome barren women, the hard varnished sawdust
dolls, the arrogant and sterile women, false in look and promise as a
hot-house peach, who walked the streets and had no curves or fruit-
fulness in them. The Jewish women waited with rich yolky cries for
him, and the news they brought him, the wisdom that they gave to him
was that he need not strangle like a mad dog in a barren dark, nor perish,
famished, unassuaged, within the wilderness beside a rusted lance—
but that there was still good earth for the plow to cleave and furrow,
deep cellars for the grain, a sheath for the shining sword, rich pockets of
spiced fertility for all the maddened lunges of desire.
They pressed around him at his table with insistent surge, and he
looked at them and saw that they were young; and sometimes they
belonged to the whole vast family of the earth: they were like all the
young people who had ever lived—they seemed clumsy, and noisy and
good, full of hope and loyalty and folly; and sometimes again, it seemed
to him that none of them had ever known youth or innocence, that they
had been born with old and weary souls, that they were born instructed
in the huge dark history of pain, the thousand mad and tortured sick-
nesses of the soul, and that the only thirst and hunger that they knew,
the desire that drove them with an insatiate lust, was for sorrow, grief,
and human misery. Had they ever cried into the howling winds at
night? Had they ever felt the sharp and tongueless ecstasy of spring,
or held their breath at night when great wheels pounded at the rail,
or trembled with a vast dark wave of pain, a wordless cry of joy, when
they heard ships calling at the harbor's mouth and thought of new lands

in the morning? Or had they always been so old and wise, so full of grief and evil?

The girls pressed in on him their sensual wave, and the boys stood farther off, behind them, waiting, and he saw the dark and furtive glances of the men pass slyly, each to each, in swift final looks of cynical communication. They waited for the women to have done, with a kind of hard and weary patience, an old and knowing agreement, a sense of acceptance, as if they had known for thousands of years that their women would betray them with a Gentile lover, and yet with a kind of triumph, as if they also knew they would regain them and be victorious in the end.

They seemed to have gained from life the terrible patience, the old and crafty skill and caution that come from long enduring of pain: as he looked at them he knew that they would never be wild and drunken, or beat their knuckles bloody on a wall, or lie beaten and senseless in the stews, but he knew that with smooth faces they would decant the bottle for some man who did, and that they would read him quietly to his desperate fate with their dark, mocking, and insatiate eyes. They had learned that a savage word would break no bones and that the wound of betrayal or a misprized love is less fatal than the stroke of the sword, the thrust of the knife: in the years that followed he saw that physically they were, for the most part, incorrupt, old and cautious, filled with skill and safety—that they had lived so long and grown so wise and crafty that their subtile, million-noted minds could do without and hold in dark contempt the clumsy imperfections of a fleshly evil—that they could evoke and live completely in a world of cruel and subtle intuitions, unphrased and unutterable intensities of cruelty, shame, and horror, without lifting a finger or turning a hand. Thus, in these years, as his own mind grew mad and twisted with the insane fabrications of a poisonous jealousy—as it immediately and without a bridge or break translated into terms of literal physical actuality an insane picture of cruelty and horror: of daughters who acted as procurers to their mothers, of sons and husbands going unperturbed to sleep in houses where their sisters, wives, and children lay quilted in the lust and evil abominations of an adulterous love, of calm untelling faces, looks and glances of a childlike purity, an air of goodness, faith and morning innocence throughout, while the whole knowledge of an unspeakable evil trembled in their hearts forever with an obscene and soundless laughter —these abominations of his fancy, this vile progeny which his mad

brain translated into literal fact, were probably for the most part only
images the cruel and subtile minds of the old, wise, patient Jews had
evoked and played with in their complex fantasy; and as he looked at
the swarm of dark insistent faces round him at the table, an overwhelming sensation of defeat and desolation drowned his spirit—their dark
looks read, and ate, and mocked at him, and yet were full of affection
and tenderness as if they loved the food they fed upon: it seemed to him
that he alone must die; that he must break his heart and smash his bones,
lie beaten, drunken, mashed and senseless in the dives, must wreck his
reason, lose his sanity, destroy his talent, and die a mad-dog howling
in the wilderness while they—they alone—these old, wise, weary, patient,
pain-devouring subtile-minded Jews—endured.

LIV

ROBERT's mistress had come to town, and Robert asked Eugene to
dine with them. In spite of the fact that Robert had talked constantly of
his love for Martha, they snapped and snarled at each other throughout
the evening. They went to a restaurant on Sixth Avenue in Greenwich
Village for dinner. During the course of the meal several people came in
whom Robert knew: the moment he saw them he would call sharply to
them, or jump up nervously and go to greet them. Then he would bring
them back to the table and, in a tone of dogged and sullen intensity,
introduce them to Martha, saying: "I want you to meet my wife."
Martha's face would flush with anger and sullen rage, but she would
acknowledge the introduction and mutter a few uncordial words of
greeting. As for the people to whom he introduced her, they at first
received the news that Martha was his wife with a look of blank stupefaction, managing, at length, to stammer: "B-b-but we didn't know you
were married, Robert! Why didn't you let some one know about it?
When did it happen?"

"About two weeks ago," he said brusquely, obviously getting a fierce
and sullen satisfaction from this absurd lie.

"Where are you living?"

"At the Leopold."

"Will you be staying there?"

"No, we're moving out soon."

"Are you going to live in New York?"

"Yes," he said doggedly, "we've taken an apartment. . . . Going to
move in Monday."

"Why, Robert!" they cried, having now recovered some fluency of speech, "we're awfully glad to know about this." And the women with some pretense at cordiality would turn to Martha, saying, "You must come to see us when you've settled down," and the men would wring Robert by the hand, slap him on the back, and dig him in the ribs. It was obvious that Robert derived a fierce and perverse pleasure from his stupid lie, but the girl was in a state of smouldering rage which blazed out at him the moment his friends had gone away. "You damn fool," she snapped, "what do you mean by telling a lie like that?"

"It's not a lie," he said, "it's the truth. You're my wife in everything but name!"

"You're a liar! Take that back! Don't you believe him," she said to Eugene, "there's not a word of truth in what he says. . . . You damned fool!" she blazed out at him. "What do you mean by telling your friends a story like that? Don't you know they're going to find out that you lied to them. And then," she added bitterly, "what are they going to say about me? You never thought of that, did you? Oh, no! You don't care if you ruin me or not! All you think of is yourself!"

"I don't care," he said with a sullen fierceness, "you're my wife and that's what I'm going to tell them all!"

"You're not!"

"I am! I'll show you if I don't!"

"I'm not your wife, and you needn't be so sure I ever will be! I got married once to a sick man, and I'll think it over a good long time, I assure you, before I get married again to a crazy man! Now, you'd better not be too sure of yourself, Mr. Weaver! You're not married to me yet by a long shot!"

A bitter quarrel broke out between them: they snarled, snapped, sneered, and wrangled—their voices rose until people at other tables began to look at them and listen curiously, but they paid no attention whatever to any one but themselves. Robert ended the argument suddenly by pushing his chair back from the table, sighing heavily, and saying feverishly and impatiently:

"All right, all right, all right! You're right! I'm wrong! Only, for God's sake, shut up and let me have a little peace!" Then they got into a taxi and went back to the hotel. They had a bottle of whiskey and they all went up to Robert's room, telephoned for ice and ginger ale, and began to drink. It was a little before midnight.

About two o'clock that night, as they sat there, a light, odd step, ap-

proaching briskly, came down the corridor and paused outside Robert's
door: then some one rapped lightly and sharply at the door, and with
this same movement of an odd, light and exuberant vitality. They
looked at one another with the sudden startled look of people who feel
the interruption of an intense silence around them—for the Leopold
for two hours had been steeped in this silence of sleep, and they now
experienced its living and animate presence for the first time. A
good many sensations of guilt—all but the real one—flashed through
their minds: that they had been drinking and making more noise
than they should, and that a guest had complained to the office about
them; or that some one had discovered that Robert had a woman
in his room, and that, in the interests of hotel decorum, she was to
be commanded to leave and go to her own quarters. The rapping
at the door was repeated, more brisk and loud. They were all very still,
Robert looked at Eugene nervously, remembering, perhaps, the sum of
his past errors at the hotel and his precarious standing there.

"You go see who it is," he said.

Eugene went to the door and opened it. A man—or rather, the wisp,
the breath, the fume of what had been a man—stood there: it was a
small figure with nothing on its skeleton of fragile bone which was
recognizable as living flesh, with only the covering, it seemed, of a
parchment-like skin so tightly drawn over the contours of the face and
head that the skull widened and flared with an impression of enormous
dome-like width and depth above a face so wizened and shrunken that
one remembered it later only as a feverish glint of teeth, an unshaved
furze of beard, and two blazing flags of red, darkened and shadowed by
the sunken depth of the sockets of the eye, where burned a stare of an
incredible size and brilliance—that and the whispering ghost of a voice,
the final, dominant, and unforgettable impression.

This wraith was clothed, or rather, engulfed, in garments which,
although of good cut and quality, it seemed never to have worn before:
they swathed it around and fell away in shapeless folds so that the body
was as indecipherable among them as a stick, and the neck emerged
from a collar through which it seemed the whole figure of the man
might have slipped as easily as through a hoop.

And yet the creature was burning with a savage energy which
coursed like an electric current through his withered body: it bore him
along at a light, odd step, capricious and buoyant as the bobbing of a

cork, and it foamed and bubbled in him now as he stood impatiently rapping at the door, and it blazed in his eyes with a corrupt and fatal glee, a mad flaming exuberance, a focal intensity of triumph, joy, and hate.

He entered the room immediately as soon as Eugene opened the door: he went in briskly at his light corky step and immediately said briskly and jovially in his whispering thread of voice: "Good evening! Are we all here? Is every one well? Did some one say something?"—he looked around inquiringly, then, with a disappointed air, continued — "No? I thought some one spoke. Well, then, come in, Mr. Upshaw. Thank you, I will. Won't you sit down? Yes, indeed!" He seated himself. "Will you have a drink? I should be delighted"—here he took the bottle, poured a stiff shot of whiskey into a glass, and drank it at one gulp. When he had finished, he looked around more quietly until his gaze rested with a kind of evil temperance on his wife: "Hello, Martha," he said casually and quietly. "How are you?" She did not answer and in a minute he repeated, still with his evil calm but with a more vicious intensity of tone, "Listen, you God-damned bitch! . . . When I ask you a question, you answer. How are you?"

"How did you get here?" she said.

"Oh!—Surprised to see me, is she?—Well, I tell you, darling, how it was. I was going to walk—I was going to walk, if necessary—now that just shows you how anxious I was to see you—I was going to walk the whole damned way from Denver, right over mountains and prairies and rivers and everything—but I didn't have to. I found a train all ready to go, darling; it was waiting for me when I got there, so 'Why walk?' I said. When I got to Kansas City I found an airplane waiting there, so I said, 'Why ride when flying's faster?' So that's the way I got here, darling."—He paused and drank again.

"How did you know where to find me?" asked Martha sullenly.

"Oh!" said Upshaw, lightly and gaily, "that was no trouble at all. Where should I find you, my dear? Where did I expect to find you? Why, right in the bedroom of my dear old pal, Mr. Robert Weaver, of course. I knew he'd look after you. I knew he wouldn't leave an innocent young girl like you to wander around all alone in the city. . . . Hi, there, Robert," he said cordially, lifting his hand in a salute of friendly greeting, as if noting Robert's presence for the first time.

"How are you, boy! I'm glad to see you. You've been looking after my wife, haven't you, Robert? You took care of her, didn't you? I'm much obliged to you. . . . You son-of-a-bitch," he added quietly and slowly, and with an accent of infinite loathing.

No one spoke, and after gazing at his wife a moment longer with this same air of evil quietness, he said, in a tone of mock surprise: "Why, what's the matter? You don't look a bit glad to see me, darling. Most men's wives would be wild about a husband who flew across the country in an aeroplane to see them, most women would be crazy about that."

"I wish," the girl said bitterly, "that you had fallen into a river and drowned."

"Now, is *that* nice! Is *that* kind!" said Upshaw in a tone of grieved reproach.

He turned toward Eugene and spoke to him for the first time. . . . "Now, I leave it to you, Mr. ——" he hesitated, "I didn't catch your name, sir, but is it all right if I call you Mr. Whipple?"

"Yes," Eugene said. "It's all right."

"Good!" he cried. "I knew it would be. The reason I say that is I used to have a friend out in Cleveland named Charley Whipple, who was just the same type of fellow that you are—*you* know," he said quietly and sneeringly, "a fine clean-cut fellow, eyes glowing with health, beautiful complexion, broad-shouldered, both feet on the ground, good to his mother.—Oh! he was a prince!—Just the same sort of looking fellow you are—so you won't mind if I call you by his name, will you? You remind me so much of him. Well, now, Mr. Whipple, I ask you if you think it's nice for a man's wife to talk to him like this? Is it kind? Is it fair?"

"She's not your wife," said Robert. "She's my wife."

For the first time Upshaw turned and faced his enemy squarely: he surveyed him slowly, up and down, with eyes which burned and glittered with their hatred. "Did you say something?" he asked.

"You heard me," said Robert.

"Did any one speak to you? Did any one say anything to you?" Upshaw whispered. He was silent a moment; then he leaned forward slightly over the table. "Let me give you some advice," he said. "The only pity about this is that you're not going to be able to use it.—But I'm going to give it to you anyway: here it is—Don't fool with a dying man, Robert. If you're going to play around with any one, play around with the living, and not with the dead. Dead men are bad people to play around with."

"All right! All right!" cried Robert in a hoarse, excited tone. "That constitutes a threat! . . . Martha, Eugene, . . . I call on you to bear witness that he threatened me! We'll just see how that sounds in a court of law."

"Courts! Law!" said Upshaw; and even as he spoke they all felt instantly how preposterous was Robert's threat and how meaningless such terms had become for this wisp of a man.

"Do you think I care one good God-damn now for all the courts and laws that ever were? . . . Do you think there has been a time for the last two years when I gave a damn whether I lived or died?"

"Except to spite Martha and me," said Robert bitterly. "You cared about that, all right!"

"Yes," said Upshaw quietly. "You're right. I would have hung on to life as long as I could gasp a breath of air into what was left of my lung, and I would have lived on without a lung to breathe with in order to spoil your filthy game—that was the way I hated the two of you. You don't understand that, do you, Robert? You don't understand a man being able to hate so hard he can keep alive on it, he can use it instead of a lung to breathe with, he can use it instead of air. You don't know anything about that, do you?"

"Yes, I do," said Robert. "I knew you hated my guts all along!"

"Your guts!" Upshaw snarled. "Why, damn you, I hated the earth you walked upon, the air you breathed, the house you lived in, the places you went to; I hated all the people who saw you or spoke to you or had ever spent an hour in your company—you polluted the atmosphere for me if I even heard the sound of your voice."

"I know you did," said Robert, nodding. "What did I tell you?" he cried to Martha, with a note of triumphant conviction.

"You *know!* You *know!*" cried Upshaw fiercely. "Why, damn you, you poor cheap imitation of a contriving rascal, you damned little drug-store Casanova, you dirty little swine of a country-club snob, you village fortune-teller, you know nothing! . . . For two years I stayed alive with not enough sound lung left in me to cover the size of a silver dollar—and do you think it was because I was afraid to die, or wanted to live? No! No!" he whispered, and his face or rather that eloquence of eye and tooth grew passionate with the bitterest disgust and loathing I have ever seen. "I've had more than thirty years of it, and Christ! it's been enough! I've had my belly full of it. . . . I'm fed up all the way to here!" he whispered, and he struck himself fiercely at the base of the throat. He coughed, suddenly, briefly, terribly, and with a swift impatient movement of his hot corded fingers he snatched a towel from the rack beside the water-basin, pressed his lowered face into it and then stared for a moment with an expression of intent and fascinated disgust into its folds, then he flung the bloodied rag away impatiently.

"You know," he said again more calmly, and for the first time now with a touch of weariness, as if the fierce flame of this incredible energy of passion which had thus far upheld him had now been spent. "Why, you know nothing. It took a *man* to hate like that," he said. . . . "—a better man than you could ever be—yes! . . . with no more lung than a rabbit, I'm still a better man than you could ever be, for you are nothing but a thing without the courage even of your own rotten convictions——

"God!" he looked with weary disgust from one to the other as they sat sullen, dumbly sodden, saying nothing. "The two of you! What a pair! . . . And to think of the time I wasted hating you . . . to think of all the time when I might have been pushing daisies in some quiet spot . . . keeping myself alive by thinking of this moment." His body was shaken again by a horrible soundless laughter. "Christ! . . . To think that I should ever have wanted to kill either of you."

"To kill us!" said Robert hoarsely, not with fear but accusingly, as if he were collecting damning evidence in a trial.

"Yes," Upshaw answered with the same weary tranquillity, "to kill you! . . . I've breathed and drunk and thought it for two years. I've lived just for this moment. I came two thousand miles across the continent to blow your brains out. . . ."

"Did you hear him?" cried Robert, jumping up from the table. "Did you hear what he said, Martha? Did you hear him threaten me?"

"Sit down!" said Upshaw quietly. "I've seen you now and I'm satisfied. I wouldn't touch you. Why, God-damn you, you're not worth it, either of you." Again he surveyed them with slow loathing, and broke into his soundless laughter. "Kill you! Why, I wouldn't do either of you so big a favor. You don't deserve such luck! I'll let you live and rot together. . . . Take her! . . . Take her!" he cried, more strongly, his eyes burning into fury. "Take her! . . . But before you do"—with a swift movement he withdrew from his pocket a small and crumpled wad of dollar bills—"here! I want to give you something!" And he flung them straight at Robert's face, "Take that . . . and go and get yourself a *good* whore while you're at it!"

Robert sat perfectly still for a moment; then he got up slowly, went over to the door, and flung it open and walked back to the table. . . . "Get out of here," he said. Upshaw did not move: he sat regarding him silently, with an intent, contemptuous, catlike stare.

"Did you hear me?" said Robert. . . . "Get out of my room!"

"Sit down," said Upshaw. "You're going to annoy me."

"Annoy you! I'll annoy you, you damned rascal," Robert cried furiously, and suddenly he slapped Upshaw in the face, shouting, "You're going out of here this minute, do you hear? . . . I'll show you if you can insult me in my own place," and he lunged viciously towards him.

What happened then was so sudden and swift that Eugene could never thereafter remember clearly the order in which all of the events occurred: as Robert plunged towards the little man, Martha spoke sharply to him, commanding him to be still, at the same moment the table and two chairs overturned with a crash of glassware . . . and Upshaw, somehow, with an incredible speed of movement was on his feet and moving backward out of the way of Robert's lunging fist. Eugene had a brief and terribly clear sensation of a gesture of catlike speed as Upshaw thrust his hand into the pocket of his coat and then the bright wicked wink of steel. Then Martha was on top of him, clinging frantically to his arm, wrestling him into the wall, and in a moment wrenching the weapon from his grasp.

For a moment there was no sound in the room whatever save the sound of three excited people breathing rapidly and heavily, and another sound, the terrible sound of Upshaw's breathing, hoarse, rattling, painful, breaking suddenly and sharply into a torn gasping cough that was thick with blood. The first words spoken came from Martha:

"Close that door!" she commanded curtly.

Robert, instead of obliging her, turned to Eugene with an awed and quieted light in his eye.

"Did you see that?" he whispered to Eugene.—"Did you see him pull that gun on me? . . . Why!" he cried with a kind of sudden astonishment, "it was assault with a deadly weapon! That's what it was! He tried to murder me!" He was beside himself with astonishment and excitement. "I'm going to get the police," and he rushed out into the hall.

"Go get that damned fool and bring him back here," she said to Eugene. *"And close that door!"*

Eugene ran out into the corridor just in time to see Robert disappearing at his long stiff stride around the corner that led to the elevators in the main building. When Eugene got there Robert was pressing· buttons feverishly, but unfortunately, because the hour was so late, and the elevator man was asleep below, his call had not yet been answered. Eugene seized him by the arm and began to pull him along back towards his room.

"Let go of me!" he said.

"You damned fool! . . . Do you want to ruin us all?"   .

He seemed to sober up and grew calmer after a moment or two of excited prayer and protest. They went back to the room quietly enough. When they got there Martha was supporting Upshaw's body against the basin of the washstand. The man, by this time, was either unconscious or semiconscious: all the savage and unholy energy which had burned for a space so incredibly that it had the power to hurl this diseased and near-dead mite across a continent, had now flared utterly out and the creature which the girl supported in her arms, with a kind of dark and sullen tenderness, seemed to have died and dwindled with it; the body was no longer discernible, it seemed to have faded, a fabric of rotten sticks, into a shapeless heap of clothing; it dangled shapelessly and grotesquely like some deflated figure, and yet from the head, from that death's-head of skull and tooth and blazing eyes, there were spurting unbelievable, incredible fountains of blood: it burst simultaneously from the mouth and nostrils in a steady torrent until his skin was laced with it, it filled the basin, it was incredible that such fountains of bright blood should pour out of this withered squirrel of a man.

Robert sat down sullenly in a chair by the table after saying, "Now, this is your last chance. . . . I've had as much as I can stand. You've got to decide between us here and now!" She did not answer him, and he said no more, relapsing into a sullen and half-drunken stupor.

The girl washed the blood away from Upshaw's face with a towel: in a moment more she asked Eugene if he would help her carry him to the bed. Eugene picked him up and put him on the bed, his body felt like a handful of light dry sticks, he weighed no more than a child of ten, already his figure seemed, under the strange and terrible chemistry of death, to shrink and wither visibly from one moment to another but his head rested above that shapeless and grotesque bundle of clothing as if it had been severed from the body—with an immense austerity of line and light, a cold, stiffening, and upthrust calm.

Eugene went down to the office and told them what had happened.

The night clerk, a fat, shuffling old man with a mild, pasty face, and the black African negro who was at the telephone-board, received the news with astonishing calmness, and matter-of-factness, and then acted with an admirable coolness, speed and quiet precision, of which Eugene often thought in the months that followed, because it revealed to him a kind of secret knowledge, a hidden seriousness in the hotel's working, and it showed, moreover, how much knowledge, ability, and decision may be stored behind the faces of inept and foolish-looking men.

Eugene looked at the clock above the office desk: it was now ten minutes after three o'clock in the morning. Within twenty minutes they had an ambulance, a doctor, and two stretcher-bearers at the hotel: the interne, a young Jew with a little mustache, walked quietly and casually into the room, with the ends of a stethoscope fastened in his ears. Eugene thought that Upshaw was already dead! His face had the upthrust marble rigidity of death, but after a moment's examination, the doctor spoke quietly to the two men with him, they put the stretcher on the floor and laid the withered little figure on it. As they started to move out of the room Upshaw's arms began to flop and jerk stiffly and grotesquely with every step they took: at another word from the doctor they put their burden on the floor again, the interne knelt swiftly, unknotted the cravat in Upshaw's collar and loosely tied his wrists together. Then they all went out, and Martha followed, holding Upshaw's hat. She rode over in the ambulance to the hospital, which was only a few blocks away in Fifteenth Street. Robert and Eugene followed in a taxi, there was no one on the streets, the buildings and the pavements had the hard, bare angularity they have early in the morning: they waited downstairs in a little room until shortly after five o'clock in the morning, when Martha came down to see them and to tell them that Upshaw had just died.

Then Eugene left Robert and Martha there together, and walked back towards the hotel. The streets were still bare, but in the east there was the first width of morning light, cold steel-gray, harsh and sharply clean: day was beginning to break, and he could hear the rumbling jingle of a milk-wagon, and the sound of hoof and wheel behind him in the lonely street.

LV

IF the hard and rugged lineaments of Abe's character had not at this time emerged out of the glutinous paste of obscure yearnings, there was no such indecision and uncertainty in the character of his mother. It was as legible as gold, as solid as a rock.

Abe's mother was an old woman, with the powerful and primitive features of the aged Jewess: she was almost toothless, a solitary blackened tooth stood mournfully in the centre of her strong ruined mouth, she had a craggy worn face, seamed and furrowed by a countless sorrow, a powerful beaked nose, and a strong convulsive mouth, a mask which was like a destiny since it seemed to have been carved and fashioned for the dirge-like wailing of eternal grief. The face of the old woman might have served not only as the painting of the whole history of her race, but as the painting of the female everywhere—not the female with her ephemeral youth, her brief snares of hair and hide, her succulent burst of rose-lips and flowing curve—but the female timeless, ageless, fixed in sorrow and fertility, as savage, as enduring, and as fecund as the earth. The old woman's face was like a worn rock at which all the waves of life had smashed and beaten: it was unmistakably the face of an old Jewess and yet the powerful and craggy features bore an astonishing resemblance to the face of a pioneer woman or of an old Indian chief.

Her life, moreover, had the agelessness of the earth, the timelessness of her race and destiny: she had not been touched at all by the furious and savage life of the city with its sensational brevities, its hard, special, temporal qualities of speech, fashion, and belief, its million ephemeral enthusiasms, briefly held and forgotten, the stunned oblivion of its memory, which, in the brutal stupefaction of a thousand days, can hold to nothing, so that even the memory of love and death cannot endure there and a man may forget his dead brother ere his flesh grow rotten 'n the grave.

The old woman did not forget: for her, as for the God she worshipped, the passing of seven thousand years was like the passing of a single day; yesterday, tomorrow, and forever, a moment at the heart of love and memory. Thus, once when Eugene had called Abe upon the telephone, a full year after the death of his oldest brother, Jacob, the old woman had answered: the old voice came feebly, brokenly, indecipherably, and was like a wail. He asked for Abe, she could not understand, she began to talk in an excited, toothless mumble—a torrent of Yiddish broken here and there by a few mangled words and scraps of English—all she knew. At length Eugene made her understand he wanted to speak to Abe: suddenly she recognized his voice and remembered him. Then, instantly, as if it had happened only the day before, and as if he had been a friend of her dead son, although he had never known him, the old woman began to wail, faintly and rhythmically, across the wire: "Jakie! . . . My Jakie! . . . Mein Sohn Jakie! . . . He is dead."

A few days later Eugene had gone home with Abe for dinner: he lived with his mother, two brothers, and Jimmy, his sister's illegitimate child, in a flat which occupied the second floor of an old four-storey red-brick house in Twelfth Street, near Second Avenue, on the East Side. The old woman had prepared a good meal for them: a thick rich soup, chopped chicken livers, chicken, cake, and a strong sweet wine: she served them but would not sit and eat with them: she came in briefly and shook hands shyly and awkwardly, mumbling incoherently, a mangled jargon of Yiddish and English. Suddenly, however, as if she had briefly mastered herself by a strong effort her old and sorrowful face was twisted by a convulsion of powerful and incurable grief, and a long, terrible, savagely wailing cry was torn from her throat: she turned blindly, and with a movement of natural and primitive sorrow, she suddenly seized the edges of her apron in her gnarled and worn hands and flung it up over her head and rushed toward the door at a blind, lunging, reeling step. She was like one demented by sorrow: the old woman began to beat her withered breasts and pull at her wispy gray hair, meanwhile running and stumbling blindly around her kitchen in a horrible and savage dementia and drunkenness of grief. Abe followed her out, and Eugene could hear his voice, low, urgent, and tender, as he spoke to her persuasively in Yiddish, and her long wailing cries subsided and he returned. His face was sad and weary-looking and in a moment he said: "Mama's breaking up fast. She's never been able to get over my brother's death. She thinks about it all the time: she can't get it off her mind."

"How long has he been dead, Abe?"

"He died over a year ago," Abe said. "But that doesn't matter: I know her—she'll never forget it now as long as she lives. She'll always feel the same about it."

This terrible and savage picture of grief was carved upon Eugene's memory unforgettably: it became a tremendous and formidable fact, a fact as ancient, timeless, and savage as the earth, a fact which neither the stupefying oblivion of the city's life, the furious chaos of the streets, the savage glare of ten thousand blind and dusty days could touch. The

old woman's grief was taller than their tallest towers, and more endùr-
ing than all their steel and stone: it would last forever when all the
city's bones were dust, and it was like the grief of all the women who
had ever beat their breasts and flung their aprons across their heads and
run, wailing, with a demented and drunken step: it filled him with
horror, anger, a sense of cruelty, disgust, and pity.

She was the fertile and enduring earth from which they sprung, and
all of them, transformed so sharply and so curiously by the city's tone
and life, drew in to her with devotion and respect: Abe, with his dreary
gray face of the man-swarm cipher, Sylvia with her feverish, electric
night-time glitter, all of the brothers and sisters, with all that was new,
sharp, alien, flashy, trivial, or material in speech, dress, manner, and
belief—all of them returned to her with love, loyalty, and reverence as
to some great broodhen of the earth. The old woman's life was rooted
in the soil of two devotions: the synagogue and the home, and all that
happened beyond the limits of this devotion was phantom and remote:
this soil was ageless, placeless, everlasting.

Abe loved his mother dearly: whenever he spoke of her, even casually, his voice was touched with a hush of respect and affection. But he
disliked his father: the few times Eugene heard him mention him he
spoke of him in a hard and bitter voice, referring to him as "that guy,"
or "that fellow," as if he were a stranger. Eugene never saw the father:
the children all felt bitterly towards him and had sent him away to room
alone. Abe told Eugene that the man was a shoemaker, and apparently
improvident and thriftless. He had never been able to earn enough
to support his family, and in addition, Abe said, he was a petty family
tyrant. Abe's childhood had been scarred by memories of privation,
tyranny and poverty—the mother and the children had had a
bitter struggle for existence, and Abe had worked since his eighth
year at a variety of hard, gray, shabby and joyless employments: he
had been a newsboy, a grocer's delivery boy, an office boy in a
broker's office, a typist in a collection agency endlessly writing out
form letters, the office man and secretary for the head-professor of
the architectural school, and one of these pallid, swarthy, greasily sweating youths of the fur and garment house districts who ceaselessly
propel through swarming and kaleidoscopic streets of trade small wheel-
trucks piled high with dresses, garments, furs, and clothes or with
the thousand travelling varieties of all that horrible nondescript junk
known under the indecisive name of "novelties." Once, also, he had

spent part of a summer in New Jersey unloading freight cars filled with Georgia watermelons, and for a considerable time he had driven a truck for his two oldest brothers, who had a zinc business in the "gas-house district" of the East Side, between Avenue A and the river and North of Fourteenth Street.

Here, once, Eugene had accompanied him at noon of a flashing day in spring, a glitter of light and flashing waters, a sparkle of gold and blue: in a large bare space near factories they had seen a ring of young thugs throwing dice, and near the river were the immense and ugly turrets of the gas tanks, and then the wharves, the great odorous piers, and the flashing waters—the vast exultant play and traffic of the river life, the powerful little tugs, the ships, and the barges laden with their strings of rusty freight cars.

As they walked away through the powerful ugliness and devastation of that district, with its wasteland rusts and rubbish, its slum-like streets of rickety tenement and shabby brick, its vast raw thrust of tank, glazed glass and factory building, and at length its clean, cold, flashing strength and joy of waters—a district scarred by that horror of unutterable desolation and ugliness and at the same time lifted by a powerful rude exultancy of light and sky and sweep and water, such as is found only in America, and for which there is yet no language—as they walked away along a street, the blue wicked shells of empty bottles began to explode on the pavements all around them: when they looked around to see from what quarter this attack was coming, the street was empty save for a young thug who leaned against the rotting edge of a closed door, hands thrust in pockets, and a look of pustulate and evil innocence upon his thin tough Irish face. The street was evil and silent and empty, but when they turned and went on again, the exploding bottles began to drop around them on the pavement in splinters of sinister blue.

Abe grinned toughly: he did not seem at all surprised or perturbed by the murderous stealth and secrecy of the attack, its obscene and cowardly uselessness. He explained that the district had been one of the worst in the city and the headquarters for one of the most criminal gangs: time and again the gangsters had broken into his brother's zinc shop and robbed it, and Abe and all his brothers, being Jews, had had to fight it out since childhood, foot and fist and tooth and nail, and club and stone, with the young Irish toughs and gangsters who infested the district. Such had been his childhood: he told Eugene many stories of bloody fights waged back and forth across these pavements, of young boys maimed, crippled, or blinded in these savage fights, of one boy who had his eye torn out of his head by his enemy's gouging thumb in a fight to a finish on one of the piers, and of another whose brains had been smashed out on the pavement below the elevated structure by a rock hurled by an enemy's hand in a fight of the neighborhood gangs. Thus, in pier and alley, on street and roof, children had learned the arts of murder, the smell of blood, the odor of brains upon the pavement. Abe told how one of his older brothers, Barney—a thickly set powerful-looking man with short thick hands and a tough meaty-looking fighter's face, gray, square, and good-humored—had to fight it out step by step with the gangsters, who had come to his shop, again and again, with demands for money—money which the merchants of the district paid them meekly and regularly for "protection" —a euphemism for graft and menace, a bribe for being left alone and for the assurance that one's shop would not be entered and one's stock smashed or stolen in the night. Barney had met all these menaces with a hard cold eye and two rock-like fists with which time and again he had beaten into a pulp the thugs who came to threaten him: he was a good man and a savage fighter and he had learned the arts of combat in the sternest and most brutal arena on earth—the city streets.

"And—oh-ho-ho-ho!"—softly, painfully, Abe lifted his widely grinning face and laughed, "how that guy loves it! Say! they picked the wrong one when they picked on him! Oh-ho-ho-ho-ho! *Can* he fight! *Does* he love it! Say! do you know what I saw him do to two of them one time—oh-ho-ho-ho-ho-ho! Gee! it was rich! They came in there to shake him down and— Oh! Ho-ho!—ho! You shoulda seen it! He picks up a keg of zinc that weighs 200 pounds and he *breaks* it—oh-ho-ho-ho!—over the first guy's head."

"And what became of the second guy?"

"Oh-ho-ho-ho! . . . Gee, it was rich! You shoulda seen that other guy get out of there! Say! He almost tore the door down in his hurry—oh-ho-ho-ho!"

Such were the various members of this family as Eugene came to know about them: each of them in his own way was marked by a decisive individuality and independence of spirit which told of their lives of combat, toil and struggle in the city streets, and yet, although indelibly marked, scarred and hardened by his life, none of them had been brutalized by it. In fact, as Eugene thought of all these people later, an extraordinary quality in them became evident. It was this: here was a family of poor East Side Jews, the children of an immigrant and thriftless shoemaker and an old orthodox Jewish woman. These children had all had to make their own way, to fight and struggle bitterly for a living: now some of them were tough, rugged and unlettered merchants, traders and mechanics, some were successful milliners and designers, and some were talented musicians, students of science, people of extraordinary intelligence and ability. And all of them, even the most unlettered, seemed to have a completely natural unaffected interest and respect for the arts, or for scholarly and intellectual attainment. This circumstance—this remarkable fusion in one poor Jewish family of elements which would have seemed almost incredible in the families of poor laboring or country people Eugene had known before—this combination of the manual, the commercial, the artistic and the scholarly in one poor family—seemed so natural both to him and to them that Eugene never found it strange or wonderful until years later.

LVI

JUNE had brought with it a blessed respite from his classes at the university. Now the summer drew on towards its close—the brutal and weary New York summer with its swelter of dead wet heats, its death of hope, its sorrow of a timeless memory. And yet, in the city's summer nights there was a kind of solemn joy, a hush of peace and light and human resignation that was so different from the wild and nameless joy and pain of spring, the sorrow of autumn, the winter's grim and stern protraction of the soul. *Then*—in these nights of waning summer—more than at any other season of the year, the immense and murmurous sound of time was audible. It was above one and around one, it was near and far, it was immense and omnipresent, and it was indefinable. It seemed to hover somewhere in the upper air, above the city's steep canyons, the giant explosions of her thousand towers, the swarming millions of her tortured and uneasy life forever waging their desperate, ugly and unprofitable strife in all her hot and tangled mazes. And that voice of time, above the ugly clamor of that tormented life, was imperturbable; immense, remote and murmurous, it seemed to have resumed into itself all of the rumors of the earth, and to comprise, out of the bitter briefness of man's days, the essence of his own eternity, and to be itself eternal, fixed, and everlasting, no matter what men lived or died.

The people of the city heard this sound of time, and on these evenings of the waning summer, their lives were subject to its spell. For the first time in many months one heard the sounds of quiet laughter in the streets at night, the voices of the people as they passed were strangely hushed, the sounds of life were immense, all murmurous as time itself. This sense of peace, of resignation, of a quiet and tranquil sorrow and joy was everywhere; it may have been some quality of the summer air that imposed on all the violence of the city's life a kind of muted harmony, but the spirit of this peace seemed to have entered the very flesh and spirit of the city, somehow to have tranquillized the feverish blood and nervous and exacerbated bodies of its people. For the first time in months their eyes were quiet and thoughtful and had lost their look of hatred and suspicion, hostility and mistrust. Their faces had lost their strained, hard, and hurried look, even their tongues had lost some of their strident, rasping, and abusive violence.

That immense and murmurous hush of time and sorrowful acceptance had touched even the life of youth. At night one still saw groups of young men walking through the streets, but even they had somehow been subdued and chastened by this spell of time. And in these bands of youth—these straggling bands of young men who struggle through the city streets at night in groups of six or eight, and who have become so much a part of our familiar experience and the city's life that they no longer seem curious to us—the change that this great spell of time had wrought was perhaps more evident than anywhere else.

Where were the songs of youth upon those city streets? Where the laughter, the wild spontaneous mirth, the passion, warmth and golden poetry of youth? Here was the great boy Jason looking for brothers in the fellowship of that inspired adventure of man's youth—the proud, deathless image of what all of us desire when young, where was it? Where were the noble thoughts and ardors of young men, the fierce and bitter desperation and the proud and foolish hopes, the grand dreams and the music of the fleeting and impossible reveries—all that makes youth lovely and desirable, and that keeps man's faith—where was it among these young men on the city streets?

It was not there. Poor sallow, dark, swarthy creatures that they were, with rasping tongues, loose mouths and ugly jeering eyes, this infamous band of youth was death-in-life itself. It had been brought still-born from its mother's womb into a world of city streets and corners, into all the waning violence of the tenement, bitterly to try to root its meagre

life into the rootless rock, meagrely to struggle in its infamous small
phlegm along the pavements, feebly to imitate the feeble objects of its
base idolatry—of which the most heroic was a gangster, the most
sagacious was a pimp, the most witty was some Broadway clown.

How often have we seen them, heard them, turned away from them
with weariness and disgust, as they straggled along at night, a meagre
shirt-sleeved band of gangling sizes, each fearful and uneasy in the
other's eye, kicking the ash-cans over as feats of derring-do, trying for
approbation with a hoarse call and a pitiable and mirthless striving after
repartee, of which the more glittering fragments ran like this:

"Hey-y . . . Eddy! . . . Holy Jeez! . . . Hey-y, youse guys! . . .
Cuh-*mahn!*"

"Ah-h, what's yer hurry? . . . Hey-y! Youse udah guys! . . . Joe's
in a hurry . . . Who's goin' t' pay duh taxi-ride?"

"Holy *Jeez!* What's keepin' yuh! . . . Youse guys, cuh-mahn!"

"Ah-h, guh-wahn. . . . What's t' hurry? Where's duh fire?"

Now in these nights of waning summer, even these raucous voices,
the pitiable sterility of these feeble jests, that meagre and constricted
speech consisting almost wholly of a few harsh cries and raucous imprecations that recurred intolerably, incredibly through all the repercussions
of an idiot monotony—all of the rootless, fearful, and horrible desolation of these young pavement lives—was somehow caught up in this
great and tragic hush and spell of time, transmitted by it, until even
their vast unloveliness of youth was given a sorrowful quality of pity
and regret.

August came, and with it already a faint and troubling premonition
of the autumn—a breath, a fragrance, and an odor—that somehow spoke
of summer's ending, the premonitory thrill and promise of the voyage.
What was it? It was one of those very strange and troubling odors
known here in America, of which our lives are all compact, which
we have lived and breathed and known with our blood, and for which
we have no language. It is, somehow—the odor of cities, cities, cities—
at the hour of evening, the scorched end of every expiring day—the
smell of evening hush and peace and of the sea in harbors. It is the
smell of old worn woods, warm resins, sultry, getting into our very
entrails somehow with its strange and nameless fragrance of sorrow
and delight; the smell of the wooden baseball bleachers, of the old
worn plankings of an amusement park, passed over by a million feet
since morning; and it is the smell of street-cars, car-barns, the faded

day-coach plush of trains, the smell of bridges and of old wharves and piers, of hot tarred roofing, and of tar out in the streets, of summer's fatigue, quietness, and summer's ending, the quiet and tranquil sorrow of memory as we remember youth, our father's voice upon the night-time summer porch, the smell of the grape-vines and the ripened grapes, the grinding screech and halt of a street-car on the hill above our father's house, and the knowledge that all this is lost, our father dead, our childhood gone, another year, our first in the great man-swarm of the city, ended—and this, the knowledge of the bitter briefness of our days, is somehow mixed with the smell of the sea in harbors, the freshening breeze of evening, the call of ships, and, somehow, God knows how, with the intolerable thrill and promise of the unknown voyage.

And with this breath of autumn and the promise of the voyage there came to Eugene the news that Starwick was at that moment in the city—would stop there briefly on his way to Europe. At this time also, Joel Pierce turned up and Eugene renewed an acquaintance that had begun in Cambridge and lapsed during the interim.

LVII

He had never met any of Joel Pierce's family, but one night towards seven o'clock when he had just returned to his room from the university, Joel telephoned him, and, saying that his father was in town, asked him if he would not go to dinner and to the theatre with them. He found Joel and his father waiting for him in the lobby. Mr. Pierce was a man of fifty years, comfortably dressed for the hot weather in a black mohair suit, and with a kind of stately yet spacious dignity of linen that was agreeably old-fashioned and that evoked a picture of an older and more leisurely generation. He was quite deaf—so deaf, in fact, that he made use of a small ear-phone—but his speech and manners, like his dress, were easy, friendly, and yet touched with an air of distinguished authority.

He took the two boys to the Lafayette for dinner, and ordered generously and with the easy and comforting assurance of a man of the world who gives every one around him a happy feeling of security and well-being. For Eugene, it was a memorable experience.

The fine restaurant—it was perhaps the finest he had yet seen—the

French waiters, the delicious food, the beautiful women, the well-dressed, prosperous and worldly-looking men and the pleasant weary languor of fading day, the huge nameless thrill and prophecy of on-coming night touched him with a feeling of joy and nameless anticipa-tion. He felt, as he had never felt before, that strange, seductive promise which the city has at evening, at the end of a day of terrible summer's heat, and which is so strangely mixed of sorrow and delight, of desola-tion and the promise of a wild and nameless joy.

And suddenly, all the horror, heat and desolation of the day was forgotten. He forgot the blind horror of the man-swarm thrusting through the mazes of the furious streets. He forgot the drowning flood of humid flesh, the pale, wet, suffering faces that thrust from nowhere out of sweltering heat, that were engulfed again into the heat-hazed distances of swarming streets in which man's life seemed more un-countable than the sands of the sea, and more blind, lost and horribly forsaken than the lives of those eyeless crawls and gropes that scuttle blindly and forever through murky ooze upon the sea's vast floor.

The old red light of evening filled his heart again with its wild prophecy, its huge and secret joy, and the great stride of oncoming night revived again, in all their magic, his childhood dreams of the enchanted city, the city of great men and glorious women, the city of unceasing joy, of power, triumph and success, and of the fortunate, good, and happy life.

As Mr. Pierce sat there with his air of quiet and urbane authority, studying the menu with a little frowning smile through the lenses of a pince-nez that dangled fashionably and casually from a black silk cord when he was not using it, the boy felt an indescribable sense of wealth and power and prosperous ease. It seemed to him that everything in the world was his for the asking, and the suave service of the waiter, hovering over Mr. Pierce with poised pencil and an attitude of devoted respect, the rich designs of snowy linen, the heavy silver, the thick car-pets, the handsome women and distinguished-looking men, all added to this feeling of wealth and happiness.

Mr. Pierce kept studying the menu with an air of good-natured seriousness, quizzing his son from time to time with gruff but genial banter:

"Joel," he would say, "what do you want? Have you any prefer-ence of your own or will you leave it to me to decide?"

"Gosh!" Joel answered in his soft, eager tone. "I don't care, Pups. Whatever you say goes with me! You know, it's all the same to me, anyway. I can eat anything you order. Only," he added laughing, "I'd prefer it if there's no meat. I'd like it much better if you ordered vegetables."

Mr. Pierce knocked the pince-nez from his nose, and turning to Eugene with an air of agreeable confidence, said:

"What's wrong with a boy who takes no more interest in his food than that? Can you make it out? It strikes me as the most astonishing thing," he went on in a gruff, distinguished way, "to see a healthy young man who has no interest in his belly. Really, Joel," he went on, turning to his son and regarding him with a kind of quizzical but good-humored sarcasm, "I'd feel so much better about you if you only liked food more. It's really tragic to see a boy of your age deliberately throwing away one of the greatest pleasures in life. Don't you think so?" he demanded, turning to the other boy again with his air of friendly confidence. "Or have you turned vegetarian, too?"

"Gosh, no!" Joel said, laughing his hushed eager, immensely agreeable laugh. "He'll agree with every word you say, Pups. He likes food even more than you do."

"Then I'm glad to hear it!" said Mr. Pierce approvingly. "I had begun to fear that this younger generation had gone utterly to hell. But if the symptoms are only local—" he frowned humorously at his son for a moment—"perhaps it's not as bad as I thought."

"You and Pups should get along together beautifully," said Joel to Eugene. "He loves to eat—he's a wonderful cook—you should come up to Rhinekill sometime and let him cook one of his meals for you."

The ordering of the meal proceeded in this agreeable fashion. Mr. Pierce ordered liberally: small pink-fleshed clams, cold, pungent and exciting in their perfect shells, a thick pea soup with little squares of toast-crust floating in it, young chicken, plump and tender, grilled so succulently that it seemed to melt away the moment that one put it in his mouth, asparagus and potatoes, and a salad of crisp lettuce, beautifully mixed, "fatigued," in a big salad bowl, iced coffee, and a dessert of ripe Camembert and salted crackers. Mr. Pierce and Eugene ate heartily and with obvious relish, but Joel, in spite of all their protests and his father's bantering ridicule, which he took with the beautiful laughing good-nature which was one of the finest traits of his character, stuck to his vegetable diet with the gentle doggedness that was also characteristic of him.

Later, when they had finished dinner, they drove uptown in a taxicab and went to one of the summer musical shows near Broadway, where an English revue was appearing. The comic actress, Beatrice Lillie, was the star of the performance. Eugene had never heard of her before, but it was evident from the fashionable and "smart" look of the audience, and the way in which Joel and other people greeted every word and gesture, that the actress was "all the rage," one of those persons who, in addition to their native talent, have some special quality that for a time makes them the darling of the cult-adepts of the world of fashion.

The revue was a clever and amusing one, but it also had a stylish quality of fashionable smartness that was more and more beginning to mark the productions of the theatre and the responses of the audience. Thus, in later years, when one had almost completely forgotten the scenes of the revue and its songs and jokes, one could still remember it for the brilliant picture of the life it evoked. And the image of that life was implied rather than portrayed. The revue was one of those productions which people were beginning to "wear" as they "wore" books or plays or a dress: people went to the revue more because it was "the thing to do," the thing that every one was talking about, than because they had a genuine desire to go, more because they had been told that it was "amusing" than from any deep conviction that they would find it so.

Thus, not only in the jokes and songs and scenes of the revue, but in the laughter and applause with which the fashionable audience greeted them, there was a quality that was somewhat strained and metallic—a new and disagreeable mirth that was coming into man's life, which seemed to have its sources not in the warm human earth and blood of humor, but to proceed from something sterile, sour and acrid in his soul. In this hard and essentially lifeless merriment there was evident the desire to wound and mock and injure. And this desire came more from fear, a need to divert attention from one's own nakedness and insecurity by an attack upon a common target, than from any real cruelty or scornful hardihood of the soul.

This fear and insecurity was evident even in the fashionable and sophisticated audience which had come to this theatre to see the smart revue. In the interval between the acts, the people streamed up the aisles and out into the lobby, and everywhere one looked, the hostile fear and insecurity of the people were apparent. For the most part the audience was fashionably dressed, the men in evening clothes, the women in expensive evening gowns, that revealed their long white arms, the velvet perfection of their breasts and long backs. It would have been difficult to find a more assured, sophisticated and wealthy-looking group of people, but in spite of this air of complete worldly assurance, their unhappiness and fear were painfully evident. Their bodies seemed to throw off and to fill the air with a feverish electric tension, the texture of their thousand voices rising all together in a braided clamor was almost hysterically high, and remembering suddenly the quiet murmurous drone of voices in a theatre twenty years before, the glamorous spell of enchantment and happiness that surrounded even the performances of some travelling company in its one-night appearance in a little town, one felt poignantly again that something old and pleasant had gone out of life, that something dissonant, painful and unwholesome had changed man's rhythm, spread a poisonous infection through the human chemistries.

One also saw, or rather powerfully felt, among these fashionable and worldly-looking men of the great city, something jaded, puny, sterile, horribly weary; a quality as if their vital energies had been depleted in an unnatural way, as if they were emptied out, dried up, sapped of their juice, and could keep going now only by a kind of lifeless dynamism, a dry electric energy which paced them to the tempo of the city's furious life, which would not let them go until it had burned them hollow to a dry gray shell.

By contrast, the vivid loveliness of the women was astonishing. The differences that distinguished these women from these men, in coloring, in the velvety texture of the skin, in the sparkling eyes, red mouths, voluptuously seductive bodies and general healthiness and glowing elasticity of figure, were so great that one was reminded of those insect species whose females are wonderfully and fatally superior in strength and beauty to their drab mates, and who finally devour them. And yet, even in the faces and figures of these lovely women, the mutilation of that hard, metallic, blunted-out stamp was also evident: one noticed that the general quality of the tone of all these mixed and intermingled voices was feminine rather than masculine, and that the feminine voice was even more assertive, arrogant and incisive in its naked penetration than the voices of the men.

In fact, even as the two young men stood in one corner of the lobby, surveying the keyed pulsations of this brilliant scene, a woman's voice could be heard, speaking with an arrogant and dogmatic assertiveness that instantly quenched denial and left no room for disagreement, however mild:

"*Yes!* I think she is *very* charming, and *very* clever, and *terribly, terribly* amusing. The dancing is *very* bad; they simply *don't know how* to train a chorus. As for the songs, I thought that one she sings about Queen Mary's hats was *awfully* funny; the rest are only fair. Of course, the décor is *abominable*—but what can you expect? That man who sings the song with her is rather good—the other one, the awful little Cockney thing, is *simply horrible!* Where do they ever find these people anyway? . . . No! No!" she said harshly and arrogantly at this point as one of the men put in a mild, low-voiced, and apologetic interjection of his own, "I do *not* agree with you! I *absolutely* do *not* agree with you: you are *absolutely* wrong! The nursemaid scene is *decidedly* the best thing in the show! The restaurant scene is *very* dull, and *very* cheap, and *terribly, terribly* vulgar! And it is *very* stupid of you not to see it!"— And having delivered herself with womanly modesty of these tolerant and generous observations, the lady turned, saw Joel, and instantly addressed him, speaking to him in the same arrogant and assertive tones she had used before, and blurting her words out through lips that she kept perfectly straight and that scarcely seemed to move or open as she spoke:

"*Joel!*" she cried. "What on earth are you doing here? . . . I thought you were at Rhinekill or in Maine? . . . And where's your mother? . . . Did she come down too? . . . No? Too bad!" she said harshly. "I want *very* much to see her. . . . Yes, I shall be in Newport the week-end after next. . . . Yes, yes," she went on with metallic harshness, "—with Alice Mortimer. . . . Is she going, too? . . . Good; then I shall see her!— My *God,* no! . . . We're not staying here. . . . We motored in to see the show. . . . No, No. . . . I've been staying at Sands Point. . . . Jerry's at Southampton. . . . But *God,* no! . . . A whole summer in this hell-hole! . . . The man's *mad!* . . . How d'ya do!" she said curtly and harshly, throwing a cold look and a curt nod towards Eugene as Joel whispered at his name, and instantly dismissing him. . . . "But do you seriously mean you're going to spend the whole summer here? . . . Not *really!* . . . But, my dear child, what in

heaven's name ever prompted you to do an idiotic thing like that?
. . . Oh! I see!" she said coldly. "Painting, eh . . ."

But now the bell for the curtain sounded, and after a few conventional
words of parting they returned to their seats.

LVIII

THE Hudson River joins the harbor. And then the harbor joins the
sea. Always the rivers run.

The Hudson River drinks from out of the inland slowly; it is like
vats that well with purple and rich wine. The Hudson River is like
purple depths of evening; it is like the flames of color on the Palisades,
elves' echoes, and old Dutch and Hallowe'en. It is like the Phantom
Horseman, the tossed boughs, and the demented winds, and it is like
the headed cider and great fires of the Dutchmen in the winter time.

The Hudson River is like old October and tawny Indians in their
camping places long ago; it is like long pipes and old tobacco; it is like
cool depths and opulence; it is like the shimmer of liquid green on summer days.

The Hudson River takes the thunder of fast trains and throws a handful of lost echoes at the hills. It is like the calls of lost men in the mountains; and it is like the country boy who is coming to the city with a
feeling of glory in his guts. It is like the green plush smell of the Pullman cars and snowy linen; it is like the kid in upper four and the good-
looking woman down below who stirs her legs slowly in starched sheets:
it is the magic river. It is like coming to the city to make money, to find
glory, fame and love, and a life more fortunate and happy than any we
have ever known. It is like the Knickerbockers and early autumn; it is
like the Rich Folks, and the River People, the Vanderbilts, the Astors,
and the Roosevelts; it is like Robert W. Chambers and the Society Folks;
it is like the younger set and Hilary, and Monica, and Garth; it is like
The Story Thus Far:

The lovely Monica Delavere the beautiful but spoiled daughter of one of
the richest men in the world meets at a party given at her father's Mount
Kisco estate in honor of her approaching marriage to a young architect
Hilary Chedester his friend Garth Montgomery a young artist just returned
from years of study abroad fascinated yet repelled by his dark passionate face
and his slender hands with the longer tapering fingers of the artist and
goaded by something enigmatic and mocking in his eyes in a moment of
mad recklessness spurred on by a twinge of jealousy at the undue attention
which she thinks Hilary is bestowing on Rita Daventry an old flame she

accepts a challenge from Garth to go for a mad dash across the night in his speedster their objective being his hunting lodge in the hills and a return before dawn arrived at the lodge however Garth coolly announces that his car is out of gasoline and that he must phone for assistance to the nearest town somewhat disturbed and reflecting for the first time now on the possible scandal her reckless exploit may cause she enters the lodge now go on with the story:

"Monica's red lips curved in a smile of mocking reproof. She made a *moue*.

" 'Hardly a place I should have chosen to spend the evening, my dear man,' she said. 'But then, perhaps it is the latest Paris fashion to take ladies to deserted places and inform them you are stranded. *C'est comme ça à Paris, hein?' "

Yes, all these things were like the Hudson River.

And above all else, the Hudson River was like the light—oh, more than anything it was the light, the light, the tone, the texture of the magic light in which he had seen the city as a child, that made the Hudson River wonderful.

The light was golden, deep and full with all rich golden lights of harvest; the light was golden like the flesh of women, lavish as their limbs, true, depthless, tender as their glorious eyes, fine-spun and maddening as their hair, as unutterable with desire as their fragrant nests of spicery, their deep melon-heavy breasts. The light was golden like a golden morning light that shines through ancient glass into a room of old dark brown. The light was brown, dark lavish brown hued with rich lights of gold; the light was rich brown shot with gold like the sultry and exultant fragrance of ground coffee; the light was lavish brown like old stone houses gulched in morning on a city street, brown like exultant breakfast smells that come from basement areas in the brownstone houses where the rich men lived; the light was blue, steep frontal blue, like morning underneath the frontal cliff of buildings, the light was vertical cool blue, hazed with thin morning mist, the light was blue, cold flowing harbor blue of clean cool waters rimed brightly with a dancing morning gold, fresh, half-rotten with the musty river stench, blue with the blue-black of the morning gulch and canyon of the city, blue-black with cool morning shadow as the ferry packed with its thousand small white staring faces turned one way, drove bluntly toward the rusty weathered slips.

The light was amber brown in vast dark chambers shuttered from young light where in great walnut beds the glorious women stirred in sensual warmth their lavish limbs. The light was brown-gold like ground coffee, merchants and the walnut houses where they lived, brown-gold like old brick buildings grimed with money and the smell of trade, brown-gold like morning in great gleaming bars of swart mahogany, the fresh wet beer-wash, lemon-rind, and the smell of angostura bitters. Then full-golden in the evening in the theatres, shining with full golden warmth and body on full golden figures of the women, on fat, red plush, and on rich, faded, slightly stale smell, and on the gilt sheaves and cupids and the cornucopias, on the fleshly, potent softly-golden smell of all the people; and in great restaurants the light was brighter gold, but full and round like warm onyx columns, smooth warmly tinted marble, old wine in dark rounded age-encrusted bottles, and the great blonde figures of naked women on rose-clouded ceilings. Then the light was full and rich, brown-golden like great fields in autumn; it was full swelling golden light like mown fields, bronze-red picketed with fat rusty golden sheaves of corn, and governed by huge barns of red and the mellow winey fragrance of the apples.—Yes, all of this had been the tone and texture of the lights that qualified his vision of the city and the river when he was a child.

Proud, cruel, everchanging and ephemeral city, to whom we came once when our hearts were high, our blood passionate and hot, our brain a particle of fire: infinite and mutable city, mercurial city, strange citadel of million-visaged time—Oh! endless river and eternal rock, in which the forms of life came, passed and changed intolerably before us, and to which we came, as every youth has come, with such enormous madness, and with so mad a hope—for what?

To eat you, branch and root and tree; to devour you, golden fruit of power and love and happiness; to consume you to your sources, river and spire and rock, down to your iron roots; to entomb within our flesh forever the huge substance of your billion-footed pavements, the intolerable web and memory of dark million-visaged time.

And what is left now of all our madness, hunger, and desire? What have you given, incredible mirage of all our million shining hopes, to those who wanted to possess you wholly to your ultimate designs, your final sources, from whom you took the strength, the passion, and the innocence of youth?

What have we taken from you, protean and phantasmal shape of time? What have we remembered of your million images, of your billion weavings out of accident and number, of the mindless fury of your dateless days, the brutal stupefaction of your thousand streets and pavements? What have we seen and known that is ours forever?

Gigantic city, we have taken nothing—not even a handful of your trampled dust—we have made no image on your iron breast and left not even the print of a heel upon your stony-hearted pavements. The possession of all things, even the air we breathed, was held from us, and the river of life and time flowed through the grasp of our hands forever, and we held nothing for our hunger and desire except the proud and trembling moments, one by one. Over the trodden and forgotten words, the rust and dusty burials of yesterday, we were born again into a thousand lives and deaths, and we were left forever with only the substance of our craving flesh, and the hauntings of an accidental memory, with all its various freight of great and little things which passed and vanished instantly and could never be forgotten, and of those unbidden and unfathomed wisps and fumes of memory that share the mind with all the proud dark images of love and death.

The tugging of a leaf upon a bough in late October, a skirl of blown papers in the street, a cloud that came and went and made its shadow in the lights of April. And the forgotten laughter of lost people in dark streets, a face that passed us in another train, the house our mistress lived in as a child, a whipping of flame at a slum's cold corner, the corded veins on an old man's hand, the feathery green of a tree, a daybreak in a city street in the month of May, a voice that cried out sharply and was silent in the night, and a song that a woman sang, a word that she spoke at dusk before she went away,—the memory of a ruined wall, the ancient empty visage of a half-demolished house in which love lay, the mark of a young man's fist in crumbling plaster, a lost relic, brief and temporal, in all the everlasting variousness of your life, as the madness, pain and anguish in the heart that caused it—these are all that we have taken from you, iron-breasted city, and they are ours and gone forever from us, even as things are lost and broken in the wind, and as the ghosts of time are lost, and as the everlasting river that flowed past us in darkness to the sea.

The river is a tide of moving waters: by night it floods the pockets of the earth. By night it drinks strange time, dark time. By night the river drinks proud potent tides of strange dark time. By night the river drains the tides, proud potent tides of time's dark waters that, with champ and lift of teeth, with lapse and reluctation of their breath, fill with a kissing glut the pockets of the earth. Sired by the horses of the sea, maned with the dark, they come.

They come! Ships call! The hooves of night, the horses of the sea, come on below their manes of darkness. And forever the river runs. Deep as the tides of time and memory, deep as the tides of sleep, the river runs.

And there are ships there! Have we not heard the ships there? (Have we not heard the great ships going down the river? Have we not heard the great ships putting out to sea?)

Great whistles blow there. Have we not heard the whistles blow there? Have we not heard the whistles blowing in the river? (A harness of bright ships is on the water. A thunder of faint hooves is on the land.)

And there is time there. (Have we not heard strange time, dark time, strange tragic time there? Have we not heard dark time, strange time, the dark, the moving tide of time as it flows down the river?)

And in the night time, in the dark there, in all the sleeping silence of the earth have we not heard the river, the rich immortal river, full of its strange dark time?

Full with the pulse of time it flows there, full with the pulse of all men living, sleeping, dying, waking, it will flow there, full with the billion dark and secret moments of our lives it flows there. Filled with all the hope, the madness and the passion of our youth it flows there, in the daytime, in the dark, drinking with ceaseless glut the land, mining into its tides the earth as it mines the hours and moments of our life into its tides, mining against the sides of ships, foaming about piled crustings of old wharves, sliding like time and silence by the vast cliff of the city, girdling the stony isle of life with moving waters—thick with the wastes of earth, dark with our stains, and heavied with our dumpings, rich, rank, beautiful, and unending as all life, all living, as it flows by us, by us, by us, to the sea!

LIX

FULL night had come when he got off the train at the town where Joel was to meet him. After the heavy rains of the afternoon, and the stormy sunset, the sky had cleared completely: a great moon blazed in the cloudless bowl of a depthless sky; after the rain, and the sultry swelter of the city streets, the tainted furnace-fumes of city breath, the air was clean and fresh, and marvellously sweet, and the great earth waited, and was still enormously, and one always knew that it was there.

The engine panted for a moment with a hoarse, metallic resonance, in the baggage-car some one threw mail-bags and thick bundles of evening papers off onto the platform, there was the swinging signal of a brakeman's lantern, the tolling of the engine bell, thick, hose-like jets of steam blew out of her, the terrific pistons moved like elbows, caught, bore down, the terrific flanges spun for a moment, the short, squat funnel belched explosive thunders of hot smoke, the train rolled past with a slow, protesting creak of ties, a hard-pressed rumble of the heavy coaches, and was on her way again.

Then the train was gone, and there was nothing but the rails, the earth, the moon, the river, and strong silence—and the haunting and immortal visage of America by night. It was there, and it was there forever, and he had always known it, and it abode there and was still, and there was something in his heart he could not utter. The rails swept northward towards the dark, and in the moon the rails were like two living strands of burning silver, and between the rails the heavy ballast rock was white as lunar marble, and the brown wooden ties were resinous and dry and very still.

Sheer beside the tracks, the low banks of the ballast-fill sloped to the edges of the mighty river. And the river blazed there in the great blank radiance of the moon, cool waters gently lapped small gluts and pockets of the shore, and in the great wink of the moon the river blazed more brightly than elves' gold. And farther off, where darkness met it, the light was broken into scallop-shells of gold, it swam and shimmered in a billion winks of fire like a school of herrings on the water, and beyond all that there was just the dark, the cool-flowing mystery of velvet-hearted night, the silent, soundless surge and coolness of the strange, the grand, the haunting, the unceasing river.

Far, far away in darkness, on the other shore—more than a mile away —the river met the fringes of the land, but where the river ended, or the land began, was hard to say. There was just *there* a greater darkness, perhaps just by a shade, a deeper, dark intensity of night—a dark, perhaps, a shade less lucent, smooth, and fluid, by an indefinable degree more solid.

Yet there were lights there—there were lights—a bracelet of a few, hard lights along the river, a gem-like incandescence, few and hard and bright, and so poignantly lost and lonely in enormous darkness as are all lights in America, sown sparsely on the enormous viewless mantle of the night, and by that pattern so defining it—a scheme of sparse, few lights, hard, bright and small, sown there upon night's enormous darkness, the great earth's secret and attentive loneliness, its huge, abiding mystery.

And forever, beyond the mysterious river's farthest shore, the great earth waited in the darkness, and was still. It waited there with the huge, attentive secrecy of night and of America, and of the wilderness of this everlasting earth on which we live; and its dark visage that we cannot see was more cruel, strange and lonely than the visage of dark death, and its rude strength more savage and destructive than a tiger's paw, and its wild, mysterious loveliness more delicate than magic, more desireful than a woman's flesh, and more thrilling, secret and seductive than a woman's love.

As he stood there, tranced in that powerful spell of silence and of night, he heard swift foot-steps running down the station stairs, he turned and saw Joel Pierce approaching. He ran forward quickly, his tall, thin figure clad in a blue coat and white flannels, alive with the swift boyish eagerness that was one of his engaging qualities.

"Gosh!" he said, in his eager whispered tone, panting a little as he came up, "—I'm sorry that I'm late: we have people staying at the house, I had to drive a woman who's been staying with us to Poughkeepsie—I tried to get you there, but your train had already gone. I drove like hell getting here.— It's good to see you!" he burst out in his eager whispering way—at once so gentle, and so friendly and spontaneous— "It's *swell* that you could come!" he whispered enthusiastically. "Come on! They're all waiting for you!"

And picking up his friend's valise, he walked swiftly across the platform and began to climb the stairs.

Although Joel Pierce would have spoken in this way to any friend—to any one for whom he had a friendly feeling, however casual—and although the other youth knew that he would have spoken this way to many other people—the words filled him with happiness, with an instinctive warmth and affection for the person who had spoken them. Indeed, the very fact that there was in Joel's words—in all his human relationships—this curious impersonality, gave what he said an enhanced value. For in this way Joel revealed instinctively what every one who knew him well felt about him—an enormous decency and radiance in his soul and character, a wonderfully generous and instinctive friendliness towards humanity—that became finer and more beautiful because of its very impersonality.

This warm, instinctive humanity was evident in all he did, it came out somehow in the most casual words and relationships with people. For example, when they went upstairs into the station waiting-room, which was completely empty, Joel paused for a moment at the ticket-seller's window and spoke to a man in shirtsleeves inside.

"Joe," he said casually yet in his eager, whispering way, "if Will comes down will you tell him not to wait? I've got every one: there'll be no one else tonight."

"All right, Mr. Pierce," the man said quietly. "If I see him, I'll tell him."

Joel's car, a small, cheap one of a popular make, was backed up against the station curb: he opened the door and put his friend's suitcase in the back, then they both got in and drove away.

About two miles back from town upon the crest of a hill that gave a good view of the great moon-wink of the noble and haunting river far below, Joel suddenly, and without slackening his reckless speed, swerved from the concrete highway into a dusty and gravel road that went off to the left. And now they were really in the heart of the deep country: on each side of them the moon-drenched fields and dreaming woods of a noble, grand and spacious land slept in the steep, white silence of the moon. From time to time, they would pass cornfields, the high and silent stature, the cool figure of the corn at night, and see a great barn, or small lights burning in some farmer's house. Then there would be only the deep, dark mystery of sleeping woods beside the road and once, in a field, a herd of cows, all faced one way, bedded down upon their forequarters, the mottled colors of their hides showing plainly in the blazing radiance of the moon. When they had gone about a mile their road swept into another one that joined it at right angles: between these roads, in the angle that they formed, there was a pleasant house—a wooden structure of eight or ten rooms, white and graceful in the moon, and surrounded by a trim, well-kept lawn and well laid-out flower-plots and gardens.

A swift and pleasurable conviction told the youth that this was Joel's house: he was therefore surprised when the car shot past without slackening its speed and then turned left upon the other road. He turned to Joel and, almost with a note of protest in his voice, said:

"Don't you live there? Isn't that your house?"

"What?" Joel whispered quickly, startled from the focal concentration of his driving. He turned to his companion with a surprised inquiring look. "—Oh, *that* house?" he went on at once. "No," he said softly. "That's not our house.— That is, it is our house," he corrected himself, "it belongs to us, but a friend of ours—Margaret Telfair—lives there now. You'll meet her tonight," he went on casually. "She's at the house now.—You'll *like* her," he whispered with soft conviction, "—she's grand! An *incredible* person!" he whispered enthusiastically.

They drove on in silence for some time: more moon-drenched fields, great barns and little farmhouses, and herds of crouching cattle more dreaming and mysterious woods, the mysterious shadows of great trees against the road, and secrecy, and sweet balsamic scents and cool-enfolding night.—They were now driving back in the direction of the river: the new road led that way.

"When do we come to your place, Joel?" the other youth asked, when they had driven on in silence for a time. "How far is it?"

"What?" Joel whispered quickly, again turning his radiant and inquiring face. "*Our* place? Oh!" he said. "We're on our place now."

"*On* it?" the other stammered, after a moment's bewildered pause. "But—but—where—I didn't see a gate or anything—when?——"

"Oh," Joel whispered, with an enlightened air. "*That!* We passed it."

"*Passed* it? Where?"

"When we turned in from the main-road," Joel whispered. "Do you remember?"

"The—the *main* road?" the other stammered. "You—you mean—that concrete highway way back there?"

"Yes," Joel whispered. "That was the entrance to our place—one of them. It's not much of an entrance," he whispered apologetically. "I don't wonder that you couldn't see it."

"Then—then—everything since then—all we passed—all this—?" the other stammered.

"Yes," Joel whispered, with his radiant, eager look, "that's it. That's our place. It's really grand country," he went on matter-of-factly. "I want to show you around tomorrow."

They swept suddenly around a curve of the gravelled road, bordered with fragrant shrubs. Before them stretched out an immense sward of velvet lawn, darkened by the grand and silent stature of great trees. The car swept forward; through the tree-barred vista of the lawn, the outline of a house appeared. It was a dream house, a house such as one sees only in a dream—the moonlight slept upon its soaring wings, its white purity, and gave the whole enormous structure an aerial delicacy, a fragile loveliness like some enchanted structure that one sees in dreams. And yet, for all this quality of dream-enchantment, there was something hauntingly familiar about it too. The car swept round the drive and halted before the moonlit façade of the house. A back porch level with the ground was flanked by tall, square columns of graceful, slender wood. To one side, far below, beyond the house, and the great moon-sweep of velvet, he could see the wink and glimmer of the Hudson River.

And suddenly that haunting sense of familiarity fused to a blind flash of recognition. The house was the house he had passed a dozen times in darkness, had seen a dozen times at morning from the windows of a speeding train along the river, as he hurtled city-wards again from those blind night passages of desire and fury in a town called Troy.

They got out of the car. Joel took his valise, and like a person walking in a dream, he followed him across the porch, into a large and dimly lit entrance-hall. Joel put his valise down in the hall, and turning, whispered:

"Look. I'll show you your room later. Mums and some other people are waiting for us on the terrace. Let's go and say hello to them first."

He nodded, unable to speak, and in silence followed his guide down the hall and through the house. Joel opened a door: the blazing moonlight fell upon the vast, swarded lawn and sleeping woods of that magic domain known as Far Field Farm. And that haunting and unearthly radiance fell as well upon the white wings of that magic house and on a group of its fortunate inhabitants who were sitting on the terrace.

The two young men went out: forms rose to greet them.

LX

A group of eight or ten people were gathered on the terrace. Joel introduced Eugene swiftly, quietly, in an eager, whispering voice, as always, with his fine, kind intuition, mindful of another person's embarrassment and confusion: the moonlit figures rose, looked toward him, passed and swam and mixed around him in a blur of names and moon-white faces and politely murmured words. Then all the figures resolved themselves again into their former positions, he was standing beside Joel's mother, looking at her with a helpless and bewildered face, she put one hand swiftly, lightly on his arm, and in a kind and quiet voice, said to him: "You sit down here, next to me."

Then she sat down again in her chair—a big, wicker chair with a vast, fan-shaped back, he sat down beside her, and sank gratefully into oblivion while the other people resumed their interrupted conversation:

"No, but—*Polly! Surely* not! You know, she actually did not go through with it?" said a strong, protesting voice, in which yet an eager curiosity was evident. "You know, they stopped the thing before she went the whole way?"

"My dear," said Polly firmly—she had evidently been well named: in the moonlight her face showed sharp and pointed, with a big nose, and the shrewd, witty, and rather malicious features of a parrot— "my dear, I *know* she *did*. I was visiting Alice Bellamy at Newport when it happened: I got the whole story straight from her. The family were perfectly frantic—they were calling Hugh Bellamy up or running in to see him a dozen times a day to find out if something could be done—how to get it annulled— But I tell you," Polly cried, shaking her head obstinately and speaking in a tone of unmistakable conviction, "—I know what I'm talking about! There's no doubt about it whatever —she *married* him—the ceremony was *actually* performed——"

"And she really *lived* with him—with this—this *stable-boy?*"

"*Lived* with him!" Polly cried. "My dear, they'd been living together for almost two weeks before old Dick Rossiter found them. Now, of course," she said piously, but with a faint, malicious smirk, "—I don't know what they'd been doing all that time—perhaps the whole affair had been quite idyllic, but—well, my dear, you can use your own imagination. My own experience with hostlers is rather limited, but I shouldn't think they were particularly renowned for their platonic virtues."

"No," said Mrs. Pierce quietly, but with an unmistakable note of level and obdurate cynicism in her voice, "—nor Ellen Rossiter either— not if I know the breed! . . . After all," she went on in a moment, in a voice that was characterized by its grimly quiet conviction, "what else could you expect out of that crowd! . . . There's bad blood there!

Bad blood in the whole lot of them," her voice rose on a formidable and powerful note of unrelenting judgment. "—Every one in Society knows that old Steve Buchanan, that girl's grandfather, was a thorough-going rotter," she bit the word off almost viciously. "His reputation was so bad that most people wouldn't even have him in their house—that was the reason he spent the last twenty years of his life in France: he had become an outcast over here, no one would speak to him —he had to get out!— But! Heavens! A *stable-boy!*" she laughed again, and this time her laugh was almost hard and ugly. "What a blow to Myra—after all her years of scheming and contriving to get Timmy Wilson and his millions into the family! . . . I knew it! I knew it!" she shook her head with formidable, obstinate conviction. "I could have told them long ago they'd have trouble with that girl before they were done with her! There's bad blood there! Of course, it was *bound* to happen, sooner or later, anyway—Myra's a fool of the first water: she never had the brains of a rabbit. But to think!—Heavens! what a let-down, after all her scheming: a stable-boy! I bet she had a fit!"

"Still," suggested a young man named Howard, at this gigantic moment, in his mincing, lisping, and effeminately mannered tone, "—as Irene Cartwright said, it was the only original thing that Ellen Rossiter ever did, and it was rather a pity to break the romance off. . . . I thought," he went on casually, "that the story they told about the hostler was rather touching—asking her to send his letters back, you know?"

"No!" cried Mrs. Pierce in an astounded tone. "Did he? . . . Well!" she went on eagerly. "And did she send them? . . . Go on, Howard!"

"But, of course," said Howard. "And the wedding ring, and everything else that he had given her. . . . I read the letter that he wrote her: it was really *too* pathetic—he said he was going with another girl—a house-maid, I believe—and he didn't want it to get out that he had paid attentions to some one else. . . . 'I have spoke it all over with my mother,' he said," Howard quoted drolly, " 'and she thinks the same as me, you ought to let me have them back' "——

"Oh, *Howard!*" Mrs. Pierce shrieked faintly. "You *know* he didn't! Simply *priceless!*"

For a moment her splendid, even teeth flashed brilliantly in the moonlight: she lifted the long cigarette-holder in her hand and took a long, deliberate puff: the fragrant, acrid smoke of Turkish tobacco

coiled upward in the moon-light air like filings of light steel. Turning
to the young man beside her, she addressed him with the somewhat
patient and dutiful kindliness of a person receiving a strange guest in her
home for the first time:

"Well," she said, "and how did you find the trip up? Did Joel
frighten you out of your wits by his driving? He does every one else."

"Well, he did go pretty fast," the youth admitted. "He had me
hanging on once or twice—when we left the main road we took the
curve on two wheels, but he seemed to know what he was doing."

"I assure you," said Mrs. Pierce, with a stern laugh, "that he does not.
I wish I could share your confidence, but I can't. I don't think he has
the faintest notion what he's doing."

"But, after all," the very quiet, pleasant, almost toneless voice of a
young man whose name was George Thornton now took up the thread
of the discussion—"after all, I should think that any reasonable man
would be content with a speed of thirty-five or forty miles an hour.
After all," he said very quietly again, "perhaps the most important
things in life are not to be got at through speed—perhaps all the
things that are most worth living for are not to be had if we always go
a mile a minute."

"That's just it, George!" Mrs. Pierce put in with decisive satisfaction.
"That's just it! Any reasonable man *would* be content with thirty-five
or forty miles an hour—but Joel is not reasonable. When he gets in a
car he's like a child that's been given a new toy to play with for the first
time."

"The greatest things in life, the highest values," George Thornton
went on in his quiet, pleasant, almost toneless voice, which now,
despite the air of telling reasonableness with which he spoke—the air of
temperance, moderation and control—was, somehow, indefinably tinged
by a sombre fatality: the tone of a man whose extreme reasonableness
comes from a fear of madness, whose temperance from some fatal impulse to insane excess—"the greatest things in life," he went on in his
quiet, toneless voice, almost as if he were talking to himself and had
not heard what Mrs. Pierce had said—"are not to be got from machinery
or speed, or any material object in the world whatever. . . . Christ,"
he continued with his quiet, utterly reasonable, and implacable finality,
"said that the greatest thing in life is love. Buddha said that the greatest
thing in life is the illumination of the human spirit. Socrates found
that man's highest duty was obedience to his country's laws. And

Confucius, after weighing life and death against each other, found
man's only reason for living in keeping as many of the conventions
of society as he could. . . . And that, Joel, perhaps is the real reason,
the only reason, why you should not drive your car at reckless speed.
. . . You break your country's law by doing so . . . and you cause
pain and worry and anxiety to other people who may love you. For that
reason, if for nothing else, you ought not to do it."

He delivered this judgment in his quiet and toneless voice, without
vanity or arrogance, but with a finality that was almost prophetic, and
that left no room for argument. When he was done speaking, there
was a deep, impersonal silence for a moment, and then the voice of
Joel's sister, Rosalind—a voice that was still the voice of a girl, but that
was also sweet and low and womanly, full of noble tenderness and
warmth—could be heard in all its affectionate young impulsiveness:

"Oh, but, George!—you're an *angel* about everything! If every one
were like you, life would be heaven!" She took his hand between her
strong, warm hands and squeezed it—an impulsive and natural gesture
with her that revealed, as much as anything else, the deep and true
affection of her nature. "—Darling," she said, "—you make all of us—
every one else—feel so mean—and small—and—ah petty. . . . I mean,"
she went on with the earnest and naïve sincerity, the spontaneous
admiration, of a generous and warm-spirited girl—"the way you live
—the way you have spent your whole life, George, in helping other
people—the way you have found out all these wonderful things about—
about—Buddha and Confucius and Socrates—you *know* so much,
George!" she cried enthusiastically—"you have learned so much, while
the rest of us were just leading an idle, stupid, empty kind of life—
and the way you give it all away to others!—the way you give your
money away to any one who needs it—the—the—way," she faltered suddenly, and her voice was choked with tears—"the way you have looked
after poor Dick all these years"—she blurted out.

"Rosalind!" Mrs. Pierce cried out sharply and warningly, yet not with
reproof so much as with apprehension.

"I don't care!" cried Rosalind impulsively—"I—I think he's wonderful! George, you're a *saint!*" she said, and clasped his hand
again.

No one spoke for a moment: George sat quietly on the terrace step,
his fine and small, bronzed head, his very still eyes, in whose steady,
quiet depths the fatal madness which would destroy him was already

legible, turned out across the great sward of moon-drenched lawn towards the shine and wink and velvet mystery of the noble river far below. In the quality of silence that held all these people, there was a sense of profound emotion—the reference to "poor Dick" had touched some sorrowful fact that all of them knew about, and one could sense this deep feeling now in the stony silence that held all of them. It was broken in a moment by Mrs. Pierce, who betrayed, by the studied matter-of-factness of her tone, the emotion which she, too, had felt:

"But it *is* an extraordinary thing, George—a simply astonishing thing —to find a young man of your age who has read and studied—and— and—*prepared* himself for life the way you have. It's *simply* astonish-ing!" she concluded, and then did what was perhaps an astonishing thing for her—quickly and vigorously she blew her nose. "But *simply* astonishing!" she said again, as she thrust the handkerchief away, and put a cigarette into her eight-inch holder.

"No, I think not," he said quietly, and without a trace of vanity or false modesty. "It would have been astonishing if I had not done it. After all, my debt to society for all that it has done for me is great enough as it is: I could not with any decency look the world in the face if I knew that I had not made some effort to repay it."

"How few rich young men feel that way about it," said Mrs. Pierce quietly. "I wish more did!"

The conversation was now turned to other, lighter channels of discus-sion: gossip, spirited but light debate. Mrs. Pierce renewed her con-versation with Howard and Polly, farther away upon the steps Rosalind, Seaholm, a dark girl named Ruth, and George Thornton talked, gossiped and laughed together with the charming intimacy of youth, and Joel and Miss Telfair were engaged in eager and excited debate— Joel, for the most part, listening with the eager, respectful, bent-forward attentiveness, the devoted courtesy of reverence, that marked all of his relations with women, and Miss Telfair doing most of the talking. She talked the way she looked and dressed and acted, the way she was: a speech fragile, empty, nervous, brittle, artificial and incisive as one of the precious bits of china, the costly, rare, enamelled little trinkets that filled up her house, her life, her interest:

"No, Joel!" she was saying with a voice that had a curious, shell-like penetration—a positive, brittle, but incisively certain voice—"you are absolutely wrong! You are *completely* mistaken about that! The thing cannot by any stretch of the imagination be called Sienese! It is *pure* Ravenna—*perfect* Ravenna—*absolutely!*" she cried, shaking her enamelled face with obdurate conviction. "It's nothing else on earth but the *purest* and *most perfect* Ravenna—and Fourteenth Century Ravenna at that! . . . No! No!" she cried incisively, cutting him off shortly, and shaking her head stubbornly as he tried to put in a smiling, whispered word of courteous doubt. "My dear child, you are dead wrong! You don't know what you're talking about! . . . I was an authority on these things before you were born. . . . I've forgotten more about Ravenna than you'll ever know! . . . No! . . . No! . . . Absolutely *not!* . . . You're *all* wrong!"

He received this stubborn, arrogant and almost insulting rebuttal as he always did—with the whispered, gracious humility of his beautiful good nature: laughing softly and enthusiastically over her arrogant and contemptuous denial, as if he were merely the victim of the most tender and high-spirited raillery.

At this moment, however, when, with a sense of resentment and displeasure he was listening to the naked and arrogant penetrations of Miss Telfair's voice, Rosalind Pierce rose from her seat on the terrace step, left the other young people there, came swiftly to where Eugene was seated, and sat down beside him.

"Why are you sitting here all by yourself—so quiet and so alone?" she said in her warm, sweet, lovely, and affectionate young voice. "Can I sit here and talk to you?" she said, and even as she spoke these words, she slipped her arm through his, and clasped him by the hand. The whole life and character of that beautiful, fine and lovely girl was in that simple, natural and spontaneous gesture. That gesture did what words could never do, explained what years of living with many people could not explain: in an instant she communicated to him the whole quality of her life, told him the kind of person she was. And the kind of person she was was unbelievably good and beautiful.

"What have you been thinking of all the time you have been sitting here?" she whispered in her low, sweet voice. "I could see you sitting here, listening, looking at us, and all the time it was just as if you were a million miles away. What were you thinking?—that we are all an idle, shallow lot, with nothing to do except to chatter and gossip about other useless people like ourselves?"

"Why—no—no," he stammered. "Why—not at all—" He looked at her with a red embarrassed face, but there was no guile or mockery in her. She was not clever enough for sarcasm or malice, not witty enough for irony: she was a creature full of innocence and ardor, without profound intelligence, but with a nature full of warmth, generous enthusiasm, and affection.

"I—I—think you're all fine," he blurted out. "I think you're great."

"Do you, darling?" she said softly. "Well, we're not." She pulled him towards her with a gesture of friendly intimacy, and said. "Come on: let's leave them all for a few minutes. I want to talk to you."

They got up, and still with her warm hand clasped in his, they walked along the terrace and around the great, moon-whitened wings of the house on to the road that swept in an oval before it.

"Do you really like us?" she said, as they walked on down the road away from the house under a deep, nocturnal mystery of great trees through which the moonlight shone and swarmed upon the earth in mottles of light. "Don't you like Joel? Don't you think he's grand?"

"I—I think he's the best fellow in the world," he said. "He's—he's just *too* good!"

"Oh, he's a saint," she said in her quiet, sweet voice. "There was never any one like him: he's the loveliest person I've ever known. . . . Aren't people wonderful?" she said, and turned and paused in the moonlit road and looked at him. "I mean, there are a lot of mean ones . . . and useless ones . . . and sort of shabby ones like . . . like—well, like some of those people there tonight . . . but there's something good in all of them—even poor little Howard Martin has something sweet and good in him: he has a kind heart—he really has—he wants to be amusing and to entertain people, he wants every one to be happy and have a good time. . . . And when you meet some one like Joel, it makes up for everything else, doesn't it? . . . Or George Thornton— don't you like him? Don't you think he's a grand person, too?"

"He—seems fine," he answered with some difficulty. "I—I never met him till tonight."

"Oh, you'll *love* him when you get to know him," the girl said earnestly. "—Everybody does. . . . He's another saint, just like Joel . . . and he's so brave, and kind, and good—and his life has been so terrible."

"Terrible? I—I thought he said——"

"Oh, he *is,* darling—he *does* have everything *that* way—money, I mean. He's terribly rich: one of the richest young men in the world. . . . Only he doesn't spend it on himself, he gives it all away and then

. . . you see, darling, George has had an unhappy life of it from the beginning. . . . His father died a raving madman, there's been insanity in his family for generations back, his mother was a horrible woman who deserted him when he was a child and ran off with a man, and he was brought up by an aunt—his father's sister—who was half cracked herself. . . . Now he lives all alone on this big place that he's inherited—he has one brother, Dick, who is two years older than he is—and he has spent practically his whole life in looking after Dick."

"Looking after him?"

"Yes," the girl said quietly, "—Dick is insane too—a raving maniac; they have guards for him, they have to watch him every minute of the time—when George comes to see him, Dick tries to kill him. . . . And George loves him, he'd give his life for him, he does everything he can to make Dick happy—and Dick hates him so that he'd kill him if he could. . . . And George has this thing hanging over him all the time, he can't forget about it for a moment, it's made his whole life wretched, and yet you'd never know it when you talk to him: he never mentions it, he's always the same to people,—always kind and good and gentle, never thinking of himself."

"I see. And is that the reason why he studies all these different philosophies—Christ and Socrates and Confucius?—"

"Yes," she said quietly. "—And Buddha. I think so. . . . He would never admit it . . . he has never said so . . . and of course no one *could* ask him. . . . But I think that's the reason. . . . There's something . . . something desperate . . . lost . . . in his eyes sometimes," she said slowly, after a pause. ". . . It's . . . it's not good to look at . . . it's . . . I imagine it's like the look you would see in the eyes of a drowning man."

"And you think that he may be afraid of . . . of insanity?"

She was silent for a moment, and did not answer him directly.

"He's been studying Buddhism for the last two years," she said. "He's had all kinds of people at the house to teach him. . . . Hindus, mystics, scholars—learned people . . . he's . . . he's become more and more . . . I don't know," she said in a puzzled tone. "—I don't know what you'd call it—sort of mystical." Again she was silent, and presently added matter-of-factly: "He's going to India next year."

"To study?"

"Yes, I think so," the girl said, and again was silent. "Somehow—it's a dreadful thought, isn't it?" she said in a low tone after a moment—

"But sometimes I have wondered if George would ever come back. . . . Perhaps," she concluded quietly, ". . . perhaps that is why we all love him so much . . . it's like loving some one who is brave and good and gentle that you know has got to die."

For some time they walked on slowly down the moon-white road without further speech.

"I want you to know Carl, too," she said. "He seems very cold and strange at first—but that is just his foreign way. He is really one of the loveliest, sweetest people that ever lived. . . . You know," she said presently, "we are going to be married in October."

"Yes, I know. Joel told me. . . . Will you live here—in this country?"

"No. I'm afraid not. . . . You see, Carl is in the diplomatic service, and they get moved around a great deal. They have to go where they get sent."

"And where will you go first? Do you know?"

"Yes, I think they are sending him to Paris next."

"Will you like that? Do you think you'll like living in Paris?"

"Of *course*," she said with her rich, warm, easy laugh. "I'm awfully easy to please—I like everything—I'm happy anywhere—wherever I am. Is that very bad of me?" she said with a kind and gently teasing smile.

"No, that's very good of you. . . . Have you ever been to Paris?"

"Yes," she cried in a rich, enthusiastic tone, "and I love it. I adore it. I studied music there. Mother and I lived there for two years before I came out."

"But now you'll have to learn Swedish and German and Italian and Spanish and Russian—all those languages—now that you're getting married to a diplomat. Won't you?"

"Yes," she said with her sweet and careless laugh— "Everything! One must become a regular little walking Berlitz school of languages—only I shan't mind very much: I'm very stupid, but my husband is so kind and clever I'm sure I'll learn in spite of everything."

"And you'll live in Paris and Rome and London and Berlin—all those places? Won't you?"

"Yes, darling," she said in her warm, sweet tone that always had something maternal and tolerantly amused in its humor, "—and in Copenhagen and Stockholm and Bucharest and Madrid—even in Pogo Pogo or in China or Peru—wherever they choose to send us. We'll be

two international hoboes, darling—that's the kind of life we'll have
to lead."

"God!" he said bluntly. "It sounds wonderful! What a thing to
happen to any one!—and to happen to you at your age! . . . But won't
it make all this—this place here—seem awfully far away, and very
strange—when you think back on it?"

"Yes," the girl said quietly, and added so softly that she seemed to
breathe the words—so softly that he could scarcely hear her, "—and quite
impossibly lovely!"

He stared at her in blank astonishment for a minute: she had clasped
her hands against her breast in a natural and simple gesture, the moon
had made an aureole of magic around the silken strands of her brown
hair, and suddenly he noticed that her eyes were bright with tears.

"Very, very far away," she said in a low tone, "and enormously beautiful. . . . You see," she said simply, "this is my home. . . . I was born
here, and I love it." She was silent for a moment longer, and then she
said quietly but in a more matter-of-fact way:

"Don't you think our place—this country here—is beautiful?"

He did not answer her for a moment: at first he was not even conscious that he had heard her. He kept staring at her with a comical expression of gape-jawed and hypnotic fascination. He was conscious of
a queer, bewildered and inappropriate feeling of surprise—a kind of
numb, absurd wonder that if he had read all the books and poems in
the world, and then tried to imagine for himself something as impossibly
lovely as this girl and the whole scene around her, he could never, by
any soaring stretch of the imagination, have come within a million
miles of it.

Behind her head the moon was making its spun aura of enchanted
light, the dress she was wearing was of some sweet gossamer stuff of
light moon-blue that seemed spun out of the very substance of the
moon itself—to float, to move like some aerial fume of magic smoke,
but the girl herself was lovely, sweet and strong as the whole earth
around her. She was herself no creature of elves' fantasy, she was not
lithe and slender, fleeting as a nymph: she was a warm, strong-bodied
girl, wide in the hips for children, a nature warm and soft and gentle
as a cow, but radiant and lovely with fair girlhood, too, and full of
sweetness, strength, and tender, jolly humor.

She stood there in the middle of the white, empty road with the
enchanted radiance of the moon upon her, and he stared at her un-

believingly, like a man who meets some vision in a dream, and does not know if he is dreaming or awake, and yet knows all the time that it is real. Then he would take his fascinated gaze away from her, and look down at the moon-white road, and stamp it with his foot, and kick and scurf the ground of the moon-white road to see if it was real, and then lift his head and look at her again, and turn and see the great, sweet fields and meadows dreaming in the moonlight, and cows down upon their knees, facing toward him with their strange and silent stare, or faced one way and grazing towards him through the moon pastures with sweet, wrenching pull of teeth; and then he would see the dark and sleeping woods of night, with all their mystery and loveliness and wild and solemn joy, and secret terror, and all the grand and casual folds and convolutions of the sleeping, moon-enchanted earth, and far away the moon-blaze and wink, the herring glamour, and the dancing scallop fires, and all the darkness, coolness, and the velvet-breasted mystery of the strange and silent river, the haunted river, the great Hudson River, drawing on forever from the dark and secret earth the sources of its depthless tides, and in the night-time, in the dark, with soundless movings of its tide, drawing on forever like time and silence past the strange and secret land, the mysterious earth, the sleeping cities and the lost and lonely little towns of dark America.

It was all so strange, so impossibly lovely, so hauntingly familiar—the grand and casual landscape of America—and it seemed past words and past belief, to be so much a part of this girl's life, and she a part of it, that all the haunting mystery of the secret earth, the silent river, and all its sweetness, fragrance and fertility, its casual homeliness, and its unuttered loveliness had entered into her, had fed her life, had shaped her to its special quality, and like a solemn music was mixed into the conduits of her blood and life and soul forever, so that now he could not bear to see her taken from it, he felt a cruel and ruinous loss and waste in this destructive separation—a loss that touched not only this girl's life, but the life of the great earth and all America as well—a loss as if a rare and glorious flower were brutally uprooted from the only earth that could produce or nurture it and which would henceforth be, by reason of its treasured loss, bereft. And feeling so, a blind and bitter resentment surged up in his heart, his whole life and spirit was set against her going, and in his soul an unforgiving and protesting voice kept saying doggedly:

"Why has she got to go? Why must she be lost? Why does she have to go and marry that damned Swede?"

In the great moon-drenched field beside the road, the cows were moving towards them slowly, grazing, pulling the fragrant meadow grass of night with sweet, cool wrenching, with rustling stir, and with whisking of dry tails.

The girl walked over to the wire fence, and one of the cows, after regarding her with its grave, gentle stare, moved slowly towards her, rattling the fence wires as it thrust its gentle, bending head across the fence and nuzzled her soft palm.

"She seems to know you," said the youth.

"Yes," the girl answered. "I know them all by name, they all know me. I gave them all their names: this one's Brindle. Aren't they lovely creatures?" she said quietly, as she stroked the cow. "Such—such—gentle pets," she said, "with their kind looks and great, soft eyes. They all know me, and will come to me when I call their names."

The other cows, indeed, were now standing still, faced toward her, looking at her with slow, gaunt, and gentle heads. Now, slowly, they started to move toward her, making a cool, sweet rustling through night grasses as they came. The moonlight burst upon their short, curved horns, it burst upon the rich bright patches of their mottled hides, upon their stringy, dung-bespattered rumps, their soft eyes, and the slow, gentle wonder of their long, gaunt heads.

And it was all so wonderful—the sleeping woods, the moon-enchanted fields, the slow, light grazings of the moonlit cows, and all the fragrance of the night, the grass, the clover and the meadow spells, and the magic warmth and loveliness of the girl, and her sweet, low voice beside him in the moonlight—that it seemed to him that all his life had been a prelude and a preparation to this wonder. He did not know what he could say, it came swelling up in a wild flood of tenderness and passion, he felt that he must tell her somehow, and he had no words for saying it; he seized her hands, and stammered:

"Look here—if I live to be a million years I'll never—the way the river was tonight, the moon, and the way Joel met me and then finding you and your mother and your friends there in the moonlight—and the river down below—and now this walk with you—this road—the field—and all these cows there in the field—and you here—why, by God!" he cried thickly, incoherently, "you are the finest girl I ever saw in all my life!—this place—tonight here—the most wonderful——"

"Come on," she said quietly, with her warm, young laugh, and took him by the arm again. "We must be going back:—the others will be waiting for us—but it *has* been lovely, hasn't it?"

"Why," he muttered thickly and seized her hand again, "—why! By God! By God!"

When they got back to the house, the guests had risen for departure, but were standing in an interested group around George Thornton, who was showing them gymnastics.

"Another thing," he was saying, in his very quiet, pleasant, toneless voice, "—another thing that you can try is this." With these words he stretched his slight and graceful figure—which was as tough as hickory and as flexible as a whip—flat out upon the bricked floor of the terrace.

"Try this some time," he continued in his quiet, even tone that had a curiously hushed, still and almost sombre penetration in the deep moon-silence of the night. "Try lying flat out on your back sometime—like this." And he lay there, small, graceful, beautifully lithe, completely relaxed.

"And then what?" said Mrs. Pierce in an interested tone. "What do you do then, George?"

"Nothing," he said with toneless quiet. "You just lie there—it relaxes you: a Hindu showed me how to do it."

"Oh, but any one could do that!" Howard Martin protested, in his mannered and rather effeminate voice. "Even I could do that, George."

"It's not as easy as you think," George said. "You see," he went on quietly, "it's really a greater effort to be relaxed than most of us realize. Most of us are all tied up in a knot—so much more tense than we know we are. The thing you've got to do," he went on with his quiet and fatal tonelessness, "is to relax—utterly relax—just let everything relax. You've got to lie so that everything—the back of your head, your shoulders, your spinal column—the whole thing—lies flat upon the floor. Like this," he said, and just lay there, small, fragile, beautifully lithe and strong, and utterly, quietly, "relaxed"—his voice coming with a quiet and strange penetration from a figure that seemed inanimate. "—It's not easy to do, but you can master it if you try."

"Oh, let me see! I'm going to try!" little Howard Martin cried with the good-natured and unself-conscious eagerness that was really one of his attractive and appealing qualities. And completely unruffled by the laughter of the group, he immediately lay down and stretched himself out beside George, his dapper little figure looking indescribably comical as he tried to follow George's instructions and imitate his posture:

"How's that, George?" he said presently, without moving. "Have I got it?"

George turned and observed him keenly for a moment:

"No," he said quietly, "you haven't got it yet, Howard. You see, you've got to flatten out completely. You've just got to let everything go limp—relax—so that your whole back is flat upon the ground."

"But I *am* flat! I *am* flat!" little Howard protested in such a mincing and comical tone of protest that every one burst out in hearty laughter, and even George smiled his fine, rare, and grave smile. "My *God!*" Howard said in an agonized tone when the laughter had subsided, "if I was any flatter I'd feel like a pancake."

"No, Howard," George Thornton said quietly after another moment of observant silence. "You haven't got it yet. You see, your back is really arched—you're not *relaxed*—your back is not upon the floor—the thing is to make yourself lie out as flat as a board—like this," and with the fingers of his strong, small, bronzed hand he gently but firmly pushed Howard's stomach down towards the floor. Howard grunted protestingly but lay there after George had taken his hand away, and George, after looking at him closely for a moment, nodded approvingly and said:

"Yes, that's better. You're getting it now. But you've really got to practice every day. It looks easy, but it's hard to do."

"But, George," Mrs. Pierce broke in, as Howard scrambled to his feet, "—what I'm interested in knowing is how you keep that beautiful, strong athlete's figure that you've got! And that dancer's *waist!* My dear sir, that is the curse of a woman's life: so if you can tell me what to do to take it off around the waist and hips I'll be eternally grateful to you."—She was, as a matter of fact, herself as lean and well-conditioned as a race-horse, but George, still lying flat upon the floor, answered quietly:

"Did you ever try this, Ida? I think you'll find it very useful for keeping the waist down.—You lie flat on your back—like this. You keep your arms flat at your sides—you mustn't raise them or lift your head. You keep your legs straight—you mustn't bend them at the knees—and then," slowly, and with a sense of infinite, hard-muscled

power and lean endurance, he suited the action to the words, "you raise
your legs to right angles with your body—straighten out again—raise—
straighten—raise—straighten—raise—straighten—if you do that a hundred times a day, when you get up and when you go to bed, I don't
think you'll ever be troubled by fat around the waist," he concluded
quietly.

"I know," Joel whispered, nodding with vigorous agreement. "I've
tried that. That's a good one. But a hundred times is a lot! It's
more than most people can do at first."

"Yes," said George quietly. "But you get used to it if you do it
every day! I can do it a hundred times with no difficulty whatever,"
he concluded quietly.

"Oh, of *course!*" Joel whispered instantly. "But then, you're hard as a
rock, George. You can do anything."

"But that doesn't look hard," Howard said again with blithe confidence. "Oh, I just *know* that I can do *that* one," he said mincingly.
And without further ado, while every one laughed, he stretched himself out again, extended his dapper flannelled legs as George instructed
him, and then slowly raised them, lowered them, raised them again
with such a painful grunt that every one burst out again in hearty
laughter. After the fourth effort he was through, admitting defeat with
a painful "Gosh! If I had to do that for a hundred times I'd be ready
for the undertaker," and scrambled to his feet again.

"Then," said George in his quiet, pleasant tone, "I think you'll find
this one good, Ida, for strengthening the muscles of the back and
stomach. You *arch,*" he said, "you arch with the neck and feet—like
this," and instantly his strong, frail, beautifully proportioned figure was
arched as lithely and gracefully as a bow, "—you come down slow like
this," he said, and sank slowly toward the ground, "you arch again like
this"—again the light and graceful human bow.

"Oh, but that looks terribly hard to do, George!" Mrs. Pierce
protested. "I could never learn to do that: it's a regular circus
stunt."

"No," he said in his quiet and toneless fashion, "you could do it,
Ida. Of course, it *is* hard at first, but it would come with practice.
. . . It makes you very strong," he went on with a completely detached
matter-of-factness. "Do you see that?" He arched his whip-cord body
again and held it in that posture—"I could keep that up indefinitely—
it makes you hard as nails," he went on quietly, and without an atom

of vanity or self-consciousness. "I could support the whole weight of a man's body there without any difficulty—and *lift* him, too."

"Not *really!*" Joel whispered in an astounded tone. "Simply incredible!"

"But not at all," said George quietly. "It's the easiest thing on earth if you're used to it. Come here, Howard," he said quietly, without moving from his arched position. "Sit down on me."

"Sit *down* on you?" said Howard, in a comically bewildered tone. "*Where,* George?"

"On my stomach," George replied. "Go on," he said, smiling his fine, grave smile at sight of Howard's hesitation. "It's all right. You won't hurt me at all. Sit down."

"Like—like this?" said Howard, and squatted gingerly and gently, settling down finally upon George's arched stomach and looking about with such a comically troubled and inquiring expression that every one burst out in hearty laughter again. "Is that all right?" he said, turning anxiously and looking down at his supporter.

"Yes, perfectly," said George. "Now draw your knees up and hold them with your arms so that your whole weight is on me. . . . Good! . . . Now! Are you ready? . . . One, two . . . One, two . . . One, two," his lithe, whip-cord figure rose and fell, arched and straightened, with little Howard sitting on top of him, and looking around with the expression of a frightened, huddled mannikin. When the demonstration was finished, both young men got to their feet, and Joel's face could be seen raised in an expression of radiant admiration, his voice could be heard in an astounded whisper, saying:

"*Simply* incredible!"

And Mrs. Pierce, her voice stronger, more powerful, and penetrating, in slow, decisive declaration:

"*George!* I—think—that—is—the—*most—astonishing*—I think—that —is—the—*most——*"

Words failed her, and as she looked at him, standing quietly composed before her, with all his beautiful, lithe grace and stillness, he smiled his grave, rare smile, and displayed his only playful raillery of the evening:

"But really, Ida," he said quietly, as he smiled his fine, slow smile at her, "if you're worried about that girlish figure you ought to try *this* sometime." With these words he bent over backward, as lithe and limber as a whip, and with his fingers arched upon the floor, suddenly, with effortless grace and speed, and without moving an inch from his position, whirled off a dozen brilliant cartwheels that would have done credit to a circus tumbler.

He came gracefully, unweariedly erect again, to standing posture, amid an ovation of breathlessly uttered wonder, frank applause.

But now the time had come for parting: there was the sound of a motor in the drive before the house, in a moment a maid-servant came quietly out upon the terrace and informed Miss Telfair that her car had come. She gathered her evening cloak about her fragile, ivory shoulders—that were somehow like a piece of her own rare porcelain—thrust her hand out towards Mrs. Pierce in swift and firm farewell, and turned saying in her crisp, incisive voice: "Well, children, I'm departing . . . Joel," she said, pausing a moment as she went, "I shall expect you and your young friend at my house for tea tomorrow."

"And are you coming to the pool tomorrow morning, Margaret?" Mrs. Pierce called after her.

"That, my dear, I couldn't tell you," she said, going. "If I do not get a call from town. We shall see what we shall see—good-night, all," and she went through the moonlit door into the house.

LXI

MRS. PIERCE stood at the foot of the stairs surveying this young stranger from the outside world with a tolerant but glacially detached smile of impersonal curiosity:

". . . Joel tells me that you like to stay up all night and prowl around. What do you do on these prowling expeditions?"

He wanted to answer her with simple eloquence and grace and warmth, he wanted to paint a picture of his midnight wanderings that would hold her there in fascinated interest, but the glacial impersonality of the woman's smile, the proud and haughty magnificence of her person, froze all the ardors of enthusiasm and conviction with which, he felt, he might have spoken, it even seemed to numb and thicken the muscles of his tongue, and he stood there gaping at her awkwardly, cutting a sorry figure, and flushing crimson with anger and vexation at his lame, stupid, halting tongue, and stammered out, replying:

"I—I walk," he mumbled. "I—I take walks."

"You—*what?*" she said kindly enough, but sharply, with a kind of peremptory authority that told him that she must already be growing weary and impatient of his stammering, incoherent speech, his mumbling awkwardness:

"Oh—*walk!*" she cried, with an air of swift enlightenment, as if her puzzled mind had just succeeded in translating his jargon. "Oh," she said quietly, and looked at him for a moment steadily with her fixed and glacial smile, "you do."

It seemed to him that those brief words were already pregnant with a cold indifferent dismissal: in them he seemed to feel the impregnable indifference of her cold detachment—the yawning gulf that separated her life from his. Already it seemed to him that she had turned away from him, dismissing him as not worthy even of such amused attention as she had given him. But after a moment, as she continued to look at him with her brilliant, glacial, detached, yet not unkindly smile, she continued:

"And what do you do on these walks? Where do you go?"

—Where? Where? Where indeed? His mind groped desperately over the whole nocturnal pattern of the city—over the lean, gaunt webbing of Manhattan with the barren angularity of its streets, the splintered, glacial soar of its terrific buildings, and the silent, frozen harshness of its streets of old brown houses, grimy brick and rusty, age-encrusted stone.

Oh, he thought that he could tell her all that could be told, that youth could know, that any man had ever known about night and time and darkness, and about the city's dark and secret heart, and what lay buried in the dark and secret heart of all America. He thought that he could tell her all that any man could ever know about the huge, attentive secrecy of night, and of man's silent heart of buried, waiting, and intolerable desire, about the thing that waits there in the nighttime in America, that lies buried at the city's secret heart of night, the mute and single tongue of man's intolerable desire, the silence of his single heart in all its overwhelming eloquence, the great tide flowing in the hearts of men, as dark and as mysterious as the great, unceasing river, the thing that waits and does not speak and is forever silent and that knows forever, and that has no words to say, no tongue to speak, and that unites six million celled and lonely sleepers at the heart of night and silence, in the great dark tide of the unceasing river, and of all our buried songs of hope and joy and wild desire that live forever in the heart of night and of America.

Yes, he thought that he could tell her all of this, but when he spoke, with thickened tongue, a numb and desperate constraint, all that he could mutter thickly was: "I—I walk."

"But *where?*" she said, a trifle more sharply, still looking at him with her glacial, curious smile. "That's what I'd like to know. Where do you go? What do you see that's so interesting? What do you find that's worth staying up all night for? Where do you go when you make these expeditions?" she again demanded. "Up to Broadway?"

"Yes," he mumbled thickly, "—sometimes—and—and sometimes—I go down town."

"Down town?" the cool incisive inflection of the voice, the glacial gray-green of the eye bored through him like a steel-blue drill. "Downtown *where?* To the Battery?"

"Y-y-yes—sometimes. . . . And—and along the East Side, too," he mumbled.

"*Where?*" she cried sharply, smiling, but manifestly impatient with his mumbled, tongue-tied answers. "*Oh*—the East Side!" she cried again, with the air of glacial enlightenment. "—In the tenement section!"

"Yes—yes," he .stumbled on desperately, "—and along Fourteenth Street and Second Avenue—and Grand Street—and—and Delancey—and—and the Bowery—and all the docks and piers and all," he blurted out, conscious of Joel's eager, radiant smile of hopeful kindness, and the miserable clown he was making of himself.

"But I should think you would find all that dreadfully boring." Mrs. Pierce's voice was now tinged with cool and mild surprise. "And awfully ugly, isn't it? . . . I mean, if you've got to prowl around at night, you might hunt for something a little more attractive than the East Side, couldn't you? . . . After all, we still have Riverside Drive—I suppose even that has changed a great deal, but in my childhood it was quite a lovely place. Or the Park?" she said, a little more kindly and persuasively. "If you want to take a walk before going to bed, why wouldn't it be better to take it in the Park—where you could see an occasional tree or a little grass. . . . Or even Fifth Avenue and around Washington Square—that used to be quite pleasant! But the East *Side!* Heavens! My dear boy, what on earth do you ever find in a place like that to interest you?"

He was absolutely speechless, congealed, actually terrified by the haughty magnificence, the glacial and almost inhuman detachment, of her person. His mouth gaped, he gulped, his lips quivered and made soundless efforts for a moment, and then he stammered:

"You—you find—you find—p-p-p-people there," he said.

"*People?*" Again, her thin eyebrows arched in fine surprise. "But of course you find people there! You find people everywhere you go. . . . Only," she added, "I shouldn't think you'd find many people anywhere at two o'clock in the morning. I should think most of them would be in bed—even on the East Side."

"They—they stay up late over there."

"But why?" she now cried with a good-natured but frank impatience. "That's just what I'm trying to find out! . . . What's it all about? What's all the *shooting* for?" she said humorously, repeating a phrase which was in current use at that time. "—What's the big attraction? What do they find to do that's so interesting that it can keep them out of bed half through the night? . . . Really," she cried, "if it's so amusing as all that, I think I'll go and have a look myself. What do they *do?*" she again insisted. "That's what I want to know."

"They—they sit around and talk."

"But *where? Where?*" she now cried with frank despair. "My dear boy, that's what I want you to tell me."

"Oh, in—in lunch-rooms—and restaurants—and speakeasies—and—and places like that."

"Yes," she nodded, with an air of satisfaction. "Good. At least, we have *that* settled. And you go to these places, too—and sit around—and watch—and listen to them. Is that it?"

"Yes," he said helplessly, nodding, her words suddenly making all this restless and unceasing explanation of the night seem reasonless, foolish, pitifully absurd, "sometimes."

"And what kind of people do you find in those places?" she said curiously. "I've often wondered what kind of people go there."

Kind? He stared at her foolishly with gaping jaw, and gaped and muttered wordlessly, and could not find a word to say to her. Kind? Great God, what word could ever shape them, what phrase could ever utter the huge swarm and impact of just one moment, out of all those million swarming memories of kaleidoscopic night! Kind? Great God, the kind of all the earth, the kind of the whole world, the unnumbered, nameless, swarming, and illimitable kind that make all living! Kind? The mongrel compost of a hundred races—the Jews, the Irish, the

Italians, and the niggers, the Swedes, the Germans, the Lithuanians and the Poles, the Russians, Czechs, and Greeks, the Syrians, Turks and Armenians, the nameless hodge-podge of the Balkans, as well as Chinese, Japs, and dapper little Filipinos—a hundred tongues, a thousand tribes, unnumbered colonies of life, all poured in through the lean gateways of the sea, all poured in upon that rock of life, to join the countless freightage of that ship of living stone, all nurtured and sustained upon the city's strong breast,—a thousand kinds, a single substance, all fused and joined there at the heart of night, all moving with that central, secret and dynamic energy, all wrought and woven in, with all their swarming variousness, into the great web of America— with all its clamor, naked struggle, blind and brutal strife, with all its violence, ignorance, and cruelty, and with its terror, joy, and mystery, its undying hope, its everlasting life.

All he could do was gape and mumble foolishly again, and stammer finally: "There—there are all kinds, I guess," and plunge on desperately, "and then—and then—there are the wharves and piers and docks— the Battery and the City Hall—and then—and then," he stumbled on, "—the Bridge—the Bridge is good."

"The Bridge?" Again the pencilled brows of arched surprise, the glacial curiosity. "What bridge?"

What bridge? Great God, the only bridge, the bridge of power, life and joy, the bridge that was a span, a cry, an ecstasy—that was America. What bridge? The bridge whose wing-like sweep that was like space and joy and ecstasy was mixed like music in his blood, would beat like flight and joy and triumph through the conduits of his life forever. What bridge? The bridge whereon at night he had walked and stood and watched a thousand times, until every fabric of its soaring web was inwrought in his memory, and every stone of its twin terrific arches was in his heart, and every living sinew of its million cabled nerves had throbbed and pulsed in his own spirit like his soul's anatomy.

"The—the Brooklyn Bridge," he mumbled. "The—the Bridge is good."

"Good? How do you mean—good?" The glacial and amused inquiry pierced his consciousness again with confusion, numb paralysis of speech, and incoherence. And at this moment Joel, seeing his agonizing embarrassment, came to his rescue with the exquisite, radiant kindliness that was the constant evidence of his fine character.

"Um. Yes," he could hear Joel whispering in a thoughtful and convinced way. "He's dead right about it, Mums. I've gone with him once or twice—and the Bridge *is* good! . . . And the East Side has good things in it, too," he whispered generously. "I saw some good bits there —street corners, a store front, alleys—there's good color—I'd like to go back sometime and paint it."

For the first time Mrs. Pierce broke into a robust, free and hearty laugh.

"Joel!" she cried. "You can get the most insane notions in your head of any boy I ever knew! If I didn't watch you, I believe you'd be painting ash-cans! . . . My dear boy," she said, laughing, "you'd better stick to what you're doing. I don't think you've had much experience with low-life—if that's what you want I'll find plenty of it for you right here in Rhinekill or on the farm. . . . If you want low-life," here she paused and laughed heartily again, "go down to Granny's tomorrow and paint the expression of those nine maids of hers when she tells them she's decided to bob their hair because it fits in so nicely with the new decoration—Hah! Hah! Hah! Hah! Hah!"—Mrs. Pierce cast back her head and laughed again, a full free hearty laugh of robust humor, in which Joel joined enthusiastically, almost suddenly, with a face radiant with glee— "I'd just like to be there when she tells them, that'll be low-life enough," she said.

"*Simply* incredible!" Joel whispered, his face still radiant with its gleeful merriment.

"But no," his mother went on more casually, and with humorous tolerance. "—You finish up what you're doing first—finish those screens you're doing for Madge Telfair—then we'll talk about low-life. . . . But I hardly think your talent lies in that direction," she said good-humoredly but with an ironically knowing smile. "I haven't been your mother all these years without finding out something about your abilities—and I hardly think they lie in that direction. So you just stick to what you're doing for the present—and if there's any low-life to be done, just let *me* do the choosing. . . . Well, then, good-night," she said quietly, kindly, and good-naturedly to the young man, as she turned to go upstairs. "Joel has told me so much about your nocturnal habits that I was curious to meet you and find out what you did. I'm glad to get the mystery cleared up. . . . I suppose," she said, with an idle and detached curiosity, "that when one is all alone and knows no one in the city, he is driven to do almost anything for amusement. . . . Where are you from?" she said curiously.

"From—from the South," he answered.

"Oh," she stared at him a moment longer with her cold, fixed smile. "Yes," she said, "I can see you are. I thought so. . . . Well, children," she said with an air of finality, "you can burn the candle at both ends if that's what you want to do—go out and bay the moon, if you like—but not too near the house," she said good-naturedly. "Your *mother's* going to bed. . . . Joel," she said quietly, "you'll be in to see me, of course, before you turn in."

"Yes, Mums," he whispered, eager, radiant, his tall, thin figure bent forward reverentially as he looked up at her, his eyebrows arching with their characteristic expression of fine surprise.—"But of course!" he said.

"Very well," she said quietly. "And now good-night to all of you."

Turning, she went swiftly up the stairs, a tall, magnificently haughty figure of a woman, holding rustling and luxurious skirts.

"And now," Joel whispered, when his mother had departed, "I'll show you your room—and how to find the kitchen—and tell you anything you want to know—and after *that*," he whispered, laughing and stroking his head, "you can do as you please, stay up as long as you like—but *I'm* going to bed."

With these words he took his guest's valise and started up the stairs. The young man followed him: he had been given a room on the second floor on the river side of the house. It was a magnificent spacious room so richly, softly carpeted that the foot sank down with velvet firmness to a noiseless tread. The quality of the room was the quality of the whole house—a kind of château-like grandeur and solidity, combined with the warmth, comfort and simplicity of a country house. Joel pressed buttons, flooding the great room with light. The wide and snowy covers of the great bed had been drawn back for the night. It was a bed fit for a king, and long and spacious enough for a man of seven feet: it waited there with a kind of still embrace, a silent and yet animate invitation that was eloquent with the promise of a strange and sweet repose.

Joel opened the door of the bathroom—it was a miracle of shining tile and creamy porcelain and gleaming silver and heavy, robe-like towels. Then Joel raised the shades, drew the curtains apart and opened the window: the fragrance of the night came in slowly, sustaining gauzy curtains on its breath of coolness like a cloud of gossamer.

And through the opened window was revealed anew the haunting loneliness of that enchanted landscape: the vast sweep of velvet-rounded lawn that slept in moonlight, and the sleeping and moon-haunted woods below and to each side, and down below them in the distance the great wink and scallop-dance and dark unceasing mystery of the lovely and immortal river—a landscape such as one might see in dreams, in dreams forever haunted by the thought of home.

The feeling of happiness that filled the youth was so grand, so wonderful and so overpowering that he could not speak. It seemed that all his life he had dreamed of one day finding such a life as this, and now that he had found it, it seemed to him that all he had dreamed was but a poor and shabby counterfeit of this reality—all he had imaged as a boy in his unceasing visions of the shining city, and of the glamorous men and women, the fortunate, good, and happy life that he would find there, seemed nothing but a shadowy and dim pre-figurement of the radiant miracle of this actuality.

It was not merely the wealth, the luxury and the comfort of the scene that filled his heart with a sense of joy and victory. Far more than this, it was the feeling that this life of wealth, and luxury and comfort was so beautiful and right and good. At the moment it seemed to him to be the life for which all men on the earth are seeking, about which all men living dream, toward which all the myriads of the earth aspire; and the thing, above all, which made this life seem so beautiful and good was the conviction that filled him at that moment of its essential incorruptible righteousness. It seemed to him to be the most wonderful and beautiful life on earth, not only because it existed for the comfort and the soul-enrichment of its choice few, but because it stood there as a beacon and a legend in the hearts of all men living—a symbol of what all life on earth should be, a promise of what every man on earth should have.

In that blind surge of youth and joy, the magic of that unbelievable discovery, he could not estimate the strange and bitter chance of destiny, nor ravel out that grievous web, that dense perplexity. He could not see how men had groped and toiled and mined, and grown blind and bent and gray, deep in the dark bowels of the earth, to wreak this moonlight loveliness upon a hill; nor know how men had sweat and women worked, how youth had struck its fire and grown old, how hope and faith and even love had died, how many nameless lives had labored, grieved, and come to naught in order that this fragile image of compacted night, this priceless distillation of its rare and chosen loveliness, should blossom to a flower of moonlight beauty on a hill.

Joel took him downstairs to the kitchen before telling him good-night. They crossed the hall, and passed through the great dining-room. It was also a noble gleaming room of white, as grand and spacious as a room in a château, but warm, and familiar, comforting as home. Then they passed through a service corridor that connected the kitchen and the pantry with the dining-room, and instantly he found himself in another part of this enchanted world—the part that cooked and served and with viewless grace, and magic stealth and instancy—performed the labors of this enchanted house.

It was such a kitchen as he had never seen before—a kitchen such as he had never dreamed possible. In its space, its order, its astounding cleanliness, it had the beauty of a great machine—a machine of tremendous power, fabulous richness and complexity—which in its ordered magnificence, its vast readiness, had the clear and glittering precision of a geometric pattern. Even the stove—a vast hooded range as large as those in a great restaurant—glittered with the groomed perfection of a racing motor. There was, as well, an enormous electric stove that was polished like a silver ornament, the pots and pans were hung in gleaming rows, in vast but orderly profusion ranging from great copper kettles big enough to roast an ox to little pans and skillets just large enough to poach an egg, but all hung there in regimented order, instant readiness, shining like mirrors, scrubbed and polished into gleaming disks, the battered cleanliness of well-used copper, seasoned iron and heavy steel.

The great cupboards were crowded with huge stacks of gleaming china ware and crockery, enough to serve the needs of a hotel. And the long kitchen table, as well as the chairs and woodwork of the room, was white and shining as a surgeon's table: the sinks and drains were blocks of creamy porcelain, clean scrubbed copper, shining steel.

It would be impossible to describe in detail the lavish variety, the orderly complexity, the gleaming cleanliness of that great room, but the effect it wrought upon his senses was instant and overwhelming. It was one of the most beautiful, spacious, thrilling, and magnificently service-able rooms that he had ever seen: everything in it was designed for use, and edged with instant readiness; there was not a single thing in the room that was not needed, and yet its total effect was to give one a feeling of power, space, comfort, rightness and abundant joy.

The pantry shelves were crowded to the ceiling with the growing treasure of a lavish victualling—an astounding variety and abundance of delicious foods, enough to stock a grocery store, or to supply an Arctic expedition—but the like of which he had never seen, or dreamed of, in a country house before.

Everything was there, from the familiar staples of a cook's necessities to every rare and toothsome dainty that the climates and the markets of the earth produce. There was food in cans, and food in tins, and food in crocks, and food in bottles. There were—in addition to such staple products of the canning art as corn, tomatoes, beans and peas, pears, plums and peaches, such rarer relishes, as herrings, sardines, olives, pickles, mustard, relishes, anchovies. There were boxes of glacéd crystalline fruits from California, and little wickered jars of sharp-spiced ginger fruit from China: there were expensive jellies green as emerald, red as rubies, smoother than whipped cream, there were fine oils and vinegars in bottles, and jars of pungent relishes of every sort, and boxes of assorted spices. There was everything that one could think of, and everywhere there was evident the same scrubbed and gleaming cleanliness with which the kitchen shone, but here there was as well, that pungent, haunting, spicy odor that pervades the atmosphere of pantries —a haunting and nostalgic fusion of delicious smells whose exact quality it is impossible to define, but which has in it the odors of cinnamon, pepper, cheese, smoked ham, and cloves.

When they got into the kitchen they found Rosalind there: she was standing by the long white table drinking a glass of milk. Joel, in the swift and correct manner with which he gave instructions, at once eager, gentle and decisive, began to show his guest around.

"And look," he whispered with his soft, and yet incisive slowness, as he opened the heavy shining doors of the great refrigerator—"here's the icebox: if you find anything there you like, just help yourself——"

Food! Food, indeed! The great icebox was crowded with such an assortment of delicious foods as he had not seen in many years: just to look at it made the mouth begin to water, and aroused the pangs of a hunger so ravenous and insatiate that it was almost more painful than the pangs of bitter want. One was so torn with desire and greedy gluttony as he looked at the maddening plenty of that feast that his will was rendered almost impotent. Even as the eye glistened and the mouth began to water at the sight of a noble roast of beef, all crisp and crackly in its cold brown succulence, the attention was diverted to a plump broiled chicken, whose brown and crackly tenderness fairly seemed to beg for the sweet and savage pillage of the tooth. But now a pungent and exciting fragrance would assail the nostrils: it was the smoked pink slices of an Austrian ham—should it be brawny bully beef, now, or the juicy breast of a white tender pullet, or should it be the smoky pungency, the half-nostalgic savor of the Austrian ham? Or that noble dish of green lima beans, now already beautifully congealed in their pervading film of melted butter; or that dish of tender stewed young cucumbers; or those tomato slices, red and thick and ripe, and heavy as a chop; or that dish of cold asparagus, say; or that dish of corn; or, say, one of those musty fragrant, deep-ribbed cantaloupes, chilled to the heart, now, in all their pink-fleshed taste and ripeness; or a round thick slab cut from the red ripe heart of that great watermelon; or a bowl of those red raspberries, most lucious and most rich with sugar, and a bottle of that thick rich cream which filled one whole compartment of that treasure-chest of gluttony, or——

What shall it be now? What shall it be? A snack! A snack! Before we prowl the meadows of the moon to-night, and soak our hearts in the moonlight's magic and the visions of our youth—what shall it be before we prowl the meadows of the moon? Oh, it shall be a snack, a snack—hah! hah!—it shall be nothing but a snack because—hah! hah!—you understand, we are not hungry and it is not well to eat too much before retiring—so we'll just investigate the icebox as we have done so oft at midnight in America—and we are the moon's man, boys—and all that it will be, I do assure you, will be something swift and quick and ready, something instant and felicitous, and quite delicate and dainty—just a snack!

I think—now let me see—h'm, now!—well, perhaps I'll have a slice or two of that pink Austrian ham that smells so sweet and pungent and looks so pretty and so delicate there in the crisp garlands of the parsley leaf!—and yes, perhaps, I'll have a slice of this roast beef, as well—h'm now!—yes, I think that's what I'm going to do—say a slice of red rare meat there at the centre—ah-h! there you are! yes, that's the stuff, that does quite nicely, thank you—with just a trifle of that crisp brown crackling there to oil the lips and make its passage easy, and a little of that cold but brown and oh—most—brawny gravy—and, yes, sir!

I think I *will*, now that it occurs to me, a slice of that plump chicken—some white meat, thank you, at the breast—ah, there it is!—how sweetly doth the noble fowl submit to the swift and keen persuasion of the knife—and now, perhaps, just for our diet's healthy balance, a spoonful of those lima beans, as gay as April and as sweet as butter, a tomato slice or two, a speared forkful of those thin-sliced cucumbers—ah! what a delicate and toothsome pickle they do make—what sorcerer invented them—a little corn perhaps, a bottle of this milk, a pint of butter and that crusty loaf of bread—and even this moon-haunted wilderness were paradise enow—with just a snack—a snack—a snack——

He was aroused from this voluptuous and hypnotic revery by the sound of Rosalind's warm sweet laugh, her tender and caressing touch upon his arm, and Joel's soundless and astonished mouth, the eager incandescence of his gleeful smile, his whole face uplifted in its fine and gentle smile, his voice cast in its frequent tone of whispering astonishment:—

"*Simply* incredible!" he was whispering to his sister. "I've never seen such an expression on *any* one's face in all my life! It's simply diabolical! When he sees food, he looks as if he's just getting ready to rape a woman!"

"Do you, darling?" said the girl, with her warm, sweet tolerance of humor. "I'm so glad to know that some one else likes food. I like it, too," she said with a warm plainness, "when I am married and start having babies I shall eat and eat and eat to my heart's content—as much as I want to, all the things I ever wanted, till I'm satisfied. . . . It's so wonderful to find some one who will eat! You don't know how hard it is to have a brother who's a vegetarian—and who tells me that I'm getting disgustingly fat—and what a horrible thing it is to eat dead animals —like eating corpses. . . . Wouldn't Joel be wonderful if he ate roast beef," she added with her warm and gentle humor, as she put her arm around her brother's waist—"he looks so thin and starved, poor thing—like a religious ascetic—doesn't he?— But then, he's such a saint as he is—isn't he?—if he liked food, as well, he'd just have everything— he'd be too perfect."

"No, sir," Joel whispered, shaking his head and laughing with his curiously boyish, almost clumsily naïve, but beautifully engaging good nature— "Not I! . . . The rest of you can eat all the dead animals you like—but you don't catch me doing it! . . . I'll stick to spinach," he whispered radiantly. "That's good enough for me."

"I know, darling," she said with a gentle and tolerant sarcasm. "You and Bernard Shaw: if he said baled hay was good for you, you'd believe him, wouldn't you?"

He laughed in his soundless, enthusiastic and beautifully generous way, his gaunt starved face lighting up with the gleeful almost diabolically brilliant radiance of his wonderful selfless good-nature.

Then, turning swiftly to his firmer manner of incisive severity—the direct and earnest concision with which he whispered his instructions —he said abruptly:

"And look, Gene . . . when you finish eating put the lights out: the switch is on the right hand by the door as you go out. . . . And stay up as long as you like, go wherever you like, do as you please— you'll bother no one," he whispered, ". . . and a good walk," he continued abruptly after a moment's pause, "—is down the road—the way you went with Ros' tonight—except that you keep on——"

"Past the cows, darling," said Rosalind gently. "Past all the lovely cows and barns and meadows of the moon."

LXII

THE two young people stopped talking instantly as Eugene came in, Joel got up and shut the door behind him, indicated an easy leather chair, where the author could read his play most comfortably, and sitting down again beside his sister, waited for the play to begin.

Eugene began to read haltingly, with the difficulty and embarrassed constraint of a young man just beginning to test his powers, exhibiting his talents to the public for the first time, and torn by all the anguish, hope, and fear, the proud incertitude, of youth.

It was a play called "Mannerhouse," a title which itself might reveal the whole nature of his error—and its subject was the decline and fall and ultimate extinction of a proud old family of the Southern aristocracy in the years that followed the Civil War, the ultimate decay of all its fortunes and the final acquisition of its proud estate, the grand old columned house that gave the play its name, by a vulgar, coarse and mean, but immensely able member of the rising "lower class."

This theme—which, in its general form and implications, was probably influenced a good deal by *The Cherry Orchard* of Chekhov— was written in a somewhat mixed mood of romantic sentiment, Byronic irony, and sardonic realism: The hero was a rather Byronic character, a fellow who concealed his dark and tender poetry under the mask of a sardonic humor; the love story was colored by defeat and envy and departure, and the hero's final return "years later," a lonely and nameless wanderer, battered by the world and the wreckage of his life, to the old ruined house in which already the rasping note of the wrecker's crew was audible, was tempered by the romantic gallantry of Cyrano. The final meeting with the girl—the woman that he loved —their ultimate gallant resignation to fate and age and destiny—was wholly Cyranoic; and the final scene, in which the gigantic faithful negro slave—now an old man, almost blind, but with the savage loyalty and majesty of a race of African beings from whom he is descended— wraps his great arms around the rotting central column of the old ruined house, snaps it in two with a last convulsion of his dying strength, and brings the whole ruined temple thundering down to bury his beloved master, his hated "poor white" enemy the new owner, and himself, beneath its ruins—was obviously a product of the Samson legend.

In spite of this, there was good stuff in the play, dramatic conflict, moving pageantry. The character of the hard, grasping but immensely able materialist of "the lower class," the newer South, was well realized —and had been derived from the character of the youth's own uncle, William Pentland. The scenes between the hero and his father—the leonic and magnificently heroic "General"—were also good; as were those between the hero and Porter, the poor-white capitalist. Even in these romantic, grandly-mannered scenes, he had already begun to use some of the powerful and inimitable materials of life itself and of his own experience: the speech of Porter was the plain, rich, pungent, earthly, strongly colored speech of his mother, of his uncle William Pentland, and of the Pentland tribe.

But the scenes between the hero and the girl were less successful: the character of the girl was shadowy and uncertain—a kind of phantasmal combination of the characters of Roxane in Cyrano, and Ophelia— and her sweet romantic loveliness, the yearning tenderness of her pure love, did not provide a convincing foil and balance for the sardonic humor, the bad and almost brutal volume of wit, with which the hero marked his pain and love and bitterness and repulsed her advances. (This scene, by the way, was undoubtedly influenced a great deal by the Hamlet and Ophelia situation.)

Likewise—in various and interesting ways, what he had read and seen and actually experienced had shaped the tone and temper of his play: the character of the pompous and banal old "Major"—the "General's" contemporary and friend and the father of the heroine— and his conversations with the hero, in which his conventional and pompous character is made the butt for the biting and sardonic gibes of the latter, were also evidently strongly colored with the influence of Polonius and Hamlet. But there was good stuff in these scenes as well, considerable originality and naturalness was shown in the characterization of the old "Major": he was, for example, trying to support the tottering fortune of a small military school, which his family had established several generations before, and whose gigantic futility, amid this decline of a ruined order and a vanquished system was, in the years after the war, ironically apparent. There was, in fact, much telling satire in this situation, and on the whole it was well managed. Moreover, its "modern" implications were evident: it suggested, for example, the Southerner's pitiable devotion to a gaudy uniform and military trappings, the profusion of ugly, trivial, cheap and brutal little "military schools" that cover the whole South, even to the present day, like an ugly rash, and whose "You furnish the boy—we send back the man" philosophy is nauseous in its hypocrisy, dishonesty, and cheap pretense.

There was much more that was good and pungent and original in these scenes between the "Major" and the hero: a great deal of the falseness, hypocrisy and sentimentality of the South was polished off in these episodes, and "the war"—the Civil War—was used effectively as a stalking horse to satirize the great World War of modern times. There was, for example, a good, and original—on the whole, a very true—variation of the Youth-and-Age, Old Man-Young Man conflict that was evident at that period, and that provided the material of so many books and plays and poems of the time.

In these scenes, it was very forcefully and amusingly shown that the conflict between youth and age had in it an element of mutual hypocrisy, a kind of mutual acceptance of a literary game about youth and age which both young and old knew in their hearts was false, but which both played.

Thus when the old "Major" would heave a melancholy sigh, and shaking his beard with a doleful and hypocritical regret, would say:

"Ah yes, my boy! . . . We old men have made a sad mess of this world. . . . We have betrayed our trust, and showed ourselves unworthy of the confidence you young men have reposed in us. . . . We were given the opportunity of making the world a better place in which to live and we have left nothing but ruin, poverty, and misery wherever we went—we have left the world in ashes. . . . Now it is for you young men of the world—for youth—glorious, brave and noble-hearted youth——"

"Ah, youth, youth," the hero would murmur at this point with a sardonic humor that of course went unnoticed by the pompous old fool to whom it was uttered—and the Major would nod his head in agreement and go on——

"Yes, youth—brave, generous and devoted youth—it remains for youth to repair the damage that we old men have done, to bind up the nation's broken wounds, to see to it that the world be made into a fit place for their children to live in, to see that——"

"Government of the people, by the people and for the people," the hero would sardonically supply.

"Yes," the old Major would agree, "—and that the children of the coming generation may not look at you, as you can look at us, and say—'What have you done, old men, with your inheritance? What kind of world are you leaving behind you for us *young* men to inherit? How can you look us in the eyes, old men, when you know that you have been unworthy of your sacred trust—that the young men of the world have been foully tricked, betrayed, dishonored by you old men'——"

"Why, Major!" the hero would now cry, in mock astonishment, as he ironically applauded. "—This is eloquence! Hear, hear! . . . And you are right! Major, you are right! The young men of the world have been betrayed and tricked! Not only tricked—but tr-r-ricked! . . . And by whom?" he would inquire with sardonic rhetoric. "Why, by these false, lying, greedy, hypocritical old men who have had the whole world in their keeping and who have reduced it to a shambles for our inheritance! . . . Major, who made the war? Who *sent* us forth to war? . . . Why, these old, false, lying, greedy men, of course! . . . And who fought the war? . . . Why, these brave, gallant, devoted, noble-spirited young men, of course! . . . And why did you old men send us forth to war, Major? . . . Why, to further your own rapacity, to protect your own ill-gotten wealth, to conquer, ravage, and invade for your own enrichment. . . . And how did we go to war, Major? Why, with faith and trust and the purity of a high conviction. . . . And how did we come back from war? With hell in our eyes. . . . We young men always go to war with faith and trust and the purity of a high conviction. . . . And we always come back with hell in our eyes! Why, Major? . . . Why, because you false, lying, greedy, selfish, and hypocritical old men of the world have lied to us. . . . You always lie to us. And how, Major, in what way do you lie to us? . . . Why, Major," he said solemnly, "you tell us that war is beautiful, ideal, and heroic—that we are going forth to fight for pure ideals, noble faith, . . . And what do we find, Major? Why," he said, as his voice sank to an ironically solemn whisper—"we find that war is really *ugly*— is really cruel—horrible—base. . . . Why, Major, do you know what we young men find when we go to war? We find that men in war actually *kill* one another. . . . Yes, sir," he would whisper solemnly, ". . . they *shoot* one another—they blow one another's brains out— *that's* what they do—why, it's murder, Major—sheer cold-blooded murder—it's not what you said it was at all—and all of it because you old greedy, lying, selfish men who make the wars have lied to us and tr-r-ricked us all along!"

"Ah, my boy," the old "Major" would answer sorrowfully—"it is a grievous charge you make against us—but I fear—I fear," here his voice would sink to a dejected whisper—"I fear that it is just."

In this way, a telling and satiric irony was derived from this scene, which was well-handled and might have been effective on the stage.

But the most effective scene of all, perhaps, was in the prologue of this play: here the scene was really splendid, thrilling in its dramatic pageantry, and undoubtedly would have been a very good and moving one upon a stage. The scene was on a hill and showed the building of the great white house—really the founding of a whole society. Before the unfinished house, a gun held cocked and ready in his hands, was standing the stern and silent figure of its founder. And before him, up and down the hill, and in and out of the unfinished house, and past its great unfinished columns, were moving two silent and unceasing files of slaves, powerful black men stripped naked to the waist, bearing upon their heads the heavy burdens of material that would go into the house. And from the house there comes a sound of constant hammering, and night comes, there are the flares of watchfires 'and the swift and cat-like passing of the great black forms. A moment's flare of insurrection, the spring of a great negro at the stern and lonely figure of the man, the flash of a knife, and the rebel falls, knocked senseless by a blow from the stock of the master's gun.

Then, another white man from the neighboring town—the minister:

the minister's low persuasive voice urging the man to see the crime of slavery, quoting the Scriptures with a telling aptness, urging him to repent, to join the life of town and church, to "come to God" . . . And the quiet and inflexible answer of the master: "I must build my home."

And nothing finally but night and dullness; the great figures of the slaves pad past in darkness, as noiseless as cats, and from the mystery of night there rises now the wailing chant of all the jungle, the lamentation of man's life of toil and grief and bitter labor, the chant of the slave.

This was a fine scene, and should have been beautiful and moving on a stage.

From this description, it will be seen how the young man's play was made up both of good and bad, how strongly it was marked by the varied influence of his reading and idolatry—by Shakespeare, Chekhov, Shaw, Rostand, the Bible—and how he had also already begun to use some of the materials of his own life and feeling and experience, how even in this groping and uncertain play, some of the real grandeur, beauty, terror, and unuttered loneliness of America, was apparent.

Thus the play, with all its faults and imitations, really did illustrate, as few things else could do, the confused incertitude and the flashes of blind but powerful intuition, which mark the artist's early life here in America, and for this reason chiefly the play was interesting.

And feeling this incertitude as he sat down to read the play— that feeling mixed of hope, of fear, of quivering apprehension which the artist feels when for the first time he releases his work from the lonely prison of creation and lets it go then, irrevocably, to stand upon its own feet, meet the naked eye of the great world without protection, and stand or fall upon its own merits—feeling this fatality of release, this irrevocable finality of action, he began to read the play in a halting, embarrassed, and almost inaudible tone, full of the proud and desperate hope, the trembling apprehension, the almost truculent hostility towards imaginary detractors which every young man feels at such a time.

He sensed quickly that his fears were groundless. No man ever had a more generous, enthusiastic and devoted following than he had that morning in the presence of these two fine young people—Joel Pierce and his sister Rosalind.

He saw—or rather *felt* at once—their rapt and fascinated attentiveness. Joel sat, his gaunt figure hinged forward on his knees, in an attitude of tense, motionless and utterly silent interest: from time to time as the young dramatist glanced up from his great sheaf of written manuscript, he could see Joel's lean gaunt face fixed on him, uplifted, with its strangely pure and radiant eagerness, and Rosalind, her warm and strong young hands clasped quietly, folded in her lap, her warm and lovely face flushed with excitement, her eyes luminous, vague and tender, as if she were really in a theatre seeing the figures in the play pass before her invested in all the magic that the stage could give to them, displayed an interest that was more relaxed and more abstracted than her brother's, but none the less absorbed.

The sense and sight and assurance of these things acted like a powerful and gloriously intoxicating liquor on his heart and mind and spirit. He felt an overpowering surge of warm affection, proud and tender gratefulness towards Joel and his sister. It seemed to him that they were the finest people he had ever known—the most generous, the truest, highest, and the loyalest—and the knowledge that they liked his play— were in fact conquered and possessed, brought out of themselves and laid under the play's power and magic—his *own* power and magic— overwhelmed him for a moment with a feeling of the purest, highest, and most glorious happiness that life can yield—the happiness that is at once the most selfish and the most selfless—the happiness of the artist when he sees that his work has been found good, has for itself a place of honor, glory, and proud esteem in the hearts of men, and has wrought upon their lives the spell of its enchantment. At that instant he saw, in one blaze of light, an image of unutterable conviction, the reason why the artist works and lives and has his being—the reward he seeks—the only reward he really cares about, without which there is nothing. It is to snare the spirits of mankind in nets of magic, to make his life prevail through his creation, to wreak the vision of his life, the rude and painful substance of his own experience, into the congruence of blazing and enchanted images that are themselves the core of life, the essential pattern whence all other things proceed, the kernel of eternity. This is the reason that the artist lives and works and has his being: that from life's clay and his own nature, and from his father's common earth of toil and sweat and violence and error and bitter anguish, he may distill the beauty of an everlasting form, enslave and conquer man by his enchantment, cast his spell across the generations, beat death down upon his knees, kill death utterly, and fix eternity with the grappling-hooks of his own art. His life is soul-hydroptic with a quenchless thirst for glory, and his spirit tortured by the anguish of possession—the intolerable desire to fix eternally in the patterns of an indestructible form a single moment of man's living, a single moment of life's beauty, passion, and unutterable eloquence, that passes, flames and goes, slipping forever through our fingers with time's sanded drop, flowing forever from our desperate grasp even as a river flows and never can be held. This is the artist, then—life's hungry man, the glutton of eternity, beauty's miser, glory's slave—and to do these things, to get the reward for which he thirsts, with his own immortality to beat and conquer life, enslave mankind, utterly to possess and capture beauty he will do anything, use anything, destroy anything—be ruthless, murderous and destructive, cold and cruel and merciless as hell to get the thing he wants, achieve the thing he values and must do or die.

He is at once life's monstrous outcast and life's beauty-drunken lover, man's bloody, ruthless, pitiless and utterly relentless enemy, and the best friend that mankind ever had: a creature compact of the most selfish, base, ignoble, vicious, cruel and unrighteous passions that man's life can fathom or the world contain, and a creature whose life with all its toil and sweat and bitter anguish is the highest, grandest, noblest, and the most unselfish, the most superbly happy, good and fortunate life that men can know, or any man attain. He is the tongue of his unuttered brothers, he is the language of man's buried heart, he is man's music and life's great discoverer, the eye that sees, the key that can unlock, the tongue that will express the buried treasure in the hearts of men, that all men know and that no man has a language for—and at the end, he is his father's son, shaped from his father's earth of blood and sweat and toil and bitter agony: he is at once therefore the parent and the son of life, and in him life and all man's nature are compact, he is most like man in his very differences, he is what all men are and what not one man in a million ever is; and he has all, knows all, sees all that any man on earth can see and hear and know.

This knowledge came to him that morning as he read the play that he had written to his two friends: as he went on with his reading, and felt with a proud triumphant joy and happiness the sense of their devotion, his voice grew strong and confident, the scenes and words and people of the play began to flame and pulse and live with his own passion—the whole play moved across his vision in flaming images of beauty, truth and loveliness, his spirit rose on the powerful wings of a jubilant conviction, a tremendous happiness, his heart beat like a hammer-stroke and seemed to ring against his ribs with every blow the music of this certitude.

It took him about two hours to read the play: when he finished he felt a sense of triumphant finality, an immense and joyful peace within him, and he waited for them to speak. For a moment there was utter stillness: Joel sat bent forward in the same position, his head supported by his lean hand; Rosalind sat quietly; neither moved an inch. In a moment Joel spoke, nodding his head and speaking with a kind of matter-of-fact assertiveness that was far more wonderful and thrilling than any idolatrous warmth of praise could have been:

"Yes," he whispered, nodding his head thoughtfully,—"it's as good as *The Cherry Orchard*—I like it better, myself—but it's as good." His manner now did take on an electric energy: he straightened sharply, and speaking almost sternly, with a blazing earnestness of conviction, he looked his friend in the eyes, and cried: "Eugene! . . . It's simply magnificent! . . . It's *easily* the greatest play any one in this country ever wrote. . . . There's nothing else to touch it . . . it's *miles* ahead of O'Neill . . . it's . . . it's as good as *Cyrano,* and you've got to admit," he said, nodding his head decisively, ". . . that's pretty great. . . . *Cyrano's* pretty swell," he whispered, ". . . And those scenes between the boy and the old 'Major' . . . they're simply grand," he whispered. "I mean, I didn't know you had it in you . . . that kind of writing, the satiric kind. . . . But it's . . . it's," his face flushed, he nodded his head doggedly, and almost grimly, as if willing to stand up for his conviction against the whole world, "it's . . . it's as good as *Shaw!*" And he laughed suddenly his radiant, soundless laugh and whispered drolly, ". . . And when I say anything's as good as Shaw . . . you've got to admit that's going pretty far for me. . . . Ros'," he said quietly, turning to the girl, "what do you think? . . . Don't you think it's pretty grand?"

For a moment she did not answer; her eyes were luminous as stars and far away.

"Oh," she said presently in her low and sweet and lovely young voice, "it's wonderful. . . . It's the most gloriously beautiful thing I ever heard. . . . Darling," she said, and took his hand between her strong, warm and living hands, as she had done the night before, ". . . you are a great man . . . a great writer. . . . I am so proud and happy to have known you . . . to be allowed to hear your play."

He felt the overpowering, thrilling happiness and joy, the blind speechless gratefulness, and the helpless and agonizing embarrassment that a young man feels at a moment like this. He did not know what to say, what to do, how to express the gratefulness, the affection, the tenderness that he felt towards them; he turned to Joel, his mouth moving wordlessly and helplessly, and could say nothing, he made a baffled and inarticulate movement of the hands, and ended up by putting his arms around Rosalind and hugging her in a clumsy, helpless fashion, which was perhaps as good a thing as he could do, and said all he wished to say.

It was not what these two young people had said to him that gave the moment a strange imperishable loveliness. Even in the blind surge of joy and happiness that swept over him and made him passionately want to believe that his play was as good as Joel and his sister said it was, that he was really the great man, the great writer they had called him, a grain of judgment remained and saved him from an utter self-deception. And curiously, for that very reason, his joy was somehow greater, his feeling of triumphant happiness sweeter than if what they had said were true. For in the very idolatry of their devotion, the enthusiastic exaggeration of their praise, there was all the blind but noble loyalty of youth, the beautiful and generous admiration of youth, that is so fine, so good, so high, so proud with faith and confidence and loyalty, and because of this, so right. It was for this reason that, even after years had passed and he had perhaps accomplished better work, earned more valid praise, he would yet remember that morning with a peculiar sense of proud and tender gratefulness. It brought back to him, as nothing else on earth could do, the beauty and the innocence of youth, the extravagance of its blind devotion that is so mistaken and so wonderful, the generous enthusiasm of its loyal faith that is so wrong and yet so right, its noble sincerity that burns brightly even in its grievous error, and that is somehow more true than fact, more real than glory, and more lasting and more precious than man's fame.

LXIII

WHEN they came out on the verandah, Joel's mother, Howard Martin, and Joel's cousin, Ruth, had just driven up before the entrance and were

getting out. They had been to the swimming pool—a small but delightful one a half mile away in a green hollow, tree-embowered—and
all three were in bathing costume. Howard Martin trod gingerly across
the drive and on to the warm brick flooring of the porch, on white
wincing well-kept feet; Mrs. Pierce and the girl wore light bathing-
robes and walked firmly, with assurance. Mrs. Pierce's figure was as
slender and as well-conditioned as the girl's—her ankles and her legs
were wonderfully graceful, strong and slender—but in comparison to her
niece's black and white voluptuousness—her dark and sullen, almost
brooding, face and her swelling creamy thighs, her lavish belly and
her melon-heavy breasts—the figure of Mrs. Pierce was lacking in
seduction: it had the strength and slenderness of youth without youth's
warmth and freshness, it had, like everything about her, a chilled and
glacial perfection that spoke of stern regimen, grim watchfulness, and
unflagging effort—"keeping fit."

As the two young men came up, Mrs. Pierce turned gracefully, her
hand upon the screen-door, and with a smile awaited them. Her teeth
were so solid, white, and perfect in their alignment that it was difficult to see where they joined together, and they sometimes suggested
twin rows of solid gleaming ivory more than individual teeth: this
circumstance also contributed to the glacial, detached and almost inhuman quality of her smile. She greeted her son's friend with a kindly
but detached "Good-morning," and without altering the rigid brilliance of her smile a jot, turned to her son, and said:

"I thought you were coming to the pool. What happened to you
and Ros'?"

These words were spoken quietly and matter-of-factly: nevertheless,
the suggestion of strong displeasure and annoyance was somehow unmistakable.

Joel answered quickly, whispering a swift concerned explanation, his
thin figure slightly bent forward, his gaunt face lifted, eagerly, radiantly
concerned, in that attitude of devoted and solicitous respect that characterized his relations with every woman, but that was extremely marked
when he spoke or listened to his mother:

"I know, Mums," he whispered swiftly, apologetically,—"I'm *terribly*
sorry—but he promised to read his play to us and that took all morning.
. . . *Mums!*" he went on in his astounded and enthusiastic whisper, "it's
simply magnificent—I wish you could have been there to hear it."

"Oh," said Mrs. Pierce quietly, and turning, for a moment she regarded her son's friend with that glacially brilliant smile of her thin and faintly carmined lips that never changed or altered in expression by an atom. "Oh," she said, "I should like to—perhaps you will read it to me sometime."

"*Simply* superb," Joel whispered, "it really is."

"And now you boys had better get ready for lunch," she said in a more warm and friendly tone. "You know how Granny hates it if people get there late."

With these words she went into the house and mounted the stairs. The young men followed her: at the foot of the stairs Joel turned and said to his visitor:

"Look—I'd hurry as much as I could! . . . We've only twenty minutes: you've just got time to bathe and dress."

Bathe and dress! The youth looked at his young host with a bewildered, uncomprehending face, and with a sinking feeling in his heart. What did they expect him to do—what, according to the formula of these strange rare people, was one supposed to do when one was invited out to lunch? He had bathed that morning when he got up, it seemed to him that he must still be very clean, and as for dressing, he had just one suit of clothes in all the world, and that was the suit he was wearing at that moment. And just one day before, when he had left New York to come to this magical, unbelievably glorious place, he had thought, in his miserable naïve ignorance, that this one suit of clothes, three shirts, three pairs of socks, and a change of underwear were abundantly sufficient to all the demands that fashion and a week-end visit could possibly make on him. At that moment, as he stared at his friend with a gaping mouth, unable to reply, the terrific impact of this new world which had stunned him the night before with its magnificence and beauty exploded in his brain in a flare of stars and rockets. And for a moment now he felt a lost, sickening desperate terror, and curiously, a feeling of blind resentment against his friend. For a moment he felt tricked and deceived— deceived by Joel's modesty, his exquisite humility, by the frayed and shabby clothes he had worn in Cambridge and New York, by the over-refinement of his breeding, which had caused him to conceal utterly his true state of life, never to suggest by a word or reference the kind of life that he came from, the wealth, the luxury, the magnificence of the world in which he had been born and lived.

"D-d-dress! . . . But . . . how—," his face reddened, he craned his neck doggedly, and suddenly blurted out:

"Dress? In what? This is the only suit I've got!"

"But of *course!*" Joel whispered, arching his eyebrows in astounded surprise. "What's wrong with that? ... You can wear a dark coat any-where—all that I meant was that you could wear white flannels with it."

"Flannels!" the other said, "I have no flannels, Joel. ... This suit is all I've got to wear; if I can't wear this, I can't go."

"But of course you can wear it!" Joel cried, concealing any surprise he may have felt with the instant impatient agreement of his tone. "It's *perfectly* all right—only," his eyes were thoughtful for a moment, he con-sidered swiftly—"Look here!" he said abruptly, "would you like to wear a pair of mine? I'm not as tall as you are, but perhaps you can make them fit. ... And if you can't," he said quickly, "it's *perfectly* all right— it doesn't matter in the slightest—it's only," and his eyes for an in-stant had a faintly perturbed expression, "—it's only that Grandfather belongs to the old school—oh, he's *swell, simply* magnificent; you'll like him the moment you see him—the only reason I dress when going there is that he's got old-fashioned standards—and he's so *grand* —I do everything I can to please him— But come on!" he whispered quickly, 'I'll give you a pair of mine, and you can wear them if they fit —and if they don't—it doesn't matter in the slightest."

They went upstairs then to Joel's room; he gave his friend a pair of striped flannel trousers, and the other departed dutifully to bathe, put on a clean shirt and collar and the flannel trousers—which proved, indeed, a very tight precarious fit, but which were made to do—and thus correctly garmented, he joined the family and the other guests, and they drove away to Mr. Joel's house.

The great rambling old house which had been so lovely in the moon-enchantment of the night before was no less beautiful by day. It sat there in the hollow of the hill, embowered in rich green and shaded by the leafy spread of its great maples, with the homely, pure, and casual loveliness that the old houses of New England have.

Old Mr. Joel himself was just as grand and imposing a personality as Joel had indicated. He was, indeed, in Joel's word, "stupendous"; a figure of leonine magnificence and gallant gentility, who might have stepped forth from a page of Thackeray. He was already past his seven-tieth year, but his body was still strongly, vigorously set: he was some-what above the middle height, but his neck and shoulders had a kind of massive strength that suggested he had been a powerfully built man in his prime. His white mane of hair was soft as silk and gave his wide brow and ruddy, pleated old man's face a kind of noble lion-like fierceness, and this impression was enhanced by his grizzled mustache and his old, rather growling, voice, which had in it nothing surly or ill-tempered, but rather a kind of old and noble masculinity, an aristocratic kind of growl that seemed perfectly adjusted to a kind of Pendennis-like language, a "Dammit-all,-sir,-it's-not-the-fellow's-drinking-that-I-mind,-it's-only-that-he's-proved-himself-incapable-of-holding-his-liquor-like-a-gentleman" kind of voice.

The inference was warranted: even as they stood there in a spacious, airy big room, the guests standing and talking in groups, drinking small glasses of a fine dry sherry, the youth could hear Joel's eager whispering voice engaged in earnest, but respectful, debate, with his leonine grand-sire, and Mr. Joel's nobly growled out answers. The conversation was about books—about the artist's right to use the materials of his own experience and conversation—and it hinged particularly upon a certain book in which the writer had apparently made use of personal letters and private documents that people he knew, a woman chiefly, had written him.

"No, sir," Mr. Joel growled, "I do not care what the circumstances may be or what the nature of the work. If I had a friend, sir, who would deliberately make public letters which a woman had written him, why, sir, I should drop him from my acquaintance—I should be forced to conclude, sir," here the old growling voice fell to an ominous whisper of irrevocable judgment, and he looked out at his grandson with a fierce glint of his old eyes under bushy brows—"I should be forced to conclude, sir, that he was nothing but a cad," old Mr. Joel whispered, and with a suddenly fierce glint of his old eyes, a sudden movement of his leonine head, he growled out in a low and savage tone: "And I should tell him so, sir. I should be compelled to tell him that he was nothing but a cad!"

"Yes, grandfather," Joel whispered eagerly, his thin figure bent forward in an attitude of devoted and attentive reverence— "But after *all,* some pretty great people have done it—Rousseau did it, and *The Confessions* are pretty great, you know— You've got to admit that.—And Byron did it in his poems—at least, every one knew who he was talking about, and then there was De Musset and George Sand."

"It makes no difference, sir," growled Mr. Joel implacably, "it makes no difference who they were or how great they may be considered in the realm of art, or how great the work they did may be—if I knew a man who did a thing like that, I should be forced to consider him a low cad—no matter how great a poet or a writer, or how great his work might be —I should consider him a cad,—and," his old growling voice fell to a whisper of boding and implacable judgment—"I should tell him so, sir. I should let him know that I considered him a cad."

Such was Joel's grandsire, Mr. Joel, and surely he was a specimen of which any group or class could well be proud: of all that Hudson River aristocracy he was justly venerated and esteemed as one of its noblest and proudest adornments. He had lived a long, honorable, and successful life; and now in his old age he had retired to the bosom of his paternal earth to spend his last years in dignity and simple ease and in calm but fruitful reflection on his rich experience. He was writing a book, and in advance it could be solemnly averred that he would make no use in it of any letters that a woman ever wrote to him.

What man, therefore, could speak with greater weight about the duties, codes and principles of man? What man was better qualified to know the rules of honor and the standards of a gentleman—and to assert a truth that might have gone unnoticed by a person of a baser spirit and a lower quality—that Rousseau was a scoundrel and De Musset and Lord Byron a couple of low cads—"because, sir, they made public letters that a woman wrote them."

It was indeed delightful to find such Thackerayan gallantry, such Olympian scorn for knavish genius and for the lives of mighty poets dead and gone, who illuminated mankind with their radiance but had their own light put out—must dwell forevermore "a couple of low cads," in outer darkness, never again to be received, acknowledged, given gracious pardon by the chivalric flower of the Hudson River rich. How wretched that stern judgment must have made Rousseau! What bitter news for Byron! What misery for De Musset!

But now a woman servant entered and announced that lunch was served. The chattering groups of people turned, and formed instinctively, and by a kind of native respect, into files of deferential waiting. until Mr. Joel had passed. He led the way, a grand and leonine old man, superbly garmented in a coat of soft, rich blue, wide loose white flannels, wound at the waist by a great sash of yellow silk—an adornment that seemed in no way inappropriate but superbly fitting the noble dignity of the old man.

At the door he paused and stood aside, with a grizzled majesty of cour-

tesy, for his wife and the other ladies of the group to pass. Then he
entered the dining room followed by his grandson and the other young
men. The dining room was another light, spacious, and graciously beautiful room in the old New England style: through the open windows
one saw the deep green and gold of trees and flowers in the embowered
magic of the setting, and the fragrance of sweet drowsy air breathed on
the curtains and flowed through the room.

The snowy table had a great bowl of fresh-cut wood flowers in the
centre: the food was also native, plain old American, and superbly
cooked: there was a thick pea-soup, fried chicken, plump and tender,
done superbly to a juicy, delicately encrusted brown: there were
candied sweet potatoes, string beans, cooked the Southern way with the
succulent sweet seasoning of pork, stewed golden corn, and creamy
mashed potatoes, a deep smooth gravy, rich and brown and thick, sliced
tomatoes and sliced cucumbers, no alcoholic beverages, but iced tea, cold
and tall and fragrant in high tinkling glasses rimed with ice, flaky bis-
cuits, smoking hot, and for dessert, fresh apple-pie, hot and crusty, hued
with cinnamon and flanked by thick fresh squares of pungent yellow
cheese.

It was, in short, a plain but wholesome and most appetizing meal, completely American in its flavor and abundance, and superbly cooked, most
fitting to this house; the simple green and natural, casual beauty of the
place, the life, the people, the homely gracious hospitality of democracy.

It is true, the meal was also rather Southern in its cooking, and its
quality—a fact that was not surprising, however, when one remembered
that Mr. Joel's present wife had been a famous Southern belle from the
bluegrass region of Kentucky.

One not only remembered this fact, it was difficult for one not to
remember it; Mrs. Joel herself made her romantic origins evident. Although she was a woman in her early sixties with white hair, she was
still remarkably preserved, and her manners, graces, dimpled smiles, her
roguish glances and her languishing soft drawl were still the familiar
stock in trade of the Dixieland coquette.

She was certainly what is called "a fine figure of a woman"; her figure
was tall, spacious, amply proportioned, her face, although beginning to
show the signs of age—a slightly wrinkled plumpness like the skin of a
full but slightly withered apple—was still almost as soft and white and
tender as a child's: she had almost all her natural teeth and they were

white and pearly, her hands were white and plump and fine, her voice had the refined and throaty burble that is familiar in the majestic American female of the upper crust, and she dimpled beautifully when she smiled.

It was rather uncomfortably evident at once that there was a strong, if suppressed, hostility between Mrs. Joel and her step-daughter, Joel's mother.

The struggle between the two was for the possession of something that neither of them any longer had—youth. Both were obviously enamored of youth—of the freshness of youth, the warmth, the charm, the grace, the vitality of youth. Both hated the idea of growing old: both bitterly and desperately refused to admit the possibility of growing old. Mrs. Joel was able to cast over her soul a spell of hypnotic deception, and by absurdly flaunting around the graces, airs and manners of a coquette, to convince herself that she was young and beautiful, able to enslave every man she met under the domination of her captivating charm.

And Mrs. Pierce felt bitterly that the older woman had had her day, that she should be willing to admit her years, gracefully submit, and take a back seat. This ugly rivalry was now apparent in almost everything they said, and gave every one at the table a feeling of tension, embarrassment and discomfort. Thus, Mrs. Joel, speaking to her step-daughter, and including the whole company, in a reference to Mrs. Pierce's strenuous pursuit of youth, her grim devotion to youth's figure and its vigorous gymnastics, now remarked in a tone of sugared venom, a malicious gaiety of fine surprise:

"But really, I do, I think it's the most astonishing thing to see a woman of your age take part in all these sports and games that only the *young* people of my generation played. . . . After all, if you were twenty—the age of Joel or this young man—I could understand it better—but at *your* age, my dear,"—she drew a fine breath of astonishment, "—really, I marvel that you don't collapse."

"Do you?" said Mrs. Pierce, smiling her glacial and inflexible smile, and in a tone of cold, impassive irony— "I confess, Mother, I see nothing at all to marvel at. . . . Please set your mind at rest—I assure you I'm not in the slightest danger of collapse. . . . I can do everything," she went on grandly, "that I could do at twenty—and I can do it better now, with less fatigue and greater skill. . . . I can hold my own with any of these young people around here, no matter what it is—whether swimming, golfing, playing tennis, or going for a walk. So you can save your sympathy, Mother," she concluded with a laugh which seemed casual and friendly enough, but which showed plainly the hard inflexibility of her antagonism, "—when I need your condolences I'll let you know."

"But, my *dear,*" said Mrs. Joel with sweet gushing malice—"I think it's ma-a-rvellous! I only wonder how you do it at your age! . . . Why, no girl of my time and generation would have *thought* of doing all the things you do every day without turning a hair— Why!" she breathed, looking around her with an air of fine amazement, "I hear Ida plays *five* sets before breakfast every morning and thinks nothing of it—but in *my* day and time, if a girl—a *young* girl, mind you—played a *single* set—she'd be positively exhausted—done up for a week."

"Perhaps, Mother," Mrs. Pierce coolly suggested, "that is why the young girls of your time were such a soft and grubby lot—and why they turned out to be such dowdy frumps later on."

Mrs. Joel's dimpled smile did not lose a single atom of its saccharine benevolence, nor did her voice alter by a shade its honied drip, but for a moment something bright and adderous passed across her eyes, and she gave her step-daughter a swift and poisonous glance that would have done credit to a snake. "—And then, of course," she went on sweetly, taking the young men at the table into her confidence with her dimpled smile—"we had such old-fashioned notions in those days, too—you boys, I know, would be amused if you could know what some of our quaint notions were—but—hah! hah! hah!"—she laughed a gay and silvery little laugh of envenomed hatred, "—my dear," she said to Joel, "—you'll have to laugh when I tell you—but do you know it was actually considered *immodest—unwomanly*—for a young girl of my time to take part in sports—*compete* in sports—against men—and as for a woman of Ida's age doing it—why, it was *unthinkable! unheard* of!—a middle-aged woman," she pronounced the words with obvious relish and for a moment there was a swift hard flexion of the muscles in Mrs. Pierce's jaw—"but a middle-aged woman in *my* day who had attempted such a thing would have been *ostracized*—an *outcast*—decent people would have had nothing to do with her!"

"Yes, I know, Mother," Mrs. Pierce said with a swift and glacial urbanity. "We've all heard about that—I think it's generally conceded now by most intelligent people that women of that generation were a pretty worthless, dull and barbarous lot."

"Ah-hah-hah!" Mrs. Joel laughed sweetly, and dimpled at her best—
"*terribly* old-fashioned, of course—but," she turned graciously to her
grandson's young guest and lavished on him her most dimpled smile,—
"*frightfully* amusing, don't you think?"

He reddened like a beet, looked helplessly at the two contesting
women, craned his neck nervously along the edges of his collar, and
finally said nothing.

Joel relieved the painful situation with his swift whispering grace of
tact and kindliness. "But really, Granny," he whispered courteously and
eagerly, "—Mums is awfully good at it, she really is. . . . She can beat
me two sets out of three in tennis, and give me ten strokes in golf—and
when it comes to *swimming*——"

"Oh," said little Howard Martin in his mincing, languishing, and
effeminate tone—"she's ma-a-rvellous! . . . Ida," he gushed, in a kind of
over-ripe ecstasy—"your diving is simply divine! . . . If you could only
show me—oh-h," he said, with gushing effeminacy—"if you could only
teach *me* how you do it—but it's *simply* perfect—*marvellous*——"

The meal now proceeded more smoothly. Mr. Joel seemed to take
small notice of the feud between the two women—his daughter and his
wife—he talked to Joel, Rosalind, and to the other young men in his
grand growling way, expressed his opinion on the candidacies of Davis
and Coolidge, and said he would vote for Davis.

"If John Davis gets in," said Mrs. Pierce with that positive worldly
assurance that characterized her opinions, "Charles Dana Gibson will
get the ambassadorship to England—oh, but *that's* settled!" she said
positively, "I happen to know that Dana Gibson can have the ambassadorship any time he wants it——"

"Providing Davis gets elected," Joel whispered, laughing. Turning to
his grandfather, he whispered respectfully, "What do you think, Grandfather? Do you think that Davis will get in?"

"No, sir," Mr. Joel growled, "I do not. I think his chances of getting
elected are *very* slight—unless some sudden upheaval turns the tide in
his direction before election day."

"And who will you vote for, sir?" Joel whispered.

"I shall vote for Davis, sir," growled Mr. Joel. "I have known him for
many years, he is a very able lawyer, a very *able* man—but, sir," his old
growling voice sank to a whisper, and he peered out fiercely from under
his grizzled eyebrows at his grandson—"his chances of election are very

slight indeed. I should not be surprised to see Coolidge win by a landslide."

"Did you hear what Alice Longworth said about him?" said Mrs. Pierce laughing, "—that he looked as if he had been weaned upon a pickle."

Every one laughed, even Mr. Joel joining with a kind of growling chuckle. As for Joel, he bent double, radiantly, gleefully convulsed with soundless laughter, snapping his fingers softly as he did so. His own humorous invention was not fertile, but his love of a good story—particularly when his mother or one of his friends told it, or quoted one of their own group—was enthusiastic. Now for a moment he bent double with this convulsed, whispering laughter: when he recovered somewhat he said softly and slowly:

"*Simply* swell . . . Gosh!" he whispered admiringly. "What a wit she's got! It's a swell story," he whispered.

"By the way, Ida," Mr. Joel growled, tugging at his short and grizzled mustache, "how is Frank? Have you been over to see them, lately?"

"Yes, Father," she answered, "we drove over last Tuesday and spent the evening with them. . . . He looks very well," she added, in answer to his question, "but, of *course*," she said decisively, "he's *never* going to be any better—they all say as much——"

"Hm," old Mr. Joel growled, tugged reflectively at his short and grizzled mustache for a moment longer, and then said: "Has he been taking any part in the campaign this summer?"

"Very little," she answered—"of course, the man has gone through hell these last few years—he's suffered agonies! He seems a little better now, but," her voice rose again on its tone of booming finality as she shook her head—"he'll never get back the use of his legs again—the man is a *permanent* cripple," she said positively—"there's no getting around it—and he himself is reconciled to it."

"Hm," growled old Mr. Joel again, as he tugged at his short mustache—"Pity! Nice fellow, Frank! Always liked him! . . . A little on the flashy order, maybe—like all his family . . . too easy-going, too agreeable . . . but great ability! . . . Pity!"

"Yes, isn't it!" Joel whispered with soft eager sympathy. "And, Grandfather," he went on with an eager enthusiasm, "—his charm is *simply* stupendous! . . . I've never known anything like it! . . . The moment that he speaks to you he makes you his friend forever—and he *knows* so much—he has such interesting things to say—really, the amount he knows is *simply* stupendous!"

"Hm, yes," old Mr. Joel agreed with a consenting growl, as he tugged thoughtfully at his grizzled gray mustache, "—but a little superficial, too. . . . The whole lot is like that . . . go hell-for-leather at everything for three weeks at a time—and then forget it. . . . Still," he muttered, ". . . an able fellow—very able. . . . Pity this thing had to happen to him just at the start of his career."

"Still, Father," Mrs. Pierce put in, "—don't you think he'd gone about as far as he was going when this thing hit him? . . . I mean, of course, he *is* a charming person—every one agrees on that. I never knew a man with more native charm than Frank— But for all his charm, don't you think there's something rather weak in his character? . . . Do you think he would have had the stamina and determination to go much further if this disease hadn't forced him to retire?"

"Um," Mr. Joel growled, as he tugged thoughtfully at his short cropped mustache. ". . . Hard to say. . . . Hard to tell what would have happened to him. . . . A little soft, perhaps, but great ability . . . great charm . . . and great opportunists, every one of them. . . . Have instinctive genius for seizing on the moment when it comes. . . . Never know what's going to happen to a man like that——"

"Well," said Mrs. Pierce, politely, but with an accent of conviction— "he might have kept on going—but I think he was through—that he'd gone as far as he could—I don't think he could have stood the gaff—I don't believe he had it in him."

"Um," Mr. Joel growled, "perhaps you're right. . . . But great pity just the same. . . . Always liked Frank. . . . Very able fellow——"

The conversation proceeded in these channels for some time, the guests discussing politics, ambassadorships, using the names of the great and celebrated people of the earth with the casual and familiar intimacy of people talking about life-long friends whom they had last seen at dinner Tuesday evening. It was the "inside" of the great world of wealth and fame and fashion—the world that the youth had read and heard about all his life—but that he had thought about, had visioned, as Olympus, mantled in celestial clouds, and forever remote from the intruding gaze of common men. Now, to hear these great names, these celestial personages, bandied about on the tip of the tongue just as familiarly as one spoke of one's own friends—to hear these people speak of the habits, the health, the conversation, and the personal home-life of this august parliament in just the same way that people spoke of their friends, acquaintances and familiars the whole world over, gave the youth a sense of living in a dream, of hearing incredible things—things incredible because of their very casual familiarity—of being the witness of an incredible event.

In this way, the meal drew to its close: Mrs. Pierce and her step-mother managed to avoid further friction, although once it threatened, when Mrs. Pierce, observing the retreating figure of one of the maid-servants—a robust and plain-featured country woman of middle age—noticed from the cropped and unnaturally white texture of her neck and skull that her hair had been cut, "bobbed" in the fashion that was to grow so popular and that was just then coming into style, and turned and questioned her step-mother about it:

"What has happened to that woman's hair, Mother?" she said. "What did she do to it?"

"Why," cried Mrs. Joel eagerly, beginning to beam and dimple around at her guests with an air of delighted satisfaction—"I had it cut off."

"*You* had it cut off?" cried Mrs. Pierce in an astounded tone.

"Why, yes, my dear," chirped Mrs. Joel eagerly, "I sent all the girls into the village one morning last week and had the barber cut their hair."

"*What!*" Mrs. Pierce boomed out in an astounded tone, and then sank back against her chair, and for a moment returned her son's stare incredulously, "you mean you herded all these girls together and *whacked* their hair off at one stroke?"

"Why, of course, my dear," said Mrs. Joel eagerly, in a rather excited and disturbed tone, "—or rather, I told them that they'd have to do it—that that was what I wanted."

"What *you* wanted?" Mrs. Pierce boomed out in the same astounded and incredulous tone.

"Why, yes"—Mrs. Joel rushed on eagerly, excitedly, taking the whole table in now with a look of beaming explanation. "—You see, I had the whole house done over this spring—redecorated—I told the decorator the *effect* I wanted," she said gushingly—"I told him everything must be done for—for—*lightness!*" she said triumphantly, "—*coolness!* . . . to do everything in light cool colors . . . get *that* effect. . . . So last week," she went on happily, "when we had that spell of *frightful* hot weather, I noticed suddenly how—how *hot*—and disagreeable all the girls looked with their long hair—how—how *out of place*," she said triumphantly, "they looked in this new scheme of things. . . . Ugh," she shuddered with a little gesture of discomfort and distaste, "—the very *sight* of them made me uncomfortable—I couldn't *bear* them! So all of a sudden it occurred to me how nice it would be—how much it would improve the —the—the general *atmosphere* of the whole house if I made them bob their hair. . . . So," she concluded, beaming around at every one with dimpled satisfaction—"that's how I came to do it—I called them all together one morning last week—Friday I think it was—and told them what I wanted—and then sent them all into the village to get it done."

There was a moment's pause while Mrs. Joel beamed at her guests with a dimpled smile of triumphant finality that seemed to say—"There! Behold my work and marvel at it! That is the way the thing was done." Her obvious satisfaction was suddenly disturbed, however, by Mrs. Pierce, who, after staring at her in astounded silence for a moment, boomed out incredulously:

"*Mother!* You *know* you didn't do a thing like *that!*"

"But—but, of course I did it, Ida," Mrs. Joel returned in a surprised and nettled tone of voice— "That's what I'm telling you. . . . What's the matter with it? . . . Don't you think the girls look nice?"

"I—think," said Mrs. Pierce slowly, after a moment's stunned reflection—"I—think—that—is—the—most—preposterous—the—most—high-handed—the—most—*God!*" she cried, and throwing her head back she fairly made the room ring with her hearty, booming, and astonished laughter: "I've heard of Catherine the Great and Marie Antoinette and the days of the Medicis—and the things they did—but I never thought I'd live to see the day their methods were adopted here in free America —Why! hah! hah! hah! hah! hah!" she fell back in her chair and fairly rocked with booming and incredulous laughter—"*whacking* the hair off those eight girls at one fell stroke because—because—" her voice choked speechlessly—"because it made you *hot* to look at them . . . because —because," her voice rose to a rich choked scream and presently she said in an almost inaudible squeak—"because she's had the house— *redecorated,*" she panted— "Why, *Mother!*" she cried strongly at last, her shoulders shaking, and her face still red with laughter, "—the King of Siam is not in it compared to you—you make absolute tyranny look like free democracy—hah! hah! hah! hah! hah!—Strike off their heads!" cried Mrs. Pierce, "—the very *sight* of them makes me perspire!" And leaning back again she surrendered herself to free, ringing, and whole-hearted laughter, in which every one save Mrs. Joel joined. When the laughter had somewhat subsided, Mrs. Joel, her plump white cheeks red with open anger, cried out in a furious voice:

"I don't agree with you! . . . I don't agree with you at all. . . . And I must say it seems very stupid of you, Ida, to take such a childish point of view."

"Childish!" Mrs. Pierce cried in a challenging tone, "you're the one who's childish! . . . If I did a thing like that to *my* girls—if I for one moment thought I had a right to take such liberties as that with other people, I'd feel like a fool! . . . Why, Mother," she cried in a strong protesting tone, "wake up! . . . What kind of a world do you live in, anyway? . . . What ever gave you the notion that you have a right to do things like that to other people—and all because you're fortunate enough to be able to keep servants and pay them wages. . . . Wake up! Wake up!" she cried in a tone of almost furious indignation, "—You're not living in the dark ages, Mother. . . . Slavery has been abolished! . . . This is the twentieth century! . . . Why, it's absurd!" she cried scornfully, and with two spots of angry color in her cheeks—"the most arrogant and high-handed thing I ever heard in all my life— The whole thing's preposterous—I only hope that no one hears about it."

"If you feel that way about it," Mrs. Joel began in a voice choked with fury, and at this moment Joel came to the rescue, and saved what really threatened to develop into an ugly, open, painful quarrel between the two women——

"Oh, but Granny," he whispered—"I'm sure the girls don't mind a bit! . . . And they look *much* nicer—and *much* cooler—without their hair than when they had it—I'm sure they feel that way about it, too."

"Well," Mrs. Joel began, still very angry but somewhat placated by her grandson's tactful intervention—"I'm glad to see that some one still has a little common sense."

And in this way the trouble was finally smoothed out by Joel's quick diplomacy, and the guests, eager to avert another painful scene between the two women, rose to go. And it was in this way that they departed, not without a final explosion of booming and astounded laughter from Mrs. Pierce as she walked out towards her car, a final hilarious reference to "redecoration," *and* the King of Siam, and the modern prototype of Catherine the Great.

LXIV

JOEL and his friend did not return immediately to the house with Joel's mother, and her other guests. Instead, leaving old Mr. Joel's house, they turned left, and struck out for a walk through the fields and slopes and wooded country of the great estate. The day was hot, the broad fields brooded in the powerful and fragrant-clovered scent of afternoon, the woods were dense with tangled mystery, immensely still and green, yet dark incredibly, and filled with drowsy silence, brooding calm, ringing with the lovely music of unnumbered birds, alive with the swift and sudden bullet-thrum of wings, and haunted with the cool and magical incantation of their hidden waters.

It was the wild, sweet, casual, savage, and incredibly lovely earth of America, and of the wilderness, and it haunted them like legends, and pierced them like a sword, and filled them with a wild and swelling prescience of joy that was like sorrow and delight.

They toiled upward through the tangled forest-jungle of a wooded slope, and down again into the cool green-gladed secrecies of a hollow, and up through the wild still music of the woods again and out into the great rude swell of unmown fields, alive with all their brooding potency, their powerful and silent energy of the hot and fragrant earth of three o'clock, the drowsy and tremulous ululation of afternoon.

Their feet trod pathways in the hot and fragrant grasses, where they trod, a million little singing things leaped up to life, and hot dry stalks brushed crudely at their knees: the earth beneath their feet gave back a firm and unsmooth evenness, a lumpy resiliency.

Once in a field before them they saw a tree dense-leaved and burnished by hot light: the sun shone on its leaves with a naked and un-green opacity, and Joel, looking towards it, whispered thoughtfully:

". . . Hm . . . It's nice, that—I mean the way the light falls on it— It would be hard to paint: I'd like to come out here and try it."

And the other assented, not, however, without a certain nameless desolation in his heart that broad and naked lights, the white and glacial opacity of brutal day aroused in him,—and wanting more the wooded grove, the green-gold magic of a wooded grass, the woodland dark and thrum and tingled mystery, and the sheer sheeting silence of the hidden water.

It was a swelling, casual, nobly lavish earth, forever haunted by a drowsy spell of time, and the unfathomed mystery of an elfin enchantment, the huge dream-sorcery of the mysterious and immortal river.

It was what he had always known it to be in his visions as a child, and he came to it with a sense of wonder and of glorious discovery, but without surprise, as one who for the first time comes into his father's country, finding it the same as he had always known it would be, and knowing always that it would be there.

And finally the whole design of that earth, with the casual and powerful surveys of its great fields, its dense still woods of moveless silence ringing with the music of the birds, its far-off hills receding into time as haunting as a dream, and the central sorcery of its shining river —that enchanted thread which ran through all, from which all swept away, and towards which all inclined—was unutterably the language of all he had ever thought or felt or known of America: the great plantation of the earth abundant to the sustenance of mighty men, and enriching all its glamorous women with the full provender of its huge compacted sweetness, an America that was so casual and rich and limitless and free, and so haunted by dark time and magic, so aching in its joy with all the bitter briefness of our days, so young, so old, so everlasting, and so triumphantly the place of man's good earth, his ripe fulfillment and of the most fortunate, good, and happy life that any man alive had ever known.

It changed, it passed, it swept around him in all its limitless surge and sweep and fold and passionate variety, and it was more strange in all its haunting loveliness than magic or a dream, and yet more near than morning, and more actual than noon.

It was a hot day: the two young men walked along with their coats flung back across their shoulders: towards five o'clock as they were coming home again, and coming down into the wooded hollow where Mr. Joel lived, Joel turned, and with a slight flush of embarrassment on his gaunt face, said:

"Look—do you mind wearing your coat when we go by Grandfather's house—you can take it off again when we get out of sight."

He said nothing, but silently did as his friend requested, and thus correctly garmented they passed the old man's great white house and crossed the little wooden bridge and stared up again out of the hollow, taking a foot-path through the woods that would lead them out into the road near Miss Telfair's house: she had invited them to tea.

And curiously, inexplicably, of all that they had said and talked about together on that walk, these two things were later all he could remember:—his friend's eyes narrowed with professional appraisal as he looked at the hot opacity of the sun-burnished tree and said, "—hm . . . It's nice, that—the light is interesting—I'd like to do it;" and the embarrassed but almost stubbornly definite way in which Joel had asked him to put on his coat as he went past "Grandfather's place." He did not know why, but that simple request aroused in him a feeling of quick and hot resentment, a desire to say,

"Good God! What kind of idol-worship is this, anyway? Surely that old man has been made of the same earth as all the rest of us—surely he's not so grand and rare and fine that he can't stand the sight of two young men in shirt-sleeves going by his house! . . . Surely there is something false, inhuman, barren in this kind of reverence—no real respect, no decent human admiration, but something cruel, empty, worthless and untrue, and against the real warmth and worth and friendliness of man!"

For a moment hot resentful words rose to his lips: that act of empty reverence seemed to him, somehow, to be arrogant and disdainful of humanity; he felt a sudden blind resentment, a choking anger against old Mr. Joel and his grand manners and his growling and magnificent old age: he wanted to bring back again the conversation he had overheard at lunch, to ask Joel bitterly who the hell he thought this old man was that he could grandly dispose of man according to his judgment as "low cads," as "gentlemen"—to inquire savagely who the hell this damned contriving, cunning old custodian of the treasures of the rich thought he was that he could arrogate unto himself the power to pronounce banishment on his betters—to call Rousseau a rascal, and De Musset and Lord Byron "a couple of low cads."

And childish, foolish as this anger was in all its blind unreason, he was to remember these two trifling episodes in later years with a feeling of regret and nameless loss. These two acts on Joel's part—the one an act of barren interest—a joyless empty interest in the blind opacity of light—and the other an act of barren joyless reverence to old age and an inhuman state—seemed to mark for him the beginning of his gradual separation from his friend, a dumb, inexplicable and sorrowful acceptation of their fatal severance. It seemed to him that here began that slow, and somehow desperately painful recognition that the enchanted world of wealth and love and beauty, of living fulfillment and of fruitful power, which he had visioned as a child in all his dreams about the fabled rich along the Hudson River—did not exist; and that he must look for that grand life in ways stranger, darker, and more painful in their labyrinthine complications than any he had ever dreamed of as a child; and that, like Moses, he must strike water from the common stone of life, and like Samson, take honey from the savage lion's maw of the great world, find all the joy of living that he lusted for in the blind swarm, the brutal stupefaction of the streets; goodness and truth in the mean hearts of common men; and beauty in the only place where it can ever be found—inextricably meshed, inwrought, and interwoven in that great web of horror, pain and sweat and bitter anguish, that great woven fabric of blind cruelty, hatred, filth and lust and tyranny and injustice, of joy, of faith, of love, of courage and devotion—that makes up life, and that resumes the world.

It was a desolating loss, a hideous acknowledgment, a cruel discovery —to know that all the haunted glory of this enchanted world, which he thought he had discovered the night before, had been just what it now seemed to him to be—moon-magic—and to know that it was gone from him forever. It was a bitter pill to know that what had seemed so grand, so strong, so right, and so inevitable at the moment of discovery was now lost to him—that some blind chemistry of man's common earth, and of his father's clay, and of genial nature, had taken from him what he seemed to possess, and that he could never make this enchanted life his own again, or ever again believe in its reality. It was a desperate and soul-sickening discovery to know that not alone through moonlight, magic, and the radiant images of their heart's desire could men find America, but that somewhere there, and far darklier and strangelier than the river, lay the thing they sought, in all the blind and brutal complications of its destiny—buried there in the grimy and illimitable jungles of its savage cities—a-prowl and raging in the desert and half-mad with hunger in the barren land, befouled and smutted with the rust and grime of its vast works and factories, warped and scarred and twisted, stunned, bewildered by the huge multitude of all its errors and blind gropings, yet still fierce with life, still savage with its hunger, still broken, slain and devoured by its terrific earth, its savage wilderness—and still, somehow, God knows how, the thing of which he was a part, that beat in every atom of his blood and brain and life, and was indestructible and everlasting, and that was America!

Miss Telfair's house, which they now entered, was just the sort of house that one would expect a woman like Miss Telfair to live in. Everywhere one looked, one saw the image of the woman's personality—and that personality was fragile, exquisite, elegant, and elaborately minute. In spite of its graceful, plain proportions, that house was not wholly a comfortable place to be in. It was filled with ten thousand little things —ten thousand little, fragile, costly, lovely and completely useless little things, and their profusion was so great, their arrangement so exquisitely right, their proximity so immediate and overwhelming that one instantly felt cramped, uneasy, and uncomfortable, fearfully apprehensive lest a sudden free and spacious movement should send a thousand rare and terribly costly little things crashing into shattered bits, the treasure of a lifetime irretrievably lost, and one's own life and work and future irretrievably mortgaged, blighted, wrecked, in one shattering instant of blind ruin. In short, in Miss Telfair's lovely, exquisite and toy-becluttered house, one felt very much like a delicate, sensitive, intelligent and highly organized bull in a horribly expensive china-shop, and this feeling was cruelly enhanced if one was twenty-three years old and six and a half feet tall, and large of hand and foot, and long of arm and leg in just proportion, and painfully embarrassed, and given to sudden and convulsive movements, and keyed and strung on the same wires as a race-horse.

It was an astonishing place, about as exquisitely feminine a place as one could imagine. One had only to take a look around to feel that no man had ever lived here, that the only man who ever came here had come as a visitor; and somehow one felt at once he knew the reason why Miss Telfair had not married—she simply did not want to have "a man about the place," a disgusting, clumsy brute of a man who would go plunging around like a wild bull, sending her vases crashing to the floor, upsetting her fragile little tables and all the precious little bric-a-brac that crowded them, sprawling out upon the voluptuously soft but elegantly arrayed cushions of the sofa, reaching for matches on the mantel and sweeping it clear of a half dozen dainty eighteenth-century clocks and plates and china shepherds with one swingeing blow, barging into dainty little stools of painted china and sending it a-teeter while Miss Telfair watched and prayed and waited with a smile of frozen apprehension, raising hell with the Wedgewood plates, the vases of Dresden and of Delft, and making the buried kings of the old Ming dynasty turn over in their graves with groans of anguish every time some brute of a bull of a man came lumbering near the dearest and most priceless treasures of their epoch.

Miss Telfair, herself the most dainty, fragile, and exquisitely inviolable ornament of the collection, was waiting for them at the centre of this fabulous clutter. She gave each of the young men a quick cool clasp of her small, frail, nail-bevarnished hand, a few crisp words of greeting, and a quick light smile, as brittle, frail, and painted as a bit of china—a smile curiously like that of Mrs. Pierce in its glacial rigidity but, like everything else about the woman, more fragile, delicate, and shell-like.

Then she turned and led the way through the house out into the sun-porch. The two young men picked their way carefully between the frail and crowded complications of a thousand costly relics and around great bowls and vases filled with flowers—great bouquets of roses, lilies and carnations, which were everywhere—and which filled the air with the clinging, dense, and overpowering sweetness of their perfumes.

The sun-parlor was a great, light place, alive and golden with bright sunlight—a magnificent room with comfortably padded wicker chairs and tables and settees, but here, as elsewhere in the house, the fabulous complication of small useless ornaments was overwhelming, and one walked with care. This room also was filled with great bowls of roses, lilies and carnations, the air was dense and heavy with their scent, and through the windows of the place one could see the smooth velvet of the lawns, trimly patterned with designs of flowers aflame with all their glorious polychrome of color, and at the end the flower-garden, which was alive with many rich and costly blooms growing in geometric designs. It was just the kind of flower-garden, just the kind of flowers, that a woman like Miss Telfair would have: their orderly, exotic and unnatural profusion suggested the cultivation of a hot-house; even the wild and lyric growth of sweet unordered nature had been made to conform to the elegant and fragile pattern of Miss Telfair's life.

She led the way to a wicker table where there were easy chairs and a comfortable settee and great flaming fragrant lights of flowers. They seated themselves and tea was brought in by a maid-servant. The service of the tea was fragile, costly, elegant, like everything else about the woman; but it was also wonderful, rich, and generous in its abundance, and this was probably like her, too. There were delicate little pastries, cubes, and crusts of things that were so flaky, rich and succulent that they melted away in the mouth; and there were little cubes and squares of sandwiches, as well, all dainty, elegant, and small, but wonderfully good. She asked them if they wanted hot-tea or iced-tea or some whiskey: the day was hot and Joel took iced-tea, refusing whiskey; the other youth took iced-tea too—she poured it for them in marvellous tall frail glasses filled with slivers of bright ice, and put in mint and lemon, doing all things deftly, beautifully, with her small, swift, china-lovely hands, and then turning to Joel's guest, with her light cool smile, her crisp incisive inquiry, in which there was somehow something good and generous, she said:

"And won't you have some whiskey, too?" and as he hesitated, and looked dubious yet consenting, added: "In your iced-tea—if you like it that way?"

He looked at her, perplexed, and said uncertainly:

"I—don't know... Does it go that way?"

Miss Telfair bent back her head—her cheeks had the delicate color of rose-tinted china, and she was pretty in the rose-tinted-china way—and laughed a thin, metallic, and yet musical and friendly laugh:

"Oh, yes!" she cried briskly and gaily, "it goes that way! . . . It goes very well that way." More seriously, she added: "Yes, it's really very good that way"—and crisply, yet encouragingly, with her fire-bright china-smile—"why don't you try it?"

He looked at Joel dubiously, not certain what to do, and not wishing to embarrass his friend, and Joel looked back, with his radiant eager smile, shaking his head in droll refusal, whispering:

"Not for me. But go on if you like. Do as you like——"

"Well, then——" he said consentingly—and Miss Telfair, smiling lightly, took a bottle of Scotch liquor off the tray, uncorked it, and poured a drink into the tea—a good stiff shot it was, too—and when he had finished the drink, she poured him out another, adding another liberal potation of the Scotch.

Thus animated and released, he felt more at ease: they talked together quickly and easily, he had a good time. She was a bright, quick, cool, inquiring kind of woman, at once detached yet friendly, coolly amused yet curious: she asked him about his work at the university, the kind of classes that he taught and the kind of people that attended them, the kind of life he had in the city, and about the play that he was writing. The detached coolness of her curiosity was much like that of Mrs. Pierce, and suggested the curiosity of a woman of a separate and privileged world hearing about the creatures who lived in the great nameless world of dust and noise and strife and swelter "down below"—and yet it was also a more friendly and eager curiosity than Mrs. Pierce had shown: it had a certain warmth of human interest in it, too.

She was obviously very fond of Joel: her relation to him was that of an old-maid friend of the family, who is so intimate and close to all the family's history that she is practically a part of it herself, and who feels for the children and all their lives and actions as much affection and interest as she could feel for her own blood. Now she turned to Joel, and began to talk to him about some decorative screens which he was painting for her: as one might expect, she knew all about decorative screens and their respective merits; she spoke of them with the exact authority, the assured conviction of the expert, she spoke her mind about them crisply, plainly, incisively, and Joel listened to her eagerly, his gaunt face lifted, turned towards her in an attitude of rapt attention and respect, while she was talking.

"The central one is excellent, Joel—really first rate, the best one you've ever done—and *decidedly* the best of the lot. The one on the right is also good—not as good as the first, it swings off-balance in the foreground. I'll show you what I mean tomorrow—but it is good, and will do."

"What about the other one—the one on the left?" he whispered eagerly. "What did you think of that?"

"I think it's very, very bad," she said coolly and incisively. "I think you've fallen down on it, and that you're going to have to do the whole thing over."

For a moment his gaunt face winced, but not with pain and disappointment, rather with swift, concerned interest, eager attentiveness: he hitched his long thin figure forward unconsciously, his large well-boned hands splayed out upon his knees, and he whispered eagerly:

"But why, Madge? . . . Tell me. Where do you think I've fallen down?"

"Well," said Miss Telfair, "in the first place, Joel, you've lost out on your design— It falls all to pieces now, you've let the whole thing get away from you: you were trying to follow it out from the one in the middle and bring it to an end, but you didn't know how to finish it— and so you put in that pavilion or summer house or whatever it is— because you didn't know what else to do."

"Don't you like that?" he whispered, smiling.

"I think it's perfectly god-awful," she answered quietly, "utterly mean-

ingless—simply terrible! It has no relation to anything else in the whole
design—it stands out like a sore thumb—and the color is atrocious.
. . . No, Joel, the whole thing is out of key, it upsets the whole design,
it has no place there."

"And what about the background?" he whispered. "What did you
think of that?"

"I think that's bad, too," she replied without a moment's hesitation.
"You've used *far, far* too much gold—almost twice as much as you did
in the other two—the proportion is very bad."

"Hm," he muttered, stroking his chin thoughtfully. "Yes," he whispered, "I see what you mean. . . . I hadn't thought about the pavilion
being out of key—perhaps you're right. . . . But," he whispered, smiling his radiantly gentle and good-natured smile, "I *don't* agree with you
spoke with a crisp but obstinate conviction, "Joel, I *know* I'm right!
argue with you about that."

"All right," she answered crisply and good-naturedly. "I'll come over
tomorrow and we'll have it out. . . . But," she shook her head, and
spoke with a crisp but obstinate conviction, "Joel, I *know* I'm right!
. . . That whole screen is out of proportion. It *won't* do. . . . You'll
have to do the whole thing over again."

They debated in this fashion of art-talk for some time, and presently
the young men rose to go. As they departed, Miss Telfair returned to
her former tone of crisp and casual friendliness, saying:

"What is Ida doing tonight? Is she going to the Pastons' for the fireworks?"

"Yes," Joel whispered. "We're all going; can't you come along?"

"No, thank you," she said, smiling. "Not this time. They're very
lovely—and very awe-inspiring—and all that—but about once every five
years is my limit. I would *not* get into that mob tonight, as hot as it is,
for a million dollars. . . . Tell Ida I expect her here for lunch tomorrow: Irene will be here. . . . And now, goodbye," she said, turning to
the other young man, and giving him a bright china smile, a swift cool
pressure of her little china hand. . . . "Come up again to see us, won't
you? . . . And bring your play along. And try going to bed some
night at ten o'clock. . . . Really!" she said with a crisp cool irony,
"—you miss very little by doing so."

As they walked away along the road towards Joel's house, Joel whispered with his radiant and admiring astonishment:

"She's *simp-ly* incredible! . . . Don't you *think* so? . . . . She *knows*

everything," he went on, without defining more exactly that large speci-
fication. "It's simply *stupendous* the things she knows! . . . And she's
such a nice person," he said quietly. "One of the *nicest* people that I ever
knew—just what an old maid ought to be—don't you think so?"

"Yes. But why is she an old maid? Why did she never get married?"

"Hm," said Joel thoughtfully, looking down the road with a detached,
abstracted stare. "I can't say. . . . She's *awfully* rich," he whispered.
"*Enormously* rich—she has loads of money—she's been able to do *just* as
she pleased all her life—she's *been* everywhere—all over the world—
and I suppose that's the reason that she never married. She never found
any one that she liked well enough to give up the kind of life she had.
. . . But she's an amazing person. . . . Don't you think so?"

"Yes," the other said.

They walked on down the road, and presently they saw the great
white shape of Joel's house, framed in the trees before them, and below
them in the light and distance of a westering sun, the shine and wink
of the great river. They entered the house.

LXV

THE Paston estate, like the Pierce estate, was situated upon the river,
but several miles farther north. To reach it, they drove through the eastern entrance of the Pierce place and through the little Dutch Colonial
village of Leydensberg, of which Joel's father was the mayor and which
the Pierce family largely owned.

"It's a pity Pups never went into politics," Joel whispered, as they
drove through the old leafy village, with its pleasant houses among
which a few of the lonely white houses of the Colonial period still
remained. "The people around here worship him: he could have anything he wanted if he ran for office."

It was the first time he had spoken of his father: with a feeling of
sharp surprise, the other youth now remembered that he had not seen
Mr. Pierce since his arrival: he wondered where he was, but did not ask.
He also now remembered that Joel's references to his father had often
been marked by a note of resignation and regret—the tone a person uses
when he speaks of some one who has possessed talents and wasted opportunities, and whose life has come to nothing.

Their road led northward from the village: they sped swiftly along a
paved highway bordered by trees and fields and woods, by houses here

and there, and presently by the solid masonry of a wall that marked the boundaries of another great estate. It was the Paston place, and presently they turned in to an entrance flanked by stone markers, and began to drive along a road arched by tall leafy trees. Night had come, the moon was not yet well up, but from time to time, there was beside the road the gleam of steel, and at times as they passed a cleared space he could plainly see the rail pattern of a tiny railway, complete in all respects—with roadbed, rock-ballast, grades, and cuts, embankments, even tunnels, but all so small in scale that it suggested a gigantic toy more than anything else. He asked what it was and Joel answered:

"It's Hunter's railway."

"*Hunter's* railway?" he asked in a puzzled tone. "But why does he need a railway here? What does he use it for?"

"Oh, he really doesn't need it for anything," Joel whispered. "It's of no use to any one. He just likes to play with it."

"Play with it? But—but what is it? . . . Isn't it a real railway?"

"Yes, of course," Joel answered, laughing at his astonishment. "It's really quite marvellous—complete in every way—with tunnels, stations, bridges, signals, round-houses, and everything else a regular railway has. Only everything is on a very small scale—like a toy."

"But the engine—the locomotive? . . . How does that run? Do you wind it up, as you do a toy, or run it by electricity, or how?"

"Oh, no," Joel answered. "It's a regular locomotive—not over two or three feet high, I should say—but runs by steam, just like a real locomotive. . . . It's really quite a fascinating thing," he whispered. "You ought to see it some time."

"But—but how does he run it? Is he able to get into anything as small as that?"

"He can, yes," said Joel, laughing again. "But usually he just runs along by the side. It's pretty cramped quarters for a grown man."

"A grown *man!* . . . Do you mean that Mr. Paston built this little railway for himself?"

"But, of *course!*" Joel turned, and looked at his friend with a surprised stare. "Who did you think I was talking about?"

"Why, I—I thought when you said—'Hunter' you meant one of his children—a boy—some child in his family who——"

"No, not at all," Joel whispered, laughing again at the astonished and bewildered look upon his companion's face. "It may be for a child, but the child is Hunter Paston himself. . . . You see," he said more quietly and seriously after a brief pause, "he's crazy about all kinds of machinery—locomotives, airplanes, motor-boats, automobiles, steam-yachts—he loves anything that has an engine in it—he always has been that way since he was a boy—and it's such a pity, too," he whispered, in the same regretful tone he had used when speaking of his father— "It's a shame he was never able to do anything with it. . . . If he hadn't had all this money, he would have made a *swell* mechanic —he really would."

But now there was a row of lights through the trees, the murmurous hum of many voices, the glittering shapes of parked machinery. They were approaching the Paston house: it was a rather gloomy-looking mansion of old brown stone, square in shape and immensely solid and imposing in its grimy magnificence, and of that style of architecture which was borrowed from France, but which went through curious and indefinable transformations on the way, so that any native grace and lightness which the style may once have had was lost: it was lumpish, ugly and involved, and somehow looked like one of the children of the New York Post Office.

A broad verandah ran around the house on all four sides, and on the side that faced the river, a large number of the friends and guests of the Paston family were now assembled. Seated on the great lawns that swept away before the house on the river side there was another larger audience composed of the people of the near-by town, and people employed on the Paston estate and the other great estates in the vicinity.

But over both groups, not only the wealthier and smaller group upon the porch, but the larger one spread out upon the lawn, there was evident a spirit of gay, happy, eager and child-like elation and expectancy that united every one in a curiously moving and high-hearted way. From the dark sweep and mystery of the lawn there rose the murmur of hundreds of excited and happy voices, all talking at once, and little bursts of laughter, sudden stirs and flurries of eager and mysterious interest.

The same spirit, the same feeling—a spirit and a feeling of plain democracy, warm friendliness, simple, eager hope and expectancy—animated the people on the porch. They were, as a group, fine-looking people: many of the young men were tall, handsome, strong and comely-looking, the girls were lovely, and many of the women were beautiful. Most of them also had a look of dignity, assurance, and character. They represented, he knew, that small group of the fabulously wealthy whose names were household words throughout the nation—and yet, whether it was due to the innate democracy of the occasion, the almost childish pleasure and anticipation which the Fourth of July and its fireworks renewed in them, and the grand and natural warmth and spaciousness of the scene—their native earth, or whether the quality of their lives was really warm and free and friendly, there was nothing at all arrogant, haughty, cold or insolently "societified" about these people. Their gathering together here upon the front porch of this gloomy old Victorian house had exactly the same quality that these summer front-porch gatherings had always had for him everywhere in little towns; with a feeling of incredulous recognition he found that the scene was instantly familiar to him, and he almost expected to hear old familiar voices—his father's voice among them, as he had heard it on the porch at home so many times, and now so long ago.

Every one in the crowd knew the Pierce family and instantly welcomed them in an eager, laughing, and excited babel of affectionate greeting. Rosalind and Joel and Mrs. Pierce went about among the crowd shaking hands and greeting people all about them, and when the greetings were over, simply and naturally found their place among those persons to whom each was most akin by virtue of friendship, age, or temperament—Mrs. Pierce among men and women of her own generation and among the older people, and Joel, Rosalind, George Thornton, and Carl Seaholm among the younger people of the gathering.

Joel introduced him quickly, casually, with his infinite grace and consideration, to several people—to several of his younger friends and to certain of the older ones who were obviously among the best-liked and most respected people there. He was introduced to Mrs. Paston, a tall and beautiful young woman, very slender, blonde, and lovely-looking: a kind of exquisite blonde icicle, and with no more human warmth or passion than an icicle of any sort would have. She gave him a few cool words of greeting, a swift cool clasp of her swift cool hand, a swift, glacial, yet not unfriendly smile, and so dismissed him, not unkindly, turning with the same cool, smiling and glacial detachment to her other guests.

Suddenly the fireworks started. Far away, at the end of the great lawn, in the obscuring darkness of the night, and among the obscuring shadows of the shrubs and trees above the hill that swept down towards the river, there was a terrific detonation—the deafening bang and flare of a gigantic rocket that whizzed up into the air in a small hurtling point of light, and exploded, illuminating heaven with a constellation of enchanted falling stars. There was a long-drawn "Oh-h!" of excitement, eagerness, and expectant joy from the crowd gathered on the lawn, the same from the people gathered on the porch, who quickly scrambled into chairs; and instantly from all the people there was utter silence, a thrilled and fascinated attentiveness, broken now and then by gasps of wonder, joy, surprise and rapture, as one giant rocket followed another in unending series, in constantly growing magnificence, until the whole universe of night was blooming with flowers of fire, alive with constellations of enchanted stars—green, red, and yellow, blue and violet and gold, that burst softly in the night with spreading glory, falling slowly to the earth like some great parachuted blossom, and cracking, puffing, bursting softly, to flower, spread, again develop in great blooms of star-enchanted fire.

Everything had the same familiar quality of America that he had always remembered, and known as a child. It brought back to him again the quiet voices of people on their summer porches, the street-car grinding to a halt on the corner of the hill above his father's house, his father's voice in darkness on the porch, and the red lifted flare of his cigar, and those Thursday nights in summer when his father took him on the street-car to the little park along the river three miles away, where there were outdoor moving-pictures on an island; later, fireworks and across the river the great flare, the receding thunder of a train. Now, curiously, that whole memory came back to him with all its vivid and unutterable poignancy: he could remember the little artificial lake there at the park—that lake just three feet deep that had seemed so vast and thrilling to him, and the boat-house with lake-water lapping at the piers, the clank of oarlocks and the dull bump and dry knocking of the boats together as they collided in the darkness, and the people, gathered there in darkness, with their dim faces upturned to the great silver dance and flicker of the moving-picture screen which was set on a little island on the lake—an island that was dense with trees and foliage, and that had seemed to him as mysterious and illimitable as the jungle. And opposite the island, on the shore, looking over the heads of the people in the boats, the greater part of the audience sat on wooden benches, all thirsty, silent, and insatiate, the petals of five hundred dim white faces all lifted to the flickering magic of the screen.

It all came back to him now as he sat there on the porch of this splendid mansion with Mrs. Pierce and Joel and the other guests, and though the place was splendid, wealthy and luxurious beyond dreams, the happy, warm, and friendly gaiety of the people, their eager looking-forward to fireworks and the Fourth of July, something free and warm and simple in their relation, recalled again those glorious expeditions of his youth to the little park upon the river, and the crowded street-cars going home, and friendly voices, laughter, and the slamming of a door, and then his father's voice upon the porch and sleep and silence —it all came back now in tones of unutterable brightness, and the Hudson River lay below him in the great fall and hush of evening light that fell across America, and even as he thought these things, a train rushed by below them on the bank of the river, was hurled instantly past in a projectile flight—a thunderbolted speed, was hurled past them citywards, and was gone at once, leaving nothing behind it but the sound of its departure, a handful of lost echoes in the hills, and the river, the mysterious river, the Hudson River in the great fall and hush of evening light, and all somehow was just as it had always been, and just as he had known he would find it, as it would always be.

LXVI

LATER that night, when the other people in the house had gone upstairs to bed, and as he was in the quiet library, making a final, longing, hungrily regretful survey of the treasure-hoard of noble books that walled the great room in their rich and mellow hues from floor to ceiling, Joel came in.

"Look," he whispered, in his abrupt and casual way, "I'm going to bed now: stay up as long as you please and sleep as late as you like tomorrow morning. . . . And look," he whispered casually—and quickly again—"what are you going to do? Do you think you have to go back to the city tomorrow?"

"Yes, Joel: I think I'll have to—I have an early class the first thing Monday morning, and if I'm going to meet it, I ought to be back by tomorrow night: I think that will be best."

"It's been nice having you," Joel whispered. "It was swell that you could come. And if you really like the place," he said simply, "I'm glad. . . . I think it's a grand place, too. . . . And Look!" he whispered quickly, casually, looking away "—I meant what I said yesterday—about that house, the gatekeeper's lodge, I mean— If you like the place, and think you'd care to live there, or come up whenever you feel like it, I wish you'd take it," he whispered. "I really do— It's no use to any one the way it stands, and we'd all be delighted if you'd come and live in it. . . . Just let me know when you are coming, just say the word, and I'll have everything ready for you— And we *wish* you would," he whispered earnestly, with his radiant smile, as if asking the other youth to do him a favor—"it would be swell."

"It's—it's pretty fine of you, Joel, too——"

"All right, sir," Joel whispered quickly, hastily, with a smile, avoiding skilfully the embarrassment of thanks: "And look, Eugene—of course I'll see you Tuesday when I get back to town—I'll be right there at the hotel the rest of the summer—except for week-ends when I come up here—but I wanted to ask you if you had made up your mind yet about going to Europe?"

"Yes, I have, Joel. At least, that's what I want to do—what I'd like to do. If I can manage it, I intend to set sail—" the two words had a glorious magic sound to him, and his pulse beat hot and hard with joy and hope as he spoke them—"to set sail in September when my work at the university is over!"

"Gosh! That's swell!" Joel whispered enthusiastically, his face lighting with radiant eagerness as if the news had given him some great and unexpected happiness— "And Frank Starwick will be glad to hear it, too. You know he's going over at the end of August; I had a letter from him just the other day."

"Yes, I know: he wrote me too."

"And he'll want to see you when he comes to town: we must all try to get together before he goes. . . . And look," he said quickly, abruptly, casually again—"if you go, how long will you be gone? How long do you intend to stay away?"

"I don't know, Joel. I'd like to go for a whole year, but I don't know if I can manage it. They've offered me an appointment for another year at the university. They want me to come back for the new term that begins in February, and maybe that's what I'll have to do. But I'd like to stay away a year!"

"I hope you can," Joel whispered. "You ought to spend a whole year over there! It would be a swell thing if you could."

"Yes; I think so, too. But I don't know how I'm going to manage it:

at the present time I don't quite see how I can. . . . You see, all I've got
to live on at the present time is what I earn as an instructor at the university—they pay me eighteen hundred dollars a year——"

"Gosh!" Joel whispered, arching his eyebrows in polite astonishment—
"That's a lot, isn't it?"

"It's not much, Joel: it amounts to $150 a month, you can get along
on that but you're not going to paint New York red on it, the way things
are to-day, especially if you've got a healthy appetite and love to eat, the
way I do."

"Yes," Joel whispered, laughing his beautiful, radiant, and almost
soundless laugh. "I can see that—that belly of yours is going to cost you
a lot of money before you get through with it. A man who loves food
the way you do ought to be a millionaire. But you see, don't you," he
said, with a flash of his rare and gentle malice—"that's what you get for
not being a vegetarian like Bernard Shaw and me. . . . Eugene," he
cried softly, laughing, after a moment's brief reflection, "—you'll love
France—the food is wonderful—but Lord!" and he laughed again his
radiant soundless laugh "—how you're going to hate England!"

"Why? Is the food bad?"

"It's unspeakable!" Joel whispered—"that is for any one who loves
food the way you do: they go through the tortures of the damned . . .
of course, for me it doesn't matter. I can eat anything—anything, that
is, so long as it's vegetables—it all tastes alike to me—but *you'll* hate it
. . . of course," he whispered earnestly, "you really won't: you'll love
the country and you'll like the English. They're swell."

"Have you been there much, Joel?"

"Only once," he whispered. "When Mums and Rosalind were there.
We had a house out in the country and we stayed there for fifteen
months. And it was grand! You'll love it. . . . Gosh! I hope you can
stay over there a whole year!" he went on eagerly. "Don't you think you
can?"

"I don't think so: you see, as I was telling you, I have only $150 a
month; when I finish up in September I'll have about five pay-checks
coming to me: that's only $750. So I figure I can get over there on that
and live for several months, but unless I can get money from my mother
—I think perhaps she'll help me—I don't see how I can get along for a
whole year."

"Then look," said Joel, speaking swiftly, and casually, and looking

away as if he were making the most matter-of-fact proposal in the world
—"Why don't you let me help you? . . . I mean," he went on hastily,
and showing his embarrassment only by two spots of color in his
gaunt face— "I'd love to do it if you'd let me—it'd be no trouble at all—
and you could pay it back whenever you like—just as soon as your play
goes on: you'll have plenty of money then, so I wish you'd take it now
when you need it. . . . You see," he whispered quickly, with a smile,
"I have loads of money—more than I can ever *possibly* use—I have no
need for it—I was twenty-one this spring, you know,—and now I'm
awfully rich," he whispered humorously, and then concluded in a
quickly apologetic whisper—"not *really,* of course—not compared to
most people—but rich, for *me,*" he whispered, smiling. "—I've got *much*
more than I need—so I really wish you'd let me help you if you need
it—Frank said he'd let me know if he needed anything and I wish you'd
do the same. . . . I think you ought to go for a whole year since you're
going—it's your first trip and *gosh!*" he whispered enthusiastically, "how
I envy you! How I wish *I* were going for the first time! It's going to be
a swell thing for you, you're going to have a grand time—and you've
simply *got* to stay for a whole year—so I wish you'd let me help you if
I can."

He had made this astoundingly generous proposal with a quick, hurried matter-of-factness that seemed to be eagerly begging for a favor,
instead of magnificently and nobly giving it. And for a moment, the
other could not answer, and when he did he did not know the reason for
his reply, for his refusal. It was as generous, as selfless, and spontaneous
an act of liberal and noble friendship as he had ever known or experienced, and for a moment, as he thought of his longed-for trip, his dire
need of money, it all seemed so magically easy, good, and wonderfully
right to him that there seemed nothing to do except instantly, gratefully and jubilantly to accept. Yet, when he opened his mouth to
speak, he found himself to his surprise refusing this miraculous and generous good-fortune. And he never knew exactly the reason why: there
was, perhaps, the growing sense of something alien and irreconcilable
in the design and purpose of their separate lives, a growing feeling of
regret, a conviction enhanced by his conversation with Joel in the studio
that morning that their lives would be lived out in separate worlds,
wrought to separate purposes, and shaped by separate beliefs, and with
that knowledge a feeling—a feeling of loneliness and finality and fare-

well—as if a great door had swung forever closed between them, as if there was something secret, buried, and essential, in the soul of each, which now could never be revealed. And, to his surprise, he heard himself saying:

"Thanks, Joel—it's mighty fine of you—about as fine as anything I ever heard—but I don't need help now. If I need it later——"

"If you do," said Joel very quickly, "I wish you'd let me know—I'd like it if you would. . . . And gosh! it's great to know that you are going," he whispered again with radiant enthusiasm. "I envy you!"

"Then I wish to God you'd come along! . . . Joel," the other burst out excitedly, with a sudden surge of eager warm conviction. "Why can't you? We'd have a great time of it—go everywhere—see everything! It would be a wonderful thing—a great experience—for you and me both. You've never seen Europe that way before, have you?—the way that you and I could see it?—you've always been with your family, your mother, haven't you?—Come on!" he cried, seizing his friend by the arm, as if they were ready to go that instant. "Let's go! We'll have the grandest trip you ever heard about!"

But Joel, laughing his radiant soundless laugh, and shaking his head with gentle but inflexible denial, said:

"No, Eugene! . . . Not for me! . . . I can't do it! I'm going to stay right here and keep on with the work I'm doing . . . besides," he added gravely, "Mums needs me. No one knows what's going to happen here in the family," he said quietly— "I mean—that thing tonight—you saw —about Mums and Pups"—he said with painful difficulty. The other nodded, and Joel concluded simply: "I've got to stay." For a moment he was silent, and suddenly the other youth noticed something starved and lonely, and almost desperately forsaken and resigned, that he had never observed in the boy's gaunt face and eyes before, and when Joel spoke again, although there was a faint smile on his face, there was something old and sad and weary in his voice that the other youth had never heard before. He said quietly:

"Perhaps you're right. . . . Perhaps you and I do belong in different worlds . . . must go different ways. . . . If that is true," Joel turned and looked directly at his friend and in his eyes there was an infinite quiet depth of regret and acceptance "—if that is true, I'm sorry. . . . At any rate, it was good to have known you. . . . And now, good-bye, Eugene—Good-night, I mean," he hastily concluded, in his former whispered, quick and casual tones, "I'll see you in the morning."

With these words he turned quickly and left him.

He stayed there long into the night in that rich room, while the great
house sank to sleep and silence all around him. And at first he moved
there quietly like a man living in an enchanted dream, almost afraid to
draw a breath lest he dispel the glory and the magic of enchantment,
and all the time the voices of the living books around him seemed to
speak to him, to say to him: "Now it is night and silence and the sleep-
time of the earth, the all-exultant time of youth and loneliness, and of
your spirit's proud accession. Now take us, plunder us and take us, for
you are alone and living in the world to-night while all the sleepers sleep,
immortal knowledge will be yours to-night, the secrets of an everlasting
and triumphal wisdom; the huge compacted treasure of the earth speaks
to you from these storied shelves, and it is yours, you are the richest
man in all the earth if you will take us, only take us, we have waited for
you long, dear friend, tonight the world is yours, and will be yours forever, if you will only take us, take us, take us."

And like a man drunk with joy, half through the night he plundered the living treasure of those shelves. They were all there—
the great chroniclers and recorders, the marvellous and enchanted lies
of old Herodotus, and Sir Thomas Malory, and the voyages of Hakluyt
and of Purchas, the histories of Mandeville and Hume. There was Bur-
ton's marvellous *Anatomy,* his staggering erudition never smelling of
the dust or of the lamp, his lusty, pungent ever-rushing-onward style,
and the annihilating irony of Gibbon's latinized sonority, and the savage, burning, somehow magic plainness of Swift's style. There was the
dark tremendous music of Sir Thomas Browne, and Hooker's sounding
and tremendous passion made great by genius and made true by faith,
and there was the giant dance, the vast storm-rounding cadence, now
demented and now strong as light, of great Carlyle; and beside the
haunting cadences of this tremendous piece, there was the pungent
worldliness of life-loving men; the keen diaries of John Evelyn, the lusty
tang and calculation and sensual rumination of old Pepys, the writing bright as noon, natural as morning, and the plain and middle-magic
of the eighteenth century, the flawless grace and faultless clearness of
Addison and Steele, and then all the pageantry of living character, the
pages crowded with the immortal flesh of Sterne, Defoe, and Smollett,
the huge comic universe of Fielding, the little one of Austen, and the
immortal and extravagant one of Charles Dickens, the magnificent

proliferation of Sir Walter Scott's tremendous gallery—and Thackeray's sentimental gallantry and magic, and all the single magics of Nathaniel Hawthorne, of Meredith, and Melville, of Landor, Peacock, Lamb, and of De Quincey, of Hazlitt, and of Poe.

There were as well, the works of all the poets, the Kelmscott Chaucers, the Dove editions, the doe-skin bindings, white and soft and velvet to the touch, the splendid bodies in all their royal pageantry of blue and gold and dense rich green—the Greek anthologies, and all the poets of antiquity, and the singing voices of the great Elizabethans—of Wyatt, Surrey, Sidney, and of Spenser, Webster, Ford and Massinger, of Kyd and Greene and Marlowe, of Beaumont, Lyly, Nash and Dekker, of Jonson, Shakespeare, Herrick, Herbert, Donne.

They were all there, from thundering Æschylus to the sweet small voice of perfect singing Herrick, from grand plain Homer to poignant Catullus, from acid and tart-humored Horace, from the lusty, vulgar and sweet-singing voice of Geoffrey Chaucer, the great bronze ring and clangorous sonority of John Dryden, to the massy gold, the choked-in richness, the haunting fall and faery, of John Keats.

They were all there—each stored there in his little niche upon the living shelves, and at first he looted them, he plundered through their golden leaves as a man who first discovers a buried and inestimable treasure, and at first is dumb with joy at his discovery, and can only plunge his hands in it with drunken joy, scoop handfuls up and pour it over him and let the massy gold leak out again in golden ruin through his spread hands; or as a man who discovers some enchanted spring of ageless youth, of ever-long immortality, and drinks of it, and can never drink enough, and drinks and feels with every drink the huge summation of earth's glory in his own enrichment, the ageless fires of its magic youth.

Then, as the night wore on, another feeling crept across his heart, the living voices of the books spoke to him with another tone. From those great tongues of life and power and soaring immortality there had now departed all the sonorous conviction of their overwhelming, all-triumphant chant. The grand and ringing tongue and joy now spoke the language of a quiet and illimitable despair, confided the legend of an inevitable defeat, an inexorable fatality.

From those high storied shelves of dense rich bindings the great voices of eternity, the tongues of mighty poets dead and gone, now seemed to speak to him out of the living and animate silence of the room. But in that living silence, in the vast and quiet spirit of sleep which filled the great house, out of the grand and overwhelming stillness of that proud power of wealth and the impregnable security of its position, even the voices of those mighty poets dead and gone now seemed somehow lonely, small, lost, and pitiful. Each in his little niche of shelf securely stored—all of the genius, richness, and whole compacted treasure of a poet's life within a foot of space, within the limits of six small dense richly-garnished volumes—all of the great poets of the earth were there, unread, unopened, and forgotten, and were somehow, terribly, the mute small symbols of a rich man's power, of the power of wealth to own everything, to take everything, to triumph over everything—even over the power and genius of the mightiest poet—to keep him there upon his little foot of shelf, unopened and forgotten, but possessed.

Thus, for the first time in his life, even the voices of the mighty poets seemed lost and small and pitifully defeated. Their great voices, which had given to the heart of youth the added fire of their triumphant magic, had borne his spirit high upon the wings of the soaring and invincible belief that no might on earth was equal to the might of poetry, no immortality could equal the immortality of a poet's life and fame, no glory touch his glory, or no strength his strength—now seemed to speak to him the mute and small and lonely judgment of defeat:

"Child, child," they said to him, "look at us and reflect: what shall it profit you to feed upon the roots of all-engulfing night, desiring glory? Do not the rats of death and age and dark oblivion feed so forever at the roots of sleep, and can you tell us where a man lies buried now, whose substance they have not devoured? Oh, child, forever in the dark old house of life to go alone, to prowl the barren avenues of night, and listen while doors swing and creak in the old house of life, and ponder on the lids of night, and ruminate the vast heart of sleep and silence and the dark, and so consume yourself—desiring what? Poor child, you son of an unlettered race, you nameless atom of the nameless wilderness, how have you let us dupe you with our fictive glories? What power is there on earth, in sea or heaven, what power have you in yourself, you son of your unuttered fathers, to find a tongue for your unuttered brothers, and to make a frame, a shape, a magic and eternal form out of the jungle of the great unuttered wilderness from which you came, of which you are a nameless and unuttered atom? What can you hope to do, poor nameless child, and would-be chronicler of the huge

unhistoried morass of the dark wilderness of America, when we, who
were the children of a hundred gold-recorded centuries and the heirs
of all the rich accumulations of tradition, have really done so little—
and have come to this? What profit do you hope to gain—what reward
could you achieve that would repay you for all the anguish, hunger, and
the desperate effort of your life? At its rare infrequent best, out of your
blind and famished gropings in the jungle depths, you may pluck out a
shining word—achieve a moment's flash of grace and intuition—a half-
heard whisper of the vast unuttered language that you seek—perhaps a
moment's taste of fame, a brief hour's flash of the imagined glory that
you thirst for. For just a moment, you, like other men, will play the
lion, will feed upon the older lion's blood, will triumph for a moment
through his defeat, will taste joy for a moment through the blood
of his despair—and then, like him, you too will be thrown to the mercy
of the coming lion, the wilderness will rise again to engulf you, your
little hour of glory for which your soul thirsts and your life is panting
will be over before it has well begun, and the myriad horde of all your
thousand mongrel races will rise with snarl and jeer and curse and
lie and mocking to do your life to death, with all the hatred of their
mongrel rancor and their own self-loathing, to kill the lion they have
crowned for just a day, to hurl you back into a nameless and dishonorable oblivion, drowned down beneath the huge mock and jibe of the
old scornmaker's pride. Therefore, short-lived, your life will soon be
ended; your youth, but just begun, will shortly be consumed, and all
the labor of your anguish and your hunger will be mocked to scorn by
the same mongrel fools who praised it, and forgotten by the very
knaves who gave it fame. Such is the infrequent good, the flash of
brief fame, to which you may aspire, the huge oblivion of failure, misery
and dishonor which will follow. But if, by miraculous good chance, you
should escape from this—be not devoured and slain and drowned out
and forgotten in the brutal swarming shades of jungle time—what
greater glory is there that you can achieve? Some such as ours, perhaps—then look at us, and see the state to which we've come. To lie
forgotten on the rich shelves of a rich man's library—to be a portion of
his idle wealth—the evidence of his arrogant possession—to rise, as all
the earth must rise—these dreaming hills and haunted woods, the
mighty river and this great moon-haunted hill where stands this house—
shout the tributes of a rich man's glory—to bow before him—to lie
bought, owned, forgotten and possessed—the greatest poets that ever

walked the earth or built, like you, great dreams of glory—to be obsequious tributes to a rich man's fame. Yes, you, even you—poor naked child
—may come to this—to reach this state, to be entombed here, bought and
idle and among the forgotten huge encumbrance of a rich man's arrogant possession—and to know at last that all the glory, genius, and
magic of a poet's life may lie condensed in six rich bindings, forgotten,
purchased and unread—and finally defeated by the only thing in life
that lusts and will triumph forever—the all-causing tyranny of wealth
that makes a slave of its great poets—that makes us the barren whores
of fame, the pimps of wealth—unused and empty on a rich man's
shelf."

So did that great treasure of unread, purchased, and forgotten books
speak to him in the silent watches of the night, as they stood there,
lonely, small and bought, on a rich man's shelf.

Towards morning, as he sat there with a great book propped upon his
knees, his mind filled with the thought of those dead, forgotten, and still-
living voices and of his rich young friend and the strange and bitter
enigma of the fatal severance which had seemed that day to close a
great door between their lives forever, he turned the pages of the
book idly, and suddenly the blurred characters on the page before him
swam legibly to view. And what those words upon the page before him
said was this:

"The young man saith unto him, All these things have I kept from my
youth up: what lack I yet?
"Jesus said unto him, If thou wilt be perfect, go and sell that thou hast,
and give to the poor, and thou shalt have treasure in heaven: and come and
follow me.
"But when the young man heard that saying, he went away sorrowful:
for he had great possessions."

LXVII

As he and Joel drove to the station it seemed to Eugene that he was
returning to a world from which he had been absent for years. And the
return was not a pleasant one. As they entered the little town, and began
to drive swiftly down a street that led to the station, the little frame
houses with their new architectures—their faded little strips of "front
yard" grass, cement walks, and cement yard walls, looked cheap, flimsy,

new and dreary—the image of a life that was itself as rootless, insecure, and drearily pretentious as the little painted frames it lived in.

It was Sunday, and as they drove up to the station, he saw before a Greek confectionery and newspaper store a group of the town sports. They were dressed up in their cheap Sunday finery, and their faces wore a smirk. As Joel got out of the car, the sports tried to look nonchalant and easy in their relations with one another, but a kind of uneasy constraint had fallen upon them, and held them until he had gone. And yet he had not noticed them or done anything that might have caused them this discomfort.

In the gravelled parking space before the station several cars were drawn up. Their shining bodies glittered in the hot sunlight like great beetles of machinery, and in the look of these great beetles, powerful and luxurious as most of them were, there was a stamped-out quality, a kind of metallic and inhuman repetition that filled his spirit, he could not say why, with a vague sense of weariness and desolation. The feeling returned to him—the feeling that had come to him so often in recent years with a troubling and haunting insistence—that "something" had come into life, "something new" which he could not define, but something that was disturbing and sinister, and which was somehow represented by the powerful, weary, and inhuman precision of these great, glittering, stamped-out beetles of machinery. And consonant to this feeling was another concerning people themselves: it seemed to him that they, too, had changed, that "something new" had come into their faces, and although he could not define it, he felt with a powerful and unmistakable intuition that it was there—that "something" had come into life that had changed the lives and faces of the people, too. And the reason this discovery was so disturbing—almost terrifying, in fact—was first of all because it was at once evident and yet indefinable; and then because he knew it had happened within the years of his own life, few and brief as they were—had happened, indeed, within "the last few years," had happened all around him while he lived and breathed and worked among these very people to whom it had happened, and that he had not observed it at the "instant" when it came. For, with an intensely literal, an almost fanatically concrete quality of imagination, it seemed to him that there must have been an "instant" —a moment of crisis, a literal fragment of recorded time in which the transition of this change came. And it was just for this reason that he now felt a nameless and disturbing sense of desolation—almost of terror;

ıt seemed to him that this change in people's lives and faces had occurred right under his nose, while he was looking on, and that he had not seen it when it came, and that now it was here, the accumulation of his knowledge had burst suddenly in this moment of perception—he saw plainly that people had worn this look for several years, and that he did not know the manner of its coming.

They were, in short, the faces of people who had been hurled ten thousand times through the roaring darkness of a subway tunnel, who had breathed foul air, and been assailed by smashing roar and grinding vibrance, until their ears were deafened, their tongues rasped and their voices made metallic, their skins and nerve-ends thickened, calloused, mercifully deprived of aching life, moulded to a stunned consonance with the crashing uproar of the world in which they lived. These were the dead, the dull, lack-lustre eyes of men who had been hurled too far, too often, in the smashing projectiles of great trains, who, in their shining beetles of machinery, had hurtled down the harsh and brutal ribbons of their concrete roads at such a savage speed that now the earth was lost forever, and they never saw the earth again: whose weary, desperate ever-seeking eyes had sought so often, seeking *man,* amid the blind horror and proliferation, the everlasting shock and flock and flooding of the million-footed crowd, that all the life and lustre and fire of youth had gone from them; and seeking so forever in the man-swarm for man's face, now saw the blind blank wall of faces, and so would never see man's living, loving, radiant, and merciful face again.

Such were the faces that he now saw waiting on the station platform of this little Hudson River town—two dozen faces from the mongrel and anonymous compost of like faces that made up America—and with a sudden blinding flash of horror and of recognition, it now came to him that they were just the faces he had seen everywhere, at a thousand times and places in "the last few years."

He had seen them in their last and greatest colony—the huge encampment of the innumerable submerged, the last and largest colony of the great mongrel and anonymous compost that makes up America: he had seen them there, hurtling forever, from the roaring arch of the great bridge, with their unceasing flight, projectile roar, unnumbered flood, in their great and desolate beetles of glittering machinery—boring forever through the huge and labyrinthine horror of that trackless jungle of uncounted ways, beneath the grime and rust

and swarm and violence and horror of Fulton Street, past all the vast
convergences, the threat and menace of the empty naked corners, the
swarming and concentric chaos of Borough Hall, and with beetling and
unceasing flight through Clinton Street, on Henry Street, through the
Bedford section, out through the flat and limitless swelter known as
"the Flatbush section," beneath the broad and humid light of solid
skies, through ten thousand rusty, grimy, nameless streets that make
up that huge and trackless swelter—and most horrible of all, a
flood of nameless faces, rootless and unnumbered lives, hurtling
blindly past forever in hot beetles of machinery along those broad,
wide, and splendidly desolate "avenues," that were flanked upon each
side by the cheap raw brick, the gaudy splendor, of unnumbered new
apartment houses, the brick and stucco atrocities of unnumbered new
cheap houses, and that cut straight and brutal as a spoke across the
labyrinthine chaos of the Brooklyn jungle—and that led to God knows
where—to Coney Island, to the beaches, to the outer districts of that
trackless web, the unknown continent of Long Island—but that, no matter where or how they led, were always crowded with the blind horror
of those unnumbered, hurtling faces, the blind horror of those great
glittering beetles of machinery drilling past forever in projectile flight,
unceasing movement and unending change, the blind horror of these
unknown nameless lives hurtling on forever, lost forever, going God
knows where!

Yes, this was the thing—blindly, desperately, unutterably though he
felt it—this was the thing that had put this look—the "new look"—
the horrible, indefinable, and abominably desolate and anonymous
look into the face of people. This was the thing that had taken all the
play and flash of passion, joy, and instant, lovely and mercurial life
out of their living faces, and that gave their faces the look of something blunted, deadened, stunned, and calloused.

This was the thing that had given people "the new look"—that
had made man what he had become—that had made all these people
waiting on the platform for the train, what they were—and now that
he had to face this thing again, now that he had to be thrust back in
it, now that, after these three days of magic, and enchantment, he must
leave this glorious world that he had just discovered—and be thrust
brutally back again into the blind and brutal stupefaction, the nameless agony and swelter of that life from which he came—it seemed to
him he could not face it, he could not go back to it again, it was too

hard, too full of pain and sweat and agony and terror, too ugly, cruel, futile, and horrible, to be endured.

No more! No more! And not be be endured! To discover for three days—three magic swift-winged days—that enchanted life that had held all his visions as a child in fee—to be for just three brief and magic days a lord of life, the valued friend, the respected and well-loved companion of great men and glorious women, to discover and possess for three haunting and intolerably lovely days the magic domain of his boyhood's "America"—the most fortunate, good and happy life that men had ever known—the most true and beautiful, the most *right*—and now to have it torn from him at the very instant of possession—and to come to this:—a nameless cipher hurtled citywards in the huge projectile of a train, with all his fellow ciphers, towards this blind and brutal stupefaction. A voice sounded far off, thundering in his ears through the battle-roar and rock of that stunned universe, as he cried:

"Joel! Joel! It was good to be here with you—Joel——"

And suddenly saw his friend's tall form recoil, shrink back, the look of something instant, startled, closed and final in his face and eye, and heard the swift incisive whisper saying quickly——

"Yes! . . . It was good that you could come! . . . And now, good-bye! . . . I shall see you——"

And so heard no more, and knew that that good-bye was final and irrevocable and could not be altered, no matter now how much or how often they should "see" each other in the future.

And at the same moment, as that door swung shut between them, and he saw that it never could be opened any more, he felt, with the knowledge of that irrevocable loss, a moment's swift and rending pity for his friend. For he saw somehow that he was lost—that there was nothing for him now but shadows on the wall—Circean make-believe —that world of moonlight, magic and painted smoke that "the river people" knew. For three days, he himself had breathed the poppied fumes of all its glorious unreality, and in those three short days the world from which he came—his father's earth of blood and sweat and stinking day and bitter agony—this world of violence and toil and strife and cruelty and terror, this swarming world of nameless lives and mongrel faces, with all its ugliness—had become phantasmal as an evil dream, until now he could scarcely endure the hot and savage swelter, the savage fury, of the unceasing city. To grope and sweat and thrust and curse his way again among the unceasing flood-tides of the grimy swarming pavements; to be buffeted, stunned, bewildered, deadened, and exhausted by the blind turmoil, the quenchless thirst and searching, the insatiate hunger and the black despair of all that bleak and fruitless struggle, that futile and unceasing strife—and to come to this! To come to this!

It was too hard, too painful, too much to be endured, he could not go!—and even as his life shrank back in all the shuddering revulsion and loathing of his desolate discovery—he heard the great train thunder on the rails—and he knew that he *must* go!

For a moment, as the train pulled out, he stood looking out the window, waved good-bye to Joel standing on the platform, and for a moment watched his tall retreating form. Then the train gained speed, was running swiftly now along the river's edge, swept round a bend, the station and the town were left behind him, and presently, just for a few brief moments as it swept along below the magic and familiar hill, he caught a vision of the great white house set proudly far away up on the hill and screened with noble trees. Then this was gone: he looked about him, up and down the grimy coach, which was dense with smoke and pungent with the smell of cheap cigars and strong tobacco.

They were all there, and instantly he knew that he had seen each one of them a million times, and had known all of them forever; the Greek from Cleveland with his cheap tan suit, his loud tan shoes, his striped tan socks, his cheap cardboard suitcase with its tan shirts and collars and its extra pair of pants, and with his hairy, seamed and pitted night-time face, his swarthy eyes, his lowering finger-breadth of forehead bent with painful patient furrowed rumination into the sensational mysteries of tabloid print. They were all there—two deafmutes talking on their fingers; a young Harlem negro and his saffron wench, togged to the nines in tan and lavender; two young Brooklyn Jews and their two girl friends grouped on turned seats; a little chorus girl from the burlesque with dyed hair of straw-blade falseness, a false, meagre, empty, painted little whore's face, and a costume of ratty finery false as all the rest of her; a young Italian with grease-black hair sleeked back in faultless patent-leather pompadour, who talked to her, eyes leering and half-lidded, with thick pale lips fixed in a slow thick smile of sensual assurance, the jaws slow-working on a wad of gum; a man with the strong, common, gaunt-jawed and anonymous visage of the working man, wearing neat, cheap, nameless clothing, and with a brown paper parcel on the rack above him; and a young dark Irishman, his tough face fierce with drink and truculence, his eyes glittering with red points of fire, his tongue snarling curses, threats, and invitations to the fight that rasped and cut with naked menace through the smoke-blue air.

The young Jews slouched with laughter, filled the car with noisy clamor, sparred glibly, swiftly, with quick, eager, and praise-asking repartee, with knowing smirk, and cynic jest, with acrid cynic wit that did not hit the mark. The little blondined whore listened to the hypnotic, slit-eyed, thick-lipped seductions of the young Italian with a small coy-bawdy smirk upon her painted face: she did not know what he meant, she had no idea what he was talking about, and with coybawdy smirk she rose, edged past his slow withdrawn knees and minced down the aisle towards the little cupboard at the end that housed the women's toilet, while with lidded sly eyes, and thick, slow-chewing and slow-smiling lips his calculating glance pursued her. The lady entered, closed the door upon a stale reek, and was gone some time. When she emerged, she arranged her clothing daintily, smoothed out her rumpled dress across her hips and came mincing down the aisle again with faint coy-bawdy smirk, and was greeted again by her gallant suitor, who welcomed her in the same manner, with lidded eyes, thick, pallid and slow-chewing lips, and slow withdrawn knees. The two deaf-mutes surveyed the scene with loathing: one was large and heavy, with the powerful shoulders of the cripple, a brutal face, a wide and cruel mouth; the other small and dark and ferret-faced—but both surveyed the scene with loathing. They looked at each and all the passengers and they dismissed each in turn upon their fingers. As they did so, their faces writhed in vicious snarls, in sneering smiles, in convulsions of disgust and hatred; they looked upon the objects of their hate and jerked cruel thumbs towards earth in gestures eloquent of annihilation and destructive sudden-death, and they drew swift fingers meaningly across their gullets with the deadly move of men who slit a throat— and all was as he had known it would be.

The working man with the strong and common face, the cheap, neat clothes, sat quietly, and looked quietly out the window, with seamed face and quiet worn eyes, and the young Irishman sweltered in strong drink and murder; the taste of blood was thick in him, his little eyes glittered with red points of fire, and ever as the train rushed on, he sowed that smoke-blue air with rasping curse, and snarling threat, with all the idiot stupefaction of a foul and idiot profanity, an obscene but limited complaint:—

"Yuh f—kin' Kikes! . . . Yuh f—kin' Jews! . . . I'll kick duh f—kin' s—t outa duh f—kin' lot of yuh, yuh f—kin' bastards, you. . . . Hey-y! You! . . . Yuh f—kin' dummies up deh talkin' on yer f—kin' fingers all duh time. . . . Hey-y! You! Inches! You f—kin' bastard, I don't give a s—t for duh whole f—kin' lot of yuh."

It was all as it had always been, as he had known it would be, as he never could have foreseen it: the young dark Irishman sowed the air with threats and foulness, he finished up his bottle, and the foulness and the old red light of murder grew. And the mongrel compost laughed and snickered as they always did, and at length grew silent when he lurched with drunken measure towards them, and the old conductor with the sour, seamed face then stopped the Irishman, and he cursed him.

And the slant light steepened in the skies, the old red light of waning day made magic fire upon the river, and the train made on forever its tremendous monotone that was like silence and forever—and now there was nothing but that tremendous monotone of time and silence and the river, the haunted river, the enchanted river that drank forever its great soundless tides from out the inland slowly, and that moved through all man's lives the magic thread of its huge haunting spell, and that linked his life to magic kingdoms and to lotus-land and to all the vision of the magic earth that he had dreamed of as a child, and that bore him on forever out of magic to all the grime and sweat and violence of the city, the unceasing city, the million-footed city, and into America.

The great river burned there in his vision in that light of fading day and it was hung there in that spell of silence and forever, and it was flowing on forever, and it was stranger than a legend, and as dark as time.

BOOK V
JASON'S VOYAGE

LXVIII

SMOKE-GOLD by day, the numb exultant secrecies of fog, a fog-numb air filled with the solemn joy of nameless and impending prophecy, an ancient yellow light, the old smoke-ochre of the morning, never coming to an open brightness—such was October in England that year. Sometimes by night in stormy skies there was the wild, the driven moon, sometimes the naked time-far loneliness, the most-oh-most familiar blazing of the stars that shine on men forever, their nameless, passionate dilemma of strong joy and empty desolation, hope and terror, home and hunger, the huge twin tyranny of their bitter governance—wandering forever and the earth again.

They are still-burning, homely particles of night, that light the huge tent of the dark with their remembered fire, recalling the familiar hill, the native earth from which we came, from which we could have laid our finger on them, and making the great earth and home seem near, most near, to wanderers; and filling them with naked desolations of doorless, houseless, timeless, and unmeasured vacancy.

And everywhere that year there was something secret, lonely, and immense that waited, that impended, that was still. Something that promised numbly, hugely, in the fog-numb air, and that never broke to any open sharpness, and that was almost keen and frosty October in remembered hills—oh, there was something there incredibly near and most familiar, only a word, a stride, a room, a door away—only a door away and never opened, only a door away and never found.

At night, in the lounging rooms of the old inn, crackling fires were blazing cheerfully, and people sat together drinking small cups of the black bitter liquid mud that they called coffee.

The people were mostly family groups who had come to visit their son or brother in the university. They were the most extraordinary, ugly, and distinguished-looking people Eugene had ever seen. There was the father, often the best looking of the lot: a man with a ruddy weathered face, a cropped white mustache, iron gray hair—an open, driving, bull-dog look of the country carried with tremendous style. The mother was very ugly with a long horse face and grimly weathered cheek flanks that seemed to have the tough consistency of well-tanned leather. Her grim bared smile shone in her weathered face and was nailed forever round the gauntness of her grinning teeth. She had a neighing voice, a shapeless figure, distinguished by the bony and angular width of the hip structure, clothed with fantastic dowdiness—fantastic because the men were dressed so well, and because everything they wore, no matter how old and used it might be, seemed beautiful and right.

The daughter had the mother's look: a tall gawky girl with a bony, weathered face and a toothy mouth, she wore an ill-fitting evening or party dress of a light unpleasant blue, with a big meaningless rosette of ruffles at the waist. She had big feet, bony legs and arms, and she was wearing pumps of dreary gray and gray silk stockings.

The son was a little fellow with ruddy apple-cheeks, crisp, fair, curly hair, and baggy gray trousers; and there was another youth, one of his college friends, of the same cut and quality, who paid a dutiful but cold attention to the daughter, which she repaid in kind, and with which every one was completely satisfied.

They had to be seen to be believed, but even then, one could only say, like the man who saw the giraffe: "I don't believe it." The young men sat stiffly on the edges of their chairs, holding their little cups of coffee in their hands, bent forward in an attitude of cold but respectful attentiveness, and the conversation that went on among them was incredible. For their manner was impregnable, they were cold, remote, and formal almost to the point of military curtness, and yet Eugene felt among them constantly an utter familiarity of affection, a strange secret warmth, past words or spoken vows, that burned in them like glacial fire.

When you got ten or fifteen feet away from them, their language could not have been more indecipherable if they had spoken in Chinese; but it was fascinating just to listen to the sounds. For there would be long mounting horse-like neighs, and then there would be reedy flute-like notes, and incisive cold finalities and clipped ejaculations and sometimes a lovely and most musical speech. But the horse-like neighs and clipped ejaculations would predominate; and suddenly Eugene understood how strange these people seemed to other races, and why Frenchmen, Germans, and Italians would sometimes stare at them with gape-mouthed stupefaction when they heard them talking.

Once when he passed by them they had the family vicar or some clergyman of their acquaintance with them. He was a mountain of a man, and he too, was hardly credible: the huge creature was at least six and a half feet tall, and he must have weighed three hundred pounds. He had a flaming moon of face and jowl, at once most animal and delicate, and he peered out keenly with luminous smoke-gray eyes beneath a bushy hedge-growth of gray brows. He was dressed in the clerical garb and his bulging grossly sensual calves were encased in buttoned gaiters. As Eugene went by, he was leaning forward with his little cup of muddy coffee held delicately in the huge mutton of his hand, peering keenly out beneath his beetling bush of brow. And what he said was this:

"Did you ever read—that is, in recent yöhs—the concluding chaptahs in 'The Vicah of Wakefield'?" Carefully he set the little cup down in its saucer. "I was reading it just the other day. It's an extraordinary thing!" he said.

It is impossible to reproduce the sound of these simple words, or the effect they wrought upon Eugene's senses

For first, the words "Did you ever" were delivered in a delicate rising-and-falling neigh, the word "read" really came out with a long reedy sound, the words "that is, in recent yöhs," in a parenthesis of sweetly gentle benevolence, the phrase "the concluding·chaptahs in 'The Vicah of Wakefield,'" in full, deliberate, satisfied tones of titular respect, the phrase "I was reading it just the other day," thoughtfully, reedily, with a subdued, gentle, and mellow reminiscence, and the final decisive phrase, "It's an extraordinary thing," with passionate conviction and sincerity that passed at the end into such an unction of worshipful admiration that the words "extraordinary thing" were not spoken, but breathed out passionately, and had the sound "'strawd'n'ry thing!"

"Ow!" the young man answered distantly, and in a rather surprised tone, with an air of coldly startled interest, "Now! I can't say that I have—not since my nursery days, at any rate!" He laughed metallically.

"You should read it again," the mountainous creature breathed unctuously. "A 'strawd'n'ry thing! A 'strawd'n'ry thing." Delicately he lifted the little cup of muddy black in his huge hand again and put it to his lips.

"But *frightfully* sentimental, down't you think?" the girl neighed sharply at this point. "I mean all the lovely-woman-stoops-to-folly sawt of thing, you now. After all, it is a bit thick to expect people to swallow *that* nowadays," she neighed, "particularly after all that's happened in the last twenty yöhs. I suppose it mattuhed in the eighteenth centureh but after all," she neighed with an impatient scorn, "who cares today? Who cares," she went on recklessly, "*what* lovely woman stoops to? I cawn't see that it makes the *slightest* difference. It's not as if it mattuhed any longah! No one cares!"

"Ow!" the young man said with his air of coldly startled interest. "Yes, I think I follow you, but I don't entirely agree. How can we be certain what *is* sentimental and what's not?"

"But it seems to me he misses the whole point!" the girl exclaimed with one full, mouth-like rush. "After all," she went on scornfully, "no one is interested in woman's folly any longah—the ruined-maiden broken-vows sawt of thing. If that was what she got she should have jolly well known what she wanted to begin with! *I'll* not waste any pity on her," she said grimly. "The greatest folly is not knowin' what you want to do! The whole point today is to live as cleveleh as possible! That's the only thing that mattahs! If you know what you want and go about it cleveleh, the rest of it will take care of itself."

"Um," the mother now remarked, her gaunt bare smile set grimly, formidably, on her weathered face. "That takes a bit of doin', *doesn't* it?" And as she spoke these quiet words her grim smile never faltered for an instant and there was a hard, an obdurate, an almost savage irony in her intonation, which left them all completely unperturbed.

"Oh, a *'strawd'n'ry* thing! A *'strawd'n'ry* thing!" the huge clerical creature whispered dreamily at this point, as if he had not heard them. And delicately he set his little cup back on the saucer.

Eugene's first impulse when he saw and heard them was to shout with an astounded laughter—and yet, somehow, one never laughed. They had a formidable and impregnable quality that silenced laughter: a quality that was so assured in its own sense of inevitable rightness that it saw no other way except its own, and was so invincibly sure in its own way that it was indifferent to all others. It could be taken among strange lands and alien faces, and to the farthest and most savage colonies on earth, and would never change or alter by a jot.

Yes, they had found a way, a door, a room to enter, and there were walls about them now, and the way was theirs. The mark of dark time and the architecture of unnumbered centuries of years were on them, and had made them what they were; and what they were, they were, and would not change.

Eugene did not know if their way was a good way, but he knew it was not his. Their door was one he could not enter. And suddenly the naked empty desolation filled his life again, and he was walking on beneath the timeless sky, and had no wall at which to hurl his strength, no door to enter by, and no purpose for the furious unemployment of his soul. And now the worm was eating at his heart again. He felt the slow interminable waste and wear of gray time all about him and his life was passing in the darkness, and all the time a voice kept saying: "Why? Why am I here now? And where shall I go?"

When Eugene got out into the High Street after dinner, the dark air would be thronging with the music of great bells, and there would be a smell of fog and smoke and old October in the air, the premonitory thrill and menace of some intolerable and nameless joy. Often at night, the visage of the sky would by some magic be released from the thick grayness that had covered it by day, and would shine forth barely, blazing with flashing and magnificent stars.

And, as the old bells thronged through the smoky air, the students would be passing along the street, singly or in groups of two or three, briskly, and with the eager haste that told of meetings to come, appointments to be kept, the expectation of some good fortune, happiness, or pleasure toward which they hurried on.

The soft glow of lights would shine from the ancient windows of the colleges, and one could hear the faint sounds of voices, laughter, sometimes music.

Then Eugene would go to different pubs and drink until the closing time. Sometimes the proctors would come into a pub where he was drinking, speak amicably to every one, and in a moment more go out again.

Somehow he always hoped that they would take him for a student. He could see them stepping up to him, as he stood there at the bar, saying courteously, yet gravely and sternly:

"Your name and college, sir?"

Then he could see the look of astonished disbelief on their grim red faces when he told them he was not a student, and at last, when he had convinced them, he could hear their crestfallen muttered-out apologies, and would graciously excuse them.

But the proctors never spoke to him, and the bar-man, seeing him look at them as they went out one night, misunderstood the look, and laughed with cheerful reassurance:

"You've nothing at all to worry about, sir. They won't bother you. It's only the gentlemen at the university they're after."

"How do they know I'm not there?"

"That I couldn't tell you, sir," he answered cheerfully, "but they 'ave a way of knowin'! Ah, yes!" he said with satisfaction, slapping a wet cloth down upon the bar. "They 'ave a way of knowin', right enough! They're a clever lot, those chaps. A very clever lot, sir, and they always 'ave a way of knowin' when you're not." And smiling cheerfully, he made a vigorous parting swipe across the wood, and put the cloth away below the counter.

Eugene's glass was almost empty and he looked at it, and wondered if he ought to have another. He thought they made them very small, and kept thinking of the governors of North and South Carolina. It was a fine, warm, open sort of pub, and there was a big fire-place just behind him, crackling smartly with a fire of blazing coals: he could feel the warmth upon his back. Outside, in the fog-numb air, people came by with lonely rapid footsteps and were lost in fog-numb air again.

At this moment the bar-maid, who had bronze-red hair and the shrewd, witty visage of a parrot, turned and called out in a cheerful, crisply peremptory tone: "Time, please, gentlemen. Closing time."

Eugene put the glass down empty on the bar again. He wondered what the way of knowing was.

It was October, about the middle of the month, at the opening of the Michaelmas term. Everywhere there was the exultant thrill and bustle of returning, of a new life, a new adventure beginning in an ancient and beautiful place that was itself enriched by the countless lives and adventures of hundreds of years which had come and gone. In the morning there was the smoky old-gold yellow of the sun, the numb excitement of the foggy air, a smell of good tobacco, beer, grilled kidneys, ham and sausages, and grilled tomatoes, a faint nostalgic smell of tea, and incredibly, somehow, in that foggy old-gold light, a smell of coffee—an intolerable, maddening, false, delusive smell, for when one went to find the coffee it would not be there: the coffee was black liquid mud, bitter, lifeless, and undrinkable.

Everything was very expensive and yet it made you feel rich yourself just to look at it. The little shops, the wine shops with their bay windows of small leaded glass, and the crusty opulence of the bottles of old port and sherry and the burgundies, the mellow homely warmth and quietness of the interior, the tailor shops, the tobacco shops with their selected grades of fine tobacco stored in ancient crocks, the little bell that tinkled thinly as you went in from the street, the decorous, courteous, yet suavely good-natured proprietor behind the counter, who had the ruddy cheeks, the flowing brown mustache and the wing-collar of the shopkeeper of solid substance, and who would hold the crock below your nose to let you smell the moist fragrance of a rare tobacco before you bought, and would offer you one of his best cigarettes before you left— all of this gave somehow to the simplest acts of life and business a ritualistic warmth and sanctity, and made you feel wealthy and secure.

And everywhere around Eugene in the morning there was the feeling of an imminent recovery, a recapture of a life that had always been his own. The buildings seemed to come from some essence of reality he had always known, but had never seen, and could scarcely believe in now, even when he put his hand upon the weathered surface of the stone.

And this look kept shining at him through the faces of the people. Sometimes it was in the faces of the college boys but more often he saw it in the people of the town. It was in the faces of tradesmen—people in butcher shops, wine shops, clothing stores—and sometimes it was in the faces of women, at once common, fine, familiar, curiously delicate and serene, going to the markets, in the foggy old-bronze light of morning, and of men who passed by wearing derby hats and with wing collars. It was in the faces of a man and his son, good-humored little red-faced bullocks, packed with life, who ran a pub in the Cowley Road near the house where, later, he went to live.

It was a look round, full, ruddy, and serene in its good-nature and had more openness and mellow humor in it than Eugene had found in the faces of the people in New England. It was more like the look of country people and small-town people in the South. Sometimes it had the open tranquil ruddiness, the bovine and self-satisfied good humor of his uncle, Crockett Pentland, and sometimes it was like Mr. Bailey, the policeman, whom the negro killed one winter's night, when snow was on the ground and all the bells began to ring. And then it was full and hearty like the face of Mr. Ernest Pegram, who was the City Plumber and lived next door to Eugene's father, or it was plump, common, kindly, invincibly provincial, ignorant and domestic, like the face of Mrs. Higginson, who lived across the street, and had herself been born in England, who had a family of eight children and three baking days a week, and was a praying, singing, and fanatic Baptist; yet on her common kindly face was the same animal, gentle, smoke-like delicacy of expression round the mouth that some of these men and women had.

It was a life that seemed so near to Eugene that he could lay his hand on it and make it his at any moment. He seemed to have returned to a room he had always known, and to have paused for a moment, without any doubt or perturbation of the soul, outside the door.

But he never found the door, or turned the knob, or stepped into the room. When he got there he couldn't find it. It was as near as his hand if he could only touch it, only as high as his heart and yet he could not reach it, only a hand's breadth off if he would span it, a word away if he would speak it. Only a stride, a move, a step away was all the peace, the certitude, the joy—and home forever—for which his life was panting, and he was drowning in the darkness.

He never found it. The old smoke-gold of morning would be full of hope and joy and imminent discovery but afternoon would come and the soft gray humid skies pressed down on him with their huge numb waste and weight and weariness of intolerable time, and the empty naked desolation filled his guts.

He would walk that legendary street past all those visible and enchanted substances of time, and see the students passing through the college gates, the unbelievable velvet green of college quads, and see the huge dark room of peace and joy that time had made, and he had no way of getting into it.

Each day he walked about the town and breathed the accursed languid softness of gray foreign air, that had no bite or sparkle in it, and went by all their fabulous age-encrusted walls of Gothic time, and wondered what in the name of God he had to do with all their walls or towers, or how he could feed his hunger on the portraits of the Spanish king, and why he was there, why he had come!

Sometimes it was just a word, the intonation of a phrase—the way they would say *"very"* or "Amer*ican*," which chilled and withered all the ardours of the heart, or the way they would say "Thank *you!*" when you paid for something, crisply, courteously, yet with a quick, cautious, and obdurate finality, as if some one had swiftly and firmly closed a door lest you should try to enter it. Eugene could listen to them talk and hear all the words, the moods and tones of life and humor that he had known all his life, until it seemed that he could foresee the very stories they were going to tell, the very situations they were going to describe—

and then in an instant all the familiar pattern of their speech would vanish, and their words could not have been stranger to him had they spoken in a foreign tongue.

Thus, as Eugene looked at the young college fellows playing in the fields below the house, their shouts and cries, the boyish roughness of their play, their strong scurfed knees, and panting breath, evoked the image of a life so familiar to him that he felt all he had to do to enter it again was to walk across the velvet width of lawn that separated him from it. But if he passed these same people two hours later in the High Street, their lives, their words were stranger than a dream, or they seemed to have an incredible fictitious quality that made everything they did or said seem false, mannered, and affected, so that when he listened to them he had a feeling of resentment and contempt for them, as if they spoke and moved with the palpable falseness of actors.

Eugene would see two young fellows before a college gate, and one, fragile of structure, with a small lean head, a sheaf of straight blonde hair and thin, sensitive features which were yet sharply and strongly marked, would be talking to another youth, his hands thrust jauntily into the pockets of his baggy gray trousers as he talked and the worn elegance of his baggy coat falling across his hands in folds of jaunty well-worn smartness.

"I say!" the youth would be saying in his crisp, rapid, sharply blurred inflections that seemed to come out of lips that barely moved. "Where *were* you last night? We missed you at the party in old Lambert's rooms, you know. Every one wondered why you didn't turn up."

"Oh," the other said (but the way he said this word sounded almost like "Ow" to Eugene). "Did they? I'm frightfully sorry to have missed it, but I simply couldn't get thöh. Had dinner with a chap I know at Magdalen. His sister's down for a day or so, and later on I simply couldn't break away.—How was the party?"

"Ow!" the other cried, casting his head back with a strong quick movement and an exultant little laugh. "Ripping! Simply ripping! What a shame you had to miss it! Old Fenton got quite squiffed along towards ten o'clock," he went on affectionately and with his exultant little laugh, "and really it was priceless! He insisted on doing an imitation of Queen Victoria sitting down to read *The Times* upon her w. c. just after modern plumbing was installed—Ow!" he cried exultantly again, casting his head up with a sharp strong movement, "the whole thing was convulsing!—To see old Fenton *settle* down!"

he cried, "to see him *look* around *suspiciously*," he whispered, still
maintaining the perfect dramatic sharpness of his inflection as he looked
around with a descriptive gesture, "to see him wait *uneasily* to see
what's going to happen—finally to see the look of *blissful* satisfaction and
contentment gradually *stealing* over his face," he whispered rapturously,
"as he settles back to read *The Times* in peace—*ow!*" he cried again, as
he cast back his small lean head with an exultant laugh, "—the whole
thing was really *too* superb!—it really was, you know! Old Lambert
was quite convulsed! We had to lift him up and stretch him out upon
the bed before he got his breath again."

In conversations such as these, in the choice and accent of the words,
the sharp crisp and yet blurred inflections of the speech, even in the
jaunty nonchalance of hands in pockets, the hang and fold of the coat,
in the exultant little laugh and the sharp strong upward movement of
the small lean head, there was something alien, suave, and old. To
Eugene it seemed to be the style of a life that was far older, more suavely
knowing and mature, than any he had ever known, so that at such a
time as this, these young boys who on the playing fields had almost the
appearance of tousled overgrown urchins, now seemed far more assured and sophisticated than he could ever be.

At the same time, the sound and inflection of their words—their assured exercise of a style of language that knew exactly where to use and
how to inflect such words as "very," "quite," "superb," "priceless," "terribly," "marvellous," and so on—this style and use seemed to Eugene
almost false, fictional, affected, and theatrical.

He felt this way chiefly because he had read about such people all his
life in books and for the most part had heard them speak in this manner
only in smart plays upon the stage. He was always connecting these
young Englishmen with actors in the theatre, and for a moment his
mind would resentfully accuse them of being nothing but cheap and
affected actors themselves and, bitterly, of "trying to talk with an English accent"—a phrase which obviously had no meaning, since they
were only speaking their own language in the way they had been taught
to speak it.

But then, at tea-time, Eugene would see these youths again in Buol's,
flirting, with the clumsy naïveté of a grubby schoolboy, with a leering
rawboned hag of a waitress, and obviously getting the thrill of their
lives from the spurious grins which this dilapidated strumpet flashed
at them through her artificial teeth. Or, as he went up the road

towards his house at night, he would pass them standing in the dark
shadows of the stormy trees, with their arms clumsily clasped around
the buttocks of a servant girl, and their lives seemed unbelievably
young, naked, and innocent again.

Around Eugene was the whole structure of an enchanted life—a life
hauntingly familiar and just the way he had always known it would be
—and now that he was there, he had no way of getting into it. The inn
itself was ancient, legendary, beautiful, elfin, like all the inns he had
ever read about, and yet all of the cheer, the warmth, the joy and comfort he had dreamed of finding in an inn was lacking.

Upstairs the halls went crazily up and down at different levels, one
mounted steps, went down again, got lost and turned around in the
bewildering design of the ancient added-on-to structure—and this was
the way he had always known it would be. But the rooms were small,
cold, dark, and dreary, the lights were dim and dismal, you stayed out
of your room as much as possible and when you went to bed at night
you crawled in trembling between clammy sheets, and huddled there
until the bed was warm. When you got up in the morning there was a
small jug of warm water at your door with which to shave, but the
jug was too small, you poured it out into the bowl and shaved yourself and added cold water from the pitcher then in order to get enough to
wash your face and hands. Then you got out of the room and went
downstairs as quickly as you could.

Downstairs it would be fine. There would be a brisk fire crackling in
the hearth, the old smoke-gold of morning and the smell of fog, the
crisp cheerful voices of the people and their ruddy competent morning
look, and the cheerful smells of breakfast, which was always liberal and
good, the best meal that they had: kidneys and ham and eggs and
sausages and toast and marmalade and tea.

But at night there would come the huge boiled-flannel splendor of
the dinner, the magnificent and prayerful service of the waiter, who
served you with such reverent grace from heavy silver platters that you
felt the food must be as good as everything looked. But it never was.

Eugene ate at a large table, in the centre of the dining-room, provided
by a thoughtful management for such isolated waifs and strays as himself. The food looked very good, and was, according to the genius of
the nation, tasteless. How they ever did it he could never tell: everything was of the highest quality and you chewed upon it mournfully,

wearily, swallowing it with the dreary patience of a man who has been condemned forever to an exclusive diet of boiled unseasoned spinach. There was a kind of evil sorcery, a desolate and fathomless mystery in the way they could take the choicest meats and vegetables and extract all the succulence and native flavor from them, and then serve them up to you magnificently with every atom of their former life reduced to the general character of stewed hay or well-boiled flannel.

There would be a thick heavy soup of dark mahogany, a piece of boiled fish covered with a nameless, tasteless sauce of glutinous white, roast beef that had been done to death in dish-water, and solid, perfect, lovely brussels sprouts for whose taste there was no name whatever. It might have been the taste of boiled wet ashes, or the taste of stewed green leaves, with all the bitterness left out, pressed almost dry of moisture, or simply the taste of boiled clouds and rain and fog. For dessert, there would be a pudding of some quivery yellow substance, beautifully moulded, which was surrounded by a thin sweetish fluid of a sticky pink. And at the end there would be a cup of black, bitter, liquid mud.

Eugene felt as if these dreary ghosts of food would also come to life at any moment, if he could only do some single simple thing—make the gesture of an incantation, or say a prayer, or speak a magic word, a word he almost had, but couldn't quite remember.

The food plagued his soul with misery, bitter disappointment, and bewilderment. For Eugene liked to eat, and they had written about food better than any one on earth. Since his childhood, there had burned in his mind a memory of the food they wrote about. It was a memory drawn from a thousand books (of which *Quentin Durward*, curiously, was one), but most of all it came from that tremendous scene in *Tom Brown at Rugby,* which described the boy's ride with his father through the frosty darkness, in an English stage-coach, the pause for breakfast at an inn, and the appearance of the host, jolly, red-faced, hospitable, who had rushed out to welcome them.

Eugene could remember with a gluttonous delight the breakfast which that hungry boy had devoured. It was a memory so touched with the magic relish of frost and darkness, smoking horses, the thrill, the ecstasy of the journey and a great adventure, the cheer, the warmth, the bustle of the inn, and the delicious abundance of the food they gave the boy, that the whole thing was evoked with blazing vividness, and now it would almost drive Eugene mad with hunger when he thought of it.

Now it seemed to him that these people had written so magnificently about good food not because they always had it, but because they had it rarely and therefore made great dreams and fantasies about it, and it seemed to him that this same quality—the quality of *lack* rather than of *possession,* of desire rather than fulfilment—had got into everything they did, and made them dream great dreams, and do heroic acts, and had enriched their lives immeasurably.

They had been the greatest poets in the world because the love and substance of great poetry were so rare among them. Their poems were so full of the essential quality of sunlight because their lives had known sunlight briefly, and so shot through with the massy substance of essential gold (a matchless triumph of light and color and material, in which they have beaten the whole world by every standard of comparison) because their lives had known so much fog and rain, so little gold. And they had spoken best of April because April was so brief with them.

Thus from the grim gray of their skies they had alchemied gold, and from their hunger, glorious food, and from the raw bleakness of their lives and weathers they had drawn magic. And what was good among them had been won sternly, sparely, bitterly, from all that was ugly, dull, and painful in their lives, and, when it came, was more rare and beautiful than anything on earth.

But that also was theirs: it was another door Eugene could not enter.

LXIX

Later, Eugene could remember everything except the way he found the house and came to live there. But a man named Morison, who was staying at the Mitre when Eugene got there, found the house and gave him the address. He was a man of twenty-eight or thirty years, but he constantly seemed younger, much younger, no older than the average college youth, an illusion that was never permanent, however, and never for a moment convincing, because one felt constantly that everything about the man was spurious.

He had been, he said, a lieutenant in the flying corps, and had just the month before resigned his commission. And he said he had resigned his commission because he had received an appointment from the government in the African colonial service, and had been sent up to the university to take a special six months' course in Colonial Administration, after which he would be "sent out" to assume his new duties in the Colonies. Finally, he was, he said, by birth, an Edinburgh Scotchman, although his family were by blood more English than Scotch, and he had lived most of his life in England. His references to his family were casual, easy, and indefinite, but carried with them, somehow, the connotations of aristocratic distinction.

He referred to his father often, but always in this casual and easy manner, as "the governor," and to his mother as "the mater," flinging in parenthetically with his easy nonchalance such a statement as "of course, my whole crowd came from Devonshire"—a statement which was unadorned and meaningless enough but that somehow—God knows how—carried with it a wonderful evocation of an ancestral seat, an ancient and distinguished name, the quiet but impregnable position of one of the "old county families."

And yet, God knows how he did it: the man said nothing about his people that might not be said of any modest little family, and probably everything he said was true. He made no open pretenses to great name or wealth or ancient lineage, but in these swift, casual, half-blurted-out references to "the governor," "the mater," and so on, he projected perfectly a legend of prestige and family that was most engaging in its sense of style and dash and recklessness.

The design of this legend was perfectly familiar to every one: Eugene had read it a thousand times in the pages of books, but he had never known any one who could evoke it so perfectly, so tellingly, and with such a non-committal economy of means, as Morison. In this casual, charming, almost nakedly simple picture of his life which he could suggest in a blurted-out phrase without giving a shred of real information about himself, or making a single admission of fact, the characters were few in number, their lineaments broadly and forcibly outlined, and their setting a familiar one.

In this setting, Morison himself played the part of the dashing young aristocrat, wild, reckless, and impetuous, always ready for fun, fight, or frolic, a bottle of Scotch, or a pretty woman, a roaring drunk, or a hot seduction—a mad hare-brained sort of fellow who plunged impetuously forward into everything, but who was somehow always saved from the odium that attaches itself to a baser sort of drunkard, brawler, or seducer, because he had in him those mysterious qualities of blood and character that made of him "a gentleman," and therefore gave his acts a faultless style, a whole immunity.

And the figure that he stroked in of his father was also a pleasant one. For "the governor," although he existed chiefly for the purpose of admonishment and reproof, as a curb upon the wild spirits of his son, was neither a sour Puritan, nor a grim-visaged household tyrant, but really a very good and understanding sort of fellow, and, within reasonable limits, as tolerant as any one could ask. The old boy, in fact, had been "a bit of a buck himself" in his younger days, and had seen his share of the flesh and the devil, and was quite willing to make allowances for the wilder escapades of youth, so long as a reasonable decorum and moderation were observed.

But there, alas, was the rub—as Morison himself would ruefully admit. He was himself such a mad, scape-grace sort of fellow that his acts sometimes passed all the bounds of decorum and propriety, and for that reason "the governor" was always "having him in upon the carpet."

There, in fact, was the whole setting. The governor existed for the sole purpose of "having him in upon the carpet"—one never saw them in any other way, but when Morison spoke about it one saw them in *this* way with blazing vividness. And this picture—the picture of Morison going in "upon the carpet"—was a very splendid one.

First, one saw Morison pacing nervously up and down in a noble and ancient hall, puffing distractedly on a cigarette and pausing from time to time in an apprehensive manner before the grim, closed barrier of an enormous seventeenth-century door which was tall and wide enough for a knight in armor to ride through without difficulty, and before whose gloomy and overwhelming front Morison looked very small and full of guilt. Then, one saw him take a last puff at his cigarette, brace his shoulders in a determined manner, knock on the panels of the mighty door, and in answer to a low growl within, open the door and advance desperately into the shadowed depths of a room so immense and magnificent that Morison looked like a single little sinner walking forlornly down the nave of a cathedral.

At the end of this terrific room, across an enormous space of carpet, sat "the governor." He was sitting behind a magnificent flat desk of ancient carved mahogany, in the vast shadowed depths behind him storied rows of old bound volumes climbed dizzily up into the upper darkness and were lost. And men in armor were standing grimly all around, and the portraits of the ancestors shone faintly in the gloom, and the old worn mellow colors of the tempered light came softly through the colored glass of narrow Gothic windows which were set far away in recessed depths of the impregnable mortared walls.

Meanwhile, "the governor" was waiting in grim silence as Morison advanced across the carpet. The governor was a man with beetling bushy eyebrows, silver hair, the lean, bitten and incisive face, the cropped mustache of a man who has seen service in old wars, and commanded garrisons in India, and after clearing his throat with a low menacing growl, he would peer fiercely out at Morison beneath his bushy brows, and say: "Well, young man?"—to which Morison would be able to make no answer, but would just stand there in a state of guilty dejection.

And the talk that then passed between the outraged father and the prodigal son was, from Morison's own account, astonishing. It was a talk that was no talk, a talk that was almost incoherent but that each understood perfectly, another language, not merely an economy of words so spare that one word was made to do the work of a hundred, but a series of grunts, blurts, oaths and ejaculations, in which almost nothing was said that was recognizable as ordered thought, but in which the meaning of everything was perfectly conveyed.

The last outrageous episode that had brought Morison in to his present position of guilt "upon the carpet" was rarely named by name or given a description. Rather, as if affronted decency and aristocratic delicacy could not endure discussion of an unmentionable offense, his fault was indicated briefly as "that sort of thing" (or simply "sort of thing," spoken fast and slurringly)—and all the other passions and emotions of anger, contrition, stern condemnation and reproof, and, at length, of exhausted relief and escape, were conveyed in a series of broken and jerky exclamations, such as: "After *all!*" "It's not as if it were the first time you had played the bloody fool!" "What I mean to say is!" "Damn it all, it's not that I mind the wine-woman-song sort of thing—young myself once—no plaster saint—never pretended that I was—man's own business if he keeps it to himself—never interfered —only when you do a thing like this and make a bloody show of yourself—you idiot!—sort of thing men can understand but women!—it's your mother I'm thinking of!" and so on.

Morison's own speech, in fact, was largely composed of phrases such as these: he blurted them out so rapidly, scarcely moving his lips and slurring his words over in such a broken and explosive way, that when one first met him it was hard to understand what he was saying:— his speech seemed to be largely a series of blurted-out phrases, such as "sort of thing," "after *all!*" "what I mean to say is!" and so on. And yet this incoherent and exclamatory style was curiously effective, for it seemed to take the listener into its confidence in rather an engaging manner which said: "of course there's no need to go into detail about all this, because I can see you are a man of the world and the same kind of fellow as I am. I know we understand each other perfectly, and the truth of what I am saying must be so self-evident that there's no point in discussing it."

In stature, he was a little below the middle height, and rather fleshy. In fact, although his jaunty and impetuous manners gave him an air of boyishness, he was already getting fat around the waist, and his neck was fat and there was a fold of flesh beneath his chin. His face was very ruddy, smooth, a little alcoholic, and he had a small blonde mustache with waxed ends. Finally, his hair was thick, sleek, of a dark taffy-colored blond which shaded off into roots of fine silken blondish white at the edges of his temples.

He could almost have passed for the average Oxford youth if it had not been for the roll of fat beneath his chin, and the blurred, veinous, and yellowed look of his eyes, and he could almost have passed for the dashing gentleman whose lineaments he could so deftly and cleverly sketch in a few boldly casual strokes had it not been that there was something spurious in his character that gave him away in everything he did or said.

And yet Eugene never knew just what this spurious quality was. He felt at once that the man was fraudulent and unfortunate, and that all he told about himself was fraudulent, and yet everything he told was not only natural and credible enough but even plausible. All he said was that he had been a lieutenant in the flying corps, and had recently resigned, and had been given an appointment in the Colonies and been sent to Oxford for a course in Colonial Administration, and that later he would be sent to Africa.

Later on, Eugene understood that all of this was probably true, but at the time it sounded like a lie. Or, if it was not a lie, he thought that there was something discreditable and shameful behind it. He thought that if Morison had been in the army flying service, as he said, he had resigned not from choice, but because he had to—because he had been caught cheating at cards, or had not paid his debts, or had been mixed up in some unwholesome mess with a woman. And he thought that if Morison was now going out to Africa it was not so much from choice as by compulsion—because he had to go. In the years that followed Eugene saw that these suspicions were probably unfounded and unjust, but that was the way Morison made him feel.

There was about him somehow the look of the ruined adventurer—shabby and run-down—the face of the actor shining through its mask of deft gentility, the face of the charlatan looking through its visage of sincerity, and the old veined yellow eyes of ruin, hopelessness, and loss looking through all his attitudes of youth, infectious spontaneity, and grace. And for this reason, somehow, the man seemed pitiably gallant, and Eugene liked him.

He and Morison would go to different pubs and drink until the closing time. Morison was using him vilely, and Eugene knew it, and did not care. Not only was he paying for three drinks of every four they drank, but he knew that Morison also sought his companionship because he thought it gave him some immunity from the college proctors, when they made their visits to a pub. And this, in fact, he admitted very frankly, and with a disarming gleefulness.

"You see," he said, "if I came in here by myself I'd get progged, but as long as I'm with you I'm probably all right."

"Why?"

"Oh," he said, with an exultant little chuckle, "because they don't know what to make of it! They've got their eye on *me*, all right," he laughed. "They've been giving me some very fishy looks—but when they see *you* here, they can't be sure—they don't know what to make of it!"

"Why don't they?"

"Oh," he said, "they're puzzled about me, but they *know* about you—they don't dare to bother you because they know you're not in the university."

"How do they know it?" he said resentfully. "I look as much like a student as these Rhodes scholars that you see—yes, and a damned sight more than most of them!"

"Yes, I know," he said tolerantly. "Still, they know you're not. They've got a way of telling."

"A way of telling! Good God, Morison, how have they got a way of telling? Do you mean to say they memorize the names and faces of all the students here, the day the term commences?"

"No, it isn't that. You see, old boy, you don't *belong* to them—I don't know what it is, but they have a way of their own of knowing."

"Do you mean that there's some damned mystery about it?—that they've got some supernatural gift of intuition that tells them when you're a student and when you're not."

"Quite!" he said. "That's just it. That's just the way they do it!" And he looked at Eugene for a moment with his blurred, veinous eyes, and laughed softly, good-naturedly, a little mockingly. "Curious, isn't it?"

"It's more than curious. It's a miracle!"

But it seemed that he was right. For sometimes the proctors would come into a pub where they were drinking, speak amicably to every one, and in a moment more go out again, but Morison would grow very quiet while they were there, and lean upon the bar, and look down at his drink until they left. And as they left they would look curiously at both men again, and their eye would pass Eugene swiftly and indifferently, and for a moment fix on Morison with a fishy and suspicious look. When they were gone he would look up again at the grinning bar-tender and, his ruddy face suffused with laughter, say exultantly:

"Oh, *priceless!* Did you see him when he looked at me?"

"I did," the man behind the counter said. "He didn't half know what to make of it, did he? The other gentleman is not a student, *is* he?"

"No!" Morison fairly shouted, his face crimson, as he pounded on the bar. "That's just the point! And they don't know what to make of it when they see me with him! They can't be sure!" he choked. "They can't be sure!"

And it was Morison who found the house out on the Ventnor road, took lodgings there himself, and gave Eugene the address.

LXX

IN the fall that year, Eugene lived about a mile out from town in a house set back from the Ventnor Road. The house was called a "farm" —Hill-top Farm, or Far-end Farm, or some such name as that— but it was really no farm at all. It was a magnificent house of the weathered gray stone they have in that country, as if in the very quality of the wet heavy air there is the soft thick gray of time itself, sternly yet beautifully soaking down forever on you—and enriching everything it touches—grass, foliage, brick, ivy, the fresh moist color of the people's faces, and old gray stone, with the incomparable weathering of time.

The house was set back off the road at a distance of several hundred yards, possibly a quarter of a mile, and one reached it by means of a road bordered by rows of tall trees which arched above the road, and which made Eugene think of home, at night when the stormy wind howled in their tossed branches. On each side of the road were the rugby fields of two of the colleges and in the afternoon he could look out and down and see the fresh moist green of the playing fields, and watch young college fellows, dressed in their shorts and jerseys, and with their bare knees scurfed with grass and turf as they twisted, struggled, swayed, and scrambled for a moment in the scrimmage-circle, and then broke free, running, dodging, passing the ball as they were tackled, filling the moist air with their sharp cries of sport. They did not have the desperate, the grimly determined, the almost professional earnestness that the college teams at home have; their scurfed and muddy knees, their swaying scrambling scrimmages, the swift breaking away and running, their panting breath and crisp clear voices gave them the appearance of grown-up boys.

Once when Eugene had come up the road in afternoon while they were playing, the ball got away from them and came bounding out into the road before him, and he ran after it to retrieve it, as he used to do when passing a field where boys were playing baseball. One of the players came over to the edge of the field and stood there waiting with his hands upon his hips while Eugene got the ball: he was panting hard, his face was flushed, and his blond hair tousled, but when Eugene threw the ball to him, he said "Thanks very much!" crisply and courteously— getting the same sound into the word *"very"* that they got in "American," a sound that always repelled Eugene a little because it seemed to have some scornful aloofness and patronage in it.

For a moment Eugene watched him as he trotted briskly away on to the field again: the players stood there waiting, panting, casual, their hands upon their hips; he passed the ball into the scrimmage, the pattern swayed, rocked, scrambled, and broke sharply out in open play again, and everything looked incredibly strange, near, and familiar.

Eugene felt that he had always known it, that it had always been his, and that it was as familiar to him as everything he had seen or known in his childhood. Even the texture of the earth looked familiar, and felt moist and firm and springy when he stepped on it, and the stormy howling of the wind in that avenue of great trees at night, was wild and desolate and demented as it had been when he was eight years old and would lie in his bed at night and hear the great oaks howling on the hill above his father's house.

The name of the people in the house was Coulson: he made arrangements with the woman at once to come and live there: she was a tall,
weathered-looking woman of middle age, they talked together in the
hall. The hall was made of marble flags and went directly out onto a
gravelled walk.

The woman was crisp, cheerful, and worldly-looking. She was still
quite handsome. She wore a well-cut skirt of woollen plaid, and a
silk blouse: when she talked she kept her arms folded because the air in
the hall was chilly, and she held a cigarette in the fingers of one hand.
A shaggy brown dog came out and nosed upward toward her hand as
she was talking and she put her hand upon its head and scratched
it gently. When Eugene told her he wanted to move in the next day,
she said briskly and cheerfully:

"Right you are! You'll find everything ready when you get here!"
Then she asked if he was at the university. He said no, and added,
with a feeling of difficulty and naked desolation, that he was a "writer,"
and was coming there to work. He was twenty-four years old.

"Then I am sure that what you do will be *very, very* good!" she
said cheerfully and decisively. "We have had several Americans in the
house before and all of them were very clever! All the Americans we
have had here were very clever people," said the woman. "I'm sure
that you will like it." Then she walked to the door with him to say
good-bye. As they stood there, there was the sound of a small motor-
car coming to a halt and in a moment a girl came swiftly across the
gravel space outside and entered the hall. She was tall, slender, very
lovely, but she had the same bright hard look in her eye that the woman
had, the same faint, hard smile around the edges of her mouth.

"Edith," the woman said in her crisp curiously incisive tone, "this
young man is an American—he is coming here tomorrow." The girl
looked at Eugene for a moment with her hard bright glance, thrust out
a small gloved hand, and shook hands briefly, a swift firm greeting.

"Oh! How d'ye do!" she said. "I hope you will like it here." Then
she went on down the hall, entered a room on the left, and closed the
door behind her.

Her voice had been crisp and certain like her mother's, but it was also
cool, young, and sweet, with music in it, and later as Eugene went down
the road, he could still hear it.

That was a wonderful house, and the people there were wonderful people. Later, he could not forget them. He seemed to have known them all his life, and to know all about their lives. They seemed as familiar to him as his own blood and he knew them with a knowledge that went deep below the roots of thought or memory. They did not talk together often, or tell any of their lives to one another. It is very hard to tell about it—the way they felt and lived together in that house—because it was one of those simple and profound experiences of life which people seem always to have known when it happens to them, but for which there is no language.

And yet, like a child's half-captured vision of some magic country he has known, and which haunts his days with strangeness and the sense of imminent, glorious re-discovery, the word that would unlock it all seemed constantly to be almost on their lips, waiting, just outside the gateway of their memory, just a shape, a phrase, a sound away, the moment that they chose to utter it—but when they tried to say the thing, something faded within their minds like fading light, and something melted within their grasp like painted smoke, and something went forever when they tried to touch it.

The nearest Eugene could come to it was this: In that house he sometimes felt the greatest peace and solitude that he had ever known. But he always knew the other people in the house were there. He could sit in his sitting-room at night and hear nothing but the stormy moaning of the wind outside in the great trees, the small gaseous flare and jet from time to time of the coal fire burning in the grate—and silence, strong living lonely silence that moved and waited in the house at night—and he would always know that they were there.

He did not have to hear them enter or go past his door, nor did he have to hear doors close or open in the house, or listen to their voices: if he had never seen them, heard them, spoken to them, it would have been the same—he would have known they were there.

It was something he had always known, and he had known it would happen to him, and now it was there with all the strangeness and dark mystery of an awaited thing. He knew them, felt them, lived among them with a familiarity that had no need of sight or word or speech. And the memory of that house and of his silent fellowship with all the people there was somehow mixed with an image of dark time. It was one of those sorrowful and unchanging images which, among all the blazing stream of images that passed constantly their stream of fire across his mind, was somehow fixed, detached, and everlasting, full of a sorrow, certitude, and mystery that he could not fathom, but that wore forever on it the old sad light of waning day—a light from which all the heat, the violence, and the substance of furious dusty day had vanished, and which was itself like time, unearthly-of-the-earth, remote, detached, and everlasting.

And that fixed and changeless image of dark time was this: In an old house of time Eugene lived alone, and yet had other people all around him, and they never spoke to him, or he to them. They came and went like silence in the house, but he always knew that they were there. He would be sitting by a window in a room, and he would know then that they were moving in the house, and darkness, sorrow, and strong silence dwelt within them, and their eyes were quiet, full of sorrow, peace, and knowledge, and their faces dark, their tongues silent, and they never spoke. Eugene could not remember how their faces looked, but they were all familiar to him as his father's face, and they had known one another forever, and they lived together in the ancient house of time, dark time; and silence, sorrow, certitude, and peace were in them. Such was the image of dark time that was to haunt his life thereafter, and into which, somehow, his life among the people in that house had passed.

In the house that year there lived, besides Eugene and Morison, the Coulsons, father and mother, and their daughter, and three men who had taken rooms together, and who were employed in a factory where motor-cars were made, two miles from town.

Perhaps the reason that Eugene could never forget these people later and seemed to know them all so well was that there was in all of them something ruined, lost, or broken—some precious and irretrievable quality which had gone out of them and which they could never get back again. Perhaps that was the reason that he liked them all so much, because with ruined people it is either love or hate: there is no middle way. The ruined people that we like are those who desperately have died, and lost their lives because they loved life dearly, and had that grandeur that makes such people spend prodigally the thing they love the best, and risk and lose their lives because life is so precious to them, and die at length because the seeds of life are in them. It is only the people that love life who die in this way—and these are the ruined people that we like.

The people in the house were people who had lost their lives because they loved the earth too well, and somehow had been slain by their hunger. And for this reason Eugene liked them all, and could not forget them later: there seemed to have been some magic which had drawn them all together to that house, as if the house itself were a magnetic centre for lost people.

Certainly, the three men who worked at the motor-car factory had been drawn together for this reason. Two were still young men in their early twenties. The third man was much older. He was a man past forty, his name was Nicholl, he had served in the army during the war and had attained the rank of captain.

He had the spare, alert, and jaunty figure that one often finds in army men, an almost professional military quality that somehow seemed to set his figure upon a horse as if he had grown there, or had spent a lifetime in the cavalry. His face also had the same lean, bitten, professional military quality: his speech, although good-natured and very friendly, was clipped, incisive, jerky, and sporadic, his lean weather-beaten face was deeply, sharply scarred and sunken in the flanks, and he wore a small cropped mustache, and displayed long frontal teeth when he smiled—a spare, gaunt, toothy, yet attractive smile.

His left arm was withered, shrunken, almost useless, part of his hand and two of the fingers had been torn away by the blast or explosion which had destroyed his arm, but it was not this mutilation of the flesh that gave one the sense of a life that had been ruined, lost, and broken irretrievably. In fact, one quickly forgot his physical injury: his figure looked so spare, lean, jaunty, well-conditioned in its energetic fitness that one never thought of him as a cripple, nor pitied him for any disability. No: the ruin that one felt in him was never of the flesh, but of the spirit. Something seemed to have been torn away from his life—it was not the nerve-centres of his arm, but of his soul, that had been destroyed. There was in the man somewhere a terrible dead vacancy and emptiness, and the spare, lean figure that he carried so well seemed only to surround this vacancy like a kind of shell.

He was always smartly dressed in clothes that sat well on his trim spruce figure. He was always in good spirits, immensely friendly in his clipped spare way, and he laughed frequently—a rather metallic cackle which came suddenly and ended as swiftly as it had begun. He seemed, somehow, to have locked the door upon dark care and worry, and to have flung the key away—to have lost, at the same time that he lost more precious things, all the fretful doubts and perturbations of conscience that most men know.

Now, in fact, he seemed to have only one serious project in his life. This was to keep himself amused, to keep himself constantly amused, to get from his life somehow the last atom of entertainment it could possibly yield, and in this project the two young men who lived with him joined in with an energy and earnestness which suggested that their employment in the motor-car factory was just a necessary evil which must be borne patiently because it yielded them the means with which to carry on a more important business, the only one in which their lives were interested—the pursuit of pleasure.

And in the way in which they conducted this pursuit, there was an element of deliberate calculation, concentrated earnestness, and focal intensity of purpose that was astounding, grotesque, and unbelievable, and that left in the mind of one who saw it a formidable and disquieting memory because there was in it almost the madness of desperation, the deliberate intent to seek oblivion, at any cost of effort, from some hideous emptiness of the soul.

Captain Nicholl and his two young companions had a little motor-car so small that it scuttled up the road, shot around and stopped in the gravel by the door with the abruptness of a wound-up toy. It was astonishing that three men could wedge themselves into this midget of a car, but wedge themselves they did, and used it to the end of its capacity, scuttling away to work in it in the morning, and scuttling back again when work was done, and scuttling away to London every Saturday, as if they were determined to wrest from this small motor, too, the last ounce of pleasure to be got from it.

Finally, Captain Nicholl and his two companions had made up an orchestra among them, and this they played in every night when they got home. One of the young men, who was a tall fellow with blond hair which went back in even corrugated waves across his head as if it had been marcelled, played the piano, the other, who was slight and dark, and had black hair, performed upon a saxophone, and Captain Nicholl himself took turns at thrumming furiously on a banjo, or rattling a tattoo upon the complex arrangement of trap drums, bass drums, and clashing cymbals that surrounded him.

They played nothing but American jazz music or sobbing crooner's rhapsodies or nigger blues. Their performance was astonishing. Although it was contrived solely for their own amusement, they hurled themselves into it with all the industrious earnestness of professional musicians employed by a night-club or dance hall to furnish dance music for the patrons. The little dark fellow who played the saxophone would bend and weave prayerfully with his grotesque instrument, as the fat gloating notes came from its unctuous throat, and from time to time he would sway in a half circle, or get up and prance forward and back in rhythm to the music, as the saxophone players in dance orchestras sometimes do.

Meanwhile the tall blond fellow at the piano would sway and bend above the keys, glancing around from time to time with little nods and smiles as if he were encouraging an orchestra of forty pieces or beaming happily at a dance floor crowded with paying customers.

While this was going on, Captain Nicholl would be thrumming madly on the strings of a banjo. He kept the instrument gripped somehow below his withered arm, fingering the end strings with his two good fingers, knocking the tune out with his good right hand, and keeping time with a beating foot. Then with a sudden violent movement he would put the banjo down, snatch up the sticks of the trap drum, and begin to rattle out a furious accompaniment, beating the bass drum with his foot meanwhile, and reaching over to smash cymbals, chimes, and metal rings from time to time. He played with a kind of desperate fury, his mouth fixed in a strange set grin, his bright eyes burning with a sharp wild glint of madness.

They sang as they played, bursting suddenly into the refrain of some popular song with the same calculated spontaneity and spurious enthusiasm of the professional orchestra, mouthing the words of negro blues and jazz with an obvious satisfaction, with an accent which was remarkably good, and yet which had something foreign and inept in it that made the familiar phrases of American music sound almost as strange in their mouths as if an orchestra of skilful patient Japanese were singing them.

They sang:

> "Yes, sir! That's my baby
> Yes, sir! Don't mean maybe
> Yes, sir! That's my baby now!"

or:

> "Oh, it ain't gonna rain no more, no more
> It ain't gonna rain no more"

or:

> "I got dose blu-u-ues"—

the young fellow at the piano rolling his eyes around in a ridiculous.
fashion, and mouthing out the word "blues" extravagantly as he sang
it, the little dark fellow bending forward in an unctuous sweep as the
note came gloating fatly from the horn, and Captain Nicholl swaying
sideways in his chair as he strummed upon the banjo strings, and im-
provising a mournful accompaniment of his own, somewhat as follows:
"I got dose blu-u-ues! Yes, suh! Oh! I got dose blues! Yes, suh! I sure
have got 'em—dose blu-u-ues—blu-u-ues—blu-u-ues!—" his mouth never
relaxing from its strange fixed grin, nor his eyes from their bright set
stare of madness as he swayed and strummed and sang the words that
came so strangely from his lips.

It was a weird scene, an incredible performance, and somehow it
pierced the heart with a wild nameless pity, an infinite sorrow and
regret.

Something precious, irrecoverable had gone out of them, and they
knew it. They fought the emptiness in them with this deliberate, formidable, and mad intensity of a calculated gaiety, a terrifying mimicry
of mirth, and the storm-wind howled around them in dark trees, and
Eugene felt that he had known them forever, and had no words to say to
them—and no door.

LXXI

Once or twice a week Eugene went into town and had tea in the
rooms of a boyhood friend whom he had known at school and who was
now a Rhodes scholar at Merton College. The name of this youth was
Johnny Park: he was a good-natured, industrious, and rather ploddy
boy, and thus far that patient, diligent and well-ordered plan of life
which he had followed since his childhood had brilliantly succeeded.
Formed in a native air, and followed out beneath familiar skies, that
plan had never been interrupted by any doubt or strangeness, by any
serious difficulty, or dark confusion of the soul, or by any of the
unforeseen surprises, shocks, or bewilderments of chance which break
upon our lives with storm-like fury and twist our precious plans awry.

Therefore, when he had been awarded the Rhodes scholarship a few
months before, during his last year at the university, it seemed that
Johnny's plan of life was marching on to its inevitable fulfilment. Every
one had known he would be appointed, it came to pass with an ordained
precision, and Johnny had announced, just as he should, that he would
study "International Law," and everything was right and proper as it

ought to be, and now he was here to march onward toward his shining goal, as he had always done.

But, for the first time in his life, something had gone wrong, something had gone terribly, appallingly amiss, and Johnny did not yet know what it was. Perhaps he never would, but now he was in the greatest trouble and confusion of his life, and he knew it. His voice was still slow, drawling, and good-natured, he was full of kindly warmth and friendliness as he had always been, he had responded quickly, dutifully, to all the customs and observances of the new life—had had gray baggy trousers and tweed coats made at the tailor's shop, had made arrangements for trips and walking-tours upon the Continent with his fellows in vacation time, had met his tutors, found out about the proctors and the penalties, learned the system of the college bills and battels, joined the Union and learned to go out dutifully for sports in the afternoon— he had even learned the mysterious ceremonial of tea and had it in his rooms each afternoon—all this he had learned and done with a punctilious thoroughness, but something had gone wrong.

Everything about Johnny was just as it had always been—his smile, his slow, good-natured voice, his amiable warmth and modesty and friendliness—all was the same with him except his eyes. But the quiet, thoughtful, tranquilly assured expression of his eyes had changed: he had in them the stunned, bewildered look, full of pain and a groping confusion, of a man who has been brutally slugged at the base of the brain, and is not yet certain what has happened to him.

His was an impossible situation, a tragic ordeal of loneliness, strangeness, and bewilderment among all the complex and alien forms of a new life for which nothing in the old had prepared him. Born in a small town in the South, going to school there and at his own State University, he had all his life breathed and lived in a familiar air, heard the familiar words of well-known voices all around him, known and seen nothing but assurance, certitude and success, in everything he planned.

And now all this, even the earth beneath his feet, had melted from him like a wisp of smoke, and he was wandering blindly about in a life as strange to him as Asia, as far as the moon, and knew nowhere to turn, nothing to grasp, no door to enter. In his whole life he had never seen or visited a great city, and then had seen New York just for a day or two, and then for seven days had known for the first time the mystery of the sea and a great ship, and now was here in the green English country, in an ancient town, hurled cruelly, suddenly, naked and unprepared for it as he was, into a life more subtle, complex and confusing than his placid soul had ever dreamed a life could be.

When Eugene asked him if he had stopped in London on his way to Oxford, the look of pain and bewilderment in his eyes had deepened, and he had answered in a slow confused voice:

"We stopped there over night but we never got to see much of it. We came on out here the next morning."

The boy was silent a moment, then he laughed good-naturedly with a troubled and uncertain note:

"It sure looked big enough from what I could see of it. I want to get down there sometime to see what it is like. I guess I've got a lot to learn," he said.

He could remember London like a man who is whirled blindly at night through a huge, limitless, smoky kaleidoscope of sound and sight and moving objects, and this memory of that enormous terrifying age-encrusted web of life—that web without end or measure, which seems blackened, soaked, and saturated not only in the gray light that falls upon it with its weight of eight million lives, but also by the gray light of compacted centuries and all the countless men who lived there and have died—that great gray web appropriately known to seafaring men as "The Smoke" had added measurably to the sense of bewilderment, terror, and naked desolation in him.

And it was pitifully the same with all the rest of them—the little group of Rhodes scholars that gathered together in Johnny's rooms every afternoon, and who seemed to huddle and cling together desperately as if they would try to shape, to resurrect, or to create some little pattern of familiar life, some small oasis of warmth and friendliness and familiar things to which they turned with desperate relief from all the alien and hostile loneliness of a life which they had never entered, which they could never make their own, which stood against them like a wall they could not pass, closed against them like a door they could not open.

Curiously, among this group of five or six Rhodes scholars, which formed the nucleus of the group which met in Johnny's rooms, only two—Johnny and his room-mate, a youth name Price—were first-year men. The others were either in the second or the final year of their appointments, but they seemed to have made no friendships with any one save with a few of the other Rhodes men, to have no other place to go, and to welcome the hospitality of these two boys with a desperate unspoken gratefulness.

There were, besides Johnny and his room-mate Price, three others who came there every day. One was a chunky, red-faced fellow, with coarse undistinguished features, who parted his short crinkly hair in the middle and had come there from Brown University, where he had been a member of the football team. He was in his second year abroad, and no longer wore his little golden football, but a good deal of his self-satisfied complacency was intact: he was thicker of hide and sense than any of the others, and evidently felt that his three years at Oxford were going to give him a kind of pick-and-choose freedom with any kind of employment when he got back home.

He asked Eugene how much he had been paid by the university in New York City where he had been employed as an instructor, and when Eugene told him, smiled tolerantly saying that he wouldn't mind "trying it for a year after I get back until I have a chance to look around." He then informed Eugene graciously that he was open to an offer, and would even be willing to work for no more than they paid *him,* while he "looked around." He added with a little smile:

"I don't imagine that I'll have much trouble: a man with an Oxford degree gets snapped up pretty quick over there, doesn't he? Still," he went on magnanimously, "I wouldn't mind living in New York a year or two until I settle down—so you can give my name to them, if you don't mind."

The other two in the group that came to Johnny's rooms were both third-year men. One was a frail, sensitive, and æsthetic-looking youth named Sterling. Although he came from one of the Western states—Arizona or New Mexico—there was nothing in him to suggest the wildness, openness, and grandeur of his native scenery. Rather, he was a most precious, a most subtle, elegantly sad, quietly bitter and disdainful fellow: he was quietly, fervently, subtly a devoted follower of Mr. T. S. Eliot, and although he revealed his theories sparely, cautiously, and by evasive indirectness, there was in all he said a quiet air of more-in-this-than-meets-the-eye, as if he were saying: "If you want to follow me you've got to learn to read between the lines and get my meaning by what is implied rather than by what is said—since there's no language that can say exactly what my meaning, which is too subtle and exact for any language, is."

He wore about him always this air of elegant, cold, and slightly disdainful restraint, and he had a habit of looking across his thin arched hands with a faint disdainful smile, and listening coldly, saying nothing, while the others talked, as if the waste-land chatter of their tongues, the waste-land vacancy of their lost waste-land souls was something that he knew he must endure, but would endure with his cold faint disdainful smile, his soul steeped in cold and patient weariness till death should mercifully release him.

The other man was a Jew named Fried and that man Eugene could never forget. Eugene didn't know where he came from, how he got there, who made him a Rhodes scholar, but he knew that of them all, save Johnny, he was the only one who had maintained his integrity, the only one who did not have a spurious, fearful, uneasily evasive quality, the only one who came out with it, the whole packed load of bitterness and hate within him, the only one who had remained himself.

Perhaps it was a bad self to remain: it was certainly a self that was lacking in charm, that had the aggressive, abusive, curiously unrighteous quality of his race—but there he was, terrifically himself and unashamed of it—with a naked formidable integrity of self that blazed with a hard and naked light of a cut jewel, and that Eugene could never forget even when the characters of the rest of them had grown blurred and shapeless and obscure.

Eugene didn't know where he came from, but he was sure it was from one of the great cities of the Atlantic seaboard—from New York, Boston, Baltimore or Philadelphia. He had seen his face, his figure, and his kind a million times upon the pavements of those cities and incredibly now, that dark unhappy face which never before had seemed to him to be a face at all, nothing but a tidal flood of nameless faces, that strident and abusive tongue which had never before seemed to him to be a single tongue, but just a common, nameless, and unnumbered ugliness of rasping voices, an anathema of bitter cries and harsh derisions— a constant phrase, a dissonance, a weather of the city's life—all that had been nameless, faceless, characterless and obscure—the look, the sound, the smell of the man-swarm ciphers of the city as dark-eyed, dark-faced, and bitter-tongued they swarmed along the pavements of the cities—all this, in that strange place, was suddenly, weirdly, resumed into a single character—a character that was hard, bitter, unforgettably itself, and that no change of sky or land or custom, nor the huge impact of all the alien and formidable pageantry of the earth, could ever alter by a jot.

Theirs was a wretched, hopeless, lonely life, a futile, feeble, barren life, an impossible, groping, wretched insecure life—and Fried was the only one of them to meet it, to admit it, to denounce it with all the bitterness of his bitter soul, and to remain himself against it. The rest were frightened, bitter, lonely, homesick, and afraid—afraid of everything, afraid of their own loneliness and their own dismal unsuccess, afraid to confess the desolation of their souls, the bitter disappointment of their hopes, afraid to laugh too loud, to show too much exuberance or enthusiasm for anything, lest some one should consider them a "hearty," and pin that feared and hated label on them.

They were afraid to express any native extravagance in dress, speech or manner lest they be branded as "bounders," afraid to talk their natural speech in their own manner lest they seem too crudely, raucously and offensively American, and afraid to imitate too studiously the language of the nation for fear that their own fellows would sneer at them for servile snobbishness, for "speaking with an English accent." Thus, caught in the web of a thousand fears, the meshes of a thousand impossible restraints, trying to maintain their lives, their characters, their native dignities even while they tried to subdue them by a thousand small half-mimicries, to be themselves even while they tried to shape themselves to something else, their characters finally, strained through the impossible weavings of this mad design, teetering frantically to maintain a crazy balance on a thousand wires, were reduced at last to the consistency of blubber—and trying to be everything, they succeeded finally in being nothing.

Oh, it was a wretched, futile, hopeless kind of life, and in their hearts they knew it, but could only speak casually, smile feebly, speak falsely, yet never lay their hearts bare boldly, and admit the truth. None of them liked Fried, they were ashamed of him, they turned on him at times in force, argued with him, denounced him, jeered at him, but at the bottom of their hearts they had a strange, secret, and unwilling respect for him, and finally grew silent and listened when he talked.

It was astonishing to watch the effect of that man's bitter tirades on that forlorn group. For where at first they would protest, remonstrate, sharply caution him, laugh uneasily and look fearfully toward the door as his harsh rasping voice mounted and grew high and snarling with its packed anathema of bitterness and hate, they would at length grow silent and look at him with fascinated eyes, and listen to that snarling and savage indictment with a kind of feeding gluttony of satisfaction, as if into that single naked and abusive tongue had been packed the whole huge weight of misery that had sweltered in their hearts, but to which they had never dared, themselves, to give utterance.

Eugene had asked Sterling how much longer he would remain abroad, and he had answered:

"Just ten months more. This is my last year. I am going home next August." He was silent for a moment, then he added with a faint, regretful smile: "In another year, I suppose, I'll be wondering if all this has ever happened. It will seem strange and beautiful," he said softly, "like some impossible dream!"

"Yeah!" snarled Fried, with a harsh interruption at this point. "An impossible dream! Jesus! An impossible nightmare!—that's what you'd better say!"

Sterling looked at him silently for a moment over his thin arched hands. He smiled faintly, disdainfully, and made no answer. In a moment he turned quietly to Eugene again, and dismissing the other man with the cold contempt of silence, continued:

"Sometimes it's hard for me to realize I ever lived there. Can there be such a place as America, I wonder?" he said with a sad faint smile. "After all this," he gestured slightly, pausing, "it will seem so strange to be a part of," he paused carefully "—*that* again. . . . Skyscrapers, subways, elevated trains—" he paused again, with a faint smile— "Tell me," he said, turning toward Eugene, "do such things *really* exist?"

"Do they *really* exist!" Fried now snarled with a jeering laugh. "Do they *really* exist! I'll tell the cock-eyed world that they exist!" he rasped. "You can bet your —— that they exist! . . . Do they exist!" he snorted to himself derisively, "Jesus!"

Sterling stared coldly at him and said nothing. For a moment Fried's hard, dark, embittered face, the feverish eyes, stared balefully at the fragile and sensitive face of the other youth, set disdainfully against him over his arched hands.

"Where do you get that stuff?" Fried said at length with harsh contempt. "You may kid these guys who never saw the place until a week ago, but you don't kid me, Sterling. Christ! I know what kind of a dream it's been—and so do you!"

Sterling did not deign to answer, but continued to look at him with cold faint disdain, and after another baleful and disgusted stare, Fried rasped out bitterly again:

"I suppose it was a dream your first term here when you tried to suck around those English guys and you thought they were going to take you right into the family, didn't you?" he sneered. "You thought you were sittin' pretty, didn't you? You were goin' to pal around with the Duke of What's-His-Name and get invited home wit' him for the Christmas holidays and make a big play for his sister, weren't you! Yes, you were!" He jeered, "You saw how far it got you, didn't you? Those guys took you for a ride and played you for a sucker, an' when they'd had all the fun wit' you they could, they dropped you like a ton of bricks! You thought that you were pretty wise, didn't you?" he snarled bitterly. "You thought that you were goin' places, didn't you? You were goin' to do something big, you were! Well, I'll tell you what you did! You handed them a laugh—see? You handed those guys a great big laugh—yes! a laugh!" he shouted violently. "And, I'll tell you something else! They're still laughin' at you! I saw you, Sterling. I know what you did. But you didn't see me, did you? Couldn't see me in those days, could you?"

"I can't see you now," said Sterling coldly. "I never could see you!"

"Is that so!" the Jew said bitterly. "Now isn't that too bad! ... Well, I'll tell you one time that you saw me, Sterling. . . . That's when those guys had left you flat. . . . You could see me then, couldn't you? You don't remember, do you?" he jeered. "Well, I'll tell you when it was. . . . It was when you came back here that year for the spring term and you found they didn't know you when you went around. It was when your tail was dragging the ground and you didn't have a friend in the world—you could see me then, all right. Couldn't you? . . . I wasn't good enough before when you were trying to break into High Society—but I was good enough to see, after they gave you the big go-by, wasn't I? . . . Sure! Sure!" he said with an air of derision, addressing himself more quietly now to the rest of the group. "I usta go by this guy when he was running around wit' his English friends— and did he see me?" he jibed savagely. "Not so you could notice it! . . . 'Who is that common person who just spoke to you, Mr. Sterling?' 'O, that! O, I cannot say, old chap—some low fellow that was on the boat wit' me when I came ovah! . . . Really cawn't recall his name! A beastly boundah, I believe!' . . . Sure! Sure!" he nodded. "That was it! High-hattin' me, you know! I wasn't good enough! And all the time these English guys were laughin' up their sleeve at him!"

They had been stunned by the snarling fury of his assault, silenced by the hypnotic compulsion of his dark, hard face, his feverish eyes, the rasping bitterness of his voice that at the end grew strident, high, and gasping from his effort to release in one explosive tirade the whole packed weight of misery, disappointment, and defeat that sweltered poisonously in his heart. Now, however, as he paused there, dark and hard and full of bitterness, surveying them balefully with toxic eyes, silenced by lack of breath rather than by lack of further curses, they gathered themselves together and went for him in a mass.

In another moment the last vestige of restraint, gentlemanly decorum, urbane and tolerant sophistication with which they had clothed themselves had vanished, and they were yelping, snarling, shouting, accusing and denying, inextricably mixed-up in one general and inglorious dog-fight; taunts, curses, insults, and indictments filled the air, all of them were shouting at the same time, and out of that roaring brawl all one could decipher was the ragged barbs and ends of their abuse—a tumult of bitter and strident voices characterized by such phrases as—"You never belonged here in the first place!" "It's fellows like you who give all the rest of us a bad name!" "Why the hell should the rest of us have to suffer for it because you talk and act like an East Side gangster?" "They think all Americans are a bunch of roughnecks because they meet a few like you." "Ah, g'wan! youse guys! You give me a pain. You all feel the same way as I do but none of you has guts enough to say so!" "You're just sore because these English boys never had anything to do with you —that's all you're sore about!" "Yeah? They had a hell of a lot to do wit' you, didn't they?—even if you did try to talk wit' an English accent." "You're a damned liar! I never tried to talk with an English accent!" "Sure you did! Everybody hoid you! You coulda cut yoeh accent wit' a hatchet! You were tryin' to suck aroun' that gang at Christ's the first year you were here!" "Who says I was?" "I say so—that's who! You an' Tommy Woodson both—" "Don't mix my name with Tommy Woodson, now! You're not going to include me with that horse's neck!" "Oh, yeah? Since when did you staht callin' him a horse's neck?" "I always called him one! He *is* one!" "Sure he is—but you didn't think so, did you, that first year that you was heah? You was pallin' around wit' him an' wouldn't have anything to do wit' the rest of us! You thought it was goin' to get you somewhere, didn't you? You saw how quick he dropped you after he got in wit' those guys at Christ's! He gave you the big go-by then, didn't he? That's when you stahted callin' him a horse's neck!" "It's a lie! I didn't!" "Sure you did!"

The snarling medley of bitter tongues rose, mounted; they vented their weight of insult, misery, and reproach on one another and at length subsided, checked by exhaustion rather than by some more charitable cause. And as the tumult died away Sterling, two spots of color burning on his pallid face, goaded completely from his former affectation of coldly elegant disdain, could be heard saying to Fried in a high, excited, almost hysterical tone:

"The kind of attack you make is simply stupid! It doesn't get you anywhere! And it's so crude! So raucous! After all, there's no reason why you've always got to be so raucous!"—the way he said the word was "raw-kus," his thin hands were trembling, and the two spots of color burned fiercely in his thin pale face; in this and the bitter way in which he said "raucous" there was finally something pitiable and futile.

And at the end, when all their strident cries had died away, the dark embittered visage of the Jew surveyed them wearily, and held them in its sway again. For as if conceding now what was most evident—that his savage, disappointed spirit had a hard integrity, an unashamed conviction, an ugly, snarling but most open courage which they lacked, they sat there, and looked at him in silence, somehow conveying by that silence a sense of bitter and unwilling respect for him, a final admission of agreement and defeat.

And he, too, when he spoke now, spoke wearily, with a bitter resignation, as if he realized the futility of his victory over them, the futility of hurling further insults, oaths, and accusations at people who knew the bitter truth of his complaint as well as he.

"Nah!" he said quietly in a moment, with this same note of bitter, weary resignation in his voice. "To hell wit' it! W'at t' hell's the use of tryin' to pretend it isn't so? You guys all know the way things are! You come over here and you think you're sittin' pretty right on top of the world! You think these guys are goin' to throw their ahms around your neck and kiss you, because they love Americans so much! And what happens?" He laughed bitterly. "Are you telling *me*? Christ! You can stay here for three years and none of them will ever give a tumble to you! You can eat your heart out for all they care, and when you leave here you'll know no more about them than when you came. And what does it getcha? What's it all about? W'at t' hell do you get out of it that's so wonderful?"

"I thought," one of the first-year men suggested mildly, and a trifle piously, as if he were quoting one of the articles of faith, "that you were supposed to get out of it a better understanding of the relations between the two great English-speaking nations."

"The two great English-speaking nations," Fried answered harshly with a jeering laugh. "Jesus! That's a good one! *What* two English-speaking nations do you mean?" he went on belligerently. "England and what other country?" he demanded. "You don't think *we* speak the same language as *they* do, do you? Christ! The first year I was here they might have been talkin' Siamese so far as I was concerned! It wasn't any language that I'd evah hoid before. . . . Yeah, I know," he went on wearily in a moment, "they fed me all that bunk, too, before I came over. . . . English-speakin' nations! . . . Goin' back to your old home! our old home. For Christ's sake!" he said bitterly. "Christ! It never was a home to me! I'd have felt more at home if they had sent me to Siberia! . . . Home! The rest of you guys can make believe it's home if you want to! . . . I know what you'll do," he muttered. "You'll stick it out and hate it like the rest of them. . . . Then you'll go back home an' high-hat every one and tell them all how wonderful it was, and what a fine time you had when you were here, and how you hated to leave it! . . . Not for me! I'm goin' home where I can see some one that I know sometime who's not too good to talk to me. . . and talk to some one who understands what I'm tryin' to say once in a while . . . and pay my little nickel for the big ride in the subway . . . and listen to the kids playin' in the street . . . an' go to sleep wit' the old elevated bangin' in my ears! . . . That's home!" he cried. "That's home enough for me."

"A hell of a home," said some one quietly.

"Don't I know it!" snarled the man. "But it's the only home I got! It's better than no home at all!"

And for a moment he smoked darkly, bitterly, in silence.

"Nah! To hell wit' it!" he muttered. "To hell wit' it! I'll be glad when it's all over! I'm sorry that I ever came!"

And he was silent then, and the others looked at him, and had no more to say, and were silent.

LXXII

THERE were four in the Coulson family: the father, a man of fifty years, the mother, somewhere in the middle forties, a son, and a daughter, Edith, a girl of twenty-two who lived in the house with her parents. Eugene never met the son: he had completed his course at Oxford a year or two before, and had gone down to London where he was now employed. During the time Eugene lived there the son did not come home.

They were a ruined family. How that ruin had fallen on them, what it was, Eugene never knew, for no one ever spoke to him about them. But the sense of their disgrace, of a shameful inexpiable dishonor, for which there was no pardon, from which there could never be redemption, was overwhelming. In the most astonishing way Eugene found out about it right away, and yet he did not know what they had done, and no one ever spoke a word against them.

Rather, the mention of their name brought silence, and in that silence there was something merciless and final, something that belonged to the temper of the country, and that was far more terrible than any open word of scorn, contempt, or bitter judgment could have been, more savage than a million strident, whispering, or abusive tongues could be, because the silence was unarguable, irrevocable, complete, as if a great door had been shut against their lives forever.

Everywhere Eugene went in town, the people knew about them, and said nothing—saying everything—when he spoke their names. He found this final, closed, relentless silence everywhere—in tobacco, wine, and tailor shops, in book stores, food stores, haberdashery stores—wherever he bought anything and gave the clerk the address to which it was to be delivered, they responded instantly with this shut finality of silence, writing the name down gravely, sometimes saying briefly, "Oh! Coulson's!" when he gave them the address, but more often saying nothing.

But whether they spoke or simply wrote the name down without a word, there was always this quality of instant recognition, this obdurate, contemptuous finality of silence, as if a door had been shut—a door that could never again be opened. Somehow Eugene disliked them more for this silence than if they had spoken evilly: there was in it something ugly, knowing, and triumphant that was far more evil than any slyly whispering confidence of slander, or any open vituperation of abuse, could be. It seemed somehow to come from all the vile and uncountable small maggotry of the earth, the cautious little hatreds of a million nameless ciphers, each puny, pallid, trivial in himself, but formidable because he added his tiny beetle's ball of dung to the mountainous accumulation of ten million others of his breed.

It was uncanny how these clerk-like faces, grave and quiet, that never spoke a word, or gave a sign, or altered their expression by a jot, when

Eugene gave them the address, could suddenly be alive with something secret, foul, and sly, could be more closed and secret than a door, and yet instantly reveal the naked, shameful, and iniquitous filth that welled up from some depthless source. He could not phrase it, give a name to it, or even see a certain sign that it was there, any more than he could put his hand upon a wisp of fading smoke, but he always knew when it was there, and somehow when he saw it his heart went hard and cold against the people who revealed it, and turned with warmth and strong affection towards the Coulson family.

There was, finally, among these grave clerk-like faces, one face that Eugene could never forget thereafter, a face that seemed to resume into its sly suave surfaces all of the nameless abomination of evil in the world, for which he had no name, for which there was no handle he could grasp, no familiar places or edges he could get his hands upon, which slid phantasmally, oilily, and smokily away whenever he tried to get his hands upon it. But it was to haunt his life for years in dreams of hatred, madness, and despair that found no frontal wall for their attack, no word for their vituperation, no door for the shoulder of his hate—an evil world of phantoms, shapes, and whispers that was yet as real as death, as ever-present as man's treachery, but that slid away from him like smoke whenever he tried to meet, or curse, or strangle it.

This face was the face of a man in a tailor shop, a fitter there, and Eugene could have battered that foul face into a bloody pulp, distilled the filthy refuse of that ugly life out of the fat swelling neck and through the murderous grip of his fingers if he could only have found a cause, a logic, and a provocation for doing it. And yet he never saw the man but twice, and briefly, and there had been nothing in his suave, sly careful speech to give offense.

Edith Coulson had sent Eugene to the tailor's shop: he needed a suit and when he asked her where to go to have it made, she had sent him to this place because her brother had his suits made there and liked it. The fitter was a heavy shambling man in his late thirties: he had receding hair, which he brushed back flat in a thick pompadour; yellowish, somewhat bulging eyes; a coarse heavy face, loose-featured, red, and sensual; a sloping meaty jaw, and large discolored buck-teeth which showed unpleasantly in a mouth that was always half open. It was, in fact, the mouth that gave his face its sensual, sly, and ugly look, for a loose and vulgar smile seemed constantly to hover about its thick coarse edges, to be deliberately, slyly restrained, but about to burst at any moment into an open, evil, foully sensual laugh. There was always about his mouth this ugly suggestion of a loose, corrupt, and evilly jubilant mirth, and yet he never laughed or smiled.

The man's speech had this same quality. It was suave and courteous, but even in its most urbane assurances, there was something non-committal, sly, and jeering, something that slid away from you, and was never to be grasped, a quality that was faithless, tricky and unwholesome. When Eugene came for the final fitting it was obvious that he had done as cheap and shoddy a job as he could do; the suit was vilely botched and skimped, sufficient cloth had not been put into it, and now it was too late to remedy the defect.

Yet, the fitter gravely pulled the vest down till it met the trousers, tugged at the coat, and pulled the thing together where it stayed until Eugene took a breath or moved a muscle, when it would all come apart again, the collar bulging outward from the shoulder, the skimpy coat and vest crawling backward from the trousers, leaving a hiatus of shirt and belly that could not now be remedied by any means.

Then, gravely he would pull the thing together again, and in his suave, yet oily, sly, and non-committal phrases say:

"Um! Seems to fit you very well."

Eugene was choking with exasperation, and knew that he had been done, because he had foolishly paid them half the bill already, and now knew no way out of it except to lose what he had paid, and get nothing for it, or take the thing, and pay the balance. He was caught in a trap, but even as he jerked at the coat and vest speechlessly, seized his shirt, and thrust the gaping collar in the fitter's face, the man said smoothly,

"Um! Yes! The collar. Should think all that will be all right. Still needs a little alteration." He made some chalk marks on Eugene. "Should think you'll find it fits you very well when the tailor makes the alterations."

"When will the suit be ready?"

"Um. Should think you ought to have it by next Tuesday. Yes. I think you'll find it ready by Tuesday."

The sly words slid away from the boy like oil: there was nothing to pin him to or grasp him by, the yellowed eyes looked casually away and would not look at Eugene, the sensual face was suavely grave, the discolored buck-teeth shone obscenely through the coarse loose mouth, and the suggestion of the foul loose smile was so pronounced now that it seemed that at any moment the man would have to turn away with heavy trembling shoulders, and stifle the evil jeering laugh that was welling up in him. But he remained suavely grave and non-committal to the end, and when Eugene asked him if he should come again to try it on, he said, in the same oily tone, never looking at him:

"Um. Shouldn't think that would be necessary. Could have it delivered to you when it's ready. What is your address?"

"The Far End Farm—it's on the Ventnor Road."

"Oh! Coulson's!" He never altered his expression, but the suggestion of the obscene smile was so pronounced that now it seemed he would have to come out with it. Instead, he only said:

"Um. Yes. Should think it could be delivered to you there on Tuesday. If you'll just wait a moment I'll ask the tailor."

Gravely, suavely, he took the coat from Eugene and walked back towards the tailor's room with the coat across his arm. In a moment, the boy heard sly voices whispering, laughing slyly, then the tailor saying:

"Where does he live?"

"Coulson's!" said the fitter chokingly, and now the foul awaited laugh did come—high, wet, slimy, it came out of that loose mouth, and choked and whispered wordlessly, and choked again, and mingled then with the tailor's voice in sly, choking, whispering intimacy, and then gasped faintly, and was silent. When the man came out again his coarse face was red and swollen with foul secret merriment, his heavy shoulders trembled slightly, he took out his handkerchief and wiped it once across his loose half-opened mouth, and with that gesture wiped the slime of laughter from his lips. Then he came toward Eugene suave, grave, and courteous, evilly composed, as he said smoothly:

"Should think we'll have that for you by next Tuesday, sir."

"Can the tailor fix it so it's going to fit?"

"Um. Should think you'll find that everything's all right. You ought to have it Tuesday afternoon."

He was not looking at Eugene: the yellowish bulging eyes were staring casually, indefinitely, away, and his words again had slid away from the boy like oil. He could not be touched, approached, or handled: there was nothing to hold him by, he had the impregnability of smoke or a ball of mercury.

As Eugene went out the door, the tailor began to speak to some one in the shop, Eugene heard low words and whispered voices, then, gasping, the word "Coulson's!" and the slimy, choking, smothered laughter as the street-door closed behind him. He never saw the man again. He never forgot his face.

That was a fine house: the people in it were exiled, lost, and ruined people, and Eugene liked them all. Later, he never knew why he felt so close to them, or remembered them with such warmth and strong affection.

He did not see the Coulsons often and rarely talked to them. Yet he felt as familiar and friendly with them all as if he had known them all his life. The house was wonderful as no other house he had ever known because they all seemed to be living in it together with this strange speechless knowledge, warmth, and familiarity, and yet each was as private, secret, and secure in his own room as if he occupied the house alone.

Coulson himself Eugene saw least of all: they sometimes passed each other going in or out the door, or in the hall: Coulson would grunt "Morning," or "Good Day," in a curt blunt manner, and go on, and yet he always left Eugene with a curious sense of warmth and friendliness. He was a stocky well-set man with iron-gray hair, bushy eyebrows, and a red weathered face which wore the open color of the country on it, but also had the hard dull flush of the steady heavy drinker.

Eugene never saw him drunk, and yet he was never sober: he was one of those men who have drunk themselves past any hope of drunkenness, who are soaked through to the bone with alcohol, saturated, tanned, weathered in it so completely that it could never be distilled out of their blood again. Yet, even in this terrible excess one felt a kind of grim control—the control of a man who is enslaved by the very thing that he controls, the control of the opium eater who cannot leave his drug but measures out his dose with a cold calculation, and finds the limit of his capacity, and stops there, day by day.

But somehow this very sense of control, this blunt ruddy style of the country gentleman which distinguished his speech, his manner, and his dress, made the ruin of his life, the desperate intemperance of drink that smouldered in him like a slow fire, steadily, nakedly apparent. It was as if, having lost everything, he still held grimly to the outer forms of a lost standard, a ruined state, when the inner substance was destroyed.

And it was this way with all of them—with Mrs. Coulson and the girl, as well: their crisp, clipped friendly speech never deviated into intimacy, and never hinted at any melting into confidence and admission. Upon the woman's weathered face there hovered, when she talked, the same faint set grin that Captain Nicholl had, and her eyes were bright and hard, a little mad, impenetrable, as were his. And the girl, although young and very lovely, sometimes had this same look when she greeted any one or paused to talk. In that look there was nothing truculent, bitter, or defiant: it was just the look of three people who had gone down together, and who felt for one another neither bitterness nor hate, but that strange companionship of a common disgrace, from which love has vanished, but which is more secret, silent, and impassively resigned to its fatal unity than love itself could be.

And that hard bright look also said this plainly to the world: "We ask for nothing from you now, we want nothing that you offer us. What is ours is ours, what we are we are, you'll not intrude nor come closer than we let you see!"

Coulson might have been a man who had been dishonored and destroyed by his women, and who took it stolidly, saying nothing, and drank steadily from morning until night, and had nothing for it now but drink and silence and acceptance. Yet Eugene never knew for certain that this was so, it just seemed inescapable, and was somehow legible not only in the slow smouldering fire that burned out through his rugged weathered face, but also in the hard bright armor of the women's eyes, the fixed set grin around their lips when they were talking—a grin that was like armor, too. And Morison, who had referred to Coulson, chuckling, as a real "bottle-a-day-man," had added quietly, casually, in his brief, indefinite, but blurted-out suggestiveness of speech:

"I think the old girl's been a bit of a bitch in her day.... Don't know, of course, but has the look, hasn't she?" In a moment he said quietly, "Have you talked to the daughter yet?"

"Once or twice. Not for long."

"Ran into a chap at Magdalen other day who knows her," he said casually. "He used to come out here to see her." He glanced swiftly, slyly at Eugene, his face reddening a little with laughter. "Pretty hot, I gather," he said quietly, smiling, and looked away. It was night: the fire burned cheerfully in the grate, the hot coals spurting in small gaseous flares from time to time. The house was very quiet all around them. Outside they could hear the stormy wind in the trees along the road. Morison flicked his cigarette into the fire, poured out a drink of whiskey into a glass, saying as he did so: "I say, old chap, you don't mind

if I take a spot of this before I go to bed, do you?" Then he shot some
seltzer in the glass, and drank. And Eugene sat there, without a
word, staring sullenly into the fire, dumbly conscious of the flood of sick
pain and horror which the casual foulness of the man's suggestion had
aroused, stubbornly trying to deny now that he was thinking of the
girl all the time.

LXXIII

One night, as Eugene was coming home along the dark road that
went up past the playing field to the house, and that was bordered on
each side by grand trees whose branches seemed to hold at night all the
mysterious and demented cadences of storm, he came upon her suddenly
standing in the shadow of a tree. It was one of the grand wild nights
that seemed to come so often in the autumn of that year: the air was
full of a fine stinging moisture, not quite rain, and above the stormy
branches of the trees he could see the sky, wild, broken, full of scudding
clouds through which at times the moon drove in and out with a kind
of haggard loneliness. By that faint, wild, and broken light, he could
see the small white oval of the girl's face—somehow even more lovely
now just because he could not see it plainly. And he could see as well
the rough gleaming bark of the tree against which she leaned.

As he approached, he saw her thrust her hand into the pocket of her
overcoat, a match flared, and for a moment he saw Edith plainly, the
small flower of her face framed in the wavering light as she lowered her
head to light her cigarette.

The light went out, he saw the small respiring glow of her cigarette before the white blur of her face, he passed her swiftly, head bent,
without speaking, his heart filled with the sense of strangeness and
wonder which the family had roused in him.

Then he walked on up the road, muttering to himself. The house
was dark when he got there, but when he entered his sitting-
room the place was still warmly and softly luminous with the glow
of hot coals in the grate. He turned the lights on, shut the door behind him, and hurled several lumps of coal upon the bedded coals. In a
moment the fire was blazing and crackling cheerfully, and getting a
kind of comfort and satisfaction from this activity, he flung off his
coat, went over to the sideboard, poured out a stiff drink of scotch
from a bottle there, and coming back to the fire, flung himself into a
chair, and began to stare sullenly into the dancing flames.

How long he sat there in this stupor of sullen and nameless fury, he did not know, but he was sharply roused at length by footsteps light and rapid on the gravel, shocked into a start of surprise by a figure that appeared suddenly at one of the French windows that opened directly from his sitting-room onto the level sward of velvet lawn before the house.

He peered through the glass for a moment with an astonished stare before he recognized the face of Edith Coulson. He opened the doors at once, she came in quickly, smiling at his surprise, and at the glass which he was holding foolishly, half-raised, in his hand.

He continued to look at her with an expression of gape-mouthed astonishment and in a moment became conscious of her smiling glance, the cool sweet assurance of her young voice.

"I say!" she was saying cheerfully, "what a lucky thing to find you up! I came away without any key—I should have had to wake the whole house up—so when I saw your light!" she concluded briskly, "—what luck! I hope you don't mind."

"Why no-o, no," Eugene stammered foolishly, still staring dumbly at her. "No—no-o—not at all," he blundered on. Then suddenly coming to himself with a burst of galvanic energy, he shut the windows, pushed another chair before the fire, and said:

"Won't you sit down and have a drink before you go?"

"Thanks," she said crisply. "I will—yes. What a jolly fire you have." As she talked she took off her coat and hat swiftly and put them on a chair. Her face was flushed and rosy, beaded with small particles of rain, and for a moment she stood before the mirror arranging her hair, which had been tousled by the wind.

The girl was slender, tall, and very lovely with the kind of beauty they have when they are beautiful—a beauty so fresh, fair, and delicate that it seems to be given to just a few of them to compensate for all the grimly weathered ugliness of the rest. Her voice was also lovely, sweet, and musical, and when she talked all the notes of tenderness and love were in it. But she had the same hard bright look in her eye that her mother had, the faint set smile around her mouth: as they stood there talking she was standing very close to him, and he could smell the fragrance of her hair, and felt an intolerable desire to put his hand upon hers and was almost certain she would not draw away. But the hard bright look was in her eye, the faint set smile around her mouth, and he did nothing.

"What'll you have?" Eugene said. "Whiskey?"

"Yes, thank you," she said with the same sweet crisp assurance with which she always spoke, "and a splash of soda." He struck a match and held it for her while she lit the cigarette she was holding in her hand, and in a moment returned to her with the drink. Then she sat down, crossed her legs, and for a moment puffed thoughtfully at her cigarette as she stared into the fire. The storm wind moaned in the great trees along the road, and near the house, and suddenly a swirl of rain and wind struck the windows with a rattling blast. The girl stirred a little in her chair, restlessly, shivered:

"Listen!" she said. "What a night! Horrible weather we have here, isn't it?"

"I don't know. I don't like the fog and rain so well. But this—the way it is tonight—" he nodded toward the window— "I like it."

She looked at him for a moment.

"Oh," she said non-committally. "You do." Then, as she sipped her drink, she looked curiously about the room, her reflective glance finally resting on his table, where there was a great stack of the ledgers in which he wrote.

"I say," she cried again, "what are you doing with all those big books there?"

"I write in them."

"Really?" she said, in a surprised tone. "I should think it'd be an awful bother carrying them around when you travel?"

"It is. But it's the best way I've found of keeping what I do together."

"Oh," she said, as before, and continued to stare curiously at him with her fair, lovely young face, the curiously hard, bright, and unrevealing glance of her eye. "I see. . . . But why do you come to such a place as this to write?" she said presently. "Do you like it here?"

"I do. As well as any place I've ever known."

"Oh! . . . I should think a writer would want a different kind of place."

"What kind?"

"Oh—I don't know—Paris—London—some place like that, where there is lots of life—people—fun—I should think you'd work better in a place like that."

"I work better here."

"But don't you get awfully fed up sitting in here all day long and writing in those enormous books?"

"I do, yes."

"I should think you would . . . I should think you'd want to get away from it sometimes."

"Yes. I do want to—every day—almost all the time."

"Then why don't you?" she said crisply. "Why don't you go off some week-end for a little spree? I should think it'd buck you up no end."

"It would—yes. Where should I go?"

"Oh, Paris, I suppose. . . . Or London! London!" she cried. "London is quite jolly if you know it."

"I'm afraid I don't know it."

"But you've *been* to London," she said in a surprised tone.

"Oh, yes. I lived there for several months."

"Then you know London," she said impatiently. "Of course you do."

"I'm afraid I don't know it very well. I don't know many people there—and after all, that's the thing that counts, isn't it?"

She looked at Eugene curiously for a moment, with the faint hard smile around the edges of her lovely mouth.

"—Should think that might be arranged," she said with a quiet, an enigmatic humor. Then, more directly, she added. "That shouldn't be difficult at all. Perhaps I could introduce you to some people."

"That would be fine. Do you know many people there?"

"Not many," she said. "I go there—whenever I can." She got up with a swift decisive movement, put her glass down on the mantel and cast her cigarette into the fire. Then she faced Eugene, looking at him with a curiously bold, an almost defiant directness, and she fixed him with this glance for a full moment before she spoke.

"Good-night," she said. "Thanks awfully for letting me in—and for the drink."

"Good-night," Eugene said, and she was gone before he could say more, and he had closed the door behind her, and he could hear her light swift footsteps going down the hall and up the steps. And then there was nothing in the house but sleep and silence, and storm and darkness in the world around him.

Mrs. Coulson came into Eugene's room just once or twice while he was there. One morning she came in, spoke crisply and cheerfully, and walked over to the window, looking out upon the velvet lawn and at the dreary, impenetrable gray of foggy air. Although the room was warm, and there was a good fire burning in the grate, she clasped her arms together as she looked, and shivered a little:

"Wretched weather, isn't it?" she said in her crisp tones, her gaunt weathered face, and toothy mouth touched by the faint fixed grin as she looked out with her bright hard stare. "Don't you find it frightfully depressing? Most Americans do," she said, getting a sharp disquieting sound into the word.

"Yes. I do, a little. We don't have this kind of weather very often. But this is the time of year you get it here, isn't it? I suppose you're used to it by now?"

"Used to it?" she said crisply, turning her gaze upon him. "Not at all. I've known it all my life but I'll never get used to it. It is a wretched climate."

"Still, you wouldn't feel at home anywhere else, would you? You wouldn't want to live outside of England?"

"No?" she said, staring at him with the faint set grin around her toothy mouth. "Why do you think so?"

"Because your home is here."

"My home? My home is where they have fine days, and where the sun is always shining."

"I wouldn't like that. I'd get tired of sunlight all the time. I'd want some gray days and some fog and snow."

"Yes, I suppose you would. But then, you've been used to having fine days all your life, haven't you? With us, it's different. I'm so fed up with fog and rain that I could do without it nicely, thank you, if I never saw it again. . . . . I don't think you could ever understand how much the sunlight means to us," she said slowly. She turned, and for a moment looked out the window. "Sunlight—warmth—fine days forever! Warmth everywhere—in the earth, the sky, in the lives of the people all around you, nothing but warmth and sunlight and fine days!"

"And where would you go to find all that? Does it exist?"

"Oh, of course!" she said crisply and good-naturedly, turning to him again. "There's only one place to live—only one country where I want to live."

"Where is that?"

"Italy," she said. "That's my real home. . . . I'd live the rest of my life there if I could." For a moment longer she looked out the window, then turned briskly, saying:

"Why don't you run over to Paris some week-end? After all, it's only seven hours from London: if you left here in the morning you'd be there in time for dinner. It would be a good change for you. I should think a little trip like that would buck you up tremendously."

Her words gave him a wonderful feeling of confidence and hope: she had travelled a great deal, and she had the casual, assured way of speaking of a voyage that made it seem very easy, and filled one with a sense of joy and adventure when she spoke about it. When Eugene tried to think of Paris by himself it had seemed very far away and hard to reach: London stood between it and him, and when he thought of the huge smoky web of London, the soft gray skies above him, and the enormous weight of lives that were hidden somewhere in that impenetrable fog, a gray desolation and weariness of the spirit filled him. It seemed to him that he must draw each breath of that soft gray air with heavy weary effort, and that every mile of his journey would be a ghastly struggle through some viscous and material substance, that weighted down his steps, and filled his heart with desolation.

But when Mrs. Coulson spoke to him about it, suddenly it all seemed wonderfully easy and good. England was magically small, the channel to be taken in a stride, and all the thrill, the joy, the mystery of Paris his again—the moment that he chose to make it his.

He looked at her gaunt weathered face, the hard bright armor of her eyes, and wondered how anything so clear, so sharp, so crisp, and so incisive could have been shaped and grown underneath these soft and humid skies that numbed him, mind and heart and body, with their thick dull substance of gray weariness and desolation.

A day or two before he left, Edith came into his room one afternoon bearing a tray with tea and jam and buttered bread. He was sitting in his chair before the fire, and had his coat off: when she came in he scrambled to his feet, reached for the coat and started to put it on. In her young crisp voice she told him not to, and put the tray down on the table, saying that the maid was having her afternoon off.

Then for a moment she stood looking at him with her faint and enigmatic smile.

"So you're leaving us?" she said presently.

"Yes. Tomorrow."

"And where will you go from here?" she said.

"To Germany, I think. Just for a short time—two or three weeks."

"And after that?"

"I'm going home."

"Home?"

"Back to America."

"Oh," she said slowly. "I see." In a moment, she added, "We shall miss you."

He wanted to talk to her more than he had ever wanted to talk to any one in his life, but when he spoke, all that he could say, lamely, muttering, was:

"I'll miss you, too."

"Will you?" She spoke so quietly that he could scarcely hear her. "I wonder for how long?" she said.

"Forever," he said, flushing miserably at the sound of the word, and yet not knowing any other word to say.

The faint hard smile about her mouth was a little deeper when she spoke again.

"Forever? That's a long time, when one is young as you," she said.

"I mean it. I'll never forget you as long as I live."

"We shall remember you," she said quietly. "And I hope you think of us sometime—back here, buried, lost, in all the fog and rain and ruin of England. How good it must be to know that you are young in a young country—where nothing that you did yesterday matters very much. How wonderful it must be to know that none of the failure of the past can pull you down—that there will always be another day for you—a new beginning. I wonder if you Americans will ever know how fortunate you are," the girl said.

"And yet you couldn't leave all this?" Eugene said with a kind of desperate hope. "This old country you've lived in, known all your life. A girl like you could never leave a place like this to live the kind of life we have in America."

"*Couldn't* I?" she said with a quiet but unmistakable passion of conviction. "There's nothing I'd like better."

Eugene stared at her blindly, dumbly for a moment; suddenly all that he wanted to say, and had not been able to say, found release in a movement of his hands. He gripped her by the shoulders and pulled her to him, and began to plead with her:

"Then why don't you? I'll take you there!—Look here—" his words were crazy and he knew it, but as he spoke them, he believed all he said

—"Look here! I haven't got much money—but in America you can make it if you want to! I'm going back there. You come, too—I'll take you when I go!"

She had not tried to free herself; she just stood there passive, unresisting, as he poured that frenzied proposal in her ears. Now, with the same passive and unyielding movement, the bright armor of her young eyes, she stepped away, and stood looking at him silently for a moment. Then slowly, with an almost imperceptible movement, she shook her head. "Oh, you'll forget all about us," she said quietly. "You'll forget about our lives here—buried in fog—and rain—and failure—and defeat."

"Failure and defeat won't last forever."

"Sometimes they do," she said with a quiet finality that froze his heart.

"Not for you—they won't!" Eugene said, and took her by the hand again with desperate entreaty. "Listen to me—" he blundered on incoherently, with the old feeling of nameless shame and horror. "You don't need to tell me what it is—I don't want to know—but whatever it is—for you, it doesn't matter—you can get the best of it."

She said nothing, but just looked at him through that hard bright armor of her eyes, the obdurate finality of her smile.

"Good-bye," she said, "I'll not forget you either." She looked at him for a moment curiously before she spoke again. "I wonder," she said slowly, "if you'll ever understand just what it was you did for me by coming here?"

"What was it?"

"You opened a door that I thought had been closed forever," she said, "a door that let me look in on a world I thought I should never see again—a new bright world, a new life and a new beginning—for us all. And I thought that was something which would never happen to any one in this house again."

"It will to you," Eugene said, and took her hand again with desperate eagerness. "It can happen to you whenever you want it to. It's yours, I'll swear it to you, if you'll only speak."

She looked at him, with an almost imperceptible movement of her head.

"I tell you I know what I'm talking about."

Again she shook her head.

"You don't know," she said. "You're young. You're an American. There are some things you'll never be old enough to know.—For some of us there's no return.—Go back," she said, "go back to the life you know—the life you understand—where there can always be a new beginning—a new life."

"And you—" Eugene said dumbly, miserably.

"Good-bye, my dear," she said so low and gently he could scarcely hear her. "Think of me sometimes, won't you—I'll not forget you." And before he could speak she kissed him once and was gone, so light and swift that he did not know it, until the door had closed behind her. And for some time, like a man in a stupor, he stood there looking out the window at the gray wet light of England.

The next day he went away, and never saw any of them again, but he could not forget them. Although he had never passed beyond the armor of their hard bright eyes, or breached the wall of their crisp, friendly, and impersonal speech, or found out anything about them, he always thought of them with warmth, with a deep and tender affection, as if he had always known them—as if, somehow, he could have lived with them or made their lives his own had he only said a word, or turned the handle of a door—a word he never knew, a door he never found.

LXXIV

THE day before he went away, the Rhodes scholars invited Eugene to lunch. That was a fine meal: they ate together in their rooms in college, they had opened their purses to the college chef, and had told him not to spare himself but to go the limit. Before the meal they drank together a bottle of good sherry wine, and as they ate they drank the college ale, strong, brown, and mellow, and when they came to coffee, they all finished off on a bottle of port apiece.

There was a fine thick seasonable soup, of the color of mahogany, and then a huge platter piled high with delicate brown-golden portions of filet of sole, and a roast of mutton, tender, fragrant, juicy and delicious as no other mutton that Eugene had ever eaten, with red currant jelly, well-seasoned sprouts, and boiled potatoes, to go with it, and at the end a fine apple-tart, thick cream, sharp cheese, and crackers.

It was a fine meal, and when they finished with it they were all happy and exultant. They were beautifully drunk and happy, with that golden, warm, full-bodied and most lovely drunkenness that can come only from good rich wine and mellow ale and glorious and abundant food—a state that we recognize instantly when it comes to us as one of the rare, the priceless, the unarguable joys of living, something stronger than philosophy, a treasure on which no price can be set, a sufficient reward for all the anguish, weariness, and disappointment of living, and a far better teacher than Aquinas ever was.

They were all young men and when they had finished they were drunk, glorious, and triumphant as only young men can be. It seemed to them now that they could do no wrong, or make no error, and that the whole earth was a pageantry of delight which had been shaped solely for their happiness, possession, and success. The Rhodes scholars no longer felt the old fear, confusion, loneliness, and bitter inferiority and desolation of the soul which they had felt since coming there.

The beauty, age, and grandeur of the life about them were revealed as they had never been before, their own fortune in living in such a place seemed impossibly good and happy, nothing in this life around them now seemed strange or alien, and they all felt that they were going to win, and make their own, a life among the highest and most fortunate people on the earth.

As for Eugene, he now thought of his departure exultantly, and with intolerable desire, not from some joy of release, but because everything around him now seemed happy, glorious, and beautiful, and a token of unspeakable joys that were to come, a thousand images of trains, of the small rich-colored joy and comfort and precision of their trains, of England, lost in fog, and swarming with its forty million lives, but suddenly not dreary, but impossibly small, and beautiful and near, to be taken at a stride, to be compassed at a bound, to enrich him, fill him, be his forever in all its joy and mystery and magic smallness.

And he thought of the huge smoky web of London with this same joy: of the suave potent ale he could get in one place there, of its squares, and ancient courts, and age-grimed mysteries, and of the fog-numb strangeness of ten million passing men and women. He thought of the swift rich projectile of the channel train, the quays, the channel boats, and darkness, night, the sudden onslaught of the savage choppy seas outside the harbor walls, and England fading, and the flashing beacon lights of France, the quays again, the little swarming figures, the excited tongues, the strange dark faces of the Frenchmen, the always-alien, magic, time-enchanted strangeness of the land, the people, and the faces; and then Paris, the nostalgic, subtle and incomparably exciting fabric of its life, its flavor, and its smell, the strange opiate of its time, the rediscovery of its food, its drink, the white, carnal, and luxurious bodies of the whores.

They were all exultant, wild, full of joy and hope and invincible belief as they thought of all these things and all the glory and the mystery that the world held treasured for their taking in the depths of its illimitable resources; and they shouted, sang, shook hands and roared with laughter, and had no doubts, or fears, or dark confusions, as they had done in other, younger, and more certain times.

Then they started out across the fields behind the colleges, and the fields were wet and green, the trees smoky-gray and blurred in magic veils of bluish mist, and the worn path felt, looked, and seemed incredibly familiar, like a field they had crossed, a path they had trod, a million times. And at length they came to their little creek-wise river, their full, flowing little river of dark time and treasured history, their quiet, narrow, deeply flowing little river, uncanny in the small perfection of its size, as it went past soundlessly among the wet fresh green of the fields that hemmed it with a sweet, kept neatness of perfection.

Then, having crossed, they went up along the river path until they came to where the crews were waiting—the Merton crew before, another college crew behind, and the students of both colleges clustered eagerly on the path beside their boats, exhorting their comrades in the shell, waiting for the signal that would start the race.

Then, even as the Rhodes scholars pounded on Eugene's back and roared at him with an exuberant affection that "You've got to run with us! You've got to root for us! You belong to Merton now!" the starting-gun cracked out, the crews bent furiously to their work, the long blades bit frantically the cold gray water, and the race was on. And they were racing lightly, nimbly now, two packs of young men running on the path, each yelping cries of sharp encouragement to his crew as he ran on beside it.

At first, as Eugene ran, he felt strong and lithe and eager. He was aware of an aerial buoyancy: his step was light, his stride was long and easy, his breath came softly, without labor, and the swift feet of the running boys thudded before, behind, around him, on the hard path, pleasantly, and he was secure in his strength and certitude again, and thought that he was one of them, and could run with them to the end of the world and back, and never feel it.

He thought he had recovered all the lean sinew and endurance of a boy, that the storm-swift flight, the speed, the hard condition, and resilient effort of a boy were his again, that he had never lost them, that they had never changed. Then a leaden heaviness began to steal along his limbs, he felt the weariness of effort for the first time, a thickening slowness in the muscles of his legs, a numb weight-like heaviness tingling at his finger-tips, and now he no longer looked so sharply and so smartly at the swinging crew below him, the nimbly running boys around him.

He began to pound ahead with dogged and deliberate effort, and his heart was pounding like a hammer at his ribs, his breath was laboring hoarsely in his throat and his tongue felt numb and thick and swollen in his mouth, and blind motes were swimming drunkenly before his eyes. He could hear his voice, unfamiliar and detached, weirdly unreal, as if some one else were speaking in him, as it panted hoarsely:

"Come on, Merton! . . . Come on, Merton! . . . Come on, Merton!"

And now the nimbler running footsteps all around him had passed, had gone ahead of him, had vanished. He could no longer see the crews nor know if they were there. He ran on blindly, desperately, hearing, seeing, saying nothing any longer, an anguished leaden creature, weighted down with a million leaden hours and weary efforts, pounding heavily, blindly, mindlessly along, beneath gray timeless skies of an immortal weariness, across the gray barren earth of some huge planetary vacancy—where there was neither shade nor stay nor shelter, where there would never be a resting place, a room, nor any door which he could enter, and where he must pound blindly, wearily along, alone, through that huge vacancy forever.

Then voices swarmed around him once again, and he could feel strong hands on him. They seized him, stopped him, and familiar faces swarmed forward at him through those swimming motes of blind gray vacancy. He could hear again the hoarse ghost-unreality of his own voice panting: "Come on, Merton!" and see his friends again, now grinning, laughing, shouting, as they shook him. "Stop! The race is over! Merton won!"

LXXV

THEIR names were Octave Feuillet, Alfred Capus, and Maurice Donnay; their names were Hermant, Courteline, and René Bazin; their names were Jules Renard, Marcelle Tinayre, and André Theuriet; and Clarétie, and Frapié and Tristan Bernard; and de Régnier and

Paul Reboux, and Lavedan; their names were Rosny, Gyp, Boylesve, and Richepin; their names were Bordeaux, Prévost, Margueritte, and Duvernois—their names, Great God, their names were countless as the sands upon the shore—and in the end, their names were only names and names and names—and nothing more.

Or, if their names were something more than names—if they sometimes shaped themselves in his mind as personalities—these personalities were faded, graceful, and phantasmal ones—each talented and secure in his position, and curiously alike—each brave and good and gentle in his trade, like lesser-known knights of the Round Table. He knew that few of them had been the hero of a generation, the leader of a century; he knew that none of them had rivalled Balzac, surpassed Stendhal, out-done Flaubert. And for this reason, their vague, phantasmal company became more haunting-strange to him than if they had.

He knew, as well, that there must be among them great differences of talent, great differences of style. His reason told him that some were good, and some were fair, and some were only cheap; even his meagre understanding of their tongue showed him that there was a great range, every kind of difference in their choice and treatment of a subject—a range that swept from the gracefully ironic sentiment of *Les Vacances d'un Jeune Homme Sage* to the stern earth-and-peasant austerity of *Le Blé qui lève;* from the dream nostalgia of *Le Passé Vivant* to the salty and difficult drolleries of *Messieurs les Ronds-de-Cuir* or *Le Train de 8h 47.*

He knew that each of these men must have had his own style, his special quality which would instantly be discerned and appraised by a French reader—he knew that some had written of the quiet life of the provinces, and that others wrote of the intrigue, the love affairs, the worldly and sophisticated gentry, of Paris; he knew that some were writers of a graceful sentiment, some delicately ironic, some drolly comic, some savagely satiric, and some grimly tragic.

But all of them seemed to come from the same place, to have the same quality, to evoke the same perfume. They were the vague and shadowy figures of a charming, beautiful, and legendary kind of life—a life that was all the more legendary to him because he was constantly groping with half-meanings, filling in his faulty understanding of the language with painful intuitions, tearing desperately at the contents of unnumbered volumes, with a tortured hunger of frustration, an aching brain, a dictionary in one hand, and one of these slick and flimsy little volumes in another.

And for this reason, perhaps, as much as any other—because of this savage struggle with an alien tongue, this agonizing, half-intuitive effort by which he groped his way to understanding through a book— the books themselves, and these graceful and shadowy figures who produced them, took on a quality that was as strange as the whole experience of these first weeks in Paris had become. Indeed, in later years, the legendary quality of his savage conflict with this world of print became indistinguishably mixed with the legendary quality of the life around him. Perhaps, even the swift, graceful, and fascinating little drawings and illustrations which dotted the pages of these books were in some measure responsible for this illusion: the pictures gave to the hard and difficult pages of a thousand fictions the illusion of an actual reality: in these little pictures he could see and recognize a thousand things that had already grown familiar to him—the narrow sidewalks and the tall and ancient houses of the Latin Quarter, the bridges of the Seine, the interior of a railway compartment, the great grilled gate of a château, people sitting at the tables in a café or on the terrace, the walls, the roofs, the chimney-pots of Paris which, no matter what changes had come about in human costume, feminine fashions, top-hats, frock-coats, or facial whiskerage, had themselves changed very little.

The most extraordinary and vividly imagined phenomenon of his desperate struggle to understand these innumerable fictions was this: Although his reason told him that all these men—all these phantasmal and haunting names—Feuillet, Capus, Donnay, Tinayre, Boylesve, Bazin, Theuriet—and all the rest of them—must have known all the sweat and anguish of hard labor, the solicitude, the grinding effort, and the desperate patience, that every artist knows, he became obsessed, haunted with the idea that the works of all this graceful, strange, and fortunate company were written without effort, with the most superb casualness and ease. It was his strange delusion that all of them were not only of an equal talent—could do all kinds of writing equally well and with equal ease—but that the reason for this marvellous endowment lay somehow in the fact that they were "French"—that by the fortunate accident of race and birth each one had somehow been constituted an artist who could do all things gracefully and well, and could do nothing wrong. Favored at birth by the great inheritance of their language, blood, and temperament, they grew up as children of a beautiful, strange, and legendary civilization whose very tongue was a guaranty of style, whose very tradition an assurance of form. These men could write nothing badly because it was not within the blood and nature of their race to do so: they must do everything gracefully, easily, and with an impeccable sense of form, because grace and ease and form were innate to them.

Finally, the most extraordinary fact of this curious obsession was his belief that all these books had been written by their authors not in the stern and lonely solitude of some midnight room, but swiftly, casually, and easily, as one might write a letter at the table of a café.

The obsession was so strong that he could see them writing at such a place—Feuillet, Capus, Donnay, Bazin—all the rest of them, each seated in the afternoon at his own inviolable table in his favorite café, each with a writing pad, a pen and ink before him, a half-emptied bock or glass of wine beside him, an adoring and devoted old waiter hovering anxiously near him—each writing steadily, rapidly, and gracefully the pages of some new and faultless story, some graceful, perfect book, filling up page after page of manuscript in their elegant, fine handwriting, without erasures or deletions, pausing thoughtfully from time to time to stare dreamily away, stroking their lank, disordered hair, their elegant French whiskers with a thin white hand, and so far from being distracted by the gaiety, the noise and clatter of the café crowd around them, deriving a renewed vitality from its sparkling stimulation, and returning to fill up page after page again.

And he could see them meeting every afternoon—that band of Bohemian immortality, that fortunate and favored company of art that could do no wrong—in some café on the Boulevards, or in some quiet, gracious old place hallowed by their patronage, in the Latin Quarter, in Montparnasse, or on the Boul St. Mich or in Montmartre.

He saw the whole scene with a blazing imagery, an exact detail, as if he had himself been present and seen and heard it all. He could hear the spirited light clamor of their conversation—like everything they did, gracious, faultless, full of ease—could see them rise to greet their famous comrades—whoever they might be—Feuillet, Capus, or Donnay, all the rest of them—could see them shake hands with the swift, firm greeting, so graceful, worldly, and so French, and hear them saying:

"Ah, my dear Maurice—how goes it with you? But—I see that I disturb you—pardon, my friend!—I see that you are busy with another of your admirable tales—Ah-h, my old one, not for the world would I disturb the flow of your so admirable genius. Parbleu! Do I wish my wretched name to become infamous to all posterity, to be heard with execration—ah, the devil! Non! The black forgetfulness of the grave is better! Eh, well, then, old comrade, till tomorrow—*Then* I hope——"

"Ah, but no, but no, but no, but no, but no! My dear Octave, you shall remain! These pages here!—Pouf! it is nothing! I am already done—Attend!" Swiftly he scrawls a line or two, and then triumphantly: "Voilà! C'est fini, old cock! A trifle I was finishing for my scoundrel of a publisher, who demands it for tomorrow.—But, tell me, my dear boy —what the devil kept you in the provinces for so long a time—so long away from this dear Pa-ree? Ah, how we have missed you: my dear fellow, Paris really never is the same unless you are here to give it grace! Tiens! Tiens! Poor Courteline has been quite inconsolable! Capus has sworn daily he would go and fetch you back! Tinayre is grouchy as a bear! My dear fellow, we have all lamented you! De Régnier was certain you had got another mistress! Boylesve insisted that she was at least a duchess—Bazin, a milkmaid——"

"And you, my old one?"

"I? My dear fellow—I knew it must be chicken-pox or measles: I was certain you would not have to stir a foot out of Pa-ree to find a wench."

"But tell me, Octave, how are all our friends? I am starved for news, I have read nothing. First of all—René——?"

"Has published another admirable work—an excellent study of life in the provinces."

"Ah, good. And Duvernois?"

"His latest comedy has been produced and is un succès fou—a charming thing—witty, naughty, quite in his best vein, my dear boy."

"Renard?"

"A comedy, a book of stories, a romance—all excellent, all doing well."

"And Courteline?"

"Une chose incomparable, my boy: a book of dialogues in his drollest vein—the public is convulsed: the police are in a towering rage about *Le Gendarme est sans Pitié*——"

"And Abel?"

"A formidable book, my lad—just what you would expect, a powerful tragedy, exact psychology, brilliant—but here he comes, all smiles—ah-h! I thought so! He sees you—My dear Abel, welcome: behold, our prodigal has come home again——"

Yes, it was so that it was done, without anguish, error, or maddening of the soul.

And far, far away from all this certain grace, this ease of form, this assured attaining of expression—there lay America—and all the dumb hunger of its hundred million tongues, its unfound form, its unborn art. Far, far away from this enchanted legend of a city—there lay America and the brutal stupefaction of its million streets, its unquiet heart, its vast incertitude, the huge sprawled welter of its life—its formless and illimitable distances.

And Great God! Great God! but it was farther, stranger than a dream —he noted its cruelty, savagery, horror, error, loss and waste of life, its murderous criminality, and its hypocritic mask of virtue, its lies, its horrible falseness, and its murderous closure of a telling tongue—and Great God! Great God! with every pulse and fibre in him, with the huge, sick ache of an intolerable homelessness, he was longing with every beating of his anguished heart for just one thing—*return!*

Day by day, hour by hour, and minute by minute, the blind hunger tore at his naked entrails with a vulture's beak. He prowled the streets of Paris like a maddened animal, he hurled himself at the protean complexities of its million-footed life like a soldier who hurls himself into a battle: he was baffled, sick with despair, wrung, trembling and depleted, finally exhausted, caught in the toils of that insatiate desire, that terrible devouring hunger that grew constantly from what it fed upon and that drove him blindly to madness. The hopeless and unprofitable struggle of the Faustian life had never been so horribly evident as it now was— the futility of his insane efforts to memorize every stone and paving brick in Paris, to burn the vision of his eyes through walls and straight into the lives and hearts of a million people, to read all the books, eat all the food, drink all the wine, to hold the whole gigantic panorama of the universe within his memory, and somehow to make "one small globe of all his being," to compact the accumulated experience of eternity into the little prism of his flesh, the small tenement of his brain, and somehow to use it all for one final, perfect, all-inclusive work—his life's purpose, his heart's last pulse and anguish, and his soul's desire.

As a result of all this anguished and frustrated struggle he began now to go about with a small notebook in his pocket, the worn stub of a chewed pencil in his hands.

And because everything went into this mad mélange, because by every

one of these scrawls of notes and sometimes incoherent words—even by
the thousands of crude drawings, swift designs which he scrawled down
in a thousand towns and places, to get the texture of a wall, the design of
a door, the shape of a table, even the sword-cut on a man's scarred face—
because in all of these shells and splinters that were thrown off from his
tormented and uneasy brain the terrible Faustian fever of his tortured
spirit was evident—no better image of his life—the life of a young man
of that period—of modern man caught in the Faustian serpent-toils of
modern life—can be given than the splintered jottings in these battered
little books afford.

Here then, picked out at random from the ferment of ten thousand
pages, and a million words—put down just as they were written, in
fragments, jots, or splintered flashes, without order or coherence—here,
with all its vanity, faith, despair, joy, and anguish, with all its falseness, error and pretension, and with all its desperate sincerity, its incredible hope, its insane desire, is a picture of a man's soul and heart—
the image of his infuriate desire—caught hot and instant, drawn flaming
from the forge of his soul's agony.

Monday, November 17, 1924: Worked over 5 hours up to present
(9:40) Cigarets and coffee—Very tired.

Tuesday: Worked 4 hours yesterday. Very tired today only an hour
—more tonight——

Wednesday: Good week's work last week—Four or five hours *actual*
writing every day—I may succeed ultimately because I'm not content
with what I do.

I was born in 1900—I am now 24 years old. During that period I think
the best writing in English has been done by James Joyce in "Ulysses"—I
think the best writing in the ballad has been done by G. K. Chesterton
in "Lepanto." The best writing in sustained narrative verse by John
Masefield—particularly in "The Dauber," "The River" and "The
Widow in The Bye Street." Who produce copiously—Arnold Bennet—
The best practitioners of the Essay—Belloc—the most gigantically
thorough realist—Theodore Dreiser—The most sparing selection and
unfailingly competent—Galsworthy—The best play for Poetry—"The
Playboy of Western World"—The best journalist—Sinclair Lewis.
The critic with the greatest subtlety—T. S. Eliot—The critic with the

greatest range and power—H. L. Mencken—The best woman writer—
May Sinclair—The next best—Virginia Woolf—The next best—Willa
Cather.

Wednesday Night—November 26, 1924: At midnight eating at Chez
Marianne—First day I have not worked for two weeks but am going
home to work after eating. Up at 12:30 today after last night felt sick—
walked to bank—found no mail—wrote and sent letters to Mama and
to University. Talked to young fellow in bank about Switzerland—had
lunch at Taverne Royale—Took taxi to Place des Vosges—Went to
Victor Hugo Museum—Walked around Square—then back to Carnavalet—at National Archives—The narrow streets, the narrow sidewalks, the great busses, taxis, autos, bicycles, trucks and the catty people
jabbering and squalling got me in a stew—Looked over distressing tons
of books at a bookshop, and went on feeling crushed—Bought two
books—Then got taxi Rue du Temple and so home through the jam of
Rue de Rivoli—Women outside pawing cheap articles at Samaritaine.
Then home to hotel where bathed went out to Deux Magots two
Apéritifs then to Apollo Revue!—Not as bad as some—one or two good
songs—but of course, on whole quite stupid.

Thursday—November 27, 1924: At one, after working till five
this morning. Dining at Drouant's—very rich, red restaurant filled with
business men talking of Les Anglais, Les Americaines, ate cinq cent
mille francs—at Drouant's—a cold consommé, a rumpsteak grille—
avec des pommes soufflées—a fond d'artichaut moray (a cheese and
cream dressing and the ends of artichokes—delicious) a coffee and a
half bottle of Nuit St. Georges couvert 4 fr. total 44 frs.
    At one table three Frenchmen of 50 or more—one of 40—one with
black beard—coal black, neatly trimmed, naked around jaws—another
a heavy distinguished man—grey beard pompadoured—grey close-
cropped moustache—high colored—nervous grey eyes shot with red—
hands white, taut and tapping constantly, while the face smiles—talks
politely—another a red gnarled satanic face—fierce with rich foods and
wines—smooth shaven—and the youngest—black hair, a black moustache—a quiet smiling, well-fleshed type. He had rich color—red shot
with richness, the satanic yet not unpleasant cast of face—the cropped
brown moustache and such pompadoured brownish hair—a Gallic type.
    LATER: Seated at the café in front of Magasin du Louvre and Palais

Royale—Heard a high even monotone that tickles the ear like a dynamo
—It made me think of a great locomotive in the yards at Altamont—
steam shut off (perhaps) and the high small ear-tickling dynamic noise
they make.

Tuesday—December 2, 1924:

MOCK LITERARY ANECDOTES:

Young mannered voice of Harvard johnny: "Oh! Simply *priceless!*
Don't you *l-o-o-ve* that?
. . . *Marvellous!*" etc.—telling what Oscar said to Whistler, and what
Whistler answered him.

A certain kind of mind collects these—pale, feeble, rootless, arty, hopeless, lost—Joel Pierce tells them, too. First time I heard them at Harvard what sophisticated raconteurs I thought them!—God, how green
I was! "You will, Oscar, you will," and all the rest of it!—Today, sitting on terrace at Taverne Royale, I made some of my own. Here they
are:

One day as Whistler was standing before a window in St. James Street
observing some prints of Battersea Lodge, he was accosted by Oscar
Wilde coming in the opposite direction. "You will, James, you will,"
said Wilde with generous impulsiveness.

"Gad," remarked the inimitable James, imperturbably adjusting his
monocle, "I wish I had said that!"

One day in June, Anatole France went to Rodin's studio for luncheon.
The talk having turned to early Greek primitives, Rodin remarked:

"Some writers have a great deal to say and an atrocious style. But
you, dear Master, have a delicious style."

"And you, Master?" queried France ironically, allowing his eyes to
rest upon the torso of The Thinker, "since when did you become a
critic?"

In the burst of laughter that followed the thrust, Rodin had to admit
himself floored for once.

A young actor who had, it must be confessed, more ambition than
talent, one day rushed excitedly up to Sir Henry Irving during the
rehearsal of "Hamlet":

"It seems to me, sir," he burst out without preliminaries, "that some
actors ruin their parts by overplaying them."

"And some," remarked Sir Henry, after an awful pause, "don't."

One day Sir James Barrie discovered Bernard Shaw while he was lunching at the Atheneum, staring somewhat disconsolate at an unsavory mess of vegetables that adorned his plate.

"I hear you are working on a new play," remarked Barrie, whimsically eyeing the contents of the platter.

For once G. B. S. had no answer ready.

Why won't these do?

(Suggestion to Young American writing Book Reviews for *New York Times* in classical, simple, god-like manner of Anatole France.)

"The new book of Monsieur Henry Spriggins, which lies before me on my desk, fills me with misgivings. The author is young and intolerant of simple things. He is full of talent, but he is proud, and has not a simple heart. What a pity!" (etc.)

Wednesday—December 3, 1924: Comédie Française tonight Les Plaideurs—and Phèdre—Respect for play grew and for actors diminished and went on—The French applauded loudly when Madame Weber ended a long declamation on a screech.

LATER: To Régence and Harry's—Bought some books along the quays—Saw Mrs. Martin at hotel today—Story of how she had been robbed—The picture galleries and antique shops of Rue des Saints Pères.

Saturday—December 6,

Young Icarus lies drowned, God knows where.

Oxford in pursuit of a woman—one of the most dreary spectacles God hath given—Buol's in the afternoon——

Foolish Question: Why are the Tories so eager to say Democracy has failed?

Hair like a copper cloud—feather and flame come back again.

The gutted plums bee-burrowed.

The poisoned inch around the heart.

The cancerous inch.

The burning inch of tongue.

The hairy grass.

The long sea-locks.

The hairy seas.

The other gate of ivory——

Ida—Cadmus—blunt drummed woodenly with blunt fingers. Sir Leoline the baron rich—Thunder-cuffing Zeus—Erasmus fed on rotten eggs—what a breath—Has an angel local motion or "The goose-soft snow."

Feathery snow—The feather-quilted snow.

Freckled eyes.

Wild Ceres through the wheat.

The slow dance of dancers.

The gull swerves seaward like hope—September full of departing leaves and wings.

He sat alone four thousand miles from home—the lonely death of seas at dawn.

The decent and untainted eyes that look on spattered death—Myself dreaming of old battles—For a child the spear goes clearly through—The musical horns beg and the battles press—The phantasy of bloody death: The cloven brain-pan—the one lost second near enough to touch its brother life, but infinitely far.

The wind-blown lights of the town.

A branch of stars.

A hen and a pig.

Quills—frills.

Mired—feathers.

The vast low stammer of the night.

By the rim—the geese go waddling to the Fair.

The minute-whirring flies buzz home to death.

"Old England will muddle through, my lads"——

She has muddled and she's through: but she's not through muddling.

Gull-cry and gull are gone.

Shadow and hawk are gone.

Shadow and hawk are gone.

Shadow and hawk are——

Friday Night—December 12, 1924:. The Fratellini Brothers: How in his rich robe I saw him—the younger brother—waiting for the act—the waiting is all over—The burlesque musical act—They were great, sad, epic—what clowns should be.

Salle Rubens with all the *meat*—All the people clustered about—dull.

Mona Ugly Lisa.

The Virgin with Saint Anne—a great picture.

Guido Reni—the sainted and sugared faces.

The Italians—Veronese—The Cana—The Gigantic three-storey canvases.

Zurberan—Goya and the Grey—Picture of a Gentleman on horseback —Nicolas Maes—Rembrandt's picture of his brother.

Sam's—The man from San Francisco with the loud, dark, debauched face.

"We had ham and eggs for lunch across at Ciro's, Anne"—the two barkeepers in Harry's, "Chip" and Bob—names of dogs and horses.

Velasquez in the Louvre.

Vetzel's again 12:30 Apéritif (X365) The arch of the opera I have never seen before, things sit like this.

(here follows drawing)

Remember Faust at The Opera.

The Promenoirs—The vast stage—click-clack of feet in the music.

I awoke this morning in a crucifixion of fear and nervousness—What if they hadn't written? What? What? What?

My agony as I approached the place—My distrust of Paris in peril— City of light disloyalties. Sun never shines more than two days (for me) here—Went to American Express—Harry's Bar—The men at Vetzel's eating——

The French are not bad but children—old men too wise and kind for hatred—but French French French and Suspicious.

How beautiful the Fratellini are! How fine a thing is a French circus! Their enormous interest in children—The lion-taming act—by far the best and finest I have ever seen—and I felt sorry for the lions—Savoir is right in this.

Monday—December 15, 1924: I am getting a new sense of control— millions of books don't annoy me so much—went along the Seine today after Louvre—most of it worthless old rubbish I must begin to put up my fences now—I can't take the world or this city with me.

Things in Paris I must see at once—*Père Lachaise*—*Also* investigate old quarter again around *Place des Vosges*—Go *there* first thing tomorrow—Go to Cluny Musée again—And up and down Rue de la Seine— Also Isle St. Louis.

Books I want: Julien Benda—New one by Soupault (?) Charles Derennes—L'Education Sexuelle. Read one of the Vautel things.

Get for inspection—and at random Le Petit Livre—Mon Livre Favori
—Bibl. Nationale—Livre Epatant—go into Court of Palais Royale—
Investigate there——
Louvre today—Mantegnas picture of St. Sebastian C.
Giotto's great picture of St. Francis D'Assisi receiving stigma from
Christ——
Gros—Pictures of Napoleon at war—The one of the leper's house at
Jaffa a good one—Huge naked leper held in kneeling position—Weight
of body.
Books I want—Go to bookstalls in Seine for books on Paris twenty
or thirty years ago with naughty illustrations.

Tuesday—December 16, 1924: Along Seine again—Looked at thousands of books and bought one—a critique on Julien Benda—Miles and
miles of books—but also, miles and miles of repetitions——
The pictures—cavaliers seducing pretty ladies; one of women half
naked embracing pillow—called Le Rêve—People in old French stage-
comedies—Then 1000's of La Chimie, La Physique, La Géologie,
L'Algèbre, Le Géometrie——
Letters—Morceaux Choisis of XVIII S. All the authors I have never
heard of—but *that* is the same at home.

Wednesday—December 17, 1924: Today bought books—Bookshop
on Rue St. Honoré—Stock's.
Bought Benda there—Along the river—Tons of Trash—L'Univers—
The Miracle of France—4 mos. in the United States, etc. etc.—Les
Cicéron, Ovide, Sénèque, etc.
Bought *Confessions of Alfred Musset*—Stall at Pont Neuf with dirty
books—*Journal d'une Masseuse.*
*Sadie Blackeyes—Lovers of The Whip—The Pleasures of Married
Life—The Galleries of The Palais Royale* where the bookshops are—
Whole series edited by Guillaume Apollinaire——
Pictures, stamps, coins—Daumier-like picture of man having tooth
pulled—Then the near dirty ones of ladies with silver wings—Silhouette-
like—Then the near XVIII Century ones.
Old Books—Seem to be millions of these too—*Essais de L'Abbé Chose
sur la Morale,* etc.
The Faustian hell again!

At La Régence: Semaine de Noël, 1924:

The people who say they "read nothing but the best," are not, as some people call them, snobs. They are fools. The battle of the Spirit is not to read and to know the best—it is to find it—The thing that has caused me so much toil and trouble has come from a deeprooted mistrust in me of all cultured authority. I hunger for the treasure that I fancy lies buried in a million forgotten books, and yet my reason tells me that the treasure that lies buried there is so small that it is not worth the pain of disinterment.

And yet nearly everything in the world of books that has touched my life most deeply has come from authority. I have not always agreed with authority that all the books called great *are* great, but nearly all the books that have seemed great to me have come from among this number.

I have not discovered for myself any obscure writer who is as great a novelist as Dostoievsky, nor any obscure poet with the genius of Samuel Taylor Coleridge.

But I have mentioned Coleridge, and although my use of his name will not, I believe, cause any protest, it may cause surprise. Why not Shelley, or Spenser, or Milton?—It is here that my war with Authority —to which I owe everything—begins again.

There are in the world of my spirit certain gigantic figures who, although great as well in the world of authority, are yet overshadowed, and in some places, loom as enormous half-ghosts—hovering upon the cloudy borderland between obscurity and living remembrance.

Such a man is Samuel Taylor Coleridge. To me, he is not one of the great English poets. He is The Poet. To me he has not to make obeisance at the throne of any other monarch—he is there by Shakespeare and Milton and Spenser.

At La Régence: Remembering the whore with rotten teeth that I talked to last night on Rue Lafayette:

My dirt is not as dirty as your dirt. My clean-ness is cleaner than your clean-ness.

If I have a hole in my sock that is cunning.

If you have a hole in your stocking love flies out of the window. Why are we like this? Boredom is the bedfellow of all the Latin peoples—the English, in spite of the phrase "bored Englishman," are not bored.

The Germans are eager and noisy about everything they are told they should be interested in.

The Americans are interested in everything for a week—a week at a time—except Sensation: they are interested in that all the time.

I have heard a great deal of the "smiling Latins," the "gay Latins," etc. I have seen few indications that the Latins are gay. They are noisy —they are really a sombre and passionate people—the Italian face when silent is rather sullen.

In New York the opportunities for learning, and acquiring a culture that shall not come out of the ruins, but belong to life, are probably greater than anywhere else in the world.

This is because America is young and rich and comparatively un-encumbered by bad things.

Tradition, which saves what is good and great in Europe, also saves what is poor, so that one wades through miles of junk to come to a great thing.

In New York books are plentiful and easy to get. The music and the theatre are the best in the world.

The great trouble with New York is that one feels uncomfortable while enjoying these things—In the daytime a man should be making money. The time to read is at night before one goes to bed. The time to hear music or go to the theatre is also at night. The time to look at a picture is on Sunday.

Another fault comes from our lack of independence. I am sure some of the most knowing people in the world, about the arts, are in America. I cannot read a magazine like *The Dial,* or *The Nation* and *The New Republic* without getting frightened. One man wrote a book called *Studies in Ten Literatures*—which of course, is foolish. We want to seem knowing about all these things because we have not enough confidence in ourselves.

We have had niggers for 300 years living all over the place—but all we did about it was to write minstrel shows, and 'coon stories, until two or three years ago when the French discovered for us how interesting they are. We let Paul Morand, and the man who wrote *Batouale,* and Soupault do it for us—Then we began to write stories about Harlem, etc.

Instead of whining, that we have no traditions, or that we must learn by keeping constantly in touch with European models, or by keeping away from them, we should get busy telling some of the stories about America that have never been told.

A book like *Main Street,* which made such a stir, is like Main Street. It is like "I've seen all Europe" tourists, who have spent two days in each country in a round-the-town bus.

In a magazine like *The American Mercury* the stories are also too much of a pattern—they're all about how the "Deacon Screwed the Methodist Minister's Wife," and how the "Town Prostitute Was Put in Jail for Coming to Church on Sunday and Mixing with the Good Folks."

When you hear people saying about *Babbitt*—that it is not the whole story and that much more can be said, you agree with them. Then they begin to talk about "the other side" and you lose hope. You see they mean by other side, Dr. Crane and Booth Tarkington.

So far from these being "the other side," there are a million other sides. And so far from *Babbitt* being too strong, the stories that may be written about America will make *Babbitt* an innocent little child's book to be read at the Christmas School entertainment along with *The Christmas Carol and* "Excelsior." The man who suggests the strangeness and variety of this life most is Sherwood Anderson. Or was. I think, he's got too fancy since he wrote *Winesburg, Ohio.*

A French writer who said there was no real variety in the life of the French because they all had red wine on the table, sat at little tables in cafés to gossip, and had mistresses, would be called a fool. Yet an American will criticize his country for standardization on no better grounds—namely that most of them are Methodists or Baptists, Democrats or Republicans, Rotarians or Kiwanians.

Babbitt is a very interesting book. But I believe it would be possible for a German writer with a talent similar to Sinclair Lewis to write a book called *Schmidt* or *Bauer* which would be just as sweeping a portrait.

Do you want to know what the gentleman looks like? He is much easier to describe than Babbitt.

Tuesday—December 23, 1924: The mystery explained! Today, at American Library, found out what it is:

"Time—that dimension of the world which we express in terms of before and after—the temporal sequence pervades mind and matter alike."

Time the form of the internal sense, and space the form of the external sense.

Theory of Relativity—the time-units of both time and space are neither points nor moments—but moments in the history of a point.

W. James—Within a definite limited interval of duration known as the specious present there is a direct perception of the temporal relations.

After an event has passed beyond the specious present it can only enter into consciousness by reproductive memory.

James "The Object of Memory is only an object imagined in the past to which the emotion of belief adheres."

Temporal experience divided into three qualitatively distinct intervals: the remembered past, the perceived specious present, and the anticipated future—By means of the tripartite division we are able to inject our present selves into the temporal stream of our own experience.

By arrangement of temporal orders of past with temporal orders of future—we can construct a temporal order of our specious presents and their contents.

Thus time has its roots in experience and yet appears to be a dimension in which experiences and their contents are to be arranged.

Thus the stuff from which time is made is of the nature of experienced data.

The Zenonian paradoxes: Achilles cannot catch up with the almost here save by occupying an infinity of positions.

A flying arrow canot remain where it is, nor be where it is not.

These things do not deal with space or time but with the properties of infinite assemblages and dense series (Americana).

Weber's at midnight: The waiters in Weber's standing in a group in their black coats and white boiled shirts——

All around the great mirrors reflecting there—for a moment a *strange* picture I thought of TIME!

The horrible monotony of the French—Weber's at midnight some Frenchmen in evening dress—the heavy eyelids—the dangling legs—the look of weary vitality——

Then in come some "Parisiennes"—God! God! All sizes and shapes and all the same—Unfit for anything else in the world, and not good

for what they are—The texture of enamelled tinted skin, the hard
avaricious noses, the chic style of coats, hair, eyebrows, etc.

The great myth that the Latins are romantic people. The Latins have
qualities and standards that we do not possess—Hence we overvalue
them.

There are many places in the world where life attains a greater variety,
interest or profundity than in Paris (viz., New York, London, Vienna,
Munich). Yet a great many Americans make their homes in Paris because they are sure it is the centre of the world's intellectual and cultural
reputations.

It is easier for a writer to secure a reputation in France than in any
other country. Many French writers have very respectable reputations
who would be laughed at in other countries. For example, Henri
Bordeaux—Some Americans who study French literature think he is a
distinguished writer. His name has a solid, respectable sound to it. On
the cover of all his books is printed "Member of the French Academy."
But you could hardly find an intellectual in America who would say a
kind word for Harold Bell Wright. Yet Harold Bell Wright—poor as
he may be—is a better writer than Henri Bordeaux. If you don't believe
it, read them. Americans are very unfair about this.

The way things go: At 6:10 A.M. the street lights of Paris go off. I sit
at a little all-night café in Grand Boulevard opposite Rue Faubourg de
Montmartre and watch light widen across the sky behind Montmartre.
At first a wide strip of blue-grey—a strip of violet light. You see the
line of the two clear and sharp. The paper trucks of Hachette, *Le Petit
Parisien,* etc., go by.

In the bar a rattling of leaden, hole-y coins—the five, ten and twenty-
five centime pieces. Taxi-drivers drinking café rhum, debating loudly
in hoarse sanguinary voices. A whore, the blonde all-night antiquity
of the quarter streets, drinking rich hot chocolate, crunching crusty
croissants at the bar. The veteran of a million lives, well known and
benevolently misprized, hoarse with iniquity and wisdom. A pox upon
you, Marianne: You have made Monsieur Le Président très triste; the
third leg of the Foreign Legion wears a sling because of you!

A swart-eyed fellow, oiled and amorous, sweetly licks with nozzly tongue his whore's rouge-varnished face: with choking secret laughter and with kissy, wetty talkie he cajoles her; she answers in swart choked whisperings with her sudden shrill whore's scream of merriment.

A morning rattle of cans and ashes on the pavements. With rich jingle-jangle and hollow clitter-clatter a Paris milk wagon passes. Suddenly, a screak of brakes: all over the world the moaning screak of brakes, and racing, starting motors.

Across the street in faint grey-bluish light the news kiosque is opening up.

"Est-ce que vous avez *Le New York 'Erald?*"

"Non, monsieur. Ce n'est pas encore arrivé."

"Et *Le Tchicago Treebune?*"

"Ça pas plus, monsieur. C'est aussi en retard ce matin."

"Merci. Alors: *Le Matin.*"

"Bien, monsieur."

Passage of leaden sous: the smell of ink-worn paper, dear to morning throughout the world. A big Hachette truck swerves up, an instant halt, the flat heavy mark of fresh-corded ink-warm paper on the pavement, a hoarse cry and instant loud departure!

Ça aussi, monsieur. Sing ye bi-i-i-rds, sing! Light up your heart, O son of man!

Sweet is the breath of morn, her rising sweet, with charm of earliest birds!

Some things will never change: some things will always be the same: brother we cannot die, we must be saved; we are united at the heart of night and morning.

A good time now, just before dawn and morning. Surfeit of sterile riches: harvests of stale bought love: the burnt-out candle-end of night, the jaded blaze of crimson light, in shuttered bars; numb weary lust—which one, which one?

The whores at daybreak, the dead brilliance of electric smiles.

Tired, tired, tired.

Tuesday: Woman who sang tonight at Concert Mayol—She was near 50—magnificent teeth—so good they made me uneasy—Those things in her head—but how? They keep them so. This comes to me—that they spend all their time looking after them: there is something filthy about this.

On the Boulevards—3.20 du matin. Reading the *Sourire* for whore-house items—I want to find me a Ballon of Champagne—First of all—préservatif right to my left around corner Rue Faubourg de Mont-martre; all-night pharmacy.

Along the quais again this afternoon to the bookstalls—Made afraid by the junk—Bought a dozen books or so, but no "prints" or "etchings" —Countless old-fashioned prints—pictures of Versailles—the Palais Royale, the Revolution—Sentimental and cheap pictures—Florid ones— "La Courtisane Passionée," etc. Stage-coach pictures, etc. Works of Eugène Scribe—The little books bound or tied, so you can't look— nothing in them—*Vie à la Campagne*—countless cheap books—ah, I have a little of it all!—Strasbourg.

Christmas Week—Colmar, Alsace-Lorraine—Written on the Spot.
The Isentheimer Altar of Mathias Grunewald in the Cloisters of the Unterlinden Museum at Colmar:
There is nothing like it in the world. I have spent over 4 months getting here—it is much more wonderful than one imagines it will be. The altar is set up *not in one piece* but in three sections in a big room with groined ceilings, a long groined room like a Dominikaner Cloister.
The first two "volets" of the altar—Everything is distorted and out of perspective. The figure of the Christ is twice as big as the other figures—the pointing finger of Saint Antoine is much too big for his body—but everything in this figure points along the joints and elbows of that arm and ends in the pointing finger.
The Lamb with its straight brisk feet, its dainty right foreleg bent delicately about the Cross and red blood spouting from its imperturba-ble heart into a goblet of rich gold, is a masterpiece of symbolic emotion that strikes far beyond intelligence.
The body of Christ, and its agony, are indescribable. The hands and the feet are enlarged to meet the agony—the hands are tendons of agony; the feet are not feet but lengths of twisted tendons driven through by a bolt and ending in bent, broken, bleeding toes. A supernatural light falls upon the immense twisted length of the body (a grey-white-green) and yet *completely solid light*—you can count the ribs, the muscles, (the head falling to the right), full of brutal agony—it is crowned with long thorns and rusty blood—it droops over, it is too big, Christ is dead.
The great figure of the woman in white comes up and breaks back-

ward at the middle and is caught in the red arms of the pitiful Saint. The fingers of the Magdalen are bent in eloquent supplication.

The blackness of hell's night behind—the unearthly greenish supernatural light upon the figures—on Christ's dead, sinewed, twisted, riven gigantic body and on the living flesh of the other figures.

The sly face of the Virgin in the wing of The Annunciation—the eyes slanting up under lowered lids in a sly leer—the fat loose sensual mouth half open, with the tongue visible—a look of sly bawdiness over all.

The enormous and demoniac intelligence that illuminates the piece in Grunewald's Altar—the angels playing instruments in "La Vierge Glorifiée par les Anges"—the faces have a *sinister golden light*—an almost unholy glee. You can hear *mad heavenly music*. This is not true with Italians—syrup and sugar.

This is the greatest and also the most "modern" picture I have ever seen.

Christmas Week—1924: Returning to Paris from Strasbourg: The approach to Paris through the Valley of the Marne—Winter—The very magnificent rainbow—the rocking clacketing train.

The suburbs of Paris—Dark—The little double-deckers rattling past loaded with people—The weary approaches to a great city—Endless repetition—monotonous endlessness—The sadness of seeing people pass you in a lighted train or subway. Why is this?

PARIS: There is nothing that I do not know about Paris—That sounds like the foolishest boast but that is true—I am sitting on the Terrace of The Taverne Royale—Rue Royale—It is winter—it is cold—but it is the same—to one hand the Madeleine—to the other the Place de la Concorde—to the right that of the Champs-Elysées—the Arc—the Bois —the fashionable quarters—the whore-houses of that district—the rue— the Troc—the Tower—the Champs de Mars—the Montparnasse section —the Latin-Quarter—the bookshops—the cafés—the Ecole—the Institute—the St. Mich—the Ile—the Notre Dame—The Old Houses—the Rue de Rivoli—the Tour St. Jacques—the Carnavalet—the Hugo— Vosges—the Bastille—the Gare de Lyon—the Gare de l'Est—Du Nord— the Montmartre—the Butte—the cafés—houses—the Rue Lepic—the Port Clignancourt—the La Villette—The Parc Monceau—the Bois— Great circle, unending universe of life, huge legend of dark time!

But unannealed by water the gaunt days sloped into the grots of time.

Paris, Saturday Night: Today has been a horrible one—I was able to sleep only the most diseased and distressed sleep (the worst sort of American-in-Europe sleep) last night after leaving Mrs. Morton. I was sick with my loss (the loss of the picture and several letters Helen sent me) and I got up sick and with the *shakes* this morning—I came to the Abiga bar—I went to the Am Ex Co—I went to Wepler's in Montmartre —At each place, as I knew they would, with mean and senile regret cut by mocking, they were sorry, sorry, sorry.

The day was of the most horrible European sort—Something that passes understanding—the wet heavy air, that deadens the soul, puts a lump of indigestible lead in the solar plexus, depresses and fatigues the flesh until one seems to lift himself leadenly through the thick wet steaming air with a kind of terrible fear—an excitement that is without hope, that awaits only the news of some further grief, failure, humiliation, and torture. There is a lassitude that enters the folds and lappings of the brain, that makes one hope for better things and better work tomorrow, but hope without belief or conviction.

The grey depression of the wet buildings—the horrible nervous pettiness of the French, swarming, honking, tooting along the narrow streets and the two-foot sidewalks, while the heavy busses beetle past——

A chapter called PARIS or So You're Going to "Paris"? (Perhaps a piece for a magazine in This.)
The fear always of the corners—you are coming out into the open, there will be waiting to thrust at you, the heavy grinding busses, the irritation of the horns, etc.

A chapter to be called "The Arithmetic of the Soul."

The music deepened like a passion.
All of our hearts are fulfilled of you, all of our souls are growing warm with you, all of our lives are beating out their breath for you, and the strange feel of our pulses is playing through our blood for you, immortal and unending living.

Sunday—Up at noon, bathed, etc. Lunch at Casenave's—Went to

Delacroix and Louvre—Something over-rich and bloody about it.—
Note how French love to paint blood (Delacroix)—then along Seine
bookstalls—found only junk—then to Lipp's for beer and *cervelas*—then
back to hotel where worked from 6:30–10.30—Then out to eat at
Taverne Royale—Walk back through Vendôme and Rue St. Honoré—
Read a little and worked from *one* to 3:00—6 hours today.

Sunday Night: I feel low—discouraged by the mass of things again
tonight. I must make some decisive action—the new web of streets
behind the dome has depressed me.

The mind grows weary with such a problem as mine, by constantly
retracing its steps, by constantly feeling around the same cylinder from
which there seems *at present* to be no escape.

The European temper is one that has learned control—that is it has
learned indifference—Each man writes his own book without worrying
very much about what the other has written—he reads little or if he
reads much, it is only a trifle—a spoonful of the ocean of print that
inundates everything—Picture Anatole France—with a reputation for
omniscience—picking daintily here and there among the bookstalls of
the Seine. To go by them affects me with horror and weariness—as it
does Paul Valéry—but I lack his power to resist. I must go by there—
and if I do again and again I cannot keep away from them.

More and more I am convinced that to be a great writer a man must
be something of an ass. I read of Tolstoi that he read no newspapers,
that he went away and lived among peasants for 7 years at a time, and
that for six years he read nothing except the novels of Dumas. Yet such
a man could write great books. I almost think it is because of this that
he did.

Bernard Shaw, one of our prophets at the present time, is worshiped
past idolatry by many people who consider that he knows everything
or practically everything.
From what I have been able to discover of his reading from his writing, I can be sure that he has read Shakespeare—not very carefully, Ibsen
very carefully, a book by Karl Marx, which made a deep impression on

him, the tracts of the Fabian Society, and the writings of Mr. and Mrs. Sidney Webb.

There is always the moment when we must begin to write. There are always the hundreds, the thousands, of struggle, of getting up, of pacing about, of sitting down, of laborious uneven accomplishment. During the time of actual work, what else besides ourselves, can help us? Can we call to mind then the contents of 20,000 books? Can we depend on anything other than ourselves for help?

At La Régence:
How certain trivial words and phrases haunt the brain—cannot be for-gotten—come back again even when years have passed. Today, have been hearing old voices, old songs, fleeting forgotten words of twenty years ago—my mother's—my father's—the voices of the summer board-ers on the porches—most of all, Dinwood Bland, sitting in pleasant back-yard of his house in Norfolk, a drink in his hand, his blind eyes blindly fixed upon the flashing sparkling waters of Hampton Roads, blindly on a white ship passing—his thin, senile, evil, strangely attractive face touched with bitterness, revulsion, and his weary disgust with life as he said:
"My father was an educated loafer."
And now, all day long, "the sound of these words rings and echoes in my mind until I can list to nothing else." And sitting here I feel like Coleridge when the rhyme for Youth and Age came to him (10 Sept. 1823 Wed. morning 10 o'clock)—"An Air," he says, "that whizzed *dia engkefalou*" (right across the character of my brain) exactly like a Hum-mel Vee—etc.
So, too, with me, all afternoon—and Dinwood Bland's haunting phrase about his father has now become:

"My father was an educated loafer,
My mother was an alcoholic bum,
My sister's name was Nelly, she had a lovely belly,
Aside from that she was a lousy scum.

"My brother Pete, he went and joined the navy,
My brother Hank, he went and caught the clap,
My little sister Anny, fell down and bruised her fanny——

Because we had an educated Pap,"—etc.

Obscure, ridiculous—but old words, old phrases, and forgotten sayings—why do they come back to haunt our meaning?

At La Régence:
On quotations—The practice of nineteenth century "good" writers was to decorate their compositions with neat little patterns of quotations. That practice still persists in a great deal of the correct writing of the present —viz., the essays and leading articles of *The Atlantic Monthly, The Spectator, Harpers, The Century, The London Mercury,* etc.—The quotation habit is generally a vicious one, often it has not even so worthy a design as to borrow from stronger and greater people an energy and clearness that we do not have, but rather serves as a sort of diploma to certify our culture—said culture consisting in our ability to quote scraps from Lamb, Dickens, John Keats, Browning, Doctor Johnson, and Matthew Arnold. The distortion this works upon the original sinew of the mind is incalculable—writing becomes a meeting of pseudo-courtliness neatly designed to arrive before Lamb with a bow and to be handed by Dickens to Lord Tennyson with a graceful flourish. The phrase "apt quotation" is one of the most misleading phrases ever invented. Most quotations so far from being apt to any purpose, are distinguished by all the ineptitude a politician displays when having spoken for twenty minutes on the Nicaraguan question, he says: "That reminds me of a little story I heard the other day. It seems there were two Irishmen whose names were Pat and Mike"—then proceeds to a discussion of the Prohibition issue, after his convulsed audience is somewhat recovered.

Europe and America are still too far apart—the "interminable" day is far too long—six days is far too long—for the intense impression— to compare and observe their essential difference——
Results: We must have them closer together—as the English and the French—as Dover and Calais—things that matter in our life cannot be recalled so easily. I have lived deeply, intensely, vividly, on the whole unhappily, for six months. Some people say that is all that matters. I do not think it is. But things cannot be called up so easily.

I am wondering in a vast *vague* about her. I love her, I think of seeing her again with a sense of strangeness and wonder; but I have no sort of

idea what it will be like, or what has happened. Why can we not remember the faces of those we love? This is true: Their faces melt into
a thousand shades and shapes and images of faces, the moment that we
try to fix them in our memory. It is only the face of a stranger we
remember there. Why?

Never has the many-ness and the much-ness of things caused me
such trouble as in the past six months. But never have I had so firm a
conviction that our lives can live upon only a few things, that we must
find them, and begin to build our fences.

All creation is the building of a fence.

But deeper study always, sharper senses, profounder living; *never* an
end to curiosity!

The fruit of all this comes later. I must think. I must mix it all
with myself and with America. I have caught much of it on paper. But
infinitely the greater part is in the wash of my brain and blood.

Shaw makes a fool of himself when he writes of Napoleon, because he
hates Napoleon and wants to make him ridiculous. But Shaw makes a
hero of himself when he writes of Cæsar; Shaw's Cæsar is the best
Cæsar I know of. It beats Shakespeare. It is as Cæsar looks (Naples
Museum) I am sure. I am sure Cæsar was like this.

But it is a mistake to suppose that Napoleon got his hair in the soup.

Dirge: Why are we unhappy?—I have no need to envy this man's
fame—nor skill to cloak myself in that man's manner—I am as naked
now as sorry—and all I ask is, Why are we so unhappy?

Why are we unhappy?

In my father's country there are yet men with quiet eyes and slow,
fond, kindly faces.

LXXVI

About four o'clock on the afternoon of New Year's Eve, 1924, as
Eugene was entering the Louvre, he met Starwick. Starwick was
elegantly dressed, as always, in casual, beautifully tailored, brown tweed
garments. He still carried a cane and twirled it indolently as he came
down the steps. He was the same old picture of bored, languorous, almost feminine grace, but instead of a shirt he was wearing a Russian
blouse of soft blue wool which snuggled around his neck in voluptuous

folds and had a kind of diamond-shaped design of crimson threads along the band.

For a moment, half-way down the gray stone steps, worn and hollowed as ancient European steps are worn and hollowed by the soft incessant eternity of feet, as the other people thronged past him, he paused, his pleasant ruddy face and cleft chin turned vaguely up towards those soft skies of time, already fading swiftly with the early wintry light.

As always, Frank looked magnificent, and with his Russian blouse, and the expression of inscrutable sorrow on his face, more mysterious and romantic than ever. Even in this foreign scene, he seemed to take possession of his surroundings with a lordly air. So far from looking like an alien, a foreigner, or a common tourist, Frank seemed to belong to the scene more than anybody there. It was as if something very frail and rare and exquisite and weary of the world—Alfred de Musset or George Moore, or the young Oscar, or Verlaine—had just come out of the Louvre, and it all seemed to belong to him.

The enormous central court of the Louvre, the soaring wings of that tremendous and graceful monument, the planned vistas of the Tuileries before him, fading into the mist-hazed air and the soft graying light— the whole tremendous scene, with all its space and strength and hauntingly aerial grace—at once as strong as ancient battlemented time, and as delicate and haunting as music on a spinet—swept together in a harmonious movement of spaciousness and majesty and graceful loveliness to form a background for the glamorous personality of Francis Starwick.

Even as he stood there, the rare and solitary distinction of his person was evident as it had never been before. People were streaming out of the museum and down the steps past him—for already it was the closing hour—and as they went by they all looked common, shabby and drearily prosaic by comparison. A middle-aged Frenchman of the middle-class, a chubby, ruddy figure of a man, dressed in cloth of the hard, ugly, ill-cut black that this class of Frenchmen wear, came by quickly with his wife, his daughter and his son. The man was driven along by the incessant, hot sugar of that energy which drives the race and which, with its unvaried repetition of oaths, ejaculations, denials, affirmations, and exactitudes, lavished at every minute upon the most trivial episodes of life, can become more drearily tedious than the most banal monotone. Compared with Starwick, his figure was thick, blunt, common in its clumsy shapelessness, and his wife had the same common, swarthy, blunted look. An American came down the steps with his wife: he was neatly dressed in the ugly light-grayish clothes that so many Americans .wear, his wife was also neatly turned out with the tedious and metallic stylishness of American apparel. They had the naked, inept and uneasy look of tourists, everything about them seemed troubled and alien to the scene, even to the breezy quality of the air, and the soft thick skies about them. When they had descended the steps, they paused a moment in a worried and undecided way, the man pulled at his watch and peered at it with his meagre prognathous face, and then said nasally:

"Well, we told them we'd be there at four-thirty. It's about that now."

All of these people, young and old, French, American, or of whatever nationality, looked dreary, dull and common, and uneasily out of place, when compared with Starwick.

After a moment's shock of stunned surprise, a drunken surge of impossible joy, Eugene ran towards him shouting, "Frank!"

Starwick turned, with a startled look upon his face: in a moment the two young men were shaking hands frantically, almost hugging each other in their excitement, both blurting out at once a torrent of words which neither heard. Finally, when they had grown quieter, Eugene found himself saying:

"But where the hell have you been, Frank? I wrote you twice: didn't you get any of my letters?—what happened to you?—where were you? —did you go down to the South of France to stay with Egan, as you said you would?"

"Ace," said Starwick—his voice had the same, strangely mannered, unearthly quality it had always had, only it was more mysterious and secretive than ever before—"Ace, I have been there."

"But why—?"—the other began, "why aren't you?—" He paused, looking at Starwick with a startled glance. "What happened, Frank?"

For, by his few quiet and non-committal words, Starwick had managed to convey perfectly the sense of sorrow and tragedy—of a grief so great it could not be spoken, a hurt so deep it could not be told. His whole personality was now pervaded mysteriously by this air of quiet, speechless and incommunicable sorrow; he looked at the other youth with the eyes of Lazarus returned from the tomb, and that glance said more eloquently than any words could ever do that he now knew and understood things which no other mortal man could ever know or understand.

"I should prefer not to talk about it," he said very quietly, and by these words Eugene understood that some tragic and unutterable event had now irrevocably sundered Starwick from Egan—though what that event might be, he saw it was not given him to know.

Immediately, however, in his old, casual, and engaging fashion, speaking between lips that barely moved, Starwick said:

"Look! What are you doing now? Is there any place you have to go?"

"No. I was just going in here. But I suppose it's too late now, anyway."

At this moment, indeed, they could hear the bells ringing in the museum, and the voices of the guards, crying impatiently:

"On ferme! On ferme, messieurs!"—and the people began to pour out in streams.

"Ace," said Starwick, "they're closing now. Besides," he added wearily, "I shouldn't think it would matter to you, anyway. . . . God!" he cried suddenly, in a high, almost womanish accent of passionate conviction, "what junk! What mountains and oceans of junk! And so bad!" he cried passionately, in his strange, unearthly tone. "So incredibly and impossibly bad. In that whole place there are just three things worth seeing—but *they!*"—his voice was high again with passionate excitement —"*they* are *unspeakably* beautiful, Eugene! God!" he cried, high and passionate again, "how *beautiful* they are! How utterly, impossibly beautiful!" Then with a resumption of his quiet, matter-of-fact tone he said, "You must come here with me some time. I will show them to you. . . . Look!" he said, in his casual tone again, "will you come to the Régence with me and have a drink?"

The whole earth seemed to come to life at once. Now that Starwick was here, this unfamiliar world, in whose alien life he had struggled like a drowning swimmer, became in a moment wonderful and good. The feeling of numb, nameless terror, rootless desolation, the intolerable sick anguish of homelessness, insecurity, and homesickness, against which he had fought since coming to Paris, and which he had been ashamed and afraid to admit, was now instantly banished. Even the strange dark faces of the French as they streamed past no longer seemed strange, but friendly and familiar, and the moist and languorous air, the soft thick grayness of the skies which had seemed to press down on his naked sides, to permeate his houseless soul like a palpable and viscous substance of numb terror and despair, were now impregnated with all the vital energies of living, with the intoxication of an unspeakable, nameless, infinitely strange and various joy. As they walked across the vast court of the Louvre towards the great arched gateway and all the brilliant traffic of the streets, the enormous dynamic murmur of the mysterious city came to him and stirred his entrails with the sensual premonitions of unknown, glamorous and seductive pleasure. Even the little taxis, boring past with wasp-like speed across the great space of the Louvre and through the sounding arches, now contributed to this sense of excitement, luxury and joy. The shrill and irritating horns sounded constantly through the humid air, and filled his heart with thoughts of New Year: already the whole city seemed astir, alive now with the great carnival of New Year's Eve.

At the Régence, they found a table on the terrace of the old café where Napoleon had played dominoes, and among the gay clatter of the crowd of waning afternoon, they drank brandy, talked passionately and with almost delirious happiness, drank brandy again, and watched the swarming and beautiful life upon the pavements and at the crowded tables all around them.

The streams of traffic up and down the whole Avenue de l'Opéra and the Place de la Comédie Française, the delicate, plain, and beautiful façade of the Comédie across the Square from them, the statue of frail De Musset, half-fainting backwards in the arms of his restoring muse —all this seemed not only part of him, but now that Starwick was here, to gain an enormous enhancement and enchantment, to be the total perfume of an incredibly good and lovely and seductive life, the whole of which, in all its infinite ramifications, seemed to be distilled into his blood like a rare liquor, and to belong to him. And so they drank and talked and drank until full dark had come, and tears stood in their eyes, and the brandy saucers were racked up eight deep upon their table.

Then, gloriously sad and happy and exultantly triumphant, and full of nameless joy and evil, they stepped into one of the shrill, exciting little taxis, and were charioted swiftly up that thronging noble street, until the great soaring masses of the Opera stood before them and the Café de la Paix was at one side.

And they were young, all-conquering and exultant, and all the magic life of strange million-footed Paris belonged to them, and all its strange and evil fragrance burned fierce and secret in their veins, and they knew

that they were young and that they would never die, that it was New
Year's Eve in Paris, and that that magic city had been created for them.
By this time they had between them about 400 francs.

Then followed the huge kaleidoscope of night: at one o'clock, leaving
a café, they got into a taxi, and vociferously demanded of the ruddy
driver, in French made eloquently confident by alcohol and joy, that
they be taken to the resorts most frequented by "nos frères—vous comprenez—les honnêtes hommes—les ouvriers."

He smilingly assented, and from that time on until dawn they made a
madman's round of little vile cafés, so mazed, so numerous, so inextricably confused in the vast web-like slum and jungle of nocturnal
Paris, that later they could never thread their way back through that
labyrinth of crooked alley-ways, and drunkenness and confusion. Their
driver took them to a region which they later thought was somewhere
in that ancient, foul and tangled quarter between the Boulevard de
Sébastopol and Les Halles. And all that night from one o'clock to dawn,
they threaded noxious alleys, beside the shuttered façades of ancient,
evil, crone-like houses, and stopped at every blaze of garish light to
enter dirty little dives, where sullen evil-visaged men surveyed them
sullenly over bistro bars, and gave them with a slimy hand cheap vile
cognac in greasy little glasses. In these places there was always the evil,
swelling, fatly unctuous and seductive music of accordions, the hoarse
bravos of applause. Here one bought metal slugs, a dozen for five francs,
and gave them to sluttish sirens with no upper teeth for the favor of a
dance; and here also there were many soldiers, Colonial negroes, black
as ebony, were most in favor; and here were men with caps and scarves
and evil, furtive eyes, who watched them steadily.

From place to place, from dive to dive, all through that huge and
noxious labyrinth of night, their wild debauch wore on. And presently
they noticed that wherever they went, two gendarmes followed them,
stood quietly at the bar, and courteously and genially took the drinks
they always bought for them, and were always there when they entered
the next place. And the ruddy and good-natured taxi-man was always
there as well, and he too always drank with them, and always said, with
robust satisfaction: "Mais, oui! Parbleu! A votre santé, messieurs!"

The gray haggard light of daybreak showed the cold gray waters of
the Seine, ancient, narrowed, flowing on between huge stone walls, the
haggard steep façades of the old shuttered houses in the Latin Quarter,
the narrow angularity of the silent streets. In Montparnasse, they got out

at the corner of the Boulevard Edgar Quinet, and demanded the reckon-
ing. All that remained to them was less than fifty francs; they took it
all, the soiled and nibbled little five-franc notes, the coppery one and
two-franc pieces, the ten and twenty-five and fifty-centime pieces, and
poured it into his hands, and stood there, guilty, silent and ashamed
before his astonished and reproachful face, because he had stood by
them well and loyally all through that blind kaleidoscope of night, and
it was New Year's Eve, and they were drunk and gay, and, he had
thought, rich Americans, and he had hired for, earned, expected, more.

"It's all we have," they said.

That ruddy robust man then did something that is perhaps rare in
the annals of French taxidom, and which they never forgot.

After an astonished moment, while he looked at the little wad of
bills and coins in his broad palm, he suddenly laughed loud and cheerfully, tossed the little wad of money in the air and caught it as it fell,
stripped off a five-franc note and pocketed the rest, handed the five-franc
note to Starwick, and said cheerfully——

"It's all right! You two boys take this and buy yourselves some breakfast to sober up on. Happy New Year!"—and with a friendly farewell
wave of the hand, drove off.

They had delicious morning crescent rolls, fresh baked and crusty,
and thick rich chocolate, at a little bakery in the Boulevard Edgar
Quinet, next to Starwick's quarters. He was living in a studio, loaned
to him, he said, by "two friends," whom he did not name, and who
were "out of town for the holidays."

The studio was one of a row of similar buildings all fronting on a
little enclosed alley-way. One entered from a street through a gate set
in the wall: one rang a bell, and presently la concierge pressed a button
which released the door. Inside, it was very quiet and still and gray with
the gray morning light of New Year's Day. And all the city was shut
out. Then they entered Starwick's studio: in the gray light a big room
with a slanting roof of gray glazed glass emerged: around the walls
were paintings, the limbs and fragments of unfinished sculptures, a
few chairs and tables, and a couch bed. At the back there was a balcony,
and steps ascending to it: here too there was a cot, and Starwick told
Eugene he could sleep up there.

Both young men were groggy with weariness and the night's debauch:
in the cold gray light, life looked black and ugly, they were exhausted
and ashamed. Starwick lay down upon the couch and went to sleep;

Eugene ascended to the balcony, pulled off his clothes and tossed them in a heap, and fell into the deep drugged sleep of drunkenness and exhaustion.

He slept till noon; and was awakened by the sound of steps below, the opening and closing of the door, and suddenly a woman's voice, light, gay, authoritative, and incisive:

"Darling, we're back again!" the gay, light voice cried out: "Welcome to our city! Happy New Year," she went on more quietly, and with a note of tender intimacy. "How have you been?"

He heard Starwick's quiet voice as it answered her, and presently the low, brief, and almost sullen tones of another woman. Starwick called sleepily up to Eugene, telling him to dress at once and come down: when he got downstairs, Starwick and the two women were waiting for him.

The one with the light, gay, incisive voice greeted him warmly and cordially, and made him feel instantly at home. She seemed to be the older of the two, and yet there was not much difference in their age. The other woman shook hands with him almost curtly, and muttered a few words of greeting. She was a big dark-haired New England sort of girl; she wore dark, drab, rusty-looking clothes, and her face had a sullen, almost heavy cast to it. While Starwick, and the other woman, whose name was Elinor, rattled gaily on together, the dark girl sat sullenly and awkwardly in her chair, and said nothing. Once or twice they spoke to her: she had a way of answering with a few curt sullen words and a short angry laugh, which went as quickly as it came, and left her face heavy and sullen again. But the moment she laughed, Eugene noticed that her mouth was very red and sweet, her teeth beautifully white, and for a moment the girl's sullen face was illuminated by a radiant tender loveliness. He heard Frank call her Ann: Starwick seemed to want to tease her, and when he spoke to her there was a little burble of malicious laughter in his voice. Turning to Eugene, his pleasant face reddening and the burble of malicious laughter playing in his throat, Frank said:

"She is *very* beautiful. You'd never think it, but she really *is*, you know."

Ann muttered something short and angry, and her face flushing, she laughed her short sudden laugh of anger and exasperation. And as she did so, her face came alive at once with its radiant loveliness, and he saw that what Starwick said of her was true.

LXXVII

THAT was a fine life that he had that year. He lived in a little hotel in the Rue des Beaux Arts. He had a good room there which cost him twelve francs a day. It was a good hotel, and was the place where Oscar Wilde had died. When any one wanted to see the celebrated death-room, he would ask to see "le chambre de Monsieur Veeld," and Monsieur Gely, the proprietor, or one of his buxom daughters, would willingly show it.

At nine o'clock in the morning the maid would come in with chocolate or coffee, bread and jam and butter, which was included in the price of the room. She put it down on a little cabinet beside his bed, which had a door and a chamber pot inside. After she went out he would get up and move it to the table, and drink the chocolate and eat some bread and jam. Then he would go back to bed and sleep until noon and sometimes later: at one o'clock, Starwick and the two women would come to take him to lunch. If they did not come, they would send him a *pneumatique* telling him where to meet them. They went to a great many different places, but the lunch was always good. Sometimes they would send a *pneumatique* telling him to meet them at the Dome or the Rotonde. When he got there, they would be sitting at a table on the terrace, and already very gay. Starwick would have a stack of saucers racked up before him on the table. On each saucer would be a numeral which said 3:50, or 5:00, or 6:00, or 7:50 francs, depending on what he had been drinking.

Usually it was cognac, but sometimes Starwick would greet him with a burble of laughter, saying in his sensuous and voluptuous voice: "Did you ever drink Amer Picon?"

"No," he would say.

"Well," said Starwick. "You ought to try it. You really ought, you know." And the soft burble would come welling up out of his throat again, and Elinor, looking at him tenderly, smiling, would say:

"Francis! You idiot! Leave the child alone!"

Then they would go to lunch. Sometimes they went to a place near by called Henriettes which Elinor had known about when she was an ambulance driver in the war. Again, they would cross the river and eat at Prunier's, Weber's, the Café Régence, Fouquet's, or at a place half way up the hill in Montmartre, which was in a Square called the Place des Martyrs, and which was called L'Ecrevisse, probably because of a little shell-fish which they sold there, and which was a specialty. That was a fine place: they always ate out on the terrace where they could see everything that was going on in the little Square, and Elinor, who had known the place for years, said how lovely it would be in spring.

Often they would eat at little places, which were not very expensive and which Elinor also knew about. She knew about everything: there was nothing about Paris she did not know. Elinor did the talking, rattling off her French like a native—or, anyway, like a native of Boston who speaks French well—trippingly off the tongue, getting the same intonations and gestures the French got, when she argued with them, saying:

"Mais non—mais non mais non mais non mais non mais non!" so rapidly that we could hardly follow her, and she could say: "Oui. C'est ça!—Mais parfaitement!—Entendu! . . . Formidable!" etc., in the same way a Frenchman could.

Yet there was a trace of gaiety and humor in everything she said and did. She had "the light touch" about everything, and understood just how it was with the French. Her attitude toward them was very much the manner of a mature and sophisticated person with a race of clamoring children. She never grew tired of observing and pointing out their quaint and curious ways: if the jolly proprietor of a restaurant came to the table and proudly tried to speak to them his garbled English, she would shake her head sharply, with a little smile, biting her lower lip as she did so, and saying with a light and tender humor:

"Oh, nice! . . . He wants to speak his English! . . . Isn't he a dear? . . . No, no," she would say quickly if any one attempted to answer him in French. "Please let him go ahead—poor dear! He's so proud of it!"

And again she would shake her head, biting her lower lip, with a tender wondering little smile, as she said so, and "Yes!" Francis would say enthusiastically and with a look of direct, serious, and almost sorrowful earnestness. "And how grand the man is about it—how simple and grand in the way he does it! . . . Did you notice the way he used his hand—I mean like some one in a painting by Cimabue—it really is, you know," he said earnestly. "The centuries of living and tradition that have gone into a single gesture—and he's quite unconscious of it. It's grand—I mean like some one in a painting by Cimabue—it really is, you know," he said with the sad, serious look of utter earnestness. "It's really quite incredible."

"Quite," said Elinor, who with a whimsical little smile had been looking at a waiter with sprouting mustaches, as he bent with prayerful reverence, stirring the ingredients in a salad bowl—"Oh, Francis, darling, look—" she whispered, nodding toward the man. "Don't you *love* it? . . . Don't you simply *adore* the way they do it! . . . I *mean*, you know! Now where? Where?" she cried, with a gesture of complete surrender—"*where* could you find anything like that in America? . . . I mean, you simply couldn't find it—that's all."

"*Quite!*" said Francis concisely. And turning to Eugene, he would say with that impressive air of absolute sad earnestness, "And it's really *most* important. It really is, you know. It's astonishing to see what they can put into a single gesture. I mean—the Whole Thing's there. It really is."

"Francis!" Elinor would say, looking at him with her gay and tender little smile, and biting her lip as she did so—"You *kid*, you! I *mean!*——"

Suddenly she put her hand strongly before her eyes, bent her head, and was rigid in a moment of powerful and secret emotion. In a moment, however, she would look up, wet-eyed, suddenly thrust her arm across the table at Eugene, and putting her hand on his arm with a slight gallant movement, say quietly:

"O, I'm sorry—you poor child! . . . After all, there's no reason why you should have to go through all this. . . . I mean, darling," she explained gently, "I have an adorable kid at home just four years old— sometimes something happens to make me think of him—you understand, don't you?"

"Yes," he said.

"Good," she said briskly and decisively, with a swift and gallant smile, as she patted his arm again. "I knew you would!"

She had left her husband and child in Boston, she had come here to join Francis, fatality was in the air, but she was always brave and gallant about it. As Francis would say to Eugene as they sat drinking alone in a café:

"It's *mad*—Boston! . . . Perfectly *mad*—Boston! . . . I mean, the kind of thing they do when they ride a horse up the steps of the State House. . . . I mean, perfectly *grand,* you know," he cried with high enthusiasm. "They stop at nothing. It's simply *swell*—it really is, you know."

Every one was being very brave and gallant and stopping at nothing, and the French were charming, charming, and Paris gave them just the background that they needed. It was a fine life.

Elinor took charge of everything. She took charge of the money, the making of plans, the driving of bargains with avaricious and shrewd-witted Frenchmen, and the ordering of food in restaurants.

"It's really astonishing, you know," said Starwick—"the way she walks in everywhere and has the whole place at her feet in four minutes. . . . Really, Gene, you should have been with us this afternoon when she made arrangements with the man at the motor agency in the Champs Elysées for renting the car. . . . Really, I felt quite sorry for him before the thing was over. . . . He kept casting those knowing and rather *bitter* glances of reproach at me," said Starwick, with his burble of soft laugher, "as if he thought I had betrayed him by not coming to his assistance. . . . There was something *very* cruel about it . . . like a great cat, playing with a mouse . . . there really was, you know," said Starwick earnestly. "She can be completely without pity when she gets that way," he added. "She really can, you know . . . which makes it all the more astonishing—I mean, when you consider what she really is—the way she let me go to sleep on her shoulder the night we were coming back from Rheims, and I was so horribly drunk and got so disgustingly sick," he said with a simple, touching earnestness. "I mean, the *compassion* of it—it was *quite* like that Chinese goddess of the Infinite Compassion, they have in Boston—it *really* was, you know. It's quite astonishing," he said earnestly, "when you consider her background, the kind of people that she came from—it really *is*, you know . . . she's a grand person, simply terrific . . . it's utterly *mad*—Boston . . . it really is."

Certainly it was very pleasant to be in the hands of such a captain. Elinor got things done with a beautiful, serene assurance that made everything seem easy. There was no difficulty of custom or language, no weird mystery and complication of traffic, trade, and commerce, so maddening and incomprehensible to most Americans, that El-inor did not understand perfectly. Sometimes, she would just shake her head and bite her lip, smiling. Sometimes she would laugh with rich astonishment, and say: *"Perfectly* insane, of course—but then, that's the way the poor dears are, and you can't change them. . . . I *know!* I *know!* . . . It's quite incredible, but they'll *always* be that way, and we've simply got to make the best of it."

She was a heavily built woman about thirty years old who seemed older than she was. She dressed very plainly and wore a rather old hat with a cockade, which gave her a look of eighteenth-century gallantry. And the impression of maturity was increased by her heavy and un-youthful figure, and the strong authority of her face which, in spite of her good-humored, gay, and whimsical smile, her light Bostonian air of raillery, indicated the controlled tension and restraint of nerves of a person of stubborn and resolute will who is resolved always to act with aristocratic grace and courage.

In spite of her heavy figure, her rough and rather unhealthy-looking skin, she was a distinguished-looking woman, and in her smile, her tone, her play of wit, and even in the swift spitefulness and violence which could flash out and strike and be gone before its victim had a chance to retort or defend himself, she was thoroughly feminine. And yet the woman made no appeal at all to sensual desire: although she had left her husband and child to follow Starwick to France, and was thought by her own family to have become his mistress, it was impossible to imagine her in such a rôle. And for this reason, perhaps, there was something ugly, dark, and sinister in their relation, which Eugene felt strongly but could not define. He felt that Elinor was lacking in the attraction or desire of the sensual woman as Starwick seemed to be lacking in the lust of the sensual man, and there was therefore something in their relation that came from the dark, the murky swamp-fires of emotion, something poisonous, perverse and evil, and full of death.

Just the same, it was fine to be with Elinor when she was gay and deft and charming, and enormously assured, and taking charge of things. At these times, everything in life seemed simple, smooth, and easy; there were no dreary complications, the whole world became an enormous oyster ready to be opened, Paris an enormous treasure-hoard of unceasing pleasure and delight. It was good to be with her in a restaurant, and to let her do the ordering.

"Now, children," she would say in her crisp, gay, and yet authoritative tone, staring at the menu with a little frowning smile of studious yet whimsical concentration—"The rest of you can order what you like, but Mother's going to start with fish and a bottle of Vouvray—I seem to remember that it's very good here—Le Vouvray est bon ici, n'est-ce pas?" she said turning to the waiter.

"Mais, oui, madame!" he said with just the right kind of earnest enthusiasm, "C'est une spécialité."

"Bon," she said crisply. "Alors, une bouteille du Vouvray pour commencer—does that go for the rest of you, mes enfants?" she said, looking around her. They nodded their agreement.

"Bon—bon, madame," the waiter said, nodding his vigorous approval, as he put the order down. "Vous serez bien content avec le Vouvray—et puis?"—He looked at her with suave respectful inquiry. "Pour manger?"

"Pour moi," said Elinor, "le poisson—le filet de sole—n'est-ce pas—Marguery?"

"Bon, bon," he said with enthusiastic approval, writing it down. "Un filet de sole—Marguery—pour Madame—et pour Monsieur?" he said turning suavely to Eugene.

"La même chose," said that linguist recklessly and even as the waiter was nodding enthusiastically, and saying:

"Bon. Bon—parfaitement! La même chose pour monsieur," and writing it down, the others had begun to laugh at him. Starwick with his bubbling laugh, Elinor with her gay little smile of raillery and even Ann, the dark and sullen beauty of her face suddenly luminous with a short and almost angry laugh as she said:

"He hasn't said his other word yet—why don't you tell him that you want some 'mawndiawnts' "—ironically she imitated his pronunciation of the word.

"What's wrong with 'mendiants'?" he said, scowling at her. "What's the joke?"

"Nothing," said Starwick bubbling with laughter. "They're very good. They really are, you know," he said earnestly. "Only we've been wondering if you wouldn't learn another word some day and order something else."

"I know lots of other words," he said angrily. "Only, how am I ever going to get a chance to use them when the rest of you make fun of me every time I open my mouth—I don't see what the great joke is," he said resentfully. "These French people understand what I want to say," he said. "Ecoute, garçon," he said appealingly to the attentive and smiling waiter.—"Vous pouvez comprendre——"

"Cawmprawndre," said Ann mockingly.

"Vous pouvez comprendre—ce-que-je-veux-dire," he blundered on painfully.

"Mais, oui, monsieur!" the waiter cried with a beautiful reassuring smile. "Parfaitement. Vous parlez très bien. Vous êtes ici à Paris depuis longtemps?"

"Depuis six semaines," he said proudly.

The waiter lifted arms and eyebrows eloquent with astounded disbelief.

"Mais c'est merveilleux!" the waiter cried, and as the others jeered Eugene said with bitter sarcasm:

"Every one can't be a fine old French scholar the way you are; after all, I'm not travelled like the rest of you—I've never had your opportunities. And even after six weeks here there are still a few words in the French language that I don't know. . . . But I'm going to speak the ones I do know," he said defiantly, "and no one's going to stop me."

"Of course you are, darling!" Elinor said quickly and smoothly, putting her hand out on his arm with a swift movement. "Don't let them tease you! . . . I think it's mean of you," she said reproachfully. "Let the poor dear speak his French if he wants to—I think it's sweet."

He looked at her with a flushed and angry face while Starwick bubbled with laughter, tried to think of something to say in reply, but, as always, she was too quick for him, and before he could think of something apt and telling, she had flashed off as light and quick as a rapier blade:

"—Now, children," she was studying the card again—"what shall it be after the fish—who wants meat—?"——

"No fish for me," said Ann, looking sullenly at the menu. "I'll take—" suddenly her dark, sullen, and nobly beautiful face was transfigured by her short and almost angry laugh again—"I'll take an 'awmlet,' " she said sarcastically, looking at Eugene.

"Well, take your 'awmlet,' " he muttered. "Only I don't say it that way."

"Pas de poisson," she said quietly to the waiter. "I want an omelette."

"Bon, bon," he nodded vigorously and wrote. "Une omelette pour Madame. Et puis après—?" he said inquiringly.

"Rien," she said.

He looked slightly surprised and hurt, but in a moment, turning to Eugene, said:

"Et pour monsieur?—Après le poisson?"

"Donnez-moi un Chateaubriand garni," he said.

And again Ann, whose head had been turned sullenly down towards the card, looked up suddenly and laughed, with that short and almost angry laugh that seemed to illuminate with accumulating but instant radiance all of the dark and noble beauty of her face.

"God!" she said. "I knew it!—If it's not mendiants, it's Chateau-briand garni."

"Don't forget the Nuits St. George," said Starwick with his bubbling laugh, "that's still to come."

"When he gets through," she said, "there won't be a steak or raisin left in France."

And she looked at Eugene for a moment, her face of noble and tender beauty transfigured by its radiant smile. But almost immediately, she dropped her head again in its customary expression that was heavy and almost sullen, and that suggested something dumb, furious, and silent locked up in her, for which she could find no release.

He looked at her for a moment with scowling, half-resentful eyes, and all of a sudden, flesh, blood, and brain, and heart, and spirit, his life went numb with love for her.

"And now, my children," Elinor was saying gaily, as she looked at the menu—"what kind of salad is it going—" she looked up swiftly and caught Starwick's eye, and instantly their gaze turned upon their two companions. The young woman was still staring down with her sullen, dark, and dumbly silent look, and the boy was devouring her with a look from which the world was lost, and which had no place in it for time or memory.

Dark Helen in my heart forever burning.

"L'écrevisse," Eugene said, staring at the menu. "What does that mean, Elinor?"

"Well, darling, I'll tell you," she said with a grave light gaiety of tone, "an écrevisse is a kind of crawfish they have over here—a delicious little crab—but *much much* better than anything we have."

"Then the name of the place really means *The Crab?*" he asked.

"*Stop* him!" she shrieked faintly. "You barbarian, you!" she went on with mild reproach. "It's not at *all* the same."

"It's really not, you know," said Starwick, turning to him seriously. "The whole quality of the thing is different. It really is. . . . Isn't it astonishing," he went on with an air of quiet frankness, "the genius they have for names? I mean, even in the simplest words they manage to get the whole spirit of the race. I mean, this Square here, even," he gestured briefly, "La Place des Martyrs. The whole thing's there. It's really quite incredible, when you think of it," he said somewhat mysteriously. "It really is."

"Quite!" said Elinor. "And, oh, my children, if it were only spring and

I could take you down the Seine to an adorable place called La Pèche Miraculeuse."

"What does that mean, Elinor?" Eugene asked again.

"Well, darling," she said with an air of patient resignation, "if you *must* have a translation I suppose you'd call it *The Miraculous Catch*— a fishing catch, you know. Only it *doesn't* mean that. It would be sacrilege to call it that. It means *La Pèche Miraculeuse* and nothing else —it's *quite* untranslatable—it really is."

"*Yes,*" cried Starwick enthusiastically, "and even their simplest names —their names of streets and towns and places: L'Etoile, for example— how grand and simple that is!" he said quietly, "and how perfect—the whole design and spatial grandeur of the thing is in it," he concluded earnestly. "It really is, you know."

"Oh, absolutely!" Elinor agreed. "You couldn't call it *The Star,* you know. That means nothing. But *L'Etoile* is perfect—it simply *couldn't* be anything else."

"*Quite!*" Starwick said concisely, and then, turning to Eugene with his air of sad instructive earnestness, he continued: "—And that woman at Le Jockey Club last night—the one who sang the songs—you know?" he said with grave malicious inquiry, his voice trembling a little and his face flushing as he spoke—"the one you kept wanting to find out about— what she was saying?—" Quiet ruddy laughter shook him.

"*Perfectly* vile, of course!" cried Elinor with gay horror. "And all the time, poor dear, he kept wanting to know what it meant. . . . I was going to throw something at you if you kept on—if I'd had to translate *that* I think I should simply have passed out on the spot——"

"I know," said Starwick burbling with laughter—"I caught the look in your eye—it was really *quite* murderous! And *terribly* amusing!" he added. Turning to his friend, he went on seriously: "But really, Gene, it *is* rather stupid to keep asking for the meaning of everything. It *is,* you know. And it's so extraordinary," he said protestingly, "that a person of your quality—your *kind* of understanding—should be so dull about it! It really is."

"Why?" the other said bluntly, and rather sullenly. "What's wrong with wanting to find out what's being said when you don't understand the language? If I don't ask, how am I going to find out?"

"But not *at all!*" Starwick protested impatiently. "That's not the point at all: you can find out nothing that way. Really you can't," he said reproachfully. "The whole point about that song last night was not the words—the meaning of the thing. If you tried to translate it into English, you'd lose the spirit of the whole thing. Don't you see," he went on earnestly, "—it's not the *meaning* of the thing—you can't translate a thing like that, you really can't—if you tried to translate it, you'd have nothing but a filthy and disgusting jingle——"

"But so long as it's French it's beautiful?" the other said sarcastically.

"But *quite!*" said Starwick impatiently. "And it's very stupid of you not to understand that, Gene. It really is. The whole spirit and quality of the thing is *so* French—so *utterly* French!" he said in a high and rather womanish tone—"that the moment you translate it you lose everything. . . . There's nothing disgusting about the song in French —the words mean nothing, you pay no attention to the words; the extraordinary thing is that you forget the words. . . . It's the whole design of the thing, the *tone,* the *quality.* . . . In a way," he added deeply, "the thing has an *enormous* innocence—it really has, you know. . . . And it's so disappointing that you fail to see this. . . . Really, Gene, these questions you keep asking about names and meanings are becoming tiresome. They really are. . . . And all these books you keep buying and trying to translate with the help of a dictionary . . . as if you're ever going to understand anything—I mean, *really* understand," he said profoundly, "in that way."

"You may get to understand the language that way," the other said.

"But not at *all!*" cried Starwick. "That's just the point—you really find out nothing: you miss the whole spirit of the thing—just as you missed the spirit of that song, and just as you missed the point when you asked Elinor to translate La Pèche Miraculeuse for you. . . . It's extraordinary that you fail to see this. . . . The next thing you know," he concluded sarcastically, a burble of malicious laughter appearing as he spoke, "you will have enrolled for a course of lessons—" he choked suddenly, his ruddy face flushing deeply with his merriment—"for a course of lectures at the Berlitz language school."

"Oh, but he's entirely capable of it!" cried Elinor, with gay conviction. "I wouldn't put it past him for a moment. . . . My *dear,*" she said drolly, turning toward him, "I have never known such a glutton for knowledge. It's simply amazing. . . . Why, the child wants to know the meaning of everything!" she said with an astonished look about her—"the confidence he has in my knowledge is rather touching—it really is—and I'm so unworthy of it, darling," she said a trifle maliciously. "I don't deserve it at all!"

"I'm sorry if I've bored you with a lot of questions, Elinor," he said.

"But you *haven't!*" she protested. "Darling, you *haven't* for a moment! I *love* to answer them! It's only that I feel *so*—so *incompetent.* . . . But listen, Gene," she went on coaxingly, "couldn't you try to forget it for a while—just sort of forget all about these words and meanings and enter into the spirit of the thing? . . . Couldn't you, dear?" she said gently, and even as he looked at her with a flushed face, unable to find a ready answer to her deft irony, she put her hand out swiftly, patted him on the arm, and nodding her head with an air of swift satisfied finality, said:

"Good! I knew you would! . . . He's really a darling when he wants to be, isn't he?"

Starwick burbled with malicious laughter at sight of Eugene's glowering and resentful face; then went on seriously:

"—But their genius for names is quite astonishing!—I mean, even in the names of their towns you get the whole thing. . . . What could be more like Paris," he said quietly, "than the name of Paris? . . . The whole quality of the place is in the name. Or Dijon, for example. Or Rheims. Or Carcassonne. The whole spirit of Provence is in the word: what name could more perfectly express Arles than the name it has—it gives you the whole place, its life, its people, its peculiar fragrance. . . . And how different we are from them in that respect. . . . I mean," his voice rose on a note of passionate conviction, "you could almost say that the whole difference between us—the thing we lack, the thing they have —the whole thing that is wrong with us, is evident in our names. . . . It really is, you know," he said earnestly, turning toward his friend again. "The whole thing's most important. . . . How harsh and meaningless most names in America are, Eugene," he went on quietly. "Like addresses printed on a thousand envelopes at once by a stamping machine —labels by which a place may be identified but without meaning. . . . Tell me," he said quietly, after a brief pause, "what was the name of that little village your father came from? You told me one time—I remember because the whole thing I'm talking about—the thing that's wrong with us—was in that name. What was it?"

"Brant's Mill," the other young man answered.

"Quite!" said Starwick with weary concision. "A man named Brant had a mill, and so they called the place Brant's Mill."

"What's wrong with that?"

"Oh, nothing, I suppose," said Starwick quietly. "The whole thing's quite perfect. . . . *Brant's* Mill," there was a note of bitterness in his voice and he made the name almost deliberately rasping as he pronounced it. "It's a name—something to call a place by—if you write it on a letter it will get there. . . . I suppose that's what a name is for. . . . Gettysburg—I suppose a man named Gettys had a house or a farm, and so they named the town after him. . . . And your mother? What was the name of the place she came from?"

"It was a place called Yancey County."

"Quite," said Starwick as before—"and the name of the town?"

"There wasn't any town, Frank. It was a kind of cross-roads settlement called The Forks of Ivy."

"No!" Elinor's light Bostonian accent of astounded merriment rang gaily forth. "Not *really!* You *know* it wasn't!"

"But not at *all!*" said Starwick in a tone of mild and serious disagreement. "The Forks of Ivy is not bad. It's really surprisingly good, when you consider most of the other names. It even has," he paused, and considered carefully, "a kind of quality. . . . But Yancey," he paused again, the burble of sudden laughter came welling up, and for a moment his pleasant ruddy face was flushed with laughter—"*Ya-a-ancey* County" —with deliberate malice he brought the word out in a rasping countrified tone—"God!" he said frankly, turning to the other boy, "isn't it awful! . . . How harsh! How stupid! How banal! . . . And what are some of the names, where you come from, Gene?" he went on quietly after a brief pause. "I'm sure you haven't yet done your worst," he said. "There must be others just as sweet as Ya-a-ancey."

"Well, yes," the boy said grinning, "we've got some good ones: there's Sandy Mush, and Hooper's Bald, and Little Hominy. And we have names like Beaverdam and Balsam, and Chimney Rock and Craggy and Pisgah and The Rat. We have names like Old Fort, Hickory, and Bryson City; we have Clingman's Dome and Little Switzerland; we have Paint Rock and Saluda Mountain and the Frying Pan Gap——"

"Stop!" shrieked Elinor, covering her ears with her shocked fingers— "The Frying Pan Gap! Oh, but that's *horrible!*"

"But how perfect!" Starwick quietly replied. "The whole thing's there. And in the great and noble region where I come from—" the note of weary bitterness in his tone grew deeper—"out where the tall caw-r-n grows we have Keokuk and Cairo and Peoria." He paused, his grave eyes fixed in a serious and reflective stare: for a moment his pleasant ruddy face was contorted by the old bestial grimace of anguish and confusion. When he spoke again, his voice was weary with a quiet bitterness of scorn. "I was born," he said, "in the great and noble town of Bloomington but—" the note of savage irony deepened—"at a very tender age I was taken to Moline. And now, thank God, I am in Paris"; he was silent a moment longer, and then continued in a quiet and almost lifeless tone: "Paris, Dijon, Provence, Arles . . . Yancey, Brant's Mill, Bloomington." He turned his quiet eyes upon the other boy. "You see what I mean, don't you? The whole thing's there."

"Yes," the boy replied, "I guess you're right."

LXXVIII

THEY were sitting at a table in one of the night places of Montmartre. The place was close and hot, full of gilt and glitter, heavy with that unwholesome and seductive fragrance of the night that comes from perfumery, wine, brandy and the erotic intoxication of a night-time pleasure place. Over everything there was a bright yet golden blaze of light that wrought on all it touched—gilt, tinsel, table linen, the natural hue and coloring of the people, the faces of men, and the flesh of the women—an evil but strangely thrilling transformation.

The orchestra had just finished playing a piece that every one in Paris was singing that year. It was a gay jigging little tune that Mistinguette had made famous; its name was Ça, c'est Paris, and one heard it everywhere. One heard lonely wayfarers whistling it as they walked home late at night through the silent narrow streets of the Latin Quarter, and one heard it hummed by taxi-drivers, waiters, and by women in cafés. It was played constantly to the tune of flutes and violins by dance orchestras in the night-clubs of Montmartre and Montparnasse. And, accompanied by the swelling rhythms of the accordion, one heard it at big dance-halls like the Bal Bullier, and in the little dives and stews and café-brothel-dancing places along noisome alleyways near the markets and the Boulevard de Sébastopol.

In spite of its gay jigging lilt, that tune had a kind of mournful fatality. It was one of those songs which seem to evoke perfectly—it is impossible to know why—the whole color, life, and fragrance of a place and time as nothing else on earth can do. For the boy, that song would haunt him ever after with the image of Paris and of his life that year, with the memory of Starwick, Elinor, and Ann.

The song had for him the fatality of something priceless, irrecoverably

lost, full of that bitter joy and anguish we can feel at twenty-four, when
the knowledge of man's brevity first comes to us, when we first
know ruin and defeat, when we first understand what we have never
known before: that for us, as for every other man alive, all passes, all
is lost, all melts before our grasp like smoke; when we know that the
moment of beauty carries in it the seeds of its own instant death, that
love is gone almost before we have it, that youth is gone before we know
it, and that, like every other man, we must grow old and die.

The orchestra had finished playing this tune, and the dancers were
going to their tables from the polished little square of floor; in a moment
Starwick called the leader of the orchestra over to the table and asked
him to play Starwick's favorite song. This was a piece called My Chile
Bon Bon; it was not new, Starwick had first heard it several years before
in Boston, but like the other piece this tune was pregnant with the
mournful fatality of a place and period; in its grotesque words and
haunting melody there was the sense of something irrevocable, an utter
surrender and a deliberate loss, a consciousness of doom. These two
pieces together evoked the whole image and quality of that year, and of
the life of these four people: for Starwick, in fact, this Chile Bon Bon
song somehow perfectly expressed the complete fatality that had now
seized his life, the sensual inertia of his will.

The orchestra leader nodded smilingly when Starwick asked him to
play the song, went back and conferred with his musicians for a moment,
and, himself taking up a violin, began to play. As the orchestra played,
the leader walked toward their table, and, bending and swaying with
the infinite ductile grace which a violin seems to give to all its per-
formers, he stood facing the two women, seeming to offer up the wailing,
hauntingly mournful and exciting music as a kind of devotion to their
loveliness.

Elinor, tapping the tune out with her fingers on the table cloth, hummed the words lightly, absently, under her breath; Ann sat quietly,
darkly, sullenly attentive; Starwick, at one end of the table, sat turned
away, his legs indolently crossed, his ruddy face flushed with emotion,
his eyes fixed in a blind stare, and a little wet.

Once, while the piece was being played, Starwick's pleasant ruddy face
was contorted again by the old bestial grimace of nameless anguish and
bewilderment which Eugene had seen so many times before, and in
which the sense of tragic defeat, frustration, the premonition of impending ruin, was legible.

When the orchestra leader had finished with the tune, Starwick
turned wearily, thrust his arm indolently across the table towards Ann
and wiggling his fingers languidly and a trifle impatiently, said quietly:
"Give me some money."

She flushed a little, opened her purse, and said sullenly:
"How much do you want?"

The weary impatience of his manner became more evident, he wiggled
his languid fingers in a more peremptory command, and, burbling a
little with laughter at sight of her sullen face, he said in a low tone of
avaricious humor:

"Give, give, give. . . . Money, money, money," he said in a low gloating tone, and burbled again, with a rich welling of humor, as he looked
at her.

Red in the face, she flung a wad of bank notes down upon the table
with almost vicious force, he accepted them languidly, stripped off 300
franc notes and handed them indolently to the orchestra leader, who
responded with a bow eloquent with adoration; and then, without
pausing to count them, Starwick thrust the remainder carelessly in his
pocket.

"Ann!" he said reproachfully. "I am *very* hurt!" He paused a
moment; the flow and burble of soft laughter came quickly, flushing his
ruddy face, and he continued as before, with a mock gravity of reproachful humor.

"I had hoped—" his shoulders trembled slightly—"that by this time
your *finer* nature—" he trembled again with secret merriment—"your
finer nature would be ready to reveal itself."

"My finer nature be damned!" Ann said angrily. "Whether you like
it or not, I think it's disgraceful the way you fling money around! Three
hundred francs to a man for playing that damned song! And you've
done the same thing at least a dozen times! God, I'm sick of hearing
about your Chile Bon Bon!" she concluded bitterly. "I wish the damned
thing had never been written."

"Ann!" again the soft mockery of sounded reproach. "And this is the
way you repay us, after all we've done for you! It's not that I'm angry
but I'm *very very* hurt," he said gently. "I really am, you know."

"Ah-h!" She made a sudden exasperated movement as if she was
going to push the table away from her and get up, and then said with
angry warning: "Now, look here, Frank, don't you start that again
about how much you've done for me. Done for me!" she said furiously.

"Done for me!" She laughed, short and hard, with angry exasperation, and was unable to find words to continue.

Starwick's burble of soft laughter answered her:

"I *know!*" he said, his face reddening a little as he spoke—"But, after all, you *are* a little *tight,* Ann"—his shoulders trembled slightly, and his ruddy face grew deeper with its hue of humor. "I think," he said gently, and paused again, trembling with quiet laughter—"I think it may be what is known as the Beacon Hill influence. And really," he continued seriously, looking at her with grave eyes, "you really ought to try to get it out of you."

"Now, Frank," cried Ann angrily, half rising from the table, "if you start that again about my being stingy—" She sat down again abruptly, and burst out with bitter resentment, "I'm not stingy and you know it! . . . It's not that I mind spending the money, giving it to you when I've got it. . . . It's only that I think every one ought to try to bear his own share. . . . If you think that's my New England stinginess you're welcome to your opinion. . . . But I've always felt that way and always will! . . . Stingy!" she muttered, "I'm not. . . . I'm just tired of being the goat all the time. . . . It seems to me the rest of you ought to share in the expense sometime!"

"But not at *all!*" cried Starwick in a tone of astonished protest. "I can't see that that makes the *slightest* difference," he went on gently. "After all, Ann, it's not as if we were four old maids from Boston doing the grand tour and putting down every cent we spend in a mutual account book," he said a trifle sarcastically. "It's not that kind of thing at all. When four people know each other the way we do, the last thing in the world that could *possibly* be of value is money. What belongs to one belongs to all. Really," he said a trifle impatiently, "I should think you'd understand that. It's *quite* astonishing to see a person of your quality with such a material—rather *grasping*—view of money. I shouldn't think it would make the *slightest* difference to you. You really ought to get it out of your system, Ann," he said quietly. "You really must. Because you *are* a *grand* person—you really are, you know."

She flushed, and then muttered sullenly:

"Ah! Grand person my eye! I've heard all that before! You can't get around it that way!"

"But you *are!*" he said, with earnest insistence. "You are a *very* grand person—that's what makes the whole thing such a pity."

She flushed again, and then sat staring at the table in sullen embarrassment.

"And, Ann," said Starwick gently, beginning to burble with his soft flow of wicked laughter, "you are really *very* beautiful in that red dress—" his sensuous mannered tone trembled again with its burble of wicked humor—"and *very* seductive—and *very*," his shoulders trembled and his face trembled as he spoke—"You are really *quite* voluptuous," he said with sensual relish, and suddenly choked with laughter. When he had composed himself, he turned his still laughter-reddened face towards Eugene, and said earnestly: "It's *quite* astonishing! She really is, you know! She's *gloriously* beautiful!"

"Frank!" she looked at him for a moment with an expression of baffled exasperation. Then, suddenly she laughed her short and angry laugh: "God!" she cried sarcastically. "It's a high price to pay for compliments, isn't it?"

But that laugh, short and angry as it was, had made radiant, as it always did, her dark and noble beauty. Instantly her face had been lifted, transfigured from its customary expression of dark and almost heavy sullenness, her cheeks, which in repose had the pendulous sagging quality of a plump child, were suffused with rose, her sweet red mouth and white teeth suddenly shone with a radiant and lovely smile, and Eugene noticed now, as he had begun to notice, that her gray eyes when she looked at Starwick were no longer hard and angry, but smoky, luminous with a depthless tenderness.

"You *are*," Starwick concluded quietly, seriously, his pleasant face still a trifle flushed with laughter. "You are one of the most *gloriously* beautiful creatures that ever lived."

What he said was the simple truth. The girl's beauty that night was almost unbelievable. She had put on a new evening dress which had been made for her by a famous designer. The dress was a glorious red, that seemed almost to float with an aerial buoyancy of filmy gauze; no dress in the world could have suited her dark beauty, or revealed the noble proportions of her figure half so well. Her hair, which was black, coarse, and fragrant, was parted simply in the middle: Eugene noted that there were already a few streaks of coarse gray in it, but her face had the dignity of her grand and honest character—the sullen plumpness of a child and the radiant sudden sweetness and happiness of her smile, combined.

And in every other respect, Ann showed this strange and lovely union of delicacy and grandeur, of the child and the woman. Her hands were long, brown, and narrow, the fingers long and delicate, the bones as fine and small as a bird's, and yet they were strong, sensitive, able-looking hands as well. Her arms were long and slender, as firm and delicate as a young girl's, but Eugene noted that her breasts were not round and firm, but the long heavy sloping breasts of a big woman. When she got up to dance with Starwick she topped him by a head, and yet, radiant with a joy and happiness she had never known before, she seemed to float there in his arms, an Amazonian figure, great of thigh and limb and breast, and a creature of a loveliness as delicate and radiant as a child's.

They danced superbly together: in deference to Starwick, the orchestra played his Chile Bon Bon song again; when they returned to the table Starwick's ruddy face was flushed with the emotion the song always aroused in him, his eyes looked wet, and in a high, passionate, almost womanish tone, he cried to Eugene:

"God! Isn't it grand! Isn't it simply superb! It's one of the great songs of the world, it really is, you know! The thing has the same quality as a great primitive—the same quality as a primitive Apollo or Cimabue's Madonna, in the Louvre. Christ!" he cried in a high womanish tone, "the whole thing's there—it really is! I think it's the greatest song that was ever written!"

He poured out a glass of champagne, cold and sparkling, and drank it thirstily, his eyes wet, his face flushed deeply with his feeling.

LXXIX

In the dull gray light of the short and swiftly waning winter's day, the two young men were leaving the museum, to spend the rest of the afternoon until the time of their appointed meeting with the women, in drink and talk at one of the innumerable and seductive cafés of the magic city. Outside the Louvre, they hailed a taxi and were driven swiftly over one of the bridges of the Seine, through the narrow streets of the Latin Quarter, and at length stopped and got out before La Closerie des Lilas, where they were to meet the two women later on.

They spent the remainder of the afternoon in the chill wintry air of the terrace, warm with drink, with argument or discussion, and with the gaiety of life and voices of people all around them, the pageant of life that passed forever on the street before them—all that priceless, rare, and uncostly pleasure and excitement of café life which seemed unbelievable and magical to these two young Americans. The dull gray air, which was at once chill and wintry, and yet languorous, filled them with the sense of some powerful, strange, and inhuman excitement that was impending for them.

And the bright gaiety of the colors, the constant flash and play of life about them and along the pavements, the smell and potent intoxication of the cognac, gave them the sensation of a whole world given over without reserve or shame to pleasure. All these elements, together with that incomparable fusion of odors—at once corrupt and sensual, subtle and obscene—which exudes from the very texture of the Paris life—odors which it is impossible to define exactly, but which seem in the dull wintry air to be compacted of the smells of costly perfumes, of wine, beer, brandy, and of the acrid and nostalgic fumes of French tobacco, of roasted chestnuts, black French coffee, mysterious liquors of a hundred brilliant and intoxicating colors, and the luxurious flesh of scented women—smote the two young men instantly with the sensual impact of this strange and fascinating world.

But in spite of all the magic of the scene, and the assurance and security which Starwick's presence always gave to him, the ghost of the old unquiet doubt would not wholly be laid at rest, the ache of the old hunger stirred in Eugene. Why was he here now? Why had he come? The lack of purpose in this present life, the dozing indolence of this existence in which no one worked, in which they sat constantly at tables in a café, and ate and drank and talked, and moved on to sit at other tables, other cafés—and, most of all, the strange dull faces of the Frenchmen, the strange and alien life of this magic city which was so seductive but so unalterably foreign to all that he had ever known—all this had now begun to weigh inexplicably upon a troubled spirit, to revive again the old feelings of naked homelessness, to stir in him the nameless sense of shame and guilt which an American feels at a life of indolence and pleasure, which is part of the very chemistry of his blood, and which he can never root out of him. And feeling the obscure but powerful insistence of these troubled thoughts within his mind, he turned suddenly to Starwick, and, without a word of explanation said:

"But do you really feel at home here?"

"What do you mean by 'feeling at home'?"

"Well, I mean don't you ever feel out of place here? Don't you ever feel as if you didn't belong to this life—that you are a foreigner?"

"But not at all!" said Starwick a trifle impatiently. "On the contrary, I think it is the first time in my life that I have *not* felt like a foreigner. I never felt at home in the Middle-West where I was born; I hated the place from my earliest childhood, I always felt out of place there, and wanted to get away from it. But I felt instantly at home in Paris from the moment I got here:—I am far closer to this life than to any other life I've ever known, for the first time in my life I feel throughly at home."

"And you don't mind being a foreigner?"

"But of course not!" Starwick said curtly. "Besides, I am *not* a foreigner. You can only be foreign in a place that is foreign to you. This place is not."

"But, after all, Frank, you are not a Frenchman. You are an American."

"Not at all," Starwick answered concisely. "I am an American only by the accident of birth; by spirit, temperament, inclination, I have always been a European."

"And you mean you could continue to lead this kind of life without ever growing tired of it?"

"What do you mean by this kind of life?" said Starwick.

His friend nodded towards the crowded and noisy terrace of the café.

"I mean sitting around at café's all day long, going to night-clubs— eating, drinking, sitting,—moving on from one place to another—spending your life that way?"

"Do you think it's such a bad way to spend your life?" said Starwick quietly. He turned, regarding his friend with serious eyes. "Don't you find it very amusing?"

"Yes, Frank, for a time. But after a while, don't you think you'd get tired of it?"

"No more tired," said Starwick, "than I would of going to an office day after day at nine o'clock and coming away at five, doing useless and dreary work that some one else could do as well. On the contrary—this kind of life—" he nodded towards the crowded tables—"seems to me much more interesting and amusing."

"But how can you feel that you belong to it?" the other said. "I should think that would make a difference to you. It does to me—the feeling that I am a stranger here, that this is not my life. that I know none of these people."

"Are you getting ready to tell me now that an American never really gets to know any French people?" said Starwick, repeating the banal phrase with a quiet sarcasm that brought a flush to the other's face.

"Well, it's not likely that he will, from what I've heard."

Starwick cast a weary look around him at the chattering group of people at the other tables.

"God!" he said quietly. "I shouldn't think he'd want to. I imagine most of them are about as dull a lot as you could find."

"If you feel that way about them, what is the great attraction Paris holds for you? How can you possibly feel that way about the people and still say you feel at home here?"

"Because Paris belongs to the world—to Europe—more than it belongs to France. One does not come here because he wants to know the French: he comes because he can find here the most pleasant, graceful and civilized life on earth."

"Yes, but there are other things that may be more important than leading a graceful and pleasant life."

"What, for instance?" said Starwick, looking at him.

"Getting your work done is one of them. For you, I should think that would be a great deal more important."

Starwick was again silent; the old bestial grimace, image of an unutterable anguish and confusion in his soul, for a moment contorted his pleasant ruddy face, developed, passed, was gone; he said quietly and with the infinite weariness of despair that had now become the image of his life:

"Getting my work done! My God, as if it mattered."

"There was a time when you thought it did, Frank."

"Yes, there was a time when I did think so," he said lifelessly.

"And now you no longer feel that way about it?"

Starwick was silent; when he spoke again, it was not to answer directly.

—"Always the old unquiet heart," he said wearily and sadly; he turned and looked silently at his friend for a moment. "Why? Since I first knew you, you have been like that, Eugene—wanting to devour the earth, lashing your soul to frenzy in this useless, hopeless and impossible search for knowledge."

"Why useless or hopeless, Frank?"

"Because it is a kind of madness in you that grows worse all the time; because you cannot cure it, or ever satisfy this hunger of yours while you have it; because it will exhaust you, break your heart, and drive you mad; and because, even if you could gratify this impossible desire to absorb the whole sum of recorded knowledge and experience in the world, you would gain nothing by it."

"There I can't agree with you."

"Do you really think," said Starwick wearily, "that if you could achieve this hopeless ambition of reading all the books that were ever printed—of knowing all the people—seeing all the places—that you would be any better off than you now are? Now, day after day, you go prowling up and down along the book-stalls on the Seine, pawing through tons of junk and rubbish until your very heart is sick with weariness and confusion. When you are not with us, you sit alone in a café with a dictionary beside you trying to decipher the meaning of some useless and meaningless book. You no longer enjoy what you read, because you are tortured by a consciousness of the vast number of books you have not read; you go to the museums—to the Louvre—and you no longer enjoy the pictures, because you torture your brain and exhaust your energy in a foolish effort to see and remember all of them. You no longer enjoy the crowd, you go out on the streets of Paris, you sit here in this crowded café—and instead of taking pleasure in all this gaiety and life about you, you are tortured by the thought that you know none of these people, that you know nothing about their lives, that there are four million people here in Paris and you do not know a dozen of them. . . . Eugene, Eugene," he said sadly, "this thing in you is growing worse all the time; if you do not master it, it is a disease that will some day drive you mad and destroy you."

"And yet, Frank, many people on this earth have had the same disease. Because of it, in order to get knowledge, Doctor Faust sold his soul to the devil."

"Alas," said Starwick, "where is the devil?" In a moment he continued quietly, as before: "Do you think that you will really gain in wisdom if you read a million books? Do you think you will find out more about life if you know a million people rather than yourself? Do you think you will get more pleasure from a thousand women than from two or three—see more if you go to a hundred countries instead of six? And finally, do you think you'll get more happiness from life by 'getting your work done' than by doing nothing? My God, Eugene—" his voice was weary with the resigned fatality of despair that had now corrupted him—"you still feel that it is important that you 'do your work,' as you

call it, but what will it matter if you do or don't? You want to lead the
artist's life, to do the artist's work, to create out of the artist's materials—
what will it matter in the end if you do this, or nothing?"

"You did not always feel so, Frank."

"No," said Starwick wearily, "there was a time when I felt differently.
There was a time when I felt that the artist's life was the finest life on
earth—the only life I would care to lead."

"And now?"

"Now—nothing—nothing," he spoke so quietly that his words were
scarcely audible. "It no longer matters. . . . I go to the Louvre and
look at that colossal mountain of junk—up and down those endless
corridors hung with the dull or worthless work of thousands of dead
men who once felt as I did—that they must create, express the image
of their soul—that art and the artist's life were all that mattered. Now
they are dead, their dreary works have been left behind as a kind of useless relic of their agony: in that whole gigantic storage-plant of worthless art—there are just three pictures I should have cared to paint—and
I know it's not in me to paint any of them. I thought I wanted to write
plays, but now I feel the same about that, too; among all the thousands
of plays I have read or seen, I doubt that there are a dozen which I
should have cared to write—and I know now that I could have written
none of them. . . . What does it matter? Why do you goad your spirit
and exhaust your mind with these frantic efforts, these useless desires to
add another book or play to the mountains of books and plays that have
already been written? Why should we break our hearts to add to that
immense accumulation of dull, fair, or trivial work that has already been
done?" He was silent a moment longer, and then the color in his ruddy
face deepening with excitement, he said in a high, passionate tone:
"What is great—what is priceless—what we would give our lives to do
—is so impossible—so utterly, damnably impossible! And if we can
never do the best—then why do anything?"

For a moment, there returned to the other a memory of the moonlit
streets of Cambridge, and of a night when Starwick, drunk with wine
and the generous and extravagant enthusiasm of youth, had turned to
him and in a voice that rung along the sleeping street, had called him
a mighty poet. And he remembered how his own heart had beat hot
with hope and joy at the sound of those proud and foolish words, and
how he had grasped Starwick's hand and wrung it with a hard grip of
passionate conviction, and told Frank what he believed at that moment

with all the ardor of his heart—that Starwick was the greatest young man of his time and generation.

And remembering now those two drunk and happy boys who stood there in the moon-still streets, and spoke to each other the compact of their devotion and belief, he wanted to ask Frank if this weary acquiescence in defeat, that had now become the very color of his life, was a better thing than the proud and foolish vision of a boy.

But he said nothing, and after a moment's silence, Starwick looked at his watch and called the waiter, saying that it was already time for their meeting with the two women at a café in Montparnasse. Therefore, they paid the bill, and departed; but what Frank had said to him that day would live in his memory in years to come. For in Frank's words were implicit every element of the resignation, despair, and growing inertia and apathy of his will.

LXXX

THE relations between these four people had now been strained to the breaking point. That month of debauch had exacted a stern tribute from them. Their exhausted bodies and frayed nerves cried out for rest, a period of curative repose when the well of their drained energy could be filled up again. But like creatures hopelessly addicted to a drug, they could not break the bonds of this tyranny of pleasure which held them. Starwick seemed to be completely enslaved by this senseless and furious quest, this frantic seeking after new sensations, this hopeless pursuit of a happiness, a fulfilment, that they never found. He seemed unable or unwilling to break the evil spell. Rather, as if a poisonous hunger was feeding on his vitals—a hunger that grew constantly from the food it fed upon, and that could not be assuaged by any means—the evil inertia of his will, the ugly impassivity of his resignation became every day more marked.

Of all of them, he alone preserved the appearance of calm. And that cold, impassive calm was maddening: he met the storms of anger, protests, reproaches, and persuasions of the others with an air of sad humility, a kind of sorrowful acceptance, a quiet agreement to every accusation or indictment, a grand manner of sweet, sorrowful contrition that was more hateful than any deliberate insult could have been. For behind this impenetrable armor of humility, this air of mysterious fatality, there was evident a hateful arrogance which said that words were useless because no words could express the fatal wisdom of his soul, and which, with a stubborn and abominable perversity, seemed deliberately resolved on ruin.

His conduct became daily more absurd, extravagant, ridiculous. He was acting like a melodramatic fool, but it was impossible to laugh at his folly because of the desperate fatality that attended it. He did unbelievable things, contrived unbelievable situations that seemed fitting only in a world of opera but were shamefully unreal and unnecessary in the real one. What was really shameful and unworthy in his conduct was this—his fatality served no purpose, his reckless and deliberate pursuit of danger did no good except to dignify the melodramatic unreality of a comic opera situation with the realities of blood and death.

He was constantly and deliberately involving himself and others in these ridiculous but perilous situations. One night, in one of the Montmartre resorts, he had a quarrel with a man that would have been farcical save for the ugly consequences it produced, the painful and shameful memory it would later evoke. The man, an unpleasant, wizened-looking little Frenchman, a creature of the night, with obscene eyes, a yellowed skin, and a pointed beard half covering the features of a rodent, had not been able to keep his ugly eyes off Ann, had measured the noble proportions of her beauty with a kind of foul leering appraisal that had in it something almost as palpable and sensual as a naked touch, and now, as the orchestra struck up another tune, he approached the table, bowed, and asked her, courteously enough, for a dance.

Ann reddened furiously in the face, looked down sullenly at the tablecloth and, before she was able to think of a reply, Starwick said:

"Mademoiselle does not care to dance. Please go away."

The cold arrogance of Starwick's tone, and his curt dismissal, enraged the Frenchman. When he replied, his lips were bared in an ugly smile that showed unpleasant fangs of yellowed teeth; he said:

"Is the lady not allowed to speak for herself?—Is Monsieur perhaps her guardian?"

"Will you please go away now?" Starwick said again, with a cold and weary impassivity. "You are boring us."

"But, it's marvellous!" The little Frenchman cast back his yellowed face and bared his fangs in a laugh of envenomed mockery. "It's Monsieur D'Artagnan come to life again, and a lady so shy and modest that she can't speak for herself! But, it's superb!" he cried again, and with an ironic bow, concluded: "Monsieur, with all my heart I thank you for this wonderful diversion! You are very droll!"

Starwick's reply to this was to pick up the seltzer bottle on the table and, without for a moment altering his air of cold impassivity, to squirt the siphon straight in the little Frenchman's yellow face.

In a moment, the place was a seething maelstrom of excitement. People all over sprang up from their tables, the dancers stopped dancing, the orchestra stopped with a crash, and the proprietor and the waiter came towards them on the run.

In a moment, they were surrounded by an excited group of gesticulating, chattering people, all trying to talk at once. Starwick was standing up now, facing his antagonist, cold and impassive save for a deeper flush of excitement on his ruddy face. As for the little Frenchman, the look of murderous hatred on his face was horrible. Without stopping to dry his dripping face with the napkin which an excited and persuasive waiter was offering him, he thrust aside the manager, who was trying to restrain him, and coming close to Starwick, snarled:

"Your name, monsieur? I demand to know your name. My representatives will call upon you in the morning."

"Good," said Starwick coldly. "I shall wait for them. Monsieur shall have whatever satisfaction he desires."

And taking a card from his purse, he wrote the studio address below his name and gave it to the man.

"Ah, good!" the Frenchman cried harshly, glancing at it. "Until tomorrow!"

And calling for his bill, and silent to all the apologies and cajoleries of the proprietor, he departed.

"But Frank, darling!" Elinor cried, when they had seated themselves again. "What do you intend to do? Surely you're not going to—" She did not finish, but stared at him with a troubled and astonished face.

"Yes," said Starwick coldly and quietly. "He has asked me to fight a duel, and if he wants it, I shall meet him."

"Oh, but don't be absurd!" cried Elinor with an impatient laugh. "What on earth do you know about fighting duels! My poor child, how can you be so ridiculous! This is the twentieth century, darling. Don't you know that people don't act that way any more?"

"Quite!" said Starwick, with a stony calm. "Nevertheless, I shall meet him if he wants me to." He looked at her with quiet eyes for a moment, and then said gravely: "I've *got* to do that. I really have, you know."

"Got to!" Elinor cried impatiently. "Why, the child is *mad!*" Her tone immediately became crisp, incisive, authoritative: she began to speak to him quietly, kindly, but in a peremptory tone, as one might speak to a child:

"Francis," she said quietly. "Listen to me! Don't be an idiot! What does it matter about that wretched little man? It's all over now! A duel! Good heavens! Don't be such a child! Who ever heard of such a thing?"

His face reddened a little from her ridicule, but he answered, in a cold impassive tone:

"Quite! Nevertheless, I shall meet him if he wants it!"

"Meet him!" Elinor cried again. "Oh, Francis, how can you be so stupid! Meet him with what?"

"With whatever weapon he wants to use," Starwick replied. "Pistols or swords—it doesn't matter!"

"Pistols or swords!" Elinor shrieked faintly, and began to laugh. "Why, you idiot, what do you know about pistols or swords? You've never had a sword in your hand in your life—and as for pistols, you wouldn't even know how to point the thing and press the trigger!"

"It doesn't matter," he said in a very quiet and fatal way. "I shall fire into the air."

In spite of the ridiculous and melodramatic quality of these foolish words, no one laughed. They saw suddenly what fatal consequences this farcical situation might have, and having felt the desperation of his soul—that terrible despair which now seemed to be driving him on to seek ruin everywhere—they knew he would do exactly as he said, if given the opportunity.

Elinor started to go: she beckoned to a waiter and called for the bill, and said persuasively:

"Come on! Let's get out of this place! You've had too much to drink! I think your head needs clearing—a little fresh air will do you good. You'll feel different about all this tomorrow!"

"But not at all!" he said patiently, and then, as she started to get up: "Will you please sit down. We're not going yet."

"But why, darling? Aren't you ready? Haven't you raised enough hell for one evening—or do you want to fight a duel with some one else? Besides, I do think you might think of Ann. I know she's wanted to go for some time."

"But *why?*" he said, turning to Ann with an air of fine surprise. "Aren't you enjoying yourself? It's a *very* good place, and the music is awfully good—it really is, you know."

"Oh, charming, charming!" she muttered sarcastically. She had been staring at the tablecloth sullenly, with a flaming face, ever since the quarrel had begun, and now looking up suddenly, with a short and angry laugh, she said:

"God! I don't know whether to walk out of here or *crawl!* I feel all—*undressed!*"

At these words, his face really did flush crimson with embarrassment. He looked at her for a moment, and then said sharply, with a note of stern reproof and anger in his voice:

"Ann! It's *very* bad and *very* wrong—and—and—very *mean* of you to talk like that."

"That's how I feel," she muttered.

"Then," he said quietly, but with two deep and angry spots of color flaming in his cheeks, "I'm *thoroughly* ashamed of you. It's *quite* unworthy of you. At a time like this, a person of your quality has got to show more—" he paused, choosing the word carefully, "more *fibre.* You really must, you know!"

"Oh, fibre my eye!" she flared up, looking at him with flushed, lovely and angry eyes. "You don't lack fibre simply because you don't want to be made a fool of! Frank, you make me tired, the way you talk! Everywhere we go now some one's always showing 'fibre'—and every one is having a rotten, awful time. For God's sake, let's not talk so much about showing fibre and let's try to enjoy ourselves and get some pleasure and some happiness from life, and act like decent, natural people for a change. I had looked forward so much to coming on this trip with Elinor—and now—" Tears of anger and disappointment glittered in her eyes, she looked down at the table sullenly in an effort to conceal them, and then muttered: "Playing the fool and making scenes and starting rows everywhere we go! Getting into trouble everywhere, making people hate us, never having any fun! Squirting siphons at some wretched little man——" she made a sudden impulsive gesture of disgust and turned away. "God! It makes me sick!"

"I'm sorry to know you feel that way," he said quietly. "I'll try to see it doesn't happen again—but, after all, Ann—the reason it did happen is because I like you so *very* much, and have so much respect for you and won't stand for any one insulting you!"

"Ah-h! Insulting me!" she said angrily. "Good heavens, Francis, do you think I need protection from a wretched little man like that? When I've been a nurse, and had to go alone to every rotten slum in Boston, and learned to handle people twice his size! Protect me!" she said bit-

terly. "Thank you for nothing! I didn't come over here to be protected
—I don't need it. I can take care of myself. Just try to act and feel like a
decent human being—let's try to be friends together and to show some
consideration for each other—and don't worry about protecting me!"

LXXXI

HE slept little that night. The quarrel in the night-club and its consequences seemed fantastic, incredible, like a nightmare. At daybreak
he got up and went to the window and stared out at the gray light just
breaking on the roofs and chimney-pots of Paris. The old buildings
emerged haggard, pale, lemony, with all the wonderful, homely prac-
ticality of dawn and morning, and looking at them, Montmartre, the
blaze of lights, the music and the drunken voices, and the quarrel with
the Frenchman—the whole strange and evil chemistry of night—seemed
farther away, more unreal and dream-like than ever. Could it have
happened? Had Starwick really been challenged to a duel? Was he
going through with it?

He got up and dressed, and with dry lips and a strange, numb lightness
in his limbs, descended to the street and hailed a passing taxi in the Rue
Bonaparte. The sounds of morning, shutters being rolled up, scrub-
women and maids down on their knees at entrances, shops being opened
—all this made the night before seem more unreal than ever.

When he got to the studio he found everybody up. Ann was already
at work making coffee, scrambling eggs for breakfast. Elinor was just
combing up her hair, Starwick was in the balcony and had not yet
come down. Elinor kept talking as she arranged her hair, and from the
balcony Starwick answered her:

"But Frank!" she was saying, "you know you wouldn't be fool enough
to do such a thing! Surely you don't mean you intend to go through
with it?"

"Ace," he said coldly from above, "I do mean to. Quite!"

"But—oh! Don't be an ass!" she cried impatiently. Turning to Ann,
with a little, frowning smile, she bit her lips, and shaking her head
slightly, cried in an astounded tone:

"Isn't it *incredible!* Did you ever hear of such an *insane* thing in all
your life!"

But in the set of her jaw, the faint smile around the corner of her
mouth, there was the look of grim decision they had all seen before.

As Eugene entered, Ann turned from the stove, and spoon in hand, stood looking at him sullenly for a moment. Suddenly she laughed her short and angry laugh, and turned away toward Elinor, saying:

"God! Here's the second! Don't they make a pair!"

"But my *dear!*" cried Elinor with a light, gay malice. "Where is the top hat? Where are the striped trousers and the morning coat? Where is the duelling case with the revolvers? . . . All right, Monsieur D'Artagnan," she called up towards the balcony ironically. "Your friend, Monsieur Porthos has arrived . . . and breakfast is ready, darling! What's that they say about an army?" she innocently inquired, "—that it ought not to fight on an empty stomach? . . . Ahem!" she cleared her throat. "Will Monsieur D'Artagnan condescend to have the company of two frail women for breakfast on the morning of the great affair . . . or does Monsieur prefer to be left alone with his devoted second to discuss—ahem! ahem! . . . the final arrangements?"

Starwick made no reply, until he had come down the steps:

"You can stay, if you want to," he said indifferently. "I shall have nothing to say to them anyway." Turning to Eugene, he said with magnificent, bored weariness: "Find out what they want. Let me know what they want to do."

"B—but, what do you want me to say to them, Frank? What shall I tell them?"

"Anything," said Starwick indifferently. "Anything you like. Say that I will meet him anywhere—on any terms—whatever they like. Let them settle it their own way."

He picked up a spoon and started to eat his orange.

"Oh, Frank, you idiot!" cried Elinor, seizing him by the hair, and shaking his head. "Don't be stupid! You know you're not going on with this farce!"

He lifted quiet, wearily patient eyes and looked at her:

"Sorry!" he said. "But I've *got* to. If that's what he wants, I really must. I owe the man that much—I really do, you know!"

Breakfast then proceeded in a painful and uneasy silence, broken only by Elinor's malicious thrusts, and maintained by Starwick's weary and impassive calm.

At ten o'clock, there were steps along the alley-way outside, some one mounted the stoop, and the studio bell jangled. The two women exchanged uneasy looks, Starwick got up quietly and turned away, and in a moment Elinor called out sharply: "Entrez."

The door opened and a man entered the room. He wore striped

trousers that were in need of pressing, a frayed and worn-looking frock coat, and he carried a briefcase under his arm. He was bald, sallow, about forty-five years old, and had a little mustache and furtive eyes. He looked at each person in the room quickly, sharply, and then said inquiringly:

"Monsieur Star-*week?*"

"Ace," said Starwick quietly, and turned.

"Ah, bon!" the little Frenchman said briskly, and smiled, showing yellow fangs of teeth. He had been bent slightly forward, holding his briefcase with thin, eager fingers, as he waited. Now he came forward swiftly, took a card out of his wallet, and presenting it to Starwick with something of a flourish, said:

"Monsieur, permettez-moi. Ma carte."

Starwick glanced at the card indifferently, and was about to put it down upon the table when the little Frenchman interrupted him. Stretching out his thin and rather grimy hand, he said courteously yet eagerly:

"S'il vous plaît, monsieur!"—took the card again, and put it back into his wallet.

Starwick indicated a chair and said:

"Won't you sit down?"

From that time on, the conversation proceeded in mutilated French and English. The little Frenchman sat down, hitched up his striped trousers carefully and with his arched fingers poised upon his bony knees, bent forward and, with another ingratiating and somewhat repulsive smile, said:

"Monsieur Star-week ees Américain, n'est-ce pas?"

"Ace," said Starwick.

"And was at Le Rat Mort last night?"

"Ace," said Starwick again.

"Et Monsieur?" He nodded inquiringly toward Eugene, "vas also zere?"

"Ace," Starwick answered.

"Et Mademoiselle . . . et Mademoiselle," he turned with courteous inquiry towards the two young women—"zey vere also zere?"

"Ace," said Starwick as before.

"Ah, bon!" the little Frenchman cried, nodding his head vigorously, and with an air of complete satisfaction. Then, rubbing his bony, little hands together dryly and briskly, he took up his thin and battered old

briefcase, which he had been holding firmly between his knees, swiftly
unfastened the straps and unlatched it, and took out a few sheets of
flaming, yellow paper covered with notations in a fine, minute hand:
"Monsieur—" he began, clearing his throat, and rattling the flimsy
sheets impressively—"Monsieur, I s'ink"—he looked up at Starwick
ingratiatingly, but with an air of sly insinuation, "—Monsieur, I s'ink,
perhaps, vas"—he shrugged his shoulders slightly, with an air of deprecation—"Monsieur vas—drink-*ing?*"

Starwick made no answer for a moment: his face reddened, he inclined his head, and said coldly, but unconcedingly:

"Oui! C'est ça, monsieur!"

"Ah-h!" the little Frenchman cried again with a dry little cackle of
satisfaction— "—an' ven one drink—espeecial*ee*, monsieur, ven ve are
yong," he laughed ingratiatingly again, "—he sometime do an' say some
t'ings zat he regret—eh?"

"But of course!" cried Elinor at this point, quickly, impatiently,
eagerly. "That's just the point! Frank was drinking—the whole thing
happened like a flash—it's all over now—we're sorry—every one is sorry:
—it was a regrettable mistake—we're sorry for it—we apologize!"

"But not at all!" cried Starwick reddening angrily, and looking resentfully towards Elinor. "Not at all! I do *not* agree with you!"

"Oh, Frank, you idiot, be quiet! Let me handle this," she cried.
Turning to the little Frenchman, she said swiftly, smoothly, with all her
coaxing and formidable persuasiveness:

"Monsieur, what can we do to remedy this regrettable mistake?"

"Comment?" said the Frenchman, in a puzzled tone.

"Monsieur Starwick," Elinor went on with coaxing persuasion, "—
Monsieur Starwick—comme vous voyez, monsieur—est très jeune. Il
a toutes les fautes de la jeunesse. Mais il est aussi un homme de grand
esprit; de grand talent. Il a le tempérament d'un artiste: d'un homme
de génie. Comme un Français, monsieur, vous," she went on flatter-
ingly, "—*vous* connaissez cette espèce d'hommes. Vous savez qu'ils
ne sont pas toujours responsables de leurs actes. C'est comme ça avec
Monsieur Starwick. Il est de bon cœur, de bon volonté: il est honnête,
généreux et sincère, mais il est aussi plein de tempérament—impulsif:—
il manque de jugement. Hier soir nous avons tous—comme on dit—
fait la noçe ensemble. Monsieur Starwick a bu beaucoup—a bu trop
—et il a été coupable d'une chose regrettable. Mais aujourdhui il se
repent très sincèrement de sa conduite.

"Il vous offre ses apologies les plus profondes. Il a déjà souffert assez. Dans ces circonstances, monsieur," she concluded, with an air of charming persuasiveness, "on peut excuser le jeune homme, n'est-ce pas?—on peut pardonner une faute si honnêtement et sincèrement regrettée."

And she paused, smiling at him with an air of hopeful finality, as if to say: "There! You agree with me, don't you? I knew you would!"

But the Frenchman was not to be so easily persuaded. Waving thin fingers sideways in the air, and shaking his head without conviction, he laughed a dry, dubious laugh, and said:

"Ah-h! I don't know—mademoiselle! Zese apologies!—"—again he waved thin dubious fingers—"eet ees all ver-ree well to meck apologies bot ze—vat you say?—ze dom-mage!—ze dom-mage is done. . . . Monsiur," he said gravely, turning to Starwick, "you have been coupable of a ver-ree gret offense. Ze—ze—vay you say?—ze assault, monsieur—ze assault ees 'ere in France—une chose très sérieuse! Vous comprenez?"

"Ace," said Starwick coldly.

"Mon client," the little Frenchman cleared his throat portentously—"—mon client, Monsieur Reynal, 'as been terriblement blessé—insulté! monsieur!" he cried sharply. "Eeet ees necessaree zu meck des réparations, n'est-ce pas?"

"Ace," said Starwick coldly. "Whatever reparation you desire."

The Frenchman stared at him a moment in an astonished way and then, in an excited and eager tone, cried:

"Ah, bon! Zen you agree?"

"Perfectly," said Starwick.

"Bon! Bon!" the little man said eagerly, rubbing his hands together with greedy satisfaction. "Monsieur est sage—ees, vat you say?—ees ver-ree wise. Monsieur est Américain—n'est-ce pas?—un étranger—comme vous, mademoiselle . . . et vous, monsieur . . . et vous, mademoiselle—you are 'ere zu meck ze tour—zu be libre—free—n'est-ce pas —zu avoid ze complications——"

"But," said Elinor, in a bewildered tone, "—what is—I don't understand——"

"Alors," the Frenchman said, "eet ees bettaire to avoid ze complications—oui! Ah," he said, with an arching glance at Starwick, "mais Monsieur est sage . . . est très, très sage! C'est toujours mieux de faire des réparations . . . et éviter les conséquences plus sérieuses."

"But!" cried Elinor again, her astonishment growing, "I don't under-stand. What reparations are you talking about?"

"Zese, madame!" the Frenchman said, and coughing portentously, he rattled the flimsy sheets of paper in his hand, held them up before his eyes, and began to read:

"Pour l'endommagement d'un veston du soir—trois cents francs!"

"What? *What?*" said Elinor in a small, chilled tone. "For—*what?*"

"Mais, oui, madame!" the Frenchman now cried passionately, for the first time rising to the heights of moral indignation, "—un veston du soir complet—ruiné, madame!—*complètement, absolument* ruiné! . . . Trois cents francs, monsieur," he said cunningly, turning to Starwick, "—c'est pas cher! . . . Pour moi, oui!—c'est cher—mais pour vous—ah-h!" he waved his dirty fingers and laughed with scornful deprecation, "—c'est rien! Rien du tout." He rattled the flimsy paper in his hands, cleared his throat, and went on:

"Pour l'endommagement d'une chemise—une chemise, n'est-ce pas, du soir?" he looked up inquiringly, "—cinquante francs"——

"But this," gasped Elinor, "this is—" She looked at Starwick with an astounded face. Starwick said nothing.

"Pour l'angoisse mentale"—the Frenchman continued.

"What?" Elinor gasped and looked at Ann. "What did he say?"

"Mental anguish," Ann answered curtly. "All right," she turned to the Frenchman, "how much is the mental anguish?"

"C'est cinq cent francs, mademoiselle."

"But this man?" cried Elinor, turning to Ann with an air of astounded enlightenment—"this man is——"

"He's a shyster lawyer, yes!" Ann said bitterly. "Couldn't you see it from the first?"

"Ah, mademoiselle,"—the Frenchman began with a reproachful gri-mace, and a little, deprecating movement of his fingers, "—you are——"

"How much?" Ann answered in her level, toneless French. "How much do you want?"

"Vous comprenez, mademoiselle——"

"How much?" she said harshly. "How much do you want?"

His furtive eyes gleamed with a sudden fox-glint of eager greed.

"Mille francs!" he said eagerly. "Mille francs pour tout ensemble! . . . Pour vous, mademoiselle"—he laughed again with scornful dep-recation as he waved his grimy fingers—"c'est rien—pour moi——"

She got up abruptly, went over to the shelf that ran around the wall and got her purse. She opened it, took out a roll of bills, and coming back tossed them on the table before him.

"But mademoiselle"—he stammered, unable to believe his good luck, his eyes glued upon the roll of bills in a stare of hypnotic fascination.

"Give me a receipt," she said.

"Comment?" he looked puzzled for a moment, then cried, "Ah-h! Un reçu! Mais oui, mais oui, mademoiselle! Tout de suite!"

Trembling with frantic haste he scrawled out a receipt on a sheet of yellow paper, gave it to her, clutched the banknotes with a trembling claw, and stuffed them in his wallet.

"Now get out," said Ann.

"Mademoiselle?" he scrambled hastily to his feet, clutched his brief-case and his hat, and looked nervously at her—"vous dites?"

"Get out of here," she said, and began to move slowly towards him.

He scrambled for the door like a frightened cat, stammering: "Mais oui . . . mais parfaitement . . . mais"—he almost stumbled going down the steps, glancing back with nervous apprehension as he went. She shut the door behind him, came back, sat down in her chair, and stared sullenly at her plate, saying nothing. Starwick was crimson in the face, but did not look at any one and did not speak. Elinor was busy with her napkin: she had lifted it to her face and was holding it firmly across her mouth. From time to time her breast and stomach and her heavy shoulders trembled in a kind of shuddering convulsion, smothered and explosive snorts and gasps came from her.

It got too much for her: they heard a faint, choked shriek, she rose and rushed blindly across the room, entered the bathroom and slammed the door behind her. And then they heard peal after peal of laughter, shrieks and whoops and yells of it, and finally a dead silence, broken at times by exhausted gasps. Ann continued to look sullenly and miserably at her plate. As for Starwick, he sat there wearily detached, impassive, magnificent as always, but his face had the hue and color of boiled lobster.

LXXXII

One night, in a small bar or *bistro* upon the hill of Montmartre, Starwick met a young Frenchman who was to become the companion of his adventures in many strange and devious ways thereafter. It was about

four o'clock in the morning: after the usual nightly circuit of the gilded
pleasure resorts, cafés and more unsavory dives and stews of the district,
Starwick had become very drunk and unruly, had quarrelled with Elinor
and Ann when they tried to take him home, and since that time had
been wandering aimlessly through the district, going from one cheap
bar to another.

The women hung on doggedly; Starwick had refused to let them accompany him, and they had asked Eugene to stay with him and try to
keep him out of trouble. Eugene, in fact, was only less drunk than his
companion, but fortified by that sense of pride and duty which a trust
imposed by two lovely women can give a young man, he hung on, keeping pace with Starwick, drink for drink, until the whole night fused
into a drunken blur, a rout of evil faces, the whole to be remembered
later as jags of splintered light upon a chain of darkness, as flying images,
fixed, instant, and intolerably bright, in the great blank of memory.
And out of all these blazing pictures of the night and the wild reel of
their debauch, one would remain forever after, to haunt his vision
mournfully. It was the memory—or rather the *consciousness*—of the two
women, Ann and Elinor, waiting in the dark, following the blind weave
of their drunken path, all through the mad kaleidoscope of night, never
approaching them, but always there. He had not seemed to look at
them, to notice them, and yet later he had always known that they were
there. And the memory fused to one final mournful image that was to
return a thousand times to haunt him in the years to come. He and
Starwick had come out of one of the bars that broke the darkness of the
long steep hill, and were reeling down past shuttered stores and old dark
houses towards the invitation of another blaze of light.

Suddenly he knew that Ann and Elinor were behind them. For a
moment he turned, and saw the two women pacing slowly after them,
alone, patient, curiously enduring. The image of that long silent street
of night, walled steeply with old houses and shuttered shops, and of the
figures of these two women pacing slowly behind them, in the darkness, seemed in later years to bear the sorrowful legend of what their
lives—of what so much of life—was to become. And for this reason
it burned forever in his memory with a mournful, dark and haunting
radiance, became in fact, detached from names and personalities and
identic histories—became something essential, everlasting and immutable in life. It was an image of fruitless love and lost devotion, of a love
that would never come to anything, and of beautiful life that must be

ruinously consumed in barren adoration of a lost soul, a cold and un-responding heart. And it was all wrought mournfully there into the scheme of night, made legible in the quiet and gracious loveliness of these two women, so strong, so patient, and so infinitely loyal, pacing slowly down behind two drunken boys in the slant steep street and emptiness of night.

Suddenly the image blazed to the structure of hard actuality: an-other bar, and all around hoarse laughter, high sanguinary voices, a sudden scheme of faces scarred with night, and livid with night's radi-ance—whores, taxi drivers, negroes, and those other nameless unmis-takable ones—who come from somewhere—God knows where—and who live somehow—God knows how—and who recede again at morn-ing into unknown cells—but who live here only, brief as moths, and bale-ful as a serpent's eye, in the unwholesome chemistry of night.

He found himself leaning heavily on the zinc counter of the bar, star-ing at a pair of whited, flabby-looking arms, the soiled apron and shirt, the soiled night-time face and dark, mistrustful eyes of night's soiled barman. The blur of hoarse voices, shouts and oaths and laughter fused around him, and suddenly beside him he heard Starwick's voice, drunken, quiet, and immensely still:

"Monsieur," it said—its very stillness cut like a knife through all the fog of sound about him—"monsieur, du feu, s'il vous plaît."

"But sairtainlee, monsieur," a droll and pleasant-sounding voice said quietly. "W'y not?"

He turned and saw Starwick, a cigarette between his lips, bending awkwardly to get the light from a proffered cigarette which a young Frenchman was holding carefully for him. At last he got it; puffing awkwardly, and straightening, he slightly raised his hat in salutation, and said with drunken gravity:

"Merci. Vous êtes bien gentil."

"But," said the young Frenchman again, drolly, and with a slight shrug of his shoulder, "not at all! Eet ees noz-zing!"

And as Starwick started to look at him with grave drunken eyes, the Frenchman returned his look with a glance that was perfectly composed, friendly, good-humored, and drolly inquiring.

"Monsieur?" he said courteously, as Starwick continued to look at him.

"I think," said Starwick slowly, with the strangely mannered and almost womanish intonation of his voice, "I think I like you *very* much.

You are *very* kind, and *very* generous, and altogether a *very* grand person. I am *enormously* grateful to you."

"But," the Frenchman said, with droll surprise, and a slight astonished movement of his shoulders, "I 'ave done noz-zing! You ask for du feu—a light—and I geev to you. I am glad eef you like—bot—" again he shrugged his shoulders with a cynical but immensely engaging humor—"eet ees not so ver-ree grand."

He was a young man, not more than thirty years old, somewhat above the middle height, with a thin, nervously active figure, and thin, pointedly Gallic features. It was a pleasant, most engaging face, full of a sharply cynical intelligence; the thin mouth was alive with humor —with the witty and politely cynical disbelief of his race, and his tone, his manner—everything about him—was eloquent with this racial quality of disbelief, a quality that was perfectly courteous, that would raise its pointed eyebrows and say politely, "You s'ink so"—but that accepted without assent, was politely non-committal without agreement.

He was dressed as many young Frenchmen of that period dressed:— a style that served to combine the sinister toughness of the Apache with a rather gaudy and cheap enhancement of the current fashions. His clothes were neat but cheaply made; he wore a felt hat with a wide brim, creased, French fashion, up the sides, an overcoat with padded shoulders, cut in sharply at the waist, his trousers had a short and skimpy look, and barely covered the tops of his shoes. He wore spats, and a rather loud-colored scarf which he knotted loosely, cravat-fashion, and which thus concealed his collar and his shirt. Finally, when he smoked a cigarette, he drew the smoke in slowly, languorously, knowingly, with lidded eyes, and a cruel and bitter convulsion of his thin lips that gave his sharp face a sinister Apache expression.

Starwick was now crying out in a high drunken tone of passionate assurance:

"But yes! Yes! Yes!—You are a *grand* person—a *swell* person—I like you *enormously*. . . ."

"I am glad," said the Frenchman politely, with another almost imperceptible movement of the shoulders.

"But yes! You are my friend!" Starwick cried in a high passionate tone. "I like you—you must drink with me."

"Eef you like—of course!" the Frenchman politely agreed. Turning to the soiled barman who continued to look at them with dark mistrustful eyes, he said, in a hard, sharp voice, "Une fine. . . . And you, monsieur?" he turned inquiringly toward Eugene, "I s'ink you have another drink?"

"No, not now"—his glass was not yet empty. "We—we have both already had something to drink."

"I can see," the Frenchman said politely, but with a swift flicker of cynical mirth across his thin mouth, that needed no translation. Raising his glass, he said courteously:

"A votre santé, messieurs," and drank.

"Look!" cried Starwick. "You are our friend now, and you must call us by our names. My name is Frank; his is Eugene—what is yours?"

"My name ees Alec," said the young Frenchman smiling. "Zat ees w'at zey call me."

"But it's perfect!" Starwick cried enthusiastically. "It's a *swell* name—a *wonderful* name! Alec!—Ecoute!" he said to the soiled barman with the ugly eye, "Juh pawnse qu'il faut—encore du cognac," he said drunkenly, making a confused and maudlin gesture with his arm. "Encore du cognac, s'il vous plaît!" And as the barman silently and sullenly filled the three glasses from a bottle on the bar, Starwick turned to Alec, shouting with dangerous hilarity: "Cognac forever, Alec!—Cognac for you and me and all of us forever!—Nothing but drunkenness—glorious drunkenness—divine poetic drunkenness forever!"

"Eef you like," said Alec, with a polite and acquiescent shrug. He raised his glass and drank.

It was four o'clock when they left the place. Arm in arm they reeled out into the street, Starwick holding onto Alec for support, and shouting drunkenly:

"Nous sommes des amis!—Nous sommes des amis éternels! Mais oui! Mais oui!"

The whole dark and silent street rang and echoed with his drunken outcry. "Alec et moi—nous sommes des frères—nous sommes des artistes! Nothing shall part us! Non—jamais! Jamais!"

A taxi, which had been waiting in the darkness several doors away, now drove up swiftly and stopped before them at the curb. Ann and Elinor were inside: Elinor opened the door and spoke gently:

"Frank, get in the taxi now, we're going home."

"Mais jamais! Jamais!" Starwick yelled hysterically. "I go nowhere without Alec!—We are brothers—friends—he has a poet's soul."

"Frank, don't be an idiot!" Elinor spoke quietly, but with crisp authority. "You're drunk; get in the taxi; we're going home."

"Mais oui!" he shouted. "Je suis ivre! I am drunk! I will always be drunk—nothing but drunkenness forever for Alec and me!"

"Listen!" Elinor spoke quietly, pleasantly to the Frenchman. "Won't you go away, please, and leave him now? He is drunk, he does not know what he is doing, he really must go home now."

"But, of course, madame," said Alec courteously, "I go now." He turned to Starwick and spoke quietly, with his thin, engaging smile: "I s'ink, Frank, eet ees bettaire eef you go home now, non?"

"But no! But no!" cried Starwick passionately. "I will go nowhere without Alec. . . . Alec!" he cried, clutching him with drunken desperation. "You cannot go! You must not go! You cannot leave me!"

"Tomorrow, perhaps," said Alec, smiling. "Ees eet not bettaire eef we go to-gezzer tomorrow?—I s'ink zen you feel motch bettaire."

"No! No! Starwick cried obstinately. "Now! Now! Alec, you cannot leave me! We are brothers, we must tell each other everything. . . . You must show me all you know, all you have seen—you must teach me to smoke opium—take me where the opium smokers go—Alec! Alec! J'ai la nostalgie pour la boue . . ."

"Oh, Frank, quit talking like a drunken idiot! Get in the car, we're going home . . ."

"But no! But no!" Starwick raved on in his high drunken voice. "Alec and I are going on together—he has promised to take me to the places that he knows—to show me the dark mysteries—the lower depths . . ."

"Oh, Frank, for God's sake get in the car; you're making a damned fool of yourself!"

"—But no! I will not go without Alec—he must come with us—he is going to show me . . ."

"But I show you, Frank," said Alec smoothly. "Tonight, non!" He spoke firmly, waved a hand. "Eet ees impossible. I wet 'ere for some one. I must meet, I 'ave engagement—yes. Tomorrow, eef you like, I meet you 'ere! Tonight, non!" His voice was harsh, sharp with irrevocable refusal. "I cannot. Eeet ees impossible."

By dint of infinite prayers and persuasions, and by Alec's promises that he would meet him next day to take him on a tour of "the lower depths," they finally got Starwick into the taxi. All the way down the hill however, as the taxi sped across Paris, through the darkened silent streets, and across the Seine into the Latin Quarter, Starwick raved on madly about his eternal friendship with Alec, from whom he could never more be parted. The taxi turned swiftly into the dark and empty little Rue des Beaux Arts and halted before Eugene's hotel. The two women waited in nervous and impatient haste for Eugene to get out, Elinor giving his arm a swift squeeze and saying:

"Good-night, darling. We'll see you tomorrow morning. Don't forget our trip to Rheims."

When he got out, however, Starwick followed him, and began to run drunkenly towards the corner, smashing at the shutters of the shops with his cane and screaming at the top of his voice:

"Alec! Alec! Où est Alec? Alec! Alec! Mon ami Alec! Où êtes-vous?"

Eugene ran after Starwick and caught him just as he was disappearing around the corner into the Rue Bonaparte, headed for the Seine. By main strength and pleading he brought him back, and managed to get him into the taxi again, which had followed his pursuit in swift watchful reverse. He slammed the door upon that raving madman, and as the taxi drove off, he heard, through a fog of drunkenness, Elinor's swift "Thank you, darling. You behaved magnificently—tomorrow—" and Starwick raving:

"Alec! Alec! Where is Alec?"

They sped off up the silent empty street, a narrow ribbon lit sparsely by a few lamps, and walled steeply with its high old shuttered houses. Eugene walked back to his hotel, rang the night bell, and was let in. As he stumbled up the circuitous and perilous ascent of five flights, he caught a moment's glimpse of the little concierge and his wife, startled from their distressful sleep, clutching each other together in a protective embrace, as they peered out at him from the miserable little alcove where they slept—a moment's vision of their pale, meagre faces and frightened eyes.

He climbed the winding flights of stairs, and let himself into his room, switching on the light, and flinging himself down upon the bed immediately in a stupor of drunken exhaustion.

It seemed to him he had not lain there five minutes before he heard Starwick smashing at the street door below, and shouting drunkenly his own name and that of Alec. In another minute he heard Starwick stumbling up the stairs; he went to the door, opened it, and caught him just as he came stumbling in. Starwick was raving, demented, no longer conscious of his acts: he began to smash and beat at the bed with his stick, crying:

"There!—And there!—And there!—Out, out, damned spot, and make an end to you. . . . The stranger—the one I never knew—the stranger you have become—out! Out! Out!"

Turning to Eugene then, he peered at him with drunken bloodshot eyes, and said:

"Who are you?—Are you the stranger?—Are you the one I never knew?—Or are you . . .?" His voice trailed off feebly, and he sank down into a chair, sobbing drunkenly.

And getting to his feet at length, he looked about him wildly, smote the bed again with his stick, and cried out loudly:

"Where is Eugene? Where is the Eugene that I knew?—Where?—Where?—Where?" He staggered to the door and flung it open, screaming: "Alec! Where are you?"

He reeled out into the hall, and for a moment hung dangerously against the stair rail, peering drunkenly down into the dizzy pit five flights below. Eugene ran after him, seized him by the arm and together, they fell or reeled to the bottom. It was a journey as distorted and demented as a dream— a descent to be remembered later as a kind of corkscrew nightmare, broken by blind lurchings into a creaking rail, by the rattling of Starwick's stick upon the banisters, by blind sprawls, and stumblings, and by blobs and blurs of frightened faces at each landing, where Monsieur Gely's more sober patrons waited in breath-caught silence at their open doors. They reached the bottom finally amid such universal thanksgiving, such prayers for their safety, as Gely's hotel had never known before.

A vast sigh, a huge and single respiration of relief rustled up the steep dark pit of the winding stairs. But another peril lay before them. At the foot of the stairs there stood a monstrous five-foot vase which, by its lustre and the loving care with which it was polished every day by Marie, the maid, must have been the pride of the establishment. Starwick reeled blindly against it as he went past, the thing rocked sickeningly, and even as it tottered slowly over, Eugene heard Madame Gely's gasp of terror, heard her low "Mon Dieu! Ça tombe, ça tombe!" and a loud united "Ah-h-h!" of thankfulness as he caught it in his hands, and gently, safely, with such inner triumph as a man may feel who leaps through space and lands safely hanging to a flying trapeze, restored it to its former position. As he looked up he saw old Gely and his wife peering from their quarters with fat perturbed faces, and the little concierge and his wife still clutched together, peering through their curtains in a covert of bright frightened eyes.

They got out into the street at last. In the Rue Bonaparte they stopped a taxi drilling through. When they reached Montmartre again the night was breaking in gray light behind the church of Sacré-Cœur. After further drinks of strong bad cognac, they piled out of the place into another taxi, and went hurtling back through Paris. By the time they arrived at the studio full light had come.

The women were waiting up for them. Starwick mumbled something and, holding his hand over his mouth, rushed across the room into the bathroom and vomited. When he was empty, he staggered out, reeled towards the couch where Ann slept, and toppled on it, and was instantly sunk in senseless sleep.

Elinor regarded him for a while with an air at once contemplative and amused. "And now," she said cheerfully, "to awake the Sleeping Beauty from his nap." She smiled her fine bright smile, but the lines about her mouth were grimly set, and her eyes were hard. She approached the couch, and looking down upon Starwick's prostrate and bedraggled form, she said sweetly: "Get up, darling. It's breakfast-time."

He groaned feebly, and rolled over on his side.

"Up, up, up, my lamb!" Her tone was dulcet, but the hand that grasped his collar and pulled him to a sitting position was by no means gentle. "We are waiting for you, darling. The day's at morn, the hour draws close, it's almost time. Remember, dear, we're starting out for Rheims at nine o'clock."

"Oh God!" groaned Starwick wretchedly. "Don't ask me to do that! Anything, anything but that. I can't! I'll go anywhere with you if you just leave me alone until tomorrow." He flopped back on the bed again.

"Sorry, precious," she said in a light and cheerful tone, as hard as granite, "but it's too late now! You should have thought of that before. Our plans are made, we're going—and *you*," suddenly her voice hardened formidably, "*you're* coming with us." She looked at him a moment longer with hard eyes, bent and grasped him by the collar, and roughly jerked him up to a sitting position again.

"Francis," she said sternly, "pull yourself together now and get up! We're going to have no more of this nonsense!"

He groaned feebly, and staggered to his feet. He seemed to be on the verge of collapse, his appearance was so pitiable that Ann, coming from the bathroom at this moment, flushed with hot sympathy as she saw him, and cried out angrily, accusingly, to Elinor:

"Oh, leave him alone! Let him sleep if he wants to. Can't you see he is half dead? Why should we drag him along to Rheims if he doesn't feel like going? We can put the trip off until tomorrow, anyway. What does it matter when we go?"

Elinor smiled firmly and shook her head with a short inflexible movement. "No, sir," she said quietly. "Nothing is going to be put off. We are going today, as we planned. And Mr. Starwick is going with us! He may go willingly or against his will, he may be conscious or unconscious when he gets there, but, alive or dead, he's going!"

At these unhappy tidings, Starwick groaned miserably again. She turned to him and, her voice deepening to the authority of indignation, she said:

"Frank! You've *got* to see this through! There's no getting out of it now! If you don't feel well, that's just too bad—but you've got to see this thing through anyway! You've known about this trip for the past week—if you chose to spend last night making the rounds of every joint in Montmartre you've no one to blame for it but yourself! But you've *got* to go. You're not going to let us down this time!"

And steeled and wakened by the challenge of her tone—that challenge which one meets so often in people who have let their whole life go to hell, and lacking stamina for life's larger consequences insist on it for trivialities—he raised his head, looked at her with angry, bloodshot eyes, and said quietly:

"Very well, I'll go. But I resent your asking it *very* much!"

"All right, my dear," she said quietly. "If you resent it, you resent it —and that's that! Only, when you make a promise to your friends they expect you to live up to it."

"Ace," said Starwick coldly. "Quite."

"And now," she spoke more kindly, "why don't you go into the bathroom, Frank, and straighten up a bit? A little cold water across your head and shoulders would do you no end of good." She turned to Ann and said quietly: "Did you finish in there?"

"Yes," said Ann curtly, "it's all right now. I've cleaned it up." For a minute she stared sullenly at the older woman, and suddenly burst into her short and angry laugh:

"God!" she said, with a rich, abrupt, and beautifully coarse humanity. "I never saw the like of it in my life! I don't see where he put it all!" Her voice trembled with a full, rich, infuriated kind of humor. "Everything was there!" she cried, "except the kitchen sink!"

Starwick flushed deeply, and looking at her, said, quietly, gravely: "I'm sorry, Ann. I'm *terribly, terribly* sorry!"

"Oh, it's all right," she said shortly, yet with a kind of tenderness. "I'm used to it. Don't forget that I served three years' training in a hospital once. You get so you don't notice those things."

"You are a *very* swell person," he said slowly and distinctly. "I'm *terribly* grateful."

She flushed, and turned away, saying curtly: "Sit down, Frank. You'll feel better when you have some coffee. I'm making it now." And in her silent and competent way she set to work.

In these few commonplace words, all that was strong, grand, and tender in Ann's soul and character was somehow made evident. Brusque and matter-of-fact as her words had been when she referred to the disgusting task just performed, their very curtness, and the rich and coarse humanity of her sudden angry laugh, had revealed a spirit of noble tenderness and strength, a spirit so strong and sweet and full of love that it had risen triumphant not only over the stale, dead and snobbish little world from which she came, but also over the squeamishness which such a task would have aroused in most of the people who made up that world.

To Starwick, she symbolized certain divinities known to his art and his experience: Maya, or one of the great Earth-Mothers of the ancients, or the goddess of Compassionate Mercy of the Chinese, to whom he often likened her.

But to the other youth, her divinity was less mythical, more racial and mundane. She seemed to fulfill in part his vision of the grand America, to make palpable the female quality of that fortunate, good, and happy life of which he had dreamed since childhood—to evoke the structure of that enchanted life of which every American has dreamed as a child. It is a life that seems forever just a hand's-breadth off and instantly to be grasped and made our own, the moment that we find the word to utter it, the key to open it. It is a world distilled of our own blood and earth, and qualified by all our million lights and weathers, and we know that it will be noble, intolerably strange and lovely, when we find it. Finally, she was the incarnation of all the secret beauty of New England, the other side of man's dark heart, the buried loveliness that all men long for.

LXXXIII

THE car which they had chartered for a four months' tour was brought around from a garage at nine o'clock. A few minutes later they were on their way to Rheims.

Elinor drove; Eugene sat beside her; Ann and Starwick were in the rear seat. The car was a good one—a Panhard—and Elinor drove swiftly, beautifully, with magnificent competence, as she did all things, getting ahead of everybody else, besting even the swerve of the taxi drivers in their wasp-like flight, and doing it all with such smooth ease that no one noticed it.

They seemed to get through the great dense web, the monumental complication of central Paris by a kind of magic. As always, Elinor communicated to every one and everything the superb confidence of her authority. In her presence, and under her governance, the strange and alien world about them became instantly familiar as the Main Street of one's native town, making even the bewildering and intricate confusion of its swarming mass wonderfully natural and easy to be grasped. Paris, in fact, under the transforming magic of this woman's touch, became curiously American, the enchantment beautifully like Eugene's own far-off visions as a child.

It was astounding. The whole city had suddenly taken on the clear and unperplexing proportions of a map—of one of those beautifully simple and comforting maps which are sold to tourists, in which everything is charming, colorful, and cosy as a toy, and where everything that need be known—all the celebrated "points of interest"—the Eiffel Tower, the Madeleine, and Notre Dame, the Trocadéro, and the Arc de Triomphe, are pictured charmingly, in vivid colors.

Paris, in fact, had this morning become a brilliant, lovely, flashing toy. It was a toy which had been miraculously created for the enjoyment of brilliant, knowing and sophisticated Americans like Elinor and himself. It was a toy which could be instantly understood, preserved and enjoyed, a toy that they could play with to their hearts' content, a toy which need confuse and puzzle none of them for a moment, particularly since Elinor was there to explain the toy and make it go.

It was incredible. Gone was all the blind confusion, the sick despair, the empty desolation of his first month in Paris. Gone was the old blind and baffled struggle against the staggering mass and number of a world too infinitely complex to be comprehended, too strange and alien to be understood. Gone were all the old sensations of the drowning horror, the feeling of atomic desolation as he blindly prowled the streets among alien and uncountable hordes of strange dark faces, the sensation of being an eyeless, grope-thing that crawled and scuttled blindly on the sea-depths of some terrible oceanic world of whose dimensions, structure, quality and purpose it could know nothing. Gone were all those feelings of strife, profitless, strange and impotent futility—those struggles that wracked the living sinews of man's life and soul with quivering exhaustion and with sick despair, the hideous feeling of being emptied out in planetary vacancy, of losing all the high hope of the spirit's purpose, the heart's integrity—of being exploded, emptied out and dissipated into hideous, hopeless nothingness where all the spirit of man's courage turned dead and rotten as a last year's apple, and all his sounding plans of work and greatness seemed feebler than the scratchings of a dog upon a wall—a horror that can seize a man in the great jungle of an unknown city and a swarming street and that is far more terrible than the unknown mystery of any Amazonian jungle of the earth could be.

It was all gone now—the devouring hunger, and the drowning horror, and the blind confusion of the old, swarm-haunted mind of man—the fruitless struggle of the Faustian life—and in its place he had the glittering toy, the toy of legend and enchantment and of quick possession.

The French, they were a charming race—so gay, so light, and so incorrigible—so childlike and so like a race of charming toys.

Elinor made their relation to all these good people swarming in the streets around them wonderfully easy, clear, and agreeable. There was nothing strange about them, their ways were unpredictable, since they were French, but they were perfectly understandable. Her attitude, expressed in a rapid, gay and half-abstracted chatter—a kind of running commentary on the life around her as she drove—made the whole thing plain. They were a quaint lot, a droll lot, an incomparable lot—they were charming, amazing, irresponsible, a race of toys and children—they were "French."

"All right, my dear," she would murmur to herself as a fat taxi driver snaked recklessly in ahead of her and came to a triumphant stop— "have it your own way, my darling—have it your own way—I shan't argue with you—God!" she would cry, throwing her head back with a sudden rich burst of laughter—"look at the old boy with the whiskers over there at the table—did you see him twirl his gay mustachios and roll his roguish eyes at that girl as she went by? *Simply* incredible!" she cried with another laugh, and bit her lips, and shook her head in fine astonishment. "Thank you!" she murmured politely, as the gendarme shrilled upon his whistle and beckoned with his small white club. "Monsieur l'Agent, vous êtes bien gentil"—as she smoothly shifted gears and shot past him.

In this wonderful and intoxicating way all of Paris defiled past them like a great glittering toy, a splendid map of rich, luxurious shops and great cafés, an animated and beautiful design of a million gay and fascinating people, all bent on pleasure, all filled with joy, all with something so vivid, bright, particular and incomparable about them that the whole vast pattern resolved itself into a thousand charming and brilliant pictures, each wonderful and unforgettable, and all fitting instantly into the single structure, the simple and magnificent clarity of the whole design.

They swept through the huge central web of Paris, and were passing through the great shabby complication of the Eastern Quarters, the ragged, ugly sprawl of the suburbs.

And now, swift as dreams, it seemed, they were out in open country, speeding along roads shaded by tall rows of poplars, under a sky of humid gray, whitened with a milky and soul-troubling light.

Elinor was very gay, mercurial, full of sudden spontaneous laughter, snatches of song, deep gravity, swift inexplicable delight. Ann maintained a sullen silence. As for Starwick, he seemed on the verge of collapse all the time. At Château-Thierry he announced that he could go no farther; they stopped, got him into a little café, and fortified him with some brandy. He sank into a stupor of exhaustion, from which they could not rouse him. To all their persuasions and entreaties he just shook his head and mumbled wearily:

"I can't!—Leave me here!—I can't go on!"

Three hours passed in this way before they succeeded in reviving him, getting him out of the café—or estaminet—and into the car again. Ann's face was flushed with resentful anger. She burst out furiously:

"You had no right to make him come along on this trip! You knew he couldn't make it; he's dead on his feet. I think we ought to take him back to Paris now."

"Sorry, my dear," said Elinor crisply, with a fine bright smile, "but there'll be no turning back! We're going on!"

"Frank can't go on!" Ann cried angrily. "You know he can't! I think it's a rotten shame for you to insist on this when you see what shape he's in."

"Nevertheless, we're going on," said Elinor with grim cheerfulness. "And Mr. Starwick is going with us. He'll see it through now to the bitter end. And if he dies upon the way, we'll give him a soldier's burial here upon the field of honor. . . . Allons, mes enfants! Avancez!" And humming gaily and lightly the tune of Malbrouck, she shifted gears and sent the car smoothly, swiftly forward again.

It was a horrible journey. One of those experiences which, by the grim and hopeless protraction of their suffering, leave their nightmare image indelibly upon the memories of every one who has experienced them. The gray light of the short winter's day was already waning rapidly when they drove out of Château-Thierry. As they approached Rheims, dark had almost come, the lights of the town had begun to twinkle, sparsely, with provincial dismalness, in the distance. No one knew the purpose of their visit; no one knew what the trip was for, what they were coming to see—no one had enquired.

It was almost dark when they entered the town. Elinor drove immediately to the cathedral, halted the car, and got out.

"Voilà, mes amis!" she said ironically. "We are here!"

And she made a magnificent flourishing gesture towards the great ruined mass, which, in the last faint gray light of day, was dimly visible as a gigantic soaring monument of shattering arches and demolished buttresses, a lacework of terrific stone looped ruggedly with splinters of faint light, the demolished façades of old saints and kings and shell-torn towers—the twilit ruins of a twilight world.

"Magnificent!" cried Elinor enthusiastically. "Superb!—Frank! Frank! You must get out and feast your eyes upon this noble monument! I have heard you speak so often of its beauty. . . . But, my dear, you *must!*" she said, answering with fine persuasion his feeble and dispirited groan. "You'd never forgive yourself, or me either, if you knew you'd come the whole way to Rheims without a single look at its cathedral."

And, despite his wearily mumbled protests, she took him by the arm and pulled him from the car. Then, for a moment, as he stared drunkenly, with blind, unseeing eyes, at the great gray twilit shape, she propped him up and held him between herself and Eugene.

Then they all got back into the car, and she drove them to the best café, the best hotel in town. Starwick almost collapsed getting out of the car. His knees buckled under him, and he would have fallen if Ann had not caught him, put her arm around him, and held him up. His condition was pitiable. He could no longer hold his head up; it lolled and wobbled drunkenly on his neck like a flower too heavy for its heavy stalk. His eyes were glazed and leaden, and as they started into the café, he had to be held up. He lifted his feet and dragged them after him like leaden weights. The café was a large and splendid one. They found a table to one side. Starwick staggered towards the cushioned seat against the wall and immediately collapsed. From that time on, he was never wholly conscious. Ann sat down beside him, put her arm around him and supported him. He sank against her shoulder like a child. The girl's face was flushed with anger, she stared at Elinor with resentful eyes, but by no word or gesture did Elinor show that she noticed anything amiss either in Ann's or Starwick's behavior.

Rather, she chatted gaily to Eugene, she kept up a witty and high-spirited discourse with every one around her, she had never been more mercurial, quick, gay and charming than she was that evening. And announcing gaily that she was the hostess that was "giving the party," she ordered lavishly—a delicious meal, with champagne from the celebrated cellars of the establishment. And every one, spurred to hunger by the cold air and their long journey, ate heartily——every one save Ann, who ate little and sat in angry silence, with one arm around Starwick's shoulders, and Starwick, who could not be roused from his deep stupor to eat anything.

It was after nine o'clock before they got up to go. Elinor paid the bill, and still chatting as gaily and as lightly as if the whole wretched expedition had brought nothing but unqualified joy to all her guests, started for the door. Starwick had to be half-carried, half-dragged out by Ann and Eugene, under the prayerful guidance of several deeply troubled waiters. They put him in the car and got in themselves. Elinor looking around lightly, and crying out cheerfully: "Are we ready, children?" started the motor for the long drive back to Paris.

That was a hideous and unforgettable journey. Before they were done with it, they thought that it would never end. Under the protraction of its ghastly horror, time lengthened out interminably, unbelievably, into centuries. It seemed to them at last that they would never arrive, that they were rolling through a spaceless vacancy without progression, that they were hung there in the horrible ethers of some planetary emptiness where their wheels spun futilely and forever in moveless movement, unsilent silence, changeless change.

From the very beginning they did not know where they were going. By the time they got out of Rheims they were completely lost. It was a cold night, late in February; a thick fog-like mist that grew steadily more impenetrable as the night wore on, had come down and blanketed the earth in white invisibility. And through this mist there were diffused two elements: the weird radiance of a submerged moon which gave to the sea of fog through which they groped, the appearance of an endless sea of milk, and the bitter clutch of a stealthy, raw, and cruelly penetrating cold which crept into man's flesh and numbed him to the bone of misery.

All through that ghastly and interminable night, they groped their way across France in the milky ocean of antarctic fog. It seemed to them that they had travelled hundreds of miles, that Paris had long since been passed, lost, forgotten in the fog, that they were approaching the outer suburbs of Lyons or Bordeaux, that presently they would see the comforting lights of the English Channel or that they had turned northwards, had crossed Belgium, and soon would strike the Rhine.

From time to time the road wound through the ghostly street of some old village; the white walls of village houses rose sheer and blank beside the road, sheeted in phantasmal mist like ghosts, and with no sound within. Then they would be groping their way out through the open countryside again—but where or in what country, no one knew, none dared to say—and suddenly, low and level, beside them to the left, they would see the moon. It would suddenly emerge in some blind hole that opened in that wall of fog, and it was such a moon as no man living ever saw before. It was an old, mad, ruined crater of a moon, an ancient, worn, and demented thing that smouldered red like an expiring coal, and that was like the old ruined moon of a fantastic dream. It hung there on their left, just at the edge of a low ridge of hills, and it was so low, so level, and so ghostly-near, it seemed to them that they could touch it.

Towards midnight they groped their way into a whited ghostly phantom of a town which Elinor at length, with the sudden recognition of a person who revisits some old scene of childhood, discovered to be Soissons. She had known the town well during the War: the ambulance unit, in which she had been for eighteen months a driver, had been stationed here. Starwick was half conscious, huddled into Ann's shoulder on the dark rear seat. He groaned pitiably and said that he could go no farther, that they must stop. They found a hotel café that was still open and half-carried, half-dragged him in. They got brandy for him, they tried to revive him; he looked like a dead man and said that he could go no farther, that they must leave him there. And for the first time Elinor's grave tone showed concern and sharp anxiety, for the first time her hard eye softened into care. She remained firm; gently, obdurately, she refused him. He collapsed again into unconsciousness; she turned her worried eyes upon the others and said quietly:

"We can't leave him here. We've got to get him back to Paris somehow."

After two ghastly hours in which they tried to revive him, persuade him to gird up his fainting limbs for final effort, they got him back into the car. Ann covered him with blankets and held him to her for the remainder of the night, as a mother might hold a child. In the faint ghost-gleam of light her face shone dark and sombre, her eyes were dark, moveless, looking straight ahead.

Armed with instructions from an anxious waiter, they set out again on the presumptive road to Paris. The interminable night wore on; the white blanket of the fog grew thicker, they passed through more ghost-villages, sheer and sudden as a dream, sheeted in the strange numb silence of that ghostly nightmare of a fog. The old red crater of the moon vanished in a ruined helve at length behind a rise of earth. They could no longer see anything, the road before was utterly blotted out, the car-lights burned against an impenetrable white wall, they groped their way in utter blindness, they crawled at a snail's pace.

Finally, they felt their way along, inch by inch and foot by foot. Eugene stood on the running-board of the car, peering blindly into that blank wall of fog, trying only to define the edges of the road. The bitter penetration of raw cold struck through the fog and pierced them like a nail. From time to time Elinor stopped the car, while he stepped down and stamped numb feet upon the road, swung frozen arms and lustily blew warmth back into numb fingers. Then that infinite groping patience of snail's progress would begin again.

Somewhere, somehow, through that blind sea of fog, there was a sense of morning in the air. The ghosts of towns and villages grew more frequent—the towns were larger now, occasionally Elinor bumped over phantom curbs before the warning shouts of her look-out could prevent her. Twice they banged into trees along unknown pavements. There was a car-track now, the bump of cobbles, the sense of greater complications in the world about them.

Suddenly, they heard the most thrilling and evocative of all earth's sounds at morning—the lonely clopping of shod hooves upon the cobbles. In the dim and ghostly sheeting of that light, they saw the horse, the market cart balanced between its two high creaking wheels, laden with sweet clean green-and-gold of carrot bunches, each neatly trimmed as a bouquet.

They could discern the faint ghost-glimmer of the driver's face, the big slow-footed animal, dappled gray, and clopping steadily towards the central markets.

They were entering Paris, and the fog was lifting. In its huge shroud of mist dispersing, the old buildings of the city, emerged ghostly, haggard, pallidly nascent in the dim gray light. A man was walking rapidly along a terraced pavement, with bent head, hands thrust in pockets— the figure of the worker since the world began. They saw at morning, in gray waking light, a waiter, his apron ends tucked up, lifting racked chairs from the tables of a café, and on light mapled fronts of bars and shops, the signs *Bière—Pâtisserie—Tabac*. Suddenly, the huge winged masses of the Louvre swept upon them, and it was gray light now, and Eugene heard Elinor's low, fervent "Thank God!"

And now the bridge, the Seine again, the frontal blank of the old buildings on the quays, faced haggardly towards light, the narrow lane of the Rue Bonaparte, and in the silent empty street at length, his own hotel.

They said good-bye quickly, hurriedly, abstractedly, as he got out; and drove away. The women were thinking of nothing, no one now, but Starwick, life's fortunate darling, the rare, the precious, the all-favored one. In the gray light, unconscious, completely swaddled in the heavy rugs, Starwick still lay pillowed on Ann's shoulder.

LXXXIV

ALL day Eugene slept the dreamless, soundless sleep of a man who has been drugged. When he awoke, night had come again. And this concatenation of night to night, of dreamless and exhausted sleep upon the strange terrific nightmare of the night before, the swift kaleidoscope of moving action which had filled his life for the past two days, now gave to that recent period a haunting and disturbing distance, and to the events that had gone before the sad finality of irrevocable time. Suddenly he felt as if his life with Ann, Elinor, and Starwick was finished, done; for some strangely troubling reason he could not define, he felt that he would never see them again.

He got up, dressed, and went downstairs. He saw old Gely and his wife, his daughters, Marie the maid, and the little concierge: it seemed to him that they looked at him strangely, curiously, with some sorrowful sad knowledge in their eyes, and a nameless numb excitement gripped him, dulled his heart. He felt the nameless apprehension that he always felt—that perhaps all men feel—when they have been away a day or two. It was a premonition of bad news, of some unknown misfortune: he wanted to ask them if some one had come for him—without knowing who could come—if they had a message for him—not knowing who might send him one—an almost feverish energy to demand that they tell him at once what unknown calamity had befallen him in his absence. But he said nothing, but still haunted by what he thought was the strange and troubling look in their eyes—a look he had often thought he observed in people, which seemed to tell of a secret knowledge, an inhuman chemistry, a communion in men's lives to which his own life was a stranger—he hurried out into the street.

Outside the streets were wet with mist, the old cobbles shone with a dull wet gleam, through the mist the lamps burned dimly, and through the fog he heard the swift and unseen passing of the taxi-cabs, the shrill tooting of their little horns.

Yet everything was ghost-like and phantasmal—the streets of Paris had the unfamiliar reality of streets that one revisits after many years of absence, or walks again after the confinement of a long and serious illness.

He ate at a little restaurant in the Rue de la Seine, and troubled by the dismal lights, the high old houses, and the empty streets of the Latin Quarter sounding only with the brief passage of some furious little taxi drilling through those narrow lanes towards the bridge of the Seine and the great blaze and gaiety of night, he finally forsook that dark quarter, which seemed to be the image of the unquiet loneliness that beset him, and crossing the bridge, he spent the remainder of the evening reading in one of the cafés near Les Magasins du Louvre.

The next morning when he awoke, a *pneumatique* was waiting for him. It was from Elinor, and read:

"Darling, where are you? Are you still recovering from the great debauch, or have you given us the go-by, or what? The suspense is awful —won't you say it ain't so, and come to lunch with us today at half-past twelve? We'll be waiting for you at the studio.—Elinor"—Below this, in a round and almost childish hand, was written: "We want to see you. We missed you yesterday.—Ann."

He read this brief and casual little note over again and again, he laughed exultantly, and smote his fist into the air, and read again. All of the old impossible joy was revived in him. He looked about the room and found everything in it good and homely. He went to the window and looked out: a lemony sunlight was falling on the old pale walls and roofs and chimney-pots of Paris: everything sparkled with health and hope and work and morning—and all because two girls from Boston in New England had written him a note.

He held the flimsy paper of the *pneumatique* tenderly, as if it were a sacred parchment too old and precious for rough handling; he even lifted it to his nose and smelled it. It seemed to him that all the subtle, sensuous femininity of the two women was in it—the seductive and thrilling fragrance, impalpable and glorious as the fragrance of a flower, which their lives seemed to irradiate and to give to everything, to every one they touched, a sense of triumph, joy and tenderness. He read the one blunt line that Ann had written him as if it were poetry of haunting magic: the level, blunt and toneless inflexibility of her voice sounded in the line as if she had spoken, he read into her simple words a thousand buried meanings—the tenderness of a profound, simple and inarticulate spirit, whose feelings were too deep for language, who had no words for them.

When he got to the studio he found the two women waiting, but Starwick was not there. Ann was quietly, bluntly matter-of-fact as usual; Elinor almost hilariously gay, but beneath her gaiety he sensed at once a deep and worried perturbation, a worn anxiety that shone nakedly from her troubled eyes.

They told him that on their return from Rheims, Starwick had left the studio to meet Alec and had not been seen since. No word from him had they had that night or the day before, and now, on the second day since his disappearance, their anxiety was evident.

But during lunch—they ate at a small restaurant in the neighborhood, near the Montparnasse railway station—Elinor kept up a gay and rapid conversation, and persisted in speaking of Starwick's disappearance as a great lark—the kind of thing to be expected from him.

"*Perfectly* insane, of course!" she cried, with a gay laugh. "But then, it's typical of him: it's just the kind of thing that kind would do. Oh, he'll turn up, of course," she said, with quiet confidence, "—he'll turn up in a day or two, after some wild adventure that no one in the world but Francis Starwick could have had. . . . I *mean!*" she cried, "picking that Frenchman—Alec—up the way he did the other night. *Utterly* mad, of course!" she said gaily. "—But then, there you *are!* It wouldn't be Frank if he didn't!"

"I see nothing very funny about it," said Ann bluntly. "It looks like a pretty rotten mess to me. We know nothing at all about that Frenchman —who he is, what he does; we don't even know his name. For all you know he may be one of the worst thugs or criminals in Paris."

"Oh, I know, my dear—but don't be absurd!" Elinor protested. "The man's all right—Frank's always picking up these people—it always turns out all right in the end—oh, but of course!" she cried, as if dispelling a troubling thought from her mind—"Of course it will! It's too ridiculous to allow yourself to be upset like this!"

But in spite of her vigorous assurance, her eyes were full of care, and of something painful and baffled, an almost naked anguish.

He left them after lunch, promising to meet them again for dinner. Starwick had not come back. When they had finished dinner, the two women went back to the studio to wait for Starwick's possible return, and Eugene went to look for him in Montmartre, promising to let them know at once if he found Starwick or got news of him. When he got to Montmartre, he made a round first of all the resorts which Starwick had liked best and frequented most, as Eugene remembered them, of course; but no one had seen him since they had last been there all together. Finally, he went to the bistro in the Rue Montmartre, where they had first encountered Alec, and asked the soiled barman with the dark mistrustful eye, if he had seen either Alec or Starwick in the past three days. The man eyed him suspiciously for a moment before answering. Then he surlily replied that he had seen neither of them. In spite of the man's denial, he stayed on, drinking one cognac after another at the bar, while it filled up, ebbed and flowed, with the mysterious rout and rabble of the night. He waited until four o'clock in the morning: neither Starwick nor Alec had appeared. He got into a taxi and was driven back across Paris to Montparnasse. When he got to the studio, the two women were still awake, waiting, and he gave them his disappointing news. Then he departed, promising to return at noon.

All through that day they waited: the apprehension of the two women was now painfully evident, and Ann spoke bluntly of calling in the police. Towards six o'clock that evening, while they were engaged in vigorous debate concerning their course of action, there were steps along the alley-way outside, and Starwick entered the studio, followed by the Frenchman, Alec.

Starwick was in excellent spirits, his eyes were clear, his ruddy face looked fresh, and had a healthy glow. In response to all their excited greetings and inquiries, he laughed gleefully, teasingly, and refused to answer. When they tried to find out from Alec where Starwick had been, he too smiled an engaging but malicious smile, shrugged his shoulders politely, and said: "I do not know, I s'ink he tells you if he v'ants—if not!" again he smiled, and shrugged politely. And this moody and secretive silence was never broken. Starwick never told them where he had been. Once or twice, during dinner, which was an hilarious one, he made casual and mysteriously hinting references to Brussels, but, in response to all of Elinor's deft, ironic cross-examination, he only laughed his burbling laugh, and refused to answer.

And she, finally defeated, laughed suddenly, a laugh of rich astonishment, crying: *"Perfectly* insane, of course! But then, what did I tell you? It's just the sort of thing that Frank *would* do!"

But, in spite of all her high light spirits, her gay swift laughter, her distinguished ease, there was in the woman's eyes something the boy had never seen before: a horrible, baffled anguish of torment and frustration. And although her manner towards the Frenchman, Alec, was gracious, gay, and charming—although she now accepted him as "one of us," and frequently said with warm enthusiasm that he was "a *perfectly* swell person—I like him *so* much!" there was often something in her eyes when she looked at him that it was not good to see.

Alec was their guest, and Starwick's constant companion, everywhere they went thereafter. And everywhere, in every way, he proved himself to be a droll, kind, courteous, witty and urbanely cynical person: a man of charming and engaging qualities, and delightful company. They never asked his name, nor inquired about his birth, his family, or his occupation. They seemed to accept his curious fellowship with Starwick as a matter-of-course: they took him on their daily round of cafés, restaurants, night-clubs, and resorts, as if he were a life-long friend of the family. And he accepted all their favors gracefully, politely, with wit and grace and charm, with a natural and distinguished dignity and ease. He, too, never asked disturbing questions; he was a diplomat by nature, a superb tactician from his birth. Nevertheless, the puzzled, doubting and inquiring expression in his eyes grew deeper day by day; his tongue was eloquently silent, but the question in his puzzled eyes could not be hidden, and constantly sought speech.

As for Eugene, he now felt for the first time an ugly, disquieting doubt: suddenly he remembered many things—words and phrases and allusions, swift, casual darts and flashes of memory that went all the way back to the Cambridge years, that had long since been forgotten—but that now returned to fill his mind. And sometimes when he looked at Starwick, he had the weird and unpleasant sensation of looking at some one he had never seen before.

LXXXV

At the last moment, when it seemed that the argosy of their battered friendship was bound to sink, it was Elinor who saved it again. Ann, in a state of sullen fury, had announced that she was sailing for home the next week; Eugene, that he was going South to "some quiet little place where"—so did his mind comfortably phrase it—"he could settle down and write." As for Starwick, he remained coldly, wearily, sorrowfully impassive; he accepted this bitter dissolution of their plans with a weary resignation at once sad and yet profoundly indifferent; his own plans were more wrapped in a mantle of mysterious and tragic secretiveness than ever before. And seeing the desperate state which their affairs had come to, and that she could not look for help from these three gloomy secessionists, Elinor instantly took charge of things again, and became the woman who had driven an ambulance in the war.

"Listen, my darlings," she said with a sweet, crisp frivolity, that was as fine, as friendly, as comforting, and as instantly authoritative as the words of a capable mother to her contrary children—"no one is going away; no one is going back home; no one is going anywhere except on the wonderful trip we've planned from the beginning. We're going to start out next week, Ann and I will do the driving, you two boys can loaf and invite your souls to your hearts' content, and when you see a place that looks like a good place to work in, we'll stop and stay until you're tired of working. Then we'll go on again."

"Where?" said Starwick in a dead and toneless voice. "Go on where?"

"Why, my dear child!" Elinor cried in a gay tone. "Anywhere! Wherever you like! That's the beauty of it! We're not going to be bound down by any program, any schedule: we shall stay where we like, and go anywhere our sweet selves desire.

"I thought, however," she continued in a more matter-of-fact way, "that we would go first to Chartres and then on to Touraine, stopping off at Orléans or Blois or Tours—anywhere we like, and staying as long as we care to. After that, we could do the Pyrenees and all that part of France: we might stop a few days at Biarritz and then strike off into the Basque country. I know *incredible* little places we could stop at."

"Could we see Spain?" asked Starwick, for the first time with a note of interest in his voice.

"But, of *course!*" she cried. "My dear child, we can see anything, everything, go anywhere your heart desires. That's the beauty of the whole arrangement. If you feel like writing, if you want to run down to Spain to get a little writing done—why, presto! chango! Alacazam!" she said gaily, snapping her fingers, "—the thing is done! There's nothing simpler!"

For a moment, no one spoke. They all sat entranced in a kind of unwilling but magical spell of wonder and delight. Elinor, with her power to make everything seem delightfully easy, and magically simple and exciting, had clothed that fantastic program with all the garments of naturalness and reason. Everything now seemed not only possible, but beautifully, persuasively practicable—even that ludicrous project of "running down to Spain to do a little writing," that hopeless delusion of "stopping off and working, anywhere you like, until you are ready to go on again"—she gave to the whole impossible adventure not only the thrilling colors of sensuous delight and happiness, but also the conviction of a serious purpose, a reasonable design.

And in a moment, Starwick, rousing himself from his abstracted and fascinated reverie, turned to Eugene and, with the old gleeful burble of laughter in his throat, remarked simply in his strangely fibred voice:

"It sounds swell, doesn't it?"

And Ann, whose sullen, baffled look had more and more been tempered by an expression of unwilling interest, now laughed her sudden angry laugh, and said:

"It *would* be swell if every one would only act like decent human beings for a change!"

In spite of her angry words, her face had a tender, radiant look of joy and happiness as she spoke, and it seemed that all her hope and belief had returned to her.

"But of course!" Elinor answered instantly, and with complete conviction. "And that's just exactly how every one *is* going to act! Eugene will be all right," she cried—"the moment that we get out of Paris! You'll see! We've gone at a perfectly *killing* pace this last month or two! No one in the world could stand it! Eugene is tired, our nerves are all on edge, we're worn out by staying up all night, and drinking, and flying about from one place to another—but a day or two of rest will fix all that. . . . And that, my children, is just exactly what we're going to do—now—at once!" She spoke firmly, kindly, with authority. "We're getting out of Paris today!"

"Where?" said Starwick. "Where are we going?"

"We're all going out to St. Germain-en-Laye to rest up for a day or two before we leave. We'll stay at your pension, Francis, and you can pack your things while we're out there, because you won't be going back again. After that we'll come back to Paris to spend the night—we won't stay here over a day at the outside: Ann and I will clear our things out of the Studio, and Eugene can get packed up at his hotel—that should mean, let's see," she tapped her lips lightly with thoughtful fingers— "we should be packed up and ready to start Monday morning, at the latest."

"Hadn't I better stay in town and do my packing now?" Eugene suggested.

"Darling," said Elinor softly, with a tender and seductive humor, putting her fingers on his arm—"you'll do nothing of the sort! You're driving out with us this afternoon! We all love you so much that we're going to take no chance on losing you at the last minute!"

And for a moment, the strange and almost noble dignity of Elinor's face was troubled by a faint smile of pleasant, tender radiance, the image of the immensely feminine, gracious, and lovely spirit which almost grotesquely seemed to animate her large and heavy body.

Thus, under the benevolent and comforting dictatorship of this capable woman, hope had been restored to them, and in gay spirits, shouting and laughing and singing, feeling an impossible happiness when they thought of the wonderful adventure before them, they drove out to St. Germain-en-Laye that afternoon. The late sun was slanting rapidly towards evening when they arrived: they left their car before an old café near the railway station, and for an hour walked together through the vast aisles of the forest, the stately, sorrowful design of that great planted forest, so different from anything in America, so different from the rude, wild sweep and savage lyricism of our terrific earth, and so haunted by the spell of time. It was the forest which Henry the Fourth had known so well, and which, in its noble planted colonnades, suggested an architecture of nature that was like a cathedral, evoked a sense of time that was ancient, stately, classical, full of sorrow and a tragical joy, and haunted forever by the pacings of noble men and women now long dead.

When they came out of the forest at the closing hour—for in this country, in this ancient noble place, even the forests were controlled, and closed and opened by the measurements of mortal time—the old red sun of waning day had almost gone.

For a time, they stood on the great sheer butte of St. Germain, and looked across the space that intervened between themselves and Paris. Below them in the valley, the Seine wound snakewise through a series of silvery silent loops, and beyond, across the fields and forests and villages, already melting swiftly into night, and twinkling with a diamond dust of lights, they saw the huge and smoking substance that was Paris, a design of elfin towers and ancient buildings and vast inhuman distances, an architecture of enchantment, smoky, lovely as a dream, seeming to be upborne, to be sustained, to float there like the vision of an impossible and unapproachable loveliness, out of a huge opalescent mist. It was a land of far Cockaigne, forever threaded by the eternity of its silver, silent river; a city of enfabled walls, like Carcassonne, and never to be reached or known.

And while they looked it seemed to them that they heard the huge, seductive, drowsy murmur of that magic and eternal city—a murmur which seemed to resume into itself all of the grief, the joy, the sorrow, the ambitions, hopes, despairs, defeats and loves of humanity. And though all life was mixed and intermingled in that distant, drowsy sound, it was itself detached, remote, eternal and undying as the voice of time. And it hovered there forever in the timeless skies of that elfin city, and was eternally the same, no matter what men lived or died. They turned, and went into the old café near the station for an apéritif before dinner. It was one of those old, pleasantly faded cafés that one finds in little French towns. The place had the comfortable look and feel of an old shoe: the old, worn leather cushions, the chairs and tables, the mirrors in their frames of faded gilt, the old stained woods conveyed a general air of use, of peace, of homely shabby comfort, which suggested the schedule of generations of quiet people who had come here as part of the ordered ritual of a day, and which was so different from the feverish pulse, the sensual flash and glitter of the cafés of Paris. The noble peace and dignity of the great forest, and the magic vision of the time-enchanted city in the evening light, the silver, shining loops of its eternal river, still haunted their spirits, and filled their hearts with wonder and a tranquil joy. And the old café seemed to possess them, to make them its own, with its homely comfort: it was one of those places that one thinks of at once, instinctively, by a powerful intuition, as being a "good" place, and yet they could not have said why. As they came in, the proprietor smiled and spoke to them in a quiet, casual, and friendly manner as if he had always known them and, in a moment, when they were seated in the comfortable old leathers against the wall, their waiter came, and smilingly waited for their order. He was one of those waiters that one often sees abroad: an old man with a sharp, worn face, full of quiet humor and intelligence, an old, thin figure worn in service, but still spry and agile, a decent "family man" with wife and children, a man seasoned in humanity, whose years of service upon thousands of people had given him a character that was wise, good, honest, gentle, and a trifle equivocal. Each ordered an apéritif, the two women a cassis-vermouth, the two young men, Pernod: they talked quietly, happily, and with the weary, friendly understanding that people have when all their passion of desire and grief and conflict is past. The world that they had lived in for the last two months—that world of night and Paris and debauch—seemed like an evil dream, and the way before them now looked clear and plain.

When they left the café, full dark had come: they got in the car and drove to the pension at the other end of town, where Elinor had already engaged rooms for all of them. It now turned out that Elinor had taken rooms for Starwick at this pension three months before, upon his arrival in Paris, but after the first two weeks he had not lived in them, although most of his clothing, books, and other belongings were still there. It

was one more of his costly, wrong, and tragically futile efforts to find a
place—some impossibly fortunate and favorable place that never would
be found—where he could "settle down and get his writing done."

When the four friends got to the pension, dinner had already begun.
A table had been reserved for them, and as they entered the dining-
room, every one stopped eating—two dozen pairs of old dead eyes
were turned mistrustfully upon the young people, and in a moment,
all over the room, at every table, the old heads bent together eagerly in
conspiratorial secrecy, a low greedy whispering went up.

Starwick and Elinor were apparently already well and unfavorably
known to the old pensionnaires. The moment they entered, in the
vast and sibilant whispering that went around the room, envenomed
fragments of conversation could be heard:

"Ah, c'est lui! . . . Et la dame aussi! . . . Ils sont revenus ensemble.
. . . Mais, oui, oui!" At the next table to them an old hag with piled
masses of dyed reddish hair, dressed in an old-fashioned dress bedecked
with a thousand little gauds, peered at them for a moment with an expression of venomous and greedy curiosity, and then, leaning half across
the table towards an old man with a swollen apoplectic face and thick
white mustaches, and a little wizened old hag with the beady eyes
of a reptile—possibly his wife—she hissed:

"Mais oui! . . . Oui! . . . C'est lui, le jeune Américain! . . . Per-
sonne ici ne l'a pas vu depuis trois mois." The old man here muttered
something in a choked and phlegmy sort of voice, and the old parrot-
visaged hag straightened, struck her bony hand sharply on the table,
and cried out in a comical booming note:

"Mais justement! . . . Justement! . . . C'est comme vous voyez!"
. . . Here she lowered her voice again, and peering around craftily
at Elinor and Frank, who were shaking with laughter, she muttered
hoarsely:

"Il n'est pas son mari! . . . Il est beaucoup plus jeune. . . . Mais non,
mais non, mais non, mais non, mais non!" she cried with a rapid and
violent impatience as the old man muttered out a question to her greedy
ear.—"Elle est déjà mariée! . . . Oui! Oui!" This last was boomed out
positively, with an indignant glance at Elinor. "Mais justement! Justement! . . . C'est comme vous voyez!"

That night Elinor was instant, swift, and happy as a flash of light.
There was nothing that she did not seem to apprehend immediately,
to interpret instantly, to understand before a word could be spoken,

and to translate at once into a mercurial hilarity which swept every one along with it, and made all share instantly in its wild swift gaiety, even when it would have been impossible to say why one was gay. The soup was served: it was a brown disquieting liquid in which were floating slices of some troubling and unknown tissue—a whitish substance of an obscenely porous texture. It was probably tripe: Eugene stared at it with a sullen and suspicious face, and as he looked up, Elinor rocked back in her chair with a gust of wild hilarity, placed her fingers across her mouth and laughed a rich and sudden laugh. Then, before he could speak, she placed light fingers swiftly on his arm, and said swiftly, gravely, in a tone of commiserating consent:

"Yes, I know darling! I quite agree with you!——"

"What is it?" he said dumbly, in a bewildered tone. "It looks like——"

"Exactly! Exactly!" Elinor cried at once, before he could finish, and was swept by that wild light gale of merriment again—"That's exactly what it looks like—and don't say another word! We all agree with you!" She looked drolly at the uneasy liquid in the soup-plate, and then said, firmly and positively: "No, I think not! . . . If you don't mind, I'd rather not!"—and then seeing his face again, was rocked with rude and sudden laughter. "God!" she cried. "Isn't it marvellous! Will you look at the poor kid's face!"—And put light fingers gravely, swiftly, tenderly upon his arm again.

The great wave of this infectious gaiety swept them along: it was a wonderful meal. Starwick's burble of gleeful, rich humorous and suggestive laughter was heard again; Ann laughed her short and sudden laugh, but her face was radiant, happy, lovelier than it had ever been, everything seemed wonderfully good and pleasant to them. Elinor called the waitress and quietly sent the troubling soup away, but the rest of the meal was excellent, and they made a banquet of it with two bottles of the best Sauterne the pension afforded. Their hilarity was touched somewhat by the scornful patronage of bright young people among their dowdy elders, and yet they did not intend to be unkind: the whole place seemed to them a museum of grotesque relics put there for their amusement, they were determined to make a wonderful occasion of it, the suspicious eyes, greedy whisperings and conferring heads of the old people set them off in gales of laughter, and Elinor, after a glance around and a sudden peal of full rich laughter, would stifle her merriment with her fingers, and say:

"Isn't it marvellous! . . . God! Isn't it wonderful! . . . Could any one have imagined it! . . . Frank. . . . Frank!" she said quietly in a small stifled tone, "will you *look!* . . . Will you *kindly* take one look at the old girl with the dyed hair and all the thingumajigs, at the next table. . . . And the major! . . . And oh! If looks could *kill!* The things they are saying about *us!* . . . I'm sure they think we're *all* living in sin together. . . . Such *goings* on!" she cried with a gay pretense of horror. "Such open barefaced goings on, my friends, right in the face of decent people! . . . Now, is that terrible or not, Monsieur Duval, I ask you! . . . Darling," she said, turning to Starwick, and speaking in a tone of droll reproach, "don't you feel a sense of guilt? . . . Do you intend to do the right thing by a girl or not? . . . Are you going to make an honest woman of me, or aren't you? . . . Come on, now, darling," she said coaxingly, bending a little towards him, "set my tortured heart at rest! Just tell me that you intend to do the right thing by me! Won't you?" she coaxed.

"Quite!" said Starwick, his ruddy face reddening with laughter as he spoke. "But what—" the burble of gleeful and malicious laughter began to play in his throat as he spoke—"just what is the right thing? . . . Do you mean?—" he trembled a little with soundless laughter, and then went on in a gravely earnest but uncertain tone—"do you mean that you want to live?"—he arched his eyebrows meaningly, and then said in a tone of droll impossibly vulgar insinuation—"you know what I mean— *really* live, you know?"

"Frank!" she shrieked, and rocked back in her chair, covering her mouth with her fingers—"But not at *all,* darling," she went on with her former ironic seriousness, "—you're talking to an innocent maid from Boston, Mass., who doesn't know what you *mean—you beast!*" she cried. "Don't you know we Boston girls cannot begin to really live until you make an honest woman of us first?"

"In that case," Starwick said quietly, his face reddening again with laughter, "I should think we could begin to live at once. It seems to me that another man has already taken care of making you an honest woman!"

"God!" shrieked Elinor, falling back in her chair with another burst of rich and sudden laughter. "Poor Harold! . . . I had forgotten him! . . . That's all this place needs to make it perfect—Harold walking in right now to glare at us over the tops of his horn-rimmed spectacles——"

"Yes," said Starwick, "and your father and mother bringing up the rear and regarding me," he choked, "—with very *bitter* looks—you know," he said, turning to Eugene, "they feel *quite* bitterly towards me —they really do, you know. It's obvious," he said, "that they regard me as an unprincipled seducer who has defiled," his voice trembled uncertainly again, "—who has defiled the virtue of their only *darter!*" he brought this word out with a droll and luscious nasality that made them howl with laughter.

"But really," he went on seriously, turning to Elinor as he wiped his laughter-reddened face with a handkerchief, "I'm sure that's how they feel about it. When your mother and father came to the Studio the other day and found me there,"—Elinor's parents were at that time in Paris—"your father *glared* at me in much the same way that Cotton Mather would look at Casanova. But *quite!* He really did, you know. I'm sure he thought you had become my concubine."

"But, darling," Elinor replied, in her playful coaxing tone, "can't I be your concubine? . . . Oh, how *mean* you are!" she said reproachfully. "I do *so* want to be somebody's concubine." She turned to Eugene protestingly. "Now is that mean or not, I ask you! Here I am, a perfectly good well-meaning female thirty years old, brought up in Boston all my life, and with the best advantages. I've been a good girl all my life and tried to do the best I could for every one, but try as I will," she sighed, "no one will help me out in my life-long ambition to be somebody's concubine. Now is that fair or not—I ask you!"

"But not at all!" said Starwick reprovingly. "Before you can realize your ambition you've got to go out first and get yourself a reputation! . . . And," he added, with a swift exuberant glance at the crafty whispering old heads and faces all around them, "—I think you're getting one very fast."

They went upstairs immediately to the rooms that Elinor had engaged. Starwick had two comfortable big rooms in one wing of the pension; in his living-room a comfortable wood-fire had been laid and was crackling away lustily. Elinor had taken a small bedroom for Eugene, and a larger room for herself and Ann. In Ann's room, a good wood-fire was also burning cheerfully. Elinor and Starwick obviously wanted to be alone to talk together—they conveyed this by a kind of mysterious more-to-this-than-meets-the-eye quietness that had been frequent with them during all these weeks. They announced that they were going for a walk.

LXXXVI

WHEN they had gone, Eugene went to Ann's door and knocked. She showed no surprise at seeing him, but stood aside sullenly until he had come in, and then closed the door behind him. Then she went back, sat down in a chair before the fire, and leaned forward upon her knees, and for some time stared dumbly and sullenly into the crackling flames.

"Where are the others?" she said presently. "Have they gone out?"

"Yes," he said. "They went for a walk. They said they'd be gone about an hour."

"Yes," she said cynically, "and they thought it would be good for me if you and I were left alone for a while. I'm such a grand person that something just *has* to be done for me. God!" she concluded bitterly, "I'm getting tired of having people do me good! I'm fed up with it!"

He made no reply to this and she said nothing more. Her big body supported by her elbows, she continued to lean forward and stare sullenly into the flames.

He had taken a seat in another chair, and at length the silence, and his position in the chair, and the girl's sullen expression became painfully awkward, unhappy and embarrassing. He got up abruptly, took a pillow from the bed, threw it upon the floor, and lay down flat beside her chair, stretched out comfortably with his head to the dancing flames. The feel of the fire, its snap and crackle, the soft flare and fall of burned wood ash, and the resinous piny smell, together with the broad old wooden planking of the floor, the silence of the house and the feel of numb silent night outside, something homelike in the look of the room—these things, together with Ann's big New England body leaned forward towards the fire, the sullen speechless integrity of her grand and lovely face, and the smell of her, which was the smell of a big healthy woman warmed by fire—all of these things filled his senses with something immensely strong, pleasant, and familiar, something latent in man's blood, which he had not felt in many years, and that now was quiet but powerfully reawakened. It filled his heart, his blood, his senses with peace and certitude, with drowsy sensual joy, and with the powerful awakening of an old perception, like the re-discovery of an ancient faith, that the sensuous integument of life was everywhere the same, that the lives of people in this little town in France were the same as the lives of people in the town he came from, the same as the lives of

people everywhere on earth. And after all the dark and alien world of
night, of Paris, and another continent, which he had known now for
several months, this re-discovery of the buried life, the fundamental
structure of the great family of earth to which all men belong, filled
him with a quiet certitude and joy.

Ann did not move; bent forward, leaning on her knees, she continued
to stare into the fire, and looking up at her warm, dark, sullen face, he
fell asleep—into a sleep which, after all the frenzy and exhaustion of
the last weeks, was as deep and soundless as if he were drugged.

How long he lay asleep there on the floor he did not know. But he
was wakened by the sound of her voice—a sullen monotone that spoke
his name—that spoke his name quietly with a toneless, brooding insistence and that at first he thought he must have dreamed. It was repeated, again and again, quietly, insistently, without change or variation
until he knew there was no doubt of it, that he no longer was asleep.
And with something slow and strange and numb beating through him
like a mighty pulse, he opened his eyes and looked up into her face.
She had bent forward still more and was looking down at him with a
kind of slow, brooding intensity, her face smoldering and drowsy as a
flower. And even as he looked at her, she returned his look with that
drowsy, brooding stare, and again, without inflection, spoke his name.

He sat up like a flash and put his arms around her. He was beside her
on his knees and he hugged her to him in a grip of speechless, impossible
desire: he kissed her on the face and neck, again and again; her face was
warm with the fire, her skin as soft and smooth as velvet; he kissed her
again and again on the face, clumsily, thickly, with that wild, impossible
desire, and with a horrible feeling of guilt and shame. He wanted to
kiss her on the mouth, and he did not dare to do it: all the time that he
kept kissing her and hugging her to him with a clumsy, crushing grip,
he wanted her more than he had ever wanted any woman in his life,
and at the same time he felt a horrible profanity in his touch, as if he
were violating a Vestal virgin, trying to rape a nun.

And he did not know why he felt this way, the reason for these
senseless feelings of guilt and shame and profanation. He had been
with so many whores, and casual loose promiscuous women, that he
would have thought it easy to make love to this big, clumsy, sullen-
looking girl, but now all he could do was to hug her to him in an awkward grip, to mutter foolishly at her, and to kiss her warm sullen face
again and again.

He tried to put his clumsy hand upon her breast, but the feeling of shame and profanation swept over him, and he could not keep it there. He put his hand upon her knee, and thrust it under the skirt: the warm flesh of her leg stung him like an electric shock and he jerked his hand away. And all the time the girl did nothing, made no attempt to resist or push him away, just yielded with a dumb sullen passiveness to his embraces, her face smoldering with a slow sullen passion that he could not fathom or define. He did not know why she had wakened him, why she had called his name, what meaning, what emotion lay behind her brooding look, her dumb and sullen passiveness, whether she yielded herself willingly to him or not.

He did not know why he should have this sense of shame and guilt and profanation when he touched her. It may have come from an intrinsic nobility and grandeur in her person and in her character that made physical familiarity almost unthinkable; it may even have come in part from a feeling of social and class inferiority—a feeling which may be base and shameful, but to which young men are fiercely sensitive—the feeling which all Americans know and have felt cruelly, even those who scornfully deny that it exists and yet have themselves done most to foster it. Certainly he had at times been bitterly conscious of the girl's "exclusiveness"—the fact that she was a member of "an old Boston family"—a wealthy, guarded, and powerfully entrenched group; he knew that a beautiful and desirable woman like Ann would have had many opportunities to pick and choose among wealthy men of her own class, and that he himself was just the son of a working-man.

But most of all, he knew that, more than anything else, the thing that checked him now, that overpowered him with its loveliness, that filled his heart with longing and impossible desire, and at the same moment kept him from possession—was the passionate and bitter enigma of that strange and lovely thing which had shaped itself into his life and could never be lost, could never be forgotten, and was never to be known: the thing he knew by these two words—"New England."

And as the knowledge came to him he felt the greatest love and hatred for this thing that he had ever known. A kind of wild cursing anger, a choking expletive of frustration and despair possessed him. He took her by the arms and jerked her to her feet, and cursed her bitterly. And she came dumbly, passively, sullenly as before, neither yielding nor resisting, as he shook her, hugged her, cursed her incoherently in that frenzy of desire and frustrate shame:

"Look here," he panted thickly, shaking her. "Say something! . . . Do something! . . . Don't stand there like a God-damned wooden Indian! . . . Who the hell do you think you are, anyway? . . . Why are you any better than any one else? . . . Ann! Ann! Look at me! . . . Speak! What is it? . . . Oh, God-damn you!" he said with a savagely unconscious humor that neither of them noticed, "—but I love you! . . . Oh, you big, dumb, beautiful Boston bitch," he panted amorously, "—just turn your face to me—and look at me—and by God! I will! I will!" he muttered savagely, and for the first time, and with a kind of desperation, kissed her on the mouth, and glared around him like a madman and, without knowing what he was doing, began to haul and drag her along toward the bed, muttering —"By God, I'll do it!—Oh, you sweet, dumb, lovely trollop of a Back Bay—Ann!" he cried exultantly. "Oh, by God, I'll thaw you out, I'll melt your ice, my girl— by God, I'll open you!—Is it her arm, now?" he began gloatingly, and lifted her long arm with a kind of slow, rending ecstacy and bit into her shoulder haunch, "or her neck, or her warm face and sullen mouth, or the good smell of her. or that lovely belly, darling—that white, lovely, fruitful Boston belly," he gloated, "good for about a dozen babies, isn't it?—or the big hips and swelling thighs, the long haunch from waist to knee—oh, you fertile, dumb, unplowed plantation of a woman—but *I'll* plant you!" he yelled exultantly—"and the big, dumb eyes of her, and her long hands and slender fingers—how did you ever get such slender, graceful hands, you delicate, big—here! give me the hands now —and all the fine, long lady-fingers"—he said with gentle, murderous desire, and suddenly felt the girl's long fingers trembling on his arm, took them in his hands and felt them there, and all her big, slow body trembling in his grasp, and was suddenly pierced with a wild and nameless feeling of pity and regret.

"Oh, Ann, don't," he said, and seized her hand, and held it prayerfully. "Don't look like that—don't be afraid—oh, look here!" he said desperately again, and put his arms around her trembling shoulders and began to pat her soothingly. "—Please don't act like that—don't tremble so—don't be afraid of me!—Oh, Ann, please don't look at me that way— I didn't mean it—I'm so God-damned sorry, Ann—Ah-h! it's going to be all right! It's going to be all right! I swear it's going to be all right!"

he stammered foolishly, and took her hand, and pleaded with her, not knowing what he was saying, and sick with guilt and shame and horror at the profanation of his act.

Her breath was fluttering, coming uncertainly, panting short and quick and breathless like a frightened child; this and her slender hands, her long trembling fingers, the sight of her hands so strangely, beautifully delicate for such a big woman, filled him with an unspeakable anguish of remorse. She began to speak, a breathless, panting, desperate kind of speech, and he found himself desperately agreeing with everything she said, even though he did not hear or understand half of it!

". . . Mustn't stay here," she panted. "Let's get out of here . . . go somewhere . . . anywhere . . . I've got to talk to you. . . . Something I've got to tell you!" she panted desperately. ". . . You don't understand . . . awful, horrible mistake!" she muttered. ". . . Got to tell you, now! . . . Come on! Let's go."

"Oh, yes—sure—anywhere, Ann. Wherever you say," he agreed eagerly to everything she said: they put on their hats and coats with trembling haste, and were preparing to leave just as Starwick and Elinor returned.

Starwick asked them where they were going: they said they were going for a walk. He said, "Oh!" non-committally. Both he and Elinor observed their flushed, excited manner, and trembling haste, with a curious and rather perturbed look, but said nothing more, and they departed.

The pension was silent: every one had already gone to bed, and when they got out into the street, it was the same. It was a night of still, cold frost, and everywhere around them there were the strange, living presences of silence and of sleep. The houses had the closed, shuttered and attentive secrecy that houses in a small French town have at night, no one else seemed to be abroad: they strode rapidly along in the direction of the railway station, saying nothing for a time, their feet sounding sharply on the frozen ground as they walked.

At length, beneath one of the sparse, infrequent street lamps, Ann paused, turned to him, and in a rapid, excited tone which was so different from her usual sullen curtness, began to speak:

"Look here!" she said, "we've got to forget about all that tonight—about everything that happened! . . . It was my fault," she muttered, with a kind of dumb, spinsterly agony of conscience which, in its evocation of the straight innocence and integrity of her kind and person, was somehow pitiably moving—"I didn't mean to lead you on," she said naïvely. "I shouldn't have let you get started."

"Oh, Ann," he said, "you didn't do anything! It wasn't your fault! You couldn't help it—I was the one who started it."

"No. No," she muttered, with a kind of sullen, miserable doggedness. "It was all my fault. . . . Could have stopped it." She turned abruptly, miserably, and began to stride on again.

"But Ann," he began, with a kind of desperate persuasiveness, as he caught up with her, "don't take it this way. . . . Don't worry about it like this! . . . We didn't do anything bad, honestly we didn't!"

"Oh," she muttered without turning her head, "it was an awful thing—an awful thing to do to you! . . . I'm *so* ashamed," she muttered. "It was a rotten thing to do!"

"But you did nothing!" he protested. "I'm the one!"

"No, no," she muttered again—"I started it . . . I don't know why. . . . But I had no right . . . there's something you don't understand."

"But what? What is it, Ann?" He didn't know whether to laugh or cry over this dumb, spinsterly integrity of New England conscience which, it seemed to him, was taking the episode so bitterly to heart.

She paused in her long stride below another street lamp, and turning, spoke sternly, desperately, to him:

"Listen!" she said. "You've got to forget everything that happened tonight. . . . I never knew you felt that way about me. . . . You've got to forget about me. . . . You must never think of me that way again!"

"Why?" he said

"Because," she muttered, "it's wrong . . . wrong."

"Why is it wrong?"

She did not answer for a moment, and then, turning, looked him straight in the eye:

"Because," she said, with quiet bluntness, "nothing can come of it. . . . I don't feel that way about you."

He could not answer for a moment, and it seemed to him that a thin film of ice had suddenly hardened round his heart.

"Oh," he said presently; and, after a moment, added, "and don't you think you ever could?"

She did not answer, but began to walk rapidly ahead. He caught up with her again, took her by the arm and pulled her around to face him. He said sharply:

"Answer me! Don't you think you ever could?"

Her face was full of dumb, sullen misery; she muttered: "There's something you don't understand—something you don't know about."

"That's not what I asked you. Answer me."

"No," she muttered sullenly. "I can't feel that way about you. . . . I never will." She turned with a miserable look in her face and began to walk again. The ring of ice kept hardening round his heart all the time; he caught up with her again, and again stopped her.

"Listen, Ann. You've got to tell me why. I've got to know."—She shook her head miserably and turned away, but he caught her, and pulled her back, saying in a sharper, more peremptory tone:

"No, now—I've got to know. Is it because—you just never could feel that way about a fellow like me—because you could never think about me in that way——?"

She didn't answer for a moment; she just stood looking at him dumbly and miserably; and finally she shook her head in a movement of denial:

"No," she said. "It's not that."

The ring of ice kept getting thicker all the time, it seemed he would not be able to speak the words, but in a moment he said:

"Well, then, is it—is it some one else?"

She made a sudden tormented movement of anguish and despair, and turning, tried to walk away. He seized her, and jerked her back to him, and said:

"Answer me, God-damn it! Is that the reason why?"

He waited a long moment before the answer came, and then she muttered it out so low he could scarcely hear it.

"Yes," she said, and wrenched her arm free. "Let me go."

He caught her again, and pulled her back. The ring of ice seemed to have frozen solid, and in that cold block he could feel his heart throbbing like a trip-hammer.

"Who is it?" he said.

She did not answer, and he shook her roughly. "You answer me. . . . Is it some one you knew back home——?"

"Let me go," she muttered. "I won't tell you."

"By God, you will," he said thickly, and held her. "Who is it? Is it some one you met back home, or not?"

"No!" she shouted, and wrenched free with a kind of stifled sob, and started ahead, almost running: "Leave me alone now! I won't tell you!"

A sudden flash of intuition, an instant flash of recognition and horror went through him like a knife. His heart seemed to have frozen solid, his breath to have stopped: he jumped for her like a cat, and whisking her around towards him, said:

"Ann! Look at me a moment!" He put his fingers underneath her chin and jerked her face up roughly: "Are you in love with Starwick?"

A long wailing note of dumb anguish and despair was torn from her; she tried to break from his grasp, and as she wrenched to get free, cried pitiably, in a terror-stricken voice:

"Leave me alone! Leave me alone!"

"Answer, God-damn you!" he snarled. "Is it Starwick or not?"

With a last frenzied effort, she wrenched free, and screamed like a wounded animal:

"Yes! Yes! . . . I've told you now! Are you satisfied? Will you leave me alone?" And with a sobbing breath, she began to run blindly.

He ran after her again, and caught up with her and took her in his arms, but not to embrace her, but just to hold her, stop her, somehow quiet, if he could, the wild, dumb, pitiable anguish of that big creature, which tore through the ventricles of his heart like a knife. He himself was sick with horror, and a kind of utter, paralyzing terror he had never felt before; he scarcely knew what he was doing, what he was saying, but the sight of that great, dumb creature's anguish, that locked and inarticulate agony of grief, was more than he could bear. And cold with terror, he began to mumble with a thickened tongue: "Oh, but Ann, Ann!—Starwick, Starwick!—it's no use! It's no use!—Christ, what a shame! What a shame!" For suddenly he knew what Starwick was, what he had never allowed himself to admit that Starwick had become, and he kept mumbling thickly, "Christ! Christ! What a pity! What a shame!" not knowing what he was saying, conscious only, with a kind of sickening horror, of the evil mischance which had with such a cruel and deliberate perversity set their lives awry, and of the horrible waste and loss which had warped forever this grand and fertile creature's life and which now would bring all her strength, her love, the noble integrity of her spirit, to barren sterile nothing.

At the moment he had only one feeling, overwhelming and intolerable, somehow to quiet her, to stop, to heal this horrible wound of grief

and love, to bring peace to her tormented spirit somehow, to do anything, use his life in any way that would give her a little peace and
comfort.

And he kept holding her, patting her on the shoulders, saying foolishly over and over again, and not knowing what he said:

"Oh, it's all right! . . . It's all right, Ann! . . . You mustn't look
like this, you mustn't act this way . . . it's going to be all right!" And
knowing miserably, horribly, that it was not all right, that the whole
design and fabric of their lives were ruinously awry, that there was a
hurt too deep ever to heal, a wrong too cruel, fatal, and perverse ever
to be righted.

She stayed there in his arms, she turned her face into his shoulder,
she put her slender, strong and lovely hands upon his arms and held on
to him desperately, and there, in the frozen, sleeping stillness of that
street in a little French town, she wept hoarsely, bitterly, dreadfully, like
some great creature horribly wounded; and all he could do was hold on
to her until the last torn cry of pain had been racked and wrenched out
of her.

When it was all over, and she had grown quiet, she dried her eyes,
and looking at him with a dumb, pleading expression, she whispered
miserably:

"You won't tell them? You won't say anything to Frank about this,
will you? You'll never let him know?"

And stabbed again by wild, rending pity, sick with horror at her
devastating terror, he told her he would not.

They walked home in silence through the frozen, sleeping streets.
It was after midnight when they got back to the pension: the whole
house was long ago asleep. As they went up the stairs a clock began to
strike.

LXXXVII

He did not see her the next morning until it was time for lunch. She
had gone out early with the big Alsatian dog, and had spent the morning walking in the forest. During the morning he told Elinor and
Starwick that he was going back to Paris. Starwick said nothing at all,
but Elinor after a moment's silence, said coldly, and with a trace of
sarcasm:

"Very well, my dear. You're the doctor. If the lure of the great city has proved too much for you, go you must." She was silent for a moment, and then said ironically, "Does this mean that we are not to have the honor of your distinguished company on our trip? . . . Really," she said curtly, "I wish you'd try to make up your mind what you're going to do. . . . The suspense, darling, is growing *quite* unbearable. If you're trying to break it to us gently," she went on poisonously, "I beg of you to let the blow fall now, and not to spare us any longer. After all," she said with a kind of evil drollery, "we may manage to survive the shock. . . . Really, I should like to know," she said sharply, as he did not answer. "If you're not going, we'll get some one else to take your place—we wanted a fourth party to help share in the expenses," she added venomously, "and I'd like to know at once what your intentions are."

He stared at her with a smoldering face and with a swelter of hot and ugly anger in his heart, but as usual, her envenomed attack was too quick and sudden for him. Before he could answer, even as his tongue was blundering at a hot reply, she turned swiftly away, and with an air of resignation, said to Starwick:

"Will you try to find out what his intentions are? I can't find out what he wants to do. *Apparently,*" she concluded in a rich, astounded voice, "—apparently, your young friend is tongue-tied." She walked away, contained and beautifully self-possessed as ever, save for two angry spots of color in her face.

When she had gone, Starwick turned to him, and said with quiet reproof:

"You ought to let her know. You really ought, you know."

"All right!" he said quickly and hotly, "I'm letting you know right now. I'm not going."

Starwick said nothing for a moment, then with a quiet, weary, and sorrowful resignation, he said:

"I'm sorry, Gene."

The other said nothing, but just stood looking at Starwick with eyes which were cold and hard and ugly with their hate. Starwick's quiet words, the almost Christ-like humility with which he uttered them, now seemed to him to be nothing but the mask of a sneering arrogance of pride and contemptuous assurance, the badge of his immeasurable good fortune. With cold, measuring eyes of hate he looked at Starwick's soft and graceful throat, the languid indolence of his soft, voluptuously graceful figure, and with murderous calculation he thought: "How easy it would be for me to twist that damned, soft neck of yours off your shoulders! How easy it would be to take that damned, soft body in my hands and break it like a rotten stick across my knees! Oh, you damned, soft, pampered makeshift of a human being—you thing of cunning tricks and words and accents—you synthetic imitation of a living artist —you dear, damned darling of æsthetic females—you Boston woman's lap-dog, you——"

The foul words thickened to a swelter of blind hate and murder in his heart, and would not give him ease, or phrase the choking and intolerable burden of his hate; the light of hate and murder burned in his naked eye, curled his hands into two rending paws of savage power in which he seemed to feel the substance of that warm, soft throat between the strangling grip of his long fingers; and all the time he felt hopelessly tricked, outwitted, beaten by the very nakedness of his surrender to his hate, beaten by something too subtle, soft and cunning for him ever to grasp, by something which, for so it now seemed, would always beat him, by something whose impossible good fortune it would always be to take from him the thing he wanted most.

A thousand times he had foreseen this thing. A thousand times, he had foreseen, as young men will foresee, the coming of the enemy— and always he had pictured him in a definite form and guise. Always he had come, armed in insolence and power, badged with the open menace of the jeering word, the sneering tongue, the brandished fist. Always he had come to strike terror to the heart with naked threat and open brag, to try to break the heart and courage of another man, to win his jeering domination of another's life, by violence and brutal courage. He had never come by stealth but always by the frontal attack, and the youth, like every youth alive, had sworn that he would be ready for him when he came, would meet him fiercely and without retreat, and would either conquer him or most desperately lie dead before he yielded to the inexpiable shame of foul dishonor.

And now the enemy had come, but in no way that he had ever known, in no guise that he had ever pictured. The enemy had come, not armed in brutal might and open brag and from the front, but subtle, soft, and infinitely cunning, and from a place, and in a way that he had never foreseen. The enemy had come behind the mask of friendship, he had come with words of praise, with avowals of proud belief and noble confidence, in an attitude of admiration and humility—had come in such a way, and even as he spoke the words of praise and proud belief in him, had taken from him what he wanted most in life, and had not seemed to take it, or to want it, or to care.

Starwick and Elinor had quarrelled again: this time it was because he too had decided to go back to Paris that afternoon. No one but Elinor knew the purpose of his going; and that purpose, whatever it was, did not please her. When Eugene entered the dining-room for his last meal with them, they were at it hammer and tongs, totally oblivious of the sensation they were causing among the whispering and conspiring old men and women all about them. Or, if not oblivious, they were indifferent to it: even in their quarrels they kept their grand and rare and special manner—a manner which more and more conceived the universe as an appropriate backdrop for the subtle and romantic complications of their own lives, and which, in its remote and lofty detachment from the common run of man, said that here was an intercourse of souls that was far too deep and rare for the dull conscience of the world to apprehend.

Elinor was talking earnestly, positively, an accent rich, yet sharp, cultivated, yet formidably assured, a well-mannered authority, positive with denial and the conviction of experience.

"You cannot do it! I tell you that you cannot *do* it! You will come a cropper if you do!"

Starwick's face was flushed deeply with anger; he answered quietly in a mannered tone filled with a sense of outrage and indignation:

"I resent that *very* much," he said. "It is *very* wrong, and *very* unfair of you to speak that way! I *resent* it!" he said quietly, but with stern reproof.

"Sorry!" she clipped the word out curt and brusque, the way the English say it. "If you resent it, you resent it—and that's *that!* But after *all,* my dear, what else do you expect? If you insist on bringing any little cut-throat you pick up in a Montmartre bistro along with you everywhere you go, your friends are going to complain about it! And they've a right to!"

"I *resent* that *very* much!" he said again, in his mannered tone.

"Sorry!" she said crisply, curtly, as before. "But that's the way I feel about it!" She looked at him for a moment, and then, suddenly shaking her head in a short and powerful movement, she said in a whispering shudder of revulsion and disgust:

"No good, Frank! . . . I'm willing to make all the allowances I can

. . . but the man's no good—no good! . . . He just won't do!" Her tone was the tone of a powerful New Englander, of "fibre," character and breeding, putting the final dogma of his judgment upon an inferior person who "just won't do."

And again, Starwick, two spots of bright color burning in his cheeks, said coldly, quietly, and with an inflexible obstinacy:

"I resent that *very* much!"

He had apparently decided that Alec, the Frenchman they had met in a Montmartre bar one night, and who had accompanied them on most of their expeditions since, should be their guest in their forthcoming travels over France. Moreover, with that arrogant secretiveness that was characteristic of him, Frank had made an appointment to meet the Frenchman in Paris that evening, and had not until that morning informed any one of his intentions. This was the cause of the quarrel.

As Eugene entered, they looked up at him indifferently, and resumed their quarrel; Ann came in a little later, sat down without speaking, and began to eat in sullen silence. It was an unpleasant meal. Elinor assumed her customary manner of gay, light raillery, but this time, in powerful contrast to her hilarious good spirits of the night before, she was full of spite and malice—the angry desire of her tormented spirit to sting and wound as if, by causing pain to others, she could in some measure assuage her own.

"Darling," she said to Eugene, in her deft, malicious way, "I do hope you're not going to forget all about me now that you're deserting me? . . . Won't you write me now and then to cheer me up? . . . Or is this going to be good-bye forever! . . . Because, darling, if it is, I want you to say so right out . . . no matter how it hurts, I'd rather know the worst right now, so that I can go out in the garden and eat worms, or howl, or beat my head against the wall, or something," she said drolly, but with a glint of spiteful motive in her eyes and in her smooth tone that left no doubt of her intention.—"Won't you say it ain't so, darling? . . . I mean, won't you remember me long enough sometime just to write a letter to me . . . I don't care how short it is if you'll just write and let me know that you still *care*," she said maliciously. ". . . Come on, darling," she added coaxingly, leaning towards him, "say you will. . . . Promise to write me just a little letter . . . just a *teeny-weeny* little one like that," she measured drolly between two fingers, and then, while he glared at her with a hot face and angry eyes, she got in the instant, deft, decisive stroke before he could think up an answer; and so concluded it:

"Good!" she said swiftly, and patted him quickly, decisively, on the arm: "God bless you, darling! I knew you would!"

They finished lunch in a sullen and unhappy silence. After lunch, Eugene went upstairs, packed and closed his valise and came down and paid his bill. When he got outside, Elinor was sitting in the car, waiting for him. Starwick had not yet come down.

"Put your suitcase in behind," she said curtly, "and do tell Frank to hurry if he's coming. There's not much time."

"Where's Ann?" he said. "Is she coming with us to the station?"

"My dear," she said coldly, "I haven't the remotest idea. Why don't you ask her yourself if you want to know?"

He flushed again; and then with a feeling of painful embarrassment and constraint, said:

"Elinor—if you don't mind—that is—I'd like——"

"What?" she said curtly, impatiently, and sharply, turning in her seat and looking at him. "You'd like *what?*"

"If you don't mind," he said, gulping with embarrassment, and at the same moment enraged that he should feel so——

"—My money!" he blurted out.

"What? . . . What?" she demanded again, in a brusque, puzzled tone. "*Oh!*" she cried with a sudden air of enlightenment. "Your *money!* . . . You mean those express checks you gave me to keep for you?"

"Yes," he said miserably, feeling an inexplicable shame and embarrassment at having to ask for his own money, and inwardly cursing the folly which, in the rush of affection that followed their recent reconciliation, had caused him to give every cent he had into her keeping—"if you don't mind—that is——"

"But of *course,* my child!" cried Elinor, with a fine air of astonishment. "You shall have it at once!"—and opening her purse she took out the thin little, black folder that contained all the money he had left —three express checks of twenty-dollar denomination. "Here you are, sir!" she said, and gave it to him in such a way that he felt again a sense of guilt and shame as if he were acting meanly towards her, or were taking something that did not belong to him.

"I'm sorry," he stammered apologetically, "—sorry to have to ask you for it, Elinor—but you see it's all I've got left."

"It is?" she said curtly. "What did you do with all the rest that you had when we met you?"

"I—I guess I spent it," he stammered.

The answer came, and buried itself in his heart, as quick, as cold, as poisonous as a striking snake:

"You did?" she said curtly. "I wonder where. I'm sure you didn't spend any of it while you were with *us.*"

He could have strangled her. The veins stood out upon his forehead like cords, his face was brick-red, and for a moment he went blind with the rush of hot, choking blood to his head. He tried to speak, his throat worked convulsively, but no words came: he just stood there goggling at her stupidly with an inflamed face, uttering a few incoherent croaks. Before he could think of anything to say, she had escaped again: Starwick and Ann were coming out of the pension, and she was speaking to them swiftly, telling them to make haste.

No one spoke during the ride to the station. He sat on the back seat beside Ann and the big Alsatian dog; Starwick and Elinor were in front. When they got to the station, the clock still lacked more than five minutes to train-time. He and Starwick bought third-class fares, and went outside where the women were still waiting for them. Starwick and Elinor walked away a few yards and began their quarrel again; Ann said nothing, but looked at him dumbly, miserably, a look that tore at him with pity and wild regret, and that made him weak and hollow with his blind, impossible desire.

They looked at each other with angry, sullen eyes, tormented with the perverse and headstrong pride of youth, unwilling to make concessions or relent, even when each desperately wanted the other to do so.

"Good-bye," he said, and held out his hand. "Good-bye, Ann."

"What do you mean—?" she began angrily. "What are you going to do?"

"I'm saying good-bye," he said doggedly.

"You mean you're not coming with us?"

For a moment he did not answer and then, nodding towards Elinor, he said bitterly:

"Your lady friend there doesn't seem to want me very much. She doesn't seem to think I bear my fair share of the expense."

"What did she say to you?" the girl asked.

"Oh, nothing," he said in a quiet, choking tone of fury. "Nothing in particular. Just one of those friendly little things I've come to look for. She just said she didn't know what I'd done with my money—that I hadn't spent any of it while I was with you."

Her face got brick-red with a heavy, smoldering flush, she looked towards Elinor with angry eyes, and then muttered:

"It was a rotten thing to say!" Turning towards him again, she said in a low tone:

"Do you mean then that you've given up the trip? You're not coming with us?"

"That's what I've told you, isn't it?" he said harshly. "What else do you expect?"

She looked at him sullenly, angrily, a moment longer; and suddenly her eyes were wet with tears.

"It's going to be a fine trip for me, isn't it?" she muttered. "I've got a lot to look forward to, haven't I?"

"Oh, you'll get along, I guess," he jeered. "I don't think you're going to miss *my* company very much." And felt a desperate hope that she would.

"Oh, it's going to be charming, charming, isn't it!" she said bitterly. "Nothing to do but hold down the back seat alone with the dog—while *they*," she nodded towards Elinor and Starwick—"are up there having their wonderful talks together—leaving me alone to watch the dog while they stay out all night together—oh, it's going to be simply wonderful, isn't it!" she said with an infuriated sarcasm.

"So that's the reason I was wanted?" he said. "To keep you company on the back seat! To take the place of the dog! To make it look good, eh—to make the party look a little more respectable back in Boston when they hear of Mr. Starwick and his two lady friends! That's why you wanted me, is it? To fill in extra space—to be a kind of damned male nurse and chaperon to you and Elinor and Frank Starwick——"

She took a step towards him and stopped, her hands clenched beside her, her eyes shot with tears, her big body trembling for a moment with baffled anger and despair:

"God-damn you!" she said in a small, choked voice; and, her hands still clenched, she turned away abruptly to hide her tears.

At this moment Starwick approached and, his ruddy face flushing as he spoke, he said quietly, casually:

"Ann, look! Will you let me have a thousand francs?"

She turned around, glared at Starwick for a moment with angry, reddened eyes and then, to his astonishment and her own, boomed out comically, and in an enraged tone:

"No—o!"

His face went crimson with embarrassment, but after looking at her steadily for a moment, he turned, and walked back to Elinor. In a moment she could be heard saying coldly, positively:

". . . I am sorry, Francis, but I cannot! . . . You should have thought about all that before! . . . If you won't stay out here and go in with us tomorrow, you'll have to do the best you can by yourself. . . . No, sir, I cannot . . . if you want to put it that way, yes; I *won't*, then! . . . I do not *like* the man. . . . I *thoroughly* disapprove of what you're doing. . . . I *will* not help you!"

Some low, excited words passed between them, and in a moment Starwick said:

"You have no right to say that! I *resent* that *very* much!"

His ruddy face was deeply flushed with anger and humiliation; he turned abruptly on his heel and walked away without farewell. At this moment the guards could be heard calling, "En voiture! En voiture, messieurs!" and Elinor, glancing towards Ann and Eugene, said curtly:

"If you're going to catch that train, you'll have to hurry!"

Eugene turned to say good-bye to Ann; she paid no attention to his outstretched hand but stood, her hands clenched, glaring angrily at him with wet eyes.

"Good-bye!" he said roughly. "Aren't you going to say good-bye?"

She made no answer, but just stood glaring at him, and then turned away.

"All right," he said angrily. "Do as you like!"

Without a word to Elinor, he picked up his valise, ran into the station and got through the gates just as the little suburban train began to move. Starwick was climbing up into a compartment, Eugene followed him, flung his valise inside, and clambered in, breathless, just as a guard with a remonstrant face slammed the door behind him.

LXXXVIII

DURING the journey back to Paris, Eugene and Starwick said little. The two young men were the sole occupants of the compartment, they sat facing each other, looking out through the windows with gloomy eyes. The gray light of the short, winter's day was fading rapidly: when they entered Paris dusk had come; as the train rattled over the switchpoints in the yard-approaches to the Gare St. Lazare, they could see lights and life and sometimes faces in the windows of the high, faded buildings near the tracks. Through one window, in a moment's glimpse, Eugene saw a room with a round table with a dark cloth upon it, and with the light of a shaded chandelier falling on it, and a dark-haired boy of ten or twelve leaning on the table, reading a book, with his face propped in his hands, and a woman moving busily about the table, laying it with plates and knives and forks. And as the train slackened speed, he saw, high up in the topmost floor of an old house that rose straight up from the tracks, a woman come to the window, look for a moment at a canary-bird cage which was hanging in the window, reach up and take it from its hook. She had the rough, blowsy, and somewhat old-fashioned look of a whore of the Renoir period; and yet she was like some one he had known all his life.

They passed long strings of silent, darkened railway compartments, and as they neared the station, several suburban trains steamed past them, loaded with people going home. Some of the trains were the queer little double-deckers that one sees in France: Eugene felt like laughing every time he saw them and yet, with their loads of Frenchmen going home, they too were like something he had always known. As the train came into the station, and slowed down to its halt, he could see a boat-train ready for departure on another track. Sleek as a panther, groomed, opulent, ready, purring softly as a cat, the train waited there like a luxurious projectile, evoking perfectly, and at once, the whole structure of the world of power and wealth and pleasure that had created it. Beyond it one saw the whole universe of pleasure—a world of great hotels, and famed resorts, the thrilling structure of the huge, white-breasted liners, and the slanting race and drive of their terrific stacks. One saw behind it the dark coast of France, the flash of beacons, the gray, fortressed harbor walls, the bracelet of their hard, spare lights, and beyond, beyond, one saw the infinite beat and swell of strong seas, the huge nocturnal slant and blaze of liners racing through immensity, and forever beyond, beyond, one saw the faint, pale coasts of morning and America, and then the spires and ramparts of the enfabled isle, the legendary and aerial smoke, the stone and steel, of the terrific city.

Now their own train had come to a full stop, and he and Starwick were walking up the quay among the buzzing crowd of people.

Starwick turned and, flushing painfully, said in a constrained and mannered tone:

"Look! Shall I be seeing you again?"

772 OF TIME AND THE RIVER

Eugene answered curtly: "I don't know. If you want to find me, I suppose I shall be at the same place, for a time."

"And after that?—Where will you go?"

"I don't know," he answered brusquely again. "I haven't thought about it yet. I've got to wait until I get money to go away on."

The flush in Starwick's ruddy face deepened perceptibly, and, after another pause, and with obvious embarrassment, he continued as before:

"Look! Where are you going now?"

"I don't know, Francis," he said curtly. "To the hotel, I suppose, to leave my suitcase and see if they've still got a room for me. If I don't see you again, I'll say good-bye to you now."

Starwick's embarrassment had become painful to watch; he did not speak for another moment, then said:

"Look! Do you mind if I come along with you?"

He did mind; he wanted to be alone; to get away as soon as he could from Starwick's presence and all the hateful memories it evoked, but he said shortly:

"You can come along if you like, of course, but I see no reason why you should. If you're going to the studio we can take a taxi and you can let me off at the hotel. But if you're meeting somebody over on this side later on, why don't you wait over here for him?"

Starwick's face was flaming with shame and humiliation; he seemed to have difficulty in pronouncing his words and when he finally turned to speak, the other youth was shocked to see in his eyes a kind of frantic, naked desperation.

"Then, look!" he said, and moistened his dry lips. "Could you let me have some—some money, please?"

Something strangely like terror and entreaty looked out of his eyes: "I've *got* to have it," he said desperately.

"How much do you want?"

Starwick was silent, and then muttered:

"I could get along with 500 francs."

The other calculated swiftly: the sum amounted at the time to about thirty dollars. It was almost half his total remaining funds but—one look at the desperate humiliation and entreaty of Starwick's face, and a surge of savage, vindictive joy swept through him—it would be worth it.

"All right," he nodded briefly, and started to walk forward again.

"You come with me while I leave this stuff at the hotel and later on we'll see if we can't get these checks cashed."

Starwick consented eagerly. From that time on, Eugene played with him as a cat plays with a mouse. They got a taxi and were driven across the Seine to his little hotel, he left Starwick below while he went upstairs with his valise, promising to "be down in a minute, after I've washed up a bit," and took a full and leisurely three-quarters of an hour. When he got downstairs, Starwick's restless manner had increased perceptibly: he was pacing up and down, smoking one cigarette after another. In the same leisurely and maddening manner, they left the hotel. Starwick asked where they were going: Eugene replied cheerfully that they were going to dinner at a modest little restaurant across the Seine. By the time they had walked across the bridge, and through the enormous arches of the Louvre, Starwick was gnawing his lips with chagrin. In the restaurant, Eugene ordered dinner and a bottle of wine; Starwick refused to eat, Eugene expressed regret and pursued his meal deliberately. By the time he had finished, and was cracking nuts, Starwick was almost frantic. He demanded impatiently to know where they were going, and the other answered chidingly:

"Now, Frank, what's the hurry? You've got the whole night ahead of you: there's no rush at all. . . . Besides, why not stay here a while? It's a good place. Don't you think so? I discovered it all by myself!"

Starwick looked about him, and said:

"Yes, the place is all right, I suppose, the food looks good—it really does, you know—but *God!*" he snarled bitterly, "how dull! how dull!"

"*Dull?*" Eugene said chidingly, and with an air of fine astonishment. "Frank, Frank, such language—and from *you!* Is this the poet and the artist, the man of feeling and of understanding, the lover of humanity? Is this *grand,* is this *fine,* is this *swell?*" he jeered. "Is this the lover of the French—the man who's more at home here than he is at home? Why, Frank, this is unworthy of you: I thought that every breath you drew was saturated with the love of France. I thought that every pulse-beat of your artist's soul beat in sympathy with the people of this noble country. I thought that you would love this place—find it *simply swell,*" he sneered, "and *very* grand and *most* amusing—and here you turn your nose up at the people and call them dull—as if they were a lot of damned Americans! *Dull!* How can they be *dull,* Frank? Don't you see they're *French?* . . . Now this boy here, for example," he pointed to a bus-boy of eighteen years who was noisily busy piling dishes from a table onto a tray.—"Isn't he a *sweet* person, Frank?" he went on with an evil, jeering mimicry—"and there's something *very* grand and *enormously* moving about the way he piles those dishes on a tray," he continued with a deliberate parody of Starwick's mannered accent. "—I *mean,* the whole thing's there—it really is, you know—it's like that painting by Cimabue in the Louvre that we both like so much—you know the one of the Madonna with the little madonnas all around her.—I mean the way he uses his hands—Look!" he crooned rapturously as the bus-boy took a thick, blunt finger and vigorously wiped his rheumy nose with it. "—Now where, *where,* Frank," he said ecstatically, "could you find anything like that in America? I *mean,* the *grace,* the *dignity,* the complete unselfconsciousness with which that boy just wiped his nose across his finger—or his finger across his nose—Hah! hah! hah!—I get all confused, Frank—*really!*—the movement is so beautiful and fluid—it's hard to say just which is which—which does the *wiping*—nose or finger—I mean, the whole thing's *quite* incredible—and *most* astonishing—the way it comes back on itself: it's like a *fugue,* you know," and looking at the other earnestly, he said deeply: "You see what I mean, don't you?"

Starwick's face had flamed crimson during the course of this jeering parody: he returned the other's look with hard eyes, and said with cold succinctness:

"Quite! . . . If you don't mind, could we go along now and,"—his flush deepened and he concluded with painful difficulty, ". . . and . . . and do what you said you would!"

"But of *course!*" the other cried, with another parody of Starwick's tone and manner. "At once! Immediately! *Tout de suite!* . . . as we say over here! . . . Now, *there* you are!" he said enthusiastically. "*There* you are, Frank! . . . *Tout de suite!*" he murmured rapturously. "*Tout de suite!* . . . Not 'at once!' Not 'right away!' Not 'immediately!' But *tout de suite!* . . . Ah, Frank, how different from our own coarse tongue! Quel charme! Quelle musique! Quelle originalité! . . . I *mean,* the whole thing's there! . . . It really is, you know!"

"Quite" said Starwick as before, and looked at him with hard, embittered eyes. "Could we go now?"

"Mais oui, mais oui, mon ami! . . . But first, I want you to meet yon noble youth who wipes his nose with such a simple unaffected dignity, and is, withal, so *French* about it! . . . I know him well, we artists have the common touch, n'est-ce pas? Many a time and oft have we talked

JASON'S VOYAGE

together. . . . Why, Frank, you're going to love him like a brother . . . the whole, great heart of France is beating underneath that waiter's jacket . . . and, ah! such grace, such flashing rapier-work of Gallic wit, such quick intelligence and humor. . . . Ecoutez, garçon!" he called; the boy turned, startled, and then, seeing the young men, his thick lips slowly wreathed themselves in a smile of amiable stupidity. He came towards them smiling eagerly, a clumsy boy of eighteen years with the thick features, the dry, thick lips, the blunted, meaty hands and encrusted nails of the peasant. It was a face of slow, wondering intelligence, thick-witted, unperceptive, flushed with strong, dark color, full of patient earnestness, and animal good-nature.

"Bonsoir, monsieur," he said, as he came up. "Vous désirez quelque-chose?" And he grinned at them slowly, with a puzzled, trustful stare.

"But yes, my boy!. . . I have been telling my friend about you, and he wants to meet you. He is, like me, an American . . . but a true friend of France. And so I told him how you loved America!"

"But yes, but yes!" the boy cried earnestly, clutching eagerly at the suggestion. "La France and l'Amérique are of the true friends, n'est-ce pas, monsieur?"

"You have reason! It's as you say!"

"Vashingtawn!" the boy cried suddenly, with a burst of happy inspiration.

"But yes! But yes! . . . Lafayette!" the other yelled enthusiastically.

"Pair-shing!" the boy cried rapturously. "La France et l'Amérique!" he passionately proclaimed, and he turned slowly to Starwick, joined his thick, blunt fingers together, and thrusting them under Starwick's nose, nodded his thick head vigorously and cried: "C'est comme ça! . . . La France et l'Amérique!"—he shook his thick, joined fingers vigorously under Starwick's nose again, and said: "Mais oui! Mais oui! . . . C'est toujours comme ça!"

"Oh, my God!" groaned Starwick, turning away, "how dull! How utterly, *unspeakably* dreary!"

"Monsieur?" the boy spoke inquiringly, and turned blunt, puzzled features at Starwick's dejected back.

Starwick's only answer was another groan: flinging a limp arm over the back of his chair, he slumped in an attitude of exhausted weariness. The boy turned a patient, troubled face to the other youth, who said, in an explanatory way:

"He is profoundly moved. . . . What you have said has touched him deeply!"

"Ah-h!" the boy cried, with an air of sudden, happy enlightenment, and thus inspired, began with renewed ardor, and many a vigorous wag of his thick and earnest beak, to proclaim:

"Mais c'est vrai! C'est comme je dis! . . . La France et l'Amérique—" he intoned anew.

"Oh, God!" groaned Starwick without turning, and waved a feeble and defeated arm. "Tell him to go away!"

"He is deeply moved! He says he can stand no more!"

The boy cast an earnest and immensely gratified look at Starwick's dejected back, and was on the point of pushing his triumph farther, when the proprietor angrily called to him, bidding him be about his work and leave the gentlemen in peace.

He departed with obvious reluctance, but not without vigorously nodding his thick head again, proclaiming that "La France et l'Amérique sont comme ça!" and shaking his thick, clasped fingers earnestly in a farewell gesture of racial amity.

When he had gone, Starwick looked around wearily, and in a dispirited tone said:

"God! What a place! How did you ever find it! . . . And how do you manage to stand it!"

"But look at him, Frank . . . I mean, don't you just lo-o-ve it?" he jibed. "I mean, there's something so grand and so simple and so unaffected about the way he did it! It's really quite astonishing! It really is, you know!"

The poor bus-boy, indeed, had been intoxicated by his sudden and unaccustomed success. Now, as he continued his work of clearing tables and stacking dishes on a tray, he could be seen nodding his thick head vigorously and muttering to himself: "Mais oui, mais oui, monsieur! . . . La France et l'Amérique. . . . Nous sommes de vrais amis!" and from time to time he would even pause in his work, to clasp his thick fingers together illustrating this, and to mutter: "C'est toujours comme ça!"

This preoccupied elation soon proved the poor boy's undoing. For even as he lifted his loaded tray and balanced it on one thick palm, he muttered "C'est comme ça," again, making a recklessly inclusive gesture with his free hand; the mountainously balanced tray was thrown off balance, he made a desperate effort to retrieve it, and as it crashed upon the floor, he pawed frantically and sprawled after it, in one general ruinous smash of broken crockery.

There was a maddened scream from the proprietor. He came running clumsily, a squat, thick figure of a bourgeois Frenchman, clothed in black, and screaming imprecations. His mustaches bristled like the quills of an enraged porcupine, and his ruddy face was swollen and suffused, an apoplectic red:

"Brute! Fool! Imbecile!" he screamed as the frightened boy clambered to his feet and stood staring at him with a face full of foolish and helpless bewilderment. ". . . Salaud! . . . Pig! . . . Architect!" he screamed out this meaningless curse in a strangling voice, and rushing at the boy, cuffed him clumsily on the side of the face, and began to thrust and drive him before him in staggering lunges.

"—And what grace, Frank!" Eugene now said cruelly. "How *grand* and *simple* and how *unselfconscious* they are in everything they do! I *mean*, the way they use their hands!" he said ironically, as the maddened proprietor gave the unfortunate boy another ugly, clumsy shove that sent him headlong. "I *mean*, it's like a fugue—like Cimabue or an early primitive—it really is, you know——"

"Assassin! Criminal!" the proprietor screamed at this moment, and gave the weeping boy a brutal shove that sent him sprawling forward upon his hands and knees:

"Traitor! Misérable scélérat!" he screamed, and kicked clumsily at the prostrate boy with one fat leg.

"Now where?—where?" Eugene said maliciously, as the wretched boy clambered to his feet, weeping bitterly, "—where, Francis, could you see anything like that in America?"

"God!" said Starwick, getting up. "It's unspeakable!" And desperately: "Let's go!"

They paid the bill and went out. As they went down the stairs, they could still hear the hoarse, choked sobs of the bus-boy, his thick face covered with his thick, blunt fingers, crying bitterly.

He didn't know what Starwick wanted the money for, but it was plain he wanted it for something, badly. His agitation was pitiable:— the bitter exasperation and open flare of temper he had displayed once or twice in the restaurant was so unnatural to him that it was evident his nerves were being badly rasped by the long delay. Now, he kept consulting his watch nervously: he turned, and looking at Eugene with a quiet but deep resentment in his eyes, he said:

"Look. If you're going to let me have the money, I wish you'd let me have it now—please. Otherwise, I shall not need it."

And Eugene, touched with a feeling of guilt at the deep and quiet resentment in his companion's face, knowing he had promised him the money, and feeling that this taunting procrastination was ungenerous and mean, said roughly:

"All right, come on. You can have it right away."

They turned into the Rue St. Honoré, turned again, and walked to the Place Vendôme, where there was a small exchange office—or "all-night bank"—where travellers' checks were cashed. They entered, he cashed his three remaining checks: the amount was something over 900 francs. He counted the money, kept out 500 francs for Starwick, stuffed the rest into his pocket, and, turning, thrust the little sheaf of banknotes into Starwick's hand, saying brutally:

"There's your money, Frank. And now, good-bye to you. I needn't detain you any longer."

He turned to go, but the implication of his sneer had not gone unnoticed:

"Just a minute," Starwick's quiet voice halted him. "What did you mean by that?"

He paused, with a slow thick anger beating in his veins:

"By what?"

"By saying you needn't detain me any longer?"

"You got what you wanted, didn't you?"

"You mean the money?"

"Yes."

Starwick looked quietly at him a moment longer, then thrust the little roll of banknotes back into his hand:

"Take it," he said.

For a moment the other could not speak. A murderous fury choked him: he ground his teeth together, and clenched his fist, he felt a moment's almost insane desire to grip that soft throat with his strangling hand, and beat the face into a bloody jelly with his fist.

"Why, God-damn you—" he grated between clenched teeth. "God-damn you for a—!"—he turned away, saying harshly: "To hell with you! . . . I'm through!"

He began to walk away across the Square at a savage stride. He heard footsteps following him: near the corner of the Rue St. Honoré, Starwick caught up with him, and said doggedly:

"No, but I'm going with you! . . . I really *must,* you know!" His voice rose and became high, almost womanish, with his passionate declaration: "If there's anything between you and me that has to be settled before you go away, you can't leave it like this . . . we've got to have it out, you know . . . we really must!"

The other youth stood stock still for a moment. Every atom of him —blood, bone, the beating of his heart, the substance of his flesh— seemed to congeal in a paralysis of cold murder. He licked his dry lips, and said thickly:

"Have it out!"—The blood swarmed through him in a choking flood, it seemed instantly to rush down through his hands and to fill him with a savage, rending strength, the curse was torn from him in a bestial cry and snarling:

"Have it out! Why, you damned rascal, we'll have it out, all right! We'll have it out, you dirty little fairy—" The foul word was out at last, in one blind expletive of murderous hate, and suddenly that tortured, impossibly tangled web of hatred, failure, and despair found its release. He reached out, caught Starwick by the throat and collar of his shirt, and endowed with that immense, incalculable strength which hatred and the sudden lust to kill can give a man, he lifted the slight figure from the ground as if it were a bundle of rags and sticks, and slammed it back against the façade of a building with such brutal violence that Starwick's head bounced and rattled on the stone. The blow knocked Starwick senseless: his hat went flying from his head, his cane fell from his grasp and rattled on the pavement with a hard, lean clatter. For a moment, his eyes rolled back and forth with the wooden, weighted movement of a doll's. Then, as Eugene released his grip, his legs buckled at the knees, his eyes closed and his head sagged, and he began to slump down towards the pavement, his back sliding all the time against the wall.

He would have fallen if Eugene had not caught him, held him, propped him up against the wall, until he could recover. And at that moment, Eugene felt an instant, overwhelming revulsion of shame, despair, and sick horror, such as he had never known before. For a moment all the blood seemed to have drained out of his heart and left it a dead shell. He thought he had killed Starwick—broken his neck or fractured his skull: even in death—or unconsciousness—Starwick's frail body retained its languorous dignity and grace. His head dropped heavily to one side, the buckling weight of the unconscious figure slumped in a movement of terrible and beautiful repose—the same movement that one sees in a great painting of Christ lowered from the cross, as if, indeed, the whole rhythm, balance and design of that art which Starwick had observed with such impassioned mimicry had left its image indelibly upon his own life, so that, even in death or senselessness, his body would portray it.

At that moment, the measure of ruin and defeat which the other young man felt was overwhelming. It seemed to him that if he had deliberately contrived to crown a ruinous career by the most shameful and calamitous act of all, he could not have been guilty of a worse crime than the one he had just committed. It was not merely the desperate, sickening terror in his heart when he thought that Starwick might be dead—that he had killed him. It was even more than this, a sense of profanation, a sense of having done something so foul and abominable that he could never recover from it, never wash its taint out of his blood. There are some people who possess such a natural dignity of person— such a strange and rare inviolability of flesh and spirit—that any familiarity, any insult, above all any act of violence upon them, is unthinkable. If such an insult be intended, if such violence be done, the act returns a thousandfold upon the one who does it: his own blow returns to deal a terrible revenge; he will relive his crime a thousand times in all the shame and terror of inexpiable memory.

Starwick was such a person: he had this quality of personal inviolability more than any one the other youth had ever known. And now, as he stood there holding Starwick propped against the wall, calling him by name, shaking him and pleading with him to recover consciousness, his feeling of shame, despair, and bitter ruinous defeat was abysmal, irremediable. It seemed to him that he could have done nothing which would more have emphasized his enemy's superiority and his own defeat than this thing which he had done. And the feeling that Starwick would always beat him, always take from him the thing he wanted most, that by no means could he ever match the other youth in any way, gain even the most trifling victory, was now overpowering in its horror. With a sick and bitter heart of misery, he cursed the wretched folly of his act. He would willingly have cut off his hand—the hand that gave the blow —if by so doing he could undo his act, but he knew that it was now too

late, and with a feeling of blind terror he reflected that this knowledge of his defeat and fear was now Starwick's also, and that as long as
Starwick lived, he would always know about it, and realize from this
alone the full measure of his victory. And this feeling of shame, horror,
and abysmal, inexpiable regret persisted even after, with a feeling of
sick relief, he saw Starwick's eyes flutter, open, and after a moment of
vague, confused bewilderment, look at him with a quiet consciousness.

Nevertheless, his feeling of relief was unspeakable. He bent, picked
up Starwick's hat and cane, and gave them to him, saying quietly:

"I'm sorry, Frank."

Starwick put on his hat, and took the cane in his hand.

"It doesn't matter. If that's the way you felt, you had to do it," he
said in a quiet, toneless and inflexible voice. "But now, before we leave
each other, we must see this through. We've got to bring this thing into
the open, find out what it is. That *must* be done, you know!" His voice
had risen with an accent of inflexible resolve, an accent which the other
had heard before, and which he knew no fear of death or violence or
any desperate consequence could ever alter by a jot. "I've got to understand what this thing is before I leave you," Starwick said. "That must
be done."

"All right!" Eugene said blindly, desperately. "Come on, then!"

And together, they strode along in silence, along the empty pavements
of the Rue St. Honoré, past shuttered shops, and old, silent buildings
which seemed to abide there and attend upon the anguish of tormented
youth with all the infinite, cruel, and impassive silence of dark time,
the unspeakable chronicle of foredone centuries, the unspeakable anguish, grief, and desperation of a million vanished, nameless, and forgotten lives.

And thus, in bitter shame and silence and despair, the demented,
drunken, carnal, and kaleidoscopic circuit of the night began.

LXXXIX

About ten o'clock the next morning some one knocked at Eugene's
door, and Starwick walked in. Without referring to the night before,
Starwick immediately, in his casual and abrupt way, said:

"Look. Elinor and Ann are here: they came in this morning."

"Where are they?" Excitement, sharp and sudden as an electric shock,
shot through him. "Here? Downstairs?"

"No: they've gone shopping. I'm meeting them at Prunier's for lunch. Ann said she might come by to see you later on."

"Before lunch?"

"Ace," said Starwick. "Look," he said again, in his casual, mannered tone, "I don't suppose you'd care to come to lunch with us?"

"Thanks," Eugene answered stiffly, "but I can't. I've got another engagement."

Starwick's face flushed crimson with the agonizing shyness and embarrassment which the effort cost him. He leaned upon his cane and looked out the window as he spoke.

"Then, look," he said, "Elinor asks to be remembered to you." He was silent a moment, and then continued with painful difficulty, "We're all going to the Louvre after lunch: I want to see the Cimabue once more before we leave."

"When are you leaving?"

"Tomorrow," Starwick said. "—Look!" he spoke carefully, looking out the window, "we're leaving the Louvre at four o'clock. . . . I thought . . . if you were going to be over that way. . . . I think Elinor would like to see you before she goes. . . . We'll be there at the main entrance." The anguish which the effort had cost him was apparent: he kept looking away out the window, leaning on his cane, and for a moment his ruddy face was contorted by the old, bestial grimace of inarticulate pain and grief which the other had noticed the first time they had met, in Cambridge, years before. Then Starwick, without glancing at Eugene, turned towards the door. For a moment he stood, back turned, idly tapping with his cane against the wall.

"It would be nice if you could meet us there. If not——"

He turned, and for the last time in life the two young men looked squarely at one another, and each let the other see, without evasion or constraint, the image of his soul. Henceforth, each might glimpse from time to time some shadow-flicker of the other's life, the destiny of each would curiously be interwoven through twinings of dark chance and tragic circumstance, but they would never see each other face to face again.

Now, looking steadily at him before he spoke, and with the deep conviction of his spirit, the true image of his life, apparent in his face, his eyes, his tone and manner, Starwick said:

"If I don't see you again, good-bye, Eugene." He was silent for a moment and, the color flaming in his face from the depth and earnestness of his feeling, he said quietly: "It was good to have known you. I shall never forget you."

"Nor I, you, Frank," the other said. "No matter what has happened —how we feel about each other now—you had a place in my life that no one else has ever had."

"And what was that?" said Starwick.

"I think it was that you were young—my own age—and that you were my friend. Last night after—after that thing happened," he went on, his own face flushing with the pain of memory, "I thought back over all the time since I have known you. And for the first time I realized that you were the first and only person of my own age that I could call my friend. You were my one true friend—the one I always turned to, believed in with unquestioning devotion. You were the only real friend that I ever had. Now something else has happened. You have taken from me something that I wanted, you have taken it without knowing that you took it, and it will always be like this. You were my brother and my friend——"

"And now?" said Starwick quietly.

"You are my mortal enemy. Good-bye."

"Good-bye, Eugene," said Starwick sadly. "But let me tell you this before I go. Whatever it was I took from you, it was something that I did not want or wish to take. And I would give it back again if I could."

"Oh, fortunate and favored Starwick," the other jeered. "To be so rich—to have such gifts and not to know he has them—to be forever victorious, and to be so meek and mild."

"And I will tell you this as well," Starwick continued. "Whatever anguish and suffering this mad hunger, this impossible desire, has caused you, however fortunate or favored you may think I am, I would give my whole life if I could change places with you for an hour—know for an hour an atom of your anguish and your hunger and your hope. . . . Oh, to feel so, suffer so, and live so!—however mistaken you may be! . . . To have come lusty, young, and living into this world . . . not to have come, like me, still-born from your mother's womb—never to know the dead heart and the passionless passion—the cold brain and the cold hopelessness of hope—to be wild, mad, furious, and tormented—but to have belief, to live in anguish, but to live,—and not to die." . . . He turned and opened the door. "I would give all I have and all you think I have, for just one hour of it. You call me fortunate and happy. *You* are the most fortunate and happy man I ever knew. Good-bye, Eugene."

"Good-bye, Frank. Good-bye, my enemy."

"And good-bye, my friend," said Starwick. He went out, and the door closed behind him.

Eugene was waiting for them at four o'clock that afternoon when they came out from the Louvre. As he saw them coming down the steps together he felt a sudden, blind rush of affection for all of them, and saw that all of them were fine people. Elinor came towards him instantly, and spoke to him warmly, kindly, and sincerely, without a trace of mannerism or affectation or concealed spitefulness. Starwick stood by quietly, while he talked to Elinor: Ann looked on sullenly and dumbly and thrust her hands in the pockets of her fur jacket. In the dull, gray light they looked like handsome, first-rate, dignified people, who had nothing mean or petty in them and with whom nothing but a spacious, high and generous kind of life was possible. By comparison, the Frenchmen coming from the museum and streaming past them looked squalid and provincial; and the Americans and other foreigners had a shabby, dull, inferior look. For a moment the bitter and passionate enigma of life pierced him with desperation and wild hope. What was wrong with life? What got into people such as these to taint their essential quality, to twist and warp and mutilate their genuine and higher purposes? What were these perverse and evil demons of cruelty and destructiveness, of anguish, error and confusion that got into them, that seemed to goad them on, with a wicked and ruinous obstinacy, deliberately to do the things they did not want to do—the things that were so shamefully unworthy of their true character and their real desire?

It was maddening because it was so ruinous, so wasteful and so useless; and because it was inexplicable. As these three wonderful, rare and even beautiful people stood there telling him good-bye, every movement, look, and word they uttered was eloquent with the quiet but passionate and impregnable conviction of the human faith. Their quiet, serious, and affectionate eyes, their gestures, their plain, clear, and yet affectionate speech, even the instinctive tenderness that they felt towards one another which seemed to join them with a unity of living warmth and was evident in the way they stood, glanced at each other, or in swift, instinctive gestures—all this with a radiant, clear, and naked loveliness seemed to speak out of them in words no one could misunderstand, to say:

"Always there comes a moment such as this when, poised here upon the ledge of furious strife, we stand and look; the marsh-veil shifts from the enfevered swamp, the phantoms are dispersed like painted smoke, and standing here together, friend, we all see clear again, our souls are tranquil and our hearts are quiet—and we have what we have, we know what we know, we are what we are."

It seemed to him that all these people now had come to such a moment, that this clear peace and knowledge rested in their hearts, and spoke out of their eyes; it seemed to him that all his life, for years, since he had first gone to the dark North and known cities—since he had first known Starwick—was now a phantasmal nightmare—a kaleidoscope of blind, furious days, and drunken and diverted nights, the measureless sea-depth of incalculable memory, an atom lost and battered in a world of monstrous shapes, and deafened in a world of senseless, stupefying war and movement and blind fury. And it seemed to him now that for the first time he—and all of them—had come to a moment of clarity and repose, and that for the first time their hearts saw and spoke the truth that lies buried in all men, that all men know.

Elinor had taken him by the hand, and was saying quietly:

"I am sorry that you will not go with us. We have had a strange and hard and desperate time together, but that is over now, Eugene: we have all been full of pain and trouble, and all of us are sorry for the things we've done. I want you to know that we all love you, and will always think of you with friendship, as our friend, and will hope that you are happy, and will rejoice in your success as if it were our own. . . . And now, good-bye, my dear; try to think of us always as we think of you—with love and kindness. Do not forget us; always remember us with a good memory, the way we shall remember you. . . . Perhaps," for a moment her face was touched with her gay, rueful smile —"perhaps when I'm an old Boston lady with a cat, a parrot, and a canary, you will come to see me. I will be a nice old lady, then—but also I will be a ruined old lady—for they don't forget—not in a life-time, not in Boston—and this time, darling, I have gone too far. So I shan't have many callers, I shall leave them all alone—and if you're not too rich, too famous, and too proper by that time, perhaps you'll come to see me. . . . Now, good-bye."

"Good-bye, Elinor," he said. "And good luck to you."

"Look," said Starwick quietly, "we're going on—Elinor and I . . . I

thought . . . if you're not doing anything else . . . perhaps you and
Ann might have dinner together."

"I'm—I'm not," he stammered, looking at Ann, "but maybe you . . ."

"No," she muttered, staring sullenly and miserably at the ground.
"I'm not either."

"Then," Starwick said, "we'll see you later, Ann. . . . And good-bye,
Eugene."

"Good-bye, Frank."

They shook hands together for the last time, and Starwick and Elinor
turned and walked away. Thus, with such brief and casual words, the
bond of friendship—all of the faith, belief and passionate avowal of their
youth—was forever broken. They saw each other once thereafter; by
chance their lives would have strange crossings; but they never spoke
to each other again.

They waited in awkward silence for a moment until they saw Starwick and Elinor get into a taxi and drive off. Then they walked away
together across the great quadrangle of the Louvre. A haze of bluish
mist, soft, smoky as a veil, hung in the air across the vistaed sweep of
the Tuileries and the Place de la Concorde. The little taxis drilled across
the great space between the vast wings of the Louvre and through the
arches, filling the air with wasp-like drone and menace, the shrill excitement of their tootling horns. And through that veil of bluish haze,
the vast mysterious voice of Paris reached their ears: it was a sound
immense and murmurous as time, fused of the strident clamors of its
four million subjects, and yet, strangely muted, seductive, sensuous,
cruel and thrilling, filled with life and death. The mysterious fragrance of that life filled Eugene with the potent intoxication of its magic.
He drew the pungent smoky air into his lungs, and it seemed freighted
with the subtle incense of the great city's hope and secret promise, with
grief and joy and terror, with a wild and nameless hunger, with intolerable desire. It numbed his entrails and his loins with sensual prescience, and it made his heart beat hard and fast; his breath came
quickly: it was mixed into the pulses of his blood and gave to grief and
joy and sorrow, the wild mixed anguish beating in his heart, its single
magic, its impalpable desire.

They walked slowly across the great Louvre court and through the
gigantic masonries of the arch into the Rue de Rivoli. The street was
swarming with its dense web of afternoon: the sensuous complications

of its life and traffic, the vast honeycomb of business and desire; the street was jammed with its brilliant snarl of motors, with shout and horn and cry, and with the throbbing menace of machinery, and on the other side, beneath arched colonnades, the crowd was swarming in unceasing flow.

They crossed the street and made their way through a thronging maze into the Place de la Comédie Française, and found a table on the terrace of La Régence. The pleasant old café was gay with all its chattering groups of afternoon, and yet, after the great boil and fury of the streets, it was strangely calm, detached, and pleasant, too. The little separate verandahs of its terrace, the tables and the old settees and walls, gave the café an incredibly familiar and intimate quality, as if one were seated in a pleasant booth that looked out on life, a box in an old theatre whose stage was the whole world.

In one of the friendly booth-like verandahs of this pleasant old café, they found a table in a corner, seats against the wall, and sat down and gave their order to the waiter. Then, for some time, as they drank their brandy, they looked out at the flashing pulsations of the street, and did not speak.

Presently Ann, without looking at him, in her level, curt, and almost grimly toneless speech, said:

"What did you and Frank do last night?"

Excitement caught him; his pulse beat faster; he glanced quickly at her, and said:

"Oh—nothing. We went out to eat—walked around a bit—that was all."

"Out all night?" she said curtly.

"No. I turned in early. I was home by twelve o'clock."

"What happened to Frank?"

He looked at her sharply, startled. "Happened? What do you mean— 'what happened to him?' "

"What did he do when you went home?"

"How should I know? He went back to the studio, I suppose. Why do you want to know?"

She made no answer for a moment, but sat looking sullenly into the street. When she spoke again, she did not look at him, her voice was level, hard, and cold, quietly, grimly inflectionless.

"Do you think it's a very manly thing for a big hulking fellow like you to jump on a boy Frank's size?"

Hot fury choked him, passed before his vision in a blinding flood. He ground his teeth, rocked gently back and forth, and said in a small, stopped voice:

"Oh, so he told you, did he? He had to come whining to you about it, did he? The damned little . . . !"

"He told us nothing," she said curtly. "Frank's not that kind; he doesn't whine. Only, we couldn't help noticing a lump on the back of his head the size of a goose egg, and it didn't take me long to figure out the rest." She turned and looked at him with a straight, unrelenting stare, and then said harshly:

"It was a wonderful thing to do, wasn't it? I suppose you think that settles everything. You can be proud of yourself, now, can't you?"

The thin fine blade of cruel jealousy pierced him suddenly, and was twisted in his heart. In a voice trembling with all the sweltering anguish and defeat that packed his overladen heart, he sneered in bitter parody:

"Come now, Frankie, dear!—Did bad naughty mans crack little Frankie's precious head?—There, there, dearie!—Mamma kiss and make it well . . . let nice big nursey-worsey kiss-um and make-um well!— Next time Frankie-pankie goes for a walk, big Boston nursey Ann will go wiv-ems, won't she, pet, to see that wuff, wuff man leave poor little Frankie be."

She reddened angrily, and said:

"No one's trying to be Frankie's nurse. He doesn't need it, and he doesn't want it. Only, I think it's a rotten shame that a big hulking lout like you should have no more decency than to maul around as fine a person as Frank is. You ought to be ashamed of yourself; it was a rotten thing to do!"

"Why, you bitch!" he said slowly, in a low, strangled tone. "You nice, neat, eighteen-carat jewel of a snobby Boston bitch!—Go back to Boston where you came from!" he snarled. "That's where you belong; that's all you're worth. . . . So I'm a big, hulking lout, am I? And that damned little affected æsthete's the finest person that you ever knew!—Why, God-damn the lot of you for the cheap, lying, fakey Boston bitches that you are!—with your 'he's a *swell* person, he really is, you know,'—'Oh, *grand! Oh, swell! Oh, fine!*'" he jeered incoherently. "Why, damn you, who do you think you are, anyway?—that you think I'm going to stand for any more of your snobby Boston backwash!—So I'm a big, hulking lout, am I?"—the words rankled bitterly in his memory. "And dear, dar- ling little Francis is too fine, too fine—oh, dearie me, now, yes—to have

his precious little head cracked up against a wall by the likes of me. . . .
Why, damn you, Ann!" he said in a grating voice, "what are you, anyway, but a damned dull lummox of a girl from Boston? Who the hell
do you think you are, anyway, that I should sit here and take your
snobby backwash and play second fiddle while two cheap Boston women
praise Starwick up to the skies all day long, and tell me what a great
genius he is and how much finer than any one else that ever lived? By
God, it is to laugh!" he raved incoherently, blind with pain and passion,
hindering his own progress by his foolish words of wounded pride.
"—To see the damned affected æsthete get it all! You're not worth it!
You're not worth it!" he cried bitterly. "—You call me a big hulking
lout—and I feel more, know more, see more, have more life and power
and understanding in me in a minute than the whole crowd of you will
ever have—why, I'm so much better than the rest of you that—that
—that—there's no comparison!" he said lamely; and concluded, "Oh,
you're not worth it! You're not worth it, Ann! Why should I get down
on my knees to you this way, and worship you, and beg you for just one
word of love and mercy—when you call me a big, hulking lout—and
you are nothing but a rich, dull Boston snob—and you're not worth it!"
he cried desperately. "Why has it got to be like this, when you're not
worth it, Ann?"

Her face flushed, and in a moment, laughing her short and angry
laugh, she said:

"God! I can see this is going to be a pleasant evening, with you raving
like a crazy man and passing out your compliments already." She
looked at him with bitter eyes, and said sarcastically, "You say such nice
things to people, don't you? Oh, charming! Charming! Simply delightful!" She laughed her sudden angry laugh again. "God! I'll never
forget some of the nice things that you said to me!"

And already tortured by remorse and shame, the huge, indefinable
swelter of anguish in his heart, he caught her hand, and pleaded miserably, humbly.

"Oh, I know! I know!—I'm sorry, Ann, and I'll do better—so help
me God, I will!"

"Then why must you carry on like this?" she said. "Why do you
curse and revile me and say such things about Francis, who is one of
the finest people that ever lived, and who has never said a word against
you?"

"Oh, I know!" he groaned miserably, and smote his brow. "—I

don't mean to—it just gets the best of me—Ann, Ann! I love you so!"

"Yes," she muttered, "a funny kind of love, when you can say such things to me!"

"And when I hear you praise up Starwick, it all comes back to me—and Christ! Christ!—why did it have to be this way? Why did it have to be Starwick that you——?"

She got up, her face flaring with anger and resentment.

"Come on!" she said curtly. "If you can't behave yourself—if you're starting in on that—I'm not going to stay——"

"Don't go! Don't go!" he whispered, grabbing her hand and holding it in a kind of dumb anguish. "You said you'd stay! It's just for a few hours longer—oh, don't go and leave me, Ann! I'm sorry! I promise I'll do better. It's only when I think of it—oh, don't go, Ann! Please don't go! I try not to talk about it but it gets the best of me! I'll be all right now. I'll not talk about it any more—if you won't go. If you'll just stay with me a little longer—it will be all right. I swear that everything will be all right if you don't go."

She stood straight and rigid, her hands clenched convulsively at her sides, her eyes shot with tears of anger and bewilderment. She made a sudden baffled movement of frustration and despair, and cried bitterly:

"God! What is it all about? Why can't people be happy, anyway?"

They made a furious circuit of the night. They went back to all the old places—to the places they had been to with Elinor and Starwick. They went to Le Rat Mort, to Le Coq et l'Ane, to Le Moulin Rouge, to Le Bal Tabarin, to La Bolée, to the Jockey Club, to the Dome and the Rotonde,—even to the Bal Bullier. They went to the big night resorts and to the little ones, to great cafés and little bars, to dive and stew and joint and hole, to places frequented exclusively by the rich and fashionable—the foreigners, the wealthy French, the tourists, the expatriates—and to other places where the rich and fashionable went to peer down into the cauldrons of the lower depths at all those creatures who inhabited the great swamp of the night—the thieves, the whores, the rogues, the pimps, the lesbians and the pederasts—the human excrement, the damned and evil swarm of sourceless evil that crawled outward from the rat-holes of the dark, lived for a period in the night's huge blaze of livid radiance, and then were gone, vanished, melted away as by an evil magic into that trackless labyrinth from which they came.

Where had it gone? That other world of just six weeks before, with all its nocturnal and unholy magic, now seemed farther off and stranger than a dream. It was impossible to believe that these shabby places of garish light, and tarnished gold, and tawdry mirrors, were the same resorts that had glowed in all their hot and close perfumes just six weeks before, had burned there in the train of night like some evil, secret and unholy temple of desire. It was all worn off now: cheap as Coney Island, tawdry, tarnished as the last year's trappings of a circus, bedraggled, shabby as a harlot's painted face at noon. All of its sinister and intoxicating magic had turned dull and pitiably sordid: its people were pathetic, and its music dead—serving only to recall the splendid evil people and the haunting music of six weeks before.

And they saw now that this was just the way it was, the way it had always been. Places, people, music—they were just the same. All that had changed had been themselves. And all through the night they went from place to place, drinking, watching, dancing, doing just the things they had always done, but it was no good—it had all gone stale— it would never be any good again. They sat there sullenly, like people at a waning carnival, haunted by the ghosts of memory and departure. The memory of Elinor and Starwick—and particularly of Starwick— haunted each place they went to like a deathshead at a feast. And again Eugene was filled with the old, choking, baffled, and inchoate anger, the sense of irretrievable and certain defeat: Starwick in absence was even more triumphantly alive than if he had been there—he alone, by the strange, rare quality in him, had been able to give magic to this sordid carnival, and now that he was gone, the magic had gone, too.

The night passed in a kaleidoscope of baffled fury, of frenzied search and frustrate desire. All night they hurtled back and forth between the two blazing poles of Montmartre and Montparnasse: later he was to remember everything like the exploded fragments of a nightmare—a vision of dark, silent streets, old shuttered houses, the straight slant and downward plunge out of Montmartre—the sudden blaze of lights at crossings, boulevards, in cafés, night-clubs, bars and avenues, the cool plunge and shock of air along dark streets again, the taxis' shrill horn tootling at space, empty reckless corners, the planted stems of light across the Seine, the bridges and the sounding arches and dark streets, the steep slant of the hill, the livid glare of night and all the night's scarred faces over again.

They did not know why they stayed, why they hung on, why they continued grimly at this barren hunt. But something held them there

792 OF TIME AND THE RIVER

together: they could not say good-bye and part. Ann hung on sullenly, angrily, in a kind of stubborn silence, saying little, ordering brandy at the bars and cafés, champagnes in the night resorts, drinking little herself, sitting by him in a sullen, angry silence while he drank.

He was like a maddened animal: he raved, stormed, shouted, cursed, implored, entreated, reviled her and made love to her at once—there was no sense, or reason, or coherence in anything he said: it came out of him in one tortured expletive, the urge of the baffled touch, that conflict of blind love and hate and speechless agony, in his tormented spirit:

"Oh, Ann! . . . You lovely bitch! . . . You big, dark, dumb, lovely, sullen Boston bitch! . . . Oh, you whore! You whore!" he groaned, and seizing her hand, he caught it to him, and said desperately, "Ann, Ann, I love you! . . . You're the greatest . . . grandest . . . best . . . most beautiful girl that ever lived . . . Ann! Look at me—you big, ox-dumb brute. . . . Oh, you bitch. . . . You Boston bitch. . . . Will it never come out of you? . . . Won't you ever let it come? . . . Can't it be thawed, melted, shaken loose? . . . Oh, you dumb, dark, sullen, lovely bitch . . . is there nothing there? . . . is this all you are? . . . Oh, Ann, you sweet, dumb whore, if you only knew how much I love you——"

"God!" she cried, with her quick, short, and angry laugh that gave her face its sudden, radiant tenderness, its indescribable loveliness and purity, "—God! But you're the gallant lover, aren't you? First you love me, then you hate me, then I'm a dumb, sullen Boston bitch, and then a whore, and then the grandest and most beautiful girl that ever lived! God, you're wonderful, you are!" She laughed bitterly. "You say such charming things."

"Oh, you bitch!" he groaned miserably. "You big, sweet, dumb, and lovely bitch—Ann, Ann, for God's sake, speak to me, talk to me!" He seized her hand and shook it frantically. "Say just one word to show me you're alive—that you've got one, single atom of life and love and beauty in you. Ann, Ann,—look at me! In God's name, tell me, what are you? Is there nothing there? Have you nothing in you? For Christ's sake, try to say a single, living word—for Christ's sake, try to show me that you're worth it, that it's not all death and codfish, Boston, Back Bay, and cold fishes' blood"—he raved on incoherently:

"Oh! Boston and cold fishes' blood, my eye!" she muttered, with an angry flush in her face.

"And you?—What are you?" he jeered. "For God's sake, what kind of woman are you? I never heard you speak a word that a child of ten could not have spoken. I never heard you say a thing that ought to be remembered. The only things I know about you are that you are a Boston spinstress—thirty—no longer very young—a few gray hairs already on your head—comfortably secure on dead investments—over here on a spree—away from father and the family and *The Boston Evening Transcript*—but never losing them: always knowing that you will return to them—in God's name, woman, is that all you are?"

She laughed her sudden, short and angry laugh, and yet there was no rancor in it.

"That's what Frank would call a brief but masterly description, isn't it? I suppose I should be grateful." She looked at him with quiet eyes, and said simply: "What of it? Even if what you say is true, what of it? As you say, I'm just a dull, ordinary kind of person, and until you and Francis came along, no one thought me anything else, or thought any the less of me for being like that. Listen," her voice was hard and straight and sullen, "what do you expect people to be, anyway? Do you think it's fair and decent to talk about how beautiful I am, when I'm not beautiful, and then to turn and curse me because I'm just an ordinary girl?" She was silent a moment, with an angry flush upon her face, and then she said: "As for my intellect, I went to Bryn Mawr, and I got through without flunking, with a C average. That's about the kind of brain I've got." She turned and looked at him with straight, angry eyes, now shut a little with tears:

"What of it?" she said. "You say that I am dull and dumb and ordinary—well, I never pretended to be anything else. You know, we all can't be great geniuses, like you and Francis," she said, and suddenly her eyes were wet, and tears began to trickle down across her flushed face.— "I'm just what I am, I've never pretended to be any different—if you think I'm dull and stupid and ordinary, you have no right to insult me like this.—Come on, I'm going home."—She started to get up, he seized her, pulled her to him:

"Oh, you bitch! . . . You big, dumb, lovely bitch! . . . Oh, Ann, Ann, you sweet whore, how I love you—I can never let you go—oh, God-damn you, Ann——"

It ended at last, at daybreak in a bistro near Les Halles, where they had often gone at dawn with Elinor and Starwick for rolls and chocolate or coffee. Outside they could hear the nightly roar and rumble of the market, the cries of the venders, and smell all the sweet smells of earth and morning, of first light, health, and joy, and day beginning.

When they left the bistro full light had come, and they at length had fallen silent. They realized that it was useless, hopeless, and impossible, that nothing could be said.

He left her at the gate outside the studio. She pressed the bell, the gate swung open, and for a moment before she left him she stood looking at him with a flushed, angry face, wet angry eyes—a look of dumb, sullen misery that tore at his heart, and for which he had no word.

"Good-bye," she said, "if I don't see you again—" She paused and clenched her fists together at her side, closed her eyes, tears spurted out, and in a choking voice she cried out:

"Oh, this will be a fine thing for me all right! This trip has just been wonderful. God! I'm sorry that I ever saw any of you——"

"Ann! Ann!"

"If you need money—if you're broke——"

"Ann!"

"God!" she cried again. "Why did I ever come!"

She was weeping bitterly, and with a blind, infuriated movement she rushed through the gate and slammed it behind her. He never saw her again.

BOOK VI

ANTÆUS: EARTH AGAIN

XC

WHEN he awoke in Chartres he was filled with a numb excitement. It was a gray wintry day with snow in the air, and he expected something to happen. He had this feeling often in the country, in France: it was a strange, mixed feeling of desolation and homelessness, of wondering with a ghostly emptiness why he was there—and of joy, and hope, and expectancy, without knowing what it was he was going to find.

In the afternoon he went down to the station and took a train that was going to Orléans. He did not know where Orléans was. The train was a mixed train, made up of goods cars and passenger compartments. He bought a third-class ticket and got into one of the compartments. Then the shrill little whistle blew, and the train rattled out of Chartres into the countryside, in the abrupt and casual way a little French train has, and which was disquieting to him.

There was a light mask of snow on the fields, and the air was smoky: the whole earth seemed to smoke and steam, and from the windows of the train one could see the wet earth and the striped, cultivated pattern of the fields, and now and then, some farm buildings. It did not look like America: the land looked fat and well kept, and even the smoky wintry woods had this well-kept appearance. Far off sometimes one could see tall lines of poplars and knew that there was water there.

In the compartment he found three people—an old peasant and his wife and daughter. The old peasant had sprouting mustaches, a seamed and weather-beaten face, and small rheumy-looking eyes. His hands had a rock-like heaviness and solidity, and he kept them clasped upon his knees. His wife's face was smooth and brown, there were fine webs of wrinkles around her eyes, and her face was like an old brown bowl. The daughter had a dark sullen face and sat away from them next the window as if she was ashamed of them. From time to time when they spoke to her she would answer them in an infuriated kind of voice without looking at them.

The peasant began to speak amiably to him when he entered the compartment. He smiled and grinned back at the man, although he did not understand a word he was saying, and the peasant kept on talking then, thinking he understood.

The peasant took from his coat a package of the cheap, powerful tobacco—the 'bleu—which the French government provides for a few cents for the poor, and prepared to stuff his pipe. The young man pulled a package of American cigarettes from his pocket, and offered them to the peasant.

"Will you have one?"

"My faith, yes!" said the peasant.

He took a cigarette clumsily from the package and held it between his great, stiff fingers, then he held it to the flame the young man offered, puffing at it in an unaccustomed way. Then he fell to examining it curiously, revolving it in his hands to read the label. He turned to his wife, who had followed every movement of this simple transaction with the glittering intent eyes of an animal, and began a rapid and excited discussion with her.

"It's American—this."

"Is it good?"

"My faith, yes—it's of good quality."

"Here, let me see! What does it call itself?"

They stared dumbly at the label.

"What do you call this?" said the peasant to the young man.

"Licky Streek," said the youth, dutifully phonetical.

"L-l-leek-ee—?" they stared doubtfully. "What does that wish to say, in French?"

"Je ne sais pas," he answered.

"Where are you going?" the peasant said, staring at the youth with rheumy little eyes of fascinated curiosity.

"Orléans."

"How?" the peasant asked, with a puzzled look on his face.

"Orléans."

"I do not understand," the peasant said.

"Orléans! Orléans!" the girl shouted in a furious tone. "The gentleman says he is going to Orléans."

"Ah!" the peasant cried, with an air of sudden illumination. "Orléans!"

It seemed to the youth that he had said the word just the same way the peasant said it, but he repeated it.

"Yes, Orléans."

"He is going to Orléans," the peasant said, turning to his wife.

"Ah-h!" she cried knowingly, with a great air of illumination, then both fell silent, and began to stare at the youth with curious, puzzled eyes again.

"What region are you from?" the peasant asked presently, still intent and puzzled, staring at him with his small eyes.

"How's that? I don't understand."

"I say—what region are you from?"

"The gentleman is not French!" the girl shouted furiously, as if exasperated by their stupidity. "He is a foreigner. Can't you see that?"

"Ah-h!" the peasant cried, after a moment, with an air of astounded enlightenment. Then, turning to his wife, he said briefly, "He is not French. He is a stranger."

"Ah-h!"

And then they both turned their small, round eyes on him and regarded him with a fixed, animal-like curiosity.

"From what country are you?" the peasant asked presently. "What are you?"

"I am an American."

"Ah-h! An American. . . . He is an American," he said, turning to his wife.

"Ah-h!"

The girl made an impatient movement, and continued to stare furiously and sullenly out the window.

Then the peasant, with the intent, puzzled curiosity of an animal began to examine his companion carefully from head to foot. He looked at his shoes, his clothes, his overcoat, and finally lifted his eyes in an intent and curious stare to the young man's valise on the rack above his head. He nudged his wife and pointed to the valise.

"That's good stuff, eh?" he said in a low voice. "It's real leather."

"Yes, it's good, that."

And both of them looked at the valise for some time and then turned their curious gaze upon the youth again. He offered the peasant another cigarette, and the old man took one, thanking him.

"It's very fine, this," he said, indicating the cigarette. "That costs dear, eh?"

"Six francs."

"Ah-h! . . . That's very dear," and he began to look at the cigarette with increased respect.

"Why are you going to Orléans?" he asked presently. "Do you know some one there?"

"No, I am just going there to see the town."

"How?" the peasant blinked at him stupidly, uncomprehendingly. "You have business there?"

"No. I am going just to visit—to see the place."

"How?" the peasant said stupidly in a moment, looking at him. "I do not understand."

"The gentleman says he is going to see the town," the girl broke in furiously. "Can't you understand anything?"

"I do not understand what he is saying," the old man said to her. "He does not speak French."

"He speaks very well," the girl said angrily. "I understand him very well. It is you who are stupid—that's all."

The peasant was silent for some time now, puffing at his cigarette, and looking at the young man with friendly, puzzled eyes.

"America is very large—eh?" he said at length—making a wide gesture with his hands.

"Yes, it is very large. Much larger than France."

"How?" the peasant said again with a puzzled, patient look. "I do not understand."

"He says America is much larger than France," the girl cried in an exasperated tone. "I understand all he says."

Then, for several minutes, there was an awkward silence: nothing was said. The peasant smoked his cigarette, seemed on the point of speaking several times, looked puzzled and said nothing. Outside, rain had begun to fall in long slanting lines across the fields, and beyond, in the gray blown sky, there was a milky radiance where the sun should be, as if it were trying to break through. When the peasant saw this, he brightened, and leaning forward to the young man in a friendly manner, he tapped him on the knee with one of his great, stiff fingers, and then pointing towards the sun, he said very slowly and distinctly, as one might instruct a child:

"Le so-leil."

And the young man obediently repeated the word as the peasant had said it:

"Le so-leil."

The old man and his wife beamed delightedly and nodded their approval, saying, "Yes. Yes. Good. Very good." Turning to his wife for confirmation, the old man said:

"He said it very well, didn't he?"

"But, yes! It was perfect!"

Then, pointing to the rain, and making a down-slanting movement with his great hands, he said again, very slowly and patiently:

"La pluie."

"La pluie," the young man repeated dutifully, and the peasant nodded vigorously, saying:

"Good, good. You are speaking very well. In a little time you will speak good French." Then, pointing to the fields outside the train, he said gently:

"La terre."

"La terre," the young man answered.

"I tell you," the girl cried angrily from her seat by the window, "he knows all these words. He speaks French very well. You are too stupid to understand him—that's all."

The old man made no reply to her, but sat looking at the young man with a kind, approving face. Then, more rapidly than before, and in succession, he pointed to the sun, the rain, the earth, saying:

"Le soleil . . . la pluie . . . la terre."

The young man repeated the words after him, and the peasant nodded vigorously with satisfaction. Then, for a long time, no one spoke, there was no sound except for the uneven rackety-clack of the little train, and the girl continued to look sullenly out the window. Outside, the rain fell across the fertile fields in long slanting lines.

Late in the afternoon, the train stopped at a little station, and every one rose to get out. This was as far as the train went: to reach Orléans it was necessary to change to another train.

The peasant, his wife and his daughter collected their bundles and got out of the train. On another track another little train was waiting, and the peasant pointed to this with his great, stiff finger, and said to the young man:

"Orléans. That's your train there."

The youth thanked him, and gave the old man the remainder of the package of cigarettes. The peasant thanked him effusively and before they parted he again pointed rapidly towards the sun, the rain, and the earth, saying with a kind and friendly smile:

"Le soleil . . . la pluie . . . la terre."

And the young man nodded to show that he understood, repeated what the old man had said. And the peasant shook his head with vigorous approval, saying:

"Yes, yes. It's very good. You will learn fast."

At these words, the girl, who with the same sullen, aloof, and shamed look had walked on ahead of her parents, now turned, and cried out in a furious and exasperated tone:

"I tell you, the gentleman knows all that! . . . Will you leave him alone now! . . . You are only making a fool of yourself!"

But the old man and old woman paid no attention to her, but stood looking at the young man, with a friendly smile, and shook hands warmly and cordially with him as he said good-bye.

Then he walked on across the tracks and got up into a compartment in the other train. When he looked out the window again, the peasant and his wife were standing on the platform looking towards him with kind and eager looks on their old faces. When the peasant caught his eye, he pointed his great finger at the sun again, and called out:

"Le so-leil. "

"Le so-leil," the young man answered.

"Yes! Yes!" the old man shouted, with a laugh. "It's very good."

Then the daughter looked toward the young man sullenly, gave a short and impatient laugh of exasperation, and turned angrily away. The train began to move, then, but the old man and woman stood looking after him as long as they could. He waved to them, and the old man waved his great hand vigorously and, laughing, pointed towards the sun. And the young man nodded his head and shouted, to show that he had understood. Meanwhile, the girl had turned her back angrily and was walking away around the station.

Then they were lost from sight, the train swiftly left the little town behind, and now there was nothing but the fields, the earth, the smoky and mysterious distances. The rain fell steadily.

XCI

FULL dark had come—the wintry darkness of a gray wet day in early March—before he got to Orléans. The train was of the variety known in France as omnibus, one of those dingy little locals that are made up of third-class compartments and that stop at every country station. As the train neared Orléans, there was a noticeable increase in the travelling public: at every station there was a noisy traffic of arriving and departing passengers. For the most part the people had the look of the country: they came stamping in and out with muddy shoes, with a great banging of compartment doors, with a great tumult of voices, with the vigorous excitement of robust and talkative people.

They were a good-natured crowd, and seemed to know one another, if not actually by name, with the even completer familiarity of race and kind and region. At the sudden pauses at dim-lit country stations, one could hear them shouting greetings and farewells, and see them streaming away along a muddy road towards the dim light and shine of a little town with all the utter, common, and dreary familiarity of March. And the train, in those abrupt and sudden halts and pauses, seemed to be almost as casual a means of transportation as a street-car: it would rattle up to a station, halt, the people would stamp in and out with a banging of doors, and with many shouts, cries, greetings, and farewells, then the shrill little whistle would make its fifing note, and the train would rattle out into the wet and wintry countryside again.

In the compartments the lights were very low and dim, and cast flickering shadows on the faces of the passengers. Somewhere in the train, in another compartment, there was a noisy and jolly crowd of soldiers and robust country people. One man in particular dominated the whole train with his jolly energy, his vulgar and high-spirited good nature. The man's rich voice was charged indescribably with the high, sanguinary vitality of the Frenchman. The voice, to a foreigner, was at once inimitably strange in accent, quality and intonation, and yet familiar as all life, all living. It was packed with the juice of life, and had the full rich qualities of a good wine.

For the youth, that voice heard there in the flickering shadows of the little train, heard with all its robust and full-blooded penetration at the casual and abrupt halts and pauses at little stations, was to be a strangely haunting one. A thousand times thereafter the tone of that rich voice would return to him and reverberate in his memory with the haunting, strange and wonderful recurrence with which the "little" things of life —a face seen one time at a window, a voice that passed in darkness and was gone, the twisting of a leaf upon a bough—come back to us out of all the violence and savage chaos of the days—the "little" things that persist so strangely, vividly, and inexplicably when the more sensational and "important" events of life have been forgotten or obscured.

So, now, the jolly voice of this unseen Frenchman, as it shouted out good-natured but derisive comments on the customs, the appearance, and the inhabitants of every little town at which they stopped, as it was answered in like fashion by the people on the station

platforms, brought back to him instantly the memory of a little country
town in the South at which, on his way to and from college, he had
stopped a dozen times at just this hour. The name of the town was
Creasman, there was a small sectarian school there which was known as
Creasman College, and it had become traditional with the university
students, who crowded the train on their journeys home or back to college, to thrust their heads out of the windows and howl with the derisive arrogance of youth: "Whoopee, girls! Creasman College!"

And this sally was usually answered by similar jibes and jeers from
the group of students, townsfolk and country people, who crowded the
platform of the station "to see the train come through."

In this Frenchman's taunts and jeers, and in the way the people at the
stations answered him, as well as in all the traffic of noisy, muddy, talking and gesticulating people who streamed in and out of the train at
every halt, there was, in spite of all the local differences, the same essential quality that had characterized the halts at the little town set there
upon the vast, raw Piedmont of the South.

Moreover, there was in the tone and texture of the Frenchman's voice
—at once so actual, living, and familiar in its high, sanguinary energy
and so foreign, alien, and troubling to a stranger's ear—the whole
warmth and vitality of centuries of living, a quality which brought the
ancient past of Europe, and of France, to life, as the pages of history
could never do.

In the same way, the boy had long ago discovered that a single tone
or shading in his mother's or his father's voice could touch the lost past
of America—the past of the Civil War, the strange mysteries of Garfield, Arthur, Harrison, and Hayes, which is, for most Americans, more
far and strange in time than the Crusades—and bring it instantly into
life.

Thus, he had never gained a living image of the Civil War until he
heard his mother speak of it one day. Until that time, all his efforts
to recapture that lost time out of the pages of books had been futile:
the men, the battles, the generals, and the lives of all the people existed
in a world of legendary unreality, and seemed, in fact, as different from
the world he knew as if they had existed on a separate planet. And
then one day he heard his mother—who had been only five years old
when the war ended—describe the return of the troops along a country
road near home. She told how the dust rose from the ragged feet of
weary marching men, and of how she sat upon her father's shoulder

as the troops went by, and of all her friends and kinsmen who were
standing near her, and of the return of a cousin—a boy of sixteen years
—starved, ragged, wearing a stove-pipe hat, and without shoes, of how
the women wept and of the boy's words of jesting and good-natured
greeting, as he came to meet them.

Now, with the full rich accents of this unseen Frenchman, at once so
strange and so familiar, all of the ancient life of France—her wars
and histories, the great chronicles of her battles, and the brilliant and
indestructible fabric of her life and energy through so many hundred years of victory and defeat, triumph and catastrophe—began to
pulse with such a living and familiar warmth that it seemed to him
as if the whole thing from the beginning had been compacted and resumed into the rich and sanguinary energies of this one Frenchman's
voice.

The man's speech, a kind of furious and high-spirited repartee, carried on against all comers with an instant's readiness, an animal vigor,
that was almost like a national intoxication, was penetrated constantly
by the exclamation "Parbleu!"

And more than anything else, it seemed to the youth, it was the tone
and quality of that ancient exclamation, delivered with such a buoyant
and animal vitality, that united the Frenchman to the distant past of
his nation's history, to millions of buried and forgotten lives, and
through him, made that distant past blaze instantly with all the warmth
and radiance of life again.

The Frenchman's speech was lewd and ribald with the open and
robust vulgarity of healthy country people; his broad jests were published without affectation in a tone loud enough for all the world to
hear, and it was evident from the roars of hearty, sensual laughter
with which his remarks were received by the soldiers, provincials, and
strapping peasant women who were with him, that his audience was
not a squeamish one.

The chief target for this robust fellow's humor, to which he loudly
returned with unwearied pertinacity, was that unfortunate man, the
station master, whose calling, for some reason, is provocative of un-
limited mirth in France. Now, at every station, the Frenchman would
publish to the world, amid roars of laughter, his narration of the
station master's unhappy lot. In particular, he sang snatches of a ribald
song entitled "Il est cocu le chef de gare"—which described movingly
the trials of a station master's life, the cuckoldries to which the nature

of the work exposes him, the conduct of his wife when he is away from home dispatching trains. And the Frenchman would garnish this ditty with certain pointed speculations of his own, directed at the station master of each town, concerning the probable whereabouts, at that moment, of the station master's wife.

Sometimes, the answer to this ribald banter would be curses, oaths and maddened imprecations from the station master; sometimes, the answer would be a good-natured one, as rough and ready in its coarse spontaneity as the Frenchman's own, but whatever the result, the Frenchman was always ready with a reply.

"Are you speaking from your own experience?" one of the station masters yelled ironically. "Is that the way your old woman behaves when you leave home?"

"Parbleu! Oui!" the Frenchman roared back cheerfully. "Why not? The meat is all the sweeter for a little extra seasoning."

This sally was rewarded by a scream of delighted laughter from the peasant women, and the jester, thus encouraged, continued:

"Parbleu! Do you think I'd play the miser with the old girl, when I've had so much myself? But, no, my friend! What the devil! My old girl's no rare canary who'll fade away the first time that you look at her. The devil, no! There's good stuff there, sound and solid as an ox, old boy, and lots more where the last batch came from!"

At this delicate sally there were roars and screams of delighted laughter from the peasant women in the train, and when the commotion had somewhat subsided, one could hear the voice of the station master from the platform, yelling back ironically:

"Good! Since there's enough for every one, I'll come around to get my share!"

"Parbleu! Why not?" the high, sanguinary voice responded instantly. "Turn about's fair play, as the saying goes—I've played the cock to many a station master's hen——"

Roars of laughter.

"And I'd be the last fellow in the world to begrudge him now—" he would conclude triumphantly, and the train would move off to the accompaniment of roars of laughter, ribaldry, and lusty and derisive banter, above which the high, rich, energy of the Frenchman's voice, crying out,—"Parbleu! Oui! Why not?" was always dominant.

He left the train at one of the little stations near Orléans, departing amid a rough but good-natured chorus of jeers, jibes, and derisive yells

which followed him as he walked away along the platform, and to all
of which he instantly responded with his ribald vitality of coarse humor,
that in its lusty ebullience was somehow like the intoxication of a sound,
rich wine.

The boy saw him for an instant as he passed by the window of
the compartment. He was a strong, stocky figure of a man, wearing
leggings, with blue eyes, a brown mustache, and a solid face full
of dark, rich color. But even after he had disappeared from sight, the
boy could hear him shouting to the other people, the sanguinary vitality
of his instant, ribald—"Parbleu! Why not!"—a tone, a voice, a word
that had evoked the past of France, in all the living textures of her
earth and blood, and that, in future years, would bring this scene to life
again—all of the faces, voices, lives of these people—as no other single
thing could do.

At one of the little stations near Orléans, a girl opened the door and
climbed up into the compartment, which was already crowded. The
country people, however, made room for her, crowding a little closer together on the wooden bench, and telling her to wedge herself in, with
the rough but good-natured familiarity that characterized their conduct
towards one another.

The girl sat down opposite the boy, beside the window, and put the
market basket which she was carrying, on her knees. She was cleanly
but plainly dressed, a very lovely and seductive girl with a slender figure
which seemed, however, already to have attained a languorous and
sensual maturity. She was wearing a broad-brimmed hat of blue that
shaded her face, from which her eyes looked out with a luminous,
troubling, and enigmatic clarity. She said nothing, but sat silently listening to the rude jovialities of the peasant people around her, and to
the ribald shouts and yells and roars of laughter that came from the
nearby compartment.

All the time, the girl gazed directly at the young man, her lovely face
traced faintly with a tender, enigmatic smile. It seemed certain to him
that if he spoke to her she would not rebuff him. The sensation of an
impossible good fortune, of some vague and unutterable happiness
that was impending for him in this strange and unknown town, returned. Desire, slow, sultry, began to beat, throbbing in his pulses and
through the conduits of his blood. He felt certain that the girl would
not rebuff him if he spoke to her. And yet he did not speak.

And presently the little train came puffing in to Orléans, all of the people got out and streamed away towards the station along the platform. He took the girl's basket and helped her down out of the train, and with the old bewildered indecision in his heart stood there looking after her as she walked away from him with a graceful, slow, and sensual stride in which every movement that she made seemed to imply reluctance to depart, an invitation to follow. And he looked after her numbly, with hot desire pounding slow and thick in pulse and blood. And he told himself, as he had told himself so many times before, that he would certainly find her again, knowing in his heart he never would.

Already the girl had been lost among the crowds of people streaming through the station, engulfed again in the everlasting web and weaving of this great earth, to leave him with a memory of another of those brief and final meetings, so poignant with their wordless ache of loss and of regret, in which, perhaps more than in the grander, longer meetings of our life, man's bitter destiny of days, his fatal brevity, are apparent.

And again the boy found himself walking along the platform towards the station after the departing people, whom he had met so briefly, and now lost forever. Again he had sought the mysterious promises of a new land, new earth, and a shining city. Again he had come to a strange place, not knowing why he had come.

Why here?

XCII

The Grand Hôtel du Monde et d'Orléans, which was situated opposite the railway station on one of the corners of the station square, was, despite its sounding title, a modest establishment of forty or fifty rooms, constructed in that style at once grandiose and solid which is peculiar to French hotel architecture. When he entered, he found two women seated in the *bureau* carrying on an animated conversation in fluent English, of which the startling substance ran somewhat as follows:

"But yes, madame. I assure you—you need have no—kalms?—kalms?" —the younger and larger of the two women said in a doubtful tone, lifting puzzled eyebrows at her older companion—"*kalms*, Comtesse, je ne comprends pas *kalms*. Qu'est-ce-que ça veut dire?"

"Mais, non. chérie," the other answered patiently. "Pas *kalms— qualms—qualms.*" She pronounced the word slowly and carefully several times, until the other woman succeeded in saying it after her, at

which the little woman nodded her meagre little head emphatically
with a movement of bird-like satisfaction, and said:

"Oui! Oui! Bon! C'est ça! *Qualms.*"

"Mais ça veut dire?" the other said inquiringly in a puzzled tone.

"Ça veut dire, chérie—you need have no qualms, madame—" the
little wren-like woman considered carefully before she spoke—"Vous
n'avez pas besoin de perturbation—n'est-ce pas?" she cried, with an
eager look of triumph.

"Ah-h!" the other cried, with an air of great enlightenment. "Oui! Je
comprends. . . . I assure you, madame, that you need have no qualms
about the plumbing arrangements."

"Bon! Bon!" the little woman nodded her head approvingly. *"Plumbing,* chérie. *Plumbing,"* she added gently as an afterthought.

"You will find everyt'ing t'oroughly modairne——"

"Thoroughly—" the other said, slowly and carefully. *"Thoroughly—*
you pronounce it this way, my dear—*th—th—"* She leaned forward,
inserting her tongue illustratively between her false teeth.

"Thoroughly," the other said, with evident difficulty, and repeated—
"thoroughly modairne——"

"Modern, dear! *Modern!"* the little wren-like woman said slowly
and carefully again, but then, nodding her head with a movement of
swift decision, she went on sharply: "Mais non! Ça va! Ça va bien!"
She nodded her head vigorously. "Laissez comme ça! Les Américains
aiment mieux comme ça—un peu d'accent, n'est-ce pas?" she said craftily. "Pour les Américains."

"Ah, oui!" the other woman responded at once, nodding seriously.
"Vous avez raison. Ce n'est pas bon de parler trop correctement. Un
peu d'accent est mieux. Ils aiment ça—les Américains."

They nodded wisely at each other, their faces comically eloquent with
that strange union of avarice, hard worldliness, and provincial naïveté
which qualifies a Frenchman's picture of the earth. Then, looking up
at the young man, who was standing awkwardly before the *bureau,* the
younger of the two women said coldly:

"Monsieur?——"

The young woman was perhaps twenty-eight years old, but her cold,
dark face, which was lean and sallow and cleft powerfully by a large
strong nose, had a maturity of cold mistrustfulness and unyielding
avarice which was incalculable. It was as if from birth her spirit had
been steeped in the hard and bitter dyes of man's iniquity, as if she had

sucked the acid nutriment of mistrust and worldly wisdom out of her mother's breast—as if her hard heart and her cold, dark eyes had never known youth, remembered innocence, or been blinded by romantic fantasies—as if, in short, she had sprung full-armored from her cradle, versed in all grim arts of seeking for one's self, clutching her first sous in a sweating palm, learning to add by numbers before she could prattle a child's prayer.

Seen so, the woman's face had a cold and stern authority of mistrust that was impregnable. The face, indeed, might have been the very image of a hotel-keeper's soul, impeccable in its perfection of bought courtesy, but hard, cold, lifeless, cruel as hell, obdurate as a block of granite, to any warming ray of mercy, pardon, or concession where another's loss and its own gain might be concerned.

And yet, for all its cold and worldly inhumanity, the face was a passionate one as well. Her strong, black brows grew straight and thick in an unbroken line above her eyes, her upper lip was dark with a sparse but unmistakable mustache of a few black hairs, her face, at once cold and hard in its mistrust, and smouldering with a dark and sinister desire, was stamped with that strange fellowship of avarice and passion he had seen in the faces of women such as this all over France.

He had seen these women everywhere—behind the cashier's desk in restaurants, shops, and stores, behind the desks in cafés, theatres, and brothels, or in the bureau of a hotel such as this. Sometimes they were alone, sometimes they were seated together behind one of those enormous tall twin desks, enthroned there like the very magistrates of gain, totting up the interminable figures in their ledgers with the slow care and minute painfulness of greed. They sat there, singly, or two abreast, behind their tall desks near the door, casting their hard eyes in a glance of cold mistrust upon the customers and at each other, conspiring broodingly together as they checked and compared each other's ledgers— seeming to be set there, in fact, not only as a watch upon the cheats and treasons of the world, but as a watch upon their own, as well.

And yet, haired darkly on their upper lips, cold, hard, mistrustful in their grasping avarice as they might be, he had always felt in them the complement of a sinister passion. He felt that when all the day's countings were over, the last entry made in the enormous ledger, the last figure added up, and the last drops of sweat wrung from the leaden visage of the final sous—then, *then,* he felt, they would pull down the shutters, bare their teeth in smiles of savage joy, and go to their appointed meeting with their lover, Jack the Ripper. Upon faces such as these, even during their day-light impassivity of cold mistrust, the ardor of their nocturnal secrecies was almost obscenely articulate; it required little effort of the imagination to see these women quilted in a vile, close darkness, a union of evil chemistries, locked in the grip of a criminal love, with teeth bared in the bite and shine of a profane and lawless ecstasy, and making savage moan.

Such, in fact, was the face of the young woman in the bureau of the hotel, who now looked up at him with the cold inquiry of mistrust, and said:

"Monsieur?——"

"I—I'd like to get a room," he stammered awkwardly, faltering before her hard, impassive stare, and speaking to her in her own language.

"Comment?" she said sharply, a little startled at being addressed so immediately in the language wherein she had just been holding—studious practice. "Vous désirez?——"

"Une chambre," he mumbled—"pas trop chère."

"Ah-h—a room! He says he wants a room, my dear," the little woman now put in, quickly and eagerly. She hopped up briskly and came towards him with an eager gleam in her sharp old eyes, an anticipating hope in her meagre face.

"You are a stranger?" she inquired, peering sharply at him. "An American?"—with a look of eager hope.

"Yes," he said.

"Ah-h!" her breath went in with a little intake of greedy satisfaction. "I thought so! . . . Yvonne! Yvonne!" she cried sharply, turning to the other woman in a state of great excitement. "He's an American— he wants a room—he must have something good—an American," she babbled, "the best you've got——"

"But yes!" cried Yvonne rising. "To be sure. At vunce!" she cried, and struck a bell, calling: "Jean! Jean!"

"But not—not," the youth stuttered, "not the best—it's just for me— I'm all alone," he appealed to the smaller woman—"something not very expensive," he said desperately.

"Ah—hah—hah!" she said, emitting a little chuckling laugh of gloating satisfaction and continuing to peer craftily up at him. "An American! And young, too.—How old are you, my boy?"

"T-t-twenty-four," he stuttered, staring at her helplessly.

"Ah—hah—hah!" Again the little gloating laugh. "I thought so—

and why are you here? . . . What are you doing here in Orléans, eh?" she said imperatively, yet coaxingly. "What brings you here, my boy?"

"Why—why—" he stammered confusedly, and then finding no adequate reason (since there was none) for being there, he blurted out—"I'm—a writer—a—a—journalist," he stammered, feeling this made his lie the less.

"Ah—hah—hah," she chuckled softly again with a kind of abstracted gluttony of satisfaction—"a journalist, eh, my boy?" in her ravenous eagerness she had begun to pat and stroke his arm with a claw-like hand, as a cook might stroke a fat turkey before killing it. "A journalist, eh? . . . Yvonne! Yvonne!" suddenly she turned to the other woman again, speaking rapidly in a burst of high excitement. "The young man is a journalist . . . an American journalist . . . he writes for *The New York Times,* Yvonne . . . the greatest newspaper in America."

"Well, not exactly that," he blundered, red in the face from confusion and embarrassment. "I never said——"

"Ah—hah—hah," the little old woman said again with her little gloating laugh, peering up at him with a crafty gleam in her sharp old eyes, and stroking his arm in her unconscious eagerness. ". . . And you've come to write about us, eh? . . . Joan of Arc, eh?" she said seducingly, with a little crafty laugh of triumph. "—The Cathedral . . . the Maid of Orléans . . . ah, my boy, you have come to the right place. . . . I will show you everything. . . . I will take care of you. . . . You are in good hands now. . . . Ah-h, we love the Americans here. . . . Yvonne! Yvonne!" she cried again, her excitement growing all the time. "He says he is here to write about Orléans for *The New York Times* . . . he will put it all in . . . the Cathedral . . . Joan of Arc . . . the hotel here . . . the greatest paper in America . . . millions of people will come here when they read it——"

"Well, now, I never said—" he began again.

"Ah—hah—hah," again she was peering up at him craftily, with old eyes of eager greed, chortling her little laugh of gloating triumph, as she stroked his arm. "Twenty-four, eh? . . . And where are you from, my boy? . . . Where is your home?"

"Why—New York, I suppose," he said hesitantly.

"Yes, yes, I know," she said impatiently—"but before that? Where were you born? . . . What State are you from?"

He stared at her for a moment with bewildered face.

"Why, I don't think you'd know where it is," he said at length. "I'm from Catawba."

"Catawba—yes!" the old woman pressed on eagerly. "And what part of Catawba? What town?"

"Why"—he stared at her, gape-jawed with amazement—"a place called Altamont."

"Altamont!" she crowed jubilantly. "Altamont—yes! Altamont—of course!"

"You *know* it?" he said incredulously. "You've *heard* of it?"

"*Heard* of it! Why, my boy, I've been there seven times!" She chuckled with triumph, then went on with a wild and incoherent eagerness. "Little Mother, they call me . . . I am known everywhere. . . . Letters . . . cablegrams . . . the Governor of Arkansas . . ." she babbled. "I gave up everything . . . spent my fortune. . . . Ah, my boy, I love the Americans. . . . They call me Little Mother. . . . Altamont! . . . A beautiful town! . . . Do you know Doctor Bradford and his family? . . . And how is Harold? . . . What's Alice doing now—has she married . . . a lovely girl. . . . And how is George Watson? . . . What's he doing, eh? . . . Is he still secretary of the Chamber of Commerce? . . . And Mrs. Morgan Hamilton. . . . And Charles McKee— ah, how I should like to see all my dear old friends in Altamont again."

"You—you know them—all those people?" he gasped, hearing as in a dream the great cathedral bells throng out upon the air of night.

"*Know* them! . . . I know every one in the town. . . . I always stay with Doctor Bradford and his family. . . . Ah, what lovely people, my boy. . . . How good they have been to me. . . . I love Americans! . . . Little Mother, they call me," she went on in a strange, tranced tone, her eyes burning feverishly as she spoke—" 'As the brave little woman who is known to thousands of Our Boys as the Little Mother of the Stars and Stripes stood before the great audience that packed the City Auditorium last night as it has never been packed before in its whole history, it is safe to say there was not a dry eye in the great'—Yvonne!" She broke sharply away from her mysterious recitation, and again addressed herself excitedly to the hotel woman—"I know his town . . . I know his family . . . I know his father and his mother . . . I have stayed at their house! . . . They are all dear friends of mine! . . . Quick! Tell Madame Vatel that an American friend of mine is here. . . . Tell her it is going to be a great thing for her . . . for Orléans . . . for all of us. . . . Tell her he is going to write about the hotel in *The New York*

Times . . . you will give him a good room . . . a good price, eh?" she said cunningly. "He will bring hundreds of people here to the hotel——"

"But yes, Countess," said Yvonne. "Perfectly."

"The best! The best!" the old woman cried. "He comes from one of the most prominent families in America—ah—hah—hah! You will see!" She chuckled with mysterious cunning. "I shall make you all rich and famous before I'm through . . . I know all the rich Americans. . . . Hah—hah. . . . They will all come here now when he has written about us. . . . *The New York Times,* Yvonne," she whispered gloatingly, "the paper all the rich Americans read. . . . Tell Madame Vatel what has happened. . . . Ah, a great thing, Yvonne. . . . a great thing for us all—see!" she whispered mysteriously, pointing towards the bewildered youth—"the head, Yvonne! The head! You can tell by the head, Yvonne," she whispered. *"What* a clever head, Yvonne. . . . *The New York Times,* eh? . . ." she chuckled craftily, "that all the clever writers write for! . . . Tell Vatel!" she whispered gloatingly, rubbing her little claw-like hands together. "Tell Madame. . . . Tell every one. . . . He must have the best," she muttered with conspiratorial secrecy. "The best."

"But yes, Countess," Yvonne said smoothly. "Monsieur shall have nothing but the best. Number Seven, I think," she said reflectively. "Oui! Number Seven!" She nodded her head decisively with satisfaction. "I am sure Monsieur will like the room. . . . Jean! Jean!" She clapped her hands sharply to the attentive porter, who now sprang forward nimbly. "Apportez les baggages de Monsieur au Numéro Sept."

"But—but—the price?" the youth said awkwardly.

"The price," said Yvonne, "to Monsieur is—twelve francs. To others —that is deeferent, eh?" she said with a significant smile and an expressive shrug. "But since Monsieur is a friend of the Countess, the price will be twelve francs."

"Cheap! Cheap!" the Countess muttered. "And now, my boy," she said coaxingly, taking him by the arm, "you must take your meals here, too. . . . The cuisine! . . . Ah-h! Merveilleuse!" she whispered, making a small rhapsodic gesture with one hand. "You will eat here, too, my boy—eh?"

He nodded dumbly, and the old woman turned immediately to Yvonne with a look of cunning triumph, saying: "Did you hear, Yvonne? . . . Do you see? . . . He will take his meals here, too. . . . Tell Vatel . . . Tell Madame . . . I know all the rich Americans. . . . They will all come now, Yvonne," she whispered. "You will see. . . . And now, my boy," she said with an air of decision, turning to him again, "have you had dinner yet? . . . No? . . . Good!" she said with satisfaction. "I shall eat with you," she took him by the arm possessively. "We shall eat together here in the hotel. . . . I shall have Pierre set a table for us . . . we shall always eat together there—just you and I. . . . Ah, you have come to the right place . . . I shall look after you and watch you like your own mother, my boy. . . . There are so many bad places here in Orléans . . . so many low resorts. I shall tell you where they are so that you can keep out of them . . . it is so easy for a young man to go astray. . . . So many young Americans who come over here get into trouble, meet with bad companions, because they have no one to guide them. . . . But have no fear, my boy . . . I will watch over you while you are here like your own mother. . . . They call me Little Mother."

He cast a distressed and perplexed glance towards Yvonne, and that capable person came instantly and suavely to his rescue.

"Perhaps, Countess," she said smoothly, "Monsieur would like to see his room and brosh up a beet after ze fatigue of his journey—eh?"

He looked at her gratefully, and the Countess, nodding her head vigorously, said instantly:

"Oui! Oui! C'est ça! . . . By all means, my boy, go up to your room and wash up a bit. . . . Ah, a lovely room! He will like it, eh, Yvonne? . . . New furnishings, hot and cold water, beautiful plumbing."

"I can assure Monsieur," said Yvonne dutifully, "that he need have no—kalms——"

"Qualms, Yvonne, qualms," the Countess corrected her gently—"a lovely room, my boy! And when you have finished come on down and we will dine together. . . . You will find me here. I will wait for you. And while you eat," she said enticingly, "I shall let you read my clippings—ah-h, I have a great book full of them. . . . You shall read it all, everything—what it says about their Little Mother," she said tenderly. "And I shall keep you company. I shall talk to you and tell you what to do in Orléans. . . . No, no, I shall eat nothing," she said hastily, as if to allay some economic apprehension on his part. "It will cost you nothing. . . . A little of your coffee, perhaps. . . . Perhaps a glass of wine—no more. Ah, my dear," the old woman went on sadly, "the food here is so lovely, and I cannot eat it . . . I can eat nothing——"

"Nothing?" he said, staring at her.

"Rien, rien, rien," she cried, waving her hand sidewise.

"The Countess is on—what you say—a diet?" said Yvonne sympathetically. "Eet ees the doctor's orders—she cannot eat."

"Rien du tout," the Countess said again. "Nothing but horse's blood, my dear," the Countess said in a sad voice. "That's all I live on now."

"*Horse's* blood!" he stared at her unbelievingly.

"Oui!" she nodded. "Sang de cheval! You see, my dear," she went on in an explanatory tone, "I have anæmia—and by the doctor's orders I take horse's blood. . . . But the food here is so lovely. Lovely. I shall wait for you, my boy, and watch you eat."

"Jean!" cried Yvonne sharply, giving the youth his freedom by one brisk act. "Les baggages de Monsieur. Numéro Sept."

She handed the key to the porter.

"Oui, monsieur," the porter said cheerfully, picking up the youth's valise. "Par ici, s'il vous plaît."

They went back and got into the little ascenseur, just big enough for two. It mounted slowly, creakingly, with slatting rope. They got off at the first flight: he followed the porter down a thickly-carpeted hall and then, while the man switched on lights, turned down the coverlet of the bed, and pulled the heavy curtains together in order to assure that atmosphere of stale nocturnal confinement without which sleep in France seems impossible, he examined the room.

The place easily lived up to all the rapturous prophesies which the Countess had made of it. It was astonishingly luxurious—with that almost indecent luxury that is characteristic of a French hotel room, and that is disquietingly similar to the luxury of a brothel. The bed was a lavish, canopied affair with crimson hangings; the floor was covered with a thick crimson carpet, completely noiseless to the tread; there was a sensually fat sofa and several fat chairs covered with fat, red plush and painted with gilt, a great gilt-rimmed mirror above the mantel, a washbowl of deep and heavy porcelain with glittering nickel fixtures, a lavish bidet the inevitable provision of a French woman's needs, and curtains of a fat, silk, quilted material whose sensual folds were now closely drawn together, completing the effect of bordello secrecy and luxury previously described.

And this oriental luxury was being provided to him for seventy cents a day on the recommendation of a mad old woman who drank horse's blood and whom he had never seen until a half hour ago. As he stood there bewildered by this new, strange turn of chance and destiny, he felt the stillness of the old town around him, and heard again the vast, sweet thronging of the cathedral bells through the dark and silent air, and felt again, as he had felt so many times, the strange and bitter miracle of life. And there was something in his heart he could not utter.

When he went downstairs again, he found the old woman waiting for him, with an eager and cunning gleam at once comical and pathetic in her sharp old eyes, and a great book of newspaper clippings in her arms.

With an air of complete possession, she took him by the arm, and thus linked, they entered the hotel restaurant together. As they went in, it was at once evident that the fame of the young journalist had preceded him. There was a great scraping of chairs around the family table and Madame Vatel, her husband, their comely married daughter, and the daughter's little girl, rose from the family soup in unison, and received him with a chorus of smiles, bows, and enchanted murmurs of greeting that alarmed him by their profuse respectfulness, and that became almost fawningly obsequious as the Countess began to publish the merits of his power and influence in a torrential French of which he could only capture occasional glittering fragments, the chief of which was the proud name of *The New York Times*—"le grand journal Américain."

Then, having muttered out a few desperate words of thanks for the overwhelming and unexpected warmth of their reception, he and the Countess were escorted by a bowing waiter to the table which had been prepared for them at the other end of the restaurant, near the street entrance. The food—a savory and wholesome country soup, broiled fish, succulent thick slices of roast beef, tender, red, and juicy as none he had ever tasted before, a crisp and tender salad of endive, and camembert and coffee—was as delicious as the Countess had predicted; the wine—a Beaujolais, of which the old woman drank half a glass—both cheap and good; the service of the old waiter suave, benevolent, and almost unctuously attentive; and his own mixed feelings of alarm, astonishment, embarrassment at the position in which he had been placed, resentment at the imposture into which the old woman had compelled him, and wild, helpless, mounting, and astounded laughter—were explosive, indescribable.

He would look up uneasily from the delicious food to see the Vatel family, heads together around their table in a congress of whispering secrecy, and with the imprint of conspiratorial greed and cunning on their faces. Then they would catch his eye, nudge one another, and bow and smile at him with fawning graciousness, and he would return to his food savagely, not knowing whether to curse or howl with laughter.

During the whole course of the meal, the Countess sat opposite him, watching like a hawk every move he made, her old eyes gleaming cunningly, and a strange, fixed smile, which he had come to recognize as being at once crafty and naïve, shrewd with guile and yet pathetically inquiring, hovering faintly upon her sharp and meagre face.

All the time while he was eating, the old woman kept up her strange, fragmentary monologue—a semi-coherent discourse which mirrored forth the very image of her soul and seemed to be addressed to herself as much as to any listener. With a ravenous attentiveness she watched him devour his food, exhorted him to waste none of it, and to sop up the sauce as well, demanded of the old waiter second helpings of the delicious roast beef, accompanying her command with a glittering account of the prosperity that would accrue to him and the hotel as a result of this solicitude; plied the boy with questions concerning his friends, his work, his future prospects, and his travels—in short, pried, probed, wormed and insinuated her way into every corner of his history, and appointed herself guide and censor of his life and conduct from this moment on.

"How long have you been over here, my boy?"—she said in her low but vibrant monotone, which had that curious, dead resonance, an almost bodiless energy that seems to come from indestructible vitality of mind or spirit when the vitality of flesh has been exhausted. It was an energy at once as bitterly tenacious as man's clutch on life, yet marked all the time by the brooding fatality of people who have lived too long and seen all things go—"How long have you been in Europe? . . . And where were you first? . . . England, yes. . . . And after England. . . . Paris? Where did you stay there? . . . How much did they charge you for your room? · . . . Twelve francs. . . . Yes, but you could do better, my boy. . . . You could do much better. . . . You should find a place for eight francs a day. . . . All the Americans spend too much money," she said sadly. "They come over here and waste their money. . . . I have seen so many Americans get stranded here. . . . During the war I had to help so many out. . . . Tell me, my boy," she leaned over and clutched his arm with her claw-like hand, "you are not going to get stranded here like other Americans, are you?" her voice had a low, hoarse, and fatal note in it. "Promise me you won't get stranded here."

He promised her.

"How much money have you got, my boy—eh?" she said, her old eyes lighted with an avaricious gleam. A sudden apprehension shocked her; she started forward, saying quickly—"You've got enough to pay your bill? You've got enough to get you out of Orléans? . . . You won't get stranded here at the hotel?"

He reassured her, and with a look of relief she continued:

"You must tell me every day how much you spend. . . . You must let me watch your money for you. . . . So few young men in America understand the value of money. . . . They throw it away as if it were dirt. . . . There are so many ways to waste your money here in France. . . . We have so many things to spend money on—it's gone before you know it—restaurants, hotels, liquor, wine, cafés—Ah, cafés, cafés!" she sighed with dead fatality. "Cafés everywhere you go," she said. "They are the curse of France. Cafés and women. . . . Have you met the women yet?" she demanded sharply. He told her that he had.

"Yes, I know," she said, her voice sad with its note of resigned fatality. "You meet them in cafés—bad women, waiting there to prey upon the young Americans. . . . Tell me—" the eager gleam awakened in her eyes again—"have you given them much of your money?"

He told her that he had.

"Ah, I know," she answered sadly. "All the young Americans waste their money in that way. . . . Don't do it, my boy," her claw-like hand went out and grasped his arm. "Promise me you will not give any more money away to those women. . . . They are *bad,* bad . . . the shame of France. . . . Get yourself a nice girl, my boy. . . . I know some nice girls here in Orléans. . . . I will introduce you—But don't go to the cafés, my boy—Or, if you go, don't talk to any of the women there. . . . No nice woman here in Orléans goes to the café . . . all the women that you meet there are bad, bad. . . . The best café," she concluded irrelevantly, "is on the Place Martroi. You will find the women there. . . . If you go, tell me tomorrow about the music. . . . They have good music there. . . . I love good music. . . . One hears so little music here in Orléans. . . . There are so few amusements for a decent woman here. . . . Sometimes I want to go to the café to hear the music, but if I did I would no longer be a decent woman. . . . I suppose you'll go to the café tonight?" she said sadly, fatally, but with an eager glint of inquiry in her old eyes. "All the Americans go to the cafés. It's the only place there is to go to here."

Towards ten o'clock, which was her hour of retiring, he escaped from her, and went to the café of which she had spoken. There was an orchestra of three pieces playing the kind of music that is played in French cafés; and many mirrors, and long seats of old worn leather around the walls; and several young whores sitting singly at tables, patiently ogling the sporting males of Orléans, who stroked their mustaches and ogled back, but spent no money on them. And there was one extremely lovely, blonde, seductive and experienced-looking whore from Paris, who ogled no one, but sat by herself at a table, frowning reflectively with half-closed eyes and with a cigarette in her mouth, studiously involved in solitaire, and completely indifferent to the gallantries of the ogling males of Orléans, although many a languishing look was cast in her direction. The men played cards or dominoes together, held their secret, sly, and whispered conversations, and then roared with laughter; the café orchestra played the music that a French café orchestra always plays; the waiters went back and forth with trays and glasses; the proprietor went from table to table talking to his regular patrons; the whores sat patiently at tables, and smiled and ogled when they caught somebody's eye; and somehow the whole scene was instantly, poignantly familiar, like something he had known all his life.

And he did not know why this was true. But something essential in the substance and the structure of the scene—the beautiful and sophisticated prostitute from Paris, the seducers and gallants of the town of Orléans, the feeling of silence, secrecy, and darkness all around him in the old sleeping town—in which this place was now the only spot of warmth and gaiety and lightness—even the occasional shrill fife and piping whistle at the railway station not far away—all these things and people had their counterpart, somehow, in the life of small towns everywhere and in the life he had known in a small town as a child, when he had lain in his bed in darkness and had heard the distant wail and thunder of a departing train, and had seen then in the central core and vision of his heart's desire, his image of the distant, the shining, the fabulous, thousand-spired, magic city, and had thought then of a lovely and seductive red-haired woman named Norah Ryan, who had that year come from the great city to live there in his mother's house, and whose coming and whose going would always be a thing of mystery and wonder to them all; and felt, then, as now, all around him the numb nocturnal stillness of the town, the impending prescience of wild joy, the heartbeats of ten thousand sleeping men.

And this feeling of unutterable loss and familiarity, of strangeness and reality, remained with him later when he left the closing café and walked home towards his hotel through a silent, cobbled street, between rows of old, still houses, the shuttered secrecy of the shops.

And later, the feeling was more strong and strange than ever, as he lay in his sumptuous bed in the hotel, reading the clippings in the Countess' books—those incredible explosions of Yankee journalese that this old woman had inspired in a thousand little towns across America— brought back here, read here now, in the midnight stillness of this ancient town as the great cathedral bells thronged through the air—the miraculous weavings of dark chance and destiny, all near as his heart and farther off than heaven, familiar as his life, and stranger than a dream.

XCIII

IN the weeks that followed, the boy discovered in the totally absurd, yet curiously persuasive illogic of the woman's mind a revealing illustration of the psychology of fraud, the self-hypnosis of the impostor. When he would protest to her at the effrontery of her representations, the staggering fiction she had now woven about him, his family, his wealth, his power, his influence, and his profession, which made an open, bare-faced use of great names and institutions of which he had no knowledge, and to which he could make no claim, the old woman would answer him at once with a series of arguments so ingeniously persuasive that for a moment he would find himself almost conquered by their hypnotic power, absurdly false though he knew them to be.

"Look here," he would say resentfully. "What do you mean by telling all these people that I represent *The New York Times?* What if *The New York Times* should hear about it and have me thrown in jail for fraud—for using their name when I had no right to do it?—You'd be safe—you would," he said bitterly. "I'd be the one to suffer—*you* could always get out of it by saying that you acted in good faith, that you really thought I *did* work for *The Times.*"

"But you *do,* don't you?" She looked at him with a surprised and puzzled face.

"No!" he shouted. "Of course I don't! And I never told you so, either! It's something you made up out of your own head five minutes after I met you, and nothing I could say would stop you.—Now you've told people all over town that I'm writing stories about Orléans for *The New York Times,* and am going to put *them* in the stories. We've accepted favors, got things at reduced prices and been entertained by these people all because you told them I am working for *The Times* and that they are going to get some free publicity out of it. Don't you realize what that is?" he said angrily, glaring at her. "That's fraud. That's getting something by false pretense. You can be put in jail for that! . . . Why the next thing I know you'll be getting money from them—collecting a commission from them for getting me to write them up. Perhaps you have already, for all I know," he concluded bitterly.

"But you did tell me that you were a journalist, my boy," the old woman said gently. "You told me that, you know."

"Well—yes," he sullenly admitted. "I did tell you that. I said that, because I want to be a writer, and I've done nothing yet—and somehow it didn't seem so big to say I was a journalist. . . . Besides," he blundered on uncertainly, "I thought the word had a kind of different meaning here from what it has at home——"

She nodded her head briskly with a satisfied air:

"Exactly. . . . A journalist is one who contributes articles and sketches on timely subjects to current publications. . . . And you've done that, haven't you?"

"Well," he conceded, "I wrote some pieces for the university magazine when I was at college——"

"Ah-h! Exactly!"—this with an air of triumph.

"And I was editor of the college newspaper."

"But of course! Just as I say!"

"And I suppose I did write news stories about the university once in a while and send them to the paper back home."

"Of course you did, my boy! Of course!"

"And I did write what they call a feature article one time and sold it to a paper. . . . And I wrote a one-act play and it was published in a book and I've had so far eight dollars royalty on it," he concluded his recital with a meagre glow of hope, a lame belief that his journalistic pretensions were not wholly fraudulent.

"But—" the Countess lifted astounded eyebrows, and looked about her with a fine gesture of the hands expressive of bewilderment—"just as I *say,* my boy! Just as I *say.* From what you tell me there's no doubt of it! You are a journalist."

"Well," he conceded gloomily, "I guess if you can establish my reputation from that, I could swear to what I've told you. . . . Oh, yes," he added ironically, "and I forgot to tell you that I got up early in the morning and carried papers, when I was a kid."

"Exactly! Exactly!" she nodded seriously—"you showed a talent for your present work right from the start. You have been trained in your profession since childhood."

"Oh, my God!" he groaned. "What's the use? Have it your own way, then. I can't argue with you. . . . Only, for God's sake, Countess, stop telling people around here that I am working for *The New York Times.*"

"Now, my boy, see here; you mustn't be so modest about things. If you don't learn to blow your own horn a little no one else will do it for you. As clever and brilliant as you are, you mustn't be so self-effacing. What if you are not yet editor of *The New York Times*——?"

"Editor! Editor, hell! I'm not even office boy!"

"But, of *course,* my dear!" she said patiently. "You will be some day. But at the present time you are a rising young journalist of great gifts, for whom all of your confrères on *The Times* are expecting a brilliant career——"

"Now, Countess, you look here——"

She waved her hand tolerantly with a dismissing gesture, and went on:

"All that will come," she said. "You are still young—no one expects you to be editor yet."

"You'll have me editor if you talk much longer," he said sarcastically. "I wouldn't put it past you. But if you're determined to tell people I'm a journalist, why drag in *The New York Times?* After all, I could pretend to be a journalist without feeling an utter fraud. So why drag in *The Times?*"

"Ah," she said. "*The Times* is a great newspaper. People have heard of *The Times.* To say you are connected with *The Times* means something, carries prestige."

"Well, if it's prestige you want, why don't you tell them I'm a college professor? You know, I did work as an instructor for a year in New York. If you told them I'm a professor I could at least feel a little less guilty."

"Oh," she said seriously, "but no one here would believe such a story as that. You are too young to be a professor. Besides," she added practically, "it is much better anyway to tell them you are working for *The Times*."

"Why?"

"Because," she patiently explained, "they can see some value in that. The power of the press is great. A professor could do nothing for them. A clever young man writing articles for *The Times* might do much."

"But, damn it," he cried, in an exasperated tone, "I've never written articles for *The Times*. Can't you understand that?"

"Now, see here, my boy," she said quietly. "Try to be reasonable about this thing. What's the use of confusing these people here with needless explanations? What does it matter if you haven't written articles for *The Times*? You *are* writing them now——"

"Oh, hell, Countess!"

"You are going to write these very brilliant and interesting articles about Orléans," she went on calmly, "and they will be published in *The New York Times,* because they will be so very clever that *The New York Times* will want to publish them. So why tell these simple people here anything more than that? It would only confuse them. I have told them nothing but the truth," she said virtuously, "I have told them you are writing a series of articles about Orléans for the great newspaper, *The New York Times,* and that, my boy, is all they need to know." She smiled tranquilly at him. He gave up.

"All right," he said. "You win. Have it your own way. I'm anything you like—the white-haired boy, the prize performer, the crown jewel of *The New York Times*."

She nodded with approval.

The farce grew more extravagant day by day. And because this fantastic chance had somewhat dulled the smothering ache that had been almost constant since his parting with Ann, Elinor, and Starwick, he stayed on from ·day to day, not knowing why he stayed or why he should depart, but held with a kind of hypnotic interest by this web of absurd circumstance in which he had so swiftly been involved.

In the morning, when he came downstairs, the old woman would be waiting for him and would sharply and eagerly catechize him about his conduct the night before.

"Did you go to the café last night, my dear? . . . How much did you have to drink? Eh? . . . A Pernod, four cognacs, coffee, a package of cigarettes. . . . What did that come to, eh? . . . How much did you spend? . . . Twenty-one francs! . . . Ah, my dear, too much, too much!" she clucked sadly and regretfully. "You will spend all your money in cafés and have nothing to go on with! . . . Tell me, now, my dear," her old eyes had an eager glint of curiosity, "were there many people there? . . . Was the place crowded? . . . Were there many women? . . . You didn't talk to any of the girls, did you?" she said sharply.

He said that he had.

"You should not have done that!" she said reproachfully. "And what did she want? She wanted you to come with her, eh?"

"No; we didn't get that far. She asked me for a cigarette."

"And did you give it to her?"

"Yes, of course."

"But no money! You didn't give her any money?" she said feverishly.

"No."

"Did you buy her a drink? . . . Was that what all the cognac was for?"

"No. It was for me."

"How much money have you left, my boy? . . . Are you keeping track of your expenses? . . . Did you get another of those express checks cashed yesterday?"

"Yes, I did."

"What kind? A ten-dollar one?"

"Yes."

"Ah, you shouldn't have done that," she said regretfully. "Once you cash it, it goes quickly." She snapped her fingers, "like that! Ça file! Ça file!—You do not watch your money as you should. You do not keep track of what you spend. . . . My boy, promise me something, will you?" she went on in a low, earnest tone. "Promise me you won't spend all your money and get stranded here. . . . You won't do that, will you? . . . How much money have you left? . . . Tell me," she said eagerly. "How many of those express checks have you left . . . Count it, count it," she demanded greedily. "Take the book out and let me see what you have left."

He took out the little leather folder of express checks and opened it. It was getting very thin. Then he thumbed rapidly through the little sheaf of checks, trying to get it over as quickly as he could because of its distasteful reminder of a harsh reality he wanted to forget. He not only lacked by nature the sense of money, he was also at the blissful period in a young man's life when one hundred dollars is as good as a million. In fact, with twenty dollars in bright, flimsy fifty-franc notes in his pocket, the pleasant terrace of a good café, a drink, the knowledge of delicious food and wine within, and the slow, sensual meditations of desire, he felt as rich as any millionaire on earth. At such a time, the whole earth lay before him in winding vistas of pleasure, joy, and mystery: in the huge unreason of this enchantment he was sure that there was nothing ahead of him but a beautiful and fortunate life, filled with success and happiness, and if by any chance he thought of money, it was only to dismiss the thought impatiently with the irrational conviction that it would always be ready when he needed it, that it would come to him miraculously and wonderfully like manna out of heaven, that he could get great sums of money in many strange, delightful ways, at any time he wanted it.

Now the Countess, by the harsh worldliness of her insistence, had jarred him back to a disquieting reality for which he had no relish. While the old woman followed every movement with greedy, avaricious eyes glued on the checks, he thumbed them over quickly and sullenly, told her curtly their amount, and thrust the book brusquely back into his pocket.

When he had finished, she shook her head at him with sad reproach: "Ah!" she said, "what extravagance! A French family could have lived comfortably for a month on what you have spent here in the last week."

He winced, and stirred restlessly, pierced suddenly with a nameless sense of guilt and shame, and personal unworthiness, a sudden evocation of the infinite toil and minute saving of his mother's life. And he felt this despite the fact that his mother had now acquired a considerable estate, a large sum of money, and, in spite of her parsimonious economies in innumerable small ways, displayed in her real estate investments a riotous extravagance that far surpassed any of his own on the sensual pleasures of food and drink and books, on voyages and women. And this curious and irrational sense of guilt and shame was, he knew, not peculiar to himself, but rooted somehow in the structure of the lives of most of the Americans he had known. It was something that went back almost past time and memory, that they had always had, that was

distilled out of their blood, and drawn from the very air they breathed:—
a feeling that any life not based on gainful labor, any life devoted openly
and nakedly to pleasure, idleness and leisure, and the gratification of
one's own desires, was, somehow, an ignoble and shameful life.

Now, suddenly torn with this old and irremediable sense of guilt, he
scowled suddenly, fidgeted restlessly in his chair, and then spoke sharply
and angrily to the old woman, who sat with her sad, reproachful gaze
upon him:

"Well, it's spent now, it's gone, it can't be helped. What do you expect people to do with money, anyway?" he said irritably. "Count it
and kiss it and say good-night to it every time they go to sleep—and
kiss it and count it over again every time they wake up, to see none
of it has got away from them in the night? What's it for anyway if
it's not to spend? What are you living for?" he said bitterly. "What
are you waiting for? Are you saving your money so you can have a nice
coffin when they bury you?"

"Yes, my boy, but you spend so much on food and drink and on the
girls," the old woman said in a sad tone. "So much of it goes on things
like that."

"And why not?" he said resentfully. "Will you please tell me what
else I should spend it on? Is there anything better than that to spend it
on?"

"Don't spend it on those girls in the café," she said. "They are bad—
bad—they will bring you nothing but misfortune and trouble. Come,"
she said, getting up briskly. "I shall take you with me this morning and
introduce you to two nice girls. You will be better off with them than
with those women in the café."

They went out, and walked along the streets of the old town, brisk
with morning life, cheerful with the thin, musty yellow of a wintry sun.
As they walked along those streets of morning, many people recognized
the old woman and spoke respectfully to her. Sometimes shopkeepers
spoke to her from doorways, smiling good-naturedly at the sight of the
little old woman trotting briskly along beside the towering height of
the young man. Sometimes she would hear their laughter and bantering
comment among themselves about the ludicrous disproportion of the
pair, and then, turning to the young man, she would laugh in an abstracted and yet pleased way, saying:

"Ah—hah—hah! They are laughing at you and me, my boy. They
think it is very funny, the way we look together. . . . Un grand garçon,

eh?" she called out to a man standing in the doorway of a shop, who was measuring the boy up and down with a look of good-natured astonishment.

"Mon Dieu!" the man cried. "Qu'il est grand! Il mange beaucoup de soupe!"

At length, they stopped before a small millinery shop, where the old woman was having a hat made, and went in. A small bell tinkled thinly as they entered, and the milliner and her assistant came out from behind some curtains to greet them. The milliner was a competent-looking woman of thirty years, dark, with a wide face, and a strong, compact, and yet seductive figure. The assistant was younger, taller, and fair in coloring. Both were attractive girls, and both greeted him with smiles and the exclamation of good-natured astonishment that he had heard upon the street. Then, for several minutes, the little shop was gay with the light, rapid French of the three women. All seemed to be talking and laughing at the same time, in excited tones; he saw that the Countess was eagerly publishing his merits to the two girls, he caught the magic phrase *The New York Times* now and then, the two girls kept glancing at him with smiling faces, and presently the older one, who was the proprietor, walked towards him, measured her height against his shoulder, and then with a little laugh of astonishment, said:

"Mon Dieu! Qu'il est grand!"

The younger of the two girls, laughing, made a reply in rapid French which he could not follow, and the Countess, with a little chuckle of satisfaction, turned towards him, saying in an explanatory manner:

"They say they need you here, my dear, to get boxes down from the top shelf. It's too tall for them."

"Mon Dieu, oui!" the younger, taller girl, who had picked up the hat she had been making for the old woman and was shaping it in her hands, now answered instantly. "He can help Hélène now with the box while you try this on. Hélène," she called to the other girl, "show Monsieur where the boxes are and have him get one down for you."

He followed Hélène back through the curtains to the rear of the shop, pursued by the laughter and chattering comment of the other two women. Upon a shelf in the rear a number of hat-boxes were stacked up, but when he looked inquiringly at Hélène, she smiled good-naturedly, and kindly said:

"Mais non, monsieur. Nous ne sommes pas sérieuses. Attendez," and got up briskly on a chair, reaching for a box herself. It was, in fact, almost out of reach; she touched it with her outstretched finger-tips, dislodged it, it came tumbling down, and he caught it as it fell. And Hélène herself came close to falling. She teetered uncertainly on her unsteady balance, swayed towards him, and he lifted her down. For a moment, her weight was strong and palpable in his arms. He put her down reluctantly, and for a moment she stood flat against him, her hands gently resting on his arms. Then, with a pleasant litttle laugh, she said:

"Oh, la, la! Qu'il est fort!"

They went out front again, the Countess finished trying on the hat, and presently, after another burst of gay and rapid talk, he and the old woman departed. As he went out, the little bell tinkled thinly and pleasantly again; he had to stoop to go through the door. He turned to say good-bye again, the two girls were looking towards him with gay and friendly smiles; he was sorry to go, and wanted some excuse for staying. Hélène looked strong and competent and desirable, she smiled at him a friendly farewell: he thought if he came back again she would be glad to see him, but he never saw her after that.

Later, the two girls stayed in his memory with a vivid, pleasant warmth: he thought of Hélène many times, her strong seductive figure, and her wide, dark face, and he wondered what her life had been, if she had married, and what time had brought to her.

XCIV

THE crowning extravagance of the Countess' misrepresentation was revealed one morning when he found a letter addressed to him in a firm, feminine, and completely unfamiliar handwriting. The Countess had spoken to him several times of a great noblewoman in the neighborhood, who lived in a magnificent château, and with whom, it was obvious, the Countess wished to improve her slight acquaintance. Now, upon opening the letter, the following message greeted his astounded eye:

Le Château de Mornaye
February 23, 1925

My dear Mr. Gant:

My old friend, La Comtesse de Caux, informs me that you are spending some time in Orléans, preparing a series of articles for the great journal you represent, *The New York Times*.

It will be a great pleasure to me if you, together with La Comtesse, will give me the honor of your presence at Mornaye for luncheon on Thursday, the twenty-sixth. La Comtesse de Caux informs me that you became acquainted with my son Paul when he visited America with Le Maréchal Foch in 1922, and that a warm friendship grew up between you at that time. I have often heard my son speak of his American tour, and of the dear friendships he made there, and I know how keen will be his regret when he hears that you were here and that he missed you. He is at present, I regret to say, at Paris, but I have written informing him of your presence here.

At any rate, it will give me great pleasure to welcome one of my son's American friends to Mornaye, and I am looking forward to your visit with the most eager anticipation. La Comtesse de Caux has already informed me of your acceptance, and my motor will be waiting for you at the village station Thursday the twenty-sixth at noon.

Until then, ever sincerely yours,
MATHILDE, MARQUISE DE MORNAYE.

He read the letter a second time, anger swelling in a hot flood as its full significance was revealed to him. When he at length found the Countess, he was so choked with exasperation that for a moment he could not speak but stood glaring at her with infuriated eyes, holding the crumpled letter in one clenched fist.

"Now, you look here," he said at length in a smothered tone, "you look here—" he held the letter out and shook it furiously under her nose. "What do you mean by a thing like this?"

She returned his furious gaze with a glance of bright inquiry, took the letter from his hand, and immediately, after looking at it, said cheerfully:

"Oh, yes! La Marquise has written you, as she said she would. Did I not tell you I had great things in store for you?" she said triumphantly. "Ah, my boy, how fortunate you were in finding me the way you did! Do you realize how few Americans ever have the opportunity you are getting? Here you are, a boy of twenty-four, being received with open arms into one of the greatest families in France. Why, there are American millionaires who would pay a fortune for the privilege!"

"Now, you see here," he said again in a choking tone. "What do you mean by doing a thing like this behind my back?"

She raised puzzled eyebrows inquiringly:

"Behind your back? What do you mean, my boy?"

"What right have you got to tell this woman I had accepted her invitation, when you never spoke to me about it?"

"But!" she said, with a small protesting gasp—"I was sure you would be delighted! It never occurred to me that you wouldn't be! I felt sure you'd jump at the opportunity!"

"Opportunity!" he jeered. "Opportunity for what? Opportunity to let you tell this woman a pack of lies about me, and try to work her with some trick or dodge that you've got up your sleeve!"

"I have no idea what you're talking about," she said, with quiet dignity.

"Oh, yes you have!" he snarled. "You know very well what I'm talking about. You've told these lying stories and misrepresented things to people ever since I met you, but you've gone too far this time. What the hell do you mean by telling this woman that I am a good friend of her son's and met him in America?" He picked up the letter and shook it in her face again. "What do you mean by telling her such a lie as that?"

"Lie!" Her brows were lifted with an air of pained surprise. "Why, my boy, you told me that you did know her son."

"*I* told you!" he fairly screamed. "I told you nothing! I never knew the woman had a son until I got this letter."

"Listen, my friend," the Countess spoke gently and patiently as she would speak to a child. "Think back a little, won't you——?"

"Think back my eye!" he said rudely. "There's nothing to think back about. It's another lying story you made up on the spur of the moment, and you know it!"

"Don't you remember," she went on in the same quiet and patient voice, "—don't you remember telling me you were a student at Harvard University?"

"Yes, I did tell you that. And that was true. What has that got to do with knowing this woman's son?"

"Wait!" she said quietly. "Don't you remember telling me that you were there at Harvard when Marshal Foch made his visit to America?"

"Yes, I did tell you that."

"And that you saw him when he visited the university? You told me that, you know."

"Of course I did! I did see him. Every one else saw him, too. He stood on the steps of the library with his aides, and saluted while they fired the cannon off!"

"Ah!—With his aides, you say?" she said eagerly.

"Yes, of course, what's wrong with that?"

"But nothing is wrong! It's all just as I said!—Among his aides, now," she said persuasively, "did you not notice a young man, with a little mustache, about twenty-five years old, dressed in the uniform of a captain in the French army?—Think now, my boy," she went on coaxingly —"a young man—much younger than the other officers on the Marshal's staff?"

"Perhaps I did," he said impatiently. "How should I remember now? What difference does it make?"

"Because that young man, my dear," the Countess patiently explained, "that you saw standing there with the Marshal is the young Marquis— this woman's son."

He stared at her with fascinated disbelief:

"And do you mean to tell me," he said presently, "that because I may have seen some one like that standing in a great crowd of people three years ago, you had the gall to tell that woman that I knew her son— that we were friends?"

"No, no," the Countess said evasively, a little nervously. "I didn't tell her that, my dear. I'm sure I didn't tell her that. She must have misunderstood me. All I said was that you *saw* her son when he was in America. I'm sure that was all I said. And that was true, wasn't it? You *did* see him, didn't you?" she said triumphantly.

He stared at her, with mouth ajar, unable for a moment to comprehend the full enormity of such deception. Then he closed his jaws with a stubborn snap, and said:

"All right. You got yourself into this, now you get out of it. I'm not going with you."

The old woman's eyes were suddenly sharp with apprehension. She leaned forward, clutched him by the arm, and said pleadingly:

"Oh, my boy, you wouldn't do a thing like that to me, would you? Think what it means to me—the humiliation you would cause me now if you refused to go."

"I can't help that. You had no right to make arrangements with the woman in the first place, before you spoke to me. Even that wouldn't matter so much if you hadn't told her that other story about her son and me. That's the reason she's inviting me—because she thinks her son and I were friends. How can I accept such an invitation—take advantage of the woman's hospitality because you told her a story that had no truth in it?"

"Oh, that doesn't matter," the Countess spoke quickly, eagerly. "If you want me to, I shall explain to her that there was a mistake—that you really do not know her son. But it makes no difference, anyway. She would want you to come just the same. —You see," she spoke carefully, and for a moment there was a gleam of furtive, cunning understanding in her eye—the wisdom of fox for fox—"I don't think it's exactly for that reason she is inviting you."

"What other reason could there be? The woman does not know me. What other interest could she have in me?"

"Well, my boy—" the Countess hesitated, and spoke carefully—"you see, it's this way. I think she wants to speak to you," she paused carefully again before she spoke—"about a certain matter—about something she's interested in—When she heard that you were connected with *The New York Times*——"

"*What!*" He stared at her again, and suddenly exploded in a short angry laugh of resignation and defeat—"Are the whole crowd of you alike? Is there a single one of you who doesn't have some scheme, some axe to grind—who doesn't hope to get something out of Americans——"

"Then you'll go?" she said eagerly.

"Yes, I'll go!" he shouted. "Tell her anything you like. It'll serve both of you right! I'll go just to see what new trick or scheme you and this other woman are framing up. All right, I'll go!"

"Good!" she nodded briskly, satisfied. "I knew you would, my boy. La Marquise will tell you all about it when she sees you."

This final grotesque episode had suddenly determined his decision to leave Orléans. For a short time, his chance meeting with this strange old woman, his instant inclusion in the curious schemes, designs and stratagems of her life, with all that it evoked of the strange and the familiar, its haunting glimpse of the million-noted web and weaving of dark chance and destiny, had struck bright sparks of interest from his mind, had fused his spirit to a brief forgetfulness and wonder.

Now, as suddenly as it had begun, that wonder died: the life of the town, the people, the old Countess and her friends, which had for a few days seemed so new, strange, and interesting, now filled him with weariness and distaste. He was suddenly fed up with the provincial tedium of the town, he felt the old dislike and boredom that all dark bloods and races could awake in him an importunate and unreasonable desire, beneath these soft, dull skies of gray, for something bright, sharp, Northern, fierce, and wild, in life—for something gold and blue and shining, the lavish flesh of great blonde women, the surge of savage drunkenness, the fatal desperation of strong joy. The dark, strange faces of the Frenchmen all around, and all the hard perfection of that life, at once so alien and so drearily familiar, the unwearied energies of their small purposes fixed there in the small perfection of their universe, so dully ignorant of the world, so certain of itself, filled him suddenly with exasperation and dislike. He was tired suddenly of their darkness, their smallness, their hardness, their cat-like nervousness, their incessant ebullience, their unwearied and yet joyless vitalities, and the dreary monotony of their timeless greed.

He was tired of Orléans, tired of the Vatels, most of all tired, with a feeling of weary disgust and dislike, of the old Countess, and all the small tricks and schemings of her life.

And with this sudden weariness and distaste, this loss of interest in a life which had for a week or two devoured his interest, the old torment and unrest of spirit had returned. Again, the old question had returned in all its naked desolation: "Why here? And where shall I go now? What shall I do?" He saw, with a return of the old naked shame, in a flash of brutal revelation, the aimless lack of purpose in his wandering. He saw that there had been no certain reason, no valid purpose, for his coming here to Orléans, and with a sense of drowning horror, as if the phial of his spirit had exploded like a flash of ether, and emptied out into the formless spaces of a planetary vacancy, he felt that there was no purpose and no reason for his going anywhere.

And yet, the demons of unrest and tortured wandering had returned with all their fury: he knew that he must leave, that he must go on to some other destination, and he knew nowhere to go. Like a drowning man who clutches at a straw, he sought for some goal or purpose in his life, some justification for his wanderings, some target for his fierce desire. A thousand plans and projects suggested themselves to him, and each one seemed more futile, hopeless, barren than the rest. He would return to Paris and "settle down and write." He would go back to England, get a room in London, go to Oxford, the Lake District, Cornwall, Devon—a thousand towns and places, evoked by a thousand fleeting memories, returned to argue some reasonable purpose for his blind wandering. Or he would go to the South of France, "to some quiet place," or to Switzerland, "to some quiet place," or to Germany, Vienna, Italy, Spain, Majorca,—always "to settle down in some quiet place"— and for what? for what? Why, always, of course, "to write," "to write" —Great God, "to write," and even as he spoke the words the old dull shame returned to make him hate his life and all these sterile, vain pretensions of his soul. "To write"—always to seek the magic skies, the golden clime, the wise and lovely people who would transform him. "To write"—always to seek in the enchanted distances, in the dreamy per- spectives of a fool's delusions, the power and certitude he could not draw out of himself. "To write"—to be that most foolish, vain, and impotent of all impostors, a man who sought the whole world over "looking for a place to write," when, he knew now with every naked, brutal penetra- tion of his life "the place to write" was Brooklyn, Boston, Hammersmith, or Kansas—anywhere on earth, so long as the heart, the power, the faith, the desperation, the bitter and unendurable necessity, and the naked courage were there inside him all the time.

Now, having agreed to accompany the Countess on her visit to the Marquise, he suddenly decided to leave Orléans at the same time, spend the night at Blois, and go on to Tours the next day, after visiting Mor- naye. And with this purpose, he packed his bag, paid his bill at the hotel, and set out on the appointed day with the old woman who for two weeks now had been his self-constituted guide and keeper.

XCV

The village of Mornaye was a small and ancient setttlement, similar to thousands of others, situated near the gate of the château from which it got its name. A man was waiting for them at the station with a motor car: they got in and were driven swiftly through the town —a dense cluster of old gray-lemon buildings with tiled roofs, a thatched one here and there, the shops of the village grocer, cobbler, baker, visible through small dormer windows, some farm buildings, a fleet- ing glimpse of the old cobbled court-yard of a barn, some wagons, and farm implements—a little universe of life, compact, unbroken, built up to the edge of the road—and then, almost immediately, the gates of the château.

They drove through the gates and down a long and stately aisle of noble trees, and presently came to a halt before the great entrance of the château. As they approached, a footman came swiftly down the steps, opened the door of the car, and bowed, and in another moment, led by the man, they had entered the hall and were being escorted into the great salon where their hostess was awaiting them.

La Marquise de Mornaye was a woman of about sixty, but from the energy and vigor of her appearance, she seemed to be in the very prime of life. She was an extraordinary figure of a woman, as tall and strong-looking as a man, with a personal quality that was almost mountain-ously impressive in its command. The image of the boy's recent dis-content had so shaped the French as a dark and swarthy people of mean stature that it was now startling to be confronted by a woman of this grand proportion.

She had a wide, round face, smooth, brown and unwrinkled, such as one often finds in peasant people, her eyes were round, bright, and shrewd, webbed minutely by fine wrinkles at the corners. She had strong, coarse hair of gray, brushed vigorously back from a wide, low forehead. She was big in foot and limb and body, everything about the woman was strong, large and vigorous except her hands. And her hands were plump, white, tiny, as useless-looking as a baby's, shockingly dis-proportionate to the power and vigor of the rest of her big frame.

The woman had on a long, brown dress that completely covered her from neck to toe: it was a strangely old-fashioned garment—or rather it did not seem to have any fashion or style whatsoever—but it was nevertheless a magnificent garment, in its plain and homely strength per-fectly appropriate to the extraordinary woman who wore it.

In every respect—in word, tone, gesture, look, and act—the woman showed a plain, forceful, and immensely able character. Her strong, brown face was friendly, yet shrewd and knowing; she greeted the Countess cordially, but it was evident from the humor in her round, bright eyes that she was no fool in the ways of the world, and perfectly able to hold her own in any worldly encounter.

She was waiting for them, erect and smiling, as they entered the great salon, a magnificent room at least forty feet in length, warm-ly, luxuriously, yet plainly furnished, and with nothing cold or repellent in its grand proportions. She greeted the Countess immediately and cordially, extending her plump little white hand in a friendly greet-ing, and bending and kissing the little wren-like woman on her withered cheek. La Marquise, in deference to her young American guest, spoke English from the beginning. And her English, like everything else about her, was plain, forceful, and direct, completely fluent, although marked with a heavy accent.

" 'Ow are you, my dear?" La Marquise said, as she kissed the other woman on the cheek. "It is good to see you again after these so many years. 'Ow long 'as it been since you were last at Mornaye?"

"Almost seven years, Marquise," the Countess answered eagerly. "The last time—do you remember?—was in the spring of 1918."

"Ah, yes," the other answered benevolently. "Now I can remember. You were here when many of our so brave Américains were quartered here at Mornaye—Monsieur," she said, using this reference as an introduction, and turning to the boy with her plump little hand extended in a movement of kindly greeting, "I am delighted. I meck apologies for my son. I know he will so much regret not seeing you."

He flushed, and stammered out his thanks: she seemed to take no notice of his embarrassment and, having completed her friendly welcome, she turned smilingly to the Countess again, and said:

"And 'ow 'ave you been, my dear? You are looking very well," she said approvingly, "and no older dan you were de lest time you were here. I s'ink," she said smilingly, including the young man now in her friendly humor—"I s'ink la Comtesse must 'ave discover—wat you call it, eh?" she shrugged—"ze se-*cret* of ze fountain of yout', eh?"

"Ah, Marquise," the Countess fawned greedily upon the grand woman, obviously elated by these signs of intimacy—"ah—hah—hah! it is so kind of you to say so—but I fear I have grown much older since I saw you last. I have known great trouble," she said sadly, "and, as you know, Marquise, my health has not been good."

"Non?" the other said with an air of solicitous inquiry. "I am so sor-*ree,*" she continued in a tone of unimpeachable regret, which nevertheless showed that the Countess' health or lack of it was really of no moment to her whatever. "Perhaps, my dear, it is ze wretchet cleemat here. I s'ink perhaps you should go Sout' in vintaire—ah, monsieur," she continued regretfully turning to the youth, "you see Mornaye at a bat season of ze year—I fear you may be disappointed by our coun-*tree*. I 'ope you vill come beck some time in sprink. Zen, I s'ink you vill agree la France is beautiful."

"I should like to," he replied.

"But oh zis vintaire! Zis *vintaire!*" La Marquise cried with passionate distaste, folding her arms and drawing herself together in a movement of chilled ardor as she looked through a tall French door across one of those magnificent and opulent vistas that one finds in France, an architecture of proud, comely space into whose proportionate dimensions even nature herself has been compelled. It was a tremendous sweep of velvet sward, that faded into misty distances and that was cut cleanly on each side by the smoky denseness of her forest parks. Her shrewd eyes ranged across this noble prospect for a moment in an expression of chilled distaste. Then, with a slight contracted shudder of her folded arms, she turned, and said wearily:

"Ah, zis vintaire! Zis *vintaire!* Sometimes I s'ink it vill nevaire end. Every day," she went on indignantly, "it rain, rain, rain! All vintaire lonk I see noz-*zing* but rain! I get up in ze mornink and look out—and it rain! I turn my beck and zen look out again—it rain! I take a nep, I get up, I go to bet—always it rain!" She shrugged her shoulders comically, and turning to the boy with a glint of shrewdly cynical humor, she said, "I s'ink if it keep on ve 'ave again—vat you call it—Noah's Floot, eh?"

The Countess clucked sympathetically at this watery chronicle of woe, and said:

"But have you been here by yourself all winter? I should think you would get awfully lonely, my dear," she went on in a tone of ingratiating commiseration. "I know how you must miss your son."

"No. I vas in Paris for two veeks in Decembaire," said La Marquise. "But it rain zere too," she said, with another shrug of comic despair, and then added vigorously, "No! I do not get lonely if it do not rain. But ven it rains—zen it is tereeble. . . . Come," she said brusquely, almost curtly, turning away from the gray prospect through the window, "let us seet here vere eet ees varm." Still clasping her arms across her breast, she led them towards a coal fire which was crackling cheerfully in a hearth at one end of the great room; they seated themselves comfortably around the fire, La Marquise rang a bell, and spoke a few words to a butler, and presently he returned, bringing glasses and a decanter of old Sherry on a tray.

They sat talking amiably then of many things. La Marquise questioned the boy about America, his stay in France, the places he had seen, referred regretfully again to the absence of her son, and of the great friendship he cherished for America and Americans as a result of his travels there with Marshal Foch. And from time to time, the Countess, with a cunning that was comically naïve in its bare-faced self-exposure, would prod him with a skinny finger, and whisper hoarsely:

"Ask her some questions, my dear. You should ask her more questions and write more in your little book. It will make a good impression."

And, although he saw from the glint of shrewd humor in the sharp eyes of La Marquise, that none of this clumsy by-play had been lost on her, and that the other woman's design was perfectly apparent to her, he responded dutifully, if awkwardly, asking respectful questions about the age and history of the château, the extent of its estate, and so on. At length, emboldened by the modest success of these beginnings, and feeling that a clever young journalist should display an intelligent curiosity about the current affairs of the nation to which he is a visitor, he asked a question about the government of the period, of which Herriot was the leader, and which was dominantly socialist.

It was, he saw, an unfortunate move; the Countess poked him sharply with a warning finger, but it was too late. He saw instantly that his question had produced a bad impression on La Marquise: for the first time, her manner of amiable and cordial friendliness vanished, her face hardened, there was an angry glint in her shrewd eyes, and in a moment she said harshly, and in a tone of arrogant impatience:

"I know nozzing about zose pipple! I pay no attention to anys'ing zey say! Zey are fools! fools!" she cried violently. "You must not believe anys'ing zey say! Zose men are traitors! . . . Charlatans! . . . Zey are ze pipple who have ruined and betrayed France!" In her agitation she got up and walked across the room. "Here!" she cried, picking up a newspaper on a table and returning with it. "Here is what you should reat if you want ze trut!" She thrust a copy of *L'Action Française* into his hands. "Zat paper—and zat alone—will tell you ze trut about ze way s'ings are in France today. Ah, monsieur!" she cried earnestly, "you do not know—ze world does not know—no one outside of France can know ze trut, because zese wretched men control ze press—and make it print vatever lies zey tell it to. But you reat *zis,* monsieur—you reat *zis,"* she struck the paper with the back of her hand as she spoke, "and you will get ze trut! Ah, zat man!" she said with a grim chuckle of admiration. "Ze rédacteur—ze—vat you say?—ze *editor* of zat paper, Léon Daudet—ah, zat man is *right!*" she said with a chuckle of satisfaction. "Zat man is sometimes coarse—he call zem bat names—he is not always très gentil—but," again she chuckled grimly "he iss *right!* He tells ze trut—he calls zem vat zey are—ze traitors and creeminals who 'ave ruined France." She was silent for a moment, and then in a voice harsh with passion, she said violently: "La France, monsieur, is a royaume—a—vat you call it?—a monarchy —a kinkdom. Ze French people must have a kink—zey are lost vitout a kink—zey cannot govern zemselves vitout a kink! . . . Zere can be no France, monsieur, vitout a kink!" she almost shouted. "Zere has been no France since ze monarchy vas destroyed by zese scélérats who 'ave betrayed La France—zere vill never be a France until ze kink is restored to his rightful office and zese creeminals and traitors 'ave been sent to ze guillotine vere zey belonk. . . . So do not ask me anys'ink about zese men, monsieur," she said with arrogant passion. "I know nozzing about zem. I pay no attention to zem! Zey are fools . . . traitors . . . creeminals," she shouted, "you reat zat paper, you vill get ze trut."

She was breathing hoarsely and her eyes glinted with hard fires of passion. At this moment, fortunately, the butler entered, bowed, and, speaking in a quiet voice, informed his mistress that luncheon was served. The words recalled the angry woman to her duties as a hostess: with an almost comical suddenness, she assumed her former manner of gracious cordiality, smiled amiably at her guests, and saying with benevolent good-nature, "After our lonk journey and our so much talk, ve are 'ongry—yes?" led the way into the dining-room.

As they went in, the little old Countess nudged her young companion again with a stealthy warning, and whispered with nervous reproach:

"You should not have asked her that, my dear. Please do not say anything more to her about the government."

The dining-room of the château was another magnificent chamber, like everything else about the château nobly harmonious with those elements of strength and grace, splendor and simplicity, warmth and delicacy united with princely dignity, which are the triumphs of this period of French architecture. In spite of the chill air of the room—for it was poorly heated—one felt its living and noble warmth immediately.

The boy, who had looked forward to this meeting with considerable awe and apprehension, now felt himself completely at home, stirred by a profound, tranquil and lovely joy at the noble beauty and simplicity of the château. Even in the sense of retrenchment, the worn uniforms of the servants, the knowledge that they served their mistress in various offices, there was something pleasant, homely, and familiar: he discovered, to his surprise, that he now felt none of the constraint and uneasiness which he experienced when Joel Pierce had taken him to his

great estate upon the Hudson River, and he had for the first time seen
the lives of the great American millionaires.

With La Marquise de Mornaye he was not conscious of that exactly
mannered style—most mannered in its very affectation of simplicity—
that vulgar arrogance which he had felt among the rich Americans
of Joel Pierce's class. La Marquise was plain as an old shoe, vigorous
and lusty as a peasant, and completely an aristocrat—magnificently herself, without an ounce of affectation—a woman Joel Pierce's people
would have fawned upon, and to whom they would have given a king's
ransom if by so doing they could have bought for son or daughter an
alliance with her family.

La Marquise seated him beside her, the Countess opposite her, and at
once they began to eat. The food was magnificent, there was a different
wine of royal vintage (brought up from the famous cellar of the château)
with every course. La Marquise left no doubt at all about the robust
nature of her appetite, and by everything she did and was—the plain
shrewdness, warmth, and sensible humanity of her nature—she made it
plain that she expected her guests to eat heartily also, and not to be too
nice and dainty about it, either.

"Ven vun is younk as you are," she said, turning with a smile to her
young guest, "he is 'ongry often—non?" she inquired. She put her soup-
spoon to her mouth, swallowed some soup, and smacking her lips with
an air of relish, turned to the youth again, and said plainly and positively:

"Eet ees good! Oui! I s'ink you will like it, too." Turning to the
Countess, who had tasted nothing, she said severely:

"Vy do you vait, my dear? Are you not 'ongry? You must eat."

"Ah—hah—hah!" the Countess said with a little undecided laugh,
her eyes greedily fixed upon the smoking soup. "—You know, my dear,
I am on a diet by the doctor's orders—sang de cheval, you know," she
chattered in a distracted tone as her greedy eyes went ravenously along
the table—"I eat almost nothing—really, my dear, I don't think I
should." She snatched up a piece of bread in one greedy little claw,
broke it with an appetizing crackle, and began to cram it into her mouth
like a starved animal—"Ah—hah—hah!" The poor starved old woman
laughed with almost hysterical delight, and tried to speak with a mouth
full of bread—"I know I shouldn't—but you always have such delicious
food, my dear." She lifted the soup-spoon, and drew in with a long slob-

bering suction. "Ah, mon Dieu! mon Dieu!" she gurgled rapturously—
"quel potage!"

And so the meal progressed. With such a lusty trencher-woman as La
Marquise beside one, it was not hard to follow suit; they polished off
the soup, which was a delicious, savory, peasant-like brew, in record
time, and, as if their hunger mounted from the delicious food it fed
on, they turned then to the chicken. The chicken, which was almost
all fat and juicy breast, was so young, crisp, tender, plump and succulent
that it seemed almost to melt in the mouth, the boy took two or three
rhapsodic swallows and the chicken was gone, at which La Marquise,
lifting her voice over his feeble and half-hearted protests, said to the
butler: "Encore du poulet pour Monsieur."

A second chicken, even plumper, crisper and more tender than the
first, was instantly provided, after which the roast and vegetables were
served. He had never tasted better food in his life—everything, haricots,
peas, beef, seemed to melt like an ambrosial ether the moment that he
put it in his mouth; there was a new wine with every course, each wine
rarer, older, richer and more delicious than the last, the butler kept
filling up their glasses, and he kept drinking the grand wine until
heart, mind, and soul, and every conduit of his life seemed infused by
its glorious warmth and fragrance. They talked little as they ate: for
some time there were no sounds except the crisp crackle of the bread,
the ring of heavy silver, the sound of wine gulped down, the delicate
chime of glasses, and the low, quiet orders of the butler speaking to
his helper, as swiftly, expertly, and noiselessly they moved around the
table, seeming to be there at one's elbow, and to read the gastronomic
hopes and wishes of each guest before he had time to open his mouth
and utter them.

La Marquise ate with robust concentration, putting down her knife
from time to time to pick up her wine-glass and take a generous swallow, after which she would put the glass down and wipe a napkin
deliberately across her mouth and pause, for a moment, breathing a little
heavily, with an air of hearty satisfaction.

As for the Countess, she ate like a famished wolf: where the movements of La Marquise were hearty and deliberate, those of the Countess
were almost frantically swift and eager. Her sharp and greedy little
eyes glittered with an almost delirious joy, she would seize a glass of
wine and drain it in one greedy gulp; at times she was so excited by
the variety and abundance of the dishes that she seemed unable to decide

what to reach for next. She reached out greedily in all directions, her eyes darting avaricious glances to and fro, chicken, meat, vegetables, salad, wine disappeared as if by magic, and were replenished, and all the time the poor old woman chuckled craftily to herself, and muttered to herself in broken monologue:

"Ah—hah—hah!"—crunch, crunch, crunch! And away went the chicken. "Mon Dieu!—But it's good!—Ah—hah—hah!" gulp, gulp, gulp; down would go the wine. "Mon Dieu! mon Dieu! Such food! Such wine!—Mais oui! Mais oui! . . . Un peu encore, s'il vous plaît! Quel boeuf! Quel boeuf!"

At which La Marquise would put down her glass, wipe her mouth, look across the table at the Countess, and say:

" 'Ow you like, eh? Good? Mais oui! Il faut manger," she said coarsely, and applied herself again to knife and fork.

By the time they got down to the cheese—which was a ripe, delicious Brie—La Marquise de Mornaye was at last fortified for conversation. Putting down her empty wine-glass with a deliberate movement, she straightened in her chair, wiped her mouth, sat upright for a moment in an attitude of solid satisfaction, and then, turning to her American guest, said:

"Do you know Patterson T. Jones—eh? 'E is an officer—a vat you call it?—a major in ze Américain army." She pronounced these words with an air of naïve confidence, as if Patterson T. Jones must be a name instantly familiar to every American. When the boy told her, however, that he did not know Major Patterson T. Jones and confessed, further, that he had never heard of him, La Marquise looked slightly astonished and disappointed; and in a moment, her shrewd eyes narrowing slightly as she spoke, she said rather grimly:

"I should like verree verree motch to see zat gentleman again. I should like verree verree motch to know vere he now iss. . . . Attendez!" she said sharply, as inspiration struck her. "Perhaps if I show you this—vat you say?—his photographie—you vill know ze man. . . . Guillaume!" she raised her voice a little in command. "Apportez-moi les photographies des officiers Américains."

"Oui, madame," the butler answered, and went swiftly and silently out of the room.

"Yes," La Marquise continued with an air of grim meditation, "I should verree verree motch like to know vere Major Patterson T. Jones iss to be found."

The butler returned with several large square photographs, bowed, and gave them to his mistress.

" 'Ere, you see," she said, taking one of them and pointing with her finger, "zis vas taken here—in zis verree room at a great ban*quet* vitch I have made for ze Americains in 1918. Zis," she said proudly, and pointing with a plump white finger—"zis is me—c'est moi, La Marquise!" she cried in a jolly tone, and laughed with satisfaction as she pointed to her own beaming likeness at the head of a long table, sumptuously adorned with fine silver, china, linen, and a forest thicket of dark, crusty-looking bottles of old wine—obviously the relics of a memorable feast. "And zis," La Marquise said more grimly, pointing again with her plump white finger, "zis is Major Patter*son* T. Jones—You know him, eh?" she said.

The boy looked at the picture for a moment and then handed it back to La Marquise, telling her that he did not recognize the face of Patterson T. Jones.

"Patter*son* T. Jones," La Marquise answered, slowly, and with an air of grim deliberation, "is a gentleman I vant verree verree motch to see. Zat is ze man," she said, "who took my picture—who told me he vould get for me oh! soch huge soms of mon-nee if he could teck my picture to America," she laughed ironically—"and so I let him teck ze picture, and I have heard nozzing from him since."

"Was—was it your own picture, Marquise? A portrait of yourself?"

"Mais non, mon ami," she said impatiently. "Dat's vat I tell you—eet vas a picture, a photographie—of Le Maréchal. Zere vas only seex sotch pictures of Le Maréchal in existence—I say to Madame Foch vun time ven I am at Paris—I see ze picture in her house—I say—'Oh, my dear, zat so lovely picture of Le Maréchal—I must have vun for myself,' I say. 'Ah,' she say, 'I do not know, Mathilde—he do not like to give away zese pictures—I have only t'ree,' she say, 'but vait. I see vat I can do—' Zen, vun night I go to dinnaire at zere house. 'Mathilde,' he say, 'for vat you vant my picture? I give it to you,' he say, 'and zen all ze ozzer girls vill vant vun, too. I meck my vife jalouse, and zen zere is no peace. I have enough of var,' he say. 'I am too old to start anozzer vit my vife!' 'You give to me zat picture,' I say. 'I am no young leddy in ze chorus,' I say, 'to meck your vife jalouse. She vant you to give it to me, too.' 'Bon,' he say. 'Here it is, zen.' . . . And he give to me ze so beautiful photographie vit his name below written out to me: 'To Mathilde, old comrade, fet'ful friend'—I bring ze picture beck ven I come beck to Mornaye,"

La Marquise continued, "and Major Patterson T. Jones he see it ven he iss here. 'How motch you vant for zat picture of Le Maréchal?' he say. 'Oh,' I say, 'I cannot say. Already I have an offer of ten s'ousand francs,' I say, 'but I vould not sell it because ze Maréchal himself, he give to me.' 'Vell,' say Major Patterson T. Jones, 'you lett me teck zat picture vit me ven I go beck to America, and I sell it for you.' 'How motch you get for me, eh?' I ask him. 'Oh,' he say, 'I get twent' s'ousand francs for you—mebbe more.' 'You sure?' I say. 'Mais oui!' say Major Patterson T. Jones. 'Absolument'—'All right,' I say. 'I give to you. If you get twenty s'ousand francs I give you five,' I say. And so he teck my picture and he go avay, and since den," La Marquise bitterly conclued, "I nevaire hear from him."

"Ah!" the Countess cried indignantly. "Le scélérat!"

"Mais oui!" the other woman now said passionately. "It is infâme! Zis man have my picture, I have nozzing—Ze lest time Madame Foch is here, she look around, she say, 'But vere, my dear,—vere iss ze picture zat Le Maréchal give you? I do not see it,' she say. What can I do?" La Marquise went on in a despairing tone. "I cannot say to her 'I lose it!' I cannot say to her 'I give it avay to an Américain who sell it for me.' I don't know vat to say, all I can say is, 'I leave it, my dear, in Paris vit my son Paul ven I vas zere. He have it, but ze next time zat he come to Mornaye he vill bring it.' But ven she come again, vat story can I tell her zen?" La Marquise demanded. "Ah! Zat scélérat! Zat Patterson T. Jones! If ever I get my fingers on zat gentleman I s'ink he vill remember me!" she said, with a glint in her eye, and a grim note in her voice, that left no doubt of her intention—"But is it not infâme, monsieur," she said with a virtuous indignation that was now ludicrous after her naïve exposure of her own avarice and greed—"is it not infâme zat somevun teck·avay a picture zat a friend give to you—and promise you motch monnee for it—and zen to hear from him no more? Scélérat! T'ief!" she muttered, "I like to get my hands on him!—But now, monsieur," she said, turning to him abruptly, with a smile of winning ingratiation, "I meck a leetle speech to you. You are—la Comtesse tells me—a younk journalist—eh?"

"Well, Marquise," he flushed, and began to blunder out an explanation —"I can't exactly say——"

"Mais oui!" the Countess swiftly interposed. "He has written many clever articles—pour les grands journaux Américains, n'est-ce pas—la tête, vous voyez?" she whispered craftily, bending over the table and nod-

ding towards him as she spoke—"C'est très intelligent, n'est-ce pas?"
"Et pour *Le Times?*" La Marquise demanded. "Il écrit tout ça pour
Le New York Times?"
"Mais oui," the Countess said glibly, before he could object. "Il est
déjà bien connu. Moi—j'ai lu beaucoup de choses de sa main——"
"Now, look here," he began, glaring angrily across the table at the
lying old woman. "You have no right——"
"Ah, oui!" La Marquise broke in, with a vigorous nod of satisfaction,
after a brief inspection of him. "C'est très évident! Il est intelligent!
Bon!" she said decisively, and turned to him with the air of a person
whose mind is made up, and whose course of action determined—"Now,
monsieur," she said, "I tell you vat I have in mind. I have beeg 'ospital—
non?" she said, smiling a little at his puzzled look. "I am—vat you
call it?—le prési*dent*—le directeur, n'est-ce pas?—of beeg 'ospital in de
Nort'—ve have zere ze soldats, n'est-ce pas—ze oh so many blessés—les
pauvres!" she said in a tone of pity—"les mutilés de la guerre. . . . Ve
have old building—eet ees no good, eet ees not beeg enough—not
moderne—and so," she added simply, "ve build anozzer—beeg, moderne—and"—the conclusion of the matter—"ve need monnee." She was
silent for a moment, beaming hopefully at him. "Monsieur," she said
presently, in an ingratiating tone, and with an air of naïve confidence
that was astounding—"I s'ink ven I tell you vat ve need—'ow much
monnee," her voice sank craftily, "you vill get for us—eh?"
He stared at her for a moment with a bewildered face, unable to
reply.
"But how," he stammered at length—"how do you think—what do
you think I can do?" he said bluntly.
"Ah!" La Marquise cried triumphantly. "C'est facile!" Again her
voice became low, confiding, crafty. "You are a journalist—eh? You
write for ze grand journal Américain—ze *New York Times*—yes? . . .
Vell, I tell you vat to say," she went on placidly. "You write ze article
for ze *Times*—you spick of zis beeg 'ospi*tal*—you tell of ze grand vork
of restauration—you tell of ze poor soldats—les blessés—les mutilés—
you say La France have nozzing—zey have no monnee—ze poor pipples
'ave lose everys'ink—you say, ve 'ave so motch—ze rich Américains—
ve must not let zis great vork die—ve must help ze poor soldats—ve must
give ze monnee for ze 'ospital. . . . You see—I show you," she cried
with a confident chuckle—"if you like I write eet out myself—and zen
all you have to do is meck—vat do you say?—la traduction."

"How—how much do you want?"

"Un million de francs," she said, dismissing this bagatelle airily. "—For ze Américains vat ees dat? Pouf! Nozzing! Mais pour les Français—ah!" she said sadly, "for ze French eet ees too motch. Un millionaire Américain—he see your story—he say 'Ve cannot let zis grand vork die' —he write vun check out for ze whole amount—and zen," her smile of satisfaction deepened, "he send to me, eh?—He meck out check to Marquise—he never miss eet—and he send to me." For a moment she was silent, smiling triumphantly at him. When she spoke again, she bent towards him, her voice became low, confiding, craftily conspiratorial— "And I tell you vat I do. . . . You write ze piece and get for me ze mon-nee . . . and I give you a fourt'—twenty-five per cent—non?"

In a moment, as he continued to stare at her with an expression of gape-mouthed astonishment, she straightened, with an air of satisfied finality, nodded her head, and then said with business-like decision: "Bon. Eet ees settled zen." She rose decisively from the table, and her guests followed her—"You come vit me," she said, as she led the way out of the dining-room, "and I give you—vat you say?—ze fects."

She was already gone, before he could blurt out a few words of bewildered protest; the Countess was at his side, prodding him sharply with a skinny finger, and muttering in a tone of reproachful entreaty: "Go on, my dear! Go on! And you should ask more questions! Don't sit there, saying nothing. It will make a good impression. And use your little book more often," the Countess whispered cunningly. "You should write more in it when she speaks to you."

"Now you see here," he burst out furiously, "I'm not going to write down anything. I'm tired of this foolishness—I'm not going to be a party any longer to your damned schemes or for this woman's, either. I'm going to tell her once and for all that I'll write no article—not for *The Times* nor any place else!"

"Oh, my boy," the old woman whispered imploringly. "You wouldn't do that! Please don't say a thing like that, I beg of you! . . . Think what it means to me," she whispered—"I am so poor, so miserable—for years I have waited for an opportunity to see this woman—it means so much to me, so little to you. Please be polite, my dear—it's only for a little time. You'll be going soon. What can it matter to you? She has her schemes like everybody else . . . keep silent if you feel you must, but be polite to her, for God's sake; pretend to listen—don't ruin everything for me now."

"All right," he muttered grimly. "I'll listen, but I'm damned if I'll write anything down in the little book."

When they returned to the salon, La Marquise had provided herself with various letters, folders, and descriptive circulars about the institution for which she was now soliciting aid. They seated themselves around the fire again, with coffee and liqueurs; by the time La Marquise had finished the description of her hospital project, the gray light of the brief wintry afternoon was fading rapidly, and the time for their departure had approached.

Before they left, she took them on a brief tour of inspection of the château, showing them the portraits of her ancestors, the great room with the huge, gold-canopied bed where King Henri IV had slept, on one of his visits to the château—unoccupied since, now closed save for museum visits such as this.

Their last visit, before departure, was to the library: it was a pleasant, warm-looking room adjacent to the grand salon, and had the appearance of being seldom used. La Marquise smiled at the eager curiosity with which the young man looked over the storied rows of books, the costly elegance and rich color of their bindings.

"You like to reat, eh?"

He told her that he did. She smiled, and said indifferently :

"I do not like so motch. It bore me ven I reat so long."

He asked her a few questions about some of the modern French writers—Proust, Gide, Romains, and Cocteau, among others—for a moment her face was hardened by the arrogant look it had worn when he had asked her about the government, and she said rather impatiently:

"I know nozzing about zose pipple. Yes, I have heard of some of zem. But I never reat zem. Zere is no good writing in France any more. Ze latest s'ing I have here,"—she nodded towards the shelves of books—"is Paul Bourget. But I never reat him, eizer."

In a few moments, they had said farewell, and were being driven away from the château. Rain had begun to fall again, the dull, gray light was almost gone and, since there was no convenient train, La Marquise had instructed her driver to take them back to Blois in the car.

During the ride back to town, he spoke seldom to the Countess. And she, as if recognizing the impatience, weariness and dislike he had come to feel towards her, the approaching end of their brief and curious relationship, was silent, too. When they got back to the hotel, he told her rather curtly he was tired and was going to his room to wash up and take a brief rest before dinner.

"But yes, my dear," she said instantly. "Of course you should. I can see that you are tired. Perhaps," she added quietly, "I shall see you again when you come down."

"Of course you will," he said shortly, almost angrily, in a tone that showed the irritable exasperation which too long association with the woman had now caused him to feel.

"Good-bye, my dear. Get some rest now. You need it."

When he got to his room, he took off his coat and shoes, lay down on his bed, and instantly fell asleep. When he awoke, he discovered he had slept almost three hours, that it was eight o'clock. Already late for dinner, washing and dressing hastily, he went down-stairs to find no one but the proprietor's wife in the *bureau*. Even before he could ask her where the Countess was, the woman had smilingly informed him that the old woman had gone, had already taken a train back to Orléans.

"Mais elle vous a remis de très affectueux adieux," the woman said with a smile. "Elle vous a fait des grands compliments."

And for a moment, when he realized that she was gone, he was conscious of a strange, mixed feeling of pity, loss and regret. He remembered suddenly the curt exasperation of his parting and something lonely, sad, and silent in the eyes of the old woman as she had said good-bye. The old loneliness had closed in around him again, he felt the sense of loss and sorrow that one feels when some one he has known a long time has gone.

BOOK VII

KRONOS AND RHEA: THE DREAM OF TIME

PLAY us a tune on an unbroken spinet, and let the bells ring, let the bells ring! Play music now: play us a tune on an unbroken spinet. Do not make echoes of forgotten tune, do not strike music from old broken keys, do not make ghosts with faded tinklings on the yellowed board; but play us a tune on an unbroken spinet, play lively music when the instrument was new, let us see Mozart playing in the parlor, and let us hear the sound of the ladies' voices. But more than that; waken the turmoil of forgotten streets, let us hear their sounds again unmuted, and unchanged by time, throw the light of Wednesday morning on the Third Crusade, and let us see Athens on an average day. Let us hear the sound of the voices of the Greeks, and observe closely if they were all wise and beautiful at ten o'clock in the morning; let us see if their limbs were all perfect, and their gestures grave and stately, also let us smell their food and observe them eating, and hear, if only once, the sound of a wheel in a street, the texture of just four forgotten moments.

Give us the sounds of Egypt on a certain day; let us hear the voice of King Menkaura and some of the words of the Lady Sennuwy; also the voices of the cotton-farmers. Let us hear the vast and casual sound of life, in these old peoples: their greetings in the street, the voices of the housewives and the merchants. And let us hear the laughter of a woman in the sixteenth century.

The cry of the wolf would always be the same; the sound of the wheel will always be the same; and the hoof of the horse on the roads of every time will be the same. But play us a tune on an unbroken spinet; and let us hear the voices of the knights at dinner. The cry of a man to his dog, and the barking of the dog; the call of the plow-driver to his horse, and the sound of the horse; the noise of the hunt, and the sound of the flowing water, will always be the same.

By the waters of life, by time, by time, play us a tune on an unbroken spinet, and let us hear the actual voices of old fairs; let us move backward through our memories, and through the memory of the race, let us relive the million forgotten moments of our lives, and let us see poor people sitting in their rooms in 1597, and let us see the rich man standing with his back before the fire, in the Middle Ages, and his wife knitting by the table, and let us hear their casual words.

Let us see the men who built the houses of Old Frankfort; let us see how they worked, and let us see them sitting on hewn timbers when they ate their lunches; let us hear their words, the sound of their voices. Unwind the fabric of lost time out of our entrails, repair the million little threads of actual circumstance until the seconds grow gray, bright and dusty with the living light, and we see the plain unfabled faces of the people; let us awake, and hear the people in the streets, and see Tobias Smollett pass our window.

Then, play us a tune on the unbroken spinet, let time be as the road to London and we a traveller on it; and let us enter London and find out what year it is there in the Mile End Road; let it be dark, and let us enter London in the dark, and hear men's voices, and let us see if we could understand them; and let us then find out what year it is, a lodging for the night, and see if they read mystery on us, or would fly away from us.

But there are times that are stranger yet, there are times that are stranger than the young knights and the horses, and the sounds of the eating taverns. The far time is the time of yesterday: it is the time of early America, it is the voices of the people on Broadway in 1841, it is the sounds of the streets in Des Moines in 1887, it is the engines of the early trains at Baltimore in 1853, it is the faces and voices of the early American people, who are lapped up in the wilderness, who are hid from us, whose faces are in mystery, whose lives are more dark and strange than the lives of the Saxon thanes.

The time that is lovely is the time of the fatness and of the bright colors; it is the elfin time of the calendars, and the sad and mysterious time of the early photographs. It is the time of the early lithographs, it is the time when the world was green and red and yellow. It is the time of the red barn and the windmill, and the house of the seven thousand gables; it is the time of the green lawn and the blue sky and the white excursion-steamer in the river, and the flags, the streamers, and gay brown-and-white buntings, the brass bands and the tumult of all the people who cry out Hurray, hurray!

It is the time of the boy rolling his hoop down the pink path, and of Mama in a bonnet and with a muff, and a stuck-out bottom, and Papa with a derby; it is the time of peace and plenty and the fair stripes of color, and the iron stag. It is the time of the lightning-rod salesman and the summer boarder, it is the time of Farmer Hayseed and of Dusty Rhodes the tramp, it is the time when boys started on the downward path through cigarettes; it is a lovely time. It is the time of the lures and snares of the wicked city and of the Great White Way; it is the time of pitfalls that await the innocent country girl with a whaleboned collar and a small waist; it is the time of Palaces of Sin or the Devil on Sunday; it is the time of the Tenderloin, of the nests of vice; it is the time of the gilded resorts with mirrors and soft carpets, where the mechanical piano played and you bought champagne, and of the High Class places and the Madam who would not stand for any ungentlemanly behavior, the time of the girls who wore evening dresses and were Perfect Ladies.

It is the time of the opera and theatre parties, and the Horse Show, and of late jolly suppers in the walnut dining-rooms; it is the time of elegant ladies with long gloves on naked arms, and Welsh rarebit in the chafing-dish; it is the time of the Four Hundred, and the great names of the millionaires—the Vanderbilts, the Astors, and the Goulds —it is the time of the powdered flunkies and the twenty-dollar favors; it is the time of Newport, and the canopied red-carpeted sidewalks, and the great mansions on Fifth Avenue, and the splendid gilt and plush marble halls, and the time of the fortune-hunting foreign noblemen (London papers please copy).

It is the time of the effeminate fop, and the lisping ass (Oh, Percy! I'll slap you on your wrist, you rough, rude thing, you!); it is the time of the Damned Dude who wears English clothes and has cuffs on his trousers (Hey, mister! Is it raining in London?), and he never did anything in his life but spend his old man's money, he never did an honest lick of work in his life, he's not worth powder enough to kill him, and if the son-of-a-bitch comes fooling around any sister of mine I'll beat the everlasting tar out of him.

When the songs that they sang were old and sweet, when the songs that they sang were like beauty's from afar, and when people sitting on their porches in the dusk could hear (O sweet and low!) the corner quartette sing, "Sweet Adeline"; when the songs that they sang were "Daisy, Daisy, Give Me Your Answer True."

It is the time of the wharves and the tangled shipping, the horse-cars by the docks, of piled-up casks and kegs of rum and molasses. There are forgotten fume-flaws of bright smoke above Manhattan; where are the lost faces that came towards us over Brooklyn bridge, where are the parted ripples and the proud forgotten ships?

By the waters of life, before we knew that we must die, before we had seen our father's face, before we had sought the print of his foot: by the waters of time (the tide! the tide!), before we had seen the shadows in the haunted woods, before lost moments lived again, before the shades were fleshed. Who are we, that must follow in the footsteps of the king? Who are we, that had no kings to follow? We are the unkinged men. Have we left shadows on forgotten walls? Have we crossed running water and lived for seven timeless years with the enchantress, and shall we find our son who is ourself, and will he know us?

Shall your voices unlock the gates of my brain? Shall I know you, though I have never seen your face? Will you know me, and will you call me "son"? Father, I know that you live, though I have never found you.

In the old town of Tours he quickly found lodging in an ancient hotel or tavern—really a congeries of old, whited buildings with separate doors, looking out on a cobbled courtyard through whose gate, in former times perhaps, the horses and post-chaise of weary travellers had often clattered. In a cold, little room in one of the buildings facing on the court, he now settled down, and there began for him one of the most extraordinary and phantasmal time-experiences of his life. Day passed into night, night merged into day again like the unbroken weaving of a magic web, and he stayed on, week after week, plunged in a strange and legendary spell of time that seemed suspended and detached from the world of measurable event, fixed in unmoving moment, unsilent silence, changeless change.

Later, it seemed to him that that strange revery and dream of time, in which his life was now so strangely fixed, had been induced by a series of causes, easy to understand in the light of experience, and almost logical in their consequence. It was five months since he had left America. After the overwhelming impact of impression and event which a new world, a new life, had brought to him in so many varied, chance, and unexpected ways—after the ship, the voyage, the enormous isolation, the whole earth-detachment of the sea (itself a life, a world, a universe of new experience), after the weeks in England, the huge web of London, the brief but poignantly illuminating days in Bristol, Bath, and Devonshire, with fleeting glimpses of something so strange, yet so familiar, so near, yet never to be touched, that it seemed to him he was looking in through a lighted window at a life which he had always known, but which he could never make his own; after the terrific impact of France and Paris—the month of bewildered, desperate and almost terror-stricken isolation in a new and hostile world—an atom, wordless, tongueless, almost drowned among the strange, dark faces of the Frenchmen; after all the confusion, grief, and error of that month—the night-time kaleidoscope of cafés, brothels, alcohol, and women, the frenzied day-time prowling through museums, bookstalls, thronging streets—the thousand monuments of an alien culture, the million faces of an alien race, until every atom of him was wrung, trembling, maddened and exhausted, sick with loss and hopelessness, weary with despair—after the huge first shock and flood-tide of immersion in an alien life—had come his meeting with Starwick, Elinor, and Ann, the brief, fatal, furious weeks of their relation, the bitter loss and waste and rankling pain of parting; and finally the sweltering and incurable ache, the blind and driven aimlessness of wandering, the chance encounter with the Countess, and the brief interlude of forgetfulness and oblivion that had come to him while he was with her—and now, blank, silent loneliness again, the blind fortuity of chance, the arbitrary halt and desperate entrenchment of his spirit in this town of Tours.

Now, after the savage kaleidoscope of these months of hope and grief and ecstasy, of desolation and despair, of passion, love, and suffering, of maddened hunger and infuriate desire, after all the restless and insatiable seeking of his goaded, driven, and unresting soul, he had come at last to a place of quietness and pause; and suddenly he was like a desperate and bewildered man who has come in from the furious street of life to seek sanctuary and repose in the numb stillness of a tomb.

Day and night now, from dawn to dark, from sleeping until waking, in that strange spell of time and silence that was neither dream nor sleep nor waking vision, but that like an enchantment was miraculously composed of all, obsessed as a man exiled, banished, or condemned by fate to live upon a desert island without possibility of escape or return—he thought of home.

In that enchanted spell of time and silence, as men who gaze in visions across misty and illimitable seas, with the terrible homelessness of a man for whom there can never be return, with the terrible homelessness of a man who longs for home and has no home—with the impossible, hopeless, incurable and unutterable homesickness of the American, who is maddened by a longing for return, and does not know to what he can return, whose brain burns night and day with the maddened hope, whose heart aches night and day with the smothering and incurable ache of the houseless, homeless, and forsaken atom of the earth who has no goal or ending for his hunger, no final dwelling-place for his desire—he thought of home.

What was it? It was the furious desire, unceasing, unassuaged, of wandering and forsaken man—the lost American—who longs forever for return—and who has no door to enter, no room to dwell in, no single handsbreadth of certain, consecrated earth upon that continent of wild houseless space, to which he can return.

An astounding—an almost incredible thing—now happened. He had come to Tours, telling himself that now at last, at last, he was going "to settle down and write," that he was going to justify his voyage by the high purpose of creation. In his mind there swarmed various projects, cloudy, vague, and grandiose in their conception, of plays, books, stories, essays he must write: with desperate resolve he sat down grimly now to shape these grand designs into the stern and toilsome masonry of words. A few impatient, fragmentary beginnings, the opening pages of a story, the beginning speeches of a play—all crumpled in a wad and impatiently tossed aside—were the final results of this ambitious purpose.

And yet, write he did. Useless, fragmentary, and inchoate as were these first abortive efforts, he began to write now like a madman—as only a madman could write—driven by an insanity of sense and soul and feeling which he no longer could master or control, tranced in a hypnosis by whose fatal and insatiate compulsions he was forced, without will, to act. Gripped by that ungovernable desire, all ordered plans, designs, coherent projects for the work he had set out to do went by the board, were burned up in the flame of a quenchless passion, like a handful of dry straw. Seated at a table in his cold, little room that overlooked the old cobbled court of the hotel, he wrote ceaselessly from dawn to dark, sometimes from darkness on to dawn again—hurling himself upon the bed to dream, in a state of comatose awareness, strange sleeping-wakeful visions, dreams mad and terrible as the blinding imagery that now swept constantly across his brain its blaze of fire.

The words were wrung out of him in a kind of bloody sweat, they poured out of his finger tips, spat out of his snarling throat like writhing snakes; he wrote them with his heart, his brain, his sweat, his guts;

he wrote them with his blood, his spirit; they were wrenched out of the last secret source and substance of his life.

And in those words was packed the whole image of his bitter homelessness, his intolerable desire, his maddened longing for return. In those wild and broken phrases was packed the whole bitter burden of his famished, driven, over-laden spirit—all the longing of the wanderer, all the impossible and unutterable homesickness that the American, or any man on earth, can know.

They were all there—without coherence, scheme, or reason—flung down upon paper like figures blasted by the spirit's lightning stroke, and in them was the huge chronicle of the billion forms, the million names, the huge, single, and incomparable substance of America.

XCVII

At morning, in a foreign land, whether upon the mournful plains of Hungary, or in some quiet square of Georgian houses, embedded in the immensity of sleeping London, he awakes, and thinks of home; or in some small provincial town of France, he starts up from his sleep at night, he starts up in the living, brooding stillness of the night, for suddenly he thinks that he has heard there the sounds of America and the wilderness, the things that are in his blood, his heart, his brain, in every atom of his flesh and tissue, the things for which he draws his breath in labor, the things that madden him with an intolerable and nameless pain.

And what are they? They are the whistle-wail of one of the great American engines as it thunders through the continent at night, the sound of the voices of the city streets—those hard, loud, slangy voices, full of violence, humor, and recklessness, now stronger and more remote than the sounds of Asia—the sounds that come up from the harbor of Manhattan in the night—that magnificent and thrilling music of escape, mystery, and joy, with the mighty orchestration of the transatlantics, the hoarse little tugs, the ferryboats and lighters, those sounds that well up from the gulf and dark immensity of night and that pierce the entrails of the listener.

For this will always be one of the immortal and living things about the land, this will be an eternal and unchanging fact about that city whose only permanence is change: there will always be the great rivers flowing around it in the darkness, the rivers that have bounded so many *nameless* lives, those rivers which have moated in so many changes, which have girdled the wilderness and so much hard, brilliant, and sensational living, so much pain, beauty, ugliness, so much lust, murder, corruption, love, and wild exultancy.

They'll build great engines yet, and grander towers, but always the rivers run, in the day, in the night, in the dark, draining immensely their imperial tides out of the wilderness, washing and flowing by the coasts of the fabulous city, by all the little ticking sounds of time, by all the million lives and deaths of the city. Always the rivers run, and always there will be great ships upon the tide, always great horns are baying at the harbor's mouth, and in the night a thousand men have died while the river, always the river, the dark eternal river, full of strange secret time, washing the city's stains away, thickened and darkened by its dumpings, is flowing by us, by us to the sea.

He awakes at morning in a foreign land, and he thinks of home. He cannot rest, his heart is wild with pain and loneliness, he sleeps, but then he knows he sleeps, he hears the dark and secret spell of time about him; in ancient towns, thick tumbling chimes of the cathedral bells are thronging through the dark, but through the passages of his diseased and unforgetful sleep the sounds and memory of America make way: now it is almost dawn, a horse has turned into a street and in America, there is the sound of wheels, the lonely clop-clop of the hooves upon deserted pavements, silence, then the banging clatter of a can.

He awakes at morning in a foreign land, he draws his breath in labor in the wool-soft air of Europe: the wool-gray air is all about him like a living substance; it is in his heart, his stomach, and his entrails; it is in the slow and vital movements of the people; it soaks down from the sodden skies into the earth, into the heavy buildings, into the limbs and hearts and brains of living men. It soaks into the spirit of the wanderer; his heart is dull with the gray weariness of despair, it aches with hunger for the wilderness, the howling of great winds, the bite and sparkle of the clear, cold air, the buzz, the tumult and the wild exultancy. The wet, woolen air is all about him, and there is no hope. It was there before William the Conqueror; it was there before Clovis and Charles "the Hammer"; it was there before Attila; it was there before Hengist and Horsa; it was there before Vercingetorix and Julius Agricola.

It was there now; it will always be there. They had it in Merry England and they had it in Gay Paree; and they were seldom merry, and they were rarely gay. The wet, woolen air is over Munich; it is over

Paris; it is over Rouen and Madame Bovary; it soaks into England; it gets into boiled mutton and the Brussels sprouts; it gets into Hammersmith on Sunday; it broods over Bloomsbury and the private hotels and the British Museum; it soaks into the land of Europe and keeps the grass green. It has always been there; it will always be there. His eyes are mad and dull; he cannot sleep without the hauntings of phantasmal memory behind the eyes; his brain is overstretched and weary, it gropes ceaselessly around the prison of the skull, it will not cease.

The years are walking in his brain, his father's voice is sounding in his ears, and in the pulses of his blood the tom-tom's beat. His living dust is stored with memory: two hundred million men are walking in his bones; he hears the howling of the wind around forgotten eaves; he cannot sleep. He walks in midnight corridors; he sees the wilderness, the moon-drenched forests; he comes to clearings in the moonlit stubble, he is lost, he has never been here, yet he is at home. His sleep is haunted with the dreams of time; wires throb above him in the whiteness, they make a humming in the noonday heat.

The rails are laid across light, hunched miles of golden wheat, the rails are wound through mountains, they curve through clay-yellow cuts, they enter tunnels, they are built up across the marshes, they hug the cliff and follow by the river's bank, they cross the plains with dust and thunder, and they leap through flatness and the dull scrub-pine to meet the sea.

Then he awakes at morning in a foreign land, and thinks of home.

For we have awaked at morning in a foreign land and heard the bitter curse of their indictment, and we know what we know, and it will always be the same.

"One time!" their voices cried, leaning upon a bar the bitter weight of all their discontent. "One time! I've been back one time—just once in seven years," they said, "and Jesus that was plenty! One time was enough! To hell with that damned country! What have they got now but a lot of cheap spaghetti joints and skyscrapers?" they said. "If you want a drink, you sneak down three back-alleyways, get the once-over from a couple of ex-prize fighters, and·then plank down a dollar for a shot of varnish that would rot the guts out of a goat! . . . And the women!"—the voices rose here with infuriated scorn—"What a nice lot of cold-blooded gold-digging bastards *they've* turned out to be! . . . I spent thirty dollars taking one of 'em to a show, and to a night-club afterward! When bedtime came do you think I got anything out of it? . . . 'You may kiss my little hand,' she says. . . . 'You may kiss my little—that's what you may do,'" the voices snarled with righteous bitterness. "When I asked her if she was goin' to come through she started to yell for the cops! . . . A woman who tried to pull one like that over here would get sent to Siberia! . . . A nice country, I don't think! . . . Now, get this! *Me,* I'm a Frenchman, see!" the voice said with a convincing earnestness. "These guys know how to *live,* see! This is my country where I belong, see! . . . Johnny, luh même chose pour mwah et m'seer! . . . Fill 'em up again, kid."

"Carpen-*teer!*" the voices then rose jeeringly, in true accents of French pugnacity. "Sure, I'm a Frenchman—but Carpen-*teer!* Where do yuh get that stuff? Christ, Dempsey could 'a' took that frog the best day that he ever saw! . . . An accident!" the voices yelled. "Whattya mean—an accident? Didn't I see the whole thing with my own eyes? Wasn't I back there then? . . . Wasn't I talkin' t' Jack himself an hour after the fight was over? . . . An accident! Jesus! The only accident was that he let him last four rounds. 'I could have taken him in the first if I wanted to,' Jack says to me. . . . Sure, I'm a Frenchman!" the voice said with belligerent loyalty. "But Carpen*teer! Jesus!* Where do you get that stuff?"

And, brother, I have heard the voices you will never hear, discussing the graces of a life more cultured than any you will ever know—and I know and I know, and yet it is still the same.

Bitterly, bitterly Boston one time more! the flying leaf, the broken cloud—"I think," said they, "that we will live here now. I think," they said, "that we are running down to Spain next week so Francis can do a little writing. . . . And really," their gay yet cultivated tones continued, "it's wonderful what you can do here if you only have a little money. . . . *Yes,* my dear!" their refined accents continued in a tone of gay conviction. "It's really quite incredible, you know. . . . I happen to know of a real honest-to-goodness château near Blois that can be had for something less than $7000! . . . It's all rather incredible, you know," those light, half-English tones went on, "when you consider what it takes to live in Brookline! . . . Francis has always felt that he would like to do a little writing, and I feel somehow the atmosphere is better here for all that sort of thing—it really is, you know. Don't you think so?" said those gay and cultivated tones of Boston which you, my brother, never yet have heard. "And after all," those cultivated tones went on in accents of a droll sincerity, "you see all the people here you really *care* to see, I *mean*, you know! They all come to Paris at one time or another—I *mean*, the trouble really is in getting a little time alone for yourself. . . . Or do you find it so?" the voices suavely, lightly, asked. . . . "Oh, look! look at that—there!" they cried with jubilant elation, "I mean that boy and his girl there, walking along with their arms around each other! . . . Don't you just a-do-o-re it? . . . Isn't it too *ma-a-rvelous?*" those refined and silvery tones went on, with patriotic tenderness. "I mean, there's something so perfectly sweet and un-self-conscious about it all!" the voices said with all the cultivated earnestness of Boston! "Now *where?*—where?—would you see anything like that at home?" the voices said triumphantly.

(Seldom in Brookline, lady. Oh, rarely, seldom, almost never in the town of Brookline, lady. But on the Esplanade—did you ever go out walking on the Esplanade at night-time, in the hot and sultry month of August, lady? They are not Frenchmen, lady: they are all Jews and Irish and Italians, lady, but the noise of their kissing is like the noise the wind makes through a leafy grove—it is like the great hooves of a hundred thousand cavalry being pulled out of the marshy places of the earth, dear lady.)

". . . I *mean*—these people really understand that sort of thing so much better than we do. . . . They're so much *simpler* about it. . . . I mean, so much more graceful with that kind of thing. . . . Il faut un peu de sentiment, n'est-ce pas? . . . Or do you think so?" said those light, those gay, those silvery, and half-English tones of cultivated Boston, which you, my brother, never yet have heard.

(I got you, lady. That was French. I know. . . . But if I felt your leg, if I began by fondling gracefully your leg, if in a somewhat graceful Gallic way I felt your leg, and said, "Chérie! Petite chérie!"—would you remember, lady, this is Paris?)

Oh, bitterly, bitterly, Boston one time more: their silvery voices speak an accent you will never know, and of their loins is marble made, but, brother, there are corn-haired girls named Neilsen out in Minnesota, and the blonde thighs of the Lindquist girl could break a bullock's back.

Oh, bitterly, bitterly, Boston one time more: the French have little ways about them that we do not have, but brother, they're still selling cradles down in Georgia, and in New Orleans their eyes are dark, their white teeth bite you to the bone.

Oh, bitterly, bitterly, Boston, one time more, and of their flesh is codfish made. Big Brother's still waiting for you with his huge, red fist, behind the barn up in the State of Maine, and they're still having shotgun marriages at home.

Oh, brother, there are voices you will never hear—ancestral voices prophesying war, my brother, and rare and radiant voices that you know not of, as they have read us into doom. The genteel voices of Oxenford broke once like chimes of weary, unenthusiastic bells across my brain, speaking to me compassionately its judgment on our corrupted lives, gently dealing with the universe, my brother, gently and without labor—gently, brother, gently, it dealt with all of us, with easy condescension and amused disdain:

"I'm afraid, old boy," the genteel voice of Oxenford remarked, "you're up against it over thöh. . . . I really am. . . . Thöh's no place thö faw the individual any longah,"—the genteel voice went on, un-individual brother. "Obviously," that tolerant voice instructed me, "obviously, thöh can be no cultuah in a country so completely lackin' in tradition as is yoähs. . . . It's all so objective—if you see what I main—thöh's no place left faw the innah life," it said, oh, outward brother! ". . . We Europeans have often obsöhved (it's *very* curious, you know) that the *Amer*ican is incapable of any real feelin'—it seems quite impawsible faw him to distinguish between true emotion an' sentimentality—an' he invayably chooses the lattah! . . . *Curious, isn't it?*—or do you think so, brother? Of co'se, thöh is yoäh beastly dreadful sex-prawblem. . . . Yoäh women! . . . Oh, deah, deah! . . . Perhaps we'd bettah say no moah . . . but, thöh you *ah!*"—right in the eye, my brother. "Yoäh country is a matriahky, my deah fellah . . . it really is, you know." . . . if you can follow us, dear brother. "The women have the men in a state of complete subjection . . . the male is rapidly becomin' moah sexless an' emasculated"—that genteel voice of doom went on—"No!— Decidedly you have quite a prawblem befoah you. . . . Obviously thöh can be no cultuah while such a condition puhsists. . . . *That* is why when my friends say to me, 'You ought to see *America*, . . . you really ought, you know.' . . . I say, 'No, thanks. . . . If you don't mind, I'd rathah not. . . . I think I'll stay at home . . . I'm sorry,'" the compassionate tones of Oxenford went on, "but that's the way I feel—it really is, you know. . . . Of co'se, I know you couldn't undahstand my feelin'—faw aftah all, you ah a Yank—but thöh you ah! Sorry!" it said regretfully, as it spoke its courteous but inexorable judgments of eternal exile, brother, and removed forever the possibility of your ever hearing it. "But that's the way I feel! I hope you don't mind," the voice said gently, with compassion.

No, sir, I don't mind. We don't mind, he, she, it, or they don't mind. Nobody minds, sir, nobody minds. Because, just as you say, sir, oceans are between us, seas have sundered us, there is a magic in you that we cannot fathom—a light, a flame, a glory—an impalpable, indefinable, incomprehensible, undeniable something-or-other, something which I can never understand or measure because—just as you say, sir—with such compassionate regret, I am—I am—a Yank.

'Tis true, my brother, we are Yanks. Oh, 'tis true, 'tis true! I am a Yank! Yet, wherefore Yank, good brother? Hath not a Yank ears? Hath not a Yank lies, truths, bowels of mercy, fears, joys, and lusts? Is he not warmed by the same sun, washed by the same ocean, rotted by the same decay, and eaten by the same worms as a German is? If you kill him, does he not die? If you sweat him, does he not stink? If you lie with his wife or his mistress, does she not whore, lie, fornicate and betray, even as a Frenchman's does? If you strip him, is he not naked as a Swede? Is his hide less white than Baudelaire's? Is his breath more foul than the King of Spain's? Is his belly bigger, his neck fatter, his face more hoggish, and his eye more shiny than a Munich brewer's? Will he not cheat, rape, thieve, whore, curse, hate, and murder like any European? Aye—Yank! But wherefore, wherefore Yank—good brother?

Brother, have we come then from a fated stock? Augured from birth, announced by two dark angels, named in our mother's womb? And for what? For what? Father-less, to grope our feelers on the sea's dark bed, among the polyped squirms, the blind sucks and crawls and sea-valves of the brain, loaded with memory that will not die? To cry our love out in the wilderness, to wake always in the night, smiting the pillow in some foreign land, thinking forever of the myriad sights and sounds of home?

"While Paris Sleeps!"—By God, while Paris sleeps, to wake and walk and not to sleep; to wake and walk and sleep and wake, and sleep again, seeing dawn come at the window-square that cast its wedge before our glazed, half-sleeping eyes, seeing soft, hated foreign light, and breathing soft, dull languid air that could not bite and tingle up the blood, seeing legend and lie and fable wither in our sight as we saw what we saw, knew what we knew.

Sons of the lost and lonely fathers, sons of the wanderers, children of hardy loins, the savage earth, the pioneers, what had we to do with all their bells and churches? Could we feed our hunger on portraits of the Spanish king? Brother, for what? For what? To kill the giant of loneliness and fear, to slay the hunger that would not rest, that would not give us rest.

Of wandering forever, and the earth again. Brother, for what? For what? For what? For the wilderness, the immense and lonely land. For the unendurable hunger, the unbearable ache, the incurable loneliness. For the exultancy whose only answer is the wild goat-cry. For a million memories, ten thousand sights and sounds and shapes and smells and names of things that only we can know.

For what? For what? Not for a nation. Not for a people, not for an empire, not for a thing we love or hate.

For what? For a cry, a space, an ecstasy. For a savage and nameless hunger. For a living and intolerable memory that may not for a second be forgotten, since it includes all the moments of our lives, includes all we do and are. For a living memory; for ten thousand memories; for a million sights and sounds and moments; for something like nothing else on earth; for something which possesses us.

For something under our feet, and around us and over us; something that is in us and part of us, and proceeds from us, that beats in all the pulses of our blood.

Brother, for what?

First for the thunder of imperial names, the names of men and battles, the names of places and great rivers, the mighty names of the States. The name of The Wilderness; and the names of Antietam, Chancellorsville, Shiloh, Bull Run, Fredericksburg, Cold Harbor, the Wheat Fields, Ball's Bluff, and the Devil's Den; the names of Cowpens, Brandywine, and Saratoga; of Death Valley, Chickamauga, and the Cumberland Gap. The names of the Nantahalahs, the Bad Lands, the Painted Desert, the Yosemite, and the Little Big Horn; the names of Yancey and Cabarrus counties; and the terrible name of Hatteras.

Then, for the continental thunder of the States: the names of Montana, Texas, Arizona, Colorado, Michigan, Maryland, Virginia, and the two Dakotas; the names of Oregon and Indiana, of Kansas and the rich Ohio; the powerful name of Pennsylvania, and the name of Old Kentucky; the undulance of Alabama; the names of Florida and North Carolina.

In the red-oak thickets, at the break of day, long hunters lay for bear—the rattle of arrows in laurel leaves, the war-cries round the painted buttes, and the majestical names of the Indian Nations: the Pawnees, the Algonquins, the Iroquois, the Comanches, the Blackfeet, the Seminoles, the Cherokees, the Sioux, the Hurons, the Mohawks, the Navajos, the Utes, the Omahas, the Onondagas, the Chippewas, the Crees, the Chickasaws, the Arapahoes, the Catawbas, the Dakotas, the Apaches, the Croatans, and the Tuscaroras; the names of Powhatan and Sitting Bull; and the name of the Great Chief, Rain-In-The-Face.

Of wandering forever, and the earth again: in red-oak thickets, at the break of day, long hunters lay for bear. The arrows rattle in the laurel leaves, and the elmroots thread the bones of buried lovers. There have been war-cries on the Western trails, and on the plains the gunstock rusts upon a handful of bleached bones. The barren earth? Was no love living in the wilderness?

The rails go westward in the dark. Brother, have you seen starlight on the rails? Have you heard the thunder of the fast express?

Of wandering forever, and the earth again—the names of the mighty rails that bind the nation, the wheeled thunder of the names that net the continent: the Pennsylvania, the Union Pacific, the Santa Fé, the Baltimore and Ohio, the Chicago and Northwestern, the Southern, the Louisiana and Northern, the Seaboard Air Line, the Chicago, Milwaukee and Saint Paul, the Lackawanna, the New York, New Haven and Hartford, the Florida East Coast, the Rock Island, and the Denver and Rio Grande.

Brother, the names of the engines, the engineers, and the sleeping-cars: the great engines of the Pacific type, the articulated Mallets with three sets of eight-yoked driving-wheels, the 400-ton thunderbolts with J. T. Cline, T. J. McRae, and the demon hawk-eyes of H. D. Campbell on the rails.

The names of the great tramps who range the nation on the fastest trains: the names of the great tramps Oklahoma Red, Fargo Pete, Dixie Joe, Iron Mike, The Frisco Kid, Nigger Dick, Red Chi, Ike the Kike, and The Jersey Dutchman.

By the waters of life, by time, by time, Lord Tennyson stood among the rocks, and stared. He had long hair, his eyes were deep and sombre, and he wore a cape; he was a poet, and there was magic and mystery in his touch, for he had heard the horns of Elfland faintly blowing. And by the waters of life, by time, by time, Lord Tennyson stood among the cold, gray rocks, and commanded the sea to break—break—break! And the sea broke, by the waters of life, by time, by time, as Lord Tennyson commanded it to do, and his heart was sad and lonely as he watched the stately ships (of the Hamburg-American Packet Company, fares forty-five dollars and up, first-class) go on to their haven under the hill, and Lord Tennyson would that his heart could utter the thoughts that arose in him.

By the waters of life, by time, by time: the names of the mighty rivers, the alluvial gluts, the chains of the continent, the throats that drink America (Sweet Thames, flow gently till I end my song). The names of the men who pass, and the myriad names of the earth that abides forever: the names of the men who are doomed to wander, and the name of that immense and lonely land on which they wander, to which they return, in which they will be buried—America! The immortal earth which waits forever, the trains that thunder on the continent, the men who wander, and the women who cry out, "Return!"

Finally, the names of the great rivers that are flowing in the darkness (Sweet Thames, flow gently till I end my song).

By the waters of life, by time, by time: the names of great mouths, the mighty maws, the vast, wet, coiling, never-glutted and unending snakes that drink the continent. Where, sons of men, and in what other land will you find others like them, and where can you match the mighty music of their names?—The Monongahela, the Colorado, the Rio Grande, the Columbia, the Tennessee, the Hudson (Sweet Thames!); the Kennebec, the Rappahannock, the Delaware, the Penobscot, the Wabash, the Chesapeake, the Swannanoa, the Indian River, the Niagara (Sweet Afton!); the Saint Lawrence, the Susquehanna, the Tombigbee, the Nantahala, the French Broad, the Chattahoochee, the Arizona, and the Potomac (Father Tiber!)—these are a few of their princely names, these are a few of their great, proud, glittering names, fit for the immense and lonely land that they inhabit.

Oh, Tiber! Father Tiber! You'd only be a suckling in that mighty land! And as for you, sweet Thames, flow gently till I end my song: flow gently, gentle Thames, be well-behaved, sweet Thames, speak softly and politely, little Thames, flow gently till I end my song.

By the waters of life, by time, by time, and of the yellow cat that smites the nation, of the belly of the snake that coils across the land—of the terrible names of the rivers in flood, the rivers that foam and welter in the dark, that smash the levees, that flood the lowlands for two thousand miles, that carry the bones of the cities seaward on their tides: of the awful names of the Tennessee, the Arkansas, the Missouri, the Mississippi, and even the little mountain rivers, brothers, in the season of the floods.

Delicately they dive for Greeks before the railway station: the canoe glides gently through the portals of the waiting-room (for whites). Full fathom five the carcass of old man Lype is lying (of his bones is coral made) and delicately they dive for lunch-room Greeks before the railway station.

Brother, what fish are these? The floatage of sunken rooms, the sodden bridal-veils of poverty, the slime of ruined parlor plush, drowned faces in the family album; and the blur of long-drowned eyes, blurred features, whited, bloated flesh.

Delicately they dive for Greeks before the railway station. The stern, good, half-drowned faces of the brothers Trade and Mark survey the tides. Cardui! Miss Lillian Leitzell twists upon one arm above the flood; the clown, half-sunken to his waist, swims upward out of swirling yellow; the tiger bares his teeth above the surges of a river he will never drink. The ragged tatters of the circus posters are plastered on soaked boards. And delicately they dive for Greeks before the railway station.

Have we not seen them, brother?

For what are we, my brother? We are a phantom flare of grieved desire, the ghostling and phosphoric flicker of immortal time, a brevity of days haunted by the eternity of the earth. We are an unspeakable utterance, an insatiable hunger, an unquenchable thirst; a lust that bursts our sinews, explodes our brains, sickens and rots our guts, and rips our hearts asunder. We are a twist of passion, a moment's flame of love and ecstasy, a sinew of bright blood and agony, a lost cry, a music of pain and joy, a haunting of brief, sharp hours, an almost captured beauty, a demon's whisper of unbodied memory. We are the dupes of time.

For, brother, what are we?

We are the sons of our father, whose face we have never seen, we are the sons of our father, whose voice we have never heard, we are the sons of our father, to whom we have cried for strength and comfort in our agony, we are the sons of our father, whose life like ours was loved, we are the sons of our father, to whom only can we speak out the strange, dark burden of our heart and spirit, we are the sons of our father, and we shall follow the print of his foot forever.

XCVIII

How long he had remained at Tours he scarcely knew: suspended in this spell of time and memory, he seemed to have detached himself not only from the infinite connections that bound him to the past, but from every project and direction that he had considered for the future. Day after day he stayed in his little room above the cobbled court of the hotel; he ate his meals there, going out at nightfall to eat and drink in a café, to walk about the streets, once or twice to go home with a woman of the town, and finally to come back to his room, to write furiously for hours, and then, stretched out in bed, nailed to the rock of a furiously wakeful sleep, to live again through the immense and spaceless images of night, in an alert but comatose hypnosis of the will.

One morning he awoke with a shock of apprehension, the foreboding of calamitous mischance. It was the first time in weeks that he had taken thought of the state of his resources, or felt any care or worry for the future. He counted his money with feverish haste, and discovered that less then 250 francs remained. For a moment he sat on the edge of the bed, holding the little wad of franc notes in his hand, stunned and bewildered by this sudden realization that his funds were exhausted, and for the moment not knowing what to do. His hotel bill for the week was due; he went at once to the bureau and asked for it; a hasty calculation assured him that when he had paid it, less than twenty francs would be left.

He knew no one in Tours to whom he could appeal for aid; one glance at the impeccable, cold courtesy of the female face, hard, dark and gallic, in the bureau of the hotel—the basalt of the eyes, the line of hair across the brows—told him that he could as soon wring milk and honey from the cobblestones as extract an ounce of charitable relief from the granite coffers of her soul. The brows drew in, the black eyes hardened with a cold narrowing of mistrust: even before he spoke he saw she had read the story of his profligate extravagance, and that from that moment the hard propriety of her suspicious soul had been turned against him with that virtuous dislike which such people feel for un-monied men. When he spoke, therefore, it was to tell her he was leav-ing that day: she inclined her dark, hard face impassively, saying: "Oui, monsieur," and asked if he would have his room vacated by twelve o'clock.

He went to the railway station and looked up rates and distances. During the whole period of his stay in Tours—in fact, during the whole course of his wanderings since leaving Paris—he had been vaguely assured that he was moving in the general direction of Provence, Mar-seilles, and the South. He now discovered, on consulting a map, that he was off this course by some hundreds of kilometers, and on the south-west road to Bordeaux, the Pyrenees, and Spain. For a moment, he was decided to take the train for Bordeaux—a post-card from Ann had been mailed from Carcassonne, and she had informed him that they were on their way to Biarritz. A brief inquiry, however, convinced him that his funds were by no means sufficient to get him even as far as Bordeaux and, over there, he felt, his case was more desperate than ever. He knew no one there and had no hope of meeting any one he knew. He dis-covered also that the lowest fare back to Paris—the third-class fare—was about thirty-four francs, almost twice as much as he possessed.

Finally, with a feeling of malevolent joy—for, curiously, a growing realization of his plight, and the dark, hard eyes of the Frenchmen fixed on him in an expression of avaricious mistrust, had now wakened in him a jubilant indifference, a desire to roar with laughter—he thought of Orléans and the Countess.

He found that his funds were sufficient for third-class fare to Orléans, which was about seventeen francs, and that a train was leaving in an hour. Returning to the hotel, he packed his valise with frenzied haste, throwing his clothing in and stamping it down with his feet, rode to the station in the hotel's horse-drawn bus, and an hour later was on his way back to Orléans.

Late March had come: the day was overcast with thin, gray clouds, an uncertain milky radiance of light; the fields and earth and forests, still bare, had a moist, thawed fertility that spoke of spring. On the way up, snow began to fall, a brief flurry of large, wet flakes that melted as they fell: it was soon over, and the sun broke through in thin, wavering gusts of light.

There were no other passengers in his compartment; he sat looking out the window across the wet fields, and from time to time, as he visualized the look of startled, crafty apprehension on the Countess' face when she saw him, he burst into wild, sudden whoops and yells of laughter that echoed loudly above the steady pounding of the wheels.

It was noon when he reached Orléans: he took his heavy bag and went limping out across the station square, pausing once to rest his aching arm and change his grip. On entering the hotel he found Yvonne in the *bureau*. She looked up from her ledger as he entered, her dark face hardening with a mistrust of cold surprise as she saw him.

"Monsieur has returned to stay?" she inquired, and looked towards his valise. "You wish a room?"

"I do not know yet," he said easily. "I shall let you know in a few minutes. At present, I should like to speak to the Countess. Is she here?"

She did not answer for a moment, her black brows gathered in a line, and her eyes grew perceptibly harder, colder, more mistrustful as she looked at him.

"Yes. I s'ink she is in her room," she said at length. "I vill see. . . . Jean!" she called sharply, and struck a bell.

The porter appeared, started with surprise when he saw the youth, and then smiled cordially and greeted him in friendly fashion. Then he turned inquiringly to Yvonne. She spoke curtly:

"Dites à Madame la Comtesse que Monsieur, le jeune Américain, est revenu. Il attend."

"Mais oui, monsieur," the porter said briskly, turning towards him. "Et **votre bagage?**" he looked inquiringly at the valise. "Vous restez ici?"

"Je ne sais pas. Je vous dirai plus tard. Merci," he said, as the porter took the valise, and put it away behind the office desk.

The porter departed with his message. Yvonne returned to her books, and he waited, pacing the hall in a state of nervous elation, until he heard the old woman's voice, sharp, startled, excited, speaking to the porter on the floor above. Then he heard her coming down the stairs, turned and faced her sharply-inquiring, apprehensive face as she came down, and was vigorously pumping her uncertain and unwilling little claw, before she had time to stammer out a greeting:

"But what—why—what brings you here?" she said. "I thought you had returned to Paris by now. Where have you been?" she asked sharply.

"In Tours," he answered.

"Tours! But what were you doing there all this time? . . . What happened to you?" she asked suspiciously.

"Ah, Countess," he said solemnly, "it is a long story." Then, with a deliberate burlesque of portentous gravity, he lowered his voice and whispered hoarsely, "I fell among thieves."

"What—?" she said in a faltering tone. "What are you saying? . . . You mean you have come back here . . . that you have no . . . how much money have you left?" she demanded sharply.

He thrust his hand into his trousers pocket, fished around and pulled out a few small coins: four two-franc pieces, a franc, two twenty-five-centime coins, a ten- and a five-centime piece——

"That's all," he said, counting them over. "Nine francs sixty-five."

"W-w-w-w-what?" she stammered. "Nine francs sixty-five—do you mean that's all you have left?"

"That's all," he said cheerfully, "but now that I'm here at last it doesn't matter."

"Here!" she gasped. "Do you mean you are going—what do you intend to do?" she said sharply.

"Oh," he said easily, "I shall wait here until I get money from America."

"And—and how long do you think that will take?" the old woman was twisting her skinny fingers with feverish apprehension.

"Oh, not long," he said airily. "I wrote my mother yesterday, and it ought not to take over four or five weeks to get an answer."

"Four or five weeks!" the old woman said hoarsely. "What are you saying? Four or five weeks, and you have nine francs sixty-five in your pockets! My God! the man is mad!"

"Oh, that part of it will be all right, I guess," he said with an easy laugh. "I told my mother all about you and Monsieur and Madame Vatel, and all my other friends here, and how good you had been to me, and how you were always befriending Americans, and how they call you Little Mother. I told her you couldn't have been kinder to me if you'd been my own mother, and that she didn't need to worry about me at all. So I guess that part of it's all right," he concluded comfortably. "I told her that I'd just put up here at the hotel, and that you and the Vatels would take good care of me until the money comes from home."

"Put up here! . . . For four or five weeks! . . . Hush, my boy! Hush!" she whispered, clutching him feverishly with her bony little claw, and casting an apprehensive glance towards Yvonne whose dark head was lowered studiously above her ledger, but who suggested, by a certain strained attentiveness of posture, that she was missing none of the conversation.

"Come," the Countess whispered feverishly again, pulling him towards the stairway as she spoke. "You come with me, my boy. I want to talk to you alone."

They went upstairs to a parlor on the first floor, deserted, closed, a little stale with its sumptuous bordello furnishings of gilt and crimson plush. There the Countess turned to him, and said directly:

"See here, my boy. What you want to do is out of the question. It will be impossible for you to stay here for four or five weeks! Impossible!" she cried, twisting her bony little hands with growing agitation. "It cannot be done!"

He looked surprised, a little pained.

"Why?" he said.

"Because," she said, and now at last her tone was simple and direct in its quiet assertion, "the Vatels will not keep you here—they will not give you credit for so long a time——"

"And you?" he said quietly.

"My friend," the old woman answered simply, "I have not got it." She raised her bony little shoulders in a shrug. "At the present moment I have nothing—not a sou! I get a little money from America on the first and fifteenth of each month—if I had it, I would give it to you, but I have nothing now. And what I get would not be nearly enough to pay your expenses here for five weeks. It cannot be done."

For the first time since his return he felt respect and sympathy for her; in face of the plain and honest directness of her confession all of his former humor of cynical mockery had vanished. He said:

"In that case, it cannot be done. You are right. I must try to get help elsewhere."

"You have friends in Paris, haven't you? You know people there—Americans?"

"Yes—I think I could get help from some one if I were in Paris."

"Then I shall try to help you to get there," she said quickly. "How much will you need?"

"I think the third-class fare from here is about seventeen francs," he said.

"And you have—how much? Nine sixty-five?" She calculated

swiftly, was silent a moment, and then with an air of decision, marked by a faint flush of painful embarrassment on her withered cheek as she thought of the unpleasant task before her, she said: "If you will wait here, I will go below and see what I can do with these people. . . . I do not know," she said shortly, the faint flush deepening as she spoke, "but I will try."

She left him, and presently he heard voices below, mixed in rapid and excited argument. In ten minutes the old woman returned. In her hand she held a ten-franc note.

"Here," she said, giving it to him. "With what you have, it will be enough to get you to Paris. I have inquired. There is a train in twenty minutes. Now, my boy," she said quickly, taking him by the arm, "you must go. You will just have time to buy your ticket and get on the train. You have no time to lose."

He had been surprised and disappointed at the meagre exactness of her loan: he had eaten nothing all day long and suddenly, with no funds to spare and the prospect of a continued and indefinite fast before him, he felt ravenously hungry. And now it was his turn to redden with embarrassment; he found it difficult to speak, and in a moment said hesitantly:

"I wonder if these people here would let me have a sandwich. . . . I've had nothing to eat."

She did not answer; he saw the faint flush deepen on her sallow cheeks again and, already sorry for the additional distress his request had caused her, he said quickly:

"No, it doesn't matter. I'll get something when I get to Paris. Besides, there's not time now, anyway. I'll have to get that train."

"Yes," she said quickly, with relief. "I think you should. That is best. . . . And now, my boy, make haste. You have no more time to lose."

"Good-bye, Countess," he said, taking her by the hand, and suddenly feeling for the old, lonely, and penniless woman the deepest affection and respect he had ever felt for her. "You have really been my friend. I'm sorry that I've had to cause you this trouble. I'll send you the money when I get to Paris. Good-bye, now, and good-luck to you."

When she answered, her voice was quiet and her old eyes were sad and tranquilly resigned:

"Ah," she said, "I was afraid that this would happen to you. I have known so many Americans—they are so reckless, so extravagant, they do not watch their money. . . . Good-bye, my boy," she now said quietly, clasping his hand. "Take care of yourself and do not get into any more trouble. . . . Let me know if all goes well with you. . . . Good-bye, good-bye. . . . Ah, you are so young, aren't you? Some day you will learn. . . . Good-bye, God bless you—you must hurry now—good-bye. Good-bye."

She followed him as he went quickly down the stairs, and stood on the stairs watching him as he departed. His valise had been put out before the *bureau,* where he could get it easily: Yvonne and Madame Vatel were waiting silently in the office. Yvonne did not speak at all; when he spoke to Madame Vatel, she cocked her head a little, and said coldly: "Monsieur."

He seized the grip and started for the door with it at a rapid limping stride. At the door he paused, turned, and saw the Countess, still standing on the stairs, and looking at him with old, sad eyes.

"Good-bye," he cried in jubilant farewell. "Good-bye, Countess."

"Good-bye, my boy," her voice was so weary, old, and sad he could scarcely hear her.

Then he limped rapidly away from the hotel, across the square, and towards the station and the train.

All through the afternoon the train roared up across the fat and fertile countryside towards Paris. A late sun broke through ragged clouds of torn gold: the light was wild and radiant with a prophecy of spring. In the compartment, his only companion was a young soldier: a boy of eighteen, tall, gawky, big of hand and foot and limb, looking even clumsier than he really was in his thick-soled army shoes, his blue-olive uniform—his long shanks coarsely wound with bands of olive cloth.

The boy had a friendly, olive-colored face, a little marred by pimples and fuzzy unshaved hair; he talked constantly, amiably indifferent to his companion's foreign speech and manner, garrulously friendly in a hoarse boy voice.

In the middle of the afternoon he began to unpack various bundles from the staggering impedimenta of military equipment with which he was surrounded. From a pocket of his overcoat he solemnly fished out an enormous tin of sardines. From another package he took out a gigantic bottle of red wine, and with the same gravity, began to unfold from its wrapping in a newspaper a three-foot loaf of crusty bread.

Then, with the same deliberate concentration, he opened the sardine tin, uncorked the wine-bottle and took a hearty preliminary swig, pulled out a clasp-knife with an evil-looking six-inch blade and, holding the loaf gripped firmly between his knees, began with a backward motion to carve a crisp and liberal slab out of the crusty loaf. This done, he put the bread aside, solemnly impaled a huge sardine upon the point of his gleaming knife, smacked it down upon the slab of bread and, furnishing himself with another hearty swig of the red wine, began to poke the sandwich happily away towards its intended destination, carrying on a choked but completely unperturbed conversation with his companion as he did so.

And his fellow traveller, gazing on that coarse but appetizing fare, felt the pangs of hunger awake in him again with such maddening insistence, that the whole legend of his starved desire must have been written on his yearning face and greedy eyes. At any rate, the young soldier, his mouth still crammed with food, uttered some inarticulate but friendly sounds, in which the word "Mangez" alone was intelligible, suddenly thrust loaf, bottle, knife, and sardine tin towards his starved companion, and with a gesture of rude encouragement, hoarsely spattered forth again:

"Mangez!"

The fellow traveller required no second bidding. He fell to ravenously on sardines, wine, and crusty loaf; they sat there cramming themselves enthusiastically, uttering choked and muffled sounds from time to time, and grinning at each other amiably.

Nothing he had ever eaten tasted as good as that coarse fare; the strong, plain wine was pulsing warmly in his veins, the food made a warm glow in his grateful belly; outside, the sun had broken through in stripes of ragged gold and bronze, above the wheels he could hear great roars of hearty country laughter from another compartment, the high, rich, sanguinary voice of a Frenchman as he cried "Parbleu!"

And he was going back to Paris again, without a penny, a prospect, or a plan, and he felt no care nor pain nor trouble any longer—nothing but wild joy and jubilant happiness such as he had never felt before. He did not know why.

XCIX

EARLY in April, money came from home, and he was on his way again. This time he started South in true earnest, hurtling southward on one of the crack trains of the P. L. M., his nose flattened against the window of the compartment, and his eyes glued on the landscape with such an unwinking intensity, a desperate and insatiate greed, that his fellow passengers stared at him curiously, and then looked at one another with quiet smiles and winks.

As it had always done, the movement and experience of the train filled him with a sense of triumph, joy, and luxury. The crack express, with its gleaming cars, its richly furnished compartments, its luxurious restaurant, warm with wine and food and opulence and suave service, together with the appearance of the passengers, who had the look of ease and wealth and cosmopolitan assurance that one finds among people who travel on such trains, awoke in him again the feeling of a nameless and impending joy, the fulfilment of some impossible happiness, the feeling of wealth and success which a train had always given him, even when he had only a few dollars in his pocket, and that now, in the groomed luxury of this European express, was immeasurably enhanced.

On such a train, indeed, the compact density of the European continent became thrilling in its magical immediacy: one felt everywhere around him—in the assured and wealthy-looking men, the lovely and seductive-looking women—even in the landscape that stretched past with its look of infinite cultivation, its beautifully checkered design of fields, its ancient scheme of towns and villages and old farm buildings —the sense of a life rich with the maturity of centuries, infinitely various and fascinating in its evocation of a world given without reserve to pleasure, love, and luxury—in short, the American's dream of "Europe," a world with all the labor, pain, and fear, the rasping care and fury of his own harsh world, left out.

At Lyons, mid-way on his journey to the South, he left the train. And again, he did not know the reason for his stopping: he had been told that "there was nothing to be seen," but the place was a great city; his old hunger for new cities conquered him, he paused to stay a day, and stayed a week.

Later, he could remember just four things that had held him there in that great provincial town. They were a river, two restaurants, and a girl. The river was the Rhône; it came foaming out of the Alps to form at Lyons its juncture with the Saône. Day after day he sat on a café terrace looking at the river; it foamed past bright and glacial, green as emerald, cold and shining, bearing in forever its message of the Alps, the thaw of crystal ice, the coming on of spring. All of the coming of the spring was somehow written in the cold, sparkling and unforgettable green loveliness of that shining water; it haunted him like something he had always known, like something he had found, like something he would one day discover.

The food in the town was incomparable. It was a native cookery, a food belonging to the region—plain, pungent, peasant-like and nobly good, there is in all the world no better cooking than can be found in the great provincial town of Lyons.

At two places there, La Mère Guy's, and La Mère Filliou's, they call their best cooks by the name of "mother." They offer eating fit for kings, yet all so reasonable and plain that almost any man can afford it. La Mère Guy's establishment is in an old house with various old rooms all used as restaurants. The floor is sanded, there are no suave carpets, no low murmuring of refined voices, no thin tinkle of musical glasses, none of the suave, worldly luxury that one finds in the great restaurants of Paris. It is a place not made for tourists—for Lyons is not a tourist town, and what tourist before ever came there to eat?—It is a place made for the Lyonnais—according to their taste—and one will find them there at Mother Guy's and Filliou's, in all their robust, straightforward eating earnestness. Mother Filliou's is a more open sort of place than Mother Guy's; it is across the river, away from the central part of Lyons, which is on an island formed by the green girdling of the Rhône and Saône. At Mother Filliou's one can look inside; when the weather permits, most people eat outside on a terrace: Mother Filliou's has more sunlight, open air, and gaiety, but the rooms at Mother Guy's have a more convenient, closed, and homely appearance. Both places are crowded with solid-looking Lyonnais of both sexes, their faces filled with sanguinary life, their voices loud and robust, their napkins tucked in under their chins, as they set heartily to work.

The food is largely chicken, beef, and fish, superbly cooked. One will never forget the chicken at Mother Guy's or Mother Filliou's: the chicken is plump and tender country chicken, fresh from the lovely countryside near Lyons, it is so crisp and succulent it almost melts away in your mouth. The beef is thick and juicy and tender, everything is cooked plainly, but with all the peasant spice and pungency; they like spicy and robust relishes, and one eats whole onions, pickled in a kind of brine. There, people drink only one wine, but that is Beaujolais, a plain, grand wine that in this town is cheaper than mineral water, and seems made by nature to wash down such victuals as these people eat.

On the opposite side of the central isle of Lyons, which is the side bounded by the Saône, there is a steep hill surmounted by the church of Notre-Dame-de-Fourvière, a famous place of pilgrimage for the devout. And there, one day, while pilgrims filed in to see the relics, and pay devotion to their saint, and while some monks were chanting from their sonorous and reverberating litany through the great spaces, he saw a girl he could not forget: she sat down across the aisle from him, looked at him, smiled drowsily. She was small, plump; her figure was erotically seductive; she raised 'her head, and seemed to listen drowsily to chanting monks, and he saw that in her neck, a warm, slow pulse was beating—slowly, slowly, richly, warmly beating. She turned her eyes, which were gray and smoky with a cat-like potency, and looked at him again, smiled drowsily, and slowly crossed her heavy legs with a slow, sensual sliding of warm silk. And all the time, the pulse beat slowly, richly, with a drowsy warmth of maddening and hot desire—and that was the last of the four things he saw, remembered, and could not forget of Lyons.

A shining river, emerald green, and magic with its Alpine prescience of spring, of known, undiscovered loveliness; the noble cooking of Mother Guy and Mother Filliou; a pulse in the throat of an unknown girl that beat its slow, warm promise of fulfilled desire—these, of a town of more than six hundred thousand lives and faces, were all that later clearly would remain.

The rest was smoke and silence—some faces here and there, a scheme of streets, an enormous square, a hill crowned with a pilgrim's church, a priest, broad-hatted, with slit mouth and gimlet eyes, some museum relics out of ancient Gaul—all fugitive and broken, gone like smoke.

. . . An emerald river, and a shining light; some glorious cookery and drink; the pulse-beat in the warm throat of a girl—these would remain. Smoke! Smoke! has it been otherwise with any man?

And again, he was hurtling southward in a train.

C

Time, please, time. . . . What time is it? . . . Gentlemen, it's closing time. . . . Time, gentlemen . . . that time of year thou may'st in me behold. . . . In the good old summer-time. . . . I keep thinking of you all the time . . . all the time . . . and all the time. . . . A long time ago the world began. . . . There goes the last bell, run, boy, run: you'll just have time. . . . There are times that make you ha-a-ap-py, there are times that make you sa-a-ad. . . . Do you remember the night you came back to the University: it was that time right after your brother's death, you had just come back that night, I know I was coming across the campus before Old East when I saw you coming up the path with a suitcase in your hand. It was raining but we both stopped and began to talk there—we stepped in under one of the oak-trees because it was raining. I can still remember the old, wet, shining bark of the tree—the reason I can remember is that you put your hand out and leaned against the tree as you talked to me and I kept thinking how tall you were—of course you didn't notice it, you weren't conscious of it but you had your head up and it must have been about eight feet above the ground. But I can remember everything we said that night—it was that time when you came back just after your brother's death: that's when it was all right, I guess that's why I can remember it so well. . . . It's time all little boys were in bed. . . . Now, boy, I'll tell you when it was: it was that time your Papa made that trip to California—the reason that I know is I had just got a letter from him that morning written from Los Angeles telling me how he had seen John Balch and old Professor Truman, and how they had both gone into the real-estate business out there, and both of them getting rich by leaps and bounds —but that's just exactly when it was, sir, the time he made that trip out there in 1906, along towards the end of February, and I had just finished reading his letter when—well as I say now . . . Garfield, Arthur, Harrison and Hayes . . . time of my father's time, life of his life. "Ah, Lord," he said, "I knew them all—and all of them are gone. I'm the only one that's left. By God, I'm getting old." . . . In the year that the locusts came, something that happened in the year the locusts came, two voices that I heard there in that year. . . . Child! Child! It seems so long ago since the year the locusts came, and all of the trees were eaten bare: so much has happened, and it seems so long ago. . . .

"To keep time with!"—To Eugene Gant, Presented to Him on the Occasion of His Twelfth Birthday, by His Brother, B. H. Gant, Oct. 3, 1912. . . . "To keep time with!" . . . Up on the mountain, down in the valley, deep, deep in the hill, Ben, cold, cold, cold.

"Ces arbres——"
"Monsieur?" a thin, waxed face of tired Gaul, professionally attentive,

the eyebrows arched perplexedly above old tired eyes, the waiter's
fatigued napkin on the arm.

"—Monsieur——?"

"Ces arbres—" he stammered, pointing helplessly— "J'ai—j'ai—mais
je les ai vu—avant——"

"Monsieur?"—the eyebrows still more patient, puzzled and concerned,
the voice wrought with attention—"vous dites, monsieur?"

"J'ai dit que—ces arbres—je les ai vu—" he blundered helplessly, and
suddenly muttered with a face gone sullen and ashamed— "Ça ne fait
rien—l'addition, s'il vous plaît."

The waiter stared at him a moment with courteous, slightly pained
astonishment, then smiled apologetically, shrugged his shoulders slightly in a movement of defeat, and saying, "Bien, monsieur," took the ten-
franc note upon the table, counted the racked saucers, and made change
for him.

When the waiter had gone, he sat for a moment staring at the trees.
It was in the month of April, it was night, he was alone on the café
terrace, and yet the chill air was touched with a fragrance that was soft,
thrilling and mysterious—a citrous fume, the smell of unknown flowers,
or perhaps not even this—but only the ghost of a perfume, the thrilling,
barren, and strangely seductive odor of Provence.

It was a street in the little town of Arles, at night—an old, worn,
rutted, curiously dirty-looking street, haunted by the trunks of immense
and dusty-looking trees. He had never been here before, the scene was
strange and haunting as a dream, and yet it was instantly and intolerably
familiar. It was, somehow, he thought, like a street he had been to in
some small town in the hot South at the faded end of summer—a South
Carolina town, he thought it must be, and he was sure that he would
hear the sound of familiar, unknown voices, the passing of feet, the
rustling of quiet, tired leaves. And then he saw again how strange it
was, and could see the tired waiter racking chairs and tables for the
night, and in the café tired lights and emptiness, and the white, tired
light upon the old dusty street, the huge haunting boles of the great
trees; and he knew that he had never been along that way before.

Then he got up and walked away, and put his hand upon the trunk
of one of the old trees: it was white and felt smooth to the touch, and
was somewhat like the sycamores at home—and yet it was not this that
haunted him with troubling memory. He felt, intolerably, that the place,
the scene, the great wreathed branches of the trees, were something he

had seen before—that he had seen it here from the same spot where now he sat—but *when, when, when?*

And suddenly, with a thrill of recognition that flashed across his brain like an electric spark, he saw that he was looking at the same trees that Van Gogh had painted in his picture of the roadmenders at their work in Arles, that the scene was the same, that he was sitting where the painter had sat before. And he noted that the trees had tall, straight, symmetrical trunks, and remembered that the trees that Vincent had painted had great, tendoned trunks that writhed and twisted like creatures in a dream—and yet were somehow more true than truth, more real than this reality. And the great vinelike trunks of these demented trees had wound and rooted in his heart, so that now he could not forget them, nor see this scene in any other way than that in which Van Gogh had painted it.

When he got up, the waiter was still racking chairs upon the tables, and the white and quiet light from the café fell like a tired stillness on the dusty street, and he walked away, haunted by unfathomed memories of home, and with something in his heart he could not utter.

In all the dreams and visions that now swarmed across his sleep, dreams and visions which can only be described as haunted fatally by the sense of time—his mind seemed to exercise the same complete control it ever had shown in all the operations of its conscious memory. He slept, and knew he slept, and saw the whole vast structure of the sleeping world about him as he slept; he dreamed, and knew he dreamed, and like a sorcerer, drew upward at his will, out of dark deeps and blue immensities of sleep, the strange, dark fish of his imagining.

Sometimes they came with elvish flakings of a hoary light, sometimes they came like magic and the promise of immortal joy, they came with victory and singing and a shout of triumph in his blood, and again he felt the strange and deathless joy of voyages: he was a passenger upon great ships again, he walked the broad, scrubbed decks exultantly, and smelled the hot, tarred roofs of powerful and ugly piers, he smelled the spermy sea-wrack of the harbor once again, the wastes of oil, the sharp, acrid and exultant smoke from busy little tugs, the odor of old, worn plankings, drenched with sunlight, and the thousand strange compacted spices of the laden piers. Again he felt the gold and sapphire loveliness of a Saturday in May, and drank the glory of the earth into his heart, and heard in lucent and lyrical air the heavy shattering "baugh" of the great ship's whistle, as it spoke gloriously, of springtime, new lands and departure. Again he saw ten thousand faces, touched with their strange admixture of sorrow and joy, swarm past the openings of the pier, and again he saw the flashing tides that girdled the city, whitened around the prows of a hundred boats, and gleaming with a million iridescent points of light. Again the great walled cliff, the crowded isle, the fabulous spires and ramparts of the city, as delicate as the hues of light that flashed around them, slid away from him, and one by one, the great ships, with the proud sweep of their breasts of white, their opulent storied superstructure, their music of power and speed, fell into line at noon on Saturday. And now, like bridled horses held in leash, with princely chafe and curvetings, they breach the mighty harbor, nose the narrows, circle slowly to brief pauses at the pilot's boat, and then, like racers set loose from the barriers, they are sent away, their engines tremble to a mighty stroke, the ships are given to the sea, to solitude, and to their proper glory once more.

And again he walked the decks, he walked the decks alone, and saw the glittering sea-flung city melt within his sight, and watched the sandy edges of the land fade away, and felt the incredible gold and sapphire glory of the day, the sparkle of dancing waters, and smelled salt, sea-borne air again, and saw upon the decks the joyful and exultant faces of the passengers, their looks of wonder, hope, and speculation, as they looked into the faces of strange men and women, now by the miracle of the voyage and chance isled with them in the loneliness of water, upon the glorious prison of a ship. And again he saw the faces of the lovely women, and saw the lights of love and passion in their eyes, and again he felt the plangent and depthless undulance, the unforgettable feeling of the fathomless might of the sea beneath a ship; a wild cry was torn from his throat, and a thousand unutterable feelings of the voyage, of white coasts and sparkling harbors and the creaking, eerie cries of gulls, of the dear, green dwelling of the earth again, and of strange, golden cities, potent wines, delicious foods, of women, love, and amber thighs spread amorously in ripe golden hay, of discovery and new lands, welled up in him like deathless song and certitude.

But just as these visions of delight and joy thronged upward through the deep marine of sleep, so, by the same fiat, the same calm order of an imperial will, the visions of a depthless shame, a faceless abomination of horror, an indefinable and impalpable corruption, returned to haunt his brain with their sentences of inexpiable guilt and ruin: under their evil spell he lay tranced upon his bed in a hypnosis of acquiescent horror, in a willing suspension of all his forces of resistance, like some creature held captive before the hypnotic rhythm of a reptile's head, the dull, envenomed fascination of its eye.

He moved on ceaselessly across a naked and accursed landscape and beneath a naked and accursed sky, an exile in the centre of a planetary vacancy that, like his guilt and shame, had neither place among things living nor among things dead, in which there was neither vengeance of lightning, nor mercy of burial, in which there was neither shade nor shelter, curve nor bend, nor hill, nor tree, nor hollow, in which—earth, air, sky, and limitless horizon—there was only one vast naked eye, inscrutable and accusing, from which there was no escape, and which bathed his naked soul in its fathomless depths of shame.

And then the vision faded, and suddenly, with the bridgeless immediacy of a dream, he found himself within the narrow canyon of a street, pacing interminably along on endless pavements where there was neither face nor footfall save his own, nor eye, nor window, nor any door that he might enter.

He thought he was walking through the harsh and endless continuity of one of those brownstone streets of which most of the city was constructed fifty years ago, and of which great broken lengths and fragments still remain. These streets, even if visited by some one in his waking hours, by some stranger in the fulness of health and sanity, and under the living and practical light of noon or, more particularly, by some man stunned with drink, who came there at some desolate and empty hour of night, might have a kind of cataleptic horror, a visionary unreality, as if some great maniac of architecture had conceived and shaped the first, harsh, ugly pattern of brown angularity, and then repeated it, without a change, into the infinity of illimitable repetition, with the mad and measureless insistence of an idiot monotony.

And forever he walked the street, under the brown and fatal light that fell upon him. He walked the street, and looked for a house there that was his own, for a door he knew that he must enter, for some one who was waiting for him in the house, and for the merciful dark wall and door that would hide and shelter him from the immense and naked eye of shame that peered upon him constantly. Forever he walked the street and searched the bleak, untelling façades for the house

he knew and had forgotten, forever he prowled along before the endless and unchanging façades of the street, and he never found it, and
at length he became aware of a vast sibilant whispering, of an immense
conspiracy of subdued and obscene laughter, and of the mockery of a
thousand evil eyes, that peered in silence from these bleak façades,
and that he could never find or see; and forever he walked the streets
alone, and heard the immense and secret whisperings and laughter, and
was bathed in the bottomless depths of a wordless shame, and could
never find the house he had lost, the door he had forgotten.

He was sitting in Marseilles, at a table on the terrace of a café on the
Canebière, when he saw them. Suddenly, above the rapid and vocifer-
ous animation of the café crowd, he heard Starwick's strangely timbred
voice, and turning, saw them seated at a table not a dozen feet away.
Starwick had just turned to Elinor and was saying something quietly,
in his tone of grave yet casual seriousness that often introduced his
drolleries, and then he could see Starwick's ruddy face suffuse and
deepen with his laughter, and Elinor's heavy shoulders begin to tremble,
and then heard her shriek of high, astounded, and protesting merriment.
Ann was seated listening, dark, silent, sullenly intent, with one long,
slender hand resting upon the neck of the big dog, who crouched quietly
beside her, and suddenly her dark and sullen face was lighted by its
rare and radiant smile that gave her features the instant configuration
of noble beauty.

The world rocked before him as if shattered by the force of an explosion: all the life seemed to have been blown out of him, and he sat
there staring at them, blind, numb, hollow, emptied to a shell, and
conscious of only one sensation—a kind of horrible fear that they would
turn and see him, a kind of horrible fear that they would not. They did
not turn or notice him: completely absorbed in one another, it seemed
to him that they had forgotten him as completely as if they had never
known him, and he was suddenly stabbed with a horrible chagrin at
sight of their free gaiety, a bitter anguish of despair because of the
triumph of their laughter. Then he was conscious of a single, blind and
overpowering desire—to get away from them, to get away unseen, to
get away somewhere—anywhere—so long as he could escape the agony
of meeting, the naked shame of revelation. He signalled to a waiter,
paid his bill, and quickly made his way out among the tables into the
noisy crowd that thronged forever past upon the pavement. He set his

face blindly away from them, and plunged ahead: it seemed to him that he could hear Starwick's shout of recognition, his voice calling to him above the thousand mixed vociferations of the crowd—and like a man pursued by devils, he set his head down blindly, and fled.

His life had passed into a state which, if not insane, was distinguished from insanity chiefly by a kind of quiescent understanding which surveyed the passage of time and his own actions with the powerless detachment of a spectator in a dream. Now, after this encounter with his three lost friends, even this sense of valuation was taken from him. In the weeks that followed, he was caught in a spell of time in which his life passed in a kind of evil dream, and later he was no more able to recall what he had done, how he had lived, where he had gone during this period, than if he had been the subject of a powerful and complete hypnosis. He was only vaguely conscious of what had happened, he felt a numb sense of horrible catastrophe, such as a drowning man might feel, or an anæsthetized patient who is bleeding to death under the surgeon's knife. He had a blind consciousness that some central governance of his life and reason had been exploded, that he was spinning down out of control like a shattered airplane—and that there was nothing he could do to save himself, that he could not get control again, that he could not "get back."

He lost the time-sense utterly—and it was his consciousness of this that filled him with numb terror. He would return to his room at night telling himself that he must work, then sleep, then rise by day and work again, and suddenly his room would be filled with light, the street below his window would be loud with all the noisy business of noon, and he would be seated at his table, with no knowledge how the time had passed.

He was now haunted constantly by a sense of the overwhelming nearness of his three lost friends. This feeling, indeed, would become so overpowering that at times the living presences of Starwick, Elinor, and Ann seemed invisibly to be with him, beside him. And the knowledge that they were here—for his conviction had become the obsession of an unshakable belief—seemed to give to the strange and sinister life of the evil and mysterious city an unutterable magic, to infect the very air he breathed with an intolerable anguish and delight. His whole life—heart and mind and spirit, and every nerve and sense and sinew of his body—was now passionately, indefatigably on the search for them. If he slept, it only brought to him an unbelievable ecstasy, an unbearable pain.

When he went out into the streets now it was only with the thought that he would find them—with an overwhelming conviction of his impending meeting with them. It seemed to him that every step he took was bringing him nearer to them, that he would meet them face to face around every corner that he turned—and this knowledge palsied his flesh with excitement, joy, and terror.

The two priests had finished eating, and provided with small cups of black coffee and small glasses of green chartreuse, they had settled back against the wall to enjoy in relaxed comfort the peace that passeth understanding. Both of the priests were Franciscans, they were on their way to Rome for the Holy Year, and apparently they had come well bestowed. Beside their table a frosty silver bucket, over the rim of which floated the gold necks of two empty champagne bottles, gave evidence of a meal from which nothing had been lacking. A waiter brought a box of Coronas and offered them prayerfully. The priests selected their cigars with an appeased and drowsy air: they bit the ends and grunted slightly at the flame the waiter offered them, then collapsing slowly against the cushioned wall, they meditated the ceiling in silence for several minutes through a blue, fragrant mist of dreamful ease.

It was a fine evening towards the end of May, and the two priests were in the best place to observe it. They had the first table on the right as you entered the café, and at this season of the year there was no door: the front was open. Just outside, the priests could see all the gaily painted little chairs and tables of the terrace, which was empty, and just beyond, the sidewalk and the Avenue de la Victoire, the chief thoroughfare of Nice. The street itself was quiet: from time to time a motor car flashed past or an old nag with clopping hooves, pulling a dilapidated-looking Victoria and urged on by a driver hunting for a fare. The trees along the street were in their full green leaf now and the air was sweet with the smell of the trees, the fragrance of earth and gardens and of unknown flowers. From time to time people came by with the strolling movement which a fine evening of this sort always seems to induce; and sometimes there would be young couples, lovers with arms around each other's waist, the women walking with a movement of voluptuous and languorous appeasement as if they were just coming from the act of love. But probably all they felt was the sensuous mystery, beauty and fragrance of the night, the smell of the trees and the earth and the flowers, which seemed to impregnate the whole continent of dark with the thrilling promises of desire almost made palpable, of unknown joys about to be realized.

It was a wonderfully seductive scene that opened from the entrance of the café, and all the more exciting because of its homely familiarity, its small framed limits into which life passed briefly with a ring of jaunting hooves, a sudden casual nearness and loudness of passing voices, and then—the fading and lonely recession of these homely sounds, a woman's burst of low and sensual laughter in the dark, the far-off dying-out of jaunting hooves—and silence.

The two priests missed nothing of the quiet scene: they drank it in with the air of men who have eaten nobly and who, fumed to contentment with the drugs of good tobacco and an old liqueur, are enormously pleased with life.

They were a strangely sorted pair and, once seen, would never be forgotten. The larger of the two was a huge tub and belly of a man, a kind of mammoth creature out of Rabelais, whose great moon of face flared fiercely, from the excess of his eating and his drinking. His fat neck and triple chin exuded over the neck-band of his robe, so that the garment he wore seemed to be stained and larded with the man's own grease. Everything about the great priest cried out with swingeing openness: his whole nature seemed to be permeated by a good humor so mountainously all-engulfing that nothing in the world could stop it: the huge red face would swell, suffuse, and purple with its choking laughter, the whole huge torso—the shoulders, arms and breast, and the great heaving belly—would shake and tremble like a hogshead full of jelly. And so far was he from being troubled by a thought of judgment, by fear of censure or the world's reproving eye, that the sight of a shocked or unconceding face was enough to send him off in a renewed paroxysm of volcanic mirth. There was no concealment in the man, there was even a kind of mountainously good-natured contempt for what the world might say or think of him, and for this reason his association with his fellow priest was all the more grotesquely humorous—a humor which was certainly not lost on this great modern Friar John of the Funnels, but which he relished to the full. For, by contrast to this great flaring, heaving, roaring, full moon of a man, it would be impossible to imagine a more cautious and hypocritic figure than the other priest cut. The second priest was a little man with a gray, bleak, meagre and incredibly sly kind of face in which his native caution and fear of self-exposure were constantly waging a grotesque and open warfare with the sly cunning, avaricious greed and sensual desire obscenely legible in his countenance. At the present moment, this tormented struggle between lust and caution was comically evident: the fellow's face was a grotesque painting of desire, and his furtive little eyes kept darting around in his head like rodents and he peered slyly right and left all around the café to see if any one had noticed the naked exposure of his passions. The reason for his confusion, the very sight of which set his huge companion off in great breast and belly-heavings of tremendous laughter, was not hard to find: at the table next to the two priests were seated two comely young whores, who had ogled and enticed the two holy men all through the evening, and whose seductive cajoleries, encouraged by the great priest's explosions of mountainous belly-gushing laughter, had now become naked, open, and outrageous. The little fellow was in a cold, gray sweat of fear and longing: afraid to look at the two women, he could yet hardly keep his eyes off them; and terrified lest his conduct be observed and followed, he was nevertheless unable to conceal the feverish eagerness of desire which held him fascinated in a kind of trance.

So, the indecent comedy proceeded: the two women, emboldened by the huge priest's mountainous heavings of laughter, passed swiftly from flirtatious raillery to proposals of a more serious character: at the end, something certain, swift and serious passed between the women and the huge fat priest: one of them spoke to him in a low hoarse tone, he lowered his great moon of face a trifle, and without looking at her, answered. In a moment the two girls rose with an elaborate casualness, the priest paid their bill, and the women sauntered out, turned left, moved slowly towards the corner and, crossing to the other side, advanced a few yards down the quiet intersecting street, where they paused and turned, waiting, in the obscuring shadow of a tree.

In a moment the huge priest called for the bill, paid it, tipped the waiter generously, and rising with a mountainous grunt, deliberately launched his huge bulk towards the street, closely followed by the sly and terror-stricken figure of the little priest. Outside the café, the great priest paused deliberately, looking both ways with a kind of huge and rotund benevolence; then turning left in the direction the girls had gone, he set out again in leisurely, imperturbed pursuit. And the little priest trotted along beside him like a frightened puppy beside an elephant; in every step, in every stride and movement that they made, the separate characters of the two men were grotesquely and powerfully evident. The huge priest barged along with a tremendous and deliberate majesty, swinging his great belly right and left before him as an elephant swings its trunk, and magnificently indifferent to what any one might think or say. But the little man trotted along in a state bordering on terror; he tried desperately to look casual and unconcerned, but his shifting eyes darted furtive glances right and left, and beneath the hem of his rough gown, his sandalled feet kept slatting up and down in a movement that was somehow comically sly and that revealed the man's whole character. At the corner the big priest paused deliberately again, turned, surveyed the scene and then, espying the white of the girls' dresses below the trees across the street, set out in deliberate pursuit. And the little priest trotted along beside, his head lowered, his eyes darting furtive glances right and left, his sandalled feet slatting slyly up and down. Then they caught up with the girls below the trees and, half obscured in darkness, they stood for a moment talking in low voices. Then each of the girls took one of the priests by the arm and they all walked off together down the street and soon were lost in leafy darkness and the mystery of the night. Then the waiter, who had served the priests and who, standing in the entrance, had observed the meeting across the street, turned and glaring at the youth, said quietly:

"C'est très joli, eh? . . . Moi," he continued, after a brief pause, "je n'ai pas le sentiment religieux." And having delivered himself without rancor or surprise of that devastating statement, he dismissed the subject from his mind completely and, turning to the table that the priests had left, he racked the saucers up, and wiped the table clean.

From a distance there came suddenly a woman's low, rich burst of sensual laughter, the receding hoof-beats of a horse, and then all around there was silence, the overpowering fragrance of the earth, the huge thrill and mystery of night, and the sense of an intolerable desire, close and palpable and lovely, and never to be grasped or found: and from the huge and haunting familiarity of all these things, a thousand receding and unuttered memories of time arose, a feeling of bitter loss, wild joy and pain—of a door that closed, a cloud-shadow that had gone forever. He thought of home.

Among the dreams that returned to haunt his waking, watchful sleep during the strange, living vision of that green spring, as he lay hearted at the pulse of time, there was one which remained ever after in his memory.

He was striding along a wide and sandy beach and by the side of a calm and tranquilly flowing sea. The waves broke quietly and evenly in a long, low roll upon the beach, rushing up the sand in small hissing eddies of foam and water. Below his feet the firm, brown sand sprang back with an elastic vitality, a warm and vital wind was blowing, and he drew into his lungs exultantly the smell of the sea, and of the warm, wet, fragrant beach, ribbed evenly with braided edges of brown seaweed.

He did not recognize the scene as one which he had ever visited before, and yet he felt an instant and complete familiarity with it, as if he had known it forever. Behind him, drumming evenly upon the hard, elastic sand, and fading away into the distance with a hard, wooden thunder of wheels, he heard the furious rhythm of pounding hooves of driven horses. He knew that he had just descended from a ship, and that he was living in one of the antique and early ages of the earth; and all of this he knew with joy and wonder, and without surprise, with the thrill of recovering something he had always known and had lost forever.

It was a scene out of the classic period of the earth, and yet it was wholly different from every image he had ever had about this earth, in his imagination. For where, in every vision of his mind and reading, that earth had come to him in a few sharp and radiant colors, in a structure of life as glowing and proportionate as one of its faultless temples, as remote from the world he lived in as all its fables, myths, and legends, this earth he now walked on was permeated with the living tones and weathers of life.

The world of Homer was the world of first light, sunlight, and of morning: the sea was wine-dark, a gold and sapphire purity of light fell on the walls of Troy, a lucent depthless purity of light welled from the eyes of Helen, as false, fatal, and innocently corrupt a woman as ever wrought destruction on the earth. The light that fell on Nausicaa and her maidens was all gold and crystal like the stream they bathed in, as lucent in purity as their limbs, as radiant as joy and morning on the earth; and even the lights of vengeance and the rout of the dread furies that fell upon the doomed and driven figure of Orestes were as fatal as blood, as relentless as an antique tragedy, as toneless as a destiny.

And in his pictures of a later time, of Athens in the period of recorded history, of Pericles and Plato and the time of the wars with Sparta, the scenes of history were bathed in these radiant and perfect lights and weathers. He knew these men were made of living, breathing flesh and subject to the errors and imperfections of mortal men, and yet when he tried to think of a slum in Athens, of people with bad teeth, blemished skins, muddy complexions—of disease, filth, and squalor among them, and of the million weary, beaten, dusty, sweating moments of their lives, he could not. Even human grief, pain, and trouble took on a color of classical perfection, of tragic grandeur, and the tortured and distressful skein of human life, with all that is ugly, trivial, and disgusting in it, took on the logical pattern of design and ordered destiny.

The light that fell upon them was of gold and sapphire, and of singing, or as ominous and fatal as a certain and inexorable doom; but now he walked this beach in one of the classical periods of the earth, and nothing was as he had tried to picture it, and yet all was as familiar as if he had known it forever.

There was no gold and sapphire in the air: it was warm and sultry, omened with some troubling, variable and exultant menace, fraught with the sulphurous promise of a storm, pregnant with mystery and discovery, touched with a hundred disturbing elements and weathers of man's soul, and scented with a thousand warm and spermy odors of the land and sea, that touched man's entrails with delight and prophecy.

And the sea also was neither lyrical with gold and blue, or wine-dark in its single harmony: the sea was dark and sultry as the sky that bent above it, murked greenly, thickly, milkily, as it rolled quietly and broke upon the beach, as omened with impalpable prophecy as the earth and air.

He did not know the reason for his being there, and yet he knew beyond a doubt that he had come there for a purpose, that some one was waiting for him there, that the greatest joy and triumph he had ever known was impending in this glorious meeting.

CI

THAT year, in June, he was sitting one day at a table before a little café that looked out across a quiet, cobbled square in the ancient city of Dijon. He was on his way to Paris from Italy and Switzerland and he had stopped here on impulse, remembering that the town was the capital of the old kingdom of Burgundy—a name which, in some way, since childhood, had flourished in his mind with a green magic, evoking images of a fair, green country, noble wine and food, a golden, drowsy legendry of old wars and heroes, women, gallantry, and knightly acts.

And he had not been disappointed. The old town with its ancient palaces—the worn and age-grimed façades of a forgotten power, a storied architecture—and the fair, green earth, the deep, familiar green of the intimate and yet enchanted hills, awoke in him all the old drowsy gold of legendry, the promise of a fair and enfabled domain, fat with plenty.

He had been here three days now, flooded with living green and gold, a willing captive in the spell of time, drinking the noblest wine, eating some of the noblest cookery he had ever known. After the dull Swiss food, the food and wine of Burgundy were good beyond belief; and everything—old town, the fair, green country and the hills—made a music in him again which was like all the green-gold magic of his childhood dream of France.

Now, he sat there at a table before a little café, already meditating with slow, lustful revery his noon-day meal at an ancient, famous inn where for eighteen francs one was served a stupendous meal—a succession of succulent native dishes such as he had dreamed about but had never thought that he would find outside of dreams or legends, in a town so small as this.

As he thought of this gourmet's heaven with a feeling of wonder and disbelief, the memory of a hundred little towns and cities in America returned to him, with the hideous and dyspeptic memory of their foods —the greasy, rancid, sodden, stale, dead, and weary foods of the Greek restaurants, of the lunchrooms, coffee shops and railroad cafeterias— hastily bolted and washed down to the inevitable miseries of dyspepsia with gulping swallows of sour, weak coffee.

Yes, even the noble food and wine had made a magic in this ancient place, and suddenly he was pierced again by the old hunger that haunts and hurts Americans—the hunger for a better life—an end of rawness, newness, sourness, distressful and exacerbated misery, the taking from the great plantation of the earth and of America our rich inheritance of splendor, ease, and abundance—good food, and sensual love, and noble cookery—the warmth of radiant color and of wine—pulse of the blood —an end of misery, bitterness, hunger and unrest upon the breast of everlasting plenty—the inheritance of exultancy and joy forever, which some foul, corrosive poison in our lives—bitter enigma that it is!—has taken from us.

Now, as he thought these things, sitting before the café and looking across the quiet square of whitened cobbles, a bell struck, and noon came. Slowly a great clock began to strike in the old town. In a cool, dark church, which he had seen the day before, a bell-rope, knotted at the ends, hung down before the altar-steps from an immense distance in the ceiling. The moment the town bell had finished its deep reverberation, a sexton walked noisily across the old flagged church-floor and took the bell-cord in his hands. Slowly, with a gentle rhythm, he began to swing upon the rope, and one could hear at first an old and heavy creaking from the upper air, but as yet no bell.

Then the sexton's body stiffened in its rhythm, he hung hard upon the knotted rope in punctual sway, and there began, far up in the church, the upper air of that old place, a sweet and ponderous beating of the bells. At first they beat in threes—ding-dong-dong; ding-dong-dong; then swiftly the man changed his rhythm, and the bells began to beat a faster double measure.

And now the youth remembered old, distant chimes upon a street at night; and the memory of his own bells came back into his heart. He remembered the great bell at college that rang the boys to classes, and how the knotted bell-rope came down into the room of the student who rang it; and how often he had rung the bell himself, and how at first there was the creaking noise in the upper air of the bell tower, there as here; and how, as the great bell far above him swung into its rhythm, he would be carried off the floor by that weight of thronging bronze; and he remembered still the lift and power of the old college bell, as he swung at the knotted rope, and the feeling of joy and power that surged up in him as he was lifted on the mighty upward stroke, and heard above him in the tower, the dark music of the grand old bell and the students running on the campus paths below the window, and then the loose rope, the bell tolling brokenly away to silence, the creaking sound again, and finally nothing but silence, the day's green spell and golden magic of the drowsy campus in the month of May.

And now the memory of that old bell, with all its host of long-forgotten things, swarmed back with living and intolerable pungency, as he sat there at noon in the old French town, and heard the sexton swinging on the bell of the old church.

He thought of home.

And now, with the sound of that old bell, everything around him burst into instant life. Although the structure of that life was foreign to him, and different from anything he had known as a child, everything instantly became incredibly living, near, and familiar, like something he had always known.

The little café before which he was sitting, was old and small, and had a warm, worn look of use and comfort. Inside, in the cool, dark depth of the place, were two old men sitting at a table playing cards—with a faded, green cloth upon the table; and two waiters. One of the old men had long, pointed mustaches, and a thin, distinguished face; the other was more ruddy and full-fleshed and had a beard. They played quietly, bending over the old, green cloth with studious deliberation, making each play slowly. Sometimes they spoke quietly to each other, only a few words at a time; sometimes the ruddy old man's thick shoulders would heave and tremble, and his face would flush rosily, with satisfaction; but the other one laughed thinly, quietly, in a more gentle, weary way.

The two waiters were polishing up the silverware, and getting the tables set and put in order for the mid-day meal. One of the waiters was an old man with the sprouting, energetic mustaches one sees so often in France, and with the weary, hawk-like, cynical, yet not ill-natured face that one often sees on old waiters. The other—really just a bus-boy—was a young, clumsy, thick-fingered and thick-featured country lad, with the wine-dark, vital, sanguinary coloring some Frenchmen have.

The young fellow was full of exuberant good spirits; he was polishing up the knives and forks and spoons with enthusiastic gusto, humming the snatches of a song as he did so, and slamming each piece of silver down into a drawer with such vigor, when he had finished, that it was obvious that he got great pleasure from the musical jingle thus created.

Meanwhile the old waiter moved quietly, softly, and yet wearily about, setting the tables. At length, however, at the end of a particularly violent and enthusiastic jingle of silverware from his polishing companion, he looked up, with a slight cynical arching of his eyebrows, and then, without ill-nature but with perfect urbanity, he said ironically:

"Ah! On fait la musique!"

This was all, but one saw the young fellow's face flush and redden with exuberant laughter; his thick shoulders rose and for a moment trembled convulsively, then he went on polishing, singing to himself, and hurling the noisy silverware into the drawer with more enthusiasm than ever.

And that brief, pleasant, and somehow poignantly unforgettable scene now seemed, like everything else, to be intolerably near and familiar to the youth, and something he had always known.

Before him, the quiet, faded, strangely pleasant square was waking briefly to its moment of noon-day life. Far off he could hear the little shrill fifing whistle of a French locomotive, and the sound of slow trains; an ice-wagon, with a tin interior and large, delicately carved cakes of ice, clattered across the cobbles of the square; and he remembered how he had seen, the day before, some barge people eating on a barge beneath the trees. From where he sat he could see workmen, wearing shapeless caps and baggy corduroy trousers streaked with lime and cement, and talking in hoarse, loud, disputatious voices as they leaned above their drinks on the zinc bar of a little bistro on the corner.

Some young, dull-looking women, wearing light-colored stockings, and light, gray-tannish overcoats, came by, with domesticity written in every movement that they made, looking, somehow, their wedded propriety, and the stern dullness of provincial places everywhere.

And then the lost, the irrevocable, the lonely sounds which he had not heard for fifteen years awoke there in the square, and suddenly he was a child, and it was noon, and he was waiting in his father's house to hear the slam of the iron gate, the great body stride up the high porch steps, knowing his father had come home again.

At first, before him, in that little whitened square, it was just the thring of the bicycle bells, the bounding of the light-wired wheels. And at first he could see some French army officers riding home upon their bicycles. They were proper and assured-looking men, with solid, wine-dark faces, and they rode solidly and well, driving the light-wired wheels beneath them with firm propulsions of their solid legs.

Then, with a thring of bells, an army sergeant came by, riding fast and smoothly on his way home to dinner. And then, with sudden rush, the thring of bells, the thrum of wheels increased: the clerks, the bank clerks, the bookkeepers—the little proper and respectable people of all sorts—were riding home across the quiet little square at noon.

On the other side of the square he could see two workmen who were still at work upon a piece of stone; one was holding an iron spike, and one a sledge, and they worked slowly, with frequent pauses.

A young buck, with a noisy, sporty little car, sped over the square, and vanished; and the youth wondered if he was one of the daring blades of Dijon, and what young women of the town's best families he had taken out in the car, and if he boasted to other young town blades in cafés of his prowess at seduction, as did the bucks before Wood's Pharmacy at home.

Then, for a moment there was a brooding silence in the square again, and presently there began the most lonely, lost and unforgettable of all sounds on earth—the solid, liquid leather-shuffle of footsteps going home one way, as men had done when they came home to lunch at noon some twenty years ago, in the green-gold and summer magic of full June, before he had seen his father's land, and when the kingdoms of this earth and the enchanted city still blazed there in the legendary magic of his boyhood vision.

They came with solid, lonely, liquid shuffle of their decent leather, going home, the merchants, workers, and good citizens of that old town of Dijon. They streamed across the cobbles of that little square; they passed, and vanished, and were gone forever—leaving silence, the brooding hush and apathy of noon, a suddenly living and intolerable memory, instant and familiar as all this life around him, of a life that he had lost, and that could never die.

It was the life of twenty years ago in the quiet, leafy streets and little towns of lost America—of an America that had been lost beneath the savage roar of its machinery, the brutal stupefaction of its days, the huge disease of its furious, ever-quickening and incurable unrest, its flood-tide horror of gray, driven faces, stolid eyes, starved, brutal nerves, and dull, dead flesh.

The memory of the lost America—the America of twenty years ago, of quiet streets, the time-enchanted spell and magic of full June, the solid, lonely, liquid shuffle of men in shirt-sleeves coming home, the leafy fragrance of the cooling turnip-greens, and screens that slammed, and sudden silence—had long since died, had been drowned beneath the brutal flood-tide, the edict stupefaction of that roaring surge and mechanic life which had succeeded it.

And now, all that lost magic had come to life again here in the little whitened square, here in this old French town, and he was closer to his childhood and his father's life of power and magnificence than he could ever be again in savage new America; and as the knowledge of these strange, these lost yet familiar things returned to him, his heart was filled with all the mystery of time, dark time, the mystery of strange, million-visaged time that haunts us with the briefness of our days.

He thought of home.

BOOK VIII

FAUST AND HELEN

CII

IMMENSE and sudden, and with the abrupt nearness, the telescopic
magic of a dream, the English ship appeared upon the coasts of France,
and approached with the strange, looming immediacy of powerful and
gigantic objects that move at great speed: there was no sense of con-
tinuous movement, of gradual and progressive enlargement, rather the
visages of the ship melted rapidly from one bigness to another as do the
visages of men in a cinema, which, by a series of fading sizes, brings these
kinematic shapes of things, like genii unstoppered from a wizard's bottle, to an overpowering command above the spectator.

At first there was only the calm endlessness of the evening sea, the
worn headlands of Europe, and the land, with its rich, green slopes, its
striped patterns of minutely cultivated earth, its ancient fortresses and
its town—the town of Cherbourg—which, from this distance, lay like a
solid pattern of old chalk at the base of the coastal indentation.

Westward, a little to the south, against the darkening bulk of the
headland, a long riband of smoke, black and low, told the position of the
ship. She was approaching fast, her bulk widened: she had been a dot,
a smudge, a shape—a tiny, hardly noticed point in the calm and immense
geography of evening. Now she was there, sliding gently in beyond
the ancient breakwater, inhabiting and dominating the universe with
the presence of her 60,000 tons, so that the vast setting of sky and sea and
earth, in which formerly she had been only an inconspicuous but living
mark, were now a background for her magnificence.

At this very moment of her arrival the sun rested upon the western
wave like a fading coal: its ancient light fell over sea and land without
violence or heat, with a remote, unearthly glow that had the delicate
tinging of old bronze. Then, swiftly, the sun sank down into the sea, the
uninhabited sky now burned with a fierce, an almost unbearable glory;
the sun's old light had faded; and the ship was there outside the harbor,
sliding softly through the water now, and quartering, in slow turn,
upon the land as she came up for anchor.

The sheer wall of her iron plates scarcely seemed to move at all now
in the water, it was as if she were fixed and foundered there among the
tides, as implacable as the headlands of the coast; yet, over her solid bows
the land was wheeling slowly. Water foamed noisily from her sides in

thick, tumbling columns: the sea-gulls swarmed around her, fluttering greedily and heavily to the water with their creaking and unearthly clamor. Then her anchors rushed out of her, and she stood still.

Meanwhile the tenders, bearing the passengers who were going to board the ship, had put out from the town even before the ship's arrival, and were now quite near. They had, in fact, cruised slowly for some time about the outer harbor, for the ship was late and the commander had wirelessed asking that there be as little delay as possible when he arrived.

Now the light faded on the land: the fierce, hard brilliance of the western sky, full of bright gold and ragged flame, had melted to an orange afterglow, the subtle, grapy bloom of dusk was melting across the land; the town, far off, was half immersed in it, its moving shadow stole across the fields and slopes, it moved upon the waters like a weft. Above the land the sky was yet full of light—of that strange, phantasmal light of evening which reveals itself to people standing in the dusk below without touching them with any of its radiance: the material and physical property of light seems to have been withdrawn from it, and it remains briefly in the sky, without substance or any living power, like the ghost of light, its soul, its spirit.

In these late skies of France, this late, evening light of waning summer had in it a quality that was high and sad, remote and full of classic repose and dignity. Beneath it, it was as if one saw people grave and beautiful move slowly homeward through long aisles of planted trees: the light was soft, lucent, delicately empearled—and all great labor was over, all strong joy and hate and love had ended, all wild desire and hope, all maddening of the flesh and heart and brain, the fever and the tumult and the fret; and the grave-eyed women in long robes walked slowly with cut flowers in their arms among the glades of trees, and night had come, and they would go to the wood no more.

Now, in this light, all over the land of France the men were coming from the fields: they had used preciously the last light of day, summer was almost over, the fields were mown, the hay was raked and stacked, and in a thousand places, along the Rhine, and along the Marne, in Burgundy, in Touraine, in Provence, the wains were lumbering slowly down the roads.

In the larger towns the nervous and swarming activity of evening had begun: the terraces of the cafés were uncomfortably crowded with noisy people, the pavements were thronged with a chattering and gesticulating tide, the streets were loud with traffic, the clatter of trams, the heavy grinding of buses, the spiteful little horns of innumerable small taxis. But over all, over the opulence of the mown fields, and the untidy and distressful throngings of the towns, hung this high, sad light of evening.

A stranger, a visitor from some newer and more exultant earth—an American, perhaps—had he seen this coast thus for the first time, might have imagined the land as inhabited by a race far different from the one that really lived here: he would have felt the opulent austerity of this earth under its dying light, and he would have been deeply troubled by it.

For such a visitor, disturbed by the profound and subtle melancholy of this scene, for which his own experience had given him no adequate understanding or preparation, because it was steeped in peace without hope, in beauty without joy, in tranquil and brooding resignation without exultancy, the sight of the ship, as she lay now, immense and immovable at her anchor, would have pierced him suddenly with a thrill of victory, a sudden renewal of his faith and hope, a belief in the happy destiny of life.

She lay there, an alien presence in those waters; she had the reality of magic, the reality that is so living and magnificent that it seems unreal. She was miraculous and true—as one looked at her, settled like some magic luminosity upon that mournful coast, a strong cry of exultancy rose up in one's throat: the sight of the ship was as if a man's mistress had laid her hand upon his loins.

The ship was now wholly anchored: she lay there in the water with the living stillness of all objects that were made to move. Although entirely motionless, outwardly as fixed and permanent as any of the headlands of the coast, the story of her power and speed was legible in every line. She glowed and pulsed with the dynamic secret of life, and although her great sides towered immense and silent as a cliff, although the great plates of her hull seemed to reach down and to be founded in the sea's bed, and only the quietly flowing waters seemed to move and eddy softly at her sides, she yet had legible upon her the story of a hundred crossings, the memory of strange seas, of suns and moons and many different lights, the approach of April on far coasts, the change of wars and histories, and the completed dramas of all her voyages, charactered by the phantoms of many thousand passengers, the life, the hate, the love, the bitterness, the jealousy, the intrigue of six-day worlds, each one complete and separate in itself, which only a ship can have, which only the sea can bound, which only the earth can begin or end.

She glowed with the radiance of all her brilliant and luminous history; and besides this, she was literally a visitant from a new world. The stranger from the new world who saw the ship would also instantly have seen this. She had been built several years after the war and was entirely a product of European construction, engineering, navigation, and diplomacy. But her spirit, the impulse that communicated itself in each of her lines, was not European, but American. It is Europeans, for the most part, who have constructed these great ships, but without America they have no meaning. These ships are alive with the supreme ecstasy of the modern world, which is the voyage to America. There is no other experience that is remotely comparable to it, in its sense of joy, its exultancy, its drunken and magnificent hope which, against reason and knowledge, soars into a heaven of fabulous conviction, which believes in the miracle and sees it invariably achieved.

In this soft, this somewhat languid air, the ship glowed like an immense and brilliant jewel. All of her lights were on, they burned row by row straight across her 900 feet of length, with the small, hard twinkle of cut gems: it was as if the vast, black cliff of her hull, which strangely suggested the glittering night-time cliff of the fabulous city that was her destination, had been sown with diamonds.

And above this, her decks were ablaze with light. Her enormous superstructure with its magnificent frontal sweep, her proud breast which was so full of power and speed, her storied decks and promenades as wide as city streets, the fabulous variety and opulence of her public rooms, her vast lounges and salons, her restaurants, grills, and cafés, her libraries, writing-rooms, ballrooms, swimming-pools, her imperial suites with broad beds, private decks, sitting-rooms, gleaming baths—all of this, made to move upon the stormy seas, leaning against eternity and the gray welter of the Atlantic at twenty-seven knots an hour, tenanted by the ghosts, impregnated by the subtle perfumes of thousands of beautiful and expensive women, alive with the memory of the silken undulance of their long backs, with the naked, living velvet of their shoulders as they paced down the decks at night—all of this, with the four great funnels that in the immense drive and energy of their slant were now cut sharp and dark against the evening sky, burned with a fierce, exultant vitality in the soft melancholy of this coast.

The ship struck joy into the spinal marrow. In her intense reality she became fabulous, a visitant from another world, a creature monstrous and magical with life, a stranger, seeming strange, to these melancholy coasts, for she was made to glitter in the hard, sharp air of a younger, more exultant land.

She was made also to quarter on the coasts of all the earth, to range powerfully on the crest and ridge of the globe, sucking continents towards her, devouring sea and land; she was made to enter European skies like some stranger from another world, to burn strangely and fabulously in the dull, gray air of Europe, to pulse and glow under the soft, wet European sky. But she was only a marvellous stranger there; she was a bright, jewelled thing; she came definitely, indubitably, wonderfully from but one place on earth, and in only that one place could she be fully seen and understood, in only that one place could she slide in to her appointed and imperial setting.

That place was America: that place was the reaches to the American coast: that place was the approaches to the American continent. That place, finally, and absolutely, was the port whither she was bound—the fabulous rock of life, the proud, masted city of the soaring towers, which was flung with a lion's port into the maw of ocean. And as the Americans who were now approaching the ship in the puffing little tender saw this mark upon her, they looked at her and knew her instantly; they felt a qualm along their loins, their flesh stirred.

"Oh, look!" cried a woman suddenly, pointing to the ship whose immense and glittering side now towered over them. "Isn't that lovely! God, but she's big! How do you suppose we're ever going to find the ocean?"

"The first thing I'm going to do, darling, is find my bed," said her companion, in a tone of languorous weariness. A tall and sensual-looking Jewess, she was seated on a pile of baggage, smoking a cigarette, her long legs indolently crossed: indifferently, with smouldering and arrogant glances, she surveyed the crowd of passengers on the tender.

The other woman could not be still: her rosy face was burning with the excitement of the voyage, she kept slipping the ring on and off her finger nervously, and moving around at her brisk little step among the heaped-up piles of baggage.

"Oh, here!" she cried out suddenly in great excitement, pointing to a bag buried at the bottom of one of the piles. "Oh, here!" she cried again to the general public. "This one's mine! Where are the others? Can't you find the others for me?" she said in a sharp, protesting voice to one of the porters, a little, brawny man with sprouting mustaches. "Hey?" she said, lifting her small hand complainingly to her ear as he answered her in a torrent of reassuring French. She turned to her companion protestingly:

"I can't get them to do anything. They don't pay a bit of attention to what I say! I can't find my trunk and two of my bags. I think it's the most dreadful thing I ever heard of. Don't you? Hey?" again she lifted her little hand to her ear, for she was somewhat deaf: her small, rosy face was crimson with excitement and earnestness—in her tone, her manner, her indignation, there was something irresistibly comic, and suddenly her companion began to laugh.

"Oh, Esther!" she said. "Lord!" and then paused abruptly, as if there were no more to say.

Esther was fair; she was fair; she had dove's eyes.

Now the woman's lovely face, like a rarer, richer, and more luminous substance, was glowing among all the other faces of the travellers, which, as the tender circled and came in close below the ship, were fixed with a single intentness upon the great hull that loomed over them with its overpowering immensity.

The great ship cast over them all her mighty spell: most of these people had made many voyages, yet the great ship caught them up again in her magic glow, she possessed and thrilled them with her presence as if they had been children. The travellers stood there silent and intent as the little boat slid in beside the big one, they stood there with uplifted faces; and for a moment it was strange and sad to see them thus, with loneliness and longing in their eyes. Their faces made small, lifted whitenesses; they shone in the gathering dark with a luminous glimmer: there was something small, naked and lonely in the glimmer of those faces, around them was the immense eternity of sea and death. They heard time.

For if, as men be dying, they can pluck one moment from the darkness into which their sense is sinking, if one moment in all the dark and mysterious forest should then live, it might well be the memory of such a moment as this which, although lacking in logical meaning, burns for an instant in the dying memory as a summary and a symbol of man's destiny on earth. The fading memory has forgotten what was said then by the passengers, the thousand tones and shadings of the living moment are forgotten, but drenched in the strange, brown light of time, the scene glows again for an instant with an intent silence: darkness has fallen upon the eternal earth, the great ship like a monstrous visitant blazes on the waters, and on the tender the faces of the travellers are lifted up like flowers in a kind of rapt and mournful ecstasy—they are weary of travel, they have wandered in strange cities among strange tongues and faces, and they have left not even the print of their foot in any town.

Their souls are naked and alone, and they are strangers upon the earth, and many of them long for a place where those weary of travel may find rest, where those who are tired of searching may cease to search, where there will be peace and quiet living, and no desire. Where shall the weary find peace? Upon what shore will the wanderer come home at last? When shall it cease—the blind groping, the false desires, the fruitless ambitions that grow despicable as soon as they are reached, the vain contest with phantoms, the maddening and agony of the brain and spirit in all the rush and glare of living, the dusty tumult, the grinding, the shouting, the idiot repetition of the streets, the sterile abundance, the sick gluttony, and the thirst which goes on drinking?

Out of one darkness the travellers have come to be taken into another, but for a moment one sees their faces, awful and still, all uplifted towards the ship. This is all: their words have vanished, all memory of the movements they made then has also vanished: one remembers only their silence and their still faces lifted in the phantasmal light of lost time; one sees them ever, still and silent, as they slide from darkness on the river of time; one sees them waiting at the ship's great side, all silent and all damned to die, with their grave, white faces lifted in a single supplication to the ship, and towards the silent row of passengers along the deck, who for a moment return their gaze with the same grave and tranquil stare. That silent meeting is a summary of all the meetings of men's lives: in the silence one hears the slow, sad breathing of humanity, one knows the human destiny.

"Oh, look!" the woman cried again. "Oh, see! Was ever anything more beautiful?" The ship's great beetling cliff swept sheer above her. She turned the small, flushed flower of her face and saw the slant and reach and swell of the great prow, and music filled her. She lifted the small, flushed flower of her face and saw the many men so little, so lonely, silent, and intent, that bent above her, looking from the ship's steep rail. She turned and saw the people all around her, the swift weave and patterned shifting of the forms, and she saw light then, ancient fading light, that fell upon the coasts of evening, and quiet waters reddened by fading day, and heard the unearthly creakings of a gull; and wonder filled her. And the strange and mortal ache of beauty, the anguish to pronounce what never could be spoken, to grasp what never could be grasped, to hold and keep forever what was gone the moment she put her hand upon it——

"Oh, these people here," she cried in a high tone—"The ship! . . . My God, the things that I could tell you all!" she cried indignantly. "The things I know—the things I have inside me here!"—she struck herself upon the breast with one clenched hand—"the way things are, the way they happen, and the beauty of the clear design—and no one ever asks me!" she cried out indignantly. "This wonderful thing is going on inside me all the time—and no one ever wants to know the way it happens!"—and stood staring at her friend accusingly a moment, a little figure of indignant loveliness until, becoming aware of people's smiles and her companion's laughter, her own face was suddenly suffused, and, casting back her head, she was swept with gale-like merriment—a full, rich, woman's yell of triumph and delight.

And yet, even as she laughed, she was pierced again by the old ache of wonder, the old anguish of unspoken desire, and saw the many men, so lonely, silent, and intent, the ship immense and sudden there above her in old evening light, and so—remembering, "Canst thou draw out leviathan with an hook? or his tongue with a cord which thou lettest down?"—was still with wonder.

Ah, strange and beautiful, the woman thought, how can I longer bear this joy intolerable, the music of this great song unpronounceable, the anguish of this glory unimaginable, which fills my life to bursting and which will not let me speak! It is too hard, too hard, and not to be endured, to feel the great vine welling in my heart, the wild, strange music swelling in my throat, the triumph of that final perfect song that aches forever there just at the gateway of my utterance—and that has no tongue to speak! Oh magic moment that are so perfect, unknown, and inevitable, to stand here at this ship's great side, here at the huge last edge of evening and return, with this still wonder in my heart and knowing only that somehow we are fulfilled of you, oh time! And see how gathered there against the rail high over us, there at the ship's

great side, are all the people, silent, lonely, and so beautiful, strange
brothers of this voyage, chance phantoms of the bitter briefness of our
days—and you, oh youth—for now she saw him there for the first time
—who bend there, lone and lean and secret, at the rail of night, why are
you there alone while these, your fellows, wait? . . . Ah secret and
alone, she thought—how lean with hunger, and how fierce with pride,
and how burning with impossible desire he bends there at the rail
of night—and he is wild and young and foolish and forsaken, and his
eyes are starved, his soul is parched with thirst, his heart is famished
with a hunger that cannot be fed, and he leans there on the rail and
dreams great dreams, and he is mad for love and is athirst for glory,
and he is so cruelly mistaken—and so right! . . . Ah, see, she thought,
how that wild light flames there upon his brow—how bright, how
burning and how beautiful—Oh passionate and proud!—how like the
wild, lost soul of youth you are, how like my wild lost father who will
not return!

He turned, and saw her then, and so finding her, was lost, and so
losing self, was found, and so seeing her, saw for a fading moment only
the pleasant image of the woman that perhaps she was, and that life
saw. He never knew: he only knew that from that moment his spirit
was impaled upon the knife of love. From that moment on he never
was again to lose her utterly, never to wholly re-possess unto himself
the lonely, wild integrity of youth which had been his. At that instant
of their meeting, that proud inviolability of youth was broken, not to be
restored. At that moment of their meeting she got into his life by some
dark magic, and before he knew it, he had her beating in the pulses of
his blood—somehow thereafter—how he never knew—to steal into the
conduits of his heart, and to inhabit the lone, inviolable tenement of his
one life; so, like love's great thief, to steal through all the adyts of his
soul, and to become a part of all he did and said and was—through this
invasion so to touch all loveliness that he might touch, through this
strange and subtle stealth of love henceforth to share all that he might
feel or make or dream, until there was for him no beauty that she did
not share, no music that did not have her being in it, no horror, madness, hatred, sickness of the soul, or grief unutterable, that was not
somehow consonant to her single image and her million forms—and
no final freedom and release, bought through the incalculable expendi-
ture of blood and anguish and despair, that would not bear upon its

brow forever the deep scar, upon its sinews the old mangling chains, of love.

After all the blind, tormented wanderings of youth, that woman would become his heart's centre and the target of his life, the image of immortal one-ness that again collected him to one, and hurled the whole collected passion, power and might of his one life into the blazing certitude, the immortal governance and unity, of love.

"Set me as a seal upon thine heart, as a seal upon thine arm: for love is strong as death; jealousy is cruel as the grave: the coals thereof are coals of fire, which hath a most vehement flame."

And now all the faces pass in through the ship's great side (the tender flower face among them). Proud, potent faces of rich Jews, alive with wealth and luxury, glow in rich, lighted cabins; the doors are closed, and the ship is given to the darkness and the sea.